I0643221

The Complete Dr. Thorndyke

Volume V:
The Mystery of Angelina Frood
The Shadow of the Wolf
The D'Arblay Mystery

The Complete Dr. Thorndyke

Volume V:
The Mystery of Angelina Frood
The Shadow of the Wolf
The D'Arblay Mystery

By

R. Austin Freeman

Edited by
David Marcum

First edition published in 2019
© Copyright 2019

The right of the individuals listed on the Copyright Information page to be identified as the authors of this work has been asserted by them in accordance with the Copyright, Designs, and Patents Act 1998.

All rights reserved. No reproduction, copy, or transmission of this publication may be made without express prior written permission. No paragraph of this publication may be reproduced, copied, or transmitted except with express prior written permission or in accordance with the provisions of the Copyright Act 1956 (as amended). Any person who commits any unauthorised act in relation to this publication may be liable to criminal prosecution and civil claims for damage.

All characters appearing in this work are fictitious or used fictitiously. Except for certain historical personages, any resemblance to real persons, living or dead, is purely coincidental. The opinions expressed herein are those of the authors and not of MX Publishing.

ISBN Hardback 978-1-78705-540-7
ISBN Paperback 978-1-78705-541-4
AUK ePub ISBN 978-1-78705-542-1
AUK PDF ISBN 978-1-78705-543-8

These works are in the Public Domain in Great Britain
Portrait of Dr. Thorndyke by H.M. Brock (1908)

Published in the UK by
MX Publishing
335 Princess Park Manor, Royal Drive,
London, N11 3GX
www.mxpublishing.co.uk

David Marcum can be reached at:
thepapersofsherlockholmes@gmail.com

Cover design by Brian Belanger
www.belangerbooks.com and *www.redbubble.com/people/zhahadun*

CONTENTS

Introductions

Adventures

The Mystery of Angelina Frood

The Shadow of the Wolf

(Continued on the next page . . . .)

The D'Arblay Mystery

The Complete Dr. Thorndyke

Volume V:
The Mystery of Angelina Frood
The Shadow of the Wolf
The D'Arblay Mystery

Dr. John Thorndyke

99

5A King's Bench Walk
in the late 1890's when
Thorndyke would have moved in

5A King's Bench Walk
Photographed by the Editor
during his
Sherlock Holmes Pilgrimage No. 3
(September 8th, 2016)

Meet Dr. Thorndyke
by R. Austin Freeman

My subject is Dr. John Thorndyke, the hero or central character of most of my detective stories. So I'll give you a short account of his real origin – of the way in which he did in fact come into existence.

To discover the origin of John Thorndyke I have to reach back into the past for at least fifty years, to the time when I was a medical student preparing for my final examination. For reasons which I need not go into I gave rather special attention to the legal aspects of medicine and the medical aspects of law. And as I read my text-books, and especially the illustrative cases, I was profoundly impressed by their dramatic quality. Medical jurisprudence deals with the human body in its relation to all kinds of legal problems. Thus its subject matter includes all sorts of crime against the person and all sorts of violent death and bodily injury: Hanging, drowning, poisons and their effects, problems of suicide and homicide, of personal identity and survivorship, and a host of other problems of the highest dramatic possibilities, though not always quite presentable for the purposes of fiction. And the reported cases which were given in illustration were often crime stories of the most thrilling interest. Cases of disputed identity such as the Tichbourne Case, famous poisoning cases such as the Rugeley Case and that of Madeline Smith, cases of mysterious disappearance or the detection of long-forgotten crimes such as that of Eugene Aram. All these, described and analysed with strict scientific accuracy, formed the matter of Medical Jurisprudence which thrilled me as I read and made an indelible impression.

But it produced no immediate results. I had to pass my examinations and get my diploma, and then look out for the means of earning my living. So all this curious lore was put away for the time being in the pigeon-holes of my mind – which Dr. Freud would call the *Unconscious* – not forgotten, but ready to come to the surface when the need for it should arise. And there it reposed for some twenty years, until failing health compelled me to abandon medical practice and take to literature as a profession.

It was then that my old studies recurred to my mind. A fellow doctor, Conan Doyle, had made a brilliant and well-deserved success by the creation of the immortal Sherlock Holmes. Considering that achievement, I asked myself whether it might not be possible to devise a

1

detective story of a slightly different kind – one based on the science of Medical Jurisprudence, in which, by the sacrifice of a certain amount of dramatic effect, one could keep entirely within the facts of real life, with nothing fictitious excepting the persons and the events. I came to the conclusion that it was, and began to turn the idea over in my mind.

But I think that the influence which finally determined the character of my detective stories, and incidentally the character of John Thorndyke, operated when I was working at the Westminster Ophthalmic Hospital. There I used to take the patients into the dark room, examine their eyes with the ophthalmoscope, estimate the errors of refraction, and construct an experimental pair of spectacles to correct those errors. When a perfect correction had been arrived at, the formula for it was embodied in a prescription which was sent to the optician who made the permanent spectacles.

Now when I was writing those prescriptions it was borne in on me that in many cases, especially the more complex, the formula for the spectacles, and consequently the spectacles themselves, furnished an infallible record of personal identity. If, for instance, such a pair of spectacles should have been found in a railway carriage, and the maker of those spectacles could be found, there would be practically conclusive evidence that a particular person had travelled by that train. About that time I drafted out a story based on a pair of spectacles, which was published some years later under the title of *The Mystery of 31 New Inn*, and the construction of that story determined, as I have said, not only the general character of my future work but of the hero around whom the plots were to be woven. But that story remained for some years in cold storage. My first published detective novel was *The Red Thumb-mark*, and in that book we may consider that John Thorndyke was born. And in passing on to describe him I may as well explain how and why he came to be the kind of person that he is.

I may begin by saying that he was not modelled after any real person. He was deliberately created to play a certain part, and the idea that was in my mind was that he should be such a person as would be likely and suitable to occupy such a position in real life. As he was to be a medico-legal expert, he had to be a doctor and a fully trained lawyer. On the physical side I endowed him with every kind of natural advantage. He is exceptionally tall, strong, and athletic because those qualities are useful in his vocation. For the same reason he has acute eyesight and hearing and considerable general manual skill, as every doctor ought to have. In appearance he is handsome and of an imposing presence, with a symmetrical face of the classical type and a Grecian nose. And here I may remark that his distinguished appearance is not merely a concession to my personal taste but is also a protest against the monsters of ugliness whom some detective writers have evolved.

These are quite opposed to natural truth. In real life a first-class man of any kind usually tends to be a good-looking man.

Mentally, Thorndyke is quite normal. He has no gifts of intuition or other supernormal mental qualities. He is just a highly intellectual man of great and varied knowledge with exceptionally acute reasoning powers and endowed with that invaluable asset, a scientific imagination (by a scientific imagination I mean that special faculty which marks the born investigator, the capacity to perceive the essential nature of a problem before the detailed evidence comes into sight). But he arrives at his conclusions by ordinary reasoning, which the reader can follow when he has been supplied with the facts, though the intricacy of the train of reasoning may at times call for an exposition at the end of the investigation.

Thorndyke has no eccentricities or oddities which might detract from the dignity of an eminent professional man, unless one excepts an unnatural liking for Trichinopoly cheroots. In manner he is quiet, reserved and self-contained, and rather markedly secretive, but of a kindly nature, though not sentimental, and addicted to occasional touches of dry humour. That is how Thorndyke appears to me.

As to his age. When he made his first bow to the reading public from the doorway of Number 4 King's Bench Walk he was between thirty-five and forty. As that was thirty years ago, he should now be over sixty-five. But he isn't. If I have to let him *grow old along with me* I need not saddle him with the infirmities of age, and I can (in his case) put the brake on the passing years. Probably he is not more than fifty after all!

Now a few words as to how Thorndyke goes to work. His methods are rather different from those of the detectives of the Sherlock Holmes school. They are more technical and more specialized. He is an investigator of crime but he is not a detective. The technique of Scotland Yard would be neither suitable nor possible to him. He is a medico-legal expert, and his methods are those of medico-legal science. In the investigation of a crime there are two entirely different methods of approach. One consists in the careful and laborious examination of a vast mass of small and commonplace detail: Inquiring into the movements of suspected and other persons, interrogating witnesses and checking their statements particularly as to times and places, tracing missing persons, and so forth – the aim being to accumulate a great body of circumstantial evidence which will ultimately disclose the solution of the problem. It is an admirable method, as the success of our police proves, and it is used with brilliant effect by at least one of our contemporary detective writers. But it is essentially a police method.

The other method consists in the search for some fact of high evidential value which can be demonstrated by physical methods and which constitutes conclusive proof of some important point. This method also is used by the police in suitable cases. Finger-prints are examples of this kind of evidence, and another instance is furnished by the Gutteridge murder. Here the microscopical examination of a cartridge-case proved conclusively that the murder had been committed with a particular revolver, a fact which incriminated the owner of that revolver and led to his conviction.

This is Thorndyke's procedure. It consists in the interrogation of things rather than persons, of the ascertainment of physical facts which can be made visible to eyes other than his own. And the facts which he seeks tend to be those which are apparent only to the trained eye of the medical practitioner.

I feel that I ought to say a few words about Thorndyke's two satellites, Jervis and Polton. As to the former, he is just the traditional narrator proper to this type of story. Some of my readers have complained that Dr. Jervis is rather slow in the uptake. But that is precisely his function. He is the expert misunderstander. His job is to observe and record all the facts, and to fail completely to perceive their significance. Thereby he gives the reader all the necessary information, and he affords Thorndyke the opportunity to expound its bearing on the case.

Polton is in a slightly different category. Although he is not drawn from any real person, he is associated in my mind with two actual individuals. One is a Mr. Pollard, who was the laboratory assistant in the hospital museum when I was a student, and who gave me many a valuable tip in matters of technique, and who, I hope, is still to the good. The other was a watch- and clock-maker of the name of Parsons – familiarly known as Uncle Parsons – who had premises in a basement near the Royal Exchange, and who was a man of boundless ingenuity and technical resource. Both of these I regard as collateral relatives, so to speak, of Nathaniel Polton. But his personality is not like either. His crinkly countenance is strictly his own copyright.

To return to Thorndyke, his rather technical methods have, for the purposes of fiction, advantages and disadvantages. The advantage is that his facts are demonstrably true, and often they are intrinsically interesting. The disadvantage is that they are frequently not matters of common knowledge, so that the reader may fail to recognize them or grasp their significance until they are explained. But this is the case with all classes of fiction. There is no type of character or story that can be made sympathetic and acceptable to every kind of reader. The personal equation affects the reading as well as the writing of a story.

R. Austin Freeman
(1862-1943)

5A King's Bench Walk
in the early 1900's when
Thorndyke was in practice

Dr. Thorndyke: In the Footsteps
of Sherlock Holmes
by David Marcum

When Sherlock Holmes began his practice as a "Consulting Detective", his ideas of scientific criminal investigations caused the London police to look upon him as a mere "theorist". He was perceived as an amateur to be tolerated, often with amusement – until, that is, his assistance was required. Then they were more than willing to come knocking upon his door, asking for whatever help that they could receive. And usually this help took the form of brilliant solutions to bizarre and otherwise insoluble problems.

Holmes espoused methods and ideas that were considered ludicrous in the late 1800's. For instance, his frustration knew no bounds when a crime scene was disturbed. Holmes realized that so much could be determined from the physical evidence – footprints, fibers, and spatters. The police were happy to trod into and disturb the evidence as if they were herds of field beasts, with the equivalent level of intelligence.

However, Holmes's methods, and the science behind catching criminals, eventually won out and became so important that it's hard to now imagine the world without them. Many of the exact same techniques and methods that he advocated are now standard practice. From being an amateur with unusual ideas, Holmes is now recognized around the world as The Great Detective. In 2002, Holmes received a posthumous Honorary Fellowship from the British Royal Society of Chemistry, based on the fact that he was beyond his time in using chemistry and chemical sciences as a means of solving crimes.

And before that, in 1985, Scotland Yard introduced *HOLMES* (*Home Office Large Major Enquiry System*), an elaborate computer system designed to process the masses of information collected and evaluated during a criminal investigation, in order to ensure that no vital clues are overlooked. This system, providing total compatibility and consistency between all the police forces of England, Scotland, Wales, and Northern Ireland, as well as the Royal Military Police, has since been upgraded by the improved *HOLMES 2* – and like the first version, there is absolutely no doubt as to who is being honored and memorialized for his work in dragging criminology out of the dark ages.

Many famous Great Detectives followed in Holmes's footsteps – Nero Wolfe and Ellery Queen, Hercule Poirot and Solar Pons – each with their own methods and techniques, but before they began their careers, and while Holmes was still in practice in Baker Street, another London consultant – Dr. John Thorndyke – opened his doors, using the scientific methods developed and perfected by Holmes and taking them to a whole new level of brilliance.

Meet Dr. Thorndyke

Dr. John Evelyn Thorndyke was born on July 4th, 1870. We don't know about where he was raised, or if he has any family. At no point will we be introduced to a more brilliant brother who sometimes *is* the British Government. He was educated at the medical school of St. Margaret's Hospital in London, and while there, he met fellow student Christopher Jervis. They became friends but, after completing school in 1895, they lost touch with one another. Over the next six years, Thorndyke remained at St. Margaret's, taking on various jobs, hanging "about the chemical and physical laboratories, the museum and *post mortem* room," and learning what he could. He obtained his M.D. and his Doctor of Sciences, and then was called to the bar in 1896.

He'd prepared himself with the hope of obtaining a position as a coroner, but he learned of the unexpected retirement of one of St. Margaret's lecturers in medical jurisprudence. He applied for the position and, rather to his own surprise, it was awarded to him. (He would continue to maintain his association with the hospital, going on to become the Medical Registrar, Pathologist, Curator of the Museum, and then Professor of Medical Jurisprudence, all while maintaining his own private consulting practice.

It was when Thorndyke was named lecturer that he obtained his chambers at 5A King's Bench Walk, in the Inner Temple, that amazing and historic area between Fleet Street and the River. Founded over eight-hundred years ago by the Knights Templar, it is one of the four Inns of Court, (along with the Middle Temple, Lincoln's Inn, and Gray's Inn.) The buildings along King's Bench Walk, and particularly No.'s 4, 5, and 6, have a great deal of historical significance – and not just because Dr. John Thorndyke practiced at 5A for a number of years.

Thorndyke was quite fortunate to obtain a suite of rooms on multiple floors at this location, which leads to speculation about his influence and resources – a question which has no answer. In any case, it was there that he opened his practice and began to wait for clients and cases. He also made the acquaintance of elderly Nathaniel Polton, that man-of-all-work with the crinkly smile who ran the household, as well as Thorndyke's upstairs laboratory.

Like Sherlock Holmes during those early years in the 1870's when he had rooms in Montague Street next to the British Museum and spent his vast amounts of free time learning his craft, Thorndyke also found a way to make the empty hours more useful. He had the unique idea of imagining increasingly complex crimes – often a murder or series of them, for instance – and then, when he had planned every single aspect of the crime, he would turn around and work out the solution from the other side. While doing this, he made extensive notes of each of these theoretical exercises, and retained them for their later usefulness when encountering real-life crimes.

His first legal case was *Regina v Gummer* in 1897. Sadly, no further information about this affair is ever revealed to us, but we may be certain that Thorndyke used his considerable skills to bring it to a satisfactory conclusion, adding to his reputation as he did so.

In the meantime, Jervis had a more unfortunate story. As his time at school ended, his funds ran out rather unexpectedly, and after paying his various fees, he was left with earning his living as a medical assistant, or sometimes serving as a *locum tenens*, moving from one low-paying and temporary job to another, with no prospects of improvement.

Jervis is unemployed on the morning of March 22nd, 1901 when he encounters Thorndyke a few doors up from 5A King's Bench Walk. The two friends are happy to see one another, and before long, Jervis is involved in an investigation that will change his life in several ways, as recounted in *The Red Thumb Mark*.

But it should not be assumed that every Thorndyke adventure is narrated by Jervis in a typical Watsonian manner. In fact, the very next book, *The Eye of Osiris*, is instead told from the perspective of one of Thorndyke's students, Dr. Paul Berkeley. It is one of several that provide a look at Thorndyke – and Jervis – from a different perspective. But Jervis returns as narrator in the third novel, *The Mystery of 31 New Inn*, and we see Thorndyke through his eyes for a good many of both the novels and short stories.

Here a word might be mentioned about the Chronology of the Thorndyke stories. For some this is an irrelevant factor, but for others – like me – understanding the correct chronological placement of the stories is very important. Like the volumes that make up the Sherlock Holmes Canon, the Thorndyke stories aren't published in chronological order – a case set in 1907 (such as "Percival Bland's Proxy") might be collected before one that occurs in 1908, ("The Missing Mortgagee"), or it might not. For instance, *The Red Thumb Mark* (1907) is set in March and April 1901. (This chronological placement, by the way, is determined by noticing that a specific date is given three times in the book – in the British fashion of day before month – *9.3.01* – or *March 9th, 1901*. The dates for the events of the rest of the book can be carefully worked out from this fixed point.)

The next book, *The Eye of Osiris* (1911) is primarily set in the summer of 1904 (with Chapter 1, something of a prologue, taking place in late 1902.) Then, the next book to follow, *The Mystery of 31 New Inn* (1912), jumps back to the spring of 1902, about a year after the events of *The Red Thumb Mark*, and before *The Eye of Osiris*. And one of the short stories, "The Man With the Nailed Shoes" occurs in September and October 1901, between the first two books. Clearly, there is a great deal of material for the chronologicist in the Thorndyke Chronicles.

As Jervis becomes a part of Thorndyke's world, following their reacquaintance in March 1901, he meets others in Thorndyke's circle, including policemen such as Superintendent Miller and Inspector Badger, lawyers like Robert Anstey, Marchmont, and Brodribb, and other physicians like Dr. Paul Berkeley and Dr. Humphrey Jardine. He also has more opportunity to learn from his friend as he begins his own studies in order to become a similar specialist in the medico-legal practice – although he'll never be another Thorndyke.

Through Jervis's eyes – as well as others along the way – we build up our knowledge of Dr. Thorndyke. In appearance, he is tall and athletic, just under six feet in height, slender, and weighing around one-hundred-and-eighty pounds. He is exceptionally handsome – and has been called the handsomest detective in literature. He has no vices, except – perhaps – that he enjoys a Trichinopoly cigar upon occasion when he is feeling especially triumphant – although there is one time when the criminal's knowledge of this fact leads to a clever attempt at Thorndyke's murder . . . .

There are several instances where Thorndyke displays a marked resemblance to Sherlock Holmes – and not just in his scientific approach to crime. The two men sometimes say similar things – such as when Holmes says "*It is quite a pretty little problem,*" (in "A Scandal in Bohemia") or ". . . *there are some pretty little problems among them*" (in "The Musgrave Ritual"). Thorndyke mimics this in *Felo de Se?* ("*There, Jervis," said he, "is quite a pretty little problem for you to excogitate*") or "*Ah, there is a very pretty little problem for you to consider*" (in *The Eye of Osiris*).

And who can forget the many instances when Holmes refers to *data*:

- *"It is a capital mistake to theorize before one has data. Insensibly one begins to twist facts to suit theories, instead of theories to suit facts."* – "A Scandal in Bohemia"
- *"I had,"* said he, *"come to an entirely erroneous conclusion which shows, my dear Watson, how dangerous it always is to reason from insufficient data."* – "The Speckled Band"
- *"No data yet,"* he answered. *"It is a capital mistake to theorize before you have all the evidence. It biases the judgment."* – *A Study in Scarlet*
- *"The temptation to form premature theories upon insufficient data is the bane of our profession."* – *The Valley of Fear*
- *"Still, it is an error to argue in front of your data."* – "Wisteria Lodge"

Thorndyke's version? *". . . believe me, it is a capital error to decide beforehand what data are to be sought for."* – from *The Mystery of 31 New Inn*. There are others.

Then there is Holmes's quote from "The Man With the Twisted Lip":

"You have a grand gift of silence, Watson," said he. *"It makes you quite invaluable as a companion."*

Here's the Thorndyke equivalent:

"It has just been borne in upon me, Jervis," said he, *"that you are the most companionable fellow in the world. You have the heaven-sent gift of silence."*

And then there is the time, in "The Anthropologist at Large", that a client – expecting a Holmes-like performance as based on "The Blue Carbuncle" – presents Thorndyke with an object for examination:

"I understand," said he, *"that by examining a hat it is possible to deduce from it, not only the bodily characteristics of the wearer, but also his mental and moral qualities, his state of health, his pecuniary position, his past history, and even his domestic relations and the peculiarities of his place of abode. Am I right in this supposition?"*
The ghost of a smile flitted across Thorndyke's face as he laid the hat upon the remains of the newspaper. "We must

11

not expect too much," he observed. "Hats, as you know, have a way of changing owners . . . ."

Another area of intersection between Holmes and Thorndyke is the assembly of information. Recall Holmes's *"ponderous commonplace books in which he placed his cuttings"* as mentioned in "The Engineer's Thumb". We find, also in "The Anthropologist at Large", that Thorndyke does the same thing:

> *[H]is method of dealing with [the morning newspaper] was characteristic. The paper was laid on the table after breakfast, together with a blue pencil and a pair of office shears. A preliminary glance through the sheets enabled him to mark with the pencil those paragraphs that were to be read, and these were presently cut out and looked through, after which they were either thrown away or set aside to be pasted in an indexed book.*

No doubt and examination of Thorndyke's lodgings at 5A King's Bench Walk would reveal – in addition to a series of indexed commonplace books filled with clippings – a number of other items and aspects that would remind one of 221b Baker Street.

Like many locations where the detective's residence is almost a character in and of itself – Sherlock Holmes's London address at 221 Baker Street, and the New York homes of Ellery Queen on West 87th Street and Nero Wolfe's Brownstone on West 35th Street – Thorndyke's rooms at 5A King's Bench Walk are a living and vibrant place – from the entry way, where a heavy door known as "The Oak" leads visitors into a most comfortable wood-paneled sitting room, located on the (British) first floor, one flight up from the ground floor. On the next floor up, Polton has his laboratory and workshop, containing everything that is needed (or what might be manufactured) in order to solve the case.

On the next floor, underneath the attic, are bedrooms belonging to Thorndyke, Jervis, and Polton. Even after Jervis has married – and now you know that he does get married! – he continues to reside a good deal of the time in King's Bench Walk. As he explains in *When Rogues Fall Out* (1932, with the U.S. title of *Dr. Thorndyke's Discovery*):

> *Here, perhaps, since my records of Thorndyke's practice have contained so little reference to my own personal affairs, I should say a few words concerning my domestic habits. As the circumstances of our practice often made it*

12

desirable for me to stay late at our chambers, I had retained there the bedroom that I had occupied before my marriage; and, as these circumstances could not always be foreseen, I had arranged with my wife the simple rule that the house closed at eleven o'clock. If I was unable to get home by that time, it was to be understood that I was staying at the Temple. It may sound like a rather undomestic arrangement, but it worked quite smoothly, and it was not without its advantages. For the brief absence gave to my homecomings a certain festive quality, and helped to keep alive the romantic element in my married life. It is possible for the most devoted husbands and wives to see too much of one another.

Thorndyke's Other Appearances

Through the years, Thorndyke's reputation continues to grow, as presented through a number of adventures. Surprisingly, in light of the tens of thousands of Post-Canonical Sherlock Holmes that have come to light over the years, as discovered by latter-day Literary Agents taking over Watson's first Literary Agent, Sir Arthur Conan Doyle, stopped literary-agenting, there have been almost no additional Thorndyke cases brought to the public's attention. The few exceptions to this statement are *Goodbye, Dr. Thorndyke* (1972) by Norman Donaldson, and *Dr. Thorndyke's Dilemma* (1974) by John H. Dirckx. Both narratives deal with Thorndyke and Jervis in their latter years, and each is written by an expert in the field of Thorndyke scholarship.

Donaldson also wrote what might be the final scholarly word on the subject, *In Search of Dr. Thorndyke* (1971). In fact, he had intended his pastiche, *Goodbye, Dr. Thorndyke*, to be published as the conclusion to this book, but it ended up appearing separately.

To my knowledge, "The Great Fathomer", as Thorndyke is sometimes known, has rarely appeared in other locations. He is mentioned in the Solar Pons tale "The Adventure of the Proper Comma" by August Derleth, which finds Dr. Parker returning "from Thorndyke & Polton with an analysis of the capsules Mrs. Buxton had carried with her . . . ."

In my own book of authorized Solar Pons stories, *The Papers of Solar Pons* (2017), Thorndyke makes two appearances. "The Adventure of the Additional Heirs" has Pons and Parker visiting King's Bench Walk:

13

>*At 5A, we learned that our friend Thorndyke, the medical juris-practitioner, was out on some investigation or other, but Pons handed the papers, sans photograph, into the care of Polton, his crinkly-faced laboratory technician, with a detailed explanation of what he wished to learn. The man nodded and smiled, and without any extraneous chit-chat, shut the door, freeing us to return to Fleet Street. We paused at the edge of the walk to look at the photograph, still in Pons's hand.*

Later Thorndyke sends Pons a detailed report that helps toward the solution of the problem. And in "The Affair of the Distasteful Society", set in July 1921, Pons and Parker attend the first meeting of a group gathered to honor Sherlock Holmes, where the following conversation occurs:

>*"I see that you invited Thorndyke, and that little Belgian over on Farraway Street," said Rath.*
>*"And Sexton Blake as well," replied Sir Amory.*
>*"Sexton Blake is a fictional character, Sir Amory," said Pons with a smile.*

In my story, "The Adventure of the Two Sisters", included in *The New Adventures of Solar Pons*, Dr. Parker writes:

>*Pons was not the only detective who offered his services to the London populace, although he might have been the most well-known. We were friends with several others, including the former Belgian policeman who lived in Farraway Street, and another rather mysterious fellow in nearby Bottle Street. And of course, Pons went way back with Thorndyke, whose chambers were across town. It wasn't unusual for Pons and the others to regularly confer on investigations, or simply to sit down and share a few drinks and professional anecdotes.*

Thorndyke doesn't just appear in some of my Solar Pons adventures. He's also been referenced off-stage in a couple of Sherlock Holmes adventures that I've pulled from Watson's Tin Dispatch Box – and it's more than likely that others will follow. In "The "London Wheel", contained in *The MX Book of New Sherlock Holmes Stories* –

Part IV: 2016 Annual (2016), Holmes, looking through some documents, states:

> *"I believe," said Holmes, "that I have enough amateur legal training that I can get a sense of the implications of the clauses in question in both of these documents." He pulled the folded pages from his pocket. "I thought about sending a message to my* protégé *Thorndyke in King's Bench Walk for his opinion, as he could have been here very quickly, should he be at home at all and not out on his own business. However, I don't believe that will be necessary.*

Perhaps it is a point of interest that Thorndyke is referred to Holmes's protégé. Possibly more information will be forthcoming, such as that which is hinted in my story, "The Coombs Contrivance" (in *The Irregular Adventures of Sherlock Holmes!*). Set in 1889, when Thorndyke was nineteen years old, Holmes and Watson are discussing a precocious Baker Street Irregular:

> *[Holmes] pinched the bridge of his nose. "Do you trust Levi's judgment, Watson?"*
> *I considered. "For an eight-year-old, he's remarkably perceptive – as much as any of the other Irregulars who have assisted you. The Wiggins family, or the Peakes, or Thorndyke, before he went away to university."*

So was Thorndyke, perhaps, a gifted Irregular who learned from The Master, and then went on to create his own successful practice, taking what he learned to a next very successful level? Possibly. In my forthcoming story "The Inner Temple Intruder", to be found in a volume of Great Detective cross-overs, such an origin story is posited. As Robert Downey, Jr. succinctly stated when playing Holmes in 2009's *Sherlock Holmes*: "Food for thought!"

Thorndyke is also mentioned in Bob Byrne's Holmes story, "The Adventure of the Parson's Son" (*The MX Book of New Sherlock Holmes Stories – Part III: 1896-1929*), wherein Holmes, examining a piece of evidence, cries:

> *"Ha! I believe we have discredited the coat entirely. Though I wish I could get Thorndyke to examine it. Would that we were back in London."*

And it isn't just Thorndyke who has appeared elsewhere. His lawyer friend Marchmont has assisted Holmes and Watson in a small way a couple of my own "The Coombs Contrivance" and the forthcoming adventure *Sherlock Holmes and The Eye of Heka.*

Although I have encouraged these Thorndyke cameos in my own stories or in Holmes and Pons books that I edit, his appearances elsewhere are much more fleeting. In the 2015 BBC radio series *The Rivals*, Inspector Lestrade, Holmes's most frequent associate at Scotland Yard, is placed into the events of the Thorndyke short story "The Moabite Cipher". And Thorndyke has only had a handful of other media appearances. In 1964, the BBC produced seven episodes (now lost) of *Thorndyke*, starring Peter Copley. The episodes were:

- "The Case of Oscar Brodski'
- "The Old Lag"
- "A Case of Premeditation"
- "The Mysterious Visitor"
- "The Case of Phyllis Annesley" – Adapted from "Phyllis Annesley's Peril"
- "Percival Bland's Brother" – Adapted from "Percival Bland's Proxy"
- "The Puzzle Lock"

From 1971 to 1973, Thames TV aired *The Rivals of Sherlock Holmes*, and two stories were adapted: "A Message from the Deep Sea" starring John Neville (who had also played Holmes in 1965's *A Study in Terror*), and "The Moabite Cipher" starring Barrie Ingram. Except for a 1963 BBC Radio adaption of *Mr. Pottermack's Oversight*, and a few on-air readings by a single performer, there have been no other Thorndyke adaptations – which is a terrible shame, as the stories certainly lend themselves to visual and audible interpretations. Perhaps a new generation will discover Thorndyke, Jervis, and the rest, and they will find popularity once again, as they did more than a century ago.

Copley, Neville, and Ingram as Thorndyke

A Few (Hundred) Words About R. Austin Freeman
Thorndyke's Chronicler

Richard Austin Freeman was born on April 11, 1862 in the Soho district of London. He was the son of a skilled tailor and the youngest of five children. As he grew, it was expected that he would become a tailor as well, but instead he had an interest in natural history and medicine, and so he obtained employment in a pharmacist's shop. While there, he qualified as an apothecary and could have gone on to manage the shop, but instead he began to study medicine at Middlesex Hospital.

Austin Freeman qualified as a physician in 1887, and in that same year he married. Faced with the twin facts of his new marital responsibilities and his very limited resources as a young doctor, he made the unusual decision to join the Colonial Service, spending the next seven years in Africa as an Assistant Colonial Surgeon. This continued until the early 1890's, when he contracted Blackwater Fever, an illness that eventually forced him to leave the service and return permanently to England.

For several years, he served as a *locum tenens* for various physicians, a bleak time in his life as he moved from job to job, his income low, and his health never quite recovered. (These experiences were reflected in the narratives of Doctors Jervis and Berkeley.) However, he supplemented his meager income and exercised his creativity during these years by beginning to write. His early publications included *Travels and Live in Ashanti and Jaman* (1898), recounting some of his African sojourns.

In 1900, Freeman obtained work as an assistant to Dr. John James Pitcairn (1860-1936) at Holloway Prison. Although he wasn't there for very long, the association between the two men was enough to turn Freeman's attention toward writing mysteries. Over the next few years, they co-wrote several under the pseudonym *Clifford Ashdown*, including *The Adventures of Romney Pringle* (1902), *The Further Adventures of Romney Pringle* (1903), *From a Surgeon's Diary* (1904-1905), and *The Queen's Treasure* (written around 1905-1906, and published posthumously in 1975.) The specifics of the two men's writing arrangement are unknown to the present day, although much research was carried out by Freeman scholar Percival Mason ("P.M.") Stone, who was actually able to confirm Pitcairn's involvement and influence. Following this association, which apparently helped to train Freeman to be a better writer and to focus on a recurring character, his luck changed,

17

and he was able, within just a few years, to abandon the practice of medicine, which had never been successful, and become a professional author.

In approximately 1904, Freeman began developing a mystery novella based on a short job that he had held at the Western Ophthalmic Hospital. This effort, "31 New Inn", was published in 1905, and it is the true first Dr. Thorndyke story. In it, we meet narrator Dr. Christopher Jervis, working as a *locum tenens*, moving from practice to practice in the same bleak existence that Freeman had experienced. Jervis becomes involved with a patient that may or may not be in danger. Unsure what to do, he recalls his former classmate, the brilliant Dr. John Thorndyke.

Curiously, this novella, (included in Volume II of this newly reissued collection *The Complete Dr. Thorndyke*), has numerous references to the events of the first Thorndyke novel, *The Red Thumb Mark*, which would not be published until 1907. Much of Freeman's life is obscure and unknown, including his writing processes and milestones, but clearly, with so much already clearly defined in this novella about Thorndyke and Jervis, he had firmly established not only fixed aspects of their histories, but the plot of *The Red Thumb Mark* as well, several years before the book's publication. One wonders why he chose to first publish "31 New Inn", since it occurs chronologically a whole year *after* the events of *The Red Thumb Mark*.

Interestingly – at least to a chronologicist such as myself – the original novella of "31 New Inn" is specifically set in April 1900, as indicated internally. However, when it was later revised to become the third Thorndyke novel, *The Mystery of 31 New Inn*, (1912, and included in Volume I of *The Complete Dr. Thorndyke*), the narrative's date is changed to 1902 – which fits, since the events definitely occur after *The Red Thumb Mark*, which takes place in March and April 1901.

Like Rex Stout's Nero Wolfe, who seemed to have sprung fully formed from his creator's brow, Thorndyke and his world are well-defined and immediately real. Although certain characters are added to the circle through the years, the basic layout – with Thorndyke, Jervis, and Polton (the man-of-all-work crinkly-smiled assistant) are always at 5A, ready to spring into action when Jervis – or one of the other varied narrators who show up throughout the series – arrive with a curious problem.

Freeman had found his voice with the Thorndyke books and short stories, and he was able to make use of his lifelong interest in medicine and natural science – often conducting extensive experiments to work out exactly how the solutions in his stories could be discovered. And in Thorndyke's early days, Freeman was able to turn the literary form inside out with the creation of the "Inverted Mystery Story", wherein the criminal is known from the beginning – the motive is explained, the planning and execution of the crime are observed, and the miscreant is left to believe that all is well and that he'll never be caught. And then, in the second part of the story, Thorndyke enters to inexorably follow the trail that is completely invisible to everyone else, scraping away, layer by layer and point by point, until the truth is inevitably revealed.

As Freeman explained:

> *Some years ago I devised, as an experiment, an inverted detective story in two parts. The first part was a minute and detailed description of a crime, setting forth the antecedents, motives, and all attendant circumstances. The reader had seen the crime committed, knew all about the criminal, and was in possession of all the facts. It would have seemed that there was nothing left to tell. But I calculated that the reader would be so occupied with the crime that he would overlook the evidence. And so it turned out. The second part, which described the investigation of the crime, had to most readers the effect of new matter.*

This format went on to be used by a great many authors through the years. For example several of the Lord Peter Wimsey narratives come close to being this type of story, and television's *Columbo* used this type of story-telling as its basis.

While these volumes are an attempt to reintroduce the modern reader to Thorndyke, and are a celebration of him and his world, it must be discussed at some point that Freeman held views that are unacceptable. Unlike Sir Arthur Conan Doyle, who spent his last decades championing spiritualism but never allowed it to creep into the Sherlock Holmes stories, Freeman sometimes did let his own prejudices make their way into the Thorndyke tales. In his book *Social Decay and Regeneration* (1921), he expressed his rather nationalistic view that England had become an "homogenized, restless, unionized working class". Worse, he inexcusably and detestably supported the eugenics movement, arguing that people with "undesirable" traits should not be allowed to reproduce by means such as "segregation, marriage restriction, and sterilization". He referred to immigrants as "Sub-Man", and argued that society needed to be protected from "degenerates of the destructive type."

Some have attempted to excuse his beliefs as being a product of his times. For instance, it has been written that he had a distrust of Jews because of the competition that his father, a tailor, had faced when Freeman was a boy. Later, he served in the Colonial Service in Africa during some of the worst years in terms of treatment of natives by the British, and as an older man, he existed in the Great Britain between the two wars when great upheavals disrupted much of what he had known and expected.

Sadly, there are occasional racial stereotypes and references in the Thorndyke books. As I explain in the *Editor's Caveat*, some of these stereotypes had to be unfortunately maintained within the story in order to accurately reflect the plot and the characters of those times. However, there are some words or phrases that were used in the original stories – vile racial epithets that have no business being repeated or perpetuated anywhere – that I have cheerfully and happily removed. (There weren't many of them, but any are too many.)

These books are intended to bring Dr. Thorndyke and his adventures to a new generation – and not to be an untouchable and sacred literary artifact, with every nasty stain preserved and archived for the historical record. As I warn in the *Caveat*, if readers find that they want to experience the original versions as they were first written, with those hateful words included, then they would be advised to go and seek out the original books, because you won't find that filth here. These versions celebrate Dr. Thorndyke and Dr. Jervis – who do not use the awful stereotyped language, I'm glad to say! – and as such, I felt no need whatsoever to include and perpetuate the objectionable and offensive material

From Thorndyke's creation until 1914, Freeman wrote four novels and two volumes of short stories. Then, with the commencement of the First World War, he entered military service. In February 1915, at the age of fifty-two, he joined the Royal Army Medical Corps. Due to his health, which had never entirely recovered from his time in Africa, he spent the duration of the war involved with various aspects of the ambulance corps, having been promoted very early to the rank of Captain. He wrote nothing about Thorndyke during this period, but he did publish one book concerning the adventures of a scoundrel, *The Exploits of Danby Croker* (1916).

Following the war, he resumed his previous life, writing approximately one Thorndyke novel per year, as well as three more volumes of Thorndyke short stories and a number of other unrelated items, until his death on September 28th, 1943 – likely related to Parkinson's Disease, which had plagued him in later years.

Upon learning the news, *Chicago Tribune* columnist Vincent Starrett wrote:

> *When all the bright young things have performed their appointed task of flatting the complexes of neurotic semi-literates, and have gone their way to oblivion, the best of the Thorndyke stories will live on – minor classics on the shelf that holds the good books the world.*

Raymond Chandler wrote in his famous essay, which initially appeared in a couple of magazines and then was published in the book of the same name, *The Simple Art of Murder* (1950):

> *This man Austin Freeman is a wonderful performer. He has no equal in his genre, and he is also a much better writer than you might think, if you were superficially inclined, because in spite of the immense leisure of his writing, he accomplishes an even suspense which is quite unexpected . . . There is even a gaslight charm about his Victorian love affairs, and those wonderful walks across London.*

In the introduction to *Great Stories of Detection, Mystery, and Horror* (1928), Dorothy L. Sayers, Chronicler of Lord Peter Wimsey, stated:

> *Thorndyke will cheerfully show you all the facts. You will be none the wiser . . . .*

Discovering Dr. Thorndyke

I first encountered Dr. Thorndyke in a rather backwards way – in passing only – and it took several decades to correct that mistake. In approximately 1980, my dad gave me Otto Penzler's *The Private Lives of Private Eyes, Spies, Crime Fighters, and Other Good Guys* (1977). This wonderful oversized book has biographies of twenty-five well-known heroes, along with lists of the original books featuring each one.

My dad bought it for me because it had a chapter about Sherlock Holmes. There were a few others in there that I recognized or had already read about– Ellery Queen and Perry Mason – and soon I would become fanatical about a few more – Nero Wolfe and Hercule Poirot.

21

Over the next few years I would also find the chapters on James Bond and Lew Archer indispensable, and later than that I would come to appreciate the entries about Philip Marlowe, Sam Spade, Miss Marple, Philo Vance, and Lord Peter Wimsey. But there were a few that, to this day, I've never bothered to read – such as Modesty Blaise or Mr. Moto – and a few others that I skimmed but otherwise ignored. And one of these was the biography of Dr. Thorndyke.

That fact was easily understandable, as throughout the entire time that I was growing up in eastern Tennessee – and in the years since as well – I've never come across a Thorndyke book for sale here in the wild, either in a new bookstore or in a used one. If I'd found one, I might have bought and read it, liked it, and then sought out others. Instead, I was bound to discover Thorndyke by way of Sherlock Holmes.

I've been collecting traditional Sherlock Holmes pastiches since the same time that I discovered the Sherlockian Canon, when I was ten years old in 1975. Since that time, I've collected, read, and chronologicized literally thousands of them. It never gets old, and I'm constantly looking for more – and that means checking Amazon to see what new releases are on the horizon.

In 2012, someone – and I've never determined who – began releasing a variety of Holmes stories for Kindle under the author name *Dr. John H. Watson.* This wasn't too unusual – there have been a number of pastiches that officially list Watson as the author, rather than putting the editor of Watson's papers first. Of course, after determining that these latest entries weren't going to be available as real books, I bought the e-versions, and then printed them on real paper. (I cannot stand e-books – ephemeral electronic blips that you lease instead of buy. I'll only buy those titles if they aren't going to be released as legitimate books – and in this case, it's a good thing that I did, as each of these Kindle stories that I found and paid for were soon withdrawn.)

As I read these latest "Holmes" stories, I noticed that each had a definite style that captured the writing from the late 1800's or early 1900's. (No matter how modern pasticheurs try to achieve that, they never quite pull it off.) But in one of the first two or three titles that I read, I caught a couple of mistakes. In one story, Holmes and Watson leave 221 Baker Street and are immediately in the area around The Temple and Fleet Street, rather than in Marylebone, where Baker Street is properly located. On another occasion, the story's policeman – who had been identified up to that point as Inspector Lestrade – was inexplicably named *Superintendent Miller* – but only in one instance. And in another place in one of the stories, Holmes's address was stated to be *5A King's Bench Walk.*

It was then that some vague memory triggered in my head, and I realized why these stories had captured the style of the late Victorian and early Edwardian eras: *It was because they had actually been written then*. I recalled – from reading Otto Penzler's book of biographies so long ago - that 5A King's Bench Walk belonged to Dr. Thorndyke, and not Sherlock Holmes. Someone was taking the original Thorndyke stories, which I had never before read, and simply changing names: Dr. Thorndyke, Dr. Jervis, and Superintendent Miller became Sherlock Holmes, Dr. Watson, and Inspector Lestrade, respectively.

Between 2012 and 2014, the anonymous author continued to load new Kindle editions on Amazon of Thorndyke-converted to-Holmes stories, and I continued to buy them. As soon as I had one, I would read it, and then try to figure out the original Thorndyke story from which it was taken. When I'd done so, I'd post a review, identifying what this editor was doing, from where he or she was taking the story, and urging that person, whoever it was, give credit to R. Austin Freeman instead of listing the author as Dr. John H. Watson.

Soon after each of my reviews would appear, the story would be withdrawn. I don't know if it was because the editor had made enough money from the initial sales, or if my reviews alerted him or her that they're game had been uncovered. In any case, I still have the printed copies of each of these converted stories – possibly the only copies that are still in existence.

For the record, over that two year period, this editor produced sixteen converted tales – four of the original Thorndyke novels, and twelve short stories. One of the original short stories, "The Mandarin's Pearl", was converted twice, with slight variations – initially published as "The Dragon Pearl", withdrawn, and later revised and reloaded as "The Oriental Pearl":

- "The Bloodied Thumbprint" – Originally the first Thorndyke novel, *The Red Thumb Mark*;
- "The Eye of Ra" – Originally the second Thorndyke novel, *The Eye of Osiris*;
- "The Cat's Eye Mystery" – Originally the sixth Thorndyke novel, *The Cat's Eye*;
- "The Julius Dalton Mystery" – Originally the ninth Thorndyke novel, *The D'Arblay Mystery*;
- "The Green Jacket Mystery" – Originally "The Green Check Jacket";
- "Mr. Crofton's Disappearance" – Originally "The Mysterious Visitor";

- "The Coded Lock" – Originally "The Puzzle Lock";
- "The Duplicated Letter" – Originally "The Stalking Horse";
- "The Bullion Robbery" – Originally "The Stolen Ingots";
- "The Talking Corpse" – Originally "The Contents of a Mare's Nest";
- "The Blue Diamond Mystery" – Originally "The Fisher of Men";
- "The Dragon Pearl" – Originally "The Mandarin's Pearl". (This story was also reworked and published again as a Holmes story under the title "The Oriental Pearl");
- "The Ingenious Murder" – Originally "The Aluminium Dagger";
- "The Bloodhound Superstition" – Originally "The Singing Bone"; *and*
- "The Magic Box" – Originally "The Magic Casket".

For quite a while, I was happy to have these as Holmes stories, and I even considered converting the rest of the Thorndyke adventures into additions to the extended Holmes Canon as well. (For at that time I cared nothing for Dr. Thorndyke.) It was partly with these converted stories in mind that I was motivated to go ahead and publish *Sherlock Holmes in Montague Street* (2014, 2016), which did the same thing to the Martin Hewitt stories, making them early adventures of Holmes before he met Watson and moved to Baker Street. I had long before decided to my own satisfaction that Martin Hewitt *was* a young Sherlock Holmes, with his identity changed through the preparations of a different literary agent than Sir Arthur Conan Doyle.

The taking of old public-domain stories featuring other detectives as the main protagonists and switching them so that Holmes is the main character has also been done by Alan Lance Andersen for his collection *The Affairs of Sherlock Holmes* (2015, 2016), wherein various non-series Sax Rohmer stories from nearly a hundred years ago were reworked as Holmes tales. Other non-Holmes authors have sometimes done the same thing. Raymond Chandler revised some of his early short stories so that the original characters' names were changed to Philip Marlowe. Ross MacDonald – (Kenneth Millar) also rewrote his old stories as well, making them into Lew Archer cases instead. More recently, the British ITV series *Marple* has taken non-Miss Marple Agatha Christie stories and converted them into episodes featuring that character.

So I had no problems with this type of change – and still don't. In fact, in my foreword to *Sherlock Holmes of Montague Street*, I wrote that I would rather have these converted Thorndyke stories as Holmes adventures, because I would rather read about Holmes than Thorndyke. But gradually my mind began to change, and I became more curious about Thorndyke, as presented in the proper fashion.

In 2013, I was able to go to London, as well as other places in England and Scotland, on the first (of three so far) Holmes Pilgrimages. For the most part, if a location wasn't related to Holmes, I didn't visit it. There were a few exceptions – I did intentionally visit Solar Pons's house at 7B Praed Street, Hercule Poirot's two residences, James Bond's flat in Chelsea – but everything else was pretty much pure Holmes.

One day, during my Holmesian rambles, I was making my way east down Fleet Street, and I visited both of the possible locations of "Pope's Court" (as featured in "The Red-Headed League"), Poppin's Court and Mitre Court. (The latter is also one of the locations where Denis Nayland Smith and Dr. Petrie had quarters in some of the Fu Manchu books.) I decided that Mitre Court was certainly the original of "Pope's Court", and I passed through it to find myself unexpectedly in The Temple.

That's the amazing thing about a Holmes Pilgrimage to London – one travels to a site and finds two more very close by. I had planned to visit The Temple, but hadn't realized that I was so close. And now here I was – and more interesting was the fact that I was walking along King's Bench Walk, which runs downhill from the Miter Court passage. I recalled that Thorndyke had lived at 5A, so I made my way there – but without too much awe on that day, because I hadn't actually read any Thorndyke adventures yet – just some converted Holmes stories.

After I returned home, the thought of that side-trip to Thorndyke's front door stuck in my mind, and I sought out and read the first novel in the series, *The Red Thumb Mark*. I was so impressed that I kept going, and discovered a wonderful series of books and stories – fascinating characters and mysteries, and very evocative descriptions of both the London and the countryside of those times.

When I returned on my second Holmes Pilgrimage in 2015, I took the second Thorndyke book with me, reading it while there – while also reading Holmes stories too, of course! This one, *The Eye of Osiris*, has a great deal of London atmosphere, and I spent part of one late afternoon tracking down locations in this book – or what's now left of them – in the area around Fetter Lane to the north of Thorndyke's home in The Temple. It was truly unforgettable.

And of course I made an intentional stop at King's Bench Walk on that 2015 trip, and again on Holmes Pilgrimage No. 3 in 2016. By that point I was a Thorndyke fan, and I took the trouble to write to the current occupiers of 5A before I traveled to see if I could step inside and perhaps spend a moment in Thorndyke's old quarters. Sadly, they did not respond – either because it was simply beneath them to do so, or possibly because they get too many people like me who want to make a literary pilgrimage to what is a functioning and thriving business location.

While making photographs at Thorndyke's old doorway, I had several chances to go inside when someone else would enter or leave – My ever-present deerstalker and I could have simply been bold enough to slip in and then talk my way onward. It worked at other places on my Holmes Pilgrimages – the laboratory at Barts where Holmes and Watson met, for instance, and the site of the (former?) Diogenes Club at No. 78 Pall Mall, where they acted just oddly enough to make me think that the club is still there. But for some reason, barging into Thorndyke's old chambers without proper permission didn't feel quite right. But if or when I make Holmes Pilgrimage No. 4, I'll definitely make an even greater effort to see the doctor's former rooms.

The Editor and his deerstalker at 5A King's Bench Walk
September 2016

With many thanks . . . .

These last few years have been an amazing ride, and I've been able to play in the Sherlockian sandbox more than I'd ever imagined. (And subsequently, the Solar Pons sandbox, and now Thorndyke, too! Along the way, I've been able to meet some incredible people, both in person and in the modern electronic way, and also I've been able to read several hundred new Holmes adventures, as well as to be able to share them with others.

Still, what is most important is my amazingly wonderful wife (of over thirty years!) Rebecca, and our truly awesome son and my friend, Dan. I love you both, and you are everything to me! I am the luckiest guy in the world.

I have all the gratitude in the world for everyone that I've encountered along the way – It's an undeniable fact that Sherlock Holmes authors are the *best* people! I'd like to thank those who offer support, encouragement, and friendship, sometimes patiently waiting on me to reply as my time is directed in many other directions. Many many thanks to (in alphabetical order): Brian Belanger, Derrick Belanger, Bob Byrne, Roger Johnson, Mark Mower, Denis Smith, Tom Turley, Dan Victor, and Marcia Wilson.

In particular, I'd also like to especially thank Steve Emecz, who is always supportive of every idea that I pitch. It's been my particular good fortune that he crossed my path – it changed my life in a way that would have never happened otherwise, and I'm grateful for every opportunity!

I hope that these books will provide pleasure to those discovering Dr. Thorndyke for the first time, and to others who have known him for a long time. As always, I approach these matters from a Sherlockian perspective, so of course these stories, to me, are a peripheral extension of Holmes's world, and as such they are just more tiny threads woven into the ongoing Great Holmes Tapestry. However, they are wonderful on their own, and however one reads them, I wish great joy upon the journey.

David Marcum
(Revised October 2019)

Questions, comments, and story submissions
may be addressed to David Marcum at
thepapersofsherlockholmes@gmail.com

5A King's Bench Walk
in the late 1890's when
Thorndyke was in residence

Editor's *Caveat*

These stories have been prepared using modern text-converting software, and as such, occasional deviations in punctuation have occurred. Those who absolutely must have the original version, down to each jot and dash, should understand that this version was created in order to present Dr. Thorndyke's adventures to a modern audience, and not to preserve an absolute pristine model for the historical archives.

Similarly, these stories were written in a time when racial prejudice and stereotypes were much more common than today. While some of these stereotypes must be unfortunately maintained within the story in order to accurately reflect the plot and the characters of those times, there are some words that were used in the original stories – vile racial epithets that have no business being repeated or perpetuated anywhere – that I have cheerfully removed. (There weren't many of them, but *any* are *too many*.)

If readers find that they want to experience the original versions as they were first written, with those hateful and ignorant words included, then they would be advised to seek out the original books. These versions celebrate Dr. Thorndyke and Dr. Jervis – who do *not* use the awful stereotyped language, I'm glad to say! – and as such, I felt no need whatsoever to include objectionable and offensive material simply for the sake of honoring or archiving the historical record.

David Marcum
Editor

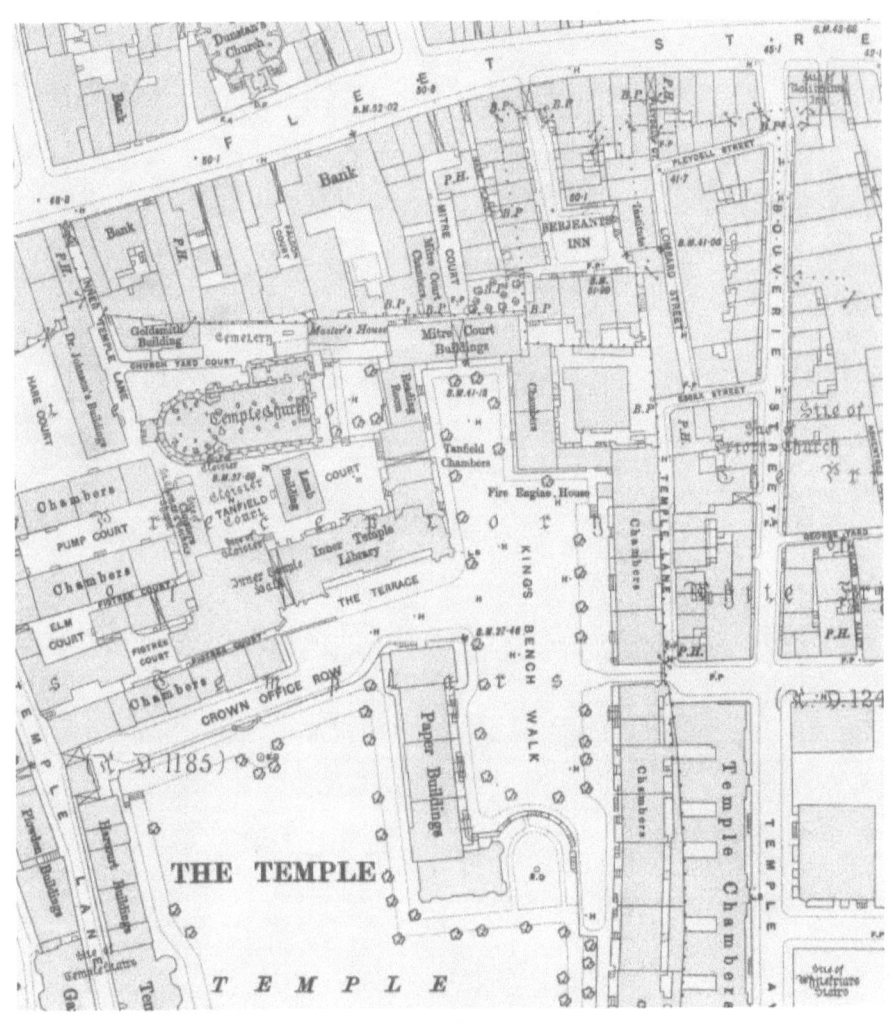

King's Bench Walk and the Temple, London
around 1900

1924 Hodder & Stoughton Cover

Chapter I
The Doper's Wife

It takes a good deal to surprise a really seasoned medical practitioner, and still more to arouse in him an abiding curiosity. But at the time when I took charge of Dr. Humphrey's practice in Osnaburgh Street, Regent's Park, I was far from being a seasoned practitioner, having, in fact, been qualified little more than a year, in which short period I had not yet developed the professional immunity from either of the above mental states. Hence the singular experience which I am about to relate not only made a deep impression on me at the time, but remained with me for long after as a matter of curious speculation.

It was close upon midnight – indeed an adjacent church clock had already struck the third quarter – when I laid aside my book and yawned profoundly, without prejudice to the author who had kept me so long from my bed. Then I rose and stretched myself, and was in the act of knocking the long-extinct ashes out of my pipe when the bell rang. As the servants had gone to bed, I went out to the door, congratulating myself on having stayed up beyond my usual bedtime, but wishing the visitor at the devil all the same. The opening of the door gave me a view of a wet street with a drizzle of rain falling, a large closed car by the kerb, and a tallish man on the doorstep, apparently about to renew his attack on the bell.

"Dr. Pumphrey?" he asked, and by that token I gathered that he was a stranger.

"No," I answered, "he is out of town, but I am looking after his practice."

"Very well," he said, somewhat brusquely. "I want you to come and see a lady who has been suddenly taken ill. She has had a rather severe shock."

"Do you mean a mental or a physical shock?" I asked.

"Well, I should say mental," he replied, but so inconclusively that I pressed him for more definite particulars.

"Has she sustained any injuries?" I inquired.

"No," he answered, but still indecisively. "No, that is, so far as I know. I think not."

"No wound, for instance?"

"No," he replied, promptly and very definitely, from which I was disposed to suspect that there was an injury of some other kind. But it

37

was of no use guessing. I hurried back into the surgery and, having snatched up the emergency bag and my stethoscope, rejoined my visitor, who forthwith hustled me into the car. The door slammed, and the vehicle moved off with the silent, easy motion of a powerful engine.

We started towards Marylebone Road and swept round into Albany Street, but after that I lost my bearings, for the fine rain had settled on the windows so that it was difficult to see through them, and I was not very familiar with the neighbourhood. It seemed quite a short journey, but a big car is very deceptive as to distance. At any rate, it occupied but a few minutes, and during that time my companion and I exchanged hardly a word. As the car slowed down I asked, "What is this lady's name?"

"Her name," he replied, in a somewhat hesitating manner, "is – She is a Mrs. Johnson."

The manner of the reply suggested a not very intimate acquaintance, which seemed odd under the circumstances, and I reflected on it rapidly as I got out of the car and followed my conductor. We seemed to be in a quiet bystreet of the better class, but it was very dark, and I had but a glimpse as I stepped from the car to the gate of the house. Of the latter, all that I was able to note was that it appeared to be of a decent, rather old-fashioned type, standing behind a small front garden, that the windows were fitted with jalousie shutters, and that the number on the door was *43*.

As we ascended the steps the door opened, and a woman was dimly discernible behind it. A lighted candle was on the hall table, and this my conductor picked up, requesting me to follow him up the stairs. When we arrived at the first floor landing, he halted and indicated a door which was slightly ajar.

"That is the room," said he, and with that he turned and retired down the stairs.

I stood for a few moments on the dark landing, deeply impressed by the oddity of the whole affair, and sensible of a growing suspicion which was not lessened when, by the thin line of light from within the room, I observed on the door-jamb one or two bruises, as if the door had been forced from without. However, this was none of my business, and thus reflecting, I was about to knock at the door when four fingers appeared round the edge of it and drew it further open, and a man's head became visible in the opening.

The fingers and the head were alike such as instantly to rivet the attention of a doctor. The former were of the kind known as "clubbed fingers", fingers with bulbous ends, of which the nails curved over like nut-shells. The head, in form like a great William pear, presented a long, coffin-shaped face with high cheek-bones, deep-set eyes with narrow, slanting eye-slits, and a lofty, square forehead surmounted by a most singular mop of mouse-coloured hair which stood straight up like the fur of a mole.

"I am the doctor," said I, having taken in these particulars in an instantaneous glance, and having further noted that the man's eyes were reddened and wet. He made no reply, but drew the door open and retired, whereupon I entered the room, closing the door behind me, and thereby becoming aware that there was something amiss with the latch.

The room was a bedroom, and on the bed lay a woman, fully clothed, and apparently in evening dress, though the upper part of her person was concealed by a cloak which was drawn up to her chin. She was a young woman – about twenty-eight, I judged – comely and, in fact, rather handsome, but deadly pale. She was not, however, unconscious, for she looked at me listlessly, though with a certain attention. In some slight embarrassment, I approached the bed and, as the man had subsided into a chair in a corner of the room, I addressed myself to the patient.

"Good evening, Mrs. Johnson. I am sorry to see you looking so ill. What is the matter? I understand that you have had some kind of shock."

As I addressed her, I seemed to detect a faint expression of surprise, but she replied at once, in a weak voice that was little more than a whisper, "Yes. I have had rather an upset. That is all. They need not really have troubled you."

"Well, you don't look very flourishing," said I, taking the wrist that was uncovered by her mantle, "and your hand is as cold as a fish."

I felt her pulse, checking it by my watch, and meanwhile looking her over critically. And not her alone. For on the wall opposite me was a mirror in which, by a little judicious adjustment of position, I was able to observe the other occupant of the room while keeping my back towards him, and what I observed was that he was sitting with his elbows on his knees, and his face buried in his hands.

"Might one inquire," I asked, as I put away my watch, "what kind of shock it is that you are suffering from?"

The faintest trace of a smile stole across her pale face as she answered, "That isn't really a medical question, Doctor, is it?"

"Perhaps it isn't," I replied, though, of course, it was.

But I thought it best to waive the question, as there seemed to be some reservation and, noting this latter fact, I again considered her attentively. Whatever her condition was, and whatever it might be due to, I had to form my opinion unassisted, for I could see that no information would be furnished, and the question that I had to settle was whether her state was purely mental, or whether it was complicated by any kind of physical injury. The waxen pallor of her face made me uneasy, and I found it difficult to interpret the expression of the set features. Some strong emotion had left its traces, but whether that emotion was grief, horror, or fear, or whether the expression denoted bodily pain, I could not determine. She had closed her eyes, and her face was like a death mask, save that it lacked the serenity of a dead face.

"Are you in any pain?" I asked, with my fingers still on the thready pulse. But she merely shook her head wearily, without opening her eyes.

It was very unsatisfactory. Her appearance was consistent with all kinds of unpleasant possibilities, as was also the strange atmosphere of secrecy about the whole affair. Nor was the attitude of that ill-favoured man whom I could see in the glass, still sitting hunched up with his face buried in his hands, at all reassuring. And gradually my attention began to focus itself upon the cloak which covered the woman's body and was drawn around her neck up to her chin. Did that cloak conceal anything? It seemed incredible, seeing that they had sent for a doctor. But the behaviour of everybody concerned was incredibly irrational. I produced my stethoscope, which was fitted with a diaphragm that enabled one to hear through the clothing and, drawing the cloak partly aside, applied the chest-piece over the heart. On this the patient opened her eyes and made a movement of her hand towards the upper part of the cloak. I listened carefully to her heart – which was organically sound, though a good deal disordered in action – and moved the stethoscope once or twice, drawing aside the cloak by degrees. Finally, with a somewhat quick movement, I turned it back completely.

"Why," I exclaimed, "what on earth have you been doing to your neck?"

"That mark?" she said in a half-whisper. "It is nothing. It was made by a gold collar that I wore yesterday. It was rather tight."

"I see," said I, truthfully enough, for the explanation of her condition was now pretty clear up to a certain point.

Of course, I did not believe her. I did not suppose that she expected me to. But it was evidently useless to dispute her statement or make any comment. The mark upon her neck was a livid bruise made by some cord or band that had been drawn tight with considerable force, and it was not more than an hour old. How or by whom the injury had been inflicted was not, in a medical sense, my concern. But I was by no means clear that I had not some responsibilities in the case other than the professional ones.

At this moment the man in the corner uttered a deep groan and exclaimed in low, intense tones, "My God! My God!" Then, to my extreme embarrassment, he began to sob audibly.

It was excessively uncomfortable. I looked from the woman – into whose ghastly face an expression of something like disgust and contempt had stolen – to the huddled figure in the glass. And as I looked, the man plunged one hand into his pocket and dragged out a handkerchief, bringing with it a little paper packet that fell to the floor. Something in the appearance of that packet, and especially in the hasty grab to recover it and the quick, furtive glance towards me that accompanied the action, made a new and sinister suggestion – a suggestion that the man's emotional, almost hysterical state supported, and that lent a certain unpleasant congruity to the otherwise inexplicable circumstances. That packet, I had little doubt, contained cocaine. The question was how did that fact – if it were a fact – bear on my patient's condition?

I inspected her afresh, and felt her pulse again. In the man's case the appearances were distinctive enough. His nerves were in rags, and even across the room I could see that the hand that held the handkerchief shook as if with a palsy. But in the woman's condition there was no positive suggestion of drugs, and something in her face – a strong, resolute face despite its expression of suffering – and her quiet, composed manner when she spoke, seemed to exclude the idea. However, there was no use in speculating. I had got all the information I was likely to get, and all that remained for me to do was to administer such treatment as my imperfect understanding of the case indicated. Accordingly I opened my emergency bag and, taking out a couple of little bottles and a measure-glass, went over to the washstand and mixed a draught in the tumbler, diluting it from the water-bottle.

In crossing the room, I passed the fireplace, where, on and above the mantelpiece, I observed a number of signed photographs, apparently of actors and actresses, including two of my patient, both of which were in character costume and unsigned – from which it seemed probable that my patient was an actress, a probability that was strengthened by the hour at which I had been summoned and by certain other appearances in the room with which Dr. Pumphrey's largely theatrical practice had made me familiar. But, as my patient would have remarked, this was not a medical question.

"Now, Mrs. Johnson," I said, when I had prepared the draught – and as I spoke she opened her eyes and looked at me with a slightly puzzled expression – "I want you to drink this."

She allowed me to sit her up enough to enable her to swallow the draught, and as her head was raised, I took the opportunity to glance at the back of her neck, where I thought I could distinctly trace the crossing of the cord or band that had been drawn round it. She sank back with a

41

sigh, but remained with her eyes open, looking at me as I repacked my bag.

"I shall send you some medicine," I said, "which you must take regularly. It is unnecessary for me to say," I added, addressing the man, "that Mrs. Johnson must be kept very quiet, and in no way agitated."

He bowed, but made no reply, and I then took my leave.

"Good night, Mrs. Johnson," I said, shaking her cold hand gently. "I hope you will be very much better in an hour or two. I think you will if you keep quite quiet and take your medicine."

She thanked me in a few softly spoken words and with a very sweet smile, of which the sad wistfulness went to my heart. I was loath to leave her, in her weak and helpless state, to the care of her unprepossessing companion, encompassed by I knew not what perils. But I was only a passing stranger, and could do no more than my professional office.

As I approached the door – with an inquisitive eye on its disordered lock and loosened striking-box – the man rose, and made as if to let me out. I wished him good-night, and he returned the salutation in a pleasant voice, and with a distinctly refined accent, quite out of character with his uncouth appearance. Feeling my way down the dark staircase, I presently encountered my first acquaintance, who came to the foot of the stairs with the candle.

"Well," he said, in his brusque way, "how is she?"

"She is very weak and shaken," I replied. "I want to send her some medicine. Shall I take the address, or are you driving me back?"

"I will take you back in the car," said he, "and you can give me the medicine."

The car was waiting at the gate, and we went out together. As I turned to close the gate after me, I cast a quick glance at the house and its surroundings, searching for some distinctive feature in case recognition of the place should be necessary later. But it was a dark night, though the rain had now ceased, and I could see no more than that the adjoining house seemed to have a sort of corner turret, crowned with a small cupola, and surmounted by a weather-vane.

During the short journey home not a word was spoken, and when the car drew up at Dr. Pumphrey's door and I let myself in with the key, my companion silently followed me in. I prepared the medicine at once, and handed it to him with a few brief instructions. He took it from me, and then asked what my fee was.

"Do I understand that I am not required to continue the attendance?" I asked.

"They will send for you, I suppose, if they want you," he replied. "But I had better pay your fee for this visit, as I came for you."

42

I named the fee and, when he had paid it, I said, "You understand that she will require very careful and tender treatment while she is so weak?"

"I do," he answered, "but I am not a member of the household. Did you make it clear to Mr. – her husband?"

I noted the significant hesitation, and replied, "I told him, but as to making it clear to him, I can't say. His mental condition was none of the most lucid. I hope she has someone more responsible to look after her."

"She has," he replied, and then he asked, "You don't think she is in any danger, I hope?"

"In a medical sense," I answered, "I think not. In other respects you know better than I do."

He gave me a quick look, and nodded slightly. Then, with a curt "Good-night," he turned and went out to the car.

When he was gone, I made a brief record of the visit in the day-book, and entered the fee in the cash column. In the case of the experienced Dr. Pumphrey, this would have been the end of the transaction. But, new as I was to medical practice, I was unable to take this matter-of-fact view of its incidents. My mind still surged with surprise, curiosity, and a deep concern for my fair patient. Filling my pipe, I sat down before the gas fire to think over the mystery to which I had suddenly become a party.

What was it that had happened in that house? Obviously, something scandalous and sinister. The secrecy alone made that manifest. Not only had the whereabouts of the house been withheld from me, but a false name had been given. I realized that when my late visitor stumbled over the name and substituted "her husband", He had forgotten what name it was that he had given on the spur of the moment. I understood, too, the look of surprise that my patient had given when I addressed her by that false name. Clearly, something had happened which had to be hushed up if possible.

What was it? The elements of the problem, and the material for solving it, were the mark on the woman's neck, the condition of the door, and a packet which I felt morally certain contained cocaine. I considered these three factors separately and together.

The mark on the neck was quite recent. Its character was unmistakable. A cord or band had been drawn tight and with considerable violence, either by the woman herself, or by some other person – that is to say, it was a case either of attempted suicide or attempted murder. To which of these alternatives did the circumstances point?

43

There was the door. It had been broken in, and had therefore been locked on the inside. That was consistent with suicide, but not inconsistent with murder. Then, by whom had it been broken in? By a murderer to get at his victim? Or by a rescuer? And if the latter, was it to avert suicide or murder?

Again, there was the drug – assumed, but almost certain.

What was the bearing of that? Could these three persons be a party of "dopers", and the tragedy the outcome of an orgy of drug-taking? I rejected this possibility at once. It was not consistent with the patient's condition nor with her appearance or manner, and the man who had fetched me and brought me back was a robust, sane-looking man who seemed quite beyond suspicion.

I next considered the persons. There were three of them: Two men and a woman. Of the men, one was a virile, fairly good-looking man of perhaps forty, the other – the "husband" – was conspicuously unprepossessing, physically degenerate, and mentally, as I judged, a hysterical poltroon. Here there seemed to be the making of trouble, especially when one considered the personal attractiveness of the woman.

I recalled her appearance very vividly. A handsome woman, not, perhaps, actually beautiful – though she might have been that if the roses of youth and health had bloomed in those cheeks that I had seen blanched with that ghastly pallor. But apart from mere comeliness, there was a suggestion of a pleasing, gracious personality. I don't know how it had been conveyed to me, excepting by the smile with which she had thanked me and bidden me farewell – a smile that had imparted a singular sweetness to her face. But I had received that impression, and also that she was a woman of decided character and intelligence.

Her appearance was rather striking. She had a great mass of dark hair, parted in the middle, and drawn down over the temples, nearly covering the ears, darkish grey eyes, and unusually strong, black, level eyebrows, that almost met above the straight, shapely nose. Perhaps it was those eyebrows that gave the strength and intensity to her expression, aided by the compressed lips – though this was probably a passing condition due to her mental state.

My cogitations were prolonged well into the small hours, but they led to nothing but an open verdict. At length I rose with a slight shiver and, dismissing the topic from my mind, crept up to bed.

But both the persons and the incident refused to accept their dismissal. For many days afterwards I was haunted by two faces, the one – ugly, coffin-shaped, surmounted by a shock of soft, furry, mouse-coloured hair – the other, sweet, appealing, mutely eloquent of tragedy

44

and sorrow. Of course, I received no further summons, and the whereabouts of the house of mystery remained a secret until almost the end of my stay in Osnaburgh Street. Indeed, it was on the very day before Dr. Pumphrey's return that I made the discovery.

I had been making a visit to a patient who lived near Regent's Park, and on my way back had taken what I assumed to be a short cut. This led me into a quiet, old fashioned residential street, of which the houses stood back behind small front gardens. As I walked along the street I seemed to be aware of a faint sense of familiarity which caused me to observe the houses with more than usual attention. Presently I observed a little way ahead on the opposite side a house with a corner turret topped by a cupola, which bore above it a weather-vane. I crossed the road as I approached it, and looked eagerly at the next house. Its identity was unmistakable. My attention was immediately attracted by the jalousies with which the windows were fitted, and on looking at the front door I observed that the number was Forty-three.

This, then, was the house of mystery – perhaps of crime.

But whatever that tragedy had been, its actors were there no longer. The windows were curtainless and blank, an air of spring-cleaning and preparation pervaded the premises, and a bill on a little notice board announced a furnished house to let, and invited inquiries. For a moment, I was tempted to accept that invitation. But I was restrained by a feeling that it would be in a way a breach of confidence. The names of those persons had been purposely withheld from me, doubtless for excellent reasons, and professional ethics seemed to forbid any unauthorized pryings into their private affairs. Wherefore, with a valedictory glance at the first-floor window, which I assumed to be that of the room that I had entered, I went on my way, telling myself that, now, the incident was really closed, and that I had looked my last on the persons who had enacted their parts in it.

In which, however, I was mistaken. The curtain was down on the first act, but the play was not over. Only the succeeding acts were yet in the unfathomed future. "*Coming events cast their shadows before them*", but who can interpret those shadows, until the shapes which cast them loom up, plain and palpable, to mock at their own unheeded premonitions.

Chapter II
Re-Enter "Mr. Johnson"

It was a good many months before the curtain rose on the second act of the drama of which this narrative is the record. Rather more than a year had passed, and in that time certain changes had taken place in my condition, of which I need refer only to the one that, indirectly, operated as the cause of my becoming once more a party to the drama aforesaid. I had come into a small property, just barely sufficient to render me independent, and to enable me to live in idleness, if idleness had been my hobby. As it was not, I betook myself to Adam Street, Adelphi, to confer with my trusty medical agent, Mr. Turcival, and from that conference was born my connexion with the strange events which will be hereafter related.

Mr. Turcival had several practices to sell, but only one that he thought quite suitable. "It is a death vacancy," said he, "at Rochester. A very small practice, and you won't get much out of it, as the late incumbent was an old man and you are a young man – and you look ten years younger since you shaved off that fine beard and moustache. But it is going for a song, and you can afford to wait, and you couldn't have a more pleasant place to wait in than Rochester. Better go down and have a look at it. I'll write to the local agents, Japp and Bundy, and they will show you the house and effects. What do you say?"

I said "Yes", and so favourably was I impressed that the very next day found me in a first-class compartment en route for Rochester, with a substantial portmanteau in the guard's van.

At Dartford it became necessary to change, and as I sauntered on the platform, waiting for the Rochester train, my attention was attracted to a man who sat, somewhat wearily and dejectedly, on a bench, rolling a cigarette. I was impressed by the swift dexterity with which he handled the paper and tobacco, a dexterity that was explained by the colour of his fingers, which were stained to the hue of mahogany. But my attention was quickly diverted from the colour of the fingers to their shape. They were clubbed fingers. At the moment when I observed the fact I was looking over his shoulder from behind, and could not see his face. But I could see that he had a large, pear-shaped head, surmounted by an enormous cap, from beneath which a mass of mouse-coloured hair stuck out like untidy thatch.

I suppose I must have halted unconsciously, for he suddenly looked round, casting at me a curious, quick, furtive, suspicious glance. He evidently did not recognize me – naturally, since my appearance was so much changed, but I recognized him instantly. He was "Mr. – , her husband", And his appearance was not improved since I had last seen him. Inspecting him from the front, I observed that he was sordidly shabby and none too clean, and that his large, rough boots were white with dust as if from a long tramp on the chalky Kentish roads.

When the train came in, I watched him saunter to a compartment a few doors from my own, rolling a fresh cigarette as he went, and at each station when we stopped, I looked out of the window to see where he got out. But he made no appearance until the train slowed down at Rochester when I alighted quickly and strolled towards his compartment. It had evidently been well filled, for a number of passengers emerged before he appeared, contesting the narrow doorway with a stout workman. As he squeezed past, the skirt of his coat caught and was drawn back, revealing a sheath-knife of the kind known to seamen as "Green River", attached to a narrow leather belt. I did not like the look of that knife. No landsman has any legitimate use for such a weapon. And the fact that this man habitually carried about him the means of inflicting lethal injuries – for it had no other purpose – threw a fresh light, if any were needed, on the sinister events of that memorable night in the quiet house near Regent's Park.

As I had to look after my luggage, I lost sight of him, and when having deposited my portmanteau in the cloak room, I walked out across the station approach and looked up and down the street, he was nowhere to be seen. Dimly wondering what this man might be doing in Rochester, and whether his handsome wife were here, too – assuming her to be still in existence – I turned and began to saunter slowly westward. I had walked but two or three-hundred yards when the door of a tavern which I was approaching opened, and a man emerged, licking his lips with uncommon satisfaction, and rolling a cigarette. It was my late fellow-traveller. He stood by the tavern door, looking about him, and glancing at the people on the footway. Just as I was passing him, he approached me and spoke.

"I wonder," said he, "if you happen to know a Mrs. Frood who lives somewhere about here."

"I am afraid I don't," I replied, thankful to be able to tell the truth – for I should have denied knowledge of her in any case. "I am a stranger to the town at present."

He thanked me and turned away, and I walked on, but no longer at a saunter, wondering who Mrs. Frood might be and keeping an eye on the numbers of the houses on the opposite side of the street.

A few minutes' walk brought into view the number I was seeking, painted in the tympanum of a handsome Georgian portico appertaining to one of a pair of pleasant old redbrick houses. I halted to inspect these architectural twins before crossing the road. Old houses always interest me, and these two were particularly engaging, as their owners apparently realized, for they were in the pink of condition, and the harmony of the quiet green woodwork and the sober red brick was no chance effect. Moreover they were painted alike to carry out the intention of the architect, who had evidently designed them to form a single composition, to which end he had very effectively placed, between the twin porticoes, a central door which gave access to a passage common to the two houses and leading, no doubt, to the back premises.

Having noted these particulars, I crossed the road and approached the twin which bore beside its doorway a brass plate, inscribed "*Japp and Bundy, Architects and Surveyors*". In the adjoining bay window, in front of a green curtain, was a list of houses to let and, as I paused for a moment to glance at this, a face decorated with a pair of colossal tortoiseshell-rimmed spectacles, rose slowly above the curtain, and then, catching my eye, popped down again with some suddenness.

I ascended the short flight of steps to the open street door and, entering the hall, opened the office door and walked in. The owner of the spectacles was perched on a high stool at a higher desk with his back to me, writing in a large book. The other occupant of the office was a small, spare, elderly man, with a pleasant wrinkly face and a cockatoo-like crest of white hair, who confronted me across a large table on which a plan was spread out. He looked up interrogatively as I entered, and I proceeded at once to announce myself.

"I am Dr. Strangeways," said I, drawing a bundle of papers from my pocket. "Mr. Turcival – the medical agent, you know – thought I had better come down and settle things up on the spot. So here I am."

"Precisely," said my new acquaintance, motioning me to a chair – it was a shield-back Heppelwhite, I noticed. "I agree with Mr. Turcival. It is all quite plain sailing. The position is this: Old Dr. Partridge died about three weeks ago, and the executor of his will, who lives in Northumberland, has instructed us to realize his estate. We have valued the furniture, fittings, and effects, have added a small amount to cover the drugs and instruments and the goodwill of the practice, and this is the premium. It is practically just the value of the effects."

"And the lease of the house?"

"Expired some years ago and we allowed Dr. Partridge to remain as a yearly tenant, which he preferred. You could do the same or you could have a lease, if you wished."

"Is the house your property?" I asked.

"No, but we manage it for the owner, a Mrs. Frood."

"Oh, it belongs to Mrs. Frood, does it?"

He looked up at me quickly, and I noticed that the gentleman at the desk had stopped writing. "Do you know Mrs. Frood?" he asked.

"No, but it happens that a man who came down by my train asked me a few minutes ago if I could give him her address. Fortunately I couldn't."

"Why fortunately?"

The question brought me, up short. My prejudice against the man was due to my knowledge of his antecedents, which I was not prepared to disclose. I therefore replied evasively, "Well, I wasn't very favourably impressed by his appearance. He was a shabby-looking customer. I suspected that he was a cadger of some kind."

"Indeed! Now, what sort of a person was he? Could you describe him?"

"He was a youngish man – from thirty-five to forty, I should say – apparently well-educated but very seedy and not particularly clean. A queer-looking man, with a big, pear-shaped head and a mop of hair like the fur of a Persian cat. His fingers are clubbed at the ends, and stained with tobacco to the knuckles. Do you know him?"

"I rather suspect I do. What do you say, Bundy?"

Mr. Bundy grunted. "Hubby, I ween," said he.

"You don't mean Mrs. Frood's husband?" I exclaimed.

"I do. And it is, as you said, very fortunate that you were not able to give him her address, as she is unable to live with him and is at present unwilling to let him know her whereabouts. It is an unfortunate affair. However, to return to your business, you had better go up and have a look at the house and see what you think of it. You might just walk up with Dr. Strangeways, Bundy."

Mr. Bundy swung round on his stool and, taking off his spectacles, stuck in his right eye a gold-rimmed monocle, through which he inspected me critically. Then he hopped off the stool and, lifting the lid of the desk, took out a velour hat and a pair of chamois gloves, the former of which he adjusted carefully on his head before a small mirror and, having taken down a labelled key from a key-board and provided himself with a smart, silver-mounted cane, announced that he was ready.

As I walked along the picturesque old street at Mr. Bundy's side, I reverted to my late fellow passenger and my prospective landlady.

49

"I gather," said I, "that Mrs. Frood's matrimonial affairs are somewhat involved."

"So do I." said Bundy. "Seems to have made a regular mucker of it. I don't know much about her, myself, but Japp knows the whole story. He's some sort of relative of hers, uncle or second cousin or something of the kind. But Japp is a bit like the sailor's parrot – he doesn't let on unnecessarily."

"What sort of a woman is Mrs. Frood?" I asked.

"Oh, quite a tidy sort of body. I've only seen her once or twice, haven't been here long myself – tallish woman, lot of black hair, thick eye-brows, rather squeaky voice. Not exactly my idea of a beauty, but Frood seems quite keen on her."

"By the way, how comes it that he doesn't know her address? She's a Rochester woman, isn't she?"

"No. I don't know where she comes from. London, I think. This property was left to her by an aunt who lived here – a cousin of Japp's. Angelina came down here a few weeks ago on the q.t. to get away from hubby, and I fancy she's been keeping pretty close."

"She's living in lodgings, then, I suppose?"

"Yes – at least she lives in a set of offices that Japp furnished for her, and the lady who rents the rest of the house looks after her. As a matter of fact, the offices are next door to ours, but you had better consider that information as confidential, at any rate while hubby is in the neighbourhood. This is your shanty."

He halted at the door of a rather small, red brick house and, while I was examining the half-obliterated inscription on the brass plate, he thrust the key into the lock and made ineffectual efforts to turn it. Suddenly there was a loud click from within, followed by the clanking of a chain and the drawing of bolts. Then the door opened slowly, and a long-faced, heavy-browed, elderly woman surveyed us with a gloomy stare.

"Why didn't you ring the bell?" she demanded, gruffly.

"Had a key," replied Bundy, extracting it, and flourishing it before her face.

"And what's the good of a key when the door was bolted and chained?"

"But, naturally, I couldn't see that the door was bolted and chained."

"I suppose you couldn't with that thing stuck in your eye. Well, what do you want?"

"I have brought this gentleman, Dr. Strangeways, to see you. He has seen your portraits in the shop windows and wished to be introduced. Also he wants to look over the house. He thinks of taking the practice."

"Well, why couldn't you say that before?" she demanded.

"Before what?" he inquired blandly.

She made no reply other than a low growl, and Bundy continued, "This lady, Dr. Strangeways, is the renowned Mrs. Dunk, more familiarly known as La Giaconda, who administered the domestic affairs of the late Dr. Partridge, and is at present functioning as custodian of the premises." He concluded the presentation by a ceremonious bow and a sweep of his hat, which Mrs. Dunk acknowledged by turning her back on him and producing a large bunch of keys, with which she proceeded to unlock the doors that opened on the hall.

"The upstairs rooms are unlocked," she said, adding, "If you want me you can ring the bell." And with this she retired to the basement stairs and vanished.

My examination of the rooms was rather perfunctory, for I had made up my mind already. The premium was absurdly small, and I could see that the house was furnished well enough for my immediate needs. As to the practice, I had no particular expectations.

"Better have a look at the books," said Bundy when we went into the little surgery, "though Mr. Turcival has been through them, and I daresay he has told you all about the practice."

"Yes," I answered, "he told me that the practice was very small and that I probably shouldn't get much of it, as Partridge was an old man and I am a young one. Still, I may as well glance through the books."

Bundy laid the day book and ledger on the desk and placed a stool by the latter, and I seated myself and began to turn over the leaves and note down a few figures on a slip of paper, while my companion beguiled the time by browsing round the surgery, taking down bottles and sniffing at their contents, pulling out drawers, and inspecting the instruments and appliances. A very brief examination of the books served to confirm Mr. Turcival's modest estimate of the practice and, when I had finished, I closed them and turned round to report to Mr. Bundy, who was, at the moment, engaged in "sounding" the surgery clock with the late Dr. Partridge's stethoscope.

"I think it will do," said I. "The practice is negligible, but the furniture and fittings are worth the money, and I daresay I shall get some patients in time. At any rate, the premises are all in going order."

"You are not dependent on the practice, then?" said he.

"No. I have enough just barely to exist on until the patients begin to arrive. But what about the house?"

51

"You can have a lease if you like, or you can go on with the arrangement that Partridge had. If I were you, I should take the house on a three years' agreement with the option of a lease later if you find that the venture turns out satisfactorily."

"Yes," I agreed, "that seems a good arrangement. And when could I have possession?"

"You've got possession now if you agree to the terms. Say yes, and I'll draft out the agreement when I get back. You and Mrs. Frood can sign it this evening. You give us a cheque and we give you your copy of the document, and the thing is $D - U - N$, done."

"And what about this old woman?"

"La Giaconda Dunkibus? I should keep her if I were you. She looks an old devil, but she's a good servant. Partridge had a great opinion of her, so Japp tells me, and you can see for yourself that the house is in apple-pie order and as clean as a new pin."

"You think she would be willing to stay?"

Bundy grinned. (He was a good deal given to grinning, and he certainly had a magnificent set of teeth). "Willing?" he exclaimed. "She's going to stay whether you want her or not. She has been here the best part of her life and nothing short of a torpedo would shift her. You'll have to take her with the fixtures, but I don't think you'll regret it."

As Bundy was speaking, I had been, half-unconsciously, looking him over, interested in the queer contrast between his almost boyish appearance and gay irresponsible manner on the one hand and, on the other, his shrewdness, his business capacity, and his quick, decisive, evidently forceful character.

To look at, he was just a young "nut" – small, spruce, dandified, and apparently not displeased with himself. His age I judged to be about twenty-five, his height about five-feet-six. In figure he was slight, but well set-up, and he seemed active and full of life and energy. He was extraordinarily well turned-out. From his close-cropped head, with the fore-lock "smarmed" back in the correct "nuttish" fashion, so that his cranium resembled a large black-topped filbert, to his immaculately polished and remarkably small shoes, there was not an inch of his person that had not received the most careful attention. He was clean-shaved, so clean that on the smooth skin nothing but the faint blue tinge on cheek and chin remained to suggest the coarse and horrid possibilities of whiskers. And his hands had evidently received the same careful attention as his face – indeed, even as he was talking to me, he produced from his pocket some kind of ridiculous little instrument with which he proceeded to polish his finger-nails.

"Shall I ring the bell?" he asked after a short pause, "and call up the spirit of the Dunklett from the vasty deep? May as well let her know her luck."

As I assented he pressed the bell-push, and in less than a minute Mrs. Dunk made her appearance and stood in the doorway, looking inquiringly at Bundy, but uttering no sound.

"Dr. Strangeways is going to take the practice, Mrs. Dunk," said Bundy, "inclusive of the house, furniture, and all effects, and he is also prepared to take you at a valuation."

As the light of battle began to gleam in Mrs. Dunk's eyes, I thought it best to intervene and conduct the negotiations myself.

"I understand from Mr. Bundy," said I, "that you were Dr. Partridge's housekeeper for many years, and it occurred to me that you might be willing to act in the same capacity for me. What do you say?"

"Very well," she replied. "When do you want to move in?"

"I propose to move in at once. My luggage is at the station."

"Have you checked the inventory?" she asked.

"No, I haven't, but I suppose nothing has been taken away?"

"No," she answered. "Everything is as it was when Dr. Partridge died."

"Then we can go over the inventory later. I will have my things sent up from the station, and I shall come in during the afternoon to unpack."

She agreed concisely to this arrangement and, when we had settled a few minor details, I departed with Bundy to make my way to the station and thereafter to go in search of lunch.

"You think," said I, as we halted opposite the station approach, "that we can get everything completed today?"

"Yes," he replied, "I will get the agreement drawn up in the terms that we have just settled on, and will make an appointment with Mrs. Frood. You had better look in at the office about half-past-six."

He turned away with a friendly nod and a flash of his white teeth, and bustled off up the street, swinging his smart cane jauntily, and looking, with his trim, well-cut clothes, his primrose-coloured gloves, and his glistening shoes, the very type of cheerful, prosperous, self-respecting and self-satisfied youth.

Chapter III
Angelina Frood

Punctually at half-past-six I presented myself at the office of Messrs. Japp and Bundy. The senior partner was seated at a writing-table covered with legal-looking documents and, as I entered, he looked up with a genial, wrinkly smile of recognition, and then turned to his junior.

"You've got Dr. Strangeways's agreement ready, haven't you, Bundy?" he asked.

"Just finished it five minutes ago," was the reply. "Here you are."

Bundy swung round on his stool and held out the two copies. "Would you mind going through it with Dr. Strangeways?" said Japp. "And then you might go with him to Mrs. Frood's and witness the signatures. I told her you were coming."

Bundy pulled out his watch, and glared at it through his great spectacles.

"By Jove!" he exclaimed, "I'm afraid I can't. There's old Baldwin, you know. I've got to be there at a quarter-to-seven."

"So you have," said Japp, "I had forgotten that. You had better be off now. I'll see to Dr. Strangeways, if he isn't in a hurry for a minute or two."

"I'm not in a hurry at all," said I. "Don't put yourself out for me."

"Well, if you really are not," said Japp, "I'll just finish what I am doing, and then I'll run in with you and get the agreement completed. You might look through it while you are waiting and see that it is all in order."

Bundy handed me the agreement and, as I sat down to study it, he removed his spectacles, stuck his eye-glass in his eye, hopped off his perch, brought forth his hat, gloves, and stick and, having presented his teeth for my inspection, took his departure.

I read through the agreement carefully to ascertain that it embodied the terms agreed on verbally and compared the two copies. Then, while Mr. Japp continued to turn over the leaves of his documents, I let my thoughts stray from the trim, orderly office to the house of mystery in London and the strange events that had befallen there on that rainy night more than a year ago. Once more I called up before the eyes of memory the face of my mysterious patient, sweet and gracious in spite of its deathly pallor. Many a time, in the months that had passed, had I recalled it – so often that it seemed, in a way, to have become familiar. In a few minutes I was going to look upon that face again – for there could be no reasonable doubt that my prospective landlady was she. I looked forward expectantly, almost with excitement, to the meeting. Would she recognize me? I wondered. And if she did not, should I make myself known? This was a difficult question, and I had come to no decision upon it when I was aroused from my reverie by a movement on the part of Mr. Japp, whose labours had apparently come to an end. Folding up the documents and securing them in little bundles with red tape, he deposited them in a cupboard with his notes, and from the same receptacle took out his hat.

"Now," said he, "if you find the agreement in order, we will proceed to execute it. Are you going to pay the premium now?"

"I have my cheque-book with me," I replied. "When we have signed the agreement, I will settle up for everything."

"Thank you," said he. "I have prepared a receipt which is, practically, an assignment of the furniture and effects and of all rights in the practice."

He held the door open and I passed out. We descended the steps, and passing the central door common to the two houses, ascended to that of the adjoining house, where Mr. Japp executed a flourish on a handsome brass knocker. In a few moments the door was opened by a woman whom I couldn't see very distinctly in the dim hall, especially as she turned about and retired up the stairs. Mr. Japp advanced to the door of the front room and rapped with his knuckles, whereupon a high, clear, feminine voice bade him come in. He accordingly entered, and I followed.

The first glance disposed of any doubts that I might have had. The lady who stood up to receive us was unquestionably my late patient, though she looked taller than I had expected. But it was the well-remembered face, less changed, indeed, than I could have wished, for it was still pale, drawn, and weary, as I could see plainly enough in spite of the rather dim light – for, although it was not yet quite dark, the curtains were drawn and a lamp lighted on a small table, beside which was a low easy-chair, on which some needlework had been thrown down.

Mr. Japp introduced me to my future landlady, who bowed and, having invited us to be seated, took up her needlework and sat down in the easy-chair.

"You are not looking quite up to the mark," Japp observed, regarding her critically, as he turned over the papers.

"No," she admitted, "I think I am a little run down."

"Hmm," said Japp. "Oughtn't to get run down at your age. Why, you are only just wound up. However, you've got a doctor for a tenant, so you will be able to take out some of the rent in medical advice. Let me see, I told you what the terms of the agreement were, but you had better look through it before you sign."

He handed her one of the documents, which she took from him and, dropping her needlework in her lap, leaned back in her chair to read it. Meanwhile, I examined her with a good deal of interest and curiosity, wondering how she had fared and what had happened to her in the months that had elapsed since I had last seen her. The light was not very favourable for a minute inspection, for the lamp on the table was the sole luminary, and that was covered by a red silk shade. But I was confirmed in my original impression of her. She was more than ordinarily good-looking, and rather striking in appearance, and I judged that under happier conditions she might have appeared even more attractive. As it was, the formally parted dark hair, the strongly marked, straight eyebrows, the firm mouth, rather compressed and a little drawn down at the corners, and the pale complexion imparted to her face a character that was somewhat intense, sombre, and even troubled. But for this I could fully account from my knowledge of her circumstances, and I was conscious of looking on her with a very sympathetic and friendly eye.

"This is quite satisfactory to me," she said at length, in the clear, high-pitched voice to which Bundy had objected, "and if it is equally so to Dr. Strangeways, I suppose I had better sign."

She laid the paper on the table and, taking the fountain-pen that Japp proffered, signed her name, *Angelina Frood*, in a bold, legible hand, and then returned the pen to its owner, who forthwith affixed his signature as witness and spread out the duplicate for me to sign. When this also was completed, he handed me the copy signed by Mrs. Frood and the receipt for the premium, and I drew a cheque for the amount and delivered it to him.

"Many thanks," said he, slipping it into a wallet and pocketing it. "That concludes our business and puts you finally in possession. I wish you every success in your practice. By the way, I mentioned to Mrs. Frood that you had seen her husband and that you know how she is placed, and she agreed with me that it was best that you should understand the position in case you should meet him again."

"Certainly," Mrs. Frood agreed. "There is no use in trying to make a secret of it. He came down with you from London, Mr. Japp tells me."

"Not from London," said I. "He got in at Dartford." Here Mr. Japp rose and stole towards the door. "Don't let me interrupt you," said he, "but I must get back to the office and hear what Bundy has to report. Don't get up. I can let myself out."

He made his exit quietly, shutting the door after him, and as soon as he was gone Mrs. Frood asked, "Do you mean that he changed into your train at Dartford?"

"No," I answered. "I think he came to Dartford on foot. He looked tired and his boots were covered with white dust."

"You are very observant, Dr. Strangeways," she said. "I wonder what made you notice him so particularly?"

"He is rather a noticeable man," I said, and then, deciding that it was better to be quite frank, I added, "But the fact is I had seen him before."

"Indeed!" said she. "Would you think me very inquisitive if I asked where you had seen him?"

"Not at all," I answered. "It was a little more than a year ago, about twelve o'clock at night, in a house near Regent's Park, to which I was taken in a closed car to see a lady."

As I spoke she dropped her needlework and sat up, gazing at me with a startled and rather puzzled expression. "But," she said, "you are not the doctor who came to see me that night?"

"I am, indeed," said I.

"Now," she exclaimed, "isn't that an extraordinary thing? I had a feeling that I had seen you somewhere before. I seemed to recognize your voice. But you don't look the same. Hadn't you a beard then?"

"Yes, I am but the shaven and shorn remnant of my former self, but I am your late medical attendant."

She looked at me with an odd, reflective, questioning expression, but without making any further comment. Presently she said, "You were very kind and sympathetic, though you were so quiet. I wonder what you thought of it all."

"I hadn't much to go on beyond the medical facts," I replied evasively.

"Oh, you needn't be so cautious," said she, "now that the cat is out of the bag."

"Well," I said, "it was pretty obvious that there had been trouble of some kind. The door had been broken open, there was one man in a state of hysterics, another man considerably upset and rather angry, and a woman with the mark on her neck of a cord or band – "

"It was a knitted silk neck-tie, to be accurate. But you put the matter in a nut-shell very neatly, and I see that you diagnosed what novelists call 'the eternal triangle'. And to a certain extent you were right, only the triangle was imaginary. If you don't mind, I will tell you just what did happen. The gentleman who came for you was a Mr. Fordyce, the lessee of one or two provincial theatres – I was on the stage then, but perhaps you guessed that."

"As a matter of fact, I did."

"Well, Mr. Fordyce had an idea of producing a play at one of his houses, and was going to give me a leading part. He had been to our house once or twice to talk the matter over with Nicholas (my husband) and me, and we were more-or-less friendly. He was quite a nice, sober kind of man, and perfectly proper and respectful. On this night he had been at the theatre where I had an engagement and, as it was a wet night, he drove me home in his car, and was coming in to have a few words with us about our business. He wanted to see a photograph of me in a particular costume, and when we arrived home I ran upstairs to fetch it. There I found Nicholas, who had seen our arrival from the window, and was in a state of furious jealousy. Directly I entered the room, he locked the door and flew at me like a wild beast. As to what followed, I think you know as much as I do, for I fainted, and when I recovered Nicholas was sobbing in a corner, and Mr. Fordyce was standing by the door, looking as black as thunder."

"Had your husband been jealous of Mr. Fordyce previously?"

"Not a bit. But on this occasion he was in a very queer state. I think he had been drinking, and taking some other things that were bad for him —"

"Such as cocaine," I suggested.

"Yes. But, dear me! What a very noticing person you are, Dr. Strangeways! But you are quite right. It was the cocaine that was the cause of the trouble. He was always a difficult man – emotional, excitable, eccentric, and not very temperate – but after he had acquired the drug habit he went to the bad completely. He became slovenly, and even dirty in his person, frightfully emotional, and gave up work of all kind, so that but for my tiny income and my small earnings we should have starved."

"So you actually supported him?"

"Latterly I did. And I daresay, if I had remained on the stage, we should have done fairly well, as I was supposed to have some talent, though I didn't like the life. But, of course, after this affair, I didn't dare to live with him. He wasn't safe. I should have been constantly in fear of my life."

"Had he ever been violent before'"

"Not seriously. He had often threatened horrible things, and I had looked on his threats as mere vapourings, but this was a different affair. I must have had a really narrow escape. So the very next day, I went into lodgings. But that didn't answer. He wouldn't agree to the separation, and was continually dogging me and making a disturbance. In the end, I had to give up my engagement and go off, leaving no address."

"I suppose you went back to your people?"

"No," she replied. "As a matter of fact, I haven't any people. My mother died when I was quite a child, and I lost my father when I was about seventeen. He died on the Gold Coast, where he held an appointment as District Commissioner."

"Ah," said I, "I thought you were in some way connected with West Africa. I noticed the zodiac ring on your finger when you were signing the agreement. When I was newly qualified, I took a trip down the West Coast as a ship's surgeon, and bought one of those rings at Cape Coast."

"They are quaint little things, aren't they?" she remarked, slipping the ring off her finger and handing it to me. "I don't often wear it, though. It is rather clumsy, and it doesn't fit very well, and I don't care much for rings."

I turned the little trinket over in my hand and examined it with reminiscent interest. It was a roughly wrought band of yellow native gold, with the conventional signs of the zodiac worked round it in raised figures. Inside I noticed that the letters *A. C.* had been engraved.

"It was given to you before you were married, I presume," said I, as I returned it to her.

"Yes," she replied, "those are the initials of my maiden name – *Angelina Carthew*." She took the ring from me, but instead of replacing it on her finger, dropped it into a little pouch-like purse with metal jaws which she had taken from her pocket.

"Your position is a very disagreeable one," said I, reverting to the main topic. "I wonder that you haven't applied for a judicial separation. There are ample grounds for making the application."

"I suppose there are. But it wouldn't help me really, even if it were granted. I shouldn't get rid of him."

"You could apply to the police if he molested you."

"No doubt. But that doesn't sound very restful, does it?"

"I am afraid it doesn't. But it would be better than being constantly molested without having any remedy or refuge."

"Perhaps it would," she agreed doubtfully, and then, with a faint smile, she added, "I suppose you are wondering what on earth made me marry him?"

"Well," I replied, "it appears to me that his good fortune was more remarkable than his personal attractions."

"He wasn't always like he is now," said she. "I married him nearly ten years ago, and he was fairly presentable then. His manners were quite nice and he had certain accomplishments that rather appealed to a young girl – I was only eighteen and rather impressionable. He was then getting a living by writing magazine stories – love stories, they were, of a highly emotional type – and occasional verses. They were second-rate stuff, really, but to me he seemed a budding genius. It was not until after we were married that the disillusionment came, and then only gradually as his bad habits developed."

"By the way, what do you suppose he has come down here for? What does he want? I suppose he wishes you to go back to him?"

"I suppose he does. But, primarily, I expect he wants money. It is a horrible position," she added, with sudden passion. "I hate the idea of hiding away from him when I suspect that the poor wretch has come down to his last few shillings. After all, he is my husband, and I am not so deadly poor now."

"He seemed to have the wherewith to provide a fair supply of tobacco, to say nothing of the cocaine and a 'modest quencher' at the tavern," I remarked drily. "At any rate, I hope he won't succeed in finding out where you live."

"I hope not," said she. "If he does, I shall have to move on, as I have had to do several times already, and I don't want to do that. I have only been here a little over two months, and it has been very pleasant and peaceful. But you see, Dr. Strangeways, that, if I am to follow Mr. Japp's advice, I shall inflict on you a very unpromising patient. There is no medical treatment for matrimonial troubles."

"No," I agreed, rising and taking up my hat, "but the physical effects may be dealt with. If I am appointed your medical advisor, I shall send you a tonic, and if I may look in now and again to see how you are getting on. I may be able to help you over some of your difficulties."

"It is very kind of you," she said, rising and shaking my hand warmly and, accepting my suggestion that she had better not come to the street door, she showed me out into the hall and dismissed me with a smile and a little bow.

When I reached the bottom of the steps, I stood irresolutely for a few moments and then, instead of making my way homeward, turned up the street towards the cathedral and the bridge, walking slowly and reflecting profoundly on the story I had just heard. It was a pitiful story, and the quiet, restrained manner of the telling made it the more impressive. All that was masculine in me rose in revolt against the useless, inexcusable wrecking of this poor woman's life. As to the man, he was, no doubt, to be pitied for being the miserable, degenerate wretch that he was. But he was doomed beyond any hope of salvation. Such wretches as he are condemned in the moment of their birth, they are born to an inheritance of misery and dishonour. But it is infamous that in their inevitable descent into the abyss – from which no one can save them – they should have the power to drag down with them sane and healthy human beings who were destined by nature to a life of happiness, of usefulness, and honour. I thought of the woman I had just left – comely, dignified, energetic, probably even talented. What was her future to be? So far as I could see, the shadow of this drug-sodden wastrel had fallen upon her, never to be lifted until merciful death should dissolve the ill-omened union.

This last reflection gave my thoughts a new turn. What was this man's purpose in pursuing her? Was he bent merely on extorting money or on sharing her modest income? Or was there some more sinister motive? I recalled his face, an evil, sly, vindictive face. I considered what I knew of him – that he had undoubtedly made one attempt to murder this woman, and that, to my knowledge, he carried about his person the means of committing murder. For what purpose could he have provided himself with that formidable weapon? It might be merely as a means of coercion, or it might be as a means of revenge.

Thus meditating, I had proceeded some distance along the street when I observed, on the opposite side, an old, three-gabled house which looked like some kind of institution. A lamp above the doorway threw its light on a stone tablet on which I could see an inscription of some length and, judging this to be an ancient almshouse, I crossed the road to inspect it more closely. A glance at the tablet told me that this was the famous rest-house established in the Sixteenth Century by worthy Richard Watts, to give a night's lodging and entertainment to six poor travellers, with the express proviso that the said travellers must be neither rogues nor proctors. I had read through the quaint inscription and was speculating, as many others have speculated, on the nature of Richard Watts's grievance against proctors as a class, when the door opened suddenly and a man rushed out with such impetuosity that he nearly collided with me. I had moved out of his way when he halted and addressed me excitedly.

"I say, governor, can you tell me where I can find a doctor?"

"You have found one," I replied. "I am a doctor. What is the matter?"

"There's a bloke in here throwing a fit," he answered, backing into the doorway and holding the door open for me. I entered, and followed him down a passage to a largish, barely furnished room, where I found four men and a woman, who looked like a hospital nurse, standing around and watching anxiously a man who lay on the floor.

"Here's a doctor, matron," said my conductor, as he ushered me in.

"Well, Simmonds," said the matron, "you haven't wasted much time."

"No, mum," replied Simmonds, "I struck it lucky. Caught him just outside."

Meanwhile I had stepped up to the prostrate man, and at the first glance I recognized him. He was Mrs. Frood's husband. And, whatever he might be "throwing", it was not a fit – in the ordinary medical sense, that is to say, it was not epilepsy or apoplexy, nor was it a fainting fit of an orthodox kind. If the patient had been a woman, one would have called it a hysterical seizure – and I could give it no other name, though I was not unmindful of the paper packet that I had seen on that former occasion. But the emotional element was obvious. The man purported to be insensible, and manifestly was not. The tightly closed eyes, the everted lips – showing a row of blackened teeth – the clutching movements of the clawlike hands – all were suggestive of at least half-conscious simulation. I stood for a while, stooping over him and watching him intently, and as I did so the bystanders watched me. Then I felt his pulse, and found it, as I had expected, quick, feeble, and irregular, and finally, producing my stethoscope, listened to his heart with as little disturbance of his clothing as possible.

"Well, Doctor," said the matron, "what do you think of him?"

"He is decidedly ill," I replied. "His heart is rather jumpy, and not very strong. Too much tobacco, I fancy, and perhaps some other things that are not very good, and possibly insufficient food."

"He told me, when he came in," said the matron, "that he was practically destitute."

"Ah," murmured Simmonds, "I expect he's been blowing all his money on Turkish baths," whereupon the other poor travellers sniggered softly, and were immediately extinguished by a reproving glance from the matron.

"Do you know what brought this attack on?" I asked.

"Yes," she replied, "he had a little dispute with Simmonds, here, and suddenly became violently excited, and then he fell down insensible, as you see him. It was all about nothing."

"I jest arsked 'im," said Simmonds, "if 'e could give me the name of the cove what done 'is 'air, 'cos I thought I'd like to 'ave mine done in the same fashionable style. That seemed to give 'im the fair pip. 'E jawed me something chronic, until I got shirty and told 'im if 'e didn't shut 'is face I'd give 'im a wipe acrost the snout. Then blow me if 'e didn't start to throw a fit."

While this lucid explanation was proceeding, I noticed that the patient was evidently listening intently, though he continued to twitch his face, exhibit his unlovely teeth, and wriggle his fingers. He was apparently waiting for my verdict with some anxiety.

"The question is," said the matron, "what is to be done with him? Do you think he is in any danger?"

62

As she spoke, we drifted towards the door, and when we were in the passage, out of earshot, I said, "The best place for that man is the infirmary. There is nothing much the matter with him but dope. He has been dosing himself with cocaine, and he has probably got some more of the stuff about him. He is in no danger now, but if he takes any more he may upset himself badly."

"It is rather late to send him to the infirmary," she said, "and I don't quite like to do it. Poor fellow, he seems fearfully down on his luck, and he is quite a superior kind of man. Do you think it would be safe for him to stay here for the night if he had a little medicine of some kind?"

"It would be safe enough," I replied, "if you could get possession of his coat and waistcoat and lock them up until the morning."

"Oh, I'll manage that," said she. "And about the medicine?"

"Let Simmonds walk up with me – I have taken Dr. Partridge's practice – and I will give it to him."

We re-entered the supper-room and found the conditions somewhat changed. Whether it was that the word "infirmary" had been wafted to the patient's attentive ears, I cannot say, but there were evident signs of recovery. Our friend was sitting up, glaring wildly about him, and inquiring where he was, to which questions Simmonds was furnishing answers of a luridly inaccurate character. When I had taken another look at the patient, and received a vacant stare of almost aggressive unrecognition, I took possession of the facetious Simmonds and, having promised to look in in the morning, wished the matron good-night and departed with my escort, who entertained me on the way home with picturesque, unflattering, and remarkably shrewd comments on the sufferer.

I had made up a stimulant mixture and, handed it to Simmonds when I remembered Mrs. Frood and that Simmonds would pass her house on his way back. For an instant, I thought of asking him to deliver her medicine for me, and then, with quite a shock, I realized what a hideous blunder it would have been. Evidently, the poor travellers gave their names, and if the man, Frood, had given his correctly, the coincidence of the names would have impressed Simmonds instantly, and then the murder would have been out, and the fat would have been in the fire properly. It was a narrow escape, and it made me realize how insecure was that unfortunate lady's position with this man lurking in the town. And, realizing this, I determined to trust the addressed bottle to nobody, but to leave it at the house myself. Accordingly, having made up the medicine and wrapped it neatly in paper, I thrust it into my pocket and, calling out to Mrs. Dunk that I should be back to supper in about half-an-hour, I set forth, and in a few minutes arrived at the little

Georgian doorway and plied the elegant brass knocker. The door was opened – rather incautiously, I thought – by Mrs. Frood herself.

"I am my own bottle-boy, you see, Mrs. Frood," said I, handing her the medicine. "I thought it safer not to send an addressed packet under the circumstances."

"But how good of you!" she exclaimed. "How kind and thoughtful! But you shouldn't have troubled about it tonight."

"It was only a matter of five minutes' walk," said I, "and besides, there was something that I thought you had better know." And hereupon I proceeded to give her a brief account of my recent adventures and the condition of her precious husband. "Is he subject to attacks of this kind?" I asked.

"Yes," she answered. "When he is put out about anything in some ways, he is rather like a hysterical woman. But, you see, I was right. He is penniless. And that – now I come to think of it – makes it rather odd that he should be here. But won't you come in for a moment?"

I entered and shut the door. "Why is it odd?" I asked.

"Because he would be getting some money tomorrow. I make him a small allowance, it is very little, but it is as much as I can possibly manage, and it is paid monthly, on the fifteenth of the month. But he has to apply for it personally at the bank or send an accredited messenger with a receipt, and as tomorrow is the fifteenth, the question is, why on earth is he down here now? I mean that it is odd that he should not have waited to collect the allowance before coming to hunt me up."

"If he is in communication with your banker," said I, "he could, I suppose, get a letter forwarded to you?"

"No," she replied, "the banker who pays him is the London agent of Mr. Japp's banker, and he doesn't know on whose behalf the payments are made. I had to make that arrangement, or he would have bombarded me with letters."

"Well," I said, "you had better keep close for a day or two. If his search for you is unsuccessful, he may get discouraged and raise the siege. I will let you know what his movements are, so far as I can."

She thanked me once more with most evident sincerity and, as I made my way to the door, she let me out with a cordial and friendly shake of the hand.

Chapter IV
Deals with Charity and Archaeology

Immediately after breakfast on the following morning, I made my way to Mr. Richard Watts's establishment, where I learned that all the poor travellers had departed with the exception of my patient, who had been allowed to stay pending my report on him.

"I shall be glad to see the back of him, poor fellow," said the matron, "for, of course, we have no arrangements for dealing with sick men."

"Do you often get cases of illness here?" I asked.

"I really don't know," she answered. "You see, I am only doing temporary duty here while the regular matron is away. But I should think not, though little ailments are apt to occur in the case of a poor man who has been on the road for a week or so."

"This man is on tramp, is he?" said I.

"Well, no," she replied. "It seems, from what he tells me, that his wife has left him, and he had reason to believe that she was staying in this town. So he came down here to try to find her. He supposed that Rochester was a little place where everybody knew everybody else, and that he would have no difficulty in discovering her whereabouts. But all his inquiries have come to nothing. Nobody seems to have heard of her. I suppose you don't happen to know the name – Frood?"

"I only came here yesterday, myself," was my evasive reply. "I am a stranger to the town. But is he certain that she is here?"

"I don't think he is. At any rate, he seems inclined to give up the search for the present, and he is very anxious to get back to London. But I don't know how he is going to manage it. He isn't fit to walk."

"Well," I said, "if it is only the railway fare that stands in the way, that difficulty can be got over. I will pay for his ticket, but I should like to be sure that he really goes."

"Oh, I'll see to that," she said, with evident relief. "I will go with him to the station, and get his ticket, and see him into the train. But you had better just have a look at him, and see that he is fit to go."

She conducted me to the supper-room, where our friend was sitting in a Windsor armchair, looking the very picture of misery and dejection.

"Here is the doctor come to see you, Mr. Frood," the matron said cheerfully, "and he is kind enough to say that, if you are well enough to travel, he will pay your fare to London. So there's an end of your difficulties."

The poor devil glanced at me for an instant, and then looked away and, to my intense discomfort, I saw that his eyes were filling.

"It is indeed good of you, sir," he murmured, shakily, but in a very pleasant voice and with a refined accent. "Most good and kind to help a lame dog over a stile in this way. I don't know how to thank you."

Here, as he showed a distinct tendency to weep, I replied hastily, "Not at all. We've all got to help one another in this world. And how are you feeling? Hand is still a little bit shaky, I see."

I put my finger on his wrist and then looked him over generally. He was a miserable wreck, but I judged that he was as well as he was ever likely to be.

"Well," I said, "you are not in first-class form, but you are up to a short railway journey. I suppose you have somewhere to go to in London?"

"Yes," he replied, dismally, "I have a room. It isn't in the Albany, but it is a shelter from the weather."

"Never mind," said I. "We must hope for better times. The matron is going to see you safely to the station and comfortably settled in the train – and – " Here I handed her a ten shilling note. " – you will get Mr. Frood's ticket, matron, and you had better give him the change. He may want a cab when he gets to town."

He glowered sulkily at this arrangement – I suspect he had run out of cigarettes – but he thanked me again and, when I had privately ascertained the time of the train which was to bear him away, I wished him *adieu*.

"I suppose," said I, "there is no likelihood of his hopping out at Strood to get a drink and losing the train?"

The matron smiled knowingly. "He will start from Strood," said she. "I shall take him over the bridge in the tram and put him into the London express there. We don't want him back here tonight."

Much relieved by the good lady's evident grasp of the situation, I turned away up the street and began to consider my next move. I had nothing to do this morning, for at present there was not a single patient on my books with the exception of Mrs. Frood, and it may have been in accordance with the prevailing belief that to persons in my condition, an individual, familiarly known as "the old gentleman", obligingly functions as employment agent, that my thoughts turned to that solitary patient. At any rate they did. Suddenly, it was borne in on me that I ought, without delay, to convey to her the glad tidings of her husband's departure. Whether the necessity would have appeared as urgent if her personal attractions had been less, I will not presume to say, nor whether had I been more self-critical, I should not have looked with some suspicion on this intense concern respecting the welfare of a woman who was almost a stranger to me. As it was, it appeared to me that I was but discharging a neighbourly duty when I executed an insinuating rat-tat on the handsome brass knocker which was adorned – somewhat inappropriately, under the circumstances – with a mask of Hypnos.

After a short interval, the door was opened by a spare, middle-aged woman of melancholic aspect, with tow-coloured hair and a somewhat anemic complexion, who regarded me inquiringly with a faded blue eye.

"Is Mrs. Frood at home?" I asked briskly.

"I am afraid she is not," was the reply, uttered in a dejected tone. "I saw her go out some time ago, and I haven't heard her come back. But I'll just see, if you will come in a moment."

I entered the hall and listened with an unaccountable feeling of disappointment as she rapped on the door first of the front room, and then of the back.

"She isn't in her rooms there," was the dispirited report, "but she may be in the basement. I'll call out and ask."

She retired to the inner hall and gave utterance to a wail like that of an afflicted sea-gull. But there was no response, and I began to feel myself infected by her melancholy.

"I am sorry you have missed her, sir," said she, and then she asked, "Are you her doctor, sir?"

I felt myself justified in affirming that I was, whereupon she exclaimed, "Ah, poor thing! It is a comfort to know that she has someone to look after her. She has been looking very sadly of late. Very sadly, she has."

I began to back cautiously towards the door, but she followed me up and continued. "I am afraid she has had a deal of trouble – a deal of trouble, poor dear. Not that she ever speaks of it to me. But I know. I can see the lines of grief and sorrow – like a worm in the bud, so to speak, sir – and it makes my heart ache. It does, indeed."

I mumbled sympathetically and continued to back towards the door.

"I don't see very much of her," she continued in a plaintive tone. "She keeps herself very close. Too close, I think. You see, she does for herself entirely. Now and again, when she asks me, which is very seldom, I put a bit of supper in her room. That is all. And I do think that it isn't good for a young woman to live so solitary, and I do hope you'll make her take a little more change."

"I suppose she goes out sometimes," said I, noting that she was out at the present moment.

"Oh, yes," was the reply. "She goes out a good deal. But always alone. She never has any society."

"And what time does she usually come in?" I asked, with a view to a later call.

"About six, or between that and seven. Then she has her supper and puts the things out on the hall table. And that is the last I usually see of her."

By this time I had reached the door and softly unfastened the latch.

"If you should see her," I said, "you might tell her that I shall look in this evening about half-past seven."

"Certainly, sir," she replied. "I shall see her at lunch-time, and I will give her your message."

I thanked her and, having now got the door open, I wished her good morning, and retreated down the steps.

As I was in the act of turning away, my eye lighted on the adjacent bay window, appertaining to the office of Messrs. Japp and Bundy, and I then perceived above the green curtain the upper half of a human face, including a pair of tortoiseshell-rimmed spectacles, an apparition which informed me that Mr. Bundy had been – to use Sam Weller's expression – "a-twigging of me." On catching my eye, the face rose higher, disclosing a broad grin, whereupon, without any apparent reason, I felt myself turning somewhat red. However, I mounted the official steps and, opening the office door, confronted the smiler and his more sedate partner.

"Ha!" said the former, "you drew a blank, Doctor. I saw the lovely Angelina go out about an hour ago. Whom did you see?"

"The lady of the house, I presume – a pale, depressed female."

"I know," said Bundy. "Looks like an undertaker's widow. That's Mrs. Gillow. Rhymes with willow – very appropriate, too," and he began to chant in an absurd, Punch-like voice, "Oh, all round my hat I'll wear the green – "

"Be quiet, Bundy," said Mr. Japp, regarding his partner with a wrinkly and indulgent smile.

Bundy clapped his hand over his mouth and blew out his cheeks, and I took the opportunity to explain. "I called on Mrs. Frood to let her know that her husband is leaving the town."

"Leaving the town, is he?" said Mr. Japp, elevating his eyebrows and thereby causing his forehead to resemble a small Venetian blind. "Do you know when?"

"He goes this morning by the ten-thirty express to London."

"Hooray!" ejaculated Bundy, with a flourish of his arms that nearly capsized his stool. He recovered himself with an effort, and then, fixing his eyes on me, proceeded to whistle the opening bars of "O! Thou that tellest good tidings to Zion!"

"That'll do, Bundy," said Mr. Japp. Then turning to me, he asked, "Where did you learn these good tidings, Doctor?"

I gave them a brief account of the happenings of the previous night and this morning's sequel, to which they listened with deep attention. When I had finished Mr. Japp said, "You have done a very great kindness to my friend Mrs. Frood. It will be an immense relief to her to know that she can walk abroad without the danger of encountering this man. Besides, if he had stayed here he would probably have found her out."

"He might even have found her at home," said Bundy, "and that would have been worse. So I propose a vote of thanks to the doctor – with musical honours. *For-hor he's a jolly good fell –* "

"There, that'll do, Bundy, that'll do," said Mr. Japp. "I never saw such a fellow. You'll have the neighbours complaining."

Bundy leaned towards me confidentially and remarked in a stage whisper, glancing at his partner, "Fidgetty old cove, regular old killjoy." Then, with a sudden change of manner, he asked, "What about that wall job, Japp? Are you going to have a look at them?"

"I can't go at present," said Japp. "Bulford will be coming in presently and I must see him. Have you got anything special to do?"

"Only old Jeff'son's lease, and that can wait. Shall I trot over and see what sort of mess they are making of things?"

"I wish you would," said Japp, whereupon Mr. Bundy removed his spectacles, stuck in his eye-glass, extracted from the desk his hat and gloves which he assumed with the aid of the looking-glass, and took his stick from the corner. Then he looked at me reflectively and asked, "Are you interested in archaeology, Doctor?"

"Somewhat," I replied. "Why do you ask?"

"Because we are putting some patches in the remains of the city wall. It isn't much to look at, and there isn't a great deal of the original Roman work left, but if you would care to have a look at it, you might walk up there with me."

I agreed readily, being, as I have said, somewhat at a loose end, and we set forth together, Bundy babbling cheerfully as we went.

"I have often thought," said he, "that there must have been something rather pleasant and restful about the old walled cities, particularly after curfew when the gates were shut – that is, provided you were inside at the time."

"Yes," said I. "An enclosed precinct has a certain agreeable quality of seclusion that you can't get in an open town or village. When I was a

69

student, I lived for a time in chambers in Staple Inn, and it was, as you say, rather pleasant, when one came home at night, and the porter had let one in at the wicket, to enter and find the gates closed, the courts all quiet and empty, and to know that all traffic was stopped and all strangers shut out until the morning. But it doesn't appear to be in accordance with modern taste, for those old Chancery Inns have nearly all gone, and there is no tendency to replace them with anything similar."

"No," Bundy agreed, stopping to look up at an old timber house. "Taste in regard to buildings, if there is any – Japp says there isn't – has changed completely in the last hundred years or so. Look at this alley we are in now. Every house has got a physiognomy of its own. But when we rebuild it, we shall fill it up with houses that will look as if they had been bought in packets like match-boxes."

Gossiping thus, we threaded our way through all sorts of queer little alleys and passages. At length Bundy stopped at a wooden gate in a high fence and, pushing it open, motioned for me to enter, and as I did so he drew out the key which was in the lock and put it in his pocket.

The place which we had entered was a space of waste land, littered with the remains of some old houses that had been demolished and enclosed on three sides by high fences. The fourth side was formed by a great mass of crumbling rubble, patched in places with rough masonry and brickwork, and showing in its lower part the remains of courses of Roman bricks. It rose to a considerable height, and was evidently of enormous thickness, as could be seen where large areas of the face had crumbled away, exposing great cavities in which wall-flowers, valerian and other rock-haunting plants, had taken up their abode. On one of these a small gang of men were at work, and it was evident that repairs on a considerable scale were contemplated, for there were several large heaps of rough stone and old bricks, and in a cart-shed in a corner of the space were a large number of barrels of lime.

As we entered, the foreman came forward to meet us, and Bundy handed him the key from the gate.

"Better keep it in your pocket," said he. "Mr. Japp is rather particular about keys that he has charge of. He doesn't like them left in doors or gates. How are the men getting on?"

"As well as you can expect of a lot of casuals like these," was the reply "There isn't a mason or a bricklayer among them, excepting that old chap that's mixing the mortar. However, it's only a rough job."

We walked over to the part of the old wall where the men were at work, and the appearances certainly justified the foreman's last remark. It was a very rough job. The method appeared to consist in building up outside the cavity a primitive wall of unhewn stone with plenty of mortar

70

and, when it had risen a foot or two, filling up the cavity inside with loose bricks, lumps of stone, shovelfuls of liquid mortar, and chunks of lime.

I ventured to remark that it did not look a very secure method of building, upon which Bundy turned his eyeglass on me and smiled knowingly.

"My dear Doctor," said he, "you don't appear to appreciate the subtlety of the method. The purpose of these activities is to create employment. That has been clearly stated by the town council. But if you want to create employment you build a wall that will tumble down and give somebody else the job of putting it up again."

Here, as a man suddenly bore down on us with a bucket of mortar, Bundy hopped back to avoid the unclean contact, and nearly sat down on a heap of smoking lime.

"You had a narrow escape that time, mister," remarked the old gentleman who presided over the mortar department, as Bundy carefully dusted his delicate shoes with his handkerchief. "That stuff would 'ave made short work of them fine clothes of yourn."

"Would it?" said Bundy, dusting his shoes yet more carefully and wiping the soles on the turf.

"Ah," rejoined the old man, "terrible stuff is quicklime. Eats up everything same as what fire does." He rested his hands on his shovel and, assuming a reminiscent air, continued, "There was a pal o' mine what was skipper of a barge. A iron barge, she was, and he had to take on a lading of lime from some kilns. The stuff was put aboard with a shoot. Well, my pal, he gets 'is barge under the shoot and then 'e goes off, leavin' 'is mate to see the lime shot into the hold. Well, it seems the mate had been takin' some stuff aboard, too. Beer, or p'raps whisky. At any rate, he'd got a skinful. Well, presently the skipper comes back, and he sees 'em a-tippin' the trucks of lime on to the shoot, and he sees the barge's hold beginning to fill, but 'e don't see 'is mate nowhere. He goes aboard, down to the cabin, but there ain't no signs of the mate there, nor yet anywheres else. Well, they gets the barge loaded and the hatch-covers on, and everything ready for sea, and still there ain't no signs of the mate. So my pal, rememberin' that the mate – his name was Bill – rememberin' that Bill seemed a bit squiffy, supposed he must 'ave gone overboard. So 'e takes on a fresh hand temporary and off 'e goes on 'is trip.

"Well, they makes their port all right and brings up alongside the wharf, but owing to a strike among the transport men they can't unload for about three weeks. However, when the strike is over, they rigs a whip and a basket and begins to get the stuff out. All goes well until they get

71

down to the bottom tier. Then one of the men brings up a bone on his shovel. 'Hallo!' says the skipper. 'What's bones a-doin' in a cargo of fresh lime?' He rakes over the stuff on the floor and up comes a skull with a hole in the top of it. 'Why, blow me,' says the skipper, 'if that don't look like Bill. He warn't as thin in the face as all that, but I seem to know them teeth.' Just then one of the men finds a clay pipe, and the skipper reckernizes it at once. 'That there's Bill's pipe,' sez he, 'and them bones is Bill's bones,' 'e sez. And so they were. They found 'is belt-buckle and 'is knife, and 'is trouser buttons and the nails out of 'is boots. And that's all there was left of Bill. He must have tumbled down into the hold and cracked his nut, and then the first truckful of lime must 'ave covered 'im up. So, if you sets any value on them 'andsome shoes o' yourn, don't you go a-treadin' in quick lime."

Bundy looked down anxiously at his shoes and, having given them an additional wipe, he moved away from the dangerous neighbourhood of the lime and we went together to examine the ancient wall.

"That was rather a tall yarn of the old man's," remarked Bundy. "Is it a fact that lime is as corrosive as he made out?"

"I don't really know very much about it," I replied. "There is a general belief that it will consume almost anything but metal. How true that is I can't say, but I remember that at the Crippen trial one of the medical experts – I think it was Pepper – said that if the body had been buried in quicklime it would have been entirely consumed – excepting the bones, of course. But it is difficult to believe that a body could disappear completely in three weeks, or thereabouts, as our friend said. How fine this old wall looks with those clumps of valerian and wallflowers growing on it! I suppose it encircled the town completely at one time?"

"Yes," he replied, "and it is a pity there isn't more of it left, or at least one or two of the gateways. A city gate is such a magnificent adornment. Think of the gates of Canterbury and Rye, and especially at Sandwich, where you actually enter the town through the barbican, and think of what Rochester must have been before all the gates were pulled down. But you must hear Japp on the subject. He's a regular architectural Jeremiah. By the way, what did you think of Mrs. Frood? You saw her last night, didn't you?"

"Yes, I was rather taken with her. She is very nice and friendly and unaffected, and good-looking, too. I thought her distinctly handsome."

"She isn't bad-looking," Bundy admitted. "But I can't stand her voice. It gets on my nerves. I hate a squeaky voice."

72

"I shouldn't call it squeaky," said I. "It is a high voice, and rather sing-song, and it isn't, somehow, quite in keeping with her appearance and manner."

"No," said Bundy, "that's what it is. She's too big for a voice like that."

I laughed at the quaint expression. "People's voices," said I, "are not like steamers' whistles, graduated in pitch according to their tonnage. Besides, Mrs. Frood is not such a very big woman."

"She is a good size," said he. "I should call her rather tall. At any rate, she is taller than I am. But I suppose you will say that she might be that without competing with the late Mrs. Bates."

"Comparisons between the heights of men and women," I said cautiously, "are rather misleading," and here I changed the subject, though I judged that Bundy was not sensitive in regard to his stature, for while he was cleaning the lime from his shoes I had noticed that he wore unusually low heels. Nor need he have been, for though on a small scale, he was quite an important-looking person.

"Don't you think," he asked, after a pause, "that it is rather queer that the man Frood should have gone off so soon? He only came down yesterday, and he can't have made much of a search for Madame."

"The queer thing is that he should have come down on that particular day," I replied. "It seems that he draws a monthly allowance on the fifteenth. That was what made him so anxious to get back, but it is odd that he didn't put off his visit here until he had collected the money."

"If he had run his wife to earth, he could have collected it from her," said Bundy. "I wonder how he found out that she was here."

"He evidently hadn't very exact information," I said, "nor did he seem quite certain that she really was here. And his failure to get any news of her appears to have discouraged him considerably. It is just possible that he has gone back to get more precise information if he can, when he has drawn his allowance."

"That is very likely," Bundy agreed, "and it is probable that we haven't seen the last of him yet."

"I have a strong suspicion that we haven't," said I.

"If he is sure she is here, and can get enough money together to come and spend a week here, he will be pretty certain to discover her whereabouts. It is a dreadful position for her. She ought to get a judicial separation."

"I doubt if she could," said he. "You may be sure he would contest that application pretty strongly, and what case would she have in support of it? He is an unclean blighter, he doesn't work, he smokes and drinks too much, and you say he takes drugs. But he doesn't seem to be violent or dangerous or threatening, or to be on questionable terms with other women – at least, I have never heard anything to that effect. Have you?"

"No," I answered. I had said nothing to him or Japp about the London incident. "He seems to have married the only woman in the world who would look at him."

Bundy grinned. "An unkind cut, that, Doctor," said he, "but I believe you're right. And here we are, back at the official premises. Are you coming in?"

I declined the invitation, and as he skipped up the steps I turned my face homewards.

Chapter V
John Thorndyke

The sexual preferences or affinities of men and women have always impressed me as very mysterious and inexplicable. I am referring to the selective choice of individuals, not to the general attraction of the sexes for one another. Why should a particular pair of human beings single one another out from the mass of their fellows as preferable to all others? Why to one particular man does one particular woman and no other become the exciting cause of the emotion of love? It is not a matter of mere physical beauty or mental excellence, for if it were, men and women would be simply classifiable into the attractive and the non-attractive, whereas we find in practice that a woman who may be to the majority of men an object of indifference, is to some one man an object of passionate love, and vice-versa. Nor is love necessarily accompanied by any delusions as to the worth of its object, for it will persist in spite of the clear recognition of personal defects and in conscious conflict with judgment and reason.

The above reflections, with others equally profound, occupied my mind as I sat on a rather uncomfortable little rush-seated chair in the nave of Rochester Cathedral, whither I had proceeded in obedience to orders from Mrs. Dunk to attend the choral afternoon service, and they were occasioned by the sudden recognition – not without surprise – of the very deep impression that had been made on me by my patient, Mrs. Frood. For the intensity of that impression I could not satisfactorily account. It is true that her circumstances were interesting and provocative of sympathy. But that was no reason for the haunting of my thoughts by her, of which I was conscious. She was not a really beautiful woman, though I thought her more than commonly good-looking, and she had evidently made no particular impression on Bundy. Yet, though I had seen her but three times, including my first meeting with her a year ago, I had to recognize that she had hardly been out of my thoughts since, and I was aware of looking forward with ridiculous expectancy to my proposed visit to her this evening.

Thus, speculations on the meaning of this preoccupation mingled themselves with other speculations – as, for instance, on the abrupt changes of intention suggested by half of an Early English arch clapped up against a Norman pier, and as my thoughts rambled on, undisturbed by a pleasant voice, intoning with soothing unintelligibility somewhere beyond the stone screen, I watched with languid curiosity the strangers who entered and stole on tiptoe to the nearest vacant chair. Presently, however, as the intoning voice gave place to the deep, pervading hum of the organ, a visitor entered who instantly attracted my attention.

He was obviously a personage – a real personage, not one of those who have achieved greatness by the free use of their elbows, or have had it thrust upon them by influential friends. This was an unmistakable thoroughbred. He was a tall man, very erect and dignified in carriage, and in spite of his iron-grey hair, evidently strong, active, and athletic. But it was his face that specially riveted my attention – not merely by reason that it was a handsome, symmetrical face, inclining to the Greek type, with level brows, a fine, straight nose, and a shapely mouth, but rather on account of its suggestion of commanding strength and intelligence. It was a strangely calm – even immobile – face, but yet it conveyed a feeling of attentiveness and concentration, and especially of power.

I watched the stranger curiously as he stepped quietly to a seat not far from me, noting how he seemed to stand out from the ordinary men who surrounded him, and wondering who he was. But I was not left to wonder very long. A few moments later another visitor arrived – but not a stranger this time, for in this newcomer I recognized an old acquaintance, a Dr. Jervis, whom I had known when I was a student and when he had taken temporary charge of my uncle's practice. Since then, as I had learned, he had qualified as a barrister and specialized in legal medicine as the coadjutor of the famous medical jurist, Dr. John Thorndyke.

For a few moments Jervis stood near the entrance looking about the nave, as if in search of someone. Then, suddenly, his eye lighted on the distinguished stranger, and he walked straight over to him and sat down by his side, from which, and from the smile of recognition with which he was greeted, I inferred that the stranger was none other than Dr. Thorndyke himself.

Jervis had apparently not seen, or at least not recognized me, but, as I observed that there was a vacant chair by his side, I determined to renew our acquaintance and secure, if possible, a presentation to his eminent colleague. Accordingly, I crossed the nave and, taking the vacant chair, introduced myself, and was greeted with a cordial handshake.

The circumstances did not admit of conversation, but presently, when the anthem appeared to be drawing to a close, Jervis glanced at his watch and whispered to me, "I want to hear all your news, Strangeways,

76

and to introduce you to Thorndyke, and we must get some tea before we go to the station. Shall we clear out now?"

As I assented he whispered to Thorndyke, and we all rose and filed silently towards the door, our exit covered by the concluding strains of the anthem. As soon as we were outside Jervis presented me to his colleague, and suggested an immediate adjournment to some place of refreshment. I proposed that they should come and have tea with me, but Jervis replied, "I'm afraid we haven't time today. There is a very comfortable teashop close to the Jasperian gate-house. You had better come there and then perhaps you can walk to the station with us."

We adopted this plan, and when we had established ourselves on a settle by the window of the ancient, low-ceiled room and given our orders to a young lady in a becoming brown costume, Jervis proceeded to interrogate.

"And what might you be doing in Rochester, Strangeways?"

"Nominally," I replied, "I am engaged in medical practice. Actually, I am a gentleman at large. I have taken a death vacancy here, and I arrived yesterday morning."

"Any patients?" he inquired.

"Two at present," I answered. "One I brought down with me and returned empty this morning. The other is his wife."

"Ha," said Jervis, "a concise statement, but obscure. It seems to require amplification."

I accordingly proceeded to amplify, describing in detail my journey from town and my subsequent dealings with my fellow-traveller. The circumstances of Mrs. Frood, being matters of professional confidence, I was at first disposed to suppress, but then, reflecting that my two friends were in a position to give expert opinions and advice, I put them in possession of all the facts that were known to me, excepting the Regent's Park incident, which I felt hardly at liberty to disclose.

"Well," said Jervis, when I had finished, "if the rest of your practice develops on similar lines, we shall have to set up a branch establishment in your neighbourhood. There are all sorts of possibilities in this case. Don't you think so, Thorndyke?"

"I should hardly say 'all sorts'," was the reply. "The possibilities seem to me to be principally of one sort, extremely disagreeable for the poor lady. She has the alternatives of allowing herself to be associated with this man – which seems to be impossible – or of spending the remainder of her life in a perpetual effort to escape from him, which is an appalling prospect for a young woman."

"Yes," agreed Jervis, "it is bad enough. But there seems to me worse possibilities with a fellow of this kind, a drinking, drug-swallowing, hysterical degenerate. You never know what a man of that type will do."

"You always hope that he will commit suicide," said Thorndyke, "and to do him justice, he does fairly often show that much perception of his proper place in nature. But, as you say, the actions of a mentally and morally abnormal man are incalculable. He may kill himself or he may kill somebody else, or he may join with other abnormals to commit incomprehensible and apparently motiveless political crimes. But we will hope that Mr. Frood will limit his activities to sponging on his wife."

The conversation now turned from my affairs to those of my friends, and I ventured to inquire what had brought them to Rochester.

"We came down," said Jervis, "to watch an inquest for one of our insurance clients. But after all it has had to be adjourned for a fortnight. So we may have the pleasure of seeing you again."

"We won't leave it to chance," said I. "Let us settle that you come to lunch with me, if that will be convenient. You can fix your own time."

My two friends consulted and, having referred to their time-table, accepted the invitation for one o'clock on that day fortnight, and when I had "booked the appointment", we finished our tea and sallied forth, making our way over the bridge to Strood Station, at the main entrance to which I wished them *adieu*.

As I turned away from the station and sauntered slowly along the shore before recrossing the bridge, I recalled the conversation of my two colleagues with a certain vague discomfort. To both of them, it was evident, the relations of my fair patient and her husband presented sinister possibilities, although I had not informed them of the actual murderous attack, and though the more cautious reticent Thorndyke had seemed to minimize them, his remarks had expressed what was already in my own mind, accentuated by what I knew. These nervy, abnormal men are never safe to deal with. Their unstable emotions may be upset in a moment and then no one can tell what will happen. It was quite possible that Frood had come to Rochester with the perfectly peaceable intention of inducing his wife to return to him. But this was far from certain, and I shuddered to think of what might follow a refusal on her part. I did not like that knife. I have a sane man's dislike of lethal weapons of all kinds, but especially do I dislike them in the hands of those whose self-control is liable to break down suddenly.

It was true that this man had not succeeded in finding his wife, and even seemed to have given up the search. But I felt pretty certain that he had not. Somehow, he had discovered that she was in the town, and from the same source he might get further information and, in any case, I felt no doubt that he would renew the pursuit, and that, in the end, he would find her. And then – but at this point I found myself opposite the house and observed Mrs. Gillow standing on the doorstep, fumbling in her pocket for the latch-key. She had just extracted it, and was in the act of inserting it into the latch when I crossed the road and made my presence known. She greeted me with a wan smile as I ascended the steps and, having by this time got the door open, admitted me to the hall.

"I gave Mrs. Frood your message at lunch-time, sir," said she, in a depressed tone, "and I believe she has come in." Here, having closed the street door, she rapped softly with her knuckles at that of the front room, whereupon the voice to which Bundy objected so much called out, "Come in, Mrs. Gillow."

The latter threw the door open. "It is the doctor, Madam," said she, and on this announcement, I walked in.

"I didn't hear you knock," said Mrs. Frood, rising, and holding out her hand.

"I didn't knock," I replied. "I sneaked in under cover of Mrs. Gillow."

"That was very secret and cautious of you," said she. "You make me feel like a sort of feminine Prince Charlie, lying perdu in the robbers' cavern, whereas I have actually been taking my walks abroad and brazenly looking in the shop windows. But I have kept a sharp lookout, all the same."

"There really wasn't any need," said I. "The siege is raised."

"You don't mean that my husband has gone?" she exclaimed.

"I do, indeed," I answered, and I gave her a brief account of the events of the morning, suppressing my unofficial part in the transaction.

"Do you think," she asked, "that the matron paid his fare out of her own pocket?"

"I am sure she didn't," I answered hastily. "She touched some local altruist for the amount – it was only a few shillings, you know."

"Still," she said, "I feel that I ought to refund those few shillings. They were really expended for my benefit."

"Well, you can't," I said with some emphasis. "You couldn't do it without disclosing your identity, and then you would have some philanthropist trying to effect a reconciliation. Your cue is to keep yourself to yourself for the present."

"For the present!" she echoed. "It seems to me that I have got to be a fugitive for the rest of my natural life. It is a horrible position, to have to live in a state of perpetual concealment, like a criminal, and never dare to make an acquaintance."

"Don't you know anyone in Rochester?" I asked.

"Not a soul," she replied, "excepting Mr. Japp, who is a relative by marriage – he was my aunt's brother-in-law – his partner, and Mrs. Gillow, and you. And you all know my position."

"Does Mrs. Gillow know the state of affairs?" I asked in some surprise.

"Yes," she answered, "I thought it best to tell her, in confidence, so that she should understand that I want to live a quiet life."

"I suppose you haven't cut yourself off completely from all your friends?" said I.

"Very nearly. I haven't many friends that I really care about much, but I keep in touch with one or two of my old comrades. But I have had to swear them to secrecy – though it looks as if the secret had leaked out in some way. Of course they all know Nicholas – my husband."

"And I suppose you have been able to learn from them how your husband views the separation?"

"Yes. Of course he thinks I have treated him abominably, and he evidently suspects that I have some motive for leaving him other than mere dislike of his unpleasant habits. The usual motive, in fact."

"What Sam Weller would call a 'priory attachment'?" I suggested.

"Yes. He is a jealous and suspicious man by nature. I had quite a lot of trouble with him in that way before that final outbreak, though I have always been most circumspect in my relations with other men. Still, a woman doesn't complain of a little jealousy. Within reason, it is a natural, masculine failing."

"I should consider a tendency to use a knitted silk necktie for purposes which I need not specify as going rather beyond ordinary masculine failings," I remarked drily, on which she laughed and admitted that perhaps it was so. There was a short pause, then, turning to a fresh subject, she asked, "Do you think you will get any of Dr. Partridge's practice?"

"I suspect not, or at any rate very little, and that reminds me that I have not yet inquired as to my patient's condition. Are you any better?"

As I asked the question, I looked at her attentively, and noted that she was still rather pale and haggard, so far as I could judge by the subdued light of the shaded lamp, and that the darkness under the eyes remained undiminished.

"I am afraid I am not doing you much credit," she replied, with a faint smile. "But you can't expect any improvement while these unsettled conditions exist. If you could induce my respected husband to elope with another woman, you would effect an immediate cure."

"I am afraid," said I, "that is beyond my powers, to say nothing of the inhumanity to the other woman. But we must persevere. You must let me look in on you from time to time, just to keep an eye on you."

"I hope you will," she replied, energetically. "If it doesn't weary you to listen to my complaints and gossip a little, please keep me on your visiting list. With the exception of Mr. Japp, you are the only human creature that I hold converse with. Mrs. Gillow is a dear, good creature, but instinct warns me not to get on conversational terms with her. She's rather lonely, too."

"Yes, you might find it difficult to turn the tap off. I am always very cautious with housekeepers and landladies."

She darted a mischievous glance at me. "Even if your landlady happens to be your patient?" she asked.

I chuckled as I remembered our dual relationship.

"That," said I "is an exceptional case. The landlady becomes merged in the patient, and the patient tends to become a friend."

"The doctor," she retorted, "tends very strongly to become a friend, and a very kind and helpful friend. I think you have been exceedingly good to me – a mere waif who has drifted across your horizon."

"Well," I said, "if you think so, far be it from me to contradict you. One may as well pick up gratefully a stray crumb of commendation that one doesn't deserve to set off against the deserved credit that one doesn't get. But I should like to think that all my good deeds in the future will be as agreeable in the doing."

She gave me a prim little smile. "We are getting monstrously polite," she remarked, upon which we both laughed.

"However," said I, "the moral of it all is that you ought to have a friendly medical eye kept on you and, as mine is the eye that happens to be available, and as you are kind enough to accept the optical supervision, I shall give myself the pleasure of looking in on you from time to time to see how you are and to hear how the world wags. What is the best time to find you at home?"

"I am nearly always at home after seven o'clock, but perhaps that is not very convenient for you. I don't know how you manage your practice."

"The fact is," said I, "that at present you are my practice, so I shall adapt my visiting round to your circumstances, and make my call at, or after, seven. I suppose you get some exercise?"

"Oh, yes. Quite a lot. I walk out in the country, and wander about Chatham and Gillingham and out to Frindsbury. I have been along the Watling Street as far as Cobham. Rochester itself I rather avoid for fear of making acquaintances, though it is a pleasant old town in spite of the improvements."

As she spoke of these solitary rambles, the idea floated into my mind that, later on, I might perchance offer to diminish their solitude. But I quickly dismissed it. Her position was, in any case, one of some delicacy – that of a young woman living apart from her husband. It would be an act the very reverse of friendly to compromise her in any way, nor would it tend at all to my own professional credit. A doctor's reputation is nearly as tender as a woman's.

Our conversation had occupied nearly three-quarters-of-an-hour and, although I would willingly have lingered, it appeared to me that I had made as long a visit as was permissible. I accordingly rose and, having given a few words of somewhat perfunctory professional advice, shook hands with my patient and let myself out.

Chapter VI
The Shadows Deepen

The coming events, whose premonitory shadows had been falling upon me unnoted since I came to Rochester, were daily drawing nearer. Perhaps it may have been that the deepening shadows began dimly to make themselves felt, that some indistinct sense of instability and insecurity had begun to steal into my consciousness. It may have been so. But, nevertheless, looking back, I can see that when the catastrophe burst upon me it found me all unsuspicious and unprepared.

Nearly a fortnight had passed since my meeting with my two friends in the Cathedral, and I was looking forward with some eagerness to their impending visit. During that fortnight little seemed to have happened, though the trivial daily occurrences were beginning to acquire a cumulative significance not entirely unperceived by me. My promise to Mrs. Frood had been carried out very thoroughly, for at least every alternate evening had found me seated by the little table with the red-shaded lamp, making the best pretence I could of being there in a professional capacity.

It was unquestionably indiscreet. The instant liking that I had taken to this woman should have warned me that here was one of those unaccountable "affinities" that are charged with such immense potentialities of blessing or disaster. The first impression should have made it clear to me that I could not safely spend much time in her society. But unfortunately the very circumstance that should have warned me to keep away was the magnet that drew me to her side.

However, there was one consoling fact: If the indiscretion was mine, so by me alone were the consequences supported. Our relations were of the most unexceptionable kind – indeed, she was not the sort of woman with whom any man would have taken a liberty. As to my feelings towards her, I could not pretend to deceive myself, but similarly, I had no delusions as to her feelings towards me. She welcomed my visits with that frank simplicity that is delightful to a friend and hopeless to a lover. It was plain to me that the bare possibility of anything beyond straightforward, honest friendship never entered her head. But this very innocence and purity, while at once a rebuke and a reassurance, but riveted my fetters the more firmly.

Such as our friendship was (and disregarding the secret reservation on my side), it grew apace – indeed, it sprang into existence at our first meeting. There was between us that ease and absence of reserve that distinguishes the intercourse of those who like and understand one another. I never had any fear of unwittingly giving offence. In our long talks and discussions, we had no need of choosing our words or phrases or of making allowances for possible prejudices. We could say plainly what we meant with the perfect assurance that it would be neither misunderstood nor resented. In short, if my feelings towards her could only have been kept at the same level as hers towards me, our friendship would have been perfect.

In the course of these long and pleasant gossiping visits, I observed my patient somewhat closely and, quite apart from the personal affinity, I became more and more favourably impressed. She was a clever woman, quick and alert in mind, and evidently well informed. She seemed to be kindly, and was certainly amiable and even-tempered, though not in the least weak or deficient in character. Probably, in happier circumstances, she would have been more gay and vivacious, for, though she was habitually rather grave and even sombre, there were occasional flashes of wit that suggested a naturally lively temperament.

As to her appearance – to repeat in more detail what I have already said – she was a rather large woman, very erect and somewhat stately in bearing, distinctly good-looking (though of this I was not, perhaps, a very good judge). Her features were regular, but not in any way striking. Her expression was, as I have said, a little sombre and severe, the mouth firmly set and slightly depressed at the corners, the eyebrows black, straight, and unusually well-marked and nearly meeting above the nose. She had an abundance of black, or nearly black, hair, parted low on the forehead and drawn back loosely, covering the ears and temples, and she wore a largish coil nearly on the top of the head, a formal, matronly style that accentuated the gravity of her expression.

Such was Angelina Frood as I looked on her in those never-to-be-forgotten evenings, as she rises before the eyes of memory as I write, and as she will remain in my recollection so long as I live.

In this fortnight, one really arresting incident had occurred. It was just a week after my meeting with Dr. Thorndyke, when, returning from a walk along the London Road as far as Gad's Hill, I stopped on Rochester Bridge to watch a barge which had just passed under, and was rehoisting her lowered mast. As I was leaning on the parapet, a man brushed past me, and I turned my head idly to look at him. Then, in an instant, I started up, for though the man's back was towards me, there was something unmistakably familiar in the gaunt figure, the seedy clothes, the great cloth cap, the shock of mouse-coloured hair, and the thick oaken stick that he swung in his hand. But I was not going to leave myself in any doubt on the subject. Cautiously I began to retrace my steps, keeping him in view but avoiding overtaking him, until he reached the western end of the bridge, when he halted and looked back. Then any possible doubt was set at rest. The man was Nicholas Frood. I don't know whether he saw me – he made no sign of recognition, and when he turned and walked on, I continued to follow, determined to make sure of his destination.

As I had hoped and expected, he took the road to the right, leading to the river bank and the station. Still following him, I noted that he walked at a fairly brisk pace and seemed to have recovered completely from his debility – if that debility had not been entirely counterfeit. Opposite the pier he turned into the station approach, and when from the corner I had watched him enter the station, I gave up the pursuit, assuming that he was returning to London.

But how long had he been in Rochester? What had he been doing, and what success had he had in his search? These were the questions that I asked myself as I walked back over the bridge. Probably he had come down for the day, and since he was returning, it was reasonable to infer that he had had no luck. As I entered the town and glanced up at the great clock that hangs out across the street from the Corn Exchange, like a sort of horological warming-pan, I saw that it was close upon eight. It was a good deal after my usual time for calling on Mrs. Frood, but the circumstances were exceptional and I felt that it was necessary to ascertain whether anything untoward had occurred. I was still debating what I should do when, as I came opposite the house, I saw Mrs. Gillow coming out of the door. Immediately I crossed the road and accosted her.

"Have you seen Mrs. Frood this evening, Mrs. Gillow?" I asked, after passing the usual compliments.

"Yes, sir," was the reply. "I left her only a few minutes ago working at one of the drawings that she does for Mr. Japp. She seems better this evening – brighter and more cheerful. I think your visits have done her good, sir. It is a lonely life for a young woman – having no one to talk to all through the long evenings. I'm always glad to hear your knock, and so, I think, is she."

"I'm pleased to hear you say so, Mrs. Gillow," said I. "However, as it is rather late, and she has something to occupy her, I don't think I will call this evening."

With this I took my leave and went on my way in better spirits. Evidently all was well so far. Nevertheless, the reappearance of this man was an uncomfortable incident. It was clear that he had not given up the pursuit and, seeing that Rochester was only some thirty miles from London, it would be quite easy for him to make periodical descents on the place to continue the search. There was no denying that Mrs. Frood's position was extremely insecure, and I could think of no plan for making it less so, excepting that of leaving Rochester, for a time at least, a solution which ought to have commended itself to me, but did not.

Perhaps it was this fact that decided me not to say anything about the incident. The obvious thing was to have told her and put her on her guard. But I persuaded myself that it would only make her anxious to no purpose, that she could not prevent him from coming nor could she take any further measures for concealment. And then there was the possibility that he might never come again.

So far as I know, he never did. During the rest of the week I perambulated the town hour after hour, looking into the shops, scanning the faces of the wayfarers in the streets and even visiting the stations at the times when the London trains were due, but never a glimpse did I catch of that ill-omened figure.

And all the time, the shadows were deepening, and that which cast them was drawing nearer.

It was nearly a week after my meeting with Nicholas Frood that an event befell at which I looked askance at the time and which was, as it turned out, the opening scene of a new act. It was on the Saturday. I am able to fix the date by an incident, trivial enough in itself, but important by reason of its forming thus a definite point of departure. My visitors were due on the following Monday, and it had occurred to me that I had better lay in a little stock of wine, and as Mr. Japp was an old resident who knew everybody in the town, I decided to consult him as to the choice of a wine merchant.

It was a little past mid-day when I arrived at the office, and as I entered I observed that some kind of conference was in progress. A man, whom I recognized as the foreman of the gang who were working on the old wall, was standing sheepishly with his knuckles resting on the table, Bundy had swung round on his stool and was glaring owlishly through his great spectacles, while Mr. Japp was sitting bolt upright, his forehead in a state of extreme corrugation and his eyes fixed severely on the foreman.

"I suppose," said Bundy, "you left it in the gate?"

"I expect Evans did," replied the foreman. "You see, I had to call in at the office, so I gave the key to Evans and told him to go on with the other men and let them in. When I got there the gate was open and the men were at work, and I forgot all about the key until it was time to come away and lock up. Then I asked Evans for it, and he said he'd left it in the gate. But when I went to look for it it wasn't there. Someone must have took it out."

"Doesn't seem very likely," said Bundy. "However, I suppose it will turn up. It had one of our wooden labels tied to it. Shall I give him the duplicate to lock up the place?"

"You must, I suppose," said Japp, "but it must be brought straight back and given to me. You understand, Smith? Bring it back at once, and deliver it to me or to Mr. Bundy. And look here, Smith. I shall offer ten shillings reward for that key, and if it is brought back and I have to pay the reward you will have to make it up among you. You understand that?"

Smith indicated grumpily that he understood, and when Bundy had handed him the duplicate key, he took his departure in dudgeon.

When he had gone I stated my business, and Bundy pricked up his ears.

"Wine, hey?" said he, removing his spectacles and assuming his eyeglass. "Tucker will be the man for him, won't he, Japp? Very superior wine merchant is Tucker. Old and crusted, round and soft, rare and curious. I'd better pop round with him and introduce him, hadn't I? You'll want to taste a few samples, I presume, Doctor?"

"I'm not giving a wholesale order," said I, smiling at his enthusiasm. "A dozen or so of claret and one or two bottles of port is all I want."

"Still," said Bundy, "you want to know what the stuff's like. Not going to buy a pig in a poke. You'll have to taste it, of course. I'll help you. Two heads are better than one. Come on. You said Tucker, didn't you, Japp?"

"As a matter of fact," said Japp, wrinkling his face up into an appreciative smile, "I didn't say anything. But Tucker will do, only he won't let you taste anything until you have bought it."

"Won't he!" said Bundy. "We shall see. Come along, Doctor."

He dragged me out of the office and down the steps, and we set forth towards the bridge, but we had not walked more than a couple of hundred yards when he suddenly shot up a narrow alley and beckoned to me mysteriously. I followed him up the alley, and as he halted I asked, "What have you come here for?"

"I want you," he replied impressively, "to take a look at this wall."

I scrutinized the wall with minute attention but failed to discover any noteworthy peculiarities in it.

"Well," I said, at length, "I don't see anything unusual about this wall."

"Neither do I," he replied, looking furtively down the alley.

"Then, what the deuce – " I began.

"It's all right," said he. "She's gone. That damsel in the pink hat. I just popped up here to let her pass. The fact is," he explained, as he emerged cautiously into the High Street, glancing up and down like an Indian on the war-path, "these women are the plague of my life, always trying to hook me for teas or bazaars or garden fetes or some sort of confounded foolishness, and that pink-hatted lady is a regular sleuth-hound."

We walked quickly along the narrow pavement, Bundy looking about him warily, until we reached the wine-merchant's premises, into which my companion dived like a harlequin and forthwith proceeded to introduce me and my requirements. Mr. Tucker was a small, elderly man, old and crusted and as dry as his own Amontillado, but he was not proof against Bundy's blandishments. Before I had had time to utter a protest, I found myself in a dark cavern at the rear of the shop, watching Mr. Tucker fill a couple of glasses from a mouldy-looking cask.

"Ha!" said Bundy, sipping the wine with a judicial air. "Hmm. Yes. Not so bad. Slightly corked, perhaps."

"Corked!" exclaimed Tucker, staring at Bundy in amazement. "How can it be corked when it is just out of the cask?"

"Well, bunged, then," Bundy corrected.

"I never heard of wine being bunged," said Tucker. "There's no such thing."

"Isn't there? Well, then, it can't be. Must be my fancy. What do you think of it, Doctor?"

"It seems quite a sound claret," said I, inwardly wishing my volatile friend at the devil, for I felt compelled, by way of soothing the wine merchant's wounded feelings, to order twice the quantity that I had intended. We had just completed the transaction, and were crossing the outer shop, when the doorway became occluded by two female figures, and Bundy uttered a half-suppressed groan. I drew aside to make way for the newcomers – two ladies whom polite persons would have described as middle-aged, on the assumption that they contemplated a somewhat extreme degree of longevity – and I was aware that Bundy was endeavouring to take cover behind me. But it was of no use. One of them espied him instantly and announced her discovery with a little squeak of ecstasy.

"Why, it's Mr. Bundy, I do declare! Now, where have you been all this long time? It's ages and ages and ages since you came to see us, isn't it, Martha? Let me see, now, when was it?" She fixed a reflective eye on her companion, while Bundy smiled a sickly smile and glanced wistfully at the open door.

88

"I know," she exclaimed, triumphantly. "It was when we had the feeble-minded children to tea, and Mr. Blote showed them the goldfish trick – at least he tried to, but the glass bowl stuck in the bag under his coat-tails and wouldn't come out, and when he tried to pull it out it broke – "

"I think you are mistaken, Marian," the other lady interrupted. "It wasn't the feeble-minded tea. It was after that, when we helped the Jewbury-Browns to get up that rumble sale – "

"Jumble sale, you mean, dear," her companion corrected.

"I mean rummage sale," the lady called Martha insisted, severely. "If you will try to recall the circumstances, you will remember that the jumble sale took place after – "

"Not after," the other lady corrected. "It was before – several days before, I should say, speaking from a somewhat imperfect memory. If you will try to recollect, Martha, dear – "

"I recollect quite distinctly," the lady called Martha interposed, a little haughtily. "There was the feeble-minded tea – that was on a Tuesday – or was it a Thursday – no, it was a Tuesday, or at least – well, at any rate, it was some days before the jum – rum – "

"Not at all," the other lady dissented emphatically. At this point, catching the eye of the lady called Marian, I crept by slow degrees out on the threshold and turned an expectant eye on Bundy. The rather broad hint took immediate effect, for the lady said to her companion, "I am afraid, Martha, dear, you are detaining Mr. Bundy and his friend. Good-bye, Mr. Bundy. Shall we see you next Friday evening? We are giving a little entertainment to the barge-boys. We are inviting them to come and bring their mouth-organs and get up a little informal concert. Do come if you can. We shall be so delighted. Good-bye."

Bundy shook hands effusively with the two ladies and darted out after me, seizing my arm and hurrying me along the pavement.

"Bit of luck for me, Doctor, having you with me. If I had been alone and unprotected I shouldn't have escaped for half-an-hour, and I should have been definitely booked for the barge-boys' pandemonium. Hallo! What's Japp up to? Oh, I see. He's sticking up the notice about that key. I ought to have done that. Japp writes a shocking fist. I must see if it is possible to make it out."

As we approached the office I glanced at the sheet of paper which Mr. Japp had just affixed to the window, and was able to read the rather crabbed heading, "*Ten Shillings Reward*". The rest of the inscription being of no interest to me, I wished Bundy *adieu* and went on my way, leaving him engaged in a critical inspection of the notice. Happening to look back a few moments later, I saw him still gazing earnestly at the paper, all unconscious of a lady in a pink hat who was tripping lightly across the road and bearing down on him with an alluring smile.

Threading my way among the foot-passengers who filled the narrow pavements, I let my thoughts ramble idly from subject to subject, from the expected visit of my two friends on the following Monday to the alarming character of the local feminine population. But always they tended to come back to my patient, Mrs. Frood. I had seen her on the preceding night and had been very ill-satisfied with her appearance. She had been paler than usual – more heavy-eyed and weary-looking, and she had impressed me as being decidedly low-spirited. It seemed as though the continual uncertainty and unrest, the abiding threat of some intolerable action on the part of her worthless husband, were becoming more than she could endure, and unwillingly I was beginning to recognize that it was my duty, both as her doctor and as her friend, to advise her to move, at least for a time, to some locality where she would be free from the constant fear of molestation.

The question was: When should I broach the subject?

And that involved the further question: When should I make my next visit? Inclination suggested the present evening, but discretion hinted that I ought to allow a decent interval between my calls, and thus oscillating between the two, I found myself in a state of indecision which lasted for the rest of the day. Eventually discretion conquered, and I decided to postpone the visit and the proposal until the following evening.

The decision was reached about the time I should have been setting forth to make the visit, and no sooner had that time definitely passed than I began to regret my resolution and to be possessed by a causeless anxiety. Restlessly I wandered from room to room, taking up books, opening them and putting them down again, and generally displaying the typical symptoms of an acute attack of fidgets until Mrs. Dunk proceeded with a determined air to lay the supper, and drew my attention to it with an emphasis which it was impossible to disregard.

I had just drawn the cork of a bottle of Mr. Tucker's claret when the door-bell rang, an event without precedent in my experience. Silently I replaced the newly-extracted cork and listened. Apparently it was a patient, for I heard the street door close and footsteps proceed to the consulting- room. A minute later Mrs. Dunk opened the dining-room door and announced, "Mrs. Frood to see you, sir."

With a slight thrill of anxiety at this unexpected visit, I strode out and, crossing the hall, entered the somewhat dingy and ill-lighted consulting room. Mrs. Frood was seated in the patients' chair, but she rose as I entered and held out her hand, and as I grasped it, I noticed how

90

tall she looked in her outdoor clothes. But I also noticed that she was looking even more pale and haggard than when I had seen her last.

"There is nothing the matter, I hope?" said I.

"No," she answered, "nothing much more than usual, but I have come to present a petition."

I looked at her inquiringly, and she continued, "I have been sleeping very badly, as you know. Last night I had practically no sleep at all, and very little the night before, and I feel that I really can't face the prospect of another sleepless night. Would you think it very immoral if I were to ask you for something that would give me a few hours' rest?"

"Certainly not," I answered, though with no great enthusiasm, for I am disposed to take hypnotics somewhat seriously. "You can't go on without sleep. I will give you one or two tablets to take before you go to bed. They will secure you a decent night's rest, and then I hope you will feel a little brighter."

"I hope so," she said, with a weary sigh.

I looked at her critically. She was, as I have said, pale and haggard, but there seemed to be something more, a certain wildness in her eyes and a suggestion or fear.

"You are not looking yourself at all to-night," I said. "What is it?"

"I don't know," she answered. "The same old thing, I suppose. But I do feel rather miserable. I seem to have come to the end of my endurance. I look into the future and it all seems dark. I am afraid of it. In fact, I seem to have – you'll think me very silly, I know – but I have a sort of presentiment of evil. Of course, it's all nonsense. But that is what I feel."

"Is there any reason for this presentiment?" I asked uneasily, for my thoughts flew at once to that ill-omened figure that I had seen on the bridge. "Has anything happened to occasion these forebodings?"

"Oh, nothing in particular," she replied. But she spoke without looking at me – an unusual thing for her to do – and I found in her answer something ambiguous and rather evasive. Could it be that she had seen her husband on that day when I had followed him? Or had he been in the town again – this very day, perhaps? Or was there something yet more significant, something even more menacing? That this deep depression of spirits, these forebodings, were not without some exciting cause I felt the strongest suspicion. But whatever the cause might be, she was evidently unwilling to speak about it.

While I was speculating thus, I found myself looking her over with a minute attention of which I was not conscious at the time, noting little trivial details of her appearance and belongings with an odd exactness of observation. My eyes travelled over the little hand-bag, stamped with her

91

initials, that rested on her lap, her dainty, high-heeled shoes with their little oval buckles of darkened bronze, the small brooch at her throat with the large opal in the middle and the surrounding circle of little pearls, and even noted that one of the pearls was missing and that the vacant place corresponded to the figure three on a clock-dial. And then they would come back to her face, to the set mouth and the downcast eyes with their expression of gloomy reverie.

I was profoundly uneasy and was on the point of opening the subject of her leaving the town. Then I decided that I would see her on the morrow and would go into the matter then. Accordingly, I went into the surgery and put a few tablets of sulphonal into a little box, and having stuck one of Dr. Partridge's labels on it, wrote the directions and then wrapped it up and sealed it.

"There," I said, giving it to her, "take a couple of those tablets and go to bed early, and let me find you looking a little more cheerful to-morrow."

She took the packet and dropped it into her bag. "It is very good of you," she said warmly. "I know you don't like doing it, and that makes it the more kind. But I will do as you tell me. I have just to go in to Chatham, but when I get back I will go to bed quite early."

I walked with her to the door, and when I had opened it she stopped and held out her hand. "Good night," she said, "and thank you so very much. I expect you will find me a great deal better to-morrow." She pressed my hand slightly, made me a little bow, smiled and, turning away, passed out, and I now noticed that the haze which had hung over the town all the afternoon had thickened into a definite fog. I stepped out on to the threshold and watched her as she walked quickly down the street, following the erect, dignified figure wistfully with my eyes as it grew more and more shadowy and unsubstantial until it faded into the fog and vanished. Then I went in to my solitary supper, with an unwonted sense of loneliness, and throughout the long evening I turned over again and again our unsatisfying talk and wondered afresh whether that presentiment of evil was but the product of insomnia and mental fatigue, or whether behind it was some sinister reality.

Chapter VII
Mrs. Gillow Sounds the Alarm

Nine o'clock on the following morning found me still seated at the breakfast table, with the debris of the meal before me and the Sunday paper propped up against the coffee-pot. It was a pleasant, sunny morning at the end of April. The birds were twittering joyously in the trees at the back of the house, a premature bluebottle perambulated the window-pane, after an unsuccessful attempt to crawl under the dish-cover, and somewhere in the town an optimistic bell-ringer was endeavouring to lure unwary loiterers out of the sunshine into the shadow of the sanctuary.

It was all very agreeable and soothing. The birds were delightful in the exuberance of their spirits, even the bluebottle was a harbinger of summer, and the solo of the bellringer, softened by distance, impinged gently on the appreciative ear, awakening a grateful sense of immunity. The sunshine and the placid sounds were favourable to reflection, which the Sunday paper was powerless to disturb. As my eye roamed inattentively down the inconsequent column of printers' errors, my mind flitted, beelike, from topic to topic, from my vague professional prospects to the visitors whom I was expecting on the morrow and from them to the rather disturbing incident of the previous evening. But here my thoughts had a tendency to stick, and I was just considering whether the proprieties admitted of my making a morning call on Mrs. Frood, with a view to clearing up the obscurity, when the street-door bell rang. The unusual sound at such an unlikely time caused me to sit up and listen with just a tinge of uneasy expectancy. A few moments later Mrs. Dunk opened the door, and having stated concisely and impassively, "Mrs. Gillow," retired, leaving the door ajar. I started up in something approaching alarm, and hurried across to the consulting room, where I found Mrs. Gillow standing by the chair with anxiety writ large on her melancholy face.

"There's nothing amiss, I hope, Mrs. Gillow?" said I.

"I am sorry to say there is, sir," she replied. "I hope you'll excuse me for disturbing you on a Sunday morning, but I thought, as you were her doctor, and a friend, too, and I may say – "

"But what has happened?" I interrupted impatiently.

"Why, sir, the fact is that she went out last night and she hasn't come back."

93

"You are quite sure she hasn't come back?"

"Perfectly. I saw her just before she went out, and she said she was coming to see you, to get something to make her sleep, and then she was just going into Chatham, and that she would be back soon, so that she could go to bed early. I sat up quite late listening for her, and before I went to bed I went down and knocked at both her doors, and as I didn't get any answer, I looked into both rooms. But she wasn't in either, and her little supper was untouched on the table in the sitting-room. I couldn't sleep a wink all night for worrying about her, and the first thing this morning I went down and, when I found the door unbolted and unchained, I went into her rooms again. But there was no sign of her. Her supper was still there, untouched, and her bed had not been slept in."

"Did you look downstairs?" I asked.

"Yes. She usually kept the door of the basement stairs locked, I think, but it was unlocked this morning, so I went down and searched all over the basement, but she wasn't there."

"It is very extraordinary, Mrs. Gillow," I said, "and rather alarming. I certainly understood that she was going home as soon as she had been to Chatham. By the way, do you know what she was going to Chatham for?"

"I don't, sir. She might have been going there to do some shopping, but it was rather late, though it was Saturday night."

"You don't know, I suppose, whether she took any things with her – though she couldn't have taken much, as she had only a little handbag with her when she came here."

"She hasn't taken any of her toilet things," said Mrs. Gillow, "because I looked over her dressing-table, and all her brushes and things were there and, as you say, she couldn't have taken much in that little bag. What do you think we had better do, sir?"

"I think," said I, "that, in the first place, I will go and see Mr. Japp. He is a relative and knows more about her than we do and, of course, it will be for him to take any measures that may seem necessary. At any rate, I will see him and hear what he says."

"Don't you think we ought to let the police know?" she asked.

"Well, Mrs. Gillow," I said, "we mustn't be too hasty. Mrs. Frood had reasons for avoiding publicity. Perhaps we had better not busy ourselves too much until we are quite certain that she has gone. She may possibly return in the course of the day."

"I am sure I hope so," she replied despondently. "But I am very much afraid she won't. I have a presentiment that something dreadful has happened to her."

"Why do you say that?" I asked. "Have you any reason for thinking so?"

"I have no actual reason," she answered, "but I have always thought that there was something behind her fear of meeting her husband."

Having no desire to discuss speculative opinions, I made no direct reply to this. Apparently Mrs. Gillow had no more to tell, and as I was anxious to see Mr. Japp and hear if he could throw any light on the mystery, I adjourned the discussion on which she would have embarked and piloted her persuasively towards the door. "I shall see you again later, Mrs. Gillow," I said, "and will let you know if I hear anything. Meanwhile, I think you had better not speak of the matter to anybody."

As soon as she was gone I made rapid preparations to go forth on my errand, and a couple of minutes later was speeding down the street at a pace dictated rather by the agitation of my mind than by any urgency of purpose. Although, by an effort of will, I had preserved a quiet, matter-of-fact demeanour while I was talking to Mrs. Gillow, her alarming news had fallen on me like a thunderbolt, and even now, as I strode forward swiftly, my thoughts seemed numbed by the suddenness of the catastrophe. That something terrible had happened I had little more doubt than had Mrs. Gillow, and a good deal more reason for my fears, for that last interview with the missing woman, looked back upon by the light of her unaccountable disappearance, now appeared full of dreadful suggestions. I had thought that she looked frightened, and she admitted to a presentiment of evil. Of whom or of what was she afraid? And what did she mean by a presentiment? Reasonable people do not have gratuitous presentiments, and I recalled her evasive reply when I asked if she had any reasons for her foreboding of evil. Now, there was little doubt that she had, that the shadow of some impending danger had fallen on her and that she knew it.

As I approached the premises of Japp and Bundy, I was assailed by a sudden doubt as to whether Mr. Japp lived there, and this doubt increased when I had executed two loud knocks at the door without eliciting any response. I was just raising my hand to make a third attack when I became aware of Bundy's head rising above the curtain of the office window, and even in my agitation I could not but notice its extremely dishevelled state. His hair – usually "smarmed" back neatly from the forehead and brushed over the crown of his head – now hung down untidily over his face like a bunch of rat's tails, and the unusualness of his appearance was increased by the fact that he wore neither spectacles nor the indispensable eyeglass. The apparition, however, was visible but for a moment, for even as I glanced at him he made a sign to me to wait and forthwith vanished.

There followed an interval of about a minute, at the end of which the door opened and I entered, discovering Bundy behind it in a dressing-gown and pyjamas, but with his hair neatly brushed and his eye-glass duly adjusted.

"Sorry to keep you waiting, Doc." said he. "Fact is, your knock woke me. The early bird catches the worm in his pyjamas."

"I apologize for disturbing your slumbers," said I, "but I wanted to see Japp. Isn't he in?"

"Japp doesn't live here," said Bundy, motioning to me to follow him upstairs. "He used to, but the house began to fill up with the business stuff and we had to make a drawing office and a store-room, so he moved off to a house on Boley Hill, and now I live here like Robinson Crusoe."

"Do you mean that you do your own cooking and housework?"

"Lord, no," he replied. "I get most of my meals at Japp's place. Prepare my own breakfast sometimes – I'm going to now, and I make tea for us both. Got a little gas-stove in the kitchen. And a charlady comes in every day to wash up and do my rooms. If you are not in a hurry, I'll walk round with you to Japp's house."

"I am in rather a hurry," said I, "at least – well, I don't know why I should be, but I am rather upset. The fact is, a very alarming thing has happened. I have just heard of it from Mrs. Gillow. It seems that Mrs. Frood went out last evening and has not come back."

Bundy whistled. "She's done a bolt," said he. "I wonder why. Do you think she can have run up against hubby in the town?"

"I don't believe for a moment that she has gone away voluntarily," said I. "She came to see me last night to get a sedative because she couldn't sleep, and she said that she was going home as soon as she had been to Chatham, and that she was going to take her medicine and go to bed early."

"That might have been a blind," suggested Bundy, "or she might have run up against her husband in Chatham."

I shook my head impatiently. "That is all nonsense, Bundy. A woman doesn't walk off into space in that fashion. Something has happened to her, I feel sure. I only hope it isn't something horrible – one doesn't dare to think of the possibilities that the circumstances suggest."

"No," said Bundy, "and it's better not to. Great mistake to let your imagination run away with you. Don't you worry, Doc. She'll probably turn up all right, or send Japp a line to say where she has gone to."

"Devil take it, Bundy!" I exclaimed irritably, "you are talking as if she were just a cat that had strayed away. If you don't care a hang what

96

becomes of her, I do. I am extremely alarmed about her. How soon will you be ready?"

"I'll run and get on my things at once," he replied, with a sudden change of manner. "You must excuse me, old chap. I didn't realize that you were so upset. I'll be with you in a few minutes and then we will start. Japp will be able to give me some breakfast."

He bustled off – to the next room, as I gathered from the sound – and left me to work off my impatience by gazing out of the window and pacing restlessly up and down the barely-furnished sitting-room. But, impatient as I was, the rapidity with which he made his toilet surprised me, for in less than ten minutes he reappeared, spick and span, complete with hat, gloves, and stick, and announced that he was ready.

"I am not usually such a sluggard," he said, as we walked quickly along the street, "but yesterday evening I got a novel. I ought not to read novels. When I do, I am apt to make a single mouthful of it, and that is what I did last night. I started the book at nine and finished it at two this morning, and the result is that I am as sleepy as an owl even now."

In illustration of this statement he gave a prodigious yawn and then turned up the steep little thoroughfare, where he presently halted at the door of a small, old-fashioned house and rang the bell. The door was opened by a middle-aged servant, from whom he learned that Mr. Japp was at home, and to whom Bundy communicated his needs in the matter of breakfast. We found Mr. Japp seated by the dining-room window, studying a newspaper with the aid of a large pipe, and Bundy proceeded to introduce me and the occasion of my visit in a few crisp sentences.

Mr. Japp's reception of the news was very different from his partner's. Starting up from his chair and taking his pipe from his mouth, he gazed at me for some seconds in silent dismay.

"I suppose," he said at length, "there is no mistake. It is really certain that she did not come back last night?"

"I am afraid there is no doubt of the fact," I replied, and I gave him the details with which Mrs. Gillow had furnished me.

"Dear! Dear!" he exclaimed. "I don't like the look of this at all. What the deuce can have happened to her?"

Here Bundy repeated the suggestion that he had made to me, but Japp shook his head. "She wouldn't have gone off without letting me or the doctor know. Why should she? We are friends, and she knew she could trust us. Besides, the thing isn't possible. A middle-class woman can't set out like a tramp without any luggage or common necessaries. There's only one possibility," he added after a pause. "She might have seen Nicholas prowling about and gone straight to the station and taken a train to London. One of her woman friends would have been able to put her up for the night."

"Or," suggested Bundy, "she might even have gone up to town with Nick himself if he met her and threatened to make a scene."

"Yes," said Japp doubtfully, "that is, I suppose, possible. But it isn't in the least likely. For that matter, nothing is likely. It is a most mysterious affair, and very disturbing, very disturbing, indeed."

"The question is," said I, "what is to be done? Do you think we ought to communicate with the police?"

"Well, no," he replied, "not immediately. If we don't hear anything, say to-morrow, I suppose we shall have to. But we had better not be precipitate. If we go to the police, we shall have to tell them everything. Let us give her time to communicate, in case she has had to make a sudden retirement – a clear forty-eight hours, as it is a week-end. But we had better make some cautious inquiries meanwhile. I suggest that we walk up to the hospital. They know me pretty well there, and I could just informally ascertain whether any accidents had been admitted, without giving any detailed reasons for the inquiry. Are you coming with us, Bundy?"

"Yes," replied Bundy, who, having been provided with a light breakfast, was despatching it with lightning speed, "I shall be ready by the time you have got your boots on."

A few minutes later we set forth together and made our way straight to the hospital. Bundy and I waited outside while Japp went in to make his inquiries and, as we walked up and down, my imagination busied itself in picturing the hideous possibilities suggested by a somewhat extensive experience of the casualty department of a general hospital. Presently Japp emerged, shaking his head.

"She is not there," said he. "There were no casualties of any kind admitted last night or since."

"Is there no other hospital?" I asked.

"None but the military hospital," he replied. "All the casualties from the district would be brought here. So we seem to be at the end of our resources, short of inquiring at the police station, and even if that were advisable, it would be useless, for if – anything had happened – anything, I mean, that we hope has not happened – Mrs. Gillow would have heard. She will be sure to have had something about her by which she could have been identified."

"She had," said I. "The little box that I gave her had her name and my address on it."

98

"Then," said Japp. "I don't see that we can do anything more. We can only wait until to-morrow evening or Tuesday morning, and if we don't get any news of her by then, notify the police."

Unwillingly I had to admit that this was so, and when I had walked back with the partners to Mr. Japp's house, I left them and proceeded to report to Mrs. Gillow and to ascertain whether, in the meantime, she had received any tidings of her missing tenant.

It was with more of fear than hope that I plied the familiar knocker, but the eager, expectant face that greeted me when the door opened, while it relieved the one, banished the other. She had heard nothing, and when I had communicated my own unsatisfactory report she groaned and shook her head.

"You are quite sure," I said, after an interval of silence, "that she did not return from Chatham?"

"I don't see how she could have done," was the reply. "You see, it was like this: I was going to see my sister at Frindsbury, and as I came down to the hall, Mrs. Frood opened her door and spoke to me. She had her hat on then, and she told me she was coming to you, and then going on to Chatham, but that she would be back pretty soon, and was going to bed early. I went out, leaving her at her room door, and took the tram to Frindsbury, and I got back home about a quarter-to-ten. Her sitting-room door was open, and I could see that she hadn't gone to bed, because her lamp was alight and her supper tray was on the table and hadn't been touched. I knocked at her bedroom door, but there was no answer, so I went upstairs and sat up listening for her, and before I went to bed I went down again, as I told you."

"What time was it when you went out?" I asked.

"About a quarter-past-eight. I told her I was going to Frindsbury, and that I should be home before ten, and I asked her not to bolt the door if she came in before me."

"Then," said I, "she must have gone out directly after you, because it was only a little after half-past eight when she called on me, and presumably she went straight on to Chatham. If we only knew what she was going there for we might be able to trace her. Did she know anybody at Chatham?"

"So far as I know," replied Mrs. Gillow, "she didn't know anybody here but you and Mr. Japp. I can't imagine what she could have been going to Chatham for."

After a little further talk, I took my leave and walked homeward in a very wretched frame of mind. Tormented as I was with a gnawing anxiety, inaction was intolerable. Yet there was nothing to be done, nothing but to wait in the feeble hope that the morning might bring some message of relief, and with a heavy foreboding that the tidings, when they came, would be evil tidings. But I found it impossible to wait passively at home. At intervals during the day I went forth to wander up and down the streets, and some impulse which I hardly dared to recognize directed my steps again and again to the wharves and foreshore that lie by the bend of the river between Rochester and Chatham.

On the following morning I betook myself as early as I decently could to the office of Japp and Bundy. No letter had arrived by the early post, nor, when I repeated my visit later, was there any news, either by post or telegram, or from Mrs. Gillow. I paid a furtive visit to the police station and glanced nervously over the bills on the notice board, and I made another perambulation of the waterside districts, which occupied me until it was time for me to repair to the station to meet the train by which my friends were expected to arrive, and did, in fact, arrive.

As we walked from the station to my house, Jervis looked at me critically from time to time. After one of these inspections he remarked, "I don't know whether it is my fancy, Strangeways, but it seems to me that the cares of medical practice are affecting your spirits. You look worried."

"I *am* worried," I replied. "There has been a very disturbing development of that case that I was telling you about."

"The doper, you mean?"

"His wife. She has disappeared. She went out on Saturday night and has not been seen since."

"That sounds rather ominous," said Jervis. "I presume the circumstances – if you know them – could be communicated without any breach of confidence."

"They will have to be made fully public if she doesn't turn up by this evening," I replied, "and I am only too glad of the chance to talk the matter over with you," and forthwith I proceeded to give a circumstantial account of the events connected with the disappearance, not omitting any detail that seemed to have the slightest bearing. And I now felt justified in relating my experience when I was acting for Dr. Pumphrey. The narrative was interrupted by our arrival at my house, but when we had taken our places at the table it was continued and listened to with intense interest by my two friends.

"Well," said Jervis, when I had finished, "it has an ugly look, especially when one considers it in connexion with that affair in London. But there is something to be said for your friend Bundy's suggestion. Don't you think so, Thorndyke?"

"Something, perhaps," Thorndyke agreed, "but not much, and if no letter arrives to-night or to-morrow morning, I should say it is excluded. This lady seems to have had complete confidence in Strangeways and in Mr. Japp. She could depend on their secrecy if she had to move suddenly to a fresh locality, and she seems to have been a responsible person who would not unnecessarily expose them to anxiety about her safety. Moreover, she would know that, if she kept them in the dark, they must unavoidably put the police on her track, which would be the last thing that she would wish."

"Can you make any suggestion as to what has probably happened?" I asked.

"It is not of much use to speculate," replied Thorndyke. "If we exclude a voluntary disappearance, an accident or sudden illness, as we apparently can, there seems to remain only the possibility of crime. But to the theory of crime – of murder, to put it bluntly – there is a manifest objection. So far as the circumstances are known to us, a murder, if it had occurred, would have been an impromptu murder, committed in a more or less public place. But the first indication of a murder of that kind is usually the discovery of the body. Here, however, thirty-six hours have elapsed, and no body has come to light. On the other hand, we have to bear in mind that there is a large, tidal river skirting the town. Into that river the missing lady might have fallen accidentally, or have been thrown, dead or alive. But it is not very profitable to speculate. We can neither form any opinion nor take any action until we have some further facts."

I must confess that, as I listened to Thorndyke thus calmly comparing the horrible possibilities, I experienced a dreadful sinking of the heart, but yet I realized that this passionless consideration of the essential evidence was more to the point, and promised more result than any amount of unskilful groping under the urge of emotion and personal feeling. And, realizing this, I formed the bold resolution of enlisting Thorndyke's aid in a regular, professional capacity, and began to cast about for the means of introducing the rather delicate subject. But while I was reflecting the opportunity was gone, at least for the present. Lunch had virtually come to an end, for Mrs. Dunk had silently and with iron visage just placed the port and the coffee on the table and retired, when, Jervis, who had observed her with evident interest, inquired, "Does that old Sphinx do the cooking, Strangeways?"

"She does everything," I answered. "I have suggested that she should get some help, but she just growled and ignored the suggestion."

"Well," said Jervis, "she doesn't give you much excuse for growling. She has turned out a lunch that would have done credit to

Delmonico's. Are you coming to the inquest with us? We shall have to be starting in a few minutes."

"I may as well," said I. "Then I can bring you back to tea. And I want to make a proposal, which we can discuss as we go along. It is with regard to the case of Mrs. Frood."

As my two friends looked at me inquiringly but made no remark, I poured out the coffee and continued, "You see, Mrs. Frood was my patient and, in a way, my friend. In fact, with the exception of Japp, I was the only friend she had in the place. Consequently I take it as my duty to ascertain what has happened to her and, if she has come to any harm, to see that the wrongdoers are brought to account. Of course, I am not competent to investigate the case myself, but I am in the position to bear any costs that the investigation would entail."

"Lucky man," said Jervis. "And what is the proposal?"

"I was wondering," I replied, a little nervously, "whether I could prevail on you to undertake the case."

Jervis glanced at his senior, and the latter replied, "It is just a little premature to speak of a 'case'. The missing lady may return or communicate with her friends. If she does not, the inquiry will fall into the hands of the police, and there is no reason to suppose that they will not be fully competent to deal with it. They have more means and facilities than we have. But if the inquiry should become necessary, and the police should be unsuccessful, Jervis and I would be prepared to render you any assistance that we could."

"On professional terms," I stipulated.

Thorndyke smiled. "The financial aspects of the case," said he, "can be considered when they arise. Now, I think, it is time for us to start."

As we walked down to the building where the inquest was to be held, we pursued the topic, and Thorndyke pointed out my position in the case.

"You notice, Strangeways," said he, "that you are the principal witness. You are the last person who saw Mrs. Frood before her disappearance, you heard her state her intended movements, you knew her circumstances, you saw and examined her husband, and you alone can give an exact description of her as she was at the time when she disappeared. I would suggest that, during the inquest, which will not interest you, you might usefully try to reconstitute that last interview and make full notes in writing of all that occurred with a very careful and detailed description of the person, clothing, and belongings of the missing lady. The police will want this information, and so shall I, if I am to give any consideration to the case."

On this suggestion I proceeded to act as soon as we had taken our places at the foot of the long table occupied by the coroner and the jury, detaching myself as well as I could from the matter of the inquest, and by the time that the deliberations were at an end and the verdict agreed upon, I had drafted out a complete set of notes and made two copies, one for the police and one for Thorndyke.

As soon as we were outside the court I presented the latter copy, which Thorndyke read through.

"This is admirable, Strangeways," said he, as he placed it in his notecase. "I must compliment you upon your powers of observation. The description of the missing lady is remarkably clear and exhaustive. And now I would suggest that you call in at Mr. Japp's office on our way back, and ascertain whether any letter has been received. If there has been no communication we shall have to regard the appearances as suspicious, and calling for investigation."

Secretly gratified at the interest which Thorndyke seemed to be developing in the mystery, I conducted my friends up the High Street until we reached the office, which I entered, leaving my colleagues outside. Mr. Japp looked up from a letter which he was writing, and Bundy, who had been peeping over the curtain, revolved on his stool and faced me.

"Any news?" I asked.

Japp shook his head gloomily. "Not a sign," said he. "I shall wait until the first post is in to-morrow morning, and then, if there are no tidings of her, I shall go across to the police station. Perhaps you had better come with me, as you are able to give the particulars that they will want."

"Very well," I said, "I will look in at half-past nine." And with this I was turning away when Bundy inquired, "Are those two toffs outside friends of yours?" and, on my replying in the affirmative, he continued, "They seem to be taking a deuce of an interest in Japp's proclamation. You might tell them that if they happen to have found that key, the money is quite safe. I will see that Japp pays up."

I promised to deliver the message and, as Bundy craned up to make a further inspection of my colleagues, I departed to join the latter.

"There is no news up to the present," I said, "but Japp proposes to wait until to-morrow morning for a last chance before applying to the police."

"Was that Japp who was inspecting us through that preposterous pair of barnacles?" Jervis asked.

"No," I answered. "That was Bundy. He suspects you of having found that key and of holding on to it until you are sure of the reward."

103

"What key is it?" asked Jervis. "The key of the strong-room? They seem to be in a rare twitter about it."

"No, it is just a gate-key belonging to a piece of waste land where they are doing some repairs to the old city wall. And, by the way, thereby hangs a tale, a horrible and tragic tale of a convivial bargee, which ought to have a special interest for a pair of medical jurists." And here I related to them the gruesome story that was told to Bundy and me by the old mortar-mixer.

They both chuckled appreciatively at the denouement, and Jervis remarked, "It would seem that the late Bill was a rather inflammable gentleman. The yarn recalls the tragic end of Mr. Krook in *Bleak House*, only that Krook went one better than Bill, for he managed to combust himself in an hour or two without any lime at all."

The story and the comment brought us to my house, which we had no sooner entered than Mrs. Dunk, who seemed to have been lying in wait for us, made her appearance with the tea, and while we were disposing of this refreshment Thorndyke reverted to the case of my missing patient.

"As I am to keep an eye on this case," said he, "I shall want to be kept in touch with it. Of course, the actual investigation – if there has to be one – will need to be conducted on the spot, which is not possible to me. What I suggest is that you write out a detailed account of everything that is known to you in connexion with it. Don't select your facts. Put down everything in any way connected with the case and say all you know about the person concerned – Mrs. Frood herself and everybody who was acquainted with her. Send this statement to me and keep a copy. Then, if any new fact becomes known, let me have it and make a note of it for your own information. You are on the spot and I shall look to you for the data, and if I want any of them amplified or confirmed I shall communicate with you.

"There is one other matter. Do not confide to anyone that you have consulted me or that I am interested in the case – neither to Mr. Japp, to the police, nor to anybody else whatsoever, and I advise you to keep your own interest in the mystery to yourself as far as possible."

"What is the need of this secrecy?" I asked, in some surprise.

"The point is," replied Thorndyke, "that when you are investigating a crime you are playing against the criminal. But if the criminal is unknown to you, you are playing against an unseen adversary. If you are visible to him he can watch your moves and reply to them. Obviously your policy is to keep out of sight and make your moves unseen. And remember that as long as you do not know who the criminal *is*, you don't know who he is *not*. Anyone may be the criminal, or may be his unconscious agent or coadjutor. If you make confidences, they may be innocently passed on to the guilty parties. So keep your own counsel rigorously. If there has been a crime, that crime has local connexions and probably a local origin. The solution of the mystery will probably be discovered here. And if you intend to take a hand in the solution let it be a lone hand, and keep me informed of everything that you do or observe, and for my part, I will give you all the help I can."

By the time we had finished our tea and our discussion the hour of my friends' departure was drawing nigh. I walked with them to the station, and when I bade them farewell I received a warm invitation to visit them at their chambers in The Temple, an invitation of which I determined to avail myself on the first favourable opportunity.

Chapter XIII
Sergeant Cobbledick Takes a Hand

Punctually at half-past-nine on the following morning, I presented myself at the office and, if I had indulged in any hopes of favourable news – which I had not – they would have been dispelled by a glance at Mr. Japp's troubled face.

"I suppose you have heard nothing?" I said, when we had exchanged brief greetings.

He shook his head gloomily as he opened the cupboard and took out his hat.

"No," he answered, "and I am afraid we never shall."

He sighed heavily and, putting on his hat, walked slowly to the door. "It is a dreadful affair," he continued, as we went out together. "How she would have hated the idea of it, poor girl! All the horrid publicity, the posters, the sensational newspaper paragraphs, the descriptions of her person and belongings. And then, at the end of it all, God knows what horror may come to light. It won't bear thinking of."

He trudged along at my side with bent head and eyes cast down, and for the remainder of the short journey neither of us spoke. On reaching the police station we made our way into a small, quiet office, the only tenant of which was a benevolent-looking, bald-headed sergeant, who was seated at a high desk and, who presented that peculiar, decapitated aspect that appertains to a police officer minus his helmet. As we entered the sergeant laid down his pen and turned to us with a benign smile.

"Good morning, Mr. Japp," said he. "What can I have the pleasure of doing for you?"

"I am sorry to say, Sergeant," replied Japp, "that I have come here on very unpleasant business," and he proceeded to give the officer a concise summary of the facts, to which our friend listened with close attention. When it was finished, the sergeant produced a sheet of blue foolscap and, having folded a wide margin on it, dipped his pen in the ink and began his examination.

"I'd better take the doctor's statement first," said he. "The lady's name is Angelina Frood, married, living apart from husband – I shall want his address presently – last seen alive by – "

"John Strangeways, M.D.," said I, "of Maidstone Road, Rochester."

The sergeant wrote this down, and continued, "Last seen at about 8:30 P.M. on Saturday, 26th April, proceeding towards Chatham, on unknown business. Can you give me a description of her?"

I described her person, assisted by Japp, and the sergeant, having committed the particulars to writing, read them out: "'*Age twenty-eight, height five feet seven inches, complexion medium, hazel eyes, abundant dark brown hair, strongly marked black eyebrows, nearly meeting over nose.*'"

"No special marks that you know of?"

"No."

"Now, Doctor, can you tell us how she was dressed?"

"She was wearing a snuff-brown coat and skirt," I replied, "and a straw hat of the same colour with a broad, dull green band. The hat was fixed on by two hat-pins with silver heads shaped like poppy-capsules. The coat had six buttons, smallish, bronze buttons – about half-an-inch in diameter – with a Tudor Rose embossed on each. Brown suede gloves with fasteners – no buttons – brown silk stockings, and brown suede shoes with small, oval bronze buckles. She had a narrow silk scarf, dull green, with three purple bands at each end – one broad band and two narrow – and knotted fringe at the ends. She wore a small circular brooch with a largish opal in the centre and a border of small pearls, of which one was missing. The missing pearl was in the position of the figure three on a clock dial. She carried a small morocco hand-bag with the initials '*A. F.*' stamped on it, which contained a little cardboard box, in which were six white tablets, the box was labelled with one of Dr. Partridge's labels, on which her name was written, and it was wrapped in white paper and sealed with sealing-wax. That is all I can say for certain. But she always wore a wedding-ring, and occasionally an African Zodiac ring, but sometimes she carried this ring in a small purse with metal jaws and a ball fastening. I believe she always carried the purse."

As I gave this description, the sergeant wrote furiously, glancing at me from time to time with an expression of surprise, while Japp sat and stared at me open-mouthed.

"Well, Doctor," said the sergeant, when he had taken down my statement and read it out, "if I find myself ailing I'm going to pop along and consult you. I reckon there isn't much that escapes your notice. With regard to that African ring now, I daresay you can't tell us what it is like."

I was, of course, able to describe it in detail, including the initials '*A. C.*' inside, and even to give a rough sketch of some of the signs embossed on it, upon which the sergeant chuckled admiringly and wagged his head as he wrote down the description and pinned the sketch on the margin of his paper. The rest of my statement dealt with the last interview and the incidents connected with Nicholas Frood's visits to Rochester, all of which the sergeant listened to with deep interest and committed to writing.

Finally, I recounted the sinister incident – now more sinister than ever – of the murderous assault in the house near Regent's Park, whereat the sergeant looked uncommonly serious and took down the statement verbatim.

"Did you know about this, Mr. Japp?" he asked.

"I knew that something unpleasant had happened," was the reply, "but I didn't know that it was as bad as this."

"Well," said the sergeant, "it gives the present affair rather an ugly look. We shall have to make some inquiries about that gentleman."

Having squeezed me dry, he turned his attention to Japp, from whom he extracted a variety of information, including the address of the banker who paid the allowance to Nicholas Frood, and that of a lady who had formerly been a theatrical colleague of Mrs. Frood's, and with whom Mr. Japp believed the latter had kept up a correspondence.

"You haven't a photograph of the missing lady, I suppose?" said the sergeant.

With evident reluctance Japp drew from his pocket an envelope and produced from it a cabinet photograph, which he looked at sadly for a few moments and then handed to me.

"I brought this photograph with me," he said, "as I knew you would want it, but I rather hope that you won't want to publish it."

"Now, why do you hope that?" the sergeant asked in a soothing and persuasive tone. "You want this lady found – or, at any rate, traced. But what better means can you suggest than publishing her portrait?"

"I suppose you are right," said Japp, "but it is a horrible thing to think of the poor girl's face looking out from posters and newspaper pages."

"It is," the sergeant agreed. "But, you see, if she is alive it is her own doing, and if she is dead it won't affect her."

While they were talking I had been looking earnestly at the beloved face, which I now felt I should never look upon again. It was an excellent likeness, showing her just as I had known her, excepting that it was free from the cloud of trouble that had saddened her expression in these latter days. As the sergeant held out his hand for it, I turned it over and read the photographer's name and address and the register number and, having made a mental note of them, I surrendered it with a sigh.

Our business was now practically concluded. When we had each read over the statements and added our respective signatures, the sergeant attested them and, having added the date, placed the documents in his desk and rose.

"I am much obliged to you, gentlemen," said he as he escorted us to the door. "If I hear anything that will interest you I will let you know, and if I should want any further information I shall take the liberty of calling on you."

"Well," said Japp, as we turned to walk back, "the fat's in the fire now. I mean to say," he added quickly, "that we've fairly committed ourselves. I hope we haven't been too precipitate. We should catch it if she came back and found that we had raised the hue-and-cry and set the whole town agog."

"I am afraid there is no hope of that," said I. "At any rate, we had no choice or discretion in the matter. A suspected crime is the business of the police."

Mr. Japp agreed that this was so, and having by this time arrived at the office, we separated, he to enter his premises and I to betake myself to Chatham with no very defined purpose, but lured thither by a vague attraction.

As I walked along the High Street, making occasional digressions into narrow alleys to explore wharves and water-side premises, I turned over the statements that had been given to the police and wondered what they conveyed to our friend, the sergeant, with his presumably extensive experience of obscure crime. To me they seemed to furnish no means whatever of starting an investigation, excepting by inquiring as to the movements of Nicholas Frood, by communicating with Angelina's late colleague, or by publishing the photograph. And here I halted to write down in my notebook before I should forget them the name and address of that lady – Miss Cumbers – and of the photographers, together with the number of the photograph, for I had decided to obtain a copy of the latter for myself, and it now occurred to me that I had better get one also for Thorndyke. And this latter reflection reminded me that I had to prepare my *précis* of the facts for him, and that I should do well to get this done at once while the matter of the two statements was fresh in my mind. Accordingly, as I paced the deck of the Sun Pier, looking up and down the busy river, with its endless procession of barges, bawleys, tugs, and cargo boats, striving ineffectually to banish the dreadful thought that, perchance, somewhere, at this very moment there was floating on its turbid waters the corpse of my dear, lost friend. I tried to recall and write down the substance of Japp's statement, as I had heard it made and had afterwards read it. At length, finding the neighbourhood of the river too disturbing, I left the pier and took my way homewards, calling in at a stationer's on the way to provide myself with a packet of sermon paper on which to write out my summary.

When Thorndyke had given me my instructions, they had appeared to me a little pedantic. The full narrative which he asked for of all the events, without selection as to relevancy, and the account of what I knew of all the persons concerned in the case, seemed an excessive formality. But when I came to write the case out the excellence of his method became apparent in two respects. In the first place, the ordered narrative put the events in their proper sequence and exhibited their connexions, and in the second, the endeavour to state all that I knew, particularly of the persons, showed me how very little that was. Of the persons in any way concerned in the case there were but five: Angelina herself, her husband, Mrs. Gillow, Mr. Japp, and Bundy. Of the first two I knew no more than what I had observed myself and what Angelina had told me, of the last three I knew practically nothing. Not that this appeared to me of the slightest importance, but I had my instructions, and in compliance with them I determined to make such cautious inquiries as would enable me to give Thorndyke at least a few particulars of them. And this during the next few days I did, and I may as well set down here the scanty and rather trivial information that my inquiries elicited, and which I duly sent on to Thorndyke in a supplementary report.

Mrs. Gillow was the wife of a mariner who was the second mate of a sailing ship that plied to Australia, who had now been away about four months, and was expected home shortly. She was a native of the locality and had known Mr. Japp for several years. She occupied the part of the house above the ground floor and kept no servant or dependent, living quite alone when her husband was at sea. She had no children. Her acquaintance with Angelina began when the latter became the tenant of the ground floor and basement, it was but a slight acquaintance, and she knew nothing of Angelina's antecedents or affairs excepting that she had left her husband.

Mr. Japp was a native of Rochester and had lived in the town all his life, having taken over his business establishment from his late partner, a Mr. Borden. He was a bachelor and was related to Angelina by marriage – his brother – now deceased – having married Angelina's aunt.

As to Bundy, he was hardly connected with the case at all, since he had seen Angelina only once or twice and had scarcely exchanged a dozen words with her. Moreover, he had but recently come to Rochester – about six weeks ago, I gathered – having answered an advertisement of Japp's for an assistant with a view to partnership, and the actual deed had not yet been executed, though the two partners were evidently quite well satisfied with one another.

110

That was all the information that I had to give Thorndyke, and with the exception of the London incident it amounted to nothing. Nevertheless, it was as well to have established the fact that if anyone were concerned in Angelina's disappearance, that person would have to be sought elsewhere than in Rochester.

Having sent off my summary and read over again and again the copy which I had kept, I began to realize the justice of Thorndyke's observation that the inquiry was essentially a matter for the police, who had both the experience and the necessary facilities, for whenever I tried to think of some plan for tracing my lost friend, I was brought up against the facts that I had nothing whatever to go on and no idea how to make a start. As to Thorndyke, he had no data but those that I had given him, and I realized clearly that these were utterly insufficient to form the basis of any investigation, and I found myself looking expectantly to the police to produce some new facts that might throw at least a glimmer of light on this dreadful and baffling mystery.

I had not very long to wait. On the Friday after our call on the sergeant, I was sitting after lunch in my dining-room with a book in my hand, while my thoughts strayed back to those memorable evenings of pleasant converse with the sweet friend who, I felt, had gone from me forever, when the doorbell rang, and Mrs. Dunk presently announced, "Sergeant Cobbledick."

"Show him in here, Mrs. Dunk," said I, laying aside my book, and rising to receive my visitor, who proved to be, as I had expected, the officer who had taken our statements. He entered with his helmet in his hand, and greeted me with a smile of concentrated benevolence.

"Sit down, Sergeant," said I, offering him an easy chair. "I hope you have some news for us."

"Yes," he replied, beaming on me. "I am glad to say we are getting on as well as we can expect. We have made quite a nice little start."

He spoke as if he had something particularly gratifying to communicate and, having carefully placed his helmet on the table, he drew from his pocket a small paper packet, which he opened with great deliberation, extracting from it a small object, which he held out in the palm of his hand.

"There, Doctor," said he, complacently, "what do you say to that?"

I looked at the object, and my heart seemed to stand still. It was Angelina's brooch! I stared at it in speechless dismay for some moments. At length I asked, huskily, "Where did you get it?"

"I found it," said the sergeant, gazing fondly at the little trinket, "where I hardly hoped to find it – in a pawnbroker's shop in Chatham."

"Did you discover who pawned it?" I asked.

111

"In a sense, yes," the sergeant replied with a bland smile.

"How do you mean – in a sense?" I inquired.

"I mean that his name was John Smith – only, of course, it wasn't, and that his address was 26, Swoffer's Alley, Chatham – only he didn't live there, because there is no such number. You see, Doctor, John Smith is the name of nearly every man who gives a false description of himself, and I went straight off to Swoffer's Alley – it was close by – and found that there wasn't any Number 26."

"Then you really don't know who pawned it?"

"We won't exactly say that," he replied. "I got a fair description of the man from the pawnbroker's wife, who made out the ticket and says she could swear to the man if she saw him. He was a seafaring man, dressed in sailor's clothes – a peaked cap and pea-jacket – a shortish fellow, rather sunburnt, with a small, stubby, dark moustache and dark hair, and a mole or wart on the left side of his nose, near the tip. She asked him where he had got the brooch, and he said it had belonged to his old woman. I should say he probably picked it up."

"Why do you think so?" I asked.

"Well, if he had – er – got it in any other way, he would hardly have popped it in Chatham forty-eight hours after the – after it was lost, with the chance that the pawnbrokers had already been notified. He pawned it on Monday night."

"Then," said I, "if he picked it up, he isn't of much importance, and in any case you don't know who he is."

"Oh, but he is of a good deal of importance," said the sergeant. "I've no doubt he picked it up, but that is only a guess. He may have got it the other way. But at any rate, he had it in his possession and he will have to give an account of how he obtained it. The importance of it is this: Taken with the disappearance, the finding of this brooch raises a strong suspicion that a crime has been committed, and if we could find out where it was picked up, we should have a clue to the place where the affair took place. I want that man very badly, and I'm going to have a good try to get him."

"I don't quite see how," said I. "You haven't much to go on."

"I've got his nose to go on," replied the sergeant.

"But there must be plenty of other men with moles on their noses."

"That's their look-out," he retorted. "If I come across a man who answers the description, I shall hang on to him until Mrs. Pawnbroker has had a look at him. Of course, if she says he's not the man, he'll be released."

"But she won't," said I. "If he has a mole on his nose, she will be perfectly certain that he is the man."

The sergeant smiled benignly. "There's something in that," he admitted. "Ladies are a bit cock-sure when it comes to identification. But you can generally check 'em by other evidence. And if this chap picked the brooch up, he would be pretty certain to tell us all about it when he heard where it came from. Still, we haven't got him yet."

For a while we sat, without speaking, each pursuing his own thoughts. To me, this dreadful discovery, though it did but materialize the vague fears that had been surging through my mind, had fallen like a thunderbolt. For, behind those fears, I now realized that there had lurked a hope that the mystery might presently be resolved by the return of the lost one. Now that hope had suddenly become extinct. I knew that she had gone out of my life forever. She was dead. This poor little waif that had drifted back into our hands brought the unmistakable message of her death, with horrible suggestions of hideous and sordid tragedy. I shuddered at the thought, and in that moment, from the grief and horror that possessed my soul, there was born a passion of hatred for the wretch who had done this thing and a craving for revenge.

"There's another queer thing that has come to light," the sergeant resumed at length. "There may be nothing in it, but it's a little queer. About the husband, Nicholas Frood."

"What about him?" I asked, eagerly.

"Why, he seems to have disappeared, too. Of course, you understand, Doctor, that what I'm telling you is confidential. We are not talking about this affair outside, and we aren't telling the Press much, at present."

"Naturally," said I. "You can trust me to keep my own counsel, and yours, too."

"I'm sure I can. Well, about this man, Frood. It seems that last Friday he went away from his lodgings for a couple of days, but he hasn't come back, and nobody knows what has become of him. He was supposed to be going to Brighton, where he has some relatives from whom he gets a little assistance occasionally, but they have seen or heard nothing of him. Quaint, isn't it? You said you saw him here on the Monday."

"Yes, and I haven't seen him since, though I have kept a look-out for him. But he may have been here, all the same. It looks decidedly suspicious."

"It is queer," the sergeant agreed, "but we've no evidence that he has been in this neighbourhood."

"Have you made any other inquiries?" I asked.

"We looked up that lady, Miss Cumbers, but we got nothing out of her. She had had a letter from Mrs. Frood on the 24th – yesterday week –

113

quite an ordinary letter, giving no hint of any intention to go away from Rochester. So there you are. The mystery seems to be concerned entirely with this neighbourhood, and I expect we shall have to solve it on the spot."

This last observation impressed me strongly. The sergeant's view of the case was the same as Thorndyke's, and expressed in almost the same words.

"Have you any theory as to what has actually happened?" I asked.

The sergeant smiled in his benignant fashion. "It isn't much use inventing theories," said he. "We've got to get the facts before we can do anything. Still, looking at the case as we find it, there are two or three things that hit us in the face. There is a strong suspicion of murder, there is no trace of the body, and there is a big tidal river close at hand. On Saturday night it was high water at half-past-eleven, so there wouldn't have been much of the shore uncovered at, say, half-past-nine, and there would have been plenty of water at any of the piers or causeways."

"Then you think it probable that she was murdered and her body flung into the river?"

"It is the likeliest thing, so far as we can judge. There is the river, and there is no sign of the body on shore. But, as I say, it is no use guessing. We've got people watching the river from Allington Lock to Sheerness, and that's all we can do in that line. The body is pretty certain to turn up, sooner or later. Of course, until it does, there is no real criminal case, and even when we've got the body, we may not be much nearer getting the murderer. Excepting the man Frood, there is no one who seems to have had any motive for making away with her, and if it was just a casual robbery with murder it is unlikely that we shall ever spot the man at all."

Having given expression to this rather pessimistic view, the sergeant rose and, picking up his helmet, took his departure, after promising to let me know of any further developments.

As soon as he was gone, I wrote down the substance of what he had said, and then embodied it in a report for Thorndyke. While I was thus occupied, the afternoon post was delivered, and included a packet from the London photographer, to whom I had written, enclosing two copies of the photograph of Angelina that Mr. Japp had handed to the sergeant. Of these, I enclosed one copy in my communication to Thorndyke, on the bare chance that it might be of some assistance to him and, having closed up the large envelope and stamped it, I went forth to drop it into the post-box.

Chapter IX
Jetsam

That portion of Chatham High Street which lies adjacent to the River Medway presents a feature that is characteristic of old riverside towns in the multitude of communications between the street and the shore. Some of these are undisguised entrances to wharves, some are courts or small thoroughfares lined with houses and leading to landing-stages, while others are mere passages or flights of steps, opening obscurely and inconspicuously on the street by narrow apertures, unnoticed by the ordinary wayfarer and suggesting the burrows of some kind of human water-rat.

In the days that followed the sergeant's visit to me I made the acquaintance of all of them. Now I would wander down the cobbled cartway that led to a wharf, there to cast a searching eye over the muddy fore-shore or scan the turbid water at high tide as it eddied between the barges and around the piles. Or I would dive into the mouths of the burrows, creeping down slimy steps and pursuing the tortuous passages through a world of uncleanness until I came out upon the shore, where the fresh smell of seaweed mingled with odours indescribable. I began to be an object of curiosity – and perhaps of some suspicion – to the denizens of the little, ruinous, timber houses that lined these alleys, and of frank interest to the children who played around the rubbish heaps or dabbled in the grey mud. But never did my roving eye light upon that which it sought with such dreadful expectation.

One afternoon, about a week after the sergeant's visit, when I was returning home from one of these explorations, I observed a man on my doorstep as I approached the house. His appearance instantly aroused my attention, for he was dressed in the amphibious style adopted by waterside dwellers, and he held something in his hand at which he looked from time to time. Before I reached the door it had opened and admitted him, and when I arrived I found him in the hall nervously explaining his business to Mrs. Dunk.

"Here is the doctor," said the latter. "You'd better tell him about it."

The man turned to me and held out an amazingly dirty fist. "I've got something here, sir," said he, "what belongs to you, I think." Here he unclosed his hand and exhibited a little cardboard box bearing one of Dr. Partridge's labels. It was smeared with mud and grime, but I recognized it instantly – indeed, when I took it with trembling fingers from his palm and looked at it closely, the name, "*Mrs. Frood*" was still decipherable under the smears of dirt.

"Where did you find this?" I asked.

"I picked it up on the strand," he replied, "about halfway betwixt the Sun Pier and the end of Ship Alley, and just below spring tide high-water mark. Is it any good?"

"Yes," I answered, "it is very important. I will get you to walk along with me to the police station."

"What for?" he demanded suspiciously. "I don't want no police stations. If it's any good, give us what you think it's worth, and have done with it."

I gave him half-a-crown to allay his suspicions, and then said, "You had better come with me to the station. I expect the police will want you to show them exactly where you found this box and help them to search the place, and I will see that you are paid for your trouble."

"But look 'ere, mister," he objected. "What's the police got to do with this 'ere box?"

I explained the position to him briefly, and then, suddenly, his face lit up. "I know," he said excitedly. "I seen the bills stuck up on the dead-'ouse door. And d'you mean to say as this 'ere box was 'ers? Cos if it was, it's worth more 'n 'arf-a-crown."

"Perhaps it is," said I. "We will hear what the sergeant thinks." And with this I opened the door and went out, and my new acquaintance now followed with the greatest alacrity, taking the opportunity, as we walked along, to remind me of my promise and to offer tentative suggestions as to the scale of remuneration for his services.

Our progress along the High Street was not unnoticed. Doubtless, we appeared a somewhat ill-assorted pair, for I observed a good many persons turn to look at us curiously, and when we passed the office, on the opposite side of the road, I saw Bundy's face rise above the curtain with an expression of undissembled curiosity.

On arriving at the station, I inquired for Sergeant Cobbledick, and was fortunate enough to find him in his office. As I entered with my companion, he bestowed on the latter a quick glance of professional interest and then greeted me with a genial smile. It was hardly necessary for me to state my business, for the single quick glance of his experienced eye at my companion had furnished the diagnosis. I had only to produce the box and indicate the finder.

"This looks like a lead," said he, reaching his helmet down from a peg. "What's your name, sonny, and where do you live?"

Sonny affirmed, with apparent reluctance, that his name was Samuel Hooper and that his abode was situated in Foul Anchor Alley, and when

116

these facts had been committed to writing by the sergeant, the latter put on his helmet and invited the said Hooper to "Come along," evidently assuming that I was to form one of the party.

As we approached the office this time I saw Bundy from afar off, and by the time we were abreast of the house he was joined by Japp, who must have stood upon tip-toe to bring his eyes above the curtain. Both men watched us with intense interest, and we had barely passed the house when Bundy's head suddenly disappeared, and a few moments later its owner emerged from the doorway and hurriedly crossed the road.

"What is in the wind, Doctor?" he asked, as he came up with us. "Japp is in a rare twitter. Have they found the body?"

"No," I answered, "only the little box that was in her hand-bag. We are going to have a look at the place where it was found."

"To see if the bag is there, too?" said he. "It probably is, unless it has been picked up already. I think I'll come along with you, if you don't object. Then I can give Japp all the news."

I did not object, nor did the sergeant – verbally, but his expression conveyed to me that he would willingly have dispensed with Mr. Bundy's society. However, he was a suave and tactful man, and he made the best of the unwelcome addition to the party, even going so far as to offer the box for Bundy's inspection.

"It is pretty dirty," the latter observed, holding it delicately in his fingers. "Wasn't it wrapped in paper when you gave it to her, Doctor?"

"It was wrapped up in paper when I found it," said Hooper, "but I took off the paper to see what was inside and, yer see, my 'ands wasn't very clean, a-grubbin' about in the mud." In conclusive confirmation of this statement, he exhibited them to us, and then gave them a perfunctory wipe on his trousers.

"What struck me," said Bundy, "was that it doesn't seem to have been in the water."

"It hadn't," said Hooper. "The outside paper was quite clean when I picked it up."

"It looks," observed the sergeant, "as if they had turned out the bag and thrown away what they didn't want, and then they probably threw away the bag, too. It is ten chances to one that it has been picked up, but if it hasn't it will probably be somewhere along the high-water mark. How are the tides, Hooper?"

"Just past the bottom of the nips," was the reply, and a few moments later our guide added, "It's down here," and plunged into what looked like an open doorway. We followed, one at a time, cautiously descending a flight of very filthy stone steps and stooping to avoid knocking our heads against the overhanging story of an ancient timber house. At the bottom we proceeded, still in single file, along a narrow, crooked passage between grimy walls and ruinous tarred fences until, after many twistings and turnings, we came to a flight of rough wooden steps, thickly coated with yellow mud and slimy sea-grass, which led down to the shore.

"Now," said the sergeant, turning up the bottoms or his trousers, "show us exactly where you picked the box up."

"It was just oppersight that there schooner," said our guide, taking his way along the muddy streak between the two lines of jetsam that corresponded to the springtide and neap-tide high-water marks, "betwixt her and the wharf."

We followed him, picking our way daintly and, having inspected the spot that he indicated, squeezed in between the schooner's bilge and the piles and raked over the rubbish that the tide had deposited on the shore.

"Was you looking for anything in partickler?" Hooper asked.

"We are looking for a small leather handbag," replied the sergeant, "or anything else we can find."

"A 'and-bag wouldn't 'ave been 'ere long," Hooper remarked. "Somebody would 'ave twigged it pretty quick, unless it got hidden under something big." He straightened himself up and gave a searching look up and down the shore, and then suddenly he started off with an air of definite purpose. Glancing in the direction towards which he was shaping his course, I observed, in the corner of a stage that jutted out from the quay, a heap of miscellaneous rubbish surmounted by the mortal remains of a large hamper. It looked a likely spot and we all followed, though not at his pace, being somewhat more fastidious as to where we stepped. Consequently he arrived considerably before us, and having flung away the hamper, began eagerly to grub among the underlying raffle. Just as we had come within a dozen yards of him, anxiously making the perilous passage over a stretch of peculiarly slimy mud, he stood up with a howl of triumph, and we all stopped to look at him. His arm was raised above his head, and from his hand hung by its handle a little morocco bag.

"There's no need to ask you to identify it, Doctor," said the sergeant, as he despoiled the water-rat of his prize. "It fits your description to a *T*."

Nevertheless, he handed it to me, drawing my attention to the initials "*A. F.*" stamped on the leather. I turned it over gloomily, noting that it showed signs of having been in the water – though not, apparently, for any considerable time – and that none of its contents remained excepting a handkerchief tucked into an inner pocket, and returned it to him without remark.

"Now, look here, Hooper," said he, "I want you to stay down here and keep an eye on this shore until I send some of our men up, and then you can stay and help them, if you like. And remember that anything that you find – no matter what it is – you keep and hand over to me or my men, and you will be paid the full value and a reward for finding it as well. Do you understand that?"

"I do," replied Hooper. "That's a fair orfer, and you can depend on me to do the square thing. I'll stay down here until your men come."

Thereupon we left him, pursuing our way along the shore and keeping an attentive eye on all the rubbish and litter that we passed, until we came to a set of rough wooden steps by the Ship Pier.

"I had no authority to offer to pay that chap," said the sergeant, as we walked up Ship Alley, "but the superintendent has put me on to work at this case, and I'm not going to lose any chances for the sake of a few shillings. It is well to keep in with these waterside people."

"Have you published a list of things that are likely to turn up?" Bundy asked.

"We've posted up a description of the missing woman with full details of her dress and belongings," replied the sergeant. "But perhaps a list of the things that might be washed up would be useful. People are such fools. Yes, it's a good idea. I'll have a list printed of everything that might get loose and be picked up, and stick it up on the wharves and waterside premises. Then there will be nothing left to their imagination."

At the top of Ship Alley he halted and, having thanked me warmly for my prompt and timely information, turned towards Chatham Town, leaving me and Bundy to retrace our steps westward.

"That was a bit of luck," the latter remarked, "finding that bag, and he hardly deserved it. He ought to have had that piece of shore under observation from the first. But he was wise to make an acceptable offer to that bodysnatcher, Hooper. I expect he lives on the shore, watching for derelict corpses and any unconsidered trifles that the river may throw up. I see there is a reward of two pounds for the body."

"You have seen the bills, then?"

"Yes. We have got one to stick up in the office window. Rather gruesome, isn't it?"

"Horrible," I said, and for a while we walked on in silence. Presently Bundy exclaimed, "By Jove! I had nearly forgotten. I have a message for you. It is from Japp. He is taking a distinguished American archaeologist for a personally conducted tour round the town to show him the antiquities, and he thought you might like to join the party."

"That is very good of him," said I. "It sounds as if it should be rather interesting."

"It will be," said Bundy. "Japp is an enthusiast in regard to architecture and ancient buildings, and he is quite an authority on the antiquities of this town. You'd better come. The American – his name is Willard – is going to charter a photographer to come round with us and take records of all the objects of interest, and we shall be able to get copies of any photographs that we want. What do you say?"

"When does the demonstration take place?"

"The day after tomorrow. We shall do the Cathedral in the morning and the castle and the town in the afternoon. Shall I tell Japp you will join the merry throng?"

"Yes, please, and convey my very warm thanks for the invitation."

"I will," said he, halting as we arrived at the office, "unless you would like to come in and convey the joyful tidings yourself."

"No," he replied, "I won't come in now. I will get home and change my boots."

"Yes, by Jingo!" Bundy agreed, with a rueful glance at his own delicate shoes. "Mudlarking calls for a special outfit. And I clean my own shoes, but I'd rather do that than face Mrs. Dunk."

With this he retired up the steps, and I turned homeward, deciding to profit by his last remark and forestall unfavourable comment by shedding my boots on the doormat.

Chapter X
Which Deals with Ancient Monuments and a Blue Boar

On arriving home, I found awaiting me a letter from Dr. Thorndyke suggesting – in response to a general invitation that I had given him some time previously – that he should come down on Saturday to spend the week-end with me. Of course, I adopted the suggestion with very great pleasure, not a little flattered at receiving so distinguished a guest, and now I was somewhat disposed to regret my engagement to attend Mr. Japp's demonstration. However, as Thorndyke was not due until lunch time, I should have an opportunity of modifying my arrangement, if necessary.

But, as events turned out, I congratulated myself warmly on not having missed the morning visit to the Cathedral. It was a really remarkable experience, and not the least interesting part of it to me was the revelation of the inner personality of my friend, Mr. Japp. That usually dry and taciturn man of business was transfigured in the presence of the things that he really loved. He glowed with enthusiasm, he exhaled the very spirit of mediaeval romance, at every pore he exuded strange and recondite knowledge. Obedient to his behest, the ancient building told the vivid story of its venerable past, presented itself in its rude and simple beginnings, exhibited the transformations that had marked the passing centuries, peopled itself with the illustrious departed, whose heirs we were and whose resting-places we looked upon, and became to us a living thing whose birth and growth we could watch, whose vicissitudes and changing conditions we could trace until they brought us to its august old age. Under his guidance we looked down the long vista of the past, from the time when simple masons scalloped the Norman capitals within, while illustrious craftsmen fashioned the wonderful west doorway, to that last upheaval that swept away the modern shoddy and restored to the old fabric its modest comeliness.

Architectural antiquities, however, are not the especial concern of this history, though they were not without a certain influence in its unfolding. Accordingly, I shall not follow our progress – attended by the indispensable photographic recording angel – through nave and aisles, form choir to transepts, and from tower to undercroft. At the close of a delightful morning I betook myself homeward, charged with new and varied knowledge, and with a cordial invitation to my guest to join the afternoon's expedition if he were archaeologically inclined.

Apparently he was, for when, shortly after his arrival, I conveyed the invitation to him he accepted at once.

"I always take the opportunity," said he, "of getting what is practically first-hand information. Your friend, Mr. Japp, is evidently an enthusiast, he has expert technical knowledge, and he has apparently filled in his detail by personal investigation. A man like that can tell you more in an hour than guide-books could tell you in a lifetime. We had better get a large-scale map of the town to enable us to follow the description, unless you have one."

"I haven't," said I, "but we can get one on the way to the rendezvous. You got my report, I suppose?"

"Yes," he replied, "I got it yesterday. That, in fact, was what determined me to come down. The discovery of that bag upon the shore dispels to some extent the ambiguity of our data. The finding of the brooch did not enlighten us much. It might simply have been dropped and picked up by some casual wayfarer. In fact, that is what the appearances suggested, for it is manifestly improbable that a person who had committed a crime would take the risk of pawning the product of robbery with violence in the very neighbourhood where the crime had been committed, and after an interval of time which would allow of the hue-and-cry having already been raised. Your sergeant is probably right in assuming that the man with the mole had nothing to do with the affair. But the finding of this bag is a different matter. It connects that disappearance with the river and it offers a strong suggestion of crime."

"Don't you think it possible that she might have fallen into the river accidentally?" I asked.

"It is possible," he admitted. "But that is where the significance of the brooch comes in. If she had fallen into the river from some wharf or pier, there does not seem to be any reason why the brooch should have become detached and fallen on land – as it apparently did. The finding of the bag where it had been thrown up by the river, and of the brooch on shore, suggests a struggle on land previous to the fall into the water. You don't happen, I suppose, to know what the bag contained?"

"I don't – excepting the packet of tablets that I gave her. When the bag was found, it was empty – at least, it contained only the handkerchief, as I mentioned in my report."

"Yes," he said reflectively. "By the way, I must compliment you on those reports. They are excellent, and with regard to this one, there are two or three rather curious circumstances. First, as to the packet of tablets. You mention that it had not been unwrapped and that, when it was found, the paper was quite clean. Therefore it had never been in the water. Therefore it had been taken out of the bag – by somebody with moderately clean hands – before the latter was dropped into the river, and it must have been thrown away on the shore above highwater mark. Incidentally, since the disappearance occurred – presumably – on the evening of the 26th of April, and the packet was found on the 7th of May, it had been lying on the shore for a full ten days. Perhaps there is nothing very remarkable in that, but the point is that Mrs. Frood was carrying the bag in her hand and she would almost certainly have dropped it if there had been any struggle. How, then, did the bag come to be in the river, and how came some of its contents to be found on the shore clean and free from any traces of submersion?"

"We can only suppose," said I, with an inward shudder – for the discussion of these hideous details made my very flesh creep – "that the murderer picked up the bag when he had thrown the body into the river, took out any articles of value, if there were any, and threw the rest on the shore."

"Yes," agreed Thorndyke, a little doubtfully, "that would seem to be what happened. And in that case, we should have to assume that the place where the packet was found was, approximately, the place where the crime was committed. For, as the packet was never immersed, it could not have been carried to that place by the tide, and one cannot think of any other agency by which it could have been moved. Its clean and unopened condition seems to exclude human agency. The question then naturally arises: Is the place where the packet was found, a place at, or near, which the tragedy could conceivably have occurred? What do you say to that?"

I considered for a few moments, recalling the intricate and obscure approach of the shore and the absence of anything in the nature of a public highway.

"I can only say," I replied at length, "that it seems perfectly inconceivable that Mrs. Frood could have been at that place, or even near it, unless she went there for some specific purpose – unless, for instance, she were lured there in some way. It is a place that is, I should say, unknown to any but the waterside people."

"We must go there and examine the place carefully," said he, "for if it is, as you say, a place to which no one could imaginably have strayed by chance, that fact has an important evidential bearing."

"Do you think it quite impossible that the package could have been carried to that place and dropped there?"

"Not impossible, of course," he replied, "but I can think of no reasonably probable way in which it could have happened, supposing the murderer to have pocketed it, and afterwards to have thrown it away. That would be a considered and deliberate act, and it is almost inconceivable that he should not have opened the packet to see what was inside, and that he should have dropped it on the dry beach when the river was close at hand. Remember that the bag was found quite near, and that it had been in the water."

"And assuming the crime to have been committed at that place, what would it prove?"

"In the first place," he replied, "it would pretty definitely exclude the theory of accidental death. Then it would suggest at least a certain amount of premeditation, since the victim would have had, as you say, to be enticed to that unlikely spot. And it would suggest that the murderer was a person acquainted with the locality."

"One of the waterside people," said I. "They are a pretty shady lot, but I don't see why any of them should want to murder her."

"It is not impossible," said he. "She was said to be shopping in Chatham, and she might have had a well-filled purse and allowed it to be seen. But that is mere speculation. The fact is that we have no data at present. We know practically nothing about Mrs. Frood. We can't say if she had any secret enemies, or if there was anyone who might have profited by her death or have had any motive for making away with her."

"We know something about her husband," said I, "and that he has disappeared in a rather mysterious fashion, and that his disappearance coincides with that of his wife."

"Yes," Thorndyke agreed, "those are significant facts. But we mustn't lose sight of the legal position. Until the body is recovered, there is no evidence of death. Until the death is proved, no charge of murder can be sustained. When the body is found it will probably furnish some evidence as to how the death occurred, if it is recovered within a reasonable time. As a matter of fact, it is rather remarkable that it has not yet been found. The death occurred – presumably – nearly a fortnight ago. Considering how very much frequented this river is, it is really rather unaccountable that the body has not come to light. But I suppose it is time that we started for the rendezvous."

I looked at my watch and decided that it was, and we accordingly set forth in the direction of the office, which was the appointed meeting-place, calling at a stationer's to provide ourselves each with a map. We chose the six-inch town plan, which contained the whole urban area, including the winding reaches of the river, folding them so as to show at an opening the peninsula on which the city of Rochester is built.

"A curious loop of the river, this," said Thorndyke, scanning the map as we went along. "Rather like that of the Thames at the Isle of

Dogs. You notice that there are quite a number of creeks on the low shore at both sides. Those will be places to watch. A floating body has rather a tendency to get carried into shallow creeks and to stay there. But I have no doubt the longshoremen are keeping an eye on them as a reward has been offered. Perhaps we might be able to go down and have a look at the shore when we have finished our perambulation of the town."

"I don't see why not," I replied, though, to tell the truth, I was not very keen on this particular exploration. To Thorndyke this quest was just an investigation to be pursued with passionless care and method. To me it was a tragedy that would colour my whole life. To him, Angelina was but a missing woman whose disappearance had to be explained by patient inquiry. To me she was a beloved friend whose loss would leave me with a life-long sorrow. Of course, he was not aware of this – he had no suspicion of the shuddering horror that his calm, impersonal examination of the evidential details produced in me. Nor did I intend that he should. It was my duty and my privilege to give him what assistance I could, and keep my emotions to myself.

"You will bear in mind," said he, as we approached the office, "that my connexion with the case of Mrs. Frood is not to be referred to. I am simply a friend staying with you for a day or two."

"I won't forget," said I, "though I don't quite see why it should matter."

"It probably doesn't matter at all," he replied. "But one never knows. Facts which might readily be spoken of before a presumably disinterested person might be withheld from one who was known to be collecting evidence for professional purposes. At any rate, I make it a rule to keep out of sight as far as possible."

These observations brought us to the office, where we found our three friends together with a young man, who was apparently acting as deputy during the absence of the partners, and the photographer. I presented Thorndyke to my friends, and when the introduction had been made Mr. Japp picked up his hat, and turned to the deputy.

"You know where to find me, Stevens," he said, "if I should be really wanted – really, you understand. But I don't particularly want to be found. Shall we start now? I propose to begin at the bridge, follow the Highstreet as far as Eastgate House, visit Restoration House, trace the city wall on the southwest side, and look over the castle. By that time we shall be ready for tea. After tea we can trace the north-east part of the wall and the gates that opened through it, and that will finish our tour of inspection."

Hereupon the procession started, Mr. Japp and his guest leading, Thorndyke, Bundy, and I following, and the photographer bringing up the rear.

"Let me see," said Bundy, looking up at Thorndyke with a sort of pert shyness. "Weren't you down here a week or two ago?"

"Yes," replied Thorndyke, "and I think I had the honour of being inspected by you while I was reading your proclamation respecting a certain lost key."

"You had," said Bundy. "In fact, I may say that you raised false hopes in my partner and me. We thought you were going to find it."

"What, for ten shillings!" exclaimed Thorndyke.

"We would have raised the fee if you had made a firm offer," said Bundy, removing his eyeglass to polish it with his handkerchief. "It was a valuable key. Belonged to a gate that encloses part of the city wall."

"Indeed!" said Thorndyke. "I don't wonder you were anxious about it considering what numbers of dishonest persons there are about. Ha! Here is the bridge. Let us hear what Mr. Japp has to say about it."

Mr. Japp's observations were concise. Having cast a venomous glance at the unlovely structure, he turned his back on it and remarked acidly, "That is the new bridge. It is, as you see, composed of iron girders. It is not an antiquity, and I hope it never will be. Let us forget it and go on to the Guildhall." He strode forward doggedly and Bundy turned to us with a grin.

"Poor old Japp," said he. "He does hate that bridge. He has an engraving of the old stone one in his rooms, and I've seen him stand in front of it and groan. And really you can't wonder. It is an awful come-down. Just think what the town must have looked like from across the river when that stone bridge was standing."

Here we halted opposite the Guildhall, and when we had read the inscription, admired the magnificent ship weathercock – said to be a model of the Rodney – and listened to Japp's observations on the architectural features of the building, the photographer was instructed to operate on its exterior while we entered to explore the Justice Room and examine the portraits. From the Guildhall we passed on to the Corn Exchange, the quaint and handsome overhanging clock of which had evidently captured Mr. Willard's fancy.

"That clock," said he, "is a stroke of genius. It gives a character to the whole street. But what in creation induced your City Fathers to allow that charming little building to be turned into a picture theatre?"

Japp shook his head and groaned. "You may well ask that," said he, glaring viciously at the inane posters and the doorway, decorated in the film taste. "If good Sir Cloudesley Shovel, who gave it to the town, could rise from his grave and look at it, now he'd – Bah! The crying need of this age is some means of protecting historic buildings from town councils. To these men an ancient building is just old-fashioned – out-of-date, a thing to be pulled down and replaced by something smart and up-to-date in the corrugated iron line." He snorted fiercely, and as the photographer dismounted his camera, he turned and led the way up the street. I lingered to help the photographer with his repacking, and meanwhile Thorndyke and Bundy walked on together, chatting amicably and suggesting to my fancy an amiable mastiff accompanied by a particularly well-groomed fox terrier.

"Do you usually give your patients a week-end holiday?" Bundy was inquiring as I overtook them.

"I haven't any patients," replied Thorndyke. "My medical practice is conducted mostly in the Law Courts."

"Good gracious!" exclaimed Bundy. "Do you mean that you live by resuscitating moribund jurymen and fattening up murderers for execution, and that sort of thing?"

"Not at all," replied Thorndyke. "Nothing so harmless. I am what is known as a Medical Expert. I give opinions on medical questions that affect legal issues."

"Then you are really a sort of lawyer?"

"Yes. A medico-legal hybrid, a sort of centaur or merman, with a doctor's head and a lawyer's tail."

"Well," said Bundy, "there are some queer professions, I once knew a chap in the furniture trade who described himself as a 'worm-eater' – drilled worm-holes in faked antiques, you know."

"And what," asked Thorndyke, "might be the analogy that you are suggesting? You don't propose to associate me with the diet of worms, I hope."

"Certainly not," said Bundy, "though I suppose your practice is sometimes connected with exhumations. But I was thinking that you must know quite a lot about crime."

"A good deal of my practice is concerned with criminal cases," Thorndyke admitted.

"Then you will be rather interested in our local mystery. Has the doctor told you about it?"

"You mean the mystery of the disappearing lady? But of what interest should it be to me? I was not acquainted with her."

"I meant a professional interest. But I suppose you are not taking a 'bus-man's holiday' – don't want to be bothered with mysteries that don't concern you. Still, I should like to hear your expert opinion on the case."

127

"You mistake my functions," said Thorndyke. "A common witness testifies to facts known to himself. An expert witness interprets facts presented to him by others. Present me your facts, and I will try to give you an interpretation of them."

"But there are no facts. That is what constitutes the mystery."

"Then there is nothing to interpret. It is a case for the police, and not for the scientific expert."

Here our conversation was interrupted by our arrival at The House of the Six Poor Travellers, and by a learned disquisition by Japp on the connotation of the word '*Proctor*' – which, it appeared, was sometimes used in the Middle Ages in the sense of a cadger or swindler. Thence we proceeded to Eastgate House, where Japp mounted his hobby and discoursed impressively on the subject of ceilings, taking as his text a specimen modelled *in situ*, and bearing the date 1590.

"The fellow who put up that ceiling," said he, "took his time about it, no doubt. But his work has lasted three-hundred-and-fifty years. That is the best way to save time. Your modern plasterer will have his ceiling up in a jiffy, and it will be down in a jiffy, and to do all over again. And never worth looking at at all."

Mr. Willard nodded. "It is very true," said he. "What is striking me in looking at all this old work is the great economy of time that is effected by taking pains and using good material, to say nothing of the beauty of the things created."

"If he goes on talking like that," whispered Bundy, "Japp'll kiss him. We must get them out of this."

Mercifully – if such a catastrophe was imminent – the ceiling discourse brought our inspection here to an end. From Eastgate House we went back to the Maidstone Road, and when we had inspected Restoration House, began to trace out the site of the city wall, which Thorndyke carefully marked on his map, to Japp's intense gratification. This perambulation brought us to the castle – which was dealt with rather summarily, as Mr. Willard had already examined it – and we then returned to the office for tea, which Bundy prepared and served with great success in his own sitting-room, while Japp dotted in with red ink on Thorndyke's map the entire city wall, including the part which we had yet to trace, and ridiculously small the ancient city looked when thus marked out on the modern town.

After tea we retraced our steps to the site of the East Gate and, having inspected a large fragment of the wall at the end of an alley, traced its line across the Highstreet, and then proceeded down Free School Lane to the fine angle-bastion at the northern corner of the lane. Thence we followed the scanty indications as far as the site of the North

Gate, and thereafter through a confused and rather unlovely neighbourhood until, on the edge of the marshes, we struck into a narrow lane, enclosed by a dilapidated tarred fence, a short distance along which we came to a closed gate, which I recognized as the one through which I had passed with Bundy on the day when we were made acquainted with the tragic history of Bill the Bargee. As Japp unlocked the gate and admitted us to the space of waste land, Bundy remarked to Thorndyke, "That is the gate that the missing key belonged to. You see there is no harm done so far. The wall is still there."

"Yes," said Thorndyke, "and not much improved in appearance by your builders' attentions. Those patches suggest the first attempts of an untalented dental student at conservation."

"They are rather a disfigurement," said Japp. "But the men had to have a job found for them, and that is the result. Perhaps they won't show so much in the photograph."

While the photographer was setting up his camera and making the exposure, Japp explained the relation of this piece of wall to the North Gate and the Gate that faced the bridge, and marked its position on Thorndyke's map.

"And that," he continued, "concludes our perambulation. The photographer is chartered by Mr. Willard, but I understand that we are at liberty to secure copies of the photographs, if we want them. Is that not so, Mr. Willard?"

"Surely," was the cordial reply, "only I stipulate that they shall be a gift from me, and I shall ask a favour in return. If there is a plate left, I should like to have a commemorative group taken, so that when I recall this pleasant day, I can also recall the pleasant society in which I spent it."

We all acknowledged the kindly compliment with a bow, and as the photographer announced that he had a spare plate, we grouped ourselves against a portion of undisfigured wall, removed our hats, and took up easy and graceful postures on either side of Mr. Willard. When the exposure had been made, and the photographer proceeded to pack up his apparatus, Thorndyke tendered his very hearty thanks to Mr. Japp and his friend for their hospitality.

"It has been a great privilege," said he, "to be allowed to share in the products of so much study and research, and I assure you it is far from being unappreciated. Whenever I revisit Rochester – which I hope to do before long – I shall think of you gratefully, and of your very kind and generous friend, Mr. Willard."

Our two hosts made suitable acknowledgments, and while these compliments were passing, I turned to Bundy.

"Can we get down to the shore from here?" I asked. "Thorndyke was saying that he would like to have a look at the river. If it is accessible from here we might take it on the way home."

"It isn't difficult to get at," replied Bundy. "If he wants to get a typical view of the river with the below-bridge traffic, by far the best place is Blue Boar Pier. It isn't very far, and it is on your way home-more or less. I'll show you the way there if you like. Japp is dining with Willard, so he won't want me."

I accepted the offer gladly, and as the exchange of compliments seemed to be completed and our party was moving towards the gate, I tendered my thanks for the day's entertainment and bade my hosts farewell, explaining that we were going riverwards. Accordingly we parted at the gate, Japp and Willard turning towards the town, while Thorndyke, Bundy, and I retraced our steps towards the marshes.

At the bottom of the lane Bundy paused to explain the topography. "That path," said he, "leads to Gas House Road and the marshes by the North Shore. But there isn't much to see there. If we take this other track we shall strike Blue Boar Lane, which will take us to the pier. From there we can get a view of the whole bend of the river right across to Chatham."

Thorndyke followed the description closely with the aid of his map, marking off our present position with a pencil. Then we struck into a rough cart-track, with the wide stretch of the marshes on our left and, following this, we presently came out into the lower part of Blue Boar Lane and turned our faces towards the river. We had not gone far when I observed a man approaching whose appearance seemed to be familiar. Bundy also observed him, for he exclaimed, "Why, that is old Cobbledick! Out of uniform, too. Very irregular. I shall have to remonstrate with him. I wonder what he has been up to. Prowling about the river bank in search of clues, I expect. And he'll suspect us of being on the same errand."

Bundy's surmise appeared to be correct, for as the sergeant drew nearer and recognized us, his face took on an expression of shrewd inquiry. But I noticed with some surprise that his curiosity seemed to be principally concerned with Thorndyke, at whom he gazed with something more than common attention. Under the circumstances I should have passed him with a friendly greeting, but he stopped and, having wished me "Good evening," said, "Could I have a few words with you, Doctor?" upon which I halted, and Thorndyke and Bundy walked on slowly. The sergeant looked after them and, turning his back to them, drew from his pocket with a mysterious air a small dirty brown bundle, which he handed to me.

130

"I wanted you just to have a look at that," he said.

I opened out the bundle, though I had already tentatively recognized it. But when it was unrolled it was unmistakable. It was poor Angelina's scarf.

"I thought there couldn't be any doubt about it," the sergeant said cheerfully when I had announced the identification. "Your description was so clear and exact. Well, this gives us a pretty fair kick-off. You can see that it has been in the water-some time, too. So we know where to look for the body. The mysterious thing is, though, that we've still got to look for it. It ought to have come up on the shore days ago. And it hasn't. There isn't a longshoreman for miles up and down that isn't on the look-out for it. You can see them prowling along the seawalls and searching the creeks in their boats. I can't think how they can have missed it. The thing is getting serious."

"Serious?" I repeated.

"Well," he explained, "there's no need for me to point out to a medical gentleman like you that bodies don't last forever, especially in mild weather such as we've been having, and in a river where the shore swarms with rats and shore-crabs. Every day that passes is making the identification more difficult."

The horrible suggestions that emerged from his explanation gave me a sensation of physical sickness. I fidgeted uneasily, but still I managed to rejoin huskily, "There's the clothing, you know."

"So there is," he agreed, "and very good means of identification in an ordinary case – accidental drowning, for instance. But this is a criminal case. I don't want to have to depend on the clothing."

"Was the scarf found floating?" I asked, a little anxious to change the subject to one less gruesome.

"No," he replied. "It was on the shore by the small creek just below Blue Boar Pier, under an empty fish-trunk. One of the Customs men from the watch-house found it. He noticed the trunk lying out on the shore as he was walking along and went out to see if there was anything in it. Then, when he found it was empty, he turned it over, and there was the scarf. He recognized it at once – there's a list of the articles stuck up on the watch-house – and kept it to bring to me. But it happened that I came down here – as I do every day – just after he'd found it. But I mustn't keep you here talking, though I'm glad I met you and got your confirmation about this scarf."

He smiled benignly and raised his hat, whereupon I wished him "Good evening" and went on my way with a sigh of relief. He was a pleasant, genial man, but his matter-of-fact way of looking at this tragedy that had eaten so deeply into my peace of mind was to me positively harrowing. But, of course, he did not understand my position in the case.

"Well," said Bundy, when I hurried up, "what's the news? Old Cobbledick was looking mighty mysterious. And wasn't he interested in us? Why he's gazing after us still. Has he had a bite? Because if he hasn't, I have. Some beastly mosquito."

"Don't rub it." said Thorndyke, as Bundy clapped his hand to his cheek. "Leave it alone. We'll put a spot of ammonia or iodine on it presently."

"Very well," replied Bundy, with a grimace expressive of resignation. "I am in the hands of the Faculty. What sort of fish was it that Isaak Walton Cobbledick had hooked? Or is it a secret?"

"I don't think there is any secrecy about it," said I. "One of the Customs men has found Mrs. Frood's scarf," and I repeated what the sergeant had told me as to the circumstances.

"It is a gruesome affair," said Bundy, "this search for these ghastly relics. Look at those ghouls down on the shore there. I suppose that is the fish-trunk."

As he spoke, we came out on the shore to the right of the pier and halted to survey the rather unlovely prospect. Outside the stunted sea-wall a level stretch of grey-green grass extended to the spring high-water mark, beyond which a smooth sheet of mud – now dry and covered with multitudinous cracks – spread out to the slimy domain of the ordinary tides. At the edge of the dry mud lay a derelict fish-trunk around which a group of bare-legged boys had gathered – and all along the shore, on the faded grass, on the dry mud and wading in the soft slime, the human water-rats were to be seen, turning over drift-rubbish, prying under stranded boats, or grubbing in the soft mud. Hard by, on the grass near the sea-wall, an old ship's long-boat had been hauled up above tide-marks to a permanent berth and turned into a habitation by the erection in it of a small house. A short ladder gave access to it from without and the resident had laid down a little causeway of flat stones leading to the wall.

"Mr. Noah seems to be at home," observed Bundy, as we approached the little amphibious residence to inspect it. He pointed to a thin wisp of smoke that issued from the iron chimney and, almost as he spoke, the door opened and an old man came out into the open stern-sheets of the boat with a steaming tin pannikin in his hand. His appearance fitted his residence to a nicety, for whereas the latter appeared to have been constructed chiefly from driftwood and wreckage, his costume suggested a collection of assorted marine salvage, with a leaning towards oil-skin.

132

"Mr. Noah" cast a malevolent glance at the searchers. Then, having fortified himself with a pull at the pannikin, he turned a filmy blue eye on us.

"Good evening," said Thorndyke. "There seems to be a lot of business-doing here," and he indicated the fish-trunk and the eager searchers.

The old man grunted contemptuously. "Parcel of fules," said he, "a-busyin' theirselves with what don't concern 'em, and lookin' in the wrong place at that."

"Still," said Bundy, "they have found something here."

"Yes," the old man admitted, "they have. And that's why they ain't goin' to find anything more." He refreshed himself with a drink of – presumably – tea, and continued, "But the things is a-beginning to come up. It's about time she come up. But she won't come up here."

"Where do you suppose she will come up?" asked Bundy.

The old man regarded him with a cunning leer. "Never you mind where she'll come up," said he. "It ain't no consarn o' yourn."

"But how do you know where she'll come up?" Bundy persisted.

"I knows," the old scarecrow replied conclusively, "becos I do. Becos I gets my livin' along-shore, and it's my business for to know."

Having made this pronouncement, Mr. Noah looked inquiringly into the pannikin, emptied it at a draught and, turning abruptly, retired into the ark, shutting the door after him with a care suited to its evident physical infirmity.

"I wonder if he really does know," said Bundy, as we walked away past the Customs watch-house.

"We can fairly take it that he doesn't," said Thorndyke, "seeing that the matter is beyond human calculation. But I have no doubt that he knows the places where bodies and other floating objects are most commonly washed ashore, and we may assume that he is proposing to devote his probably extensive leisure to the exploration of those places. It wouldn't be amiss to put the sergeant in communication with him."

"Probably the sergeant knows him," said I, "but I will mention the matter the next time I see him."

At the top of Blue Boar Lane Bundy halted and held out his hand to Thorndyke. "This is the parting of the ways," said he.

"Oh, no, it isn't," replied Thorndyke. "You've got to have your mosquito-bite treated. Never neglect an insect-bite, especially on the face."

"As a matter of fact," said I, "you have got to come and have dinner with us. We can't let you break up the party in this way."

"It's very nice of you to ask me," he began, hesitatingly, a little shy, as I guessed, of intruding on me and my visitor, but I cut him short and, hooking my arm through his, led him off, an obviously willing captive. And if his presence hindered me from discussing with Thorndyke the problem that had occasioned his visit, that was of no consequence, since we should have the following day to ourselves, and he certainly contributed not a little to the cheerfulness of the proceedings. Indeed, I seemed to find in his high spirits something a little pathetic, a suggestion that the company of two live men – one of them a man of outstanding intellect – was an unusual treat, and that his life with old Japp and the predatory females might be a trifle dull. He took to Thorndyke amazingly, treating him with a sort of respectful cheekiness, like a schoolboy dining with a favourite head-master, while Thorndyke, fully appreciative of his irresponsible gaiety, developed a quiet humour and playfulness which rather took me by surprise. The solemn farce of the diagnosis and treatment of the mosquito bite was an instance, when Thorndyke, having seated the patient in the surgery chair and invested him with a large towel, covered the table with an assortment of preposterous instruments and bottles of reagents, and proceeded gravely to examine the bite through a lens until Bundy was as nervous as a cat, and then to apply the remedy with meticulous precision on the point of a fine sable brush.

It was a pleasant evening, pervaded by a sense of frivolous gaiety that was felt gratefully by the two elder revellers and was even viewed indulgently by Mrs. Dunk. As to Bundy, his high spirits flowed unceasingly – but, I may add, with faultless good manners – and when, at length, he took his departure, he shook our hands with a warmth which, again, I found slightly pathetic.

"I have had a jolly evening!" he exclaimed, looking at me with a queer sort of wistfulness. "It has been a red-letter day", and with this he turned abruptly and walked away.

We watched him from the threshold, bustling jauntily along the pavement, and as I looked at him, there came unbidden to my mind the recollection of that other figure that I had watched from this same threshold, walking away in the fading light – walking into the fog that was to swallow her up and hide her from my sight forever.

From these gloomy reflections I was recalled by Thorndyke's voice.

"A nice youngster, that, Strangeways. Gay and sprightly, but not in the least shallow. I often think that there was a great deal of wisdom in that observation of Spencer's, that happy people are the greatest benefactors to mankind. Your friend, Bundy, has helped me to renew my youth, and who could have done one a greater service?"

Chapter XI
The Man with the Mole

When I had seen my guest off by the last train on Saturday night, I walked homeward slowly, cogitating on the results of his visit. It seemed to me that they were very insignificant. In the morning we had explored the piece of shore on which the bag and the box of tablets had been found, making our way to it by the narrow and intricate alleys which seemed to be the only approach, and we had reached the same conclusion. It was an impossible place.

"If we assume," said Thorndyke, "as we must, on the apparent probabilities, that the tragedy occurred here, we must assume that there are some significant circumstances that are unknown to us. Mrs. Frood could not have strayed here by chance. We can think of no business that could have brought her here, and since she was neither a child nor a fool, she could not have been enticed into such an obviously sinister locality without some plausible pretext. There is evidently something more than meets the eye."

"Something, you mean, connected with her past life and the people she knew?"

"Exactly. I am having careful inquiries made on the subject in likely quarters, including the various theatrical photographers. They form quite a promising source of information, as they are not only able to give addresses but they can furnish us with photographs of members of the companies who would have been colleagues and, at least, acquaintances."

"If you come across any photographs of Mrs. Frood," I said, "I should like to see them."

"You shall," he replied. "I shall certainly collect all I can get, on the chance that they may help us with the identification of the body, which may possibly present some difficulty."

Here I was reminded of Cobbledick's observations and, distasteful as they were, I repeated them to Thorndyke.

"The sergeant is quite right," said he. "This is apparently a criminal case, involving a charge of wilful murder. To sustain that charge, the prosecution will have to produce incontestable evidence as to the identity of the deceased. Clothing alone would not be sufficient to secure a conviction. The body would have to be identified. And the sergeant's anxiety is quite justified. Have you had any experiences of bodies recovered from the water?"

"Yes," I replied, "and I don't like to think of them." I shuddered as I spoke, for his question had recalled to my memory the incidents of a professional visit to Poplar Mortuary. There rose before my eyes the picture of a long black, box with a small glass window in the lid, and of a thing that appeared at that window, a huge, bloated, green and purple thing, with groups or radiating wrinkles, and in the middle a button-like object that looked like the tip of a nose. It was a frightful picture, and yet I knew that when the river that we stood by should give up its dead –

I put the thought away with a shiver and asked faintly, "About the man Frood. Don't you think that his disappearance throws some light on the mystery?"

"It doesn't throw much light," replied Thorndyke, "because nothing is known about it. Obviously the coincidence in time of the disappearance, added to the known character of the man and his relations with his wife, make him an object of deep suspicion. His whereabouts will have to be traced and his time accounted for. But I have ascertained that the police know nothing about him, and my own inquiries have come to nothing, so far. He seems to have disappeared without leaving a trace. But I shall persevere. Your object – and mine – is to clear up the mystery, and if a crime has been committed, to bring the criminal to justice."

So that was how the matter stood, and it did not appear to me that much progress had been made towards the elucidation of the mystery. As to the perpetrator or that crime, he remained a totally unknown quantity, unless the deed could be fixed on the missing man, Frood. And so matters remained for some days. Then an event occurred which seemed to promise some illumination of the darkness, a promise that it failed to fulfil.

It was about a week after Thorndyke's visit. I had gone out after lunch to post off to him the set of photographs which had been delivered to me by the photographer with my own set. I went into the post-office to register the package, and here I found Bundy in the act of sending off a parcel. When we had transacted our business we strolled out together, and he asked, "What are you going to do now, Doctor?"

"I was going to walk down to Blue Boar Pier," said I, "to see if anything further has been discovered."

"Should I be in the way if I walked there with you?" he asked. "I've got nothing to do at the moment. But perhaps you would rather go alone. You've had a good deal of my society lately."

"Not more than I wanted, Bundy," I answered. "You are my only chum here, and you are not unappreciated, I can assure you."

"It's nice of you to say that," he rejoined, with some emotion. "I've sometimes felt that I was rather thrusting my friendship on you."

"Then don't ever feel it again," said I. "It has been a bit of luck for me to find a man here whom I could like and chum in with."

He murmured a few words of thanks, and we walked on for a while without speaking. Presently, as we turned into the lane by the Blue Boar Inn, he said, a little hesitatingly. "Don't you think, Doc, that it is rather a mistake to let your mind run so much on this dreadful affair? It seems to be always in your thoughts. And it isn't good for you to think so much about it. I've noticed you quite a lot, and you haven't been the same since – since it happened. You have looked worried and depressed."

"I haven't felt the same," said I. "It has been a great grief to me."

"But," he urged, "don't you think you should try to forget it? After all, she was little more than an acquaintance."

"She was a great deal more than that, Bundy," said I. "While she was alive, I would not admit even to myself that my feeling towards her was anything more than ordinary friendship. But it was, and now that she is gone, there can be no harm in recognizing the fact, or even in confessing it to you, as we are friends."

"Do you mean, Doc," he said in a low voice, "that you were in love with her?"

"That is what it comes to, I suppose," I answered. "She was the only woman I had ever really cared for."

"And did she know it?" he asked.

"Of course she didn't," I replied indignantly. "She was a lady and a woman of honour. Of course she never dreamed that I cared for her, or she would never have let me visit her."

For a few moments he walked at my side in silence. Then he slipped his arm through mine, and pressing it gently with his hand, said softly and very earnestly, "I'm awfully sorry, Doc. It is frightfully hard luck for you, though it couldn't have been much better even if – but it's no use talking of that. I am sorry, old chap. But still, you know, you ought to try to put it away. She wouldn't have wished you to make yourself unhappy about her."

"I know," said I. "But I feel that the office belongs to me, who cared most for her, to see that the mystery of her death is cleared up and that whoever wronged her is brought to justice."

He made no reply to this but walked at my side with his arm linked in mine, meditating with an air of unwonted gravity.

When we reached the head of the pier the place was deserted excepting for one man, a sea-faring person, apparently, who was standing with his back to us, studying intently the bills that were stuck on the wall of the lookout. As we were passing, my eye caught the word "*Wanted*" on a new bill, and pausing to read it over the man's shoulder, I found that it was a description of the unknown man – "*with a mole on the left side of his nose*" – who had pawned the opal brooch. Bundy read it, too, and as we walked away he remarked, "They are rather late in putting out those bills. I should think that gentleman will have left the locality long ago, unless he was a local person", an opinion with which I was disposed to agree.

After a glance round the shore and at "The Ark" – which was closed but of which the chimney emitted a cheerful smoke suggestive of culinary activities on the part of "Mr. Noah" – we sauntered up past the head of the creek, along the rough path by the foundry, and out upon the upper shore.

"Well, I'm hanged!" exclaimed Bundy, glancing back at the watch-house, "that chap is still reading that bill. He must be a mighty slow reader, or he must find it more thrilling than I did. Perhaps he knows somebody with a mole on his nose."

I looked back at the motionless figure, and at that moment another figure appeared and advanced, as we had done, to look over the reader's shoulder.

"Why, that looks like old Cobbledick – come to admire his own literary productions. There's vanity for you. Hallo! What's up now?"

As Bundy spoke, the reader had turned to move away and had come face-to-face with the sergeant. For a moment both men had stood stock still, then there was a sudden, confused movement on both sides, with the final result that the sergeant fell, or was knocked, down and that the stranger raced off, apparently in our direction. He disappeared at once, being hidden from us by the foundry buildings, and we advanced towards the end of the fenced lane by which we had come, to intercept him, waiting by the edge of a trench or dry ditch.

"Here he comes," said Bundy, a trifle nervously, as rapid footfalls became audible in the narrow, crooked lane. Suddenly the man appeared, running furiously, and as he caught sight of us, he whipped out a large knife and, flourishing it with a menacing air, charged straight at us. I watched an opportunity to trip him up, but as he approached Bundy pulled me back with such energy that he and I staggered on the brink of the ditch, capsized, and rolled together to the bottom. By the time we had managed to scramble up, the man had disappeared into the wilderness of

138

sheds, scrap-heaps, derelict boilers, and stray railway-waggons that filled the area of land between the foundry and the coal-wharves and jetties.

"Come on, Bundy," said I, as my companion stood tenderly rubbing various projecting portions of his person, "we mustn't lose sight of him."

But Bundy showed no enthusiasm, and at this moment a rapid crescendo of heavy foot-falls was followed by the emergence of the sergeant, purple-faced and panting, from the end of the lane.

"Which way did he go?" gasped Cobbledick.

I indicated the wilderness, briefly explaining how the fugitive had escaped us, whereupon the sergeant started forward at a lumbering trot and we followed. But it was an unfavourable hunting-ground, for the bulky litter – the heaps of coal-dust, the wagons, the cranes, the piles of condemned machinery, mingled with clumps of bushes – gave the fugitive every opportunity to disappear. And, in fact, he had disappeared without leaving a trace. Presently we came out on a wharf beside which a schooner was berthed, a trim-looking little craft with a white under-body and black top-sides, bearing a single big yard on her fore-mast and the name *Anna* on her counter. She was all ready for sea and was apparently waiting for high water, for her deck was all clear and a man on it was engaged in placidly coiling a rope on the battened hatch while another watched him from the door of the deckhouse. On this peaceful scene the sergeant burst suddenly and hailing the rope-coiler demanded, "Have you seen a man run past here?"

The mariner dropped the rope, and looking up drowsily, repeated, "Have I seen a mahn?"

"Yes, a sea-faring man with a mole on his nose."

The mariner brightened up perceptibly. "Please?" said he.

"A sailor-man with a mole on his nose."

"*Ach!*" exclaimed the mariner. "Vos it tied on?"

"Tied on!" the sergeant snorted impatiently. "Of course it wasn't. It grew there."

Here the second mariner apparently asked some question, for our friend turned to him and replied, "*Ja. Maulwurf*", on which I heard Bundy snigger softly.

"No, no," I interposed, "not that sort of mole. A kind of wart, you know. *Das Mal.*"

On this the second mariner fell out of the deckhouse door, and the pair burst into yells of laughter, rolling about the deck in agonies of mirth, wiping their eyes, muttering *Maulwurf, Maulwurf,* and screeching like demented hyenas.

"Well," Cobbledick demanded impatiently, "have you seen him?"

The mariner shook his head. "No," he replied, shakily. "I have not any mahn seen."

"Well, why couldn't you say so at first," the sergeant growled.

"I vos zo zubbraised," the mariner explained, glancing at his shipmate, and the pair burst out into fresh howls of laughter.

The sergant turned away with a sort of benevolent contempt and ran his eye despairingly over the wilderness. "I suppose we had better search this place," said he, "though he is pretty certain to have got away."

At his suggestion, we separated and examined the possible hiding-places systematically, but, of course, with no result. Once only I had a momentary hope that we had not lost our quarry, when the sergeant suddenly stooped and began cautiously to stalk an abandoned boiler surrounded by a clump of bushes, but when the grinning countenance of Bundy appeared at the opposite end and that reprobate crept out stealthily and proceeded to stalk the sergeant, the last hope faded.

"I certainly thought I saw someone moving in those bushes," said Cobbledick, with a disappointed air.

"So did Mr. Bundy," said I "You must have seen one another."

The sergeant glanced suspiciously at our colleague, but made no remark, and we continued our rather perfunctory search. At length we gave it up and slowly returned to the neighbourhood of the pier. By this time the tide had turned, and a few loiterers were standing about watching the procession of barges moving downstream on the ebb. Among them was a grave-looking, sandy-haired man who leaned against the watch-house, smoking reflectively as he surveyed the river. To this philosopher Cobbledick addressed himself, explaining, as he was in plain clothes, "Good afternoon. I am a police officer and I am looking for a man who is described on that bill." Here he indicated the poster.

The philosopher turned a pale grey, and somewhat suspicious eye on him, and having removed his pipe, expectorated thoughtfully but made no comment on the statement.

"A sea-faring man," continued the sergeant, "with a mole on the left side of his nose." He looked enquiringly at the philosopher, who replied impassively, "*Nhm – nhm.*"

"Do you happen to have seen a man answering that description?"

"*Nhm – nhm,*" was the slightly ambiguous reply.

"You have seen him?" the sergeant asked, eagerly.

"Aye."

"Do you know if he belongs to any of the craft that trade here?"

"*Nhm – nhm.*"

"Do you happen to know which particular vessel he belongs to?"

"Aye," was the answer, accompanied by a grave nod.

140

"Can you tell me," the sergeant asked patiently, "which vessel that is, and where she is at present?"

Our friend replaced his pipe and took a long draw at it, gazing meditatively at a schooner which was moving swiftly down the river under the power of an auxiliary motor, and setting her sails as she went. I had noticed her already, and observed that she had a white underbody and black top-sides, and that she carried a single long yard on her foremast. At length our friend removed his pipe, expectorated, and nodded gravely at the schooner.

"Yon," said he, and replaced his pipe, as a precaution, I supposed, against unnecessary loquacity.

Cobbledick gazed wistfully at the receding schooner. "Pity," said he. "I should have liked to have a look at that fellow."

"You could get the schooner held up at Sheerness, couldn't you?" I asked.

"Yes, I could send a 'phone message to Garrison Point Fort. But, you see, she's a foreigner. Might make trouble. And he is probably not the man we want. After all, it's only a matter of a mole."

"Maulwurf," murmured Bundy.

"Yes," said the sergeant, with a faint grin, "those beggars were laughing at us. Well, it can't be helped."

We stood for a moment or two watching the schooner set one sail after another. Presently Bundy observed, "Methinks, Sergeant, that Mr. Noah is trying to attract your attention."

We glanced towards The Ark, the tenant of which was seated in the stern-sheets, scrubbing a length of rusty chain. As he caught the sergeant's eye, he beckoned mysteriously, whereupon we descended the bank and, picking our way across the muddy grass by his little causeway of stepping-stones, approached the foot of the short ladder.

"Well, Israel," said the sergeant, resting his hands on the gunwale of the old boat as he made a rapid survey of the interior, "giving the family plate a bit of a polish, eh?"

"Plate!" exclaimed the old man, holding up the chain, which, as I now saw, had a number of double hooks linked to it, "this ain't plate. 'Tis what we calls a creeper."

"A creeper," repeated the sergeant, looking at it with renewed interest. "Ha, yes, hmm. A creeper, hey? Well, Israel, what's a-doing? Have you got something to show us?"

The old man laid down the creeper and the scrubbing-brush – which had a strong suggestion of salvage in its appearance – and moved towards the door of the Ark. "Come along inside," said he.

141

Cobbledick mounted the ladder and motioned me to follow, which I did, while Bundy discretely sauntered away and sat down on the bank. On entering, I observed that the Ark followed closely the constructional traditions. Like its classical prototype, it was *"pitched with pitch, within and without"* and was furnished with a single small window, let into the door and hermetically sealed.

Seeing that our host looked at me with some disfavour, the tactful sergeant hastened to make us known to one another.

"This is Dr. Strangeways, Israel. He was Mrs. Frood's doctor, and he knows all about this affair. This, Doctor, is Mr. Israel Bangs, the eminent long-shoreman, a sort of hereditary Grand Duke of the Rochester foreshore."

I bowed ceremoniously, and the Grand Duke acknowledged the introduction with a sour grin. Then, lifting the greasy lid of a locker, he dived into it and came to the surface, as it were, with a small shoe in his hand.

"What do you say to that?" he demanded, holding the shoe under the sergeant's nose. The sergeant said nothing, but looked at me, and I, suddenly conscious of the familiar sickening sensation, could do no more than nod in reply. Soiled, muddy and sodden as it was, the poor little relic instantly and vividly recalled the occasion when I had last seen it, then all trim and smart, peeping coyly beneath the hem of the neat brown skirt.

"Where did you find it, Israel?" asked Cobbledick.

"Ah," said Bangs, with a sly leer, "that's tellin', that is. Never you mind where I found it. There's the shoe."

"Don't be a fool, Israel," said the sergeant. "What use do you suppose the shoe is to me if I don't know where you found it? I've got to put it in evidence, you know."

"You can put it where you like, so long as you pays for it," the old rascal replied, doggedly. "The findin' of it's my business."

There ensued a lengthy wrangle, but the sergeant, though patient and polite, was firm. Eventually Israel gave way.

"Well," he said, "if you undertakes not to let on to Sam Hooper or any of his lot, I'll tell you. I found it on the mud, side of the long crik betwixt Blue Boar Head and Gas-'us Point."

The sergeant made a note of the locality and, after having sworn not to divulge the secret to Sam Hooper or any other of the shore-rat fraternity, and having ascertained that Israel had no further information to dispose of, rose to depart and, I noticed that, as we passed out towards the ladder, he seemed to bestow a glance of friendly recognition on the creeper.

142

"Well," said Bundy, when we rejoined him, "what had Mr. Noah to say? I hope you remembered me kindly to my old friends, Shem, Ham, and Japhet."

"He has found one of Mrs. Frood's shoes," answered the sergeant, producing it from his pocket and offering it for inspection. Bundy glanced at it indifferently, and then remarked, "It seems to answer the description, but, for my part, I don't quite see the use of all this searching and prying. It only proves what we all know. There's no doubt that she fell into the river. The question is, how did she get there? It is not likely that it was an accident and, if it wasn't, it must have been a crime. What we want to know is, who is the criminal?"

Cobbledick pocketed the shoe with an impatient gesture. "That's the way they always talk," said he. "They will always begin at the wrong end. The question, 'Who is the murderer?' does not arise until it is certain that there has *been* a murder, and it can't be certain that there has been a murder until it is certain that the missing person is dead. And that certainty can hardly be established until the body is found. But, in the meantime, these articles are evidence enough to justify us in making other inquiries, and they may give us a hint where to look for the body. They do, in fact. They suggest that the body is probably not very far away, and more likely to be up-stream than down."

"I don't see how they do," said Bundy.

"I do," retorted the sergeant, "and that's enough for me."

Bundy, with his customary discretion, took this as closing the discussion, and further – as I guessed – surmising that the sergeant might wish to have a few words with me alone, took his leave of us when we reached the vicinity of the office.

"That is not a bad idea of old Israel's," said Cobbledick, when Bundy had gone. "The creeper, I mean."

"What about it?" I asked.

"You know what a creeper is used for, I suppose," said he. "In the old days, the revenue boats used to trail them along over the bottom in shallow water where they suspected that the smugglers had sunk their tubs. You see they couldn't always get a chance to land the stuff. Then they used to fill the spirits into a lot of little ankers or tubs, lash them together into a sort of raft and sink the raft close in-shore, on a dark night, in a marked place where their pals could go some other night and fish them up. Well the revenue cutters knew most of those places and used to go there and drift over them trailing creepers. Of course, if there were any tubs there, the creepers hooked on to the lashings and up they came."

"But what do you suppose is Israel's idea?" I asked.

143

"Why, as the body ought to have come up long before this, and it hasn't, he thinks it has been sunk. It might have been taken up the river in a boat, and sunk in mid-stream with a weight of some sort. Or it might have got caught by a lost anchor or on some old moorings. That would account for its not coming up and for these oddments getting detached and drifting ashore. So old Israel is going to get to work with a creeper. I expect he spends his nights creeping over the likely spots, and that is what makes him so deuced secret about the place where he found that shoe. He reckons that the body is somewhere thereabouts."

I made no comment on this rather horrible communication. Of course, it was necessary that the body should be searched for, since its discovery was the indispensable condition of the search for the murderer. But I did not want to hear more of the dreadful details than was absolutely unavoidable.

When we reached the Guildhall, I halted and was about to take leave of the sergeant when he said, somewhat hesitatingly, "Do you remember, Doctor, when you met me last Saturday, you had a gentleman with you?"

"I remember," said I.

"Now, I wonder if you would think I was taking a liberty if I were to ask what that gentleman's name was. I had an idea that I knew his face."

"Of course it wouldn't be a liberty," I replied. "His name is Thorndyke, Dr. John Thorndyke."

"Ah!" exclaimed Cobbledick, "I thought I couldn't be mistaken. It isn't the sort of face that one would forget. I once heard him give evidence at the Old Bailey. Wonderful evidence it was, too. Since then I've read reports of his investigations from time to time. He's a marvellous man. The way he has of raking up evidence from nowhere is perfectly astonishing. Did you happen to talk to him about this case at all?"

"Well, you see, Sergeant," I answered, rather evasively, "he had come down here for the week-end as my guest – "

"Exactly, exactly," Cobbledick interrupted, unconsciously helping me to avoid answering his question, "he came down for a rest and a change, and wouldn't want to be bothered with professional matters. Still, you know, I think he would be interested in this case. It is quite in his own line. It is a queer case, a very queer case in some respects."

"In what respects?" I asked.

It was Cobbledick's turn to be evasive. He had apparently said more than he had intended, and now drew in his horns perceptibly.

"Why," he replied, "when you come to think of – of the – er – the character of the lady, for instance. Why should anyone want to do her any harm? And then there is the mystery as to how it happened, and the place, and – in fact, there are a number of things that are difficult to understand. But I mustn't keep you standing here. If you should happen to see Dr. Thorndyke again, it might be as well to tell him about the case. It would be sure to interest him, and if he should, by any chance, want to know anything that you are not in a position to tell him, why, you know where I am to be found. I shouldn't want to make any secrets with him. And he might spot something that we haven't noticed."

I promised to follow the sergeant's advice and, having bid him *adieu*, turned back, and walked slowly homeward. As I went I reflected profoundly on my conversation with Cobbledick, from which, as it seemed to me, two conclusions emerged. First, there were elements in this mystery that were unknown to me. I had supposed that the essence of the mystery was the mere absence of data. But it now appeared from the sergeant's utterances, and still more from his evasions, that he saw farther into the affair than I did, either because he had more facts, or because, by reason of his greater experience, the facts meant more to him than they did to me. The second conclusion was that he was in some way in difficulties, that he was conscious of an inability to interpret satisfactorily the facts that were known to him. His evident eagerness to get into touch with Thorndyke made this pretty clear, and the two conclusions together suggested a further question. How much did Thorndyke know? Did he know all that the sergeant knew? Did he perchance know more? From the scanty data with which I had supplied him, might he possibly have drawn some illuminating inferences that had carried his understanding of the case beyond either mine or Cobbledick's? It was quite possible. Thorndyke's great reputation rested upon his extraordinary power of inference and constructive reasoning from apparently unilluminating facts. The facts in this case seemed unilluminating enough. But they might not be so to him. And again I recalled how both he and the sergeant seemed to look to the finding of the body as probably furnishing the solution of the mystery.

Chapter XII
The Prints of a
Vanished Hand

Mr. Bundy's opinion that no particular significance attached to the finding of further relics of the missing woman was one that I was myself disposed to adopt. The disappearance of poor Angelina was an undeniable fact, and there seemed to be no doubt that her body had fallen, or been cast, into the river. On these facts, the recovery of further articles belonging to her, and presumably detached from the body, shed no additional light. From the body itself, whenever it should be surrendered by the river, one hoped that something fresh might be learned. But all that anyone could say was that Angelina Frood had disappeared, that her disappearance was almost certainly connected with a crime, and that the agents of that crime and their motives for committing it were alike an impenetrable mystery, a mystery that the finding of further detached articles tended in no way to solve.

I shall, therefore, pass somewhat lightly over the incidents of the succeeding discoveries, notwithstanding the keen interest in them displayed by Sergeant Cobbledick and even by Thorndyke. On Monday, the 25th of May, the second shoe was found (to Israel Bangs' unspeakable indignation) by Samuel Hooper of Foul Anchor Alley, who discovered it shortly after high-water, lying on the gridiron close to Gashouse Point, and brought it in triumph to the police station.

After this, there followed a long interval, occupied by a feverish contest between Israel Bangs and Samuel Hooper. But the luck fell to the experienced Israel. On Saturday, the 20th of June, that investigator, having grounded his boat below a wharf between Gas-house Point and the bridge, discovered a silver-headed hat-pin lying on the shore between two of the piles of the wharf. Its identity was unmistakable. The silver poppy-head that crowned the pin was no trade production that might have had thousands of indistinguishable fellows. It was an individual work wrought by an artist in metal, and excepting its fellow, there was probably not another like it in the world.

The discovery of this object roused a positive frenzy of search. The stretch of muddy shore between Gas-house Point and the bridge literally swarmed with human shore-rats, male and female, adult and juvenile. Every day, and all the day, excepting at high-water, Israel Bangs hovered in his oozy little basket of a boat on the extreme edge of the mud,

146

scanning every inch of slime, and glowering fiercely at the poachers ashore who were raking over his preserves. But nothing came of it. Day after day passed. The black and odorous mud was churned up by countless feet, the pebbles were sorted out severally by innumerable filthy hands, every derelict pot, pan, box, or meat-tin was picked up again and again, and explored to its inmost recesses. But in vain. Not a single relic of any kind was brought to light by all those searchings and grubbings in the mud. Presently the searchers began to grow discouraged. Some of them gave up the search, others migrated to the shore beyond the bridge, and were to be seen wading in the mud below the Esplanade, the cricket-ground, or the boat-building yards. So the month of June ran out, and the third month began. And still there was no sign of the body.

Meanwhile I watched the two professional investigators, and noted a certain similarity in their outlook and methods. Both were keenly interested in the discoveries, and both, I observed, personally examined the localities of the finds. The sergeant conducted me to each spot in turn, making appropriate, but not very illuminating, comments, and I perceived that he was keeping a careful account of time and place. So, too, with Thorndyke, who had now taken to coming down regularly each weekend. He visited each spot where anything had been found, marking it carefully on his map, together with a reference number, and inquiring minutely as to the character of the object, its condition, and the state of the tide and the hour of the day when it was discovered, all of which particulars he entered in his note-book under the appropriate reference number.

Both of my friends, too, expressed increasing surprise and uneasiness at the non-appearance of the body. The sergeant was really worried, and he expressed his sentiments in a tone of complaint as if he felt that he was not being fairly treated.

"It's getting very serious, Doctor," he protested. "Nearly three months gone – three summer months, mind you – and not a sign of it. I don't like the look of things at all. This case means a lot to me. It's my chance. It's a detective-inspector's job, and if I bring it off it'll be a big feather in my cap. I want to get a conviction, and so far I haven't got the material for a coroner's verdict. I've half-a-mind to do a bit of creeping myself."

Thorndyke's observations on the case were much to the same effect. Discussing it one Saturday afternoon at the beginning of July, when I had met him at Strood Station and was walking with him into Rochester, he said, "My feeling is that the crux of this case is going to be the question of identity – if the body ever comes to light. Of course, if it doesn't, there

147

is no case – it is simply an unexplained disappearance. But if the body is found and is unrecognizable excepting by clothing and other extrinsic evidence, it will be hard to get a conviction even if the unrecognizable corpse should give some clue to the circumstances of death."

"I suppose," said I, "the police are searching for Nicholas Frood."

"I doubt it," he replied. "They are not likely to be wasting efforts to find a murderer when there is no evidence that a murder has been committed. What could they do if they did find him? The woman was not in his custody or even living with him. And his previous conduct is not relevant in the absence of evidence of his wife's death."

"You said you were making some inquiries yourself."

"So I am. And I am not without hopes of picking up his tracks. But that is a secondary matter. What we have to settle beyond the shadow of a doubt is the question, 'What has become of Angelina Frood?' Is she dead? And, if she is, what was the cause and what were the circumstances of her death?' The evidence in our possession points to the conclusion that she is dead, and that she met her death by foul means. That is the belief that the known facts produce. But we have got to turn that belief into certainty. Then it will be time to inquire as to the identity of the criminal."

"Do you suppose the body would be unrecognizable now?"

"I feel no doubt that it would be quite unrecognizable by ordinary means if it has been in the water all this time. But it would still be identifiable in the scientific sense, if we could only obtain the necessary data. It could, for instance, be tested by the Bertillon measurements, if we had them, and it would probably yield finger-prints, clear enough to recognize, long after the disappearance of all facial character or bodily traits."

"Would it really?" I exclaimed.

"Certainly," he replied. "Even if the whole outer skin of the hand had come off bodily, like a glove, as it commonly does in long-submerged bodies, that glove-like cast would yield fairly clear finger-prints if property treated – with dilute formalin, for instance. And then the fingers from which the outer skin had become detached would still yield recognizable finger-prints, if similarly treated, for you must remember that the papillary ridges which form the finger-print pattern, are in the true skin. The outer skin is merely moulded on them. But, unfortunately, the question is one of merely academic interest to us as we have no original finger-prints of Mrs. Frood's by which to test the body. The only method of scientific identification that seems to be available is that of anthropometric measurements, as employed by Bertillon."

"But," I objected, "the Bertillon system is based on the existence of a record of the measurements of the person to be identified. We have no record of the measurements of Mrs. Frood."

"True," he agreed. "But you may remember that Dr. George Bertillon was accustomed to apply his system, not only to suspected persons who had been arrested, but also to stray garments, hat, gloves, shoes, and so forth, that came into the possession of the police. But it is clear that, if such garments can be compared with a table of recorded measurements, they can be used as standards of comparison to determine the identity of a dead body. Of course, the measurements would have to be taken, both of the garments and of the body, by someone having an expert knowledge of anthropometrical methods."

"Of course," I agreed. "But it seems a sound method. I must mention it to Cobbledick. He has the undoubted shoes, and I have no doubt that he could get a supply of worn garments from Mrs. Gillow."

"Yes," said Thorndyke. "And, speaking of Mrs. Gillow reminds me of another point that I have been intending to inquire into. You mentioned to me that Mrs. Gillow told you, at the time of the disappearance, that she had been expecting a tragedy of some kind. She must have had some grounds for that expectation."

"She said it was nothing but a vague, general impression."

"Still, there must have been something that gave her that impression. Don't you think it would be well to question her a little more closely?"

"Perhaps it might," said I, not very enthusiastically. "We are close to the house now. We can call in and see her, if you like."

"I think we ought to leave no stone unturned," said he, and a minute or two later, when we arrived opposite the office, he remarked, looking across attentively at the two houses, "I don't see our friend Bundy's face at the window."

"No," I replied, "he is playing tennis somewhere up at the Vines. But here is Mrs. Gillow, herself, all dressed up and evidently going out visiting."

The landlady had appeared at the door just as we were crossing the road. Perceiving that we were bearing down on her, she paused, holding the door ajar. I ran up the steps, and having wished her "Good afternoon" asked if she had time to answer one or two questions.

"Certainly," she replied, "though I mustn't stay long because I have promised to go to tea with my sister at Frinsbury. I usually go there on a Saturday. Perhaps we had better go into poor Mrs. Frood's room."

She opened the door of the sitting-room, and we all went in and sat down.

"I have been talking over this mysterious affair, Mrs. Gillow," said I, "with my friend, Dr. Thorndyke, who is a lawyer, and he suggested that you might be able to throw some light on it. You remember that you had had some forebodings of some sort of trouble or disaster."

"I had," she replied, dismally, "but that was only because she always seemed so worried and depressed, poor dear. And, of course, I knew about that good-for-nothing husband of hers. That was all. Sergeant Cobbledick asked me the same question, but I had nothing to tell him."

"Did the sergeant examine the rooms?" asked Thorndyke.

"Yes, he looked over the place, and he opened her little davenport – it isn't locked – and read through one or two letters that he found there, but he didn't take them away. All he took with him was a few torn-up letters that he found in the waste-paper basket."

"If those other letters are still in the davenport," said Thorndyke, "I think it would be well for us to look through them carefully, if you don't mind, Mrs. Gillow."

"I don't see that there could be any harm in it," she replied. "I've never touched anything in her rooms, myself, since she went away. I thought it better not to. I haven't even washed up her tea-things. There they are, just as she left them, poor lamb. But if you are going to look through those letters, I will ask you to excuse me, or I shall keep my sister waiting for tea."

"Certainly, Mrs. Gillow," said I. "Don't let us detain you. And, by the way," I added, as I walked with her to the door, "it would be as well not to say anything to anybody about my having come here with my friend."

"Very well, sir," she replied. "I think you are right. The least said, the soonest mended." And with this profound generalization, she went out and I shut the street door after her.

When I returned to the sitting-room, I found Thorndyke engaged in a minute examination of the tea-things, and in particular of the spoon. I proceeded at once to the davenport and, finding it unlocked, lifted the desk-lid and peered into the interior. It contained a supply of papers and envelopes, neatly stacked, and one or two letters, which I took out. They all appeared to be from the same person – the Miss Cumbers, of whom I had heard – and a rapid glance at the contents showed that they were of no use as a source of information. I passed them to Thorndyke – who had laid down the spoon and was now looking inquisitively about the room – who scanned them rapidly and returned them to me.

"There is nothing in them," said he. "Possibly the contents of the waste-paper basket were more illuminating. But I suspect not, as the

150

sergeant appears to be as much in the dark as we are. Shall we have a look at the bedroom before we go?"

I saw no particular reason for doing so, but, assuming that he knew best, I made no objection. Going out into the hall, we entered the deserted bedroom, the door of which was locked, though the key had not been removed. At the threshold Thorndyke paused and stood for nearly half-a-minute looking about the room in the same queer, inquisitive way that I had noticed in the other room, as if he were trying to fix a mental picture of it. Meanwhile, full of the Bertillon system, I had walked across to the wardrobe to see what garments were available for measurement. I had my hand on the knob of the door when my glance fell on two objects on the dressing-table, an empty tumbler and a small water-bottle, half-full. There was nothing very remarkable about these objects, taken by themselves, but, even from where I stood, I could see that both bore a number of finger-marks which stood out conspicuously on the plain glass.

"By Jove!" I exclaimed. "Here is the very thing that you were speaking of. Do you see what it is?"

Apparently he had, for he had already taken his gloves out of his pocket and was putting them on.

"Don't touch them, Strangeways," said he, as I was approaching to inspect them more closely. "If these are Mrs. Frood's finger-prints they may be invaluable. We mustn't confuse them by adding our own."

"Whose else could they be?" I asked.

"They might be Sergeant Cobbledick's," he replied. "The sergeant has been in here." He drew a chair up to the table and, taking a lens from his pocket, began systematically to examine the markings.

"They are a remarkably fine set," he remarked, "and a complete set – the whole ten digits. Whoever made them held the bottle in the right hand and the tumbler in the left. And I don't think they are the sergeant's. They are too small and too clear and delicate."

"No," I agreed, "and the probabilities are against their being his. There is no reason why he should have wanted to take a drink of water during the few minutes that he spent here. It would have been different if it had been a beer bottle. But it would have been quite natural for Mrs. Frood to drink a glass of water while she was dressing or before she started out."

"Yes," said he. "Those are the obvious probabilities. But we must turn them into certainties if we can. Probabilities are not good data to work from. But the question is now, what are we to do? I have a small camera with me, but it would not be very convenient to take the photographs here, and it would occupy a good deal of time. On the other hand, these things would be difficult to pack without smearing the finger-prints. We want a couple of small boxes."

"Perhaps," said I, "we may find something that will do if we take a look round."

"Yes," he agreed, "we must explore the place. Meanwhile, I think I will develop up these prints for our immediate information, as we have to try to find some others to verify them."

He went back to the sitting-room, where he had put down the two cases that he always brought with him – a small suit-case that contained his toilet necessaries and a similar-sized case covered with green canvas which had been rather a mystery to me. I had never seen it open, and had occasionally speculated on the nature of its contents. My curiosity was now to be satisfied, for, when he returned with it in his hand he explained, "This is what I call my research-case. It contains the materials and appliances for nearly every kind of medico-legal investigation, and I hardly ever travel without it."

He placed it on a chair and opened it, when I saw that it formed a complete portable laboratory, containing – among other things – a diminutive microscope, a little folding camera, and an insufflator, or powder-spray. The latter he now took from its compartment and, lifting the tumbler with his gloved hand, stood it on a corner of the mantelpiece and blew over it with the insufflator a cloud of impalpably fine white powder, which settled evenly on the surface of the glass. He then tapped the tumbler gently once or twice with a lead pencil, when most of the powder coating either jarred off or crept down the surface. Finally, he blew at it lightly, which removed the rest of the powder, leaving the finger-prints standing out on the clear glass as if they had been painted on with Chinese white.

While he was operating in the same manner on the water-bottle – having first emptied it into the ewer – I examined the tumbler with the aid of his lens. The markings were amazingly clear and distinct. Through the lens I could see, not only the whole of the curious, complicated ridge-pattern, but even the rows of little round spots that marked the orifices of the sweat glands. For the first time, I realized what a perfect means of identification these remarkable imprints furnished.

"Now," said Thorndyke, when he had finished with the bottle, "the two questions are, where shall we look for confirmatory finger-prints, and where are we to get the boxes that we want for packing these things? You said that Mrs. Frood had a kitchen."

"Yes. But won't you try the furniture here, the wardrobe door, for instance. The dark, polished mahogany ought to give good prints."

"An excellent suggestion, Strangeways," said he. "We might even find the sergeant's finger-prints, as he has probably had the wardrobe open."

He sprayed the three doors of the wardrobe, and when he had tapped them and blown away the surplus powder, there appeared near the edge of each a number of finger-marks, mostly rather indistinct, and none of them nearly so clear as those on the glass.

"This is very satisfactory," said Thorndyke. "They are poor prints, but you can see quite plainly that there are two pairs of hands, one pair much larger than the other, and the prints of the larger hands are evidently not the same pattern as those on the glass, whereas those of the smaller ones are quite recognizable as the same, in spite of their indistinctness. As the large ones are almost certainly Cobbledick's, the small ones are pretty certainly Mrs. Frood's. But we mustn't take anything for granted. Let us go down to the kitchen. We shall have a better chance there."

The door of the basement staircase was still unlocked, as Mrs. Gillow had described it. I threw it open, and we descended together, I carrying the insufflator and he bearing the tumbler and bottle in his gloved hands. When he had put the two articles down on the kitchen table, he proceeded to powder first the kitchen door and then the side-door that gave on to the passage between the two houses. Both of them were painted a dark green and both yielded obvious finger-marks, and though these were mere oval smudges, devoid of any trace of pattern, their size and their groupings showed clearly enough that they appertained to a small hand. But we got more conclusive confirmation from a small aluminium frying-pan that had been left on the gas stove, for, on powdering the handle, Thorndyke brought into view a remarkably clear thumbprint, which was obviously identical with that on the water-bottle.

"I think," said he, "that settles the question. If Mrs. Gillow has not touched anything in these premises – as she assures us that she has not – then we can safely assume that these are Mrs. Frood's finger-prints."

"Are you going to annex the frying-pan to produce in evidence?" I asked.

"No," he replied. "This verification is for our own information – to secure us against the chance of producing Cobbledick's finger-prints to identify the body. I propose, for the present, to say nothing to anyone as to our possessing this knowledge. When the time comes we can tell what we know. Until then we shall keep our own counsel."

Once more I found myself dimly surprised at my friend's apparently unnecessary secrecy, but, assuming that he knew best, I made no

153

comment, but watched with somewhat puzzled curiosity his further proceedings. His interest in the place was extraordinary. In a queer, catlike fashion he prowled about the premises, examining the most trivial objects with almost ludicrous attention. He went carefully through the cooking appliances and the glass and china. He peered into cupboards, particularly into a large, deep cupboard in which spare crockery was stored, and which was, oddly enough, provided with a Yale lock. He sorted out the meagre contents of the refuse-bin, and incidentally salved from it a couple of cardboard boxes that had originally contained groceries, and he explored the now-somewhat unsavoury, larder.

"I suppose," he said reflectively, "the dustman must have used the side door. Do you happen to know?"

"I don't," said I, inwardly wondering what the deuce the dustman had to do with the case. "I understand that the door of the passage was not used."

"But she couldn't have had the dust-bin carried up the stairs and out at the front door," he objected.

"I should think not," said I. "Perhaps we could judge better if we had a look at the passage."

He adopted the suggestion and we opened the side-door – which had a Yale night-latch – and went out into the covered passage that was common to the two houses. The door that opened on to the street was bolted on the inside, but the bolts were in good working order, as we ascertained by drawing them gently, so this gave no evidence one way or the other. Then Thorndyke carefully examined the hard gravel floor of the passage, apparently searching for dropped fragments, or the dustman's foot-prints, but though there were traces suggesting that the side-doors had been used, there were no perceptible tracks leading to the street or in any way specifically suggestive of dustmen.

"Japp seems fond of Yale locks," observed Thorndyke, indicating the second side-door, which was also fitted with one. "I wonder where he keeps his dust-bin."

"Would it be worthwhile to ask him?" said I, more and more mystified by this extraordinary investigation.

"No," he replied, very definitely. "A question often gives more information than it elicits."

"It might easily do that in my case," I remarked with a grin, upon which he laughed softly and led the way back into the house. There I gathered up the two boxes and the insufflator and made my way up to the bedroom, he following with the tumbler and the water-bottle. Then came the critical business of packing these two precious objects in the boxes in such a way as to protect the finger-prints from contact with the sides,

154

which was accomplished very neatly with the aid of a number of balls or plasticine from the inexhaustible research-case.

"This is a little disappointing," said Thorndyke, looking at the hair-brush and comb as he took off his gloves. "I had hoped to collect a useful sample of hair. But her excessive tidiness defeats us. There seems to be only one or two short hairs and one full length. However, we may as well have them. They won't be of much use for comparison with the naked eye, but even a single hair can be used as a colour control under the microscope."

He combed the brush until the last hair was extracted from it, and then drew the little collection from the comb and arranged it on a sheet of paper. There were six short hairs, from two to four inches long, and one long hair, which seemed to have been broken off, as it had no bulb.

"Many ladies keep a combing-bag," he remarked, as, he bestowed the collection in a seed-envelope from the research-case, "but I gather from your description that Mrs. Frood's hair was luxuriant enough to render that economy unnecessary. At any rate, there doesn't seem to be such a bag. And now I think we have finished, and we haven't done so badly."

"We have certainly got an excellent set of finger-prints," said I. "But it seems rather doubtful whether there will ever be an opportunity of using them, and if there isn't, we shan't be much more forward for our exploration. Of course, there is the hair."

"Yes," said Thorndyke, "there is the hair. That may be quite valuable. And perhaps there are some other matters – but time will show."

With this somewhat cryptic conclusion he proceeded with great care to pack the two boxes in his suit-case, wedging them with his pyjamas so that they should not get shaken in transit.

As we walked home I reflected on Thorndyke's last remark. It seemed to contain a suggestion that the mystery of Angelina's death was not so complete to him as it was to me. For my own part, I could see no glimmer of light in any direction. She seemed to have vanished without leaving a trace excepting those few derelict objects which had been washed ashore and which told us nothing. But was it possible that those objects bore some significance that I had overlooked? That they were charged with some message that I had failed to decipher? I recalled a certain reticence on the part of Cobbledick which had made me suspect him of concealing from me some knowledge that he held or some inferences that he had drawn, and now there was this cryptic remark of Thorndyke's, offering the same suggestion. Might it possibly be that the profound obscurity was only in my own mind, the product of my inexperience, and that to these skilled investigators the problem presented a more intelligible aspect? It might easily be. I determined cautiously to approach the question.

"You seemed," said I, "to imply, just now, that there are certain data for forming hypotheses as to the solution of this mystery that envelops the disappearance of Mrs. Frood. But I am not aware of any such data. Are you?"

"Your question, Strangeways," he replied, "turns on the meaning of the word 'aware'. If two men, one literate and the other illiterate, look at a page of a printed book, both may be said to be aware of it – that is to say that in both it produces a retinal image which makes them conscious of it as a visible object having certain optical properties. In the case of the illiterate man, the perception of the optical properties is the total effect. But the literate man has something in his consciousness already, and this something combines, as it were, with the optical perception, and makes him aware of certain secondary properties of the printed characters. To both, the page yields a visual impression, but to one only does it yield what we may call a psychical impression. Are they both aware of the page?"

"I appreciate your point," said I, with a sour smile, "and I seem to be aware of a rather skilful evasion of my question."

He smiled in his turn and rejoined, "Your question was a little indirect. Shall we have it in a more direct form?"

"What I wanted to know," said I, "though I suppose I have no right to ask, is whether there appears to you to be any prospect whatever of finding any solution of the mystery of Mrs. Frood's death."

"The answer to that question," he replied, "is furnished by my own proceedings. I am not a communicative man, as you may have noticed, but I will say this much: That I have taken, and am taking, a good deal of trouble with this case, and am prepared to take more, and that I do not usually waste my efforts on problems that appear to be unsolvable. I am not disposed to say more than that, excepting to refer you again to the instance of the printed page and to remind you that whatever I know I have either learned from you or from the observation, in your company, of objects equally visible to both of us."

This reply, if not very illuminating, at least answered my question, as it conveyed to me that I was not likely to get much more information out of my secretive friend. Nevertheless, I asked, "About the man Frood: You were saying that you had some hopes of running him to earth."

"Yes, I have made a start. I have ascertained that he did apparently set out for Brighton the day before Mrs. Frood's disappearance, but he never arrived there. That is all I know at present. He was seen getting into the Brighton train, but he did not appear at the Brighton barrier – my informant had the curiosity to watch all the passengers go through – and he never made the visit which was the ostensible object of his journey. So he must have got out at an intermediate station. It may be difficult to trace him, but I am not without hope of succeeding eventually. Obviously, his whereabouts on the fatal day are a matter that has to be settled. At present he is the obvious suspect, but if an alibi should be proved in his case, a search would have to be initiated in some other direction."

This conversation brought us to my house in time to relieve Mrs. Dunk's anxieties on the subject of dinner, and as the daylight was already gone, the photographic operations were postponed until the following morning. Indeed, Thorndyke had thought of taking the objects to his chambers, where a more efficient outfit was available, but, on reflection, he decided to take the photographs in my presence so that I could, if necessary, attest their genuineness on oath. Accordingly, on the following morning, we very carefully extracted the tumbler and the bottle from their respective boxes and set them up, with a black coat of mine for a background, at the end of a table. Then Thorndyke produced his small folding camera – which pulled out to a surprising length – and, having fitted it with a short-focus objective, made the exposures, and developed the plates in a dark cupboard by the light of a little red lamp from the research case. When the plates were dry we inspected them through a lens and found them microscopically sharp. Finally, at Thorndyke's suggestion, I scratched my initials with a needle in the corner of each plate.

"Well," I said, when he had finished, "you have got the evidence that you wanted, and in a very complete form. It remains to be seen now whether you will ever get an opportunity to use it."

"Don't be pessimistic, Strangeways," said he. "We have had exceptional luck in getting this splendid series of finger-prints. Let us hope that Fortune will not desert us after making us these gifts."

"What is to be done with the originals?" I asked.

"Shall I put them back where we found them?"

"I think not," he replied. "If you have a safe or a secure lock-up cupboard, where they could be put away, out of sight, and from whence they could be produced if necessary, I will ask you to take charge of them."

There was a cupboard with a good lock in the old bureau that I had found in my bedroom, and to this I conveyed the precious objects and locked them in. And so ended – at least, for the present – the episode of our raid on poor Angelina's abode.

Chapter XIII
The Discovery in
Black Boy Lane

On a fine, sunny afternoon, about ten days after our raid on Angelina's rooms (it was Tuesday, the 14th of July, to be exact), I was sitting in my dining-room, from which the traces of lunch had just been removed, idly glancing over the paper, and considering the advisability of taking a walk, when I heard the door-bell ring. There was a short interval, then the door was opened, and the sounds of strife and wrangling that followed this phenomenon informed me that the visitor was Mr. Bundy, between whom and Mrs. Dunk there existed a state of chronic warfare. Presently the dining-room door opened – in time for me to catch a concluding growl of defiance from Mrs. Dunk – and that lady announced gruffly, "Mr. Bundy."

My visitor tripped in smilingly, "all teeth and eyeglass" as his inveterate enemy had once expressed it, holding a Panama hat, which had temporarily superseded the velour.

"Well, John," said he, "coming out to play?" He had lately taken to calling me John – in fact, a very close and pleasant intimacy had sprung up between us. It dated from the occasion when I had confided to him my unfortunate passion for poor Angelina. That confidence he had evidently taken as a great compliment, and the matter of it had struck a sympathetic chord in his kindly nature. From that moment there had been a sensible change in his manner towards me. Beneath his habitual flippancy there was an undertone of gentleness and sympathy, and even of affection. Nor had I been unresponsive. Like Thorndyke, I found in his sunny temperament, his invariable cheerfulness and high spirits, a communicable quality that took effect on my own state of mind. And then I had early recognized that, in spite of his apparent giddiness, Bundy was a man of excellent intelligence and considerable strength of character. So the friendship had ripened naturally enough.

I rose from my chair and, dropping the paper, stretched myself. "You are an idle young dog," said I. "Why aren't you at work?"

"Nothing doing at the office except some specifications. Japp is doing them. Come out and have a roll round."

"Well, Jimmy," said I. "Your name is Jimmy, isn't it?"

158

"No, it is not," he replied with dignity. "I am called Peter – like the Bishop of Rumtifoo and, by a curious coincidence, for the very same reason."

"Let me see," said I, falling instantly into the trap, "what was that reason?"

"Why, you see," he replied impressively, "the Bishop was called Peter because that was his name."

"Look here, young fellow my lad," said I, "you'll get yourself into trouble if you come up here pulling your elder's legs."

"It was only a gentle tweak, old chap," said he. "Besides, you aren't so blooming senile, after all. You are only cutting your first crop of whiskers. Are you coming out? I saw old Cobbledick just now, turning down Blue Boar Lane and looking as miserable as a wet cat."

"What was he looking miserable about?"

"The slump in relics, I expect. He is making no headway with his investigation. I fancy he had reckoned on getting an inspectorship out of this case, whereas, if he doesn't reach some sort of conclusion, he is likely to get his rapples knucked, as old Miss Barman would say. I suspect he was on his way to the Ark to confer with Mr. Noah. What do you say to a stroll in the direction of Mount Ararat?"

It was a cunning suggestion on the part of Bundy, for it drew me instantly. Repulsive as old Israel's activities were to me, the presence of those finger-prints, securely locked up in my bureau, had created in me a fresh anxiety to see the first state of the investigation completed so that the search for the murderer could be commenced in earnest. Not that my presence would help the sergeant, but that I was eager to hear the tidings of any new discovery.

Bundy's inference had been quite correct. We arrived at the head of the Blue Boar pier just in time to see the sergeant slowly descending the ladder, watched gloomily by Israel Bangs. As the former reached *terra firma* he turned round and then observed us.

"Any news, Sergeant?" I asked, as he approached across the grass.

He shook his head discontentedly. "No," he replied, "not a sign, not a vestige. It's a most mysterious affair. The things seemed to be coming up quite regularly until that hat-pin was found. Then everything came to an end. Not a trace of anything for nigh upon a month. And what, in the name of Fortune, can have become of the body? That's what I can't make out. If this goes on much longer, there won't be any body, and then we shall be done. The case will have to be dropped."

He took off his hat (He was in plain clothes as usual) and wiped his forehead, looking blankly first at me and then at Bundy. The latter also took off his hat and whisked out his handkerchief, bringing with it a little

159

telescope which fell to the ground and was immediately picked up by the sergeant. "Neat little glass, this," he remarked, dusting it with his handkerchief. "It's lucky it fell on the turf." He took off the cap and, pulling out the tubes, peered vaguely through it up and down the river. Presently he handed it to me. "Look at those craft down below the dockyard," said he.

I took the little instrument from him and pointed it at the group of small, cutter-rigged vessels that he had indicated, of which the telescope, small as it was, gave a brilliantly sharp picture.

"What are they?" I asked. "Oyster dredgers?"

"No," he replied. "They are bawleys with their shrimp-trawls down. But there are plenty of oyster dredgers in the lower river and out in the estuary, and what beats me is why none of them ever brings up anything in the trawls or dredges – anything in our line, I mean."

"What did you expect them to bring up?" Bundy asked.

"Well, there are the things that have washed ashore, and there are the other things that haven't washed ashore yet. And then there is the body."

"Mr. Noah would have something to say if they brought that up," said Bundy. "By the way, what had he got to say when you called on him?"

"Old Bangs? Why he is getting a bit shirty. Wants me to pay him for all the time he has lost on creeping and searching. Of course, I can't do that, I didn't employ him."

"Did he find the hat-pin that you spoke of?" Bundy asked.

"Yes, and he has been grubbing round the place where he found it ever since, as if he thought hat-pins grew there."

"Still," said Bundy, "it is not so unreasonable. A hat-pin couldn't have floated ashore. If the hat came off, the two hat-pins must have fallen out at pretty much the same time and place."

"Yes," the sergeant agreed, reflectively, "that seems to be common sense and, if it is, the other hat-pin ought to be lying somewhere close by. I must go and have a look there myself." He again reflected for a few moments and then asked, "Would you like to see the place where Israel found the pin?"

As I had seen the place already and had shown it to Thorndyke, I left Bundy to answer.

"Why not?" he assented – rather, I suspected, to humour the sergeant than because he felt any particular interest in the place. Thereupon Cobbledick, whose enthusiasm appeared to have been revived by Bundy's remark, led the way briskly towards the wilderness by the coal-wharves, through that desolate region and along a cart-track that

160

skirted the marshes until we came out into a sort of lesser wilderness to the west of Gas-House Road. Here the sergeant slipped through a large hole in a corrugated iron fence which gave access to a wharf littered with the unpresentable debris resulting from the activities of a firm of ship-knackers. Advancing to the edge of the wharf, Cobbledick stood for a while looking down wistfully at the expanse of unspeakable mud that the receding tide had uncovered.

"I suppose it is too dirty to go down," he said in a regretful tone.

Bundy's assent to this proposition was most emphatic and unqualified, and the sergeant had to content himself with a bird's-eye view. But he made a very thorough inspection, walking along the edge of the wharf, scrutinizing its base, pile by pile, and giving separate attention to each pot, tin, or scrap of driftwood on the slimy surface. He even borrowed Bundy's telescope to enable him to examine the more distant parts of the mud, until the owner of the instrument was reduced to the necessity of standing behind him, for politeness' sake, to get a comfortable yawn.

"Well," said Cobbledick, at long last, handing back the telescope, "I suppose we must give it up. But it's disappointing."

"I don't quite see why," said Bundy. "You have found enough to prove that the body is in the river, and no number of further relics would prove any more."

"No, there's some truth in that," Cobbledick agreed. "But I don't like the way that everything seems to have come to a stop." He crawled dejectedly through the hole in the fence and walked on for a minute or two without speaking. Presently he halted and looked about him. "I suppose Black Boy Lane will be our best way," he remarked.

"Which is Black Boy Lane?" I asked.

"It is the lane we came down after we left Japp and Willard that day," Bundy explained.

"I remember," said I, "but I didn't know it had a name."

"It was named after a little inn that used to stand somewhere near the top, but it was pulled down years ago. Here's the lane."

We entered the little, tortuous alley that wound between the high, tarred fences, and as it was too narrow for us to walk abreast, Bundy dropped behind. A little way up the lane I noticed an old hat lying on the high grass at the foot of the fence. Bundy apparently noticed it, too, for just after we had passed it I heard the sound of a kick, and the hat flew over my shoulder. At the same moment, and impelled by the same kick, a small object, which I at first thought to be a pebble, hopped swiftly along the ground in front of us, then rolled a little way, and finally came to rest, when I saw that it was a button. I should probably have passed it without further notice, having no use for stray buttons. But the more thrifty sergeant stooped and picked it up, and the instant that he looked at it he stopped dead.

"My God! Doctor," he exclaimed, holding it out towards me. "Look at this!"

I took it from him, though I had recognized it at a glance. It was a small bronze button with a Tudor Rose embossed on it.

"This is a most amazing thing," said Cobbledick.

"There can't be any doubt as to what it is."

"Not the slightest," I agreed. "It is certainly one of the buttons from Mrs. Frood's coat. The question is, how on earth did it get here?"

"Yes," said the sergeant, "that is the question, and a very difficult question, too."

"Aren't you taking rather a lot for granted?" suggested Bundy, to whom I had passed the little object for inspection. "It doesn't do to jump at conclusions too much. Mrs. Frood isn't likely to have had her buttons made to order. She must have bought them somewhere. She might even have bought them in Rochester. In any case, there must be thousands of others like them."

"I suppose there must be," I admitted, "though I have never seen any buttons like them."

"Neither have I," said Cobbledick, "and I am going to stick to the obvious probabilities. The missing woman wore buttons like this, and I shall assume that this is one of her buttons unless someone can prove that it isn't."

"But how do you account for one of her buttons being *here*?" Bundy objected.

"I don't account for it," retorted Cobbledick. "It's a regular puzzle. Of course, someone – a child, for instance – might have picked it up on the shore and dropped it here. But that is a mere guess, and not a very likely one. The obvious thing to do is to search this lane thoroughly and see if there are any other traces, and that is what I am going to do now. But don't let me detain you two gentlemen if you had rather not stay."

"I shall certainly stay and help you, Sergeant," said I, and Bundy, assuming the virtue of enthusiasm, if he had it not, elected also to stay and join in the search.

"We had better go back to the bottom of the lane," said Cobbledick, "and go through the grass at the foot of the fence from end to end. I will take the right hand side and you take the left."

We retraced our steps to the bottom of the lane and began a systematic search, turning over the grass and weeds and exposing the earth inch by inch. It was a slow process and would have appeared a singular proceeding had any wayfarer passed through and observed us, but fortunately it was an unfrequented place, and no one came to spy upon us. We had traversed nearly half the lane when Bundy stood up and stretched himself. "I don't know what your back is made of, John," said he. "Mine feels as if it was made of broken bottles. How much more have we got to do?"

"We haven't done half yet," I replied, also standing up and rubbing my lumbar region, and at this moment the sergeant, who was a few yards ahead, hailed us with a triumphant shout. We both turned quickly and beheld him standing with one arm raised aloft and the hand grasping a silver-topped hat-pin.

"What do you say to that, Mr. Bundy?" he demanded as we hurried forward to examine the new 'find'. "Shall we be jumping at conclusions if we say that this hat-pin is Mrs. Frood's?"

"No," Bundy admitted after a glance at the silver poppy-head. "This seems quite distinctive and, of course, it confirms the button. But I don't understand it in the least. How can they have come here?"

"We won't go into that," said the sergeant, in a tone of suppressed excitement that showed me pretty clearly that he had already gone into it. "They are here. And now the question arises, what became of the hat? It couldn't have dropped off down at the wharf, or this hat-pin wouldn't be here, but it must have fallen off when both hat-pins were gone. Now what can have become of it?"

"It might have been picked up and taken possession of by some woman," I suggested. "It was a good hat, and if the body was brought here soon after the crime, as it must have been, it wouldn't have been much damaged. But why trouble about the hat? Appearances suggest that the body was either brought up or taken down this lane. That is the new and astonishing fact that needs explaining."

"We don't want to do any explaining now," said Cobbledick. "We are here to collect facts. If we can find out what became of the hat, that may help us when we come to consider the explanations."

"Well, it obviously isn't here," said I.

"No," he agreed, "and it wouldn't have been left here. A murderer mightn't have noticed the button, or even the hat-pin, on a dark, foggy night. But he'd have noticed the hat, and he wouldn't have left it where it must have been seen, and probably led to inquiries. He might have taken it with him, or he might have got rid of it. I should say he would have got rid of it. What is on the other side of these fences?"

We all hitched ourselves up the respective fences far enough to look over. On the one side was a space of bare, gravelly ground with thin patches of grass and numerous heaps of cinder, on the other was an area

163

of old waste land thickly covered with thistles, ragwort, and other weeds. The sergeant elected to begin with the latter, as the less frequented and therefore more probably undisturbed. Setting his foot on the buttress of a post, he went over the fence with surprising agility, considering his figure, and was lost to view, but we could hear him raking about among the herbage close to the fence, and from time to time I stood on the buttress and was able to witness his proceedings. First he went to the bottom of the lane and from that point returned by the fence, searching eagerly among the high weeds. I saw him thus proceed, apparently to the top of the lane in the neighbourhood of the remains of the city wall. Thence he came back, but now at a greater distance from the fence, and as he was still eagerly peering and probing amongst the weeds, it was evident that he had had no success. Suddenly, when he was but a few yards away, he uttered an exclamation and ran forward. Then I saw him stoop, and the next moment he fairly ran towards me holding the unmistakable brown straw hat with the dull green ribbon.

"That tells us what we wanted to know," he said breathlessly, handing the hat to me as he climbed over the fence. "At least, I think it does. I'll tell you what I mean – but not now," he added in a lower tone, though not unheard by Bundy, as I inferred later.

"I suppose we need hardly go on with the search any further?" I suggested, having had enough of groping amongst the grass.

"Well, no," he replied. "I shall go over it again later on, but we've got enough to think about for the present. By the way, Mr. Bundy, I've found something belonging to you. Isn't this your property?"

He produced from his pocket a largish key, to which was attached a wooden label legibly inscribed "*Japp and Bundy, High Street, Rochester*".

"By Jove!" exclaimed Bundy, "it is Japp's precious key! Where on earth did you find it, Sergeant?"

"Right up at the top," was the reply. "Close to the old wall."

"Now, I wonder how the deuce it got there," said Bundy. "Some fool must have thrown it over the fence from pure mischief. However, here it is. You know there was a reward of ten shillings for finding it, Sergeant. I had better settle up at once. You needn't make any difficulties about it," he added, as the sergeant seemed disposed to decline the payment. "It won't come out of my pocket. It is the firm's business."

On this understanding, Cobbledick pocketed the proffered note and we walked on up the lane, the sergeant slightly embarrassed, as we approached the town, by the palpably unconcealable hat. Very little was said by any of us, for these new discoveries, with the amazing inferences that they suggested, gave us all abundant material for thought. The

164

sergeant walked with eyes bent on the ground, evidently cogitating profoundly, my mind surged with new speculations and hypotheses, while Bundy, if not similarly preoccupied, refrained from breaking in on our meditations.

When, at length, by devious ways, we reached the Highstreet in the neighbourhood of the Corn Exchange, we halted, and the sergeant looked at me as if framing a question. Bundy glanced up at the quaint old clock, and remarked. "It is about time I got back to the office. Mustn't leave poor old Japp to do all the work, though he never grumbles. So I will leave you here."

I realized that this was only a polite excuse to enable the sergeant to have a few words with me alone, and I accepted it as such.

"Good-bye, then," said I, "if you must be off, and in case I don't see you before, I shall expect you to dinner on Saturday if you've got the evening free. Dr. Thorndyke is coming down for the week-end, and I know you enjoy ragging him."

"He is pretty difficult to get a rise out of, all the same," said Bundy, brightening up perceptibly at the invitation. "But I shall turn up with very great pleasure." He bestowed a mock ceremonious salute on me and the sergeant and, turning away, bustled off in the direction of the office. As soon as he was out of earshot Cobbledick opened the subject of the new discoveries.

"This is an extraordinary development of our case, Doctor," said he. "I didn't want to discuss it before Mr. Bundy, though he is really quite a discreet gentleman, and pretty much on the spot, too. But he isn't a party to the case, and it is better not to talk too freely. You see the points that these fresh finds raise?"

"I see that they put a new complexion on the affair, but to me they only make the mystery deeper and more incomprehensible."

"In a way they do," Cobbledick agreed, "but, on the other hand, they put the case on a more satisfactory footing. For instance, we understand now why the body has never come to light. It was never in the river at all. Then as to the perpetrator, he was a local man – or, at least, there was a local man in it, a man who knew the town and the waterside neighbourhood thoroughly. No stranger would have found Black Boy Lane. Very few Rochester people know it."

"But," I asked, "what does the finding of these things suggest to you?"

"Well," he replied, "it suggests several questions. Let me just put these things away in my office, and then we can talk the matter over." He went into his office, and shortly returned relieved – very much relieved – of the conspicuous hat. We turned towards the bridge, and he resumed,

"The first question and the most important one is, which way was the body travelling? It is obvious that it was carried through Black Boy Lane. But in which direction? Towards the town or towards the river? When you think of the circumstances, when you recall that it was a foggy night when she disappeared, it seems at first more probable that the crime might have been committed in, or near, the lane, and the body carried down to the river. But when you consider all the facts, that doesn't seem possible. There is that box of tablets, picked up dry and clean on Chatham Hard. That seems to fix the locality where the crime occurred."

"And there is the brooch," said I.

"I don't attach much importance to that," he replied. "It might have been picked up anywhere. But the box of tablets couldn't have got from Black Boy Lane to Chatham except by the river, and it hadn't been in the river. But the hat seems to me to settle the question. You see, one hat-pin was found on the shore and the other in the lane near the hat. Now, one hat-pin might have dropped out and left the hat still fixed on the head. But when the hat came off, the pins must have come off with it. The hat came off near the top of the lane. If both the pins had been in it they would both have come out there.

"But one pin was found on the shore, therefore when the body was at the shore the hat must have been still on the head, though it had probably got loosened by all the dragging about in the boat and in landing the body. You agree to that, Doctor?"

"Yes, it seems undeniable," I answered.

"Very well," said he. "Then the body was being carried up the lane. The next question is: Was it being carried by one person or by more than one? Well, I think you will agree with me, Doctor, that it could hardly have been done by one man. It is quite a considerable distance from the shore to the top of the lane. She was a goodsized woman, and a dead body is a mighty awkward thing to carry at the best of times. I should say there must have been at least two men."

"It certainly does seem probable," I admitted.

"I think so," said he. "Then we come to another question. Was it really a dead body? Or might the woman have been merely *insensible*?"

"Good God, Sergeant!" I exclaimed. "You don't think it possible that it could have been a case of forcible abduction, and that Mrs Frood is still alive?"

"I wouldn't say it was impossible," he replied, "but I certainly don't think it is the case. You see, nearly three months have passed and there is no sign of her. But in modern England you can't hide a full-grown, able-bodied woman who has got all her wits about her. No, Doctor, I am

166

afraid we must take the view that the woman who was carried up Black Boy Lane was a dead woman. All I want to point out is that the other view is a bare possibility, and that we mustn't forget it."

"But," I urged, "don't you think that the fact that she was being carried towards the town strongly suggests that she was alive? Why on earth should a murderer bring a body, at great risk of discovery, from the river, where it could easily have been disposed of, up into the town? It seems incredible."

"It does," he agreed. "It's a regular facer. But, on the other hand, suppose she was alive. What could they have done with her? How could they have kept her out of sight all this time? And why should they have done it?"

"As to the motive," said I, "that is incomprehensible in any case. But what do you suppose actually happened?"

"My theory of it is," he replied, "that two men, at least, did the job. Both may have been local waterside men, or there may have been a stranger with a water-rat in his pay. I imagine the crime was committed at Chatham, somewhere near the Sun Pier, and that the body was put in a boat and brought up here. It was a densely foggy night, you remember, so there would have been no great difficulty, and there wouldn't be many people about. The part of it that beats me is what they meant to do with the body. They seem to have brought it deliberately from Chatham right up into Rochester Town, and they have got rid of it somehow. They must have had some place ready to stow it in, but what that place can have been, I can't form the ghost of a guess. It's a fair knock-out."

"You don't suppose old Israel Bangs knows anything about it?" I suggested.

The sergeant shook his head. "I've no reason to suppose he does," he replied. "And it is a bad plan to make guesses and name names."

We walked up and down the Esplanade for nearly an hour, discussing various possibilities, but we could make nothing of the incredible thing that seemed to have happened in spite of its incredibility. At last we gave it up and returned to the Guildhall, where, as we parted, he said a little hesitatingly, "I heard you tell Mr. Bundy that Dr. Thorndyke was coming down for the week-end. It wouldn't be amiss if you were to put the facts of the case before him. It's quite in his line, and I think he would be interested to hear about it, and he might see something that I have missed. But, of course, it must be in strict confidence."

I promised to try to find an opportunity to get Thorndyke's opinion on the case, and with this we separated, the sergeant retiring to his office and I making my way homeward to prepare a report for dispatch by the last post.

Chapter XIV
Sergeant Cobbledick is Enlightened

The custom which had grown upon my part of meeting Thorndyke at the station on the occasion of his visits was duly honoured on the present occasion, for the surprising discoveries in Black Boy Lane, which I had described in my report to him, made me eager to hear his comments. Unfortunately, on this occasion, he had come down by an unusually late train, and the opportunity for discussion was limited to the time occupied by the short walk from Rochester Station to my house, for it was close upon dinner time, and I rather expected to find Bundy awaiting us.

"Your report was quite a thrilling document," he remarked, as we came out of the station approach. "These new discoveries seem to launch us on a fresh phase of the investigation."

"Do they seem to you to offer any intelligible suggestions?" I asked.

"There is no lack of suggestions," he replied. "To a person of ordinary powers of imagination, a number of hypotheses must present themselves. But, of course, the first thing to consider is not what *might* have happened, but what *did* happen, and what we can safely infer from those happenings. We can apparently take it as proved that the body was carried through the lane, and everything goes to show that it was carried from the river towards the town. The first clear inference is that we can completely exclude accident, pure and simple. The body – living or dead – may be assumed to have been carried by some person or persons. We can dismiss the idea that the woman walked up the lane. But if someone carried the body, someone is definitely implicated. The affair comes unquestionably into the category of crime."

"That doesn't carry us very far," I said, with a sense of disappointment.

"It carries us a stage farther than our previous data did, for it excludes accident, which they did not. Then it suggests not only premeditation, but arrangement. If the body was brought up from the river, there must have been some place known to, and probably prepared by, those who brought it, in which it could be deposited, and that place must have been more secure than the river from which it was brought. But the river, itself, was a very secure hiding-place, especially if the body had been sunk with weights. Now, this is all very remarkable. If you consider the extraordinary procedure, the seizure of the victim at

Chatham, the conveyance of the body from thence to this considerable distance, the landing of it at the wharf, the conveyance of it by an apparently selected route – at enormous risk of discovery, in spite of the fog to an appointed destination – I say, Strangeways, that if you consider this astounding procedure, you cannot fail to be convinced that there was some definite purpose behind it."

"Yes," I agreed, "that seems to be so. But what could the purpose be? It appears perfectly incomprehensible. It only makes the mystery more unsolvable than ever."

"Not at all," he rejoined. "There is nothing so hopeless to investigate as the perfectly obvious and commonplace. As soon as an apparently incomprehensible motive appears, we are within sight of a solution. There may be innumerable explanations of a common-place action, but an outrageously unreasonable action, pursued with definite and considered purpose, can admit of but one or two. The action, with its underlying purpose, must be adjusted to some unusual conditions. We have only to consider to what conditions it could be adjusted, and which, if any, of those conditions actually exist, and the explanation of the apparently incomprehensible action comes into view. But here we are at our destination, and there is our friend, Bundy, standing on the doorstep. By the way, I have brought one or two photographs of Mrs. Frood for you to look at."

We arrived in time to intervene and put an end to a preliminary skirmish between the irrepressible Bundy and Mrs. Dunk, and when greetings had been exchanged, Thorndyke went up to his room to wash and deposit his luggage.

"Well, John," said Bundy, when he had hung up his hat, "it is very pleasant to see my old friend after this long separation. Very good of him, too, to invite an insignificant outsider like me to meet his distinguished colleague. You are a benefactor to me, John."

"Don't talk nonsense, Peterkin," said I. "You know we are always glad to see you. I invite you for my own pleasure and Thorndyke's, not for yours."

Bundy gave my arm a grateful squeeze. "Good old John," said he. "Nothing like doing it handsomely. But here is the great man himself," he added, as Thorndyke entered the dining-room, carrying a cardboard box, "with instruments of magic. He's going to do a conjuring trick."

Thorndyke opened the box and delicately picked out four photographs, all mounted and all of cabinet size, which he stood up in a row on the mantelpiece. Two of them were from the same negative, one being printed in red carbon, the other in sepia. The remaining two were ordinary silver prints of the conventional trade type.

Bundy looked at the collection with not unnatural surprise.

"Where did these things come from?" he asked.

"They came from London," replied Thorndyke, "where things of this kind grow. Strangeways asked me to get him some samples. How do you like them? My own preference is for the carbons, and of the two I think I like the red chalk print the better."

I ran my eye along the row and found myself in strong agreement with Thorndyke. It was not only that the carbon prints had the advantage of the finer medium. The treatment was altogether more artistic, and the likeness seemed better, in spite of a rather over-strong top-lighting.

"Yes," I said, "the carbons are infinitely superior to the silver prints, and of the two I think the red is the better because it emphasises the shadows less."

"Is the likeness as good as in the silver prints?" Thorndyke asked.

"Better, I think. The expression is more natural and spontaneous. What do you say, Peter?"

As I spoke I looked at him, not for the first time, for I had already been struck by the intense concentration with which he had been examining the two carbons. And it was not only concentration. There was a curious expression of surprise, as if something in the appearance of the portraits puzzled him.

He looked up with a perplexed frown. "As to the likeness," said he, "I don't know that I am a particularly good judge. I only saw her once or twice. But, as far as I remember, it seems to be quite a good likeness, and there can be no question as to the superiority, in an artistic sense, of the carbons. And I agree with you that the shadows are less harsh in the red than in the sepia. Who is the photographer?"

He picked up the red print and, turning it over, looked at the back. Then, finding that the back of the card was blank, he picked up the sepia print and inspected it in the same way, but with the same result. There was no photographer's name either on the back or front.

"I have an impression," said Thorndyke, "that the carbons were done a City photographer. But my man will know. He got them for me."

Bundy set the two photographs back in their places – still, as it seemed to me, with the air of a man who is trying vainly to remember something. But, at this moment, Mrs. Dunk entered with the soup tureen, and we forthwith took our places at the table.

We had finished our soup, and I was proceeding to effect the dismemberment of an enormous sole when Bundy, having fortified himself with a sip of Chablis, cast a malignant glance at Thorndyke.

"I have got some bad news for you, Doctor," said he.

"Which doctor are you addressing?" Thorndyke asked.

"There's only one now," replied Bundy. "T'other one has been degraded to the rank of John."

"That happens to be my rank, too," observed Thorndyke.

"Oh, but I couldn't think of taking such a liberty," Bundy protested, "though it is very gracious and condescending of you to suggest it. No, your rank and tine will continue to be that of doctor."

"And what is your bad news??'

"It is a case of a lost opportunity," said Bundy. "'Of all the sad words of tongue or pen,' and so on. It might have been ten shillings. But it never will now. Cobbledick has got your ten bob."

"Do you mean that Cobbledick has found the missing key?"

"Even so, alackaday! The chance is gone forever."

"Where did he find it?" Thorndyke asked.

"Ah!" exclaimed Bundy. "There it is again. The tragedy of it! He wasn't looking for it at all. He just fell over it in a field where he was searching for relics of Mrs. Frood."

"Your description," said Thorndyke "is deficient in geographical exactitude. Could you bring your ideas of locality to a somewhat sharper focus? There are probably several fields in the neighbourhood of Rochester."

"So there are," said Bundy. "Quite a lot. But this particular field lies on the right, or starboard, side of a small thoroughfare called Black Boy Lane."

"Let me see," said Thorndyke. "Isn't that the lane that we went down after leaving our friends on the day of the Great Perambulation?"

"Yes," replied Bundy, looking at him in astonishment, "but how did you know its name?" (He was, of course, not aware of my report to Thorndyke describing the discoveries and the place.)

"That," said Thorndyke "is an irrelevant question. Now when you say 'the right-hand side' – "

"I mean the right-hand side looking towards the town, of course. As a matter of fact, Cobbledick found the key among the thistles near to the fence, and quite close to the outside of the city wall."

"How do you suppose it got there?" Thorndyke asked.

"I've no idea. Someone must have taken it out of the gate and thrown it over the fence. That is obvious. But who could have done it I can't imagine. Of course, you suspect Cobbledick, but that is only jealousy."

The exchange of schoolboy repartee continued without a sensible pause on either side. But yet I seemed to detect in Thorndyke's manner a certain reflectiveness underlying the levity of his verbal conflict with Bundy, a reflectiveness that seemed to have had its origin in the "news" that the latter had communicated. Of course, I had said nothing, in my report, about the finding of the key. Why should I? Those reports referred exclusively to matters connected with the disappearance of poor Angelina. The loss and the recovery of the key were items of mere local gossip with which Thorndyke could have no concern excepting in connexion with Bundy's facetious fiction. And yet it had seemed to me that Thorndyke showed quite a serious interest in the announcement. However, he made no further reference to the matter, and the conversation drifted to other topics.

It was almost inevitable that, sooner or later, some reference should be made to the discoveries in the lane. It was Bundy, of course, who introduced the subject, and I was amazed by the adroit way in which Thorndyke conveyed the impression of complete ignorance, without making any statement, and the patient manner in which he listened to the account of the adventure, and even elicited amplified details by judicious questions. But he eluded all Bundy's efforts to extract an opinion on the significance of the discoveries.

"But," the latter protested, "you said that if I would give you the facts, you would give me the explanation."

"The explanation is obvious," said Thorndyke. "If you found these objects in the lane, they must have been dropped there."

"Well, of course they must," said Bundy. "That is quite obvious."

"Exactly," agreed Thorndyke. "That is what I am pointing out."

"But why was the body being carried up the lane? And where was it being carried to?"

"Ah," protested Thorndyke, "but now you are going beyond your facts. You haven't proved that there was any body there at all."

"But there must have been, or the things couldn't have dropped off it."

"But you haven't proved that they did drop off it. They may have, or they may not. That is a question of fact, and as I impressed on you on a previous occasion, evidence as to fact is the function of the common witness. The expert witness explains the significance of facts furnished by others. I have explained the facts that you have produced, and now you ask me to explain something that isn't a fact at all. But that is not my function. I am an expert."

"I see," said Bundy, "and now I understand why judges are so down on expert witnesses. It is my belief that they are a parcel of impostors. Wasn't Captain Bunsby an expert witness? Or was he only an oracle?"

"It is a distinction without a difference," replied Thorndyke. "Captain Bunsby is the classical instance of oracular safety. It was impossible to dispute the correctness of his pronouncements."

"Principally," said I, "because no one could make head or tail of them."

"But that was the subtlety of the method," said Thorndyke. "A statement cannot be contested until it is understood. From which it follows that if you would deliver a judgment that cannot be disputed, you must take proper precautions against the risk of being understood."

Bundy adjusted his eye-glass and fixed on Thorndyke a glare of counterfeit defiance. "I am going to take an early opportunity of seeing you in the witness-box," said he. "It will be the treat of my life."

"I must try to give you that treat," replied Thorndyke. "I am sure you will be highly entertained, but I don't think you will be able to dispute my evidence."

"I don't suppose I shall," Bundy retorted with a grin, "if it is of the same brand as the sample that I have heard."

Here the arrival of Mrs. Dunk with the coffee ushered in a truce between the disputants, and when I had filled the cups Thorndyke changed the subject by recalling the incidents of our perambulation with Japp and Mr. Willard, and Bundy, apparently considering that enough chaff had been cut for one evening, entered into a discussion on the conditions of life in mediaeval Rochester with a zest and earnestness that came as a refreshing change, after so much frivolity. So the evening passed pleasantly away until ten o'clock, when Bundy rose to depart.

"Shall we see him home, Thorndyke?" said I. "We can do with a walk after our pow-wow."

"Somebody ought to see him home," said Thorndyke. "He looks comparatively sober now, but wait till he gets out into the air." (Bundy's almost ascetic abstemiousness in respect of wine, I should explain, had become a mild joke between us.) "But I think I won't join the bacchanalian procession. I have a letter to write, and I can get it done and posted by the time you come back."

As we walked towards the office arm-in-arm – Bundy keeping up the fiction of a slight unsteadiness of gait – my guest once more expressed enjoyment of our little festivals.

"I suppose," said he, "Dr. Thorndyke is really quite a big bug in his way."

"Yes," I replied, "he is in the very front rank, in fact, I should say that he is the greatest living authority on his subject."

"Yes," said Bundy, thoughtfully, "one feels that he is a great man, although he is so friendly and so perfectly free from side. I hope I don't cheek him too much."

"He doesn't seem to resent it," I answered, "and he certainly doesn't object to your society. He expressly said, when he wrote last, that he hoped to see something of you."

"That was awfully nice of him," Bundy said with very evident gratification, and he added, after a pause, "Lord! John, what a windfall it was for me when you came down with that letter from old Turcival. It has made life a different thing for me."

"I am glad to hear it, Peter," said I, "but you haven't got all the benefit. It was a bit of luck for me to strike a live bishop in my new habitat, and a Rumtifoozlish one at that. But here we are at the episcopal palace. Shall I assist your lordship up the steps?"

We carried out the farce to its foolish end, staggering together up the steps, at the top of which I propped him securely against the door and rang the bell, with the comfortable certainty that there was no one in the house to disturb.

"Good night, John, old chap," he said cordially, as I retired.

"Good night, Peter, my child," I responded, and so took my way homeward to my other guest.

I arrived at my house in time to meet Thorndyke returning from the adjacent pillar-box, and we went in together.

"Well," said he, "I suppose we had better turn in, according to what is, I believe, the custom of this household, and turn out betimes in the morning, for a visit, perhaps, to Black Boy Lane."

"Yes," I replied, "we may as well turn in now. You are not going to leave these photographs there, are you?"

"They are your photographs," he replied. "That is, if you care to have them. I brought them down for you."

I thanked him very warmly for the gift and gathered up the portraits carefully, replacing them, for the present, in their box. Then we turned out the lights and made our way up to our respective bedrooms.

At breakfast on the following morning Thorndyke opened the subject of our investigation by cross-examining me on the matter of my report, and the more detailed account that Bundy had given.

"What does Sergeant Cobbledick think of the new developments?" he asked, when I had given him all the detail that I could.

"In a way he is encouraged. He is glad to get something more definite to work on. But for the present he seems to be high and dry. He gave me quite a learned exposition of the possibilities of the case, but he had to admit when he had finished that he was still in the dark so far as any final conclusion was concerned. He even suggested that I should put the facts before you – he recognized you when we met him on the road near Blue Boar Pier – and ask if you could make any suggestion."

"Can you recall the sergeant's exposition of the case?"

"I think so. It made rather an impression on me at the time," and here I repeated, as well as I could remember them, the various inferences that Cobbledick had drawn from the presence in the lane of the things that we had found. Thorndyke listened with deep attention, nodding his head approvingly as each point was made.

"A very admirable analysis, Strangeways," he said when I had finished. "It does the sergeant great credit. So far as it goes, it is an excellent interpretation of the facts that are in his possession. There are, perhaps, one or two points that he has overlooked."

"If there are," said I, "it would be a great kindness to draw his attention to them. He is naturally anxious to get on with the case, and he has taken endless trouble over it."

"I shall be very glad to give him a hint or two," said Thorndyke. "After breakfast I should like to go over the ground with you, and then we might go along to the station and see if he is in his office."

I agreed to this program, and as soon as we had finished our breakfast we went forth, making our way by Free School Lane and The Common to the marshes west of Gas House Road. From there we entered Black Boy Lane at the lower end and slowly followed its windings, Thorndyke looking about him attentively, and occasionally peering over the fences, which his stature enabled him to do without climbing. At the top of the lane, where it opened into a paved thoroughfare, we observed no less a personage than Sergeant Cobbledick, standing on the pavement and looking at the few adjacent houses with an expression of profound speculation. His speculative attitude changed suddenly to one of eager interest when he saw us, and on my presenting him to Thorndyke, he stood stiffly at "attention" and raised his hat with an air that I can only describe as reverent.

"Dr. Strangeways was telling me, just now," said Thorndyke, "of your very interesting observations on these new developments. He also said that you would like to talk the matter over with me."

"I should, indeed, sir," the sergeant said, earnestly, "and if I might suggest it, my office will be very quiet, being Sunday, and I could show you the things that have been found, if you would like to see them."

"As to the things that have been found," said Thorndyke, "I am prepared to take them as read. They have been properly identified. But we could certainly talk more conveniently in your office."

In a few minutes we turned into a narrow street which brought us to the side of the Guildhall, and the sergeant, having shown us into his office and given some instructions to a constable, entered and locked the door.

176

"Now, Sergeant," said Thorndyke, "tell us what your difficulty is."

"I've got several difficulties, sir," replied Cobbledick. "In the first place, here is a body being carried up the lane. You agree with me, sir, that it was going up and not down?"

"Yes, your reasons seem quite conclusive."

"Well, then, sir, the next question is, was this a dead body, or was the woman drugged or insensible? The fact that she was being taken from the river towards the town suggests that she was alive and being taken to some house where she could be hidden, but, of course, a dead body might be taken to a house to be destroyed by burning or to be dismembered or even buried, say under the cellar. I must say my own feeling is that it was a dead body."

"The reasons you gave Dr. Strangeways for thinking so seem to be quite sound. Let us proceed on the assumption that it was a dead body."

"Well, sir," said Cobble dick, gloomily, "there you are. That's all. We have got a body brought up from the river. We can trace it up to near the top of the lane. But there we lose it. It seems to have vanished into smoke. It was being taken up into the town, but where? There's nothing to show. We come out into the paved streets and, of course, there isn't a trace. We seem to have come to the end of our clues, and I am very much afraid that we shan't get any more."

"There," said Thorndyke, "I am inclined to agree with you, Sergeant. You won't get any more clues for the simple reason that you have got them all."

"Got them all!" exclaimed Cobbledick, staring in amazement at Thorndyke.

"Yes," was the calm reply, "at least, that is how it appears to me. Your business now is not to search for more clues but to extract the meaning from the facts that you possess. Come, now, Sergeant," he continued, "let us take a bird's-eye view of the case, as it were, reconstructing the investigation in a sort of synopsis. I will read the entries from my note-book."

"On Saturday, the 26th of April, Mrs. Frood disappeared. On the 1st of May the brooch was found at the pawn-brokers. On the 7th of May the box of tablets and the bag were found on the shore at Chatham, apparently fixing the place of the crime. On the 9th of May the scarf was found at Blue Boar Head. On the 15th of May a shoe was found in the creek between Blue Boar Head and Gas House Point. On the 25th of May the second shoe was found on the gridiron near Gas House Point. On the 20th of June a hat-pin was found on the shore a little west of the last spot, always creeping steadily up the river, you notice."

"Yes," said Cobbledick, "I noticed that, and I'm hanged if I can account for it in any way."

"Never mind," said Thorndyke. "Just note the fact. Then on the 14th of July four articles were found, near the bottom of the lane a button, near the middle of the lane a hat-pin and abreast of it in the field, the hat itself. Finally, at the top of the lane, in the field, you found the missing key."

"I don't see what the key has got to do with it," said the sergeant. "It don't seem to me to be in the picture."

"Doesn't it?" said Thorndyke. "Just consider a moment, Sergeant. But perhaps you have forgotten the date on which the key disappeared?"

"I don't know that I ever noticed when it was lost."

"It wasn't lost," said Thorndyke. "It was taken away – probably out of the gate – and afterwards thrown over the fence. But I daresay Dr. Strangeways can give you the date."

I reflected for a few moments. "Let me see," said I. "It was a good while ago, and I remember that it was a Saturday, because the men who were filling the holes in the city wall had knocked off at noon for a week-end. Now when was it? I went to the wine merchant's that day, and – " I paused with a sudden shock of recollection. "Why!" I exclaimed. "It was the Saturday, the day Mrs. Frood disappeared!"

Cobbledick seemed to stiffen in his chair as he suddenly turned a startled look at Thorndyke.

"Yes," agreed the latter, "the key disappeared during the morning of the 26th of April and Mrs. Frood disappeared on the evening of the same day. That is a coincidence in time. And if you consider what gate it was that this key unlocked, that it gave entrance – and also excluded entrance – to an isolated, enclosed area of waste land in which excavations and fillings-in are actually taking place, I think you will agree that there is matter for investigation."

As Thorndyke was speaking Cobbledick's eyes opened wider and wider, and his mouth exhibited a like change.

"Good Lord, Sir!" he exclaimed at length, "you mean to say – "

"No, I don't," Thorndyke interrupted with a smile. "I am merely drawing your attention to certain facts which seem to have escaped it. You said that there was no hint of a place to which the body could have been conveyed, I point out a hint which you have overlooked. That is all."

"It is a pretty broad hint, too," said Cobbledick, "and I am going to lose no time in acting on it. Do you happen to know, Doctor, who employed the workmen?"

"I gathered that Japp and Bundy had the contract to repair the wall. At any rate, they were supervising the work, and they will be able to tell you where to find the foreman. Probably they have a complete record of the progress of the work. You know Mr. Japp's address on Boley Hill, I suppose, and Mr. Bundy lives over the office."

"I'll call on him at once," said Cobbledick, "and see if he can give me the particulars, and I'll get him to lend me the key. I suppose you two gentlemen wouldn't care to come and have a look at the place with me?"

"I don't see why not," said Thorndyke. "But I particularly wish not to appear in connexion with the case, so I will ask you to say nothing to anyone of your having spoken to me about it and, of course, we go to the place alone."

"Certainly," the sergeant agreed emphatically. "We don't want any outsiders with us. Then if you will wait for me here I will get back as quickly as I can. I hope Mr. Bundy is at home."

He snatched up his hat and darted out of the office, full of hope and high spirits. Thorndyke's suggestion had rejuvenated him.

"It seems to me," I said, when he had gone, "a rather remarkable thing that you should have remembered all the circumstances of the loss of this key."

"It isn't really remarkable at all," he replied. "I heard of it after the woman had disappeared. But as soon as she had disappeared, the loss of this particular key at this particular time became a fact of possible evidential importance. It was a fact that had to be noted and remembered. The connexion of the tragedy with the river seemed to exclude it for a time, but the discoveries in the lane at once revived its importance. The fundamental rule, Strangeways, of all criminal investigation is to note everything, relevant or irrelevant, and forget nothing."

"It is an excellent rule," said I, "but it must be a mighty difficult one to carry out." And for a while we sat, each immersed in his own reflections.

The sergeant returned in an incredibly short space of time, and he burst into the office with a beaming face, flourishing the key. "I found him at home," said he, "and I've got all the necessary particulars, so we can take a preliminary look round." He held the door open, and when we had passed out, he led the way down the little street at a pace that would have done credit to a sporting lamp-lighter. A very few minutes brought us to the gate, and when he had opened it and locked it behind us, he stood looking round the weed-grown enclosure as if doubtful where to begin.

"Which patch in the wall is the one they were working at when the key disappeared?" Thorndyke asked.

179

"The last but one to the left," was the reply.

"Then we had better have a look at that, first," said Thorndyke. "It was a ready-made excavation."

We advanced towards the ragged patch in the wall, and as we drew near I looked at it with a tumult of emotions that swamped mere anxiety and expectation. I could see what Thorndyke thought, and that perception amounted almost to conviction. Meanwhile, my colleague and the sergeant stepped close up to the patch and minutely examined the rough and slovenly joints of the stonework.

"There is no trace of its having been opened," said Thorndyke. "But there wouldn't be. I think we had better scrape up the earth at the foot of the wall. Something might easily have been dropped and trodden in in the darkness." He looked towards the shed, in which a couple of empty lime barrels still remained and, perceiving there a decrepit shovel, he went and fetched it. Returning with it, he proceeded to turn up the surface of the ground at the foot of the wall, depositing each shovelful of earth on a bare spot, and spreading it out carefully. For some time there was no result, but he continued methodically, working from one end of the patch towards the other. Suddenly Cobbledick uttered an exclamation and stooped over a freshly deposited shovelful.

"By the Lord!" he ejaculated, "it is a true bill! You were quite right, sir." He stood up, holding out between his finger and thumb a small bronze button bearing an embossed Tudor Rose. Thorndyke glanced at me as I took the button from the sergeant and examined it.

"Yes," I said, "it is unquestionably one of her buttons."

"Then," said he, "we have got our answer. The solution of the mystery is contained in that patch of new rubble."

The sergeant's delight and gratitude were quite pathetic. Again and again he reiterated his thanks, regardless of Thorndyke's disclaimers and commendations of the officer's own skilful and patient investigation.

"All the same," said Cobbledick, as he locked the gate and pocketed the key, "we haven't solved the whole problem. We may say that we have found the body, but the problem of the crime and the criminal remains. I suppose, sir, you don't see any glimmer of light in that direction?"

"A glimmer, perhaps," replied Thorndyke, "but it may turn out to be but a mirage. Let us see the body. It may have a clearer message for us than we expect."

Beyond this rather cryptic suggestion he refused to commit himself, nor, when we had parted from the sergeant, could I get anything more definite out of him.

180

"It is useless to speculate," he said, by way of closing the subject. "We think that we know what is inside that wall. We may be right, but we may possibly be wrong. A few hours will settle our doubts. If the body is there, it may tell us all that we want to know."

This last observation left me more puzzled than ever.

The condition of the body might, and probably would, reveal the cause of death and the nature of the crime, but it was difficult to see how it could point out the identity of the murderer. However, the subject was closed for the time being, and Thorndyke resolutely refused to reopen it until the fresh data were available.

Chapter XV
The End of the Trail

Shortly after breakfast on the following morning Sergeant Cobbledick made his appearance at my house. I found him in the consulting room, walking about on tip-toe with his hat balanced in his hands, and evidently in a state of extreme nervous tension.

"I have got everything in train, Doctor," said he, declining a seat. "I dug up the foreman yesterday evening and he dug up one of his mates to give him a hand, if necessary, and I have the authority to open the wall. So we are all ready to begin. The two men have gone down to the place with their tools, and Mr. Bundy has gone with them to let them in. He didn't much want to go, but I thought it best that either he or Mr. Japp should be present. It is their wall, so to speak. I suppose you are coming to see the job done."

"Is there any need for me to be there?" I asked. Cobbledick looked at me in surprise. He had evidently assumed that I should be eager to see what happened.

"Well," he replied, "you are the principal witness to the identity of the remains. You saw her last, you know. What is your objection, Doctor?"

I was not in a position to answer this question. I could not tell him what this last and most horrible search meant to me, and apart from my personal feelings in regard to poor Angelina, there was no objection at all, but, on the contrary, every reason why I should be present.

"It isn't a very pleasant affair," I replied, "seeing that I knew the lady rather well. However, if you think I had better be there, I will come down with you."

"I certainly think your presence would be a help," said he. "We don't know what may turn up, and you know more about her than anybody else."

Accordingly, I walked down with him, and when he had admitted me with his key – Bundy had presumably used the duplicate – he closed the gate and locked it from within. The actual operations had not yet commenced, but the foreman and his mate were standing by the wall, conversing affably with Bundy, who looked nervous and uncomfortable, evidently relishing his position no more than I did mine.

"This is a gruesome affair, John, isn't it?" he said in a low voice. "I don't see why old Cobbledick wanted to drag us into it. It will be an awful moment when they uncover her, if she is really there. I'm frightfully sorry for you, old chap."

"I should have had to see the body in any case," said I, "and this is less horrible than the river."

Here my attention was attracted by the foreman, who had just drawn a long, horizontal chalk line across the patch of new rubble, a little below the middle.

"That's about the place where we left off that Saturday, so far as I remember," he said. "We had built up the outer case, and we filled in the hollow with loose bricks and stones, but we didn't put any mortar to them until Monday morning. Then we mixed up a lot of mortar, quite thin, so that it would run, and poured it on top of the loose stuff."

"Rum way of building a wall isn't it?" observed Cobbledick.

The foreman grinned. "It ain't what you'd call the highest class of masonry," he admitted. "But what can you expect to do with a gang of corner-boys who've never done a job of real work in their lives?"

"No, that's true," said the Sergeant. "But you made a soft job for the grave-diggers, didn't you? Why they'd only got to pick out the loose stuff and then dump it back on top when they'd put the body in. Then you came along on Monday morning and finished the job for them with one or two bucketsful of liquid mortar. How long would it have taken to pick out that loose stuff?"

"Lord bless yer," was the answer, "one man who meant business could have picked the whole lot out by hand in an hour, and he could have chucked it back in less. As you say, Sergeant, it was a soft job."

While they had been talking, the foreman's familiar demon had been making a tentative attack on the outer casing with a great, chisel-ended steel bar and a mason's hammer. The foreman now came to his aid with a sledge hammer, the first stroke of which caused the shoddy masonry to crack in all directions like pie-crust. Then the fractured pieces of the outer shell were prised off, revealing the "loose stuff" within. And uncommonly loose it was, so loose that the unjoined bricks and stones, with their adherent gouts of mortar, came away at the lightest touch of the great crow-bar.

As soon as a breach had been made at the top of the patch, the labourer climbed up and began flinging out the separated bricks and stones. Then he attacked a fresh course of the outer shell with a pick, and so exposed a fresh layer of the loose filling.

"There'll be a fresh job for the unemployed to build this up again," the sergeant observed with a sardonic smile.

"Ah," replied the foreman, "there generally is a fresh job when you take on a crowd of casuals. Wonderful provident men are casuals. Don't they take no thought for the morrow! What O!"

At this moment the labourer stood upright on his perch and laid down his pick. "Well, I'm blowed!" he exclaimed. "This is a rum go, this is."

"What's a rum go?" demanded the foreman.

"Why, here's a whole bed of dry quick-lime," was the reply.

"Ha!" exclaimed the sergeant, knitting his brows anxiously.

The foreman scrambled up, and after a brief inspection confirmed the man's statement. "Quick-lime it is, sure enough. Just hand me up that shovel, Sergeant."

"Be careful," Cobbledick admonished, as he passed the shovel up. "Don't forget what there probably is underneath."

The foreman took the shovel and began very cautiously to scrape away the surface, flinging the scrapings of lime out on to the ground, where they were eagerly scrutinized by the sergeant, while the labourer picked out the larger lumps and cast them down. Thus the work went on for about a quarter-of-an-hour, without any result beyond the accumulation on the ground below of a small heap of lime. At length I noticed the foreman pause and look attentively at the lime that he had just scraped up in his shovel.

"Here's something that I don't fancy any of our men put in," he said, picking the object out and handing it down to the Sergeant. The latter took it from him and held it out for me to see. It was another of Angelina's coat buttons.

In the course of the next few minutes two more buttons came to light, and almost immediately afterwards I saw the labourer stoop suddenly and stare down at the lime with an expression that made my flesh creep, as he pointed something out to the foreman.

"Ah!" the latter exclaimed. "Here she is! But, my word! There ain't much left of her. Look at this, Sergeant."

Very gingerly, and with an air of shuddering distaste, he picked something out of the lime and held it up, and even at that distance I could see that it was a human ulna. Cobbledick took it from him with the same distasteful and almost fearful manner, and held it towards me for inspection. I glanced at it and looked away. "Yes," I said, "It is a human arm bone."

On this, Cobbledick beckoned for the labourer to come down and, taking out his official note-book, wrote something in pencil and tore out the leaf.

184

"Take this down to the station and give it to Sergeant Brown. He will tell you what else to do." He gave the paper to the man, and having let him out of the gate, came back and climbed up to the exposed surface of the excavation, where I saw him draw on a pair of gloves and then stoop and begin to pick over the lime.

"This is a horrid business, isn't it?" said Bundy. "Why the deuce couldn't Cobbledick carry on by himself? I don't see that it is our affair. Do you think we need stay?"

"I don't see why you need. You have finished your part of the business. You have seen the wall opened. I am afraid I must stay a little longer, as Cobbledick may want me to identify some of the other objects that may be found. But I shan't stay very long. There is really no question of the identity of the body, and there is no doubt now that the body is there. Detailed identification is a matter for the coroner."

As we were speaking, we walked slowly away from the wall among the mounds of rubbish, now beginning to be hidden under a dense growth of nettles, ragwort, and thistles. It was a desolate, neglected place, sordid of aspect and contrasting unpleasantly in its modern squalor with the dignified decay of the ancient wall. We had reached the further fence and were just turning about when the sergeant hailed me with a note of excitement in his voice. I hurried across and found him standing up with his eyes fixed on something that lay in the palm of his gloved hand.

"This seems to be the ring that you described to me, Doctor," said he. "Will you just take a look at it?"

He reached down and I received in my hand the little trinket of deep-toned, yellow gold that I remembered so well. I turned it over in my palm, and as I looked on its mystical signs, its crude, barbaric workmanship and the initials "*A. C.*" scratched inside, the scene in that dimly lighted room – years ago, it seemed to me now – rose before me like a vision. I saw the gracious figure in the red glow of the lamp and heard the voice that was never again to sound in my ears, telling the story of the little bauble, and for a few moments, the dreadful present faded into the irredeemable past.

"There isn't any doubt about it, is there, Doctor?" the sergeant asked anxiously.

"None, whatever," I replied. "It is unquestionably Mrs. Frood's ring."

"That's a mercy," said Cobbledick, "because we shall want every atom of identification that we can get. The body isn't going to help us much. This lime has done its work to a finish. There's nothing left, so far as I can see, but the skeleton and the bits of metal belonging to the

185

clothing. Would you like to come up and have a look, Doctor? There isn't much to see yet, but I have uncovered some of the bones."

"I don't think I will come up, Sergeant, thank you," said I. "When you have finished, I shall have to look over what has been found, as I shall have to give evidence at the inquest. And I think I need hardly stay any longer. There is no doubt now about the identity, so far as we are concerned, at any rate."

"No," he agreed. "There is no doubt in my mind, so I need not keep you any longer if you want to be off. But, before you go, there is one little matter that I should like to speak to you about." He climbed down to the ground and, walking away with me a little distance, continued, "You see, Doctor, some medical man will have to examine the remains, so as to give evidence before the coroner. If it is impossible to identify them as the remains of Mrs. Frood, it will have to be given in evidence that they are the remains of a person who might have been Mrs. Frood – that they are the remains of a woman of about her size and age, I mean. Of course, the choice of the medical witness doesn't rest with the police, but if you would care to take on the job, our recommendation would have weight with the coroner. You see, you are the most suitable person to make the examination, as you actually knew her."

I shook my head emphatically. "For that very reason, Sergeant, I couldn't possibly undertake the duty. Even doctors have feelings, you know. Just imagine how you would feel, yourself, pawing over the bones of a woman who had once been your friend."

Cobbledick looked disappointed. "Yes," he admitted, "I suppose there is something in what you say. But I didn't think doctors troubled about such things very much, and you have got such an eye for detail – and such a memory. However, if you'd rather not, there is an end of the matter."

He climbed back regretfully to the opening in the wall, and I rejoined Bundy. "I have finished here now," said I. "That was a ring of hers that Cobbledick had found. Are you staying any longer?"

"Not if you are going away," he replied. "I am not wanted now, and I can't stick this charnel-house atmosphere. It is getting on my nerves. Let us clear out."

We walked towards the entrance with a feeling of relief at escaping from the gruesome place, and had arrived within a few yards of it when there came a loud knocking at the gate, at which Bundy started visibly.

"Good Lord!" he exclaimed, "it's like Macbeth. Here, take my key and let the beggars in, whoever they are."

I unlocked the gate and threw it open, when I saw, standing in the lane, two men, bearing on their shoulders a rough, unpainted coffin, and

186

accompanied by the labourer, who carried a large sieve. I stood aside to let them pass in, and when they had entered, Bundy and I walked out, shutting and locking the gate after us. We made our way up the lane in silence, for there was little to say but much to think about – indeed, I would sooner have been alone, but the gruesome atmosphere of the place we had come from seemed to have affected Bundy's spirits so much that I thought it only kind to ask him to come back to lunch with me, an invitation that he accepted with avidity.

During lunch we discussed the tragic discovery, and Bundy, now that he had escaped from physical contact with the relics of mortality, showed his usual shrewd common sense.

"Well," he said, "the mystery of poor Angelina Frood is solved at last – at least, so far as it is ever likely to be."

"I hope not," I replied, "for the essential point of the mystery is not solved at all. It has only just been completely propounded. We now know beyond a doubt that she was murdered, and that the murder was a deliberate crime, planned in advance. What we want to know – at least, what I want to know, and shall never rest until I do know – is, who committed this diabolical crime?"

"I am afraid you never will know, John," said he. "There doesn't seem to be the faintest clue."

"What do you mean?" I demanded. "You seem to have forgotten Nicholas Frood."

Bundy shook his head. "You are deluding yourself, John. Nicholas seems, from your account of him, to be quite capable of having murdered his wife. But is there anything to connect him with the crime? If there is, you have never told me of it. And the law demands positive evidence. You can't charge a man with murder because he seems a likely person and you don't know of anybody else. What have you got against him in connexion with this present affair?"

"Well, for instance, I know that he was prowling about this town, and that he was trying to find out where she lived."

"But why not?" demanded Bundy. "She was a runaway wife, and he was her husband."

"Then I happen to have noticed that he carried a sheath-knife."

"But do you know that she was killed with a sheath-knife?"

"No, I don't," I answered savagely. "But I say again that I shall never rest until the price of her death has been paid. There must be some clue. The murder could not have been committed without a motive, and it must be possible to discover what that motive was. Somebody must have stood to benefit in some way by her death, and I am going to find that person, or those persons, if I give up the rest of my life to the search."

"I am sorry to hear you say that, John," he said as he rose to depart. "It sounds as if you were prepared to spend the rest of your life chasing a will-o'-the-wisp. But we are premature. The inquest may bring to light some new evidence that will put the police on the murderer's track. You must remember that they have been engaged in tracing the body up to now. When the inquest has been held and the facts are known they will be able to begin the search for the murderers. And I wish them and you good luck."

I was rather glad when he was gone, for his dispassionate estimate of the difficulties of the case only served to confirm my own secret hopelessness. For I could not deny that these wretches seemed to have covered up their tracks completely. In the three months that had passed no whisper of any suspicious circumstance had been heard.

From the moment when poor Angelina had faded from my sight into the fog to that of her dreadful reappearance in the old wall, no human eye seemed to have seen her. And now that she had come back, what had she to tell us of the events of that awful night? The very body, on which Thorndyke had relied for evidence, at least, of the manner of the crime, had dwindled to a mere skeleton such as might have been exhumed from some ancient tomb. The cunning of the murderer had outwitted even Thorndyke.

The thought of my friend reminded me that I had to report to him the results of the opening of the wall, results very different from what he had anticipated when he had given the sergeant the too-fruitful hint. I accordingly wrote out a detailed report, so far as my information went, but I held it back until the last post in case anything further should come to my knowledge. And it was just as well that I did, for about eight o'clock, Cobbledick called to give me the latest tidings.

"Well, Doctor," he said, with a smile of concentrated benevolence, "I have got everything in going order. I have seen the coroner and made out a list of witnesses. You are one of them, of course – in fact, you are the star witness. You were the last person to see her alive, and you were present at the exhumation. Dr. Baines – he's rather a scientific gentleman – is to make the *post mortem* examination, and tell us the cause of death, if he can. He won't have much to go on. The lime has eaten up everything – it would, naturally, after three months – but the bones look quite uninjured, so far as I could judge."

"When does the inquest open?" I asked.

"The day after to-morrow. I've got your summons with me, and I may as well give it to you now."

I looked at the little blue paper and put it in my pocketbook. "Do you think the coroner will get through the case in one day?" I asked.

"No, I am sure he won't," replied Cobbledick. "It is an important case, and there will be a lot of witnesses. There will be the evidence as to the building of the wall, then the opening of it and the description of what we found in it, then the identification of the remains – that is you, principally, and then there will be all the other evidence, the pawnbroker, Israel Bangs, Hooper, and the others. And then, of course, there will be the question as to the guilty parties. That is the most important of all."

"I didn't know you had any evidence on that subject," said I.

"I haven't much," he replied. "From the time when she disappeared nobody saw her alive or dead and, of course, nothing has ever been heard of any occurrence that might indicate a crime. All we have to go on – and it is mighty little – is the fact that she was hiding from her husband, and that he was trying to find her. Also that he had made one attempt on her life. That is where your evidence will come in, and that of the matron at the Poor Travellers. I've had a talk with her."

"Do you know anything of Frood's movements about the time of the disappearance?"

"Practically nothing, excepting that he went away from his lodgings the day before. You see, we were not in a position to start tracing possible criminals. We had no real evidence of any crime. We knew that the woman had disappeared, and she appeared to have got into the river. But there was nothing to show how. It looked suspicious, but it wasn't a case. So long as no body was forthcoming there was no evidence of death, and nobody could have been charged. Even if we had found the body in the river, unless there had been distinct traces of violence, it would have been merely a case of 'found dead' or 'found drowned'. But now the affair is on a different footing entirely. The body has been discovered under conditions which furnish *prima facie* evidence of murder, whatever the cause of death may turn out to have been. There is sure to be a verdict of wilful murder – not that the police are dependent on the coroner's verdict. So now we can get a move on and look for the murderer."

"What chance do you think there is of finding him?" I asked.

"Well," said Cobbledick with a benevolent smile, "we mustn't be too cock-sure. But, leaving the husband out of the question and taking the broad facts, it doesn't look so unpromising. This wasn't a casual crime – fortunately. There's nothing so hopeless as a casual crime, done for mere petty robbery. But this crime was thought out. The place of burial was selected in advance. The key of the place was obtained, so that the murderer could not only get in but could lock himself – or more probably *themselves* – in and work secure from chance disturbance. And the time seems to have been selected, a week-end, with two whole nights to do the job in. All this points to very definite premeditation, and that points to a very definite motive. The person who planned this crime had something considerable to gain by Mrs. Frood's death. It may have been profit or it may have been the satisfaction of revenge.

"Well, that is a pretty good start. When we know what property she had, who comes into it at her death, if any of it is missing, and if so, what has become of it, we can judge concerning the first case. And if we find that she had any enemies besides her husband, anyone whom she had injured or who owed her a grudge, then we can judge of the second case.

"Then there is another set of facts. This murderer couldn't have been a complete stranger to the place. He knew about the wall and what was going on there. He knew the river and he possessed, or had command of, a boat. He knew the waterside premises and he knew his way – or had someone to show him the way – across the marshes and up Black Boy Lane. One, at least, of the persons concerned in this affair was a local man who knew the place well. So you see, Doctor, we have got something to go on, after all."

I listened to the sergeant's exposition with deep interest and no little revival of my drooping hopes. It was a most able summary of the case, and I felt that I should have liked Thorndyke to hear it. In fact, I determined to embody it in the amplification of my report. With the facts thus fully and lucidly collated, it did really seem as though the perpetrator of this foul crime must inevitably fall into our hands. Having refreshed the sergeant with a couple of glasses of port, I shook his hand warmly and wished him the best of success in the investigation that he was conducting with so much ability.

When he had gone I wrote a full account of our interview to add to my previous report, and expressed the hope that Thorndyke would be able to be present at the inquest, when I myself should "be and appear" at the appointed place to give evidence on the day after the morrow.

Chapter XVI
The Inquiry and a Surprise

On the morning of the inquest I started from my house well in advance of time, and in a distinctly uncomfortable frame of mind. Perhaps it was that the formal inquiry brought home to me with extra vividness the certainty that my beloved friend was gone from me forever, and that she had died in circumstances of tragedy and horror. Not that I had ever had any doubt, but now the realization was more intense. Again, I should have to give evidence. I should have to reconstitute for the information of strangers scenes and events that had for me a certain sacred intimacy. And then, above all, I should have to view – and that not cursorily – the decayed remains of the woman who had been so much to me. That would be naturally expected from a medical man and no one would guess at what it would cost me to bring myself to this last dreadful meeting.

Walking down the High Street thus wrapped in gloomy reflections, it was with mixed feelings that I observed Bundy advancing slowly towards me, having evidently awaited my arrival. In some respects I would sooner have been alone, and yet his kindly, sympathetic companionship was not altogether unwelcome.

"Good morning, John," said he. "I hope I am not *de trop*. It is a melancholy errand for you, poor old chap, and I can't do much to make it less so, but I thought we might walk down together. You know how sorry I am for you, John."

"Yes, I know and appreciate, and I am always glad to see you, Peter. But why are you going there! Have you had a summons?"

"No, I have no information to give. But I am interested in the case, of course, so I am going to attend as a spectator. So is Japp, though he is really a legitimately interested party. In fact, I am rather surprised they didn't summon him as a witness."

"So am I. He really knows more about the poor girl than I do. But, of course, he knows nothing of the circumstances of her death."

By this time we had arrived at the Guildhall, and here we encountered Sergeant Cobbledick, who was evidently on the look-out for me.

"I am glad you came early, Doctor," said he. "I want you just to pop round to the mortuary. You know the way. There's a tray by the side of the coffin with all her belongings on it. I'll get you to take a careful look at them, so that you can tell the jury that they are really her things. And you had better run your eye over the remains. You might be able to spot something of importance. At any rate, they will expect you to have viewed the body, as you are the principal witness to its identity. I've told the constable on duty to let you in. And, of course, you can go in, too, Mr. Bundy, if you want to."

"I don't think I do, thank you," replied Bundy. But he walked round with me to the mortuary, where the constable unlocked the door as he saw us approaching. I mentioned my name to the officer, but he knew me by sight, and now held the door open and followed me in, while Bundy halted at the threshold, and stood, rather pale and awe-stricken, looking in at the long table and its gruesome burden.

The tray of which Cobbledick had spoken was covered with a white table-cloth, and on this the various objects were arranged symmetrically like the exhibits in a museum. At the top was the hat, flanked on either side by a silver-headed hat-pin. The carefully smoothed scarf was spread across horizontally, the six coat-buttons were arranged in a straight vertical line, and the two shoes were placed at the bottom centre. At one side was the hand-bag, and at the other, to balance it, the handkerchief with its neatly embroidered initials, and on this were placed the Zodiac ring, the wedding ring, the box of tablets, and the brooch. On the lateral spaces the various other objects were arranged with the same meticulous care for symmetrical effect: A neat row of hair pins, a row of hooks and eyes, one or two rows of buttons from the dress and under garments, the little metal jaws of the purse, two rows of coins, silver and bronze, a pair of glove-fasteners with scorched fragments of leather adhering, a little pearl handled knife, a number of metal clasps and fastenings and other small metallic objects derived from the various garments, and a few fragments of textiles, scorched as if by fire, a couple of brown shreds, apparently from the stockings, a cindery fragment of the brown coat, and a few charred and brittle tatters of linen.

I looked over the pitiful collection while the constable stood near the door and probably watched me. There was something unspeakably pathetic in the spectacle of these poor fragments of wreckage, thus laid out, and seeming, in the almost grotesque symmetry of their disposal, to make a mute appeal for remembrance and justice. This was all that was left of her, this and what was in the coffin.

So moved was I by the sight of these relics, thus assembled and presented in a sort of tragic synopsis, that it was some time before I could summon the resolution to look upon her very self, or at least upon such vestiges of her as had survived the touch of "decay's effacing fingers". But the time was passing, and it had to be. At last I turned to the coffin and, lifting the unfastened lid, looked in.

It could have been no different from what I had expected, but yet the shock of its appearance seemed to strike me a palpable blow. Someone had arranged the bones in their anatomical order, and there the skeleton lay on the bottom of the coffin – dry, dusty, whitened with the powder of lime, such a relic as might have been brought to light by the spade of some excavator in an ancient barrow or prehistoric tomb. And yet this thing was she – *Angelina!* That grisly skull had once been clothed by her rich, abundant hair! That grinning range of long white teeth had once sustained the sweet, pensive mouth that I remembered so well. It was incredible. It was horrible. And yet it was true.

For some moments I stood as if petrified, holding up the coffin lid and gazing at the fearful shape in a trance of horror. And then suddenly I felt, as it were, a clutching at my throat and the vision faded into a blur as my eyes filled. Hastily I clapped down the coffin lid and strode towards the door with the tears streaming down my face.

Vaguely I was aware of Bundy taking my arm and pressing it to his side, of his voice as he murmured shakily, "Poor old John!" Passively I allowed him to lead me to a quiet corner above a flight of steps leading down to the river, where I halted to wipe my eyes, faintly surprised to note that he was wiping his eyes too, and that his face was pale and troubled. But if I was surprised, I was grateful, too, and never had my heart inclined more affectionately towards him than in this moment of trial that had been lightened by his unobtrusive sympathy and perfect understanding.

We stayed for a few minutes, looking down on the river and talking of the dead woman and the sad and troubled life from which this hideous crime had snatched her. Then, as the appointed time approached, we made our way to the room in which the inquiry was to be held. As we entered, a pleasant-looking, shrewd-faced man who looked like a barrister and who had been standing by a constable, approached and accosted me.

"Dr. Strangeways? My name is Anstey. I do most of the court work in connexion with Thorndyke's cases, and I am representing him here to-day. He had hoped to come down himself, but he had to go into the country on some important business, so I have to come to keep the nest warm – to watch the proceedings and make a summary of the evidence. You mentioned to him that the case would take more than one day."

"Yes," I answered, "that is what I understand. Will Dr. Thorndyke be here to-morrow?"

"Yes, he has arranged definitely to attend to-morrow. And I think he expects by then to have some information of importance to communicate."

"Indeed!" I said eagerly. "Do you happen to know the nature of it?"

Anstey laughed. "My dear Doctor," said he, "you have met Thorndyke, and you must know by now that he is about as communicative as a Whitstable native. No one ever knows what cards he holds."

"Yes," I agreed, "he is extraordinarily secretive. Unnecessarily so, it has seemed to me."

Anstey shook his head. "He is perfectly right, Doctor. He knows his own peculiar job to a finish. He is, in a way, like some highly-specialized animal, such as the three-toed sloth, for instance, which seems an abnormal sort of beast until you see it doing, with unapproachable perfection, the thing that nature intended it to do. Thorndyke is a case of perfect adaptation to a special environment."

"Still," I objected, "I don't see the use of such extreme secrecy."

"You would if you followed his cases. A secret move is a move against which the other player – if there is one – can make no provision or defence or counter-move. Thorndyke plays with a wooden face and without speaking. No one knows what his next move will be. But when it comes, he puts down his piece and says 'Check', and you'll find it is mate."

"But," I still objected, "you are talking of an adversary and of counter-moves. Is there any adversary in this case?"

"Well, isn't there?" said he. "There has been a crime committed. Someone has committed it, and that someone is not advertising his identity. But you can take it that he has been keeping a watchful eye on his pursuers, ready, if necessary, to give them a lead in the wrong direction. But it is time for us to take our places. I see the jury have come back from viewing the body."

We took our places at the long table, one side of which was allocated to the jury and the other to witnesses in waiting, the police officers, the press-men, and other persons interested in the case. A few minutes later, the coroner opened the proceedings by giving a very brief statement of the circumstances which had occasioned the inquiry, and then proceeded to call the witnesses.

The first witness was Sergeant Cobbledick, whose evidence took the form of a statement covering the whole history of the case, beginning with Mr. Japp's notification of the disappearance of Mrs Frood and ending with the opening of the wall and the discovery of the remains. The latter part of the evidence was given in minute detail and included a complete list of the objects found with the remains.

"Does any juryman wish to ask the witness any questions?" the Coroner inquired when the lengthy statement was concluded. He looked from one to the other, and when nobody answered he called the next witness. This was Dr. Baines, a somewhat dry-looking gentleman, who gave his evidence clearly, concisely, and with due scientific caution.

"You have examined the remains which form the subject of this inquiry?" the coroner asked.

"Yes. I have examined the skeleton which is now lying in the mortuary. It is that of a rather strongly-built woman, five-feet-seven inches in height, and about thirty years of age."

"Were you able to form any opinion as to the cause of death?"

"No, there were no signs of any injury nor of disease."

"Are we to understand," asked one of the jurymen, "that you consider deceased to have died a natural death?"

"I have no means of forming any opinion on the subject."

"But if she died from violence, wouldn't there be some signs of it?"

"That would depend on the nature of the violence."

"Supposing she had been shot with a revolver."

"In that case there might be a fracture of one or more bones, but there might be no fracture at all. Of course, there would be a bullet."

"Did you find a bullet?"

"No. I did not see the bones until they had been brought to the mortuary."

"There has been no mention of a bullet having been found," the coroner interposed, "and you heard Sergeant Cobbledick say that the lime had all been sifted through a fine sieve. We must take it that there was no bullet. But," he continued, addressing the witness, "the conditions that you found would not exclude violence, I presume?"

"Not at all. Only violence that would cause injury to the bones."

"What kinds of violence would be unaccompanied by injury to the bones?"

"Drowning, hanging, strangling, suffocation, stabbing and, of course, poisoning usually leaves no traces on the bones."

"Can you give us no suggestion as to the cause of death?"

"None whatever," was the firm reply.

"You have heard the description of the missing woman, Mrs. Frood. Do these remains correspond with that description?"

"They are the remains of a woman of similar stature and age to Mrs. Frood, so far as I can judge. I can't say more than that. The description of Mrs. Frood was only approximate, and the estimate of the stature, and especially the age, of a skeleton can only be approximate."

This being all that could be got out of the witness, who was concerned only with the skeleton, and naturally refused to budge from that position, the coroner glanced at his list and then called my name. I

195

rose and took my place at the top corner of the table, when I was duly sworn, and gave my name and description.

"You heard Sergeant Cobbledick's description of the articles which have been found, and which are now lying in the mortuary?" the coroner began.

I replied "Yes," and he continued, "Have you examined those articles and, if so, can you tell us anything about them?"

"I have examined the articles in the mortuary, and I recognized them as things I know to have been the property of Mrs. Angelina Frood."

Here I described the articles in detail, and stated when and where I had seen them in her possession.

"You have inspected the remains of deceased in the mortuary. Can you identify them as the remains of any particular person?"

"No. They are quite unrecognizable."

"Have you any doubt as to whose remains they are?" asked the juryman who had spoken before.

"That question, Mr. Pilley," said the coroner "is not quite in order. The witness has said that he was not able to identify the remains. Inferences as to the identity of deceased, drawn from the evidence, are for the jury. We must not ask witnesses to interpret the evidence. When did you last see Mrs. Frood alive, Doctor?"

"On the 26th of April," I replied, and here I described that last interview, recalling our conversation almost verbatim. When I came to her expressions of uneasiness and foreboding, the attention of the listeners became more and more intense, and it was evident that they were deeply impressed. Particularly attentive was the foreman of the jury, a keen-faced, alert-looking man, who kept his eyes riveted on me and, when I had finished this part of my evidence, asked, "So far as you know, Doctor, had Mrs. Frood any enemies? Was there anyone whom she had reason to be afraid of?"

This was a rather awkward question. It is one thing to entertain a suspicion privately, but quite another thing to give public expression to it. Besides, I was giving sworn evidence as to facts actually within my knowledge.

"I can't say, positively," I replied after some hesitation, "that I know of any enemy or anyone whom she had reason to fear."

The coroner saw the difficulty, and interposed with a discreet question.

"What do you know of her domestic affairs, of her relations with her husband, for instance?"

This put the matter on the basis of fact, and I was able to state what I knew of her unhappy married life in Rochester and previously in

196

London, and further questions elicited my personal observations as to the character and personality of her husband. My meeting with him at Dartford Station, the incidents in the Poor Travellers' rest-house, the meeting with him on the bridge, all were given in full detail and devoured eagerly by the jury. And from their questions and their demeanour it became clear to me that they were in full cry after Nicholas Frood.

The conclusion of my evidence brought us to the luncheon hour. I had, of course, to take Mr. Anstey back to lunch with me, and a certain wistfulness in Bundy's face made me feel that I ought to ask him, too. I accordingly presented them to one another and issued the invitation.

"I am delighted to meet you, Mr. Bundy," Anstey said heartily. "I have heard of you from my friend Thorndyke, who regards you with respectful admiration."

"Does he?" said Bundy, blushing with pleasure, but looking somewhat surprised. "I can't imagine why. But are you an expert, too?"

"Bless you, no," laughed Anstey. "I am a mere lawyer and, on this occasion, what is known technically as a devil – technically, you understand. I am watching this case for Thorndyke."

"But I didn't know that Dr. Thorndyke was interested in the case," said Bundy, in evident perplexity.

"He is interested in everything of a criminal and horrid nature," replied Anstey. "He never lets a really juicy crime mystery pass without getting all the details, if possible. You see, they are his stock in trade."

"But he never would discuss this case – not seriously," objected Bundy.

"Probably not," said Anstey. "Perhaps there wasn't much to discuss. But wait till the case is finished. Then he will tell you all about it."

"I see," said Bundy. "He is one of those prophets who predict after the event."

"And the proper time, too," retorted Anstey. "It is no use being premature."

The conversation proceeded on this plane of playful repartee until we arrived at my house, where Mrs. Dunk, having bestowed a wooden glance of curiosity at Anstey and a glare of defiance at Bundy, handed me a telegram addressed to R. Anstey, K.C., care of Dr. Strangeways. I passed it to Anstey, who opened it and glanced through it.

"What shall I say in answer?" he asked, placing it in my hand.

I read the message and was not a little puzzled by it.

"*Ask Strangeways come back with you to-night. Very urgent. Reply time and place.*"

"What do you suppose he wants me for?" I asked.

"I never suppose in regard to Thorndyke," he replied.

"But if he says it is urgent, it is urgent. Can you come up with me?"

"Yes, if it is necessary."

"It is. Then I'll say yes. And you had better arrange to stay the night – there is a spare bedroom at his chambers – and come down with him in the morning. Can you manage that?"

"Yes," I replied, "and you can say that we shall be at Charing Cross by seven-fifteen."

I could see that this transaction was as surprising to Bundy as it was to me. But, of course, he asked no questions, nor could I have answered them if he had. Moreover, there was not much time for discussion as we had to be back in the court room by two o'clock, and what talk there was consisted mainly of humorous comments by Anstey on the witnesses and the jury.

Having sent off the telegram on our way down, we took our places once more, and the proceedings were resumed punctually by the calling of the foreman of the repairing gang, who deposed to the date on which the particular patch of rubble was commenced and finished and its condition when the men knocked off work on Saturday, the 26th of April. He also mentioned the loss of the key, but could give no particulars. The cross-examination elicited the facts that he had communicated to Cobbledick and me as to the state of the loose filling.

"How many men," the coroner asked, "would it have taken to bury the body in the way in which it was buried, and how long?"

"One man could have done it easily in one night, if he could have got the body there. The stuff in the wall was all loose, and it was small stuff, easy to handle. No building had to be done. It was just a matter of shovelling the lime in and then chucking the loose stuff in on top. And the lime was handy to get at in the shed, and one of the barrels was open."

"Can you say certainly when the body was buried?"

"It must have been buried on the night of the 26th of April or on the 27th, because on Monday morning, the 28th, we ran the mortar in, and by that evening we had got the patch finished."

The next witness was the labourer, Thomas Evans, who had lost the key. His account of the affair was as follows:

"On the morning of Saturday, the 26th of April, the foreman gave me the key, because he had to go to the office. I took the key and opened the gate, and I left the key in the lock for him to take when he came. Then I forgot all about it, and I suppose he did, too, because he didn't say anything about it until we had knocked off work and were going out. Then he asks me where the key was, and I said it was in the gate. Then

198

he went and looked but it wasn't there. So we searched about a bit in the grounds and out in the lane, but we couldn't see nothing of it nowhere."

"When you let yourself in, did you leave the gate open or shut it?"

"I shut the gate, but, of course, it was unlocked. The key was outside."

"So that anyone passing up the lane could have taken it out without your noticing?"

"Yes. We was working the other side of the grounds, so we shouldn't have heard anything if anybody had took it."

That completed the evidence as to the key, and when Evans was dismissed the matron of the Poor Travellers was called. As she took her place, a general straightening of backs and air of expectancy on the part of the jury suggested that her evidence was looked forward to with more than common interest. And so it turned out to be. Her admirably clear and vivid presentment of the man, Nicholas Frood, his quarrelsome, emotional temperament, his shabby condition, his abnormal appearance, the evidences of his addiction to drink and drugs, his apparently destitute state and, above all, the formidable sheath-knife that he wore under his coat, were listened to with breathless attention, and followed by a fusilade of eager, and often highly improper, questions. But the coroner was a wise and tactful man, and he unobtrusively intervened to prevent any irregularities, as, for instance, "It is not permissible," he observed, blandly, "to ask a witness if a certain individual seemed to be a likely person to commit a crime. And a coroner's court is not a criminal court. It is not our function to establish any person's guilt, but to ascertain how deceased met with her death. If the evidence shows that she was murdered, we shall say so in our verdict. If the evidence points clearly to a particular person as the murderer, we shall name that person in the verdict. But we are not primarily investigating a crime, we are investigating a death. The criminal investigation is for the police."

This reminder cooled the ardour of the criminal investigators somewhat, but there were signs of a fresh outbreak when Mrs. Gillow gave her evidence, for that lady having a somewhat more lively imagination than the matron, tended to lure enterprising jurymen on to fresh indiscretions. She certainly enjoyed herself amazingly, and occupied a most unnecessary amount of time before she at length retired, dejected but triumphant, to the manifest relief of the coroner.

This brought the day's proceedings to a close. There were a few more witnesses on the list, and the coroner hoped to take their evidence and complete the inquiry on the following day. As soon as the court rose, Anstey and I with Bundy proceeded to a tea-shop hard by and, having refreshed ourselves with a light tea, set forth to catch our train at Strood

Station. Thither Bundy accompanied us at my invitation, but though I suspected that he was bursting with curiosity as to the object of my mysterious journey, he made no reference to it, nor did I or Anstey.

At the barrier at Charing Cross we found Thorndyke awaiting us, and Anstey, having delivered me into his custody and seen us into a taxi-cab that had already been chartered, wished us success and took his leave. Then the driver, who apparently had his instructions, started and moved out of the station.

"I don't know," said I, "whether I may now ask what I am wanted for."

"I should rather not go into particulars," he replied. "I want your opinion on something that I am going to show you, and I especially want it to be an impromptu opinion. Previous consideration might create a bias which would detract from the conclusiveness of your decision. However, you have only a few minutes to wait."

In those few minutes I could not refrain from cudgelling my brains, even at the risk of creating a bias, and was still doing so – quite unproductively – when the cab approached the hospital of St. Barnabas and gave me a hint. But it swept past the main, entrance and, turning up a side street, slowed down and stopped opposite the entrance of the medical school. Here we got out and, leaving the cab waiting, entered the hall, where Thorndyke inquired for a person of the name of Farrow. In a minute or two this individual made his appearance in the form of a somewhat frowsy, elderly man, whom, from the multitude of warts on his hands, I inferred to be the *post mortem* porter or dissecting-room attendant. He appeared to be a taciturn man, and he, too, evidently had his instructions, for he merely looked at us and then walked away slowly, leaving us to follow. Thus silently he conducted us down a long corridor, across a quadrangle beyond which rose the conical roof of a theatre, along a curved passage which followed the wall of the circular building, and down a flight of stone steps which let into a dim, cement-floored basement, lighted by sparse electric bulbs and pervaded by a faint, distinctive odour that memory associated with the science of anatomy. From the main basement room Farrow turned into a short passage, where he stopped at a door and, having unlocked it, threw it open and switched on the light, when we entered and I looked around. It was a large, cellar-like room, lighted by a single powerful electric bulb fitted with a basin-like metal reflector and attached to a long, movable arm. The activities usually carried on in it were evident from the great tins of red lead on the shelves, from a large brass syringe fitted with a stop-cock and smeared with red paint, and from a range of oblong slate tanks or coffers furnished with massive wooden lids.

200

Still without uttering a word, the taciturn Farrow swung the powerful lamp over one of the coffers, and then drew off the lid. I stepped forward and looked in. The coffer was occupied by the body of a man, evidently – from the shaven head and the traces of red paint – prepared as an anatomical "subject." I looked at it curiously, thinking how unhuman, how artificial it seemed, how like to a somewhat dingy waxwork figure. But as I looked I was dimly conscious of some sense of familiarity stealing into my mind. Some chord of memory seemed to be touched. I stooped and looked more closely, and then, suddenly, I started up.

"Good God!" I exclaimed. "It is Nicholas Frood!"

"Are you sure?" asked Thorndyke.

"Yes, quite," I answered. "It was the shaved head that put me off – the absence of that mop of hair. I have no doubt at all. Still – let us have a look at the hands."

Farrow lifted up the hands one after the other, and then, if there could have been any doubt, it was set at rest. The mahogany-coloured stain was still visible, but much more conclusive were the bulbous finger-tips and the misshapen, nutshell-like nails. There could be no possible doubt.

"This is certainly the man I saw at Rochester," said I. "I am fully prepared to swear to that. But oughtn't he to have been identified by somebody who knew him better?"

"The body has been identified this afternoon by his late landlady," replied Thorndyke, "but I wanted your confirmation, and I wanted you as a witness at the inquest. The identification is important in relation to the inquiry and the possible verdict."

"Yes, by Jove!" I agreed, with a vivid recollection of the questions put to Mrs. Gillow. "This will come as a thunder-bolt to the jury. But how, in the name of Fortune, did he come here?"

"I'll tell you about that presently," replied Thorndyke.

He tendered a fee to the exhibitor, and when the latter had replaced the lid of the coffer, he conducted us back to our starting-point, and saw us into the waiting cab.

"5A, King's Bench Walk," Thorndyke instructed the driver, and as the cab started, he began his explanation.

"This has been a long and weary search, with a stroke of unexpected good luck at the end. We have had to go through endless records of hospitals, police-courts, poorhouses, infirmaries, and inquests. It was the records of an inquest that put us at last on the track, an inquest on an unknown man, supposed to be a tramp. Roughly, the history of the affair is this:

201

"Frood seems to have started for Brighton on the 25th of April, but for some unexplained reason, he broke his journey and got out at Horwell. What happened to him there is not clear. He may have over-dosed himself with cocaine, but at any rate, he was found dead in a meadow, close to a hedge, on the morning of the 26th. He was therefore dead before his wife disappeared. The body was taken to the mortuary and there carefully examined. But there was not the faintest clue to his identity. His pockets were searched, but there was not a vestige of property of any kind about him, not even the knife of which you have spoken. The probability is that he had been robbed by some tramp of everything that he had about him, either while he was insensible or after he was dead. In any case he appeared to be completely destitute, and this fact, together with his decidedly dirty and neglected condition, led naturally to the conclusion that he was a tramp. An inquest was held, but of course, no expensive and troublesome measures were taken to trace his identity. Examinations showed that he had not died from the effects of violence, so it was assumed that he had died from exposure, and a verdict to that effect was returned. He was about to be given a pauper's funeral when Providence intervened on our behalf. It happened that the Demonstrator of Anatomy at St. Barnabas resides at Horwell, and it happened that the presence of an unclaimed body in the mortuary came to his knowledge. Thereupon he applied to the authorities, on behalf of his school, for the use of it as an anatomical subject. His application was granted and the body was conveyed to St. Barnabas, where it was at once embalmed and prepared and then put aside for use during the next winter session."

"Was that quite in order – legally, I mean?"

"That is not for us to ask," he replied. "It was not in any way contrary to public policy, and it has been our salvation in respect of our particular inquiry."

"I suppose it has," I said, not, however, quite seeing it in that light. "Of course, it disposes of the question of his guilt."

"It does a good deal more than that as matters have turned out," said he. "However, here we are in the precincts of The Temple. Let us dismiss Nicholas Frood from our minds for the time being, and turn our attention to the more attractive subject of dinner."

The cab stopped opposite a tall house with a fine carved-brick portico and, when Thorndyke had paid the driver, we ascended the steps and made our way up a couple of flights of oaken stairs to the first floor. Here, at the door of my friend's chambers, we encountered a small, clerical-looking gentleman with an extremely wrinkly, smiling face, who reminded me somewhat of Mr. Japp. "This is Mr. Polton, Strangeways," said Thorndyke, presenting him to me, "who relieves me of all the physical labour of laboratory work. He is a specialist in everything, including cookery, and if my nose does not mislead me – ha! Does it, Polton?"

"That depends, sir, on which way you follow it," replied Polton, with a smile of labyrinthine wrinkliness. "But you will want to wash, and Dr. Strangeways's room is ready for him."

On this hint, Thorndyke conducted me to an upper floor, and to a pleasant bedroom with an outlook on plane trees and ancient, red-tiled roofs, where I washed and brushed up, and from whence I presently descended to the sitting-room, whither Thorndyke's nose had already led him – and to good purpose, too.

"Mr. Polton has missed his vocation," I remarked, as I attacked his productions with appreciative gusto. "He ought to have been the manager of a West End club or a high-class restaurant."

Thorndyke regarded me severely. "I am shocked at you, Strangeways," he said. "Do you suggest that a man who can make anything from an astronomical clock to a microscope objective, who is an expert in every branch of photographic technique, a fair analytical chemist, a microscopist, and general handicraftsman, should be degraded to the office of a mere superintendent cook? It is a dreadful thought!"

"I didn't understand that he was a man of so many talents and accomplishments," I said apologetically.

"He is a most remarkable man," said Thorndyke, "and I take it as a great condescension that he is willing to prepare my meals. It is his own choice – an expression of personal devotion. He doesn't like me to take my food at restaurants or clubs. And, of course, he does it well because he is incapable of doing anything otherwise than well. You must come up and see the laboratories and workshop after dinner."

We went up when we had finished our meal and discovered Polton in the act of cutting transverse sections of hairs and mounting them to add to the great collection of microscopic objects that Thorndyke had accumulated. He left this occupation to show me the great standing camera for copying, enlarging, reducing, and microphotography, to demonstrate the capabilities of a fine back-geared lathe, and to exhibit the elaborate outfit for analysis and assay work.

"I had no idea," said I, as we returned to the sitting room, "that medico-legal practice involved the use of all these complicated appliances."

"The truth is," Thorndyke replied, "that Medical Jurisprudence is not a single subject, concerned with one order of knowledge. It represents the application of every kind of knowledge to the solution of an infinite variety of legal problems. And that reminds me that I haven't yet looked through Anstey's abstract of the evidence at the inquest, which I saw that he had left for me. Shall we go through it now? It won't take us very long. Then we can have a stroll round The Temple or on the Embankment before we turn in."

"You are coming down to Rochester to-morrow?" I asked.

"Yes," he replied. "The facts concerning Nicholas Frood will have to be communicated to the coroner, and it is possible that some other points may arise."

"Now that Frood is definitely out of the picture," said I, "do you see any possibility of solving the mystery of this crime? I mean as to the identity of the guilty parties?"

He reflected awhile. "I am inclined to think," he replied, at length, "that I may be able to offer a suggestion. But, of course, I have not yet seen the remains."

"There isn't much to be gleaned from them, I am afraid," said I.

"Perhaps not," he answered. "But we shall be able to judge better when we have read the evidence of the medical witness."

"He wasn't able to offer any opinion as to the cause of death," I said.

"Then," he replied, "we may take it that there are no obvious signs. However, it is useless to speculate. We must suspend our judgment until to-morrow." And with this he opened Anstey's summary and read through it rapidly, asking me a question now and again to amplify some point. When he had finished the abstract – which appeared to be very brief and condensed – he put it in his pocket and suggested that we should start for our proposed walk and, though I made one or two attempts to reopen the subject of the inquiry, he was not to be drawn into any further statements. Apparently there was some point that he hoped to clear up by personal observation, and meanwhile he held his judgment in suspense.

Chapter XVII
Thorndyke Puts Down
His Piece

The journey down to Rochester would have been more agreeable and interesting under different circumstances. Thorndyke kept up a flow of lively conversation to which I should ordinarily have listened with the keenest pleasure. But he persistently avoided any reference to the object of our journey, and as this was the subject that engrossed my thoughts and from which I was unable to detach them, his conversational efforts were expended on somewhat inattentive ears. In common politeness I tried to make a show of listening and even of some sort of response, but the instant a pause occurred, my thoughts flew back to the engrossing subject and the round of fruitless speculation begun again.

What was it that Thorndyke had in his mind? He was not making this journey to inform the coroner of Frood's death. That could have been done by letter, and moreover, I was the actual witness to the dead man's identity. There was some point that he expected to be able to elucidate, some evidence that had been overlooked. And that evidence seemed to be connected with that dreadful, pitiful thing that lay in the coffin – crying out, indeed, to Heaven for retribution, but crying in a voice all inarticulate. But would it be inarticulate to him? He had seemed to imply an expectation of being able to infer from the appearance of those mouldering bones the cause and manner of death, and even – so it had appeared to me – the very identity of the murderer. But how could this be possible? Dr. Baines had said that the bones showed no signs of injury. The soft structures of the body had disappeared utterly. What suggestion as to the cause of death could the bones offer? Chronic mineral poisoning might be ascertainable from examination of the skeleton, but not from a mere ocular inspection, and the question of chronic poisoning did not arise. Angelina was alive on the Saturday evening, before the Monday morning her body was in the wall. Again and again I dismissed the problem as an impenetrable mystery, and still it presented itself afresh for consideration.

A few words of explanation to the constable on duty at the mortuary secured our admission – or, rather Thorndyke's, for I did not go in, but stood in the doorway, watching him inquisitively. He looked over the objects set out on the tray and seemed to be mentally checking them. Then he put on a pair of pince-nez and examined some of them more closely. From the tray he presently turned to the coffin and, lifting off the lid, stood for a while, with his pince-nez in his hand, looking intently at the awful relics of the dead woman. From his face I could gather nothing. It was at all times a rather immobile face, in accordance with his calm, even temperament. Now it expressed nothing but interest and close attention. He inspected the whole skeleton methodically, as I could see by the way his eyes travelled slowly from the head to the foot of the coffin. Then, once more, he put on his reading-glasses and stooped to examine more I closely something in the upper part of the coffin – I judged it to be the skull. At length he stood up, put away his glasses, replaced the coffin-lid, and rejoined me.

"Has the sitting of the Court begun yet?" he asked the constable.

"They began about five minutes ago, sir," was the reply, on which we made our way to the court-room, where Thorndyke, having secured a place at the table, beckoned to the coroner's officer.

"Will you hand that to the coroner, please?" said he, producing from his pocket a note in an official-looking blue envelope. The officer took the note and laid it down before the coroner, who glanced at it and nodded and then looked with sudden interest at Thorndyke. The witness who was being examined at the moment was the pawnbroker's daughter, and her account of the mysterious man with the mole on his nose was engaging the attention of the jury. While the examination was proceeding, the coroner glanced from time to time at the note. Presently he took it up and opened the envelope, and in a pause in the evidence, took out the note and turned it over to look at the signature. Then he ran his eyes over the contents, and I saw his eyebrows go up. But at that moment one of the jurymen asked a question and the note was laid down while the answer was entered in the depositions. At length the evidence of this witness was completed, and the witness dismissed, when the coroner took up the note and read it through carefully.

"Before we take the evidence of Israel Bangs, gentlemen," said he, "we had better consider some new facts which I think you will regard as highly important. I have just received a communication from Dr. John Thorndyke, who is a very eminent authority on medico-legal evidence. He informs me that the husband of the deceased, Nicholas Frood, is dead. It appears that he died about three months ago, but his body was not identified until yesterday, when it was seen by Frood's landlady and by Dr. Strangeways, who is here and can give evidence as to the identity. I propose that we first recall Dr. Strangeways and then ask Dr. Thorndyke, who is also present, to give us the further particulars."

The jury agreed warmly to the suggestion, and I was at once recalled, and as I took my place at the coroner's left hand I felt that I was fully justifying Cobbledick's description of me as the "star witness," for not only was I the object of eager interest on the part of the jury and the sergeant himself, but also of Bundy, whose eyes were riveted on me with devouring curiosity.

There is no need for me to repeat my evidence. It was quite short. I just briefly described the body and its situation. As to how it came to the hospital, I had no personal knowledge, but I affirmed that it was undoubtedly the body of Nicholas Frood. Of that I was quite certain.

No questions were asked. There was a good deal of whispered comment, and one indiscreet juryman remarked audibly that "this fellow seemed to have cheated the hangman." Then the coroner deferentially requested Thorndyke to give the Court any information that was available, and my friend advanced to the head of the table, where the coroner's officer placed a chair for him, and took the oath.

"What a perfectly awful thing this is about poor old Nicholas!" whispered Bundy, who had crept into the chair that Thorndyke had just vacated. "It makes one's flesh creep to think of it."

"It was rather horrible," I agreed, noting that my description of the scene had evidently made his flesh creep, for he was as pale as a ghost. But there was no time to discuss the matter further, for Thorndyke, having been sworn, and started by a general question from the coroner, now began to give his evidence, in the form of a narrative similar to that which I had heard from him, and accompanied by the production of documents relating to the inquest and the transfer of the body of the unknown deceased to the medical school.

"There is no doubt, I suppose, as to the date of this man's death?" the coroner asked.

"Practically none. He was seen alive on the 25th of April, and he was found dead on the morning of the 26th. I have put in a copy of the depositions at the inquest, which give the date and time of the finding of the body."

"Then, as his death occurred before the disappearance of his wife, this inquiry is not concerned with him any further."

Here the foreman of the jury interposed with a question. "It seems that Dr. Thorndyke took a great deal of trouble to trace this man, Frood. Was he acting for the police?"

"I don't know that that is strictly our concern," said the coroner, looking at Thorndyke, nevertheless, with a somewhat inquiring expression.

"I was acting," said Thorndyke, "in pursuance of instructions from a private client to investigate the circumstances of Mrs. Frood's disappearance, to ascertain whether a crime had been committed and, if so, to endeavour to find the guilty party or parties."

"He never told us that," murmured Bundy, "at least – did you know, John?"

"I did, as a matter of fact, but I was sworn to secrecy." Bundy looked at me a little reproachfully, I thought, and I caught a queer glance from Cobbledick. But just then the coroner spoke again.

"Have you seen the evidence that was given yesterday?"

"Yes, I have a summary of it, which I have read."

"Can you, from your investigations, tell us anything that was not disclosed by that evidence?"

"Yes. I have just examined the remains of the deceased and the articles which have been found from time to time. I think I can give some additional information concerning them."

"From your examination of the remains," the coroner said somewhat eagerly, "can you give any opinion as to the cause of death?"

"No," replied Thorndyke. "My examination had reference chiefly to the identity of the remains."

The coroner looked disappointed. "The identity of the remains," said he, "is not in question. They have been clearly identified as those of Angelina Frood."

"Then," said Thorndyke, "they have been wrongly identified. I can swear positively that they are not the remains of Angelina Frood."

At this statement a sudden hush fell on the Court, broken incongruously by an audible whistle from Sergeant Cobbledick. On me the declaration fell like a thunderbolt and, on looking round at Bundy, I could see that he was petrified with astonishment. There was a silence of some seconds' duration. Then the coroner said, with a distinctly puzzled air, "This is a very remarkable statement, Dr. Thorndyke. It seems to be quite at variance with all the facts – and it appears almost incredible that you should be able to speak with such certainty, having regard to the condition of the remains and in spite of the extraordinary effect of the lime."

"It is on account of the effect of the lime that I am able to speak with so much certainty and confidence," Thorndyke replied.

"I don't quite follow that," said the coroner. "Would you kindly tell us how you were able to determine that these remains are not those of Angelina Frood?"

"It is a matter of simple inference," replied Thorndyke. "On the 26th of April last, Mrs. Frood is known to have been alive. It has been assumed that on that night or the next her body was built up in the wall.

208

If that had really happened, when the wall was opened on the 20th of July, the body would have been found intact and perfectly recognizable!"

"You are not overlooking the circumstance that it was buried in a bed of quick-lime?" said the coroner.

"No," replied Thorndyke, "in fact that is the circumstance that makes it quite certain that these remains are not those of Angelina Frood. There is," he continued, "a widely prevalent belief that quick-lime has the property of completely consuming and destroying organic substances such as a dead human body. But that belief is quite erroneous. Quick-lime has no such properties. On the contrary, it has a strongly preservative effect on organic matter. Putrefaction is a change in organic matter which occurs only when that matter is more or less moist. If such matter is completely dried, putrefaction is prevented or arrested, and such dried, or mummified, matter will remain undecomposed almost indefinitely, as we see in the case of Egyptian mummies. But quick-lime has the property of abstracting the water from organic substances with which it is in contact, of rendering them completely dry. It thus acts as a very efficient preservative. If Mrs. Frood's body had been buried, when recently dead, three months ago in fresh quick-lime, it would by now have been reduced more or less to the condition of a mummy. It would not have been even partially destroyed, and it would have been easily recognizable."

To this statement everyone present listened with profound attention and equally profound surprise, and a glance at the faces of the jurymen was sufficient to show that it had failed utterly to produce conviction. Even the coroner was evidently not satisfied and, after a few moments' reflection with knitted brows, he stated his objection.

"The belief in the destructive properties of lime," he said, "can hardly be accepted as a mere popular error. In the Crippen trial, you may remember that the question was raised, and one of the expert witnesses – no less an authority than Professor Pepper – gave it as his considered opinion that quick-lime has these destructive properties, and that if a body were buried in a sufficient quantity of quick-lime, that body would be entirely destroyed. You will agree, I think, that great weight attaches to the opinion of a man of Professor Pepper's great reputation."

"Undoubtedly," Thorndyke agreed. "He was one of our greatest medico-legal authorities, though, on this subject, I think, his views differed from those generally held by medical jurists. But the point is that this was an opinion, and that no undeniable facts were then available. But since that time, the matter has been put to the test of actual experiment, and the results of those experiments are definite facts. It is no longer a matter of opinion but one of incontestable fact."

"What are the experiments that you refer to'"

"The first practical investigation was carried out by Mr. A. Lucas, the Director of the Government Analytical Laboratory and Assay Office at Cairo. He felt that the question was one of great medico-legal importance, and that it ought to be settled definitely. He accordingly carried out a number of experiments, of which he published the particulars in his treatise on *Forensic Chemistry*. I produce a copy of this book, with your permission."

"Is this evidence admissible?" the foreman asked. "The witness can't swear to another man's experiments."

"It is admissible in a coroner's court," was the reply. "We are not bound as rigidly by the rules of evidence as a criminal court, for instance. It is relevant to the inquiry, and I think we had better hear it."

"I may say," said Thorndyke, "that I have repeated and confirmed these experiments, but I suggest that, as the published cases are the recognized authority, I be allowed to quote them before describing my confirmatory experiments."

The coroner having agreed to this course, he continued, "The tests were made with the fresh bodies of young pigeons, which were plucked but not opened, and which were buried in boxes with loosely-fitted covers, filled respectively with dry earth, slaked lime, chlorinated lime, quick-lime, and quick-lime suddenly slaked with water. These bodies were left thus buried for six months, the boxes being placed on the laboratory roof at Cairo. At the end of that period the bodies were disinterred and examined with the following results: The body which had been buried in dry earth was found to be in a very bad condition. There was a considerable smell of putrefaction and a large part of the flesh had disappeared. The body which had been buried in quick-lime was found to be in good condition. It was dry and hard, the skin was unbroken, but the body was naturally shrunken. The other three bodies do not concern us, but I may say that none of them was as completely preserved as the one that was buried in quick-lime.

"On reading the account of these experiments I decided to repeat them, partly for confirmation and partly to enable me to give direct evidence as to the effect of lime on dead bodies. I used freshly-killed rabbits from which the fur was removed by shaving, and buried them in roomy boxes in the same materials as were used in the published experiments. They were left undisturbed during the six summer months, and were then exhumed and examined. The rabbit which had been buried in dry earth was in an advanced stage of putrefaction, the one which had been buried in quick-lime was free from any odour of decomposition, the skin was intact, and the body unaltered excepting that it was dry and rather shrivelled – mummified, in fact. It was more completely preserved than any of the others."

The conclusion of this statement was followed by a slightly uncomfortable silence. The coroner stroked his chin reflectively, and the jurymen looked at one another with obvious doubt and distrust. At length Mr. Pilley gave voice to the collective sentiments.

"It's all very well, sir, for this learned gentleman to explain to us that the lime couldn't have eaten up the body of the deceased. But it has. We've seen the bare bones with our own eyes. What's the use of saying a thing is impossible when it has happened?"

Here Thorndyke produced from his pocket a sheet of notepaper and a fountain pen, and began to write rapidly, noting down, as I supposed, the jurymen's objections, which, however, the coroner proceeded to answer.

"Dr. Thorndyke's statement was that these bones are not the bones of Angelina Frood. That the body was not her body."

"Still," said the foreman, "it was somebody's body, you know. And the lime seems to have eaten it up pretty clean, possible or impossible."

"Exactly," said the coroner. "The destruction of this particular body appears to be an undeniable fact, and we may assume that one body is very much like another – in a chemical sense, at least. What do you say, doctor?"

"My statement," replied Thorndyke, "had reference to Angelina Frood, who is known to have been alive on a certain date. Of the condition of the unknown body that was buried in the wall, I can give no opinion."

Again there was an uncomfortable silence, during which Thorndyke, having finished writing, folded the sheet of notepaper, tucked the end in securely, and wrote an address on the back. Then he handed it to his neighbour, who passed it on until it reached me. I was on the point of opening it when I observed with astonishment that it was addressed to Peter Bundy, Esq., to whom I immediately handed it. But my astonishment was nothing to Bundy's. He seemed positively thunderstruck. Indeed, his aspect was so extraordinary as he sat gazing wildly at the opened note, that I forgot my manners and frankly stared at him. First he turned scarlet, then he grew deathly pale, and then he turned scarlet again. And, for the first and only time in my life, I saw him look really angry. But this was only a passing manifestation. For a few moments his eyes flashed and his mouth set hard. Then, quite suddenly, the wrath faded from his face and gave place to a whimsical smile. He tore off the fly-leaf of the note and, scribbling a few words on it, folded it up small, addressed it to Dr. Thorndyke, and handed it to me for transmission by the return route.

When it reached Thorndyke, he opened it and, having read the brief message, nodded gravely to Bundy, and once more turned his attention to the foreman, who was addressing the coroner at greater length.

"The jury wish to say, sir, that this evidence is not satisfactory. It can't be reconciled with the other evidence. The facts before the jury are these: On the 26th of April Angelina Frood disappeared, and was never afterwards seen alive. On the night that she disappeared, or on the next night, a dead body was buried in the wall. Three months later that body was found in the wall, packed in quick-lime, and eaten away to a skeleton. That skeleton has been examined by an expert, and found to be that of a woman of similar size and age to Angelina Frood. With that skeleton were found articles of clothing, jewellery, and ornaments which have been proved to have been the clothing and property of Angelina Frood. Other articles of clothing have been recovered from the river, and those articles were missing from the body when it was found in the wall. On these facts, the jury feel that it is impossible to doubt that the remains found in the wall are the remains of Angelina Frood."

As the foreman concluded the coroner turned to Thorndyke with a slightly puzzled smile. "Of course, Doctor," said he, "you have considered those facts that the foreman has summarized so admirably. What do you say to his conclusion?"

"I must still contest it," replied Thorndyke. "The foreman's summary of the evidence, masterly as it was, furnishes no answer to the objection – based on established chemical facts – that the condition of the remains when found is irreconcilable with the alleged circumstances of the burial."

The coroner raised his eyebrows and pursed up his lips.

"I appreciate your point, Doctor," said he. "But we are on the horns of a dilemma. We are between the Devil of observed fact and the Deep Sea of scientific demonstration. Can you suggest any way out of the difficulty?"

"I think," said Thorndyke, "that if you were to call Mr. Bundy, he might be able to help you out of your dilemma."

"Mr. Bundy!" exclaimed the coroner. "I didn't know he was concerned in the case. Can you give us any information, Mr. Bundy?"

"Yes," replied Bundy, looking somewhat shy and nervous. "I think I could throw a little light on the case."

"I wish to goodness you had said so before. However, better late than never. We will take your evidence at once."

On this Thorndyke returned to his seat at the table and Bundy took his place, standing by the chair which Thorndyke had resigned.

"Let me see, Mr. Bundy," said the coroner, "your Christian name is — "

"The witness has not been sworn," interrupted Thorndyke.

The coroner smiled. "We are in the hands of the regular practitioners," he chuckled. "We must mind our *P*'s and *Q*'s. Still you are quite right, Doctor. The name is part of the evidence."

The witness was accordingly sworn, and the coroner then proceeded, smilingly, "Now, Mr. Bundy, be very careful. You are making a sworn statement, remember. What is your Christian name?"

"Angelina," was the astounding reply.

"Angelina!" bawled Pilley. "It can't be. Why, it's a woman's name."

"We must presume that the witness knows his own name," said the coroner, writing it down. "Angelina Bundy."

"No, sir," said the witness. "Angelina Frood."

The coroner suddenly stiffened with the upraised pen poised in the air, and so everyone in the room, including myself, underwent an instantaneous arrest of movement as if we had been turned into stone, and I noticed that the process of petrifaction had caught us all with our mouths open. But whereas the fixed faces on which I looked, expressed amazement qualified by incredulity, my own astonishment was coupled with conviction. Astounding as the statement was, the moment that it was made I knew that it was true. In spite of the discrepancies of appearance, I realized in a flash of enlightenment, the nature of that subtle influence that had drawn me to Bundy with a tenderness hardly congruous with mere male friendship. Outwardly I had been deceived, but my sub-conscious self had recognized Angelina all the time.

The interval of breathless silence, during which the witness calmly surveyed the court through his – or rather her – eyeglass, was at length broken by the coroner, who asked gravely, "This is not a joke? You affirm seriously that you are Angelina Frood?"

"Yes, I am Angelina Frood," was the reply.

Here Mr. Pilley recovered himself and demanded excitedly, "Do we understand this gentleman to say that he is the deceased?"

"Well," replied the coroner, "he is obviously not deceased, and he states that he is not a gentleman. He has declared that he is a lady."

"But," protested Pilley, "he says that she – at least she says that he – "

"You are getting mixed, Pilley," interrupted the foreman. "This appears to be a woman masquerading as a man and playing practical

213

jokes on a coroner's jury. I suggest, sir, that we ought to have evidence of identity."

"I agree with you, emphatically," said the coroner.

"The identification is indispensable. Is there anyone present who can swear to the identity of this – *er* – person! Mr. Japp, for instance?"

"I'd rather you didn't bring Mr. Japp into it," said Angelina, hastily. "It isn't really necessary. If you will allow me to run home and change my clothes, Mrs. Gillow and Dr. Strangeways will be able to identify me. And I can bring some photographs to show the jury."

"That seems quite a good suggestion," said the coroner. "Don't you think so, gentlemen?"

"It is a very proper suggestion," said the foreman, severely. "Let her go away and clothe herself decently. How long will she be gone?"

"I shall be back in less than half-an-hour," said Angelina, and on this understanding she was given permission to retire. I watched her with a tumult of mixed emotions as she took up her hat, gloves, and stick, and strolled jauntily towards the door. There she paused for an instant and shot at me a single, swift, whimsical glance through her monocle. Then she went out, and with her disappeared forever the familiar figure of Peter Bundy.

Chapter XVIII
The Uncontrite Penitent

As the door closed on Angelina, a buzz of excited talk broke out. The astonished jurymen put their heads together and eagerly discussed the new turn of events, while the coroner sat with a deeply cogitative expression, evidently thinking hard and casting an occasional speculative glance in Thorndyke's direction. Meanwhile Cobbledick edged up to my side and presented his views in a soft undertone.

"This is a facer, Doctor, isn't it? Regular do. My word! Just think of the artfulness of that young woman, toting us round and helping us to find the things that she had just popped down for us to find. I call it a masterpiece." He chuckled admiringly, and added in a lower tone, "I hope she hasn't got herself into any kind of mess."

I looked at Cobbledick with renewed appreciation. I had always liked the sergeant. He was a capable man and a kindly one, and now he was showing a largeness of soul that won my respect and my gratitude, too. A small man would have been furious with Angelina, but Cobbledick took her performances in a proper sporting spirit. He was only amused and admiring. Not for nothing had Nature imprinted on his face that benevolent smile.

Presently Mr. Pilley, who seemed to have a special gift for the expression of erroneous opinions, addressed himself to the coroner.

"Well, Mr. Chairman," he said cheerfully, "I suppose we can consider the inquest practically over."

"Over!" exclaimed the astonished coroner.

"Yes. We were inquiring into the death of Angelina Frood. But if Mrs. Frood is alive after all, why, there's an end to the matter."

"What about the body in the mortuary?" demanded the foreman.

"Oh, ah," said Pilley. "I had forgotten about that." He looked owlishly at the coroner and then exclaimed, "But that is the body of Mrs. Frood!"

"It can't be if Mrs. Frood is alive," the coroner reminded him.

"But it must be," persisted Pilley. "It has been identified as her, and it had her clothes and ring on. Mr. Bundy must have been pulling our legs."

"There is certainly something very mysterious about that body," said the coroner. "It was dressed in Mrs. Frood's clothes, as Mr. Pilley points out, and it appears that Mrs. Frood must be in some way connected with it."

"There's no doubt about that," agreed the foreman.

"She must know who that dead person is and how the body came to be in the place where it was found, and she will have to give an account of it."

"Yes," said the coroner. "But it is a mysterious affair. I wonder if Dr. Thorndyke could enlighten us. He seems to know more about the matter than anybody else."

But Thorndyke was not to be drawn into any statement.

"It would be merely a conjecture on my part," he said. "Presumably Mrs. Frood knows how the remains got into the wall, and I must leave her to give the necessary explanations."

"I don't see what explanations she can give," said the foreman. "It looks like a clear case of wilful murder. And it is against her."

To this view the coroner gave a guarded assent, and indeed it was the obvious view. There was the body, in Angelina's clothing, and everything pointed clearly to Angelina's complicity in the crime, if there had really been a crime committed. And what other explanation was possible?

As I reflected on the foreman's ominous words, I was sensible of a growing alarm. What if Angelina had been, as it were, snatched from the grave only to be placed in the dock on a charge of murder? That she could possibly be guilty of a crime did not enter my mind. But there was evidently some sort of criminal entanglement from which she might find it hard to escape. The appearances were sinister in the extreme, her simulated disappearance, her disguise, her suspicious silence during the inquiry, to any eye but mine they were conclusive evidence of her guilt. And the more I thought about it, the more deadly did the sum of that evidence appear, until, as the time ran on, I became positively sick with terror.

The opening of a door and a sudden murmur of surprise caused me to turn, and there was Angelina herself. But not quite the Angelina that I remembered. Gone were the pallid complexion, the weary, dark-circled eyes, the down-cast mouth, the sad and pensive countenance, the dark, strong eye-brows. Rosy-cheeked, smiling, confident, and looking strangely tall and imposing, she stepped composedly over to the head of the table, and stood there gazing with calm self-possession, and the trace of a smile at the stupefied jurymen.

"Your name is – ?" said the coroner, gazing at her in astonishment.

"Angelina Frood," was the quiet reply, and the voice was Bundy's voice.

216

Here Pilley rose, bubbling with excitement. "This isn't the same person!" he exclaimed. "Why, he was a little man, and she's a tall woman. And his hair was short, and just look at hers! You can't grow a head of hair like that in twenty minutes."

"No," Angelina agreed, suavely. "I wish you could."

"The objection is not relevant, Mr. Pilley," said the coroner, suppressing a smile. "We are not concerned with the identity of Mr. Bundy but with that of Angelina Frood. Can anyone identify this lady?"

"I can," said I. "I swear that she is Angelina Frood."

"And Mrs. Gillow?"

Mrs. Gillow could and did identify her late lodger, and furthermore, burst into tears and filled the court-room with "yoops" of hysterical joy. When she had been pacified and gently restrained by the coroner's officer from an attempt to embrace the witness, the coroner proceeded.

"Now, Mrs. Frood, the jury require certain explanations from you, in regard to the body of a woman which is at present lying in the mortuary and which was found buried in the city wall with certain articles of clothing and jewellery which have been identified as your property. Did you know that that body had been buried in the wall?"

"Yes," replied Angelina.

"Do you know how it came to be in the wall?"

"Yes. I put it there."

"*You* put it there!" roared Pilley, amidst a chorus of exclamations from the jurymen. The coroner held up his hand to enjoin silence and asked, as he gazed in astonishment at Angelina.

"Can you tell us who this deceased person was?"

"I'm afraid I can't," Angelina replied, apologetically. "I don't think her name was known."

"But – er – " the astounded coroner inquired, "how did she come by her death?"

"I'm afraid I can't tell you that either," replied Angelina. "The fact is, I never asked."

"You never asked!" the coroner repeated, in a tone of bewilderment. "But – er – are we to understand that in short, did you or did you not cause the death of this person by your own act? Of course," he added hastily, "you are not bound to answer that question."

Angelina smiled at him engagingly. "I will answer with pleasure. I did not cause the death of this person."

"Then are we to understand that she was already dead when you found her?"

217

"I didn't find her. I bought her, at a shop in Great St. Andrew Street. I gave four pounds, fourteen-and-three-pence for her, including two-and-three-pence to Carter Paterson's. I've brought the bill with me."

She produced the bill from her pocket and handed it to the coroner, who read it with a portentous frown and a perceptible twitching at the corners of his mouth.

"I will read this document to you, gentlemen," he said in a slightly unsteady voice. "It is dated the 19th of April, and reads, '*Bought of Oscar Hammerstein, Dealer in Human and Comparative Osteology, Great St. Andrew Street, London, W. C., one complete set superfine human osteology, disarticulated and unbleached (female), as selected by purchaser, four-pounds-eight-shillings-and-sixpence. Replacing and cementing missing teeth, one-shilling-and-sixpence. Packing case, two shillings. Carriage, two-and-three pence. Total, four pounds, fourteen-and-three-pence. Received with thanks, O. Hammerstein.*' Perhaps you would like to see the bill, yourselves, gentlemen."

He passed it to the foreman, taking a quick glance out of the corners of his eyes at the bland and impassive Angelina, and the jury studied it in a deep silence, which was broken only by a soft, gurgling sound, from somewhere behind me, which, I discovered, on looking round, to proceed from Sergeant Cobbledick, whose crimsoned face was partly hidden by a large handkerchief and whose shoulders moved convulsively.

Presently the coroner addressed Thorndyke. "In continuation of your evidence, Doctor, does Mrs. Frood's explanation agree with any conclusions that you had arrived at from your inspection of the remains?"

"It agrees with them completely," Thorndyke replied with a grim smile.

The coroner entered the answer in the depositions, and then turned once more to Angelina.

"With regard to the objects that were found with the skeleton, did you put them there?"

"Yes. I put in the metal things and a few pieces of scorched rag to give a realistic effect – on account of the lime, you know."

"And the articles that were recovered from the river, too, I suppose?"

"Yes, I put them down – with proper precautions, of course."

"What do you mean by proper precautions?"

"Well, I couldn't afford to waste any of the things, so I used to keep a lookout with a telescope, and then, when I saw a likely person coming along, I put one of the things down where it could be seen."

"And were they always seen?"

"No. Some people are very unobservant. In that case I picked it up when the coast was clear and saved it for another time."

The coroner chuckled. "It was all very ingenious and complete. But now, Mrs. Frood, we have to ask you what was the object of these extraordinary proceedings. It was not a joke, I presume?"

"Oh, not at all," replied Angelina. "It was a perfectly serious affair. You have heard what sort of husband I had. I couldn't possibly live with him. I made several attempts to get away and live by myself, but he always followed me and found me out. So I determined to disappear altogether."

"You could have applied for a separation," said the coroner.

"I shouldn't have got it," replied Angelina, "and even if I had, of what use would it have been? I should have been bound to him for life. I couldn't have married anyone else. My whole life would have been spoilt. So I decided to disappear completely and for good, and start life afresh in a new place and under a new name. And in order that there should be no mistake about it, I thought I would leave the – er – the material for a coroner's inquest and a will directing that a suitable monument should be put up over my grave. Then, if I had ever married again, there would have been no danger of a charge of bigamy. If anyone had made any such suggestion, I could have referred them to the registrar of deaths and to the tombstone of Angelina Frood in Rochester churchyard."

"And as to a birth certificate under your new name?" the coroner asked with a twinkle of his eye.

Angelina smiled a prim little smile. "I think that could have been managed," she said.

"Well," said the coroner, "it was an ingenious scheme. But apparently Dr. Thorndyke knew who Mr. Bundy was. How do you suppose he discovered your identity?"

"That is just what I should like to know," she replied.

"So should I," said the coroner, with a broad smile, "but, of course, it isn't my affair or that of the jury. We are concerned with this skeleton that you have planted on us. I suppose you can give us no idea as to where it came from originally?"

"The dealer said it had been found in a barrow – not a wheelbarrow, you know, an ancient burial-place. Of course, I don't know whether he was speaking the truth."

"What do you think, Dr. Thorndyke?" the coroner asked.

"I think it is an ancient skeleton, though very well preserved. Some of the teeth – the original ones – show more wear than one expects to find in a modern skull. But I only made a cursory inspection."

"I think the evidence is sufficient for our purpose," said the coroner, "and that really concludes the case, so we need not detain you any longer, Mrs. Frood. I don't know exactly what your legal position is, whether you have committed any legal offence. If you have, it is not our business, and I think I am expressing the sentiments of the jury if I say that I hope that the authorities will not make it their business. No one has been injured, and no action seems to be called for."

With these sentiments the jury concurred warmly, as also did Sergeant Cobbledick, who was heard, very audibly and regardless of the proprieties, to murmur "Hear, hear!" We waited to learn the nature of the verdict, and when this had been pronounced (to the effect that the skeleton was that of an unknown woman, concerning the circumstances of whose death no evidence was available), the court rose and we prepared to depart.

"You are coming back to lunch with us, Angelina?" said I.

"I should love to," she replied, "but there is Mr. Japp. Do you think you could ask him, too?"

"Of course," I replied, with a sudden perception of the advantage of even numbers. "We shouldn't be complete without him."

Japp accepted with enthusiasm and, after a hasty farewell to Cobbledick, we went forth into the High Street, by no means unobserved of the populace. As we approached the neighbourhood of the office Angelina said, "I must run into my rooms for a few moments just to tidy myself up a little. It was such a very hurried toilette. I won't be more than a few minutes. You needn't wait for me."

"I suggest," said Thorndyke, "that Mr. Japp and I go on and break the news to Mrs. Dunk that there is a lady guest, and that Strangeways remains behind to escort the prisoner."

I fell in readily with this admirable suggestion, and as the two men walked on, I followed Angelina up the steps and waited while she plied her latch-key. We entered the hall together and then went into the sitting-room, where she stood for a moment, looking round with deep satisfaction.

"It's nice to be home again," she said, "and to feel that all that fuss is over."

"I daresay it is," said I. "But now that you are home, what have you got to say for yourself? You are a nice little baggage, aren't you?"

"I am a little beast, John," she replied. "I've been a perfect pig to you. But I didn't mean to be, and I really couldn't help it. You'll try to forgive me, won't you?"

"The fact is, Angelina," I said, "I am afraid I am in love with you."

220

"Oh, I hope to goodness you are, John," she exclaimed. "If I thought you weren't I should wish myself a skeleton again. Do you think you really are?"

She crept closer to me with such a sweet, wheedlesome air that I suddenly caught her in my arms and kissed her.

"It does seem as if you were," she admitted with a roguish smile, and then − such unaccountable creatures are women − she laid her head on my shoulder and began to sob. But this was only a passing shower. Another kiss brought back the sunshine and then she tripped away to spread fresh entanglements for the masculine heart.

In a few minutes she returned, further adorned and looking to my eyes the very picture of womanly sweetness and grace. When I had given confirmatory evidence of my sentiments towards her, we went out, just in time to encounter Mrs. Gillow and acquaint her with the program.

"I suppose," said Angelina, glancing furtively at a little party of women who were glancing, not at all furtively, at her, "one should be gratified at the interest shown by one's fellow towns-people, but don't you think the back streets would be preferable to the High Street?"

"It is no use, my dear," I replied. "We've got to face it. Take no notice. Regard these bipeds that infest the footways as mere samples of the local fauna. Let them stare and ignore them. For my part, I rather like them. They impress on me the admirable bargain that I have made in swapping Peter Bundy for a beautiful lady."

"Poor Peter," she said, pensively. "He was a sad boy sometimes when he looked at his big, handsome John and thought that mere friendship was all that he could hope for when his poor little heart was starving for love. Your deal isn't the only successful one, John, so you needn't be so conceited. But here we are home − really home, this time, for this has been my real home, John, dear. And there − Oh! Moses I − there is Mrs. Dunk, waiting to receive us!"

"What used you to do to Mrs. Dunk," I asked, "to make her so furious?"

"I only used to inquire after her health," Angelina replied plaintively. "But mum's the word. She'll spot my voice as soon as I speak."

Mrs. Dunk held the door open ceremoniously and curtsied as we entered. She was a gruff old woman, but she had a deep respect for "gentlefolk", as is apt to be the way with old servants. Angelina acknowledged her salutation with a gracious smile and followed her meekly up the stairs to the room that Mrs. Dunk had allotted to her.

I found Thorndyke and Japp established in the library − Dr. Partridge had dispensed with a drawing-room and I followed his excellent example – and here presently Angelina joined us, sailing majestically into the room and marching up to Thorndyke with an air at once hostile and defiant.

"Serpent," said Angelina.

"Not at all," Thorndyke dissented with a smile. "You should be grateful to me for having rescued you from your own barbed-wire entanglements."

"Serpent, I repeat," persisted Angelina. "To let me sit in that court-room watching all the innocents walking into my trap one after another, and then, just as I thought they were all inside, to hand me a thing like that!" and she produced, dramatically, a small sheet of paper, which I recognized as the remainder of Thorndyke's note. I took it from her, and read, *"You see whither the evidence is leading. The deception cannot be maintained, nor is there any need, now that your husband is dead. Explanations must be given either by you or by me. For your own sake I urge you to explain everything and clear yourself. Let me know what you will do."*

"This is an extraordinary document," I said, passing it to Japp. "How in the name of Fortune did you know that Bundy was Angelina?"

"Yes, how did you?" the latter demanded. "It is for you to give an explanation now."

"We will have the explanations after lunch," said he. "Mutual explanations. I want to hear how far I was correct in details."

"Very well," agreed Angelina, "we will both explain. But you will have the first innings. You are not going to listen to my explanation and then say you knew all about it. And that reminds me, John, that you had better tell Mrs. Dunk. She is sure to recognize my voice."

I quite agreed with Angelina and hurried away to intercept Mrs. Dunk and let her know the position. She was at first decidedly shocked, but a vivid and detailed description of the late Mr. Frood produced a complete revulsion – so complete, in fact, as to lead me to speculate on the personal characteristics of the late Mr. Dunk. But her curiosity was aroused to such an extent that, while waiting at table, she hardly removed her eyes from Angelina, until the latter, finding the scrutiny unbearable, suddenly produced the hated eye-glass and, sticking it in her eye, directed a stern glance at the old woman, who instantly backed towards the door with a growl of alarm, and then sniggered hoarsely.

It was a festive occasion, for we were all in exuberant spirits, including Mr. Japp, who, if he said little, made up the deficiency in smiles of forty-wrinkle power, which, together with his upstanding tuft of white hair, made him look like a convivial cockatoo.

"Do you remember our last meeting at this table?" said Angelina, "when I jeered at the famous expert and pulled his reverend leg, thinking what a smart young fellow I was, and how beautifully I was bamboozling him? And all the while he knew! He knew! And '*Not a word said the hard-boiled egg.*' Oh, serpent! Serpent!"

Thorndyke chuckled. "You didn't leave the hardboiled egg much to say," he observed.

"No. But why were you so secret? Why didn't you let on, just a little, to give poor Bundy a hint as to where he was plunging?"

"My dear Mrs. Frood – "

"Oh, call me Angelina," she interrupted.

"Thank you," said he. "Well, my dear Angelina, you are forgetting that I didn't know what was in the wall."

"My goodness!" she exclaimed. "I had overlooked that. Of course, it might have been – Good gracious! How awful!" She paused with her eyes fixed on Thorndyke, and then asked, "Supposing it had been?"

"I refuse to suppose anything of the kind," he replied. "My explanations will deal with the actual, not with the hypothetical."

There was silence for a minute or two. Like Angelina, I was speculating on what Thorndyke would have done if the remains had been real remains – and those of a man. He had evidently sympathized warmly with the hunted wife, but if her defence had taken the form of a crime, would he have exposed her? It was useless to ask him. I have often thought about it since, but have never reached a conclusion.

"You will have to answer questions better than that presently," said Angelina, "but I won't ask you any more now. You shall finish your lunch in peace, and then – into the witness-box you go. I am going to have satisfaction for that note."

The little festival went on, unhurried, with an abundance of cheerful and rather frivolous talk. But at last, like all fugitive things, it came to an end. The table was cleared, and garnished with the port decanter and the coffee service, and Mrs. Dunk, with a final glower, half-defiant and half-admiring, at Angelina, took her departure.

"Now," said Angelina, as I poured out the coffee, "the time has come to talk of many things, but especially of expert investigations into the identity of Peter Bundy. Your lead, sir."

Chapter XIX
Explanations

"The investigation of this case," Thorndyke began, "falls naturally into two separate inquiries: That relating to the crime and that which is concerned with what we may conveniently call the personation. They make certain contacts, but they are best considered separately. Let us begin with the crime.

"Now, to a person having experience of real crime, there was, in this case, from the very beginning, something rather abnormal. A woman of good social position had disappeared. There was a suggestion that she had been murdered, and the murder had apparently been committed in some public place – that is to say, not in a house. But in such cases, normally, the first evidence of the crime is furnished by the discovery of the body. It is true that, in this case, there was a suggestion that the body had been flung into the river, and this, at first, masked the abnormality to some extent. But even then there was the discrepancy that the brooch, which was attached to the person, appeared to have been found on land, while the bag, which was not attached to the person, was picked up at the water's edge. The bag itself, and the box which had been in it, presented several inconsistencies.

"They had apparently been lying unnoticed for eleven days on a piece of shore that was crowded with small craft and frequently by numbers of seamen and labourers, and that formed a play-ground for the waterside children. The clean state of the box when found showed that it had neither been handled nor immersed, and as the wrapping-paper was intact, the person who had taken it out of the bag must have thrown it away without opening it to see what it contained. The bag was found under some light rubbish. That rubbish had not been thrown on it by the water, or the bag would have been soaked, and no one could have thrown the rubbish on it without seeing the bag, which was an article of some value. Again, the bag had not been carried to this place by the water, as was proved by its condition.

"Therefore, either this was the place where the crime had been committed, or someone had brought the bag to this place and thrown it away. But neither supposition was reasonably probable. It was inconceivable that a person like Mrs. Frood should have been in this remote, inaccessible, disreputable place at such an hour. The bag could not have been brought here by an innocent person, for no such person would have thrown it away. It was quite a valuable bag. And a guilty person would have thrown it in the river, and probably put a stone in it to sink it. So you see that these first clues were strikingly abnormal. They prepared one to consider the possibility of false tracks. Even the brooch incident had a faint suggestion of the same kind when considered with the other clues. The man who pawned the brooch had a mole on his nose. Such an adornment can be easily produced artificially. It is highly distinctive of the person who possesses it, and it is equally distinctive – negatively – of the person who does not possess it. Then there was the character of the person who had disappeared. She was a woman who was seeking to escape from her husband, and hitherto she had not succeeded because she had not hidden herself securely enough. She was a person of a somewhat disappearing tendency. She had an understandable motive for disappearing.

"From the very beginning, therefore, the possibility of voluntary disappearance had to be borne in mind. And when it was, each new clue seemed to support it. There was the scarf, for instance. It was found under a fish-trunk, an unlikely place for it to have got by chance, but an excellent one for a 'plant'. The scarf was not baldly exposed, but someone was sure to turn the trunk over and find it. And at this point another peculiarity began to develop. There was a noticeable tendency for the successive 'finds' to creep up the river from Chatham towards Rochester Bridge. It was not yet very remarkable, but I noticed it, as I entered each find on my map. The brooch was associated with Chatham, the bag and box with the Chatham shore a little farther up, the scarf with the Rochester shore at Blue Boar Head. As I say, it attracted my attention, and when the first shoe was found above Blue Boar Head, the second shoe farther up still, and the hat-pin yet farther up towards the bridge, it became impossible to ignore it. There was no natural explanation. Whether the body were floating or stationary, the constancy of direction was inexplicable, for the tide sweeps up and down twice daily, and objects detached from the body would be carried up or down stream, according to the direction of the tide when they became detached. This regular order was a most suspicious circumstance. Later, when the objects were found in Black Boy Lane, it became absurd. It was a mere paper-chase. Just look at my map."

He exhibited the large-scale map, on which each "find" was marked by a small circle. The series of circles, joined by a connecting line, proceeded directly from near Sun Pier, Chatham, along the shore, and up Black Boy Lane to the gate of the waste ground, and across it to the wall.

Angelina giggled. "You can't say I didn't make it as easy as I could for poor old Cobbledick," she said. "Of course, I never reckoned on

225

anyone bringing up the heavy guns. By the way, I wonder who your private client was. Do you know, John?" she added, with a sudden glance of suspicion and as I grinned sheepishly, she exclaimed, "Well! I wouldn't have believed it. It was a regular conspiracy. But I am interrupting the expert. Proceed, my Lord."

"Well," Thorndyke resumed, "we have considered the aspect of the crime problem taken by itself, as it appeared to an experienced investigator. From the first there was a suspicion that the clues were counterfeit, and with each new clue this suspicion deepened. And you will notice an important corollary. If the case was a fraud, that fraud was being worked by someone on the spot. Keep that point in mind, for it has a most significant bearing on the other problem, that of the personation, to which we will now turn our attention. But before we go into details, there are certain general considerations that we ought to note, in order that we may understand more clearly how the deception became possible.

"The subject of personation and disguise is often misunderstood. It is apt to be supposed that a disguise effects a complete transformation resulting in a complete resemblance to the individual personated – or, as in this case, a complete disappearance of the identity of the disguised person. But no such transformation is possible. All disguise is a form of bluff. It acts by suggestion. And the suggestion is effected by a set of misleading circumstances which produce in the dupe a state of mind in which a very imperfect disguise serves to produce conviction. That is the psychology of personation, and I can only express my admiration of the way in which Angelina had grasped it. Her conduct of this delicate deception was really masterly. Let us consider it in more detail.

"Mr. Bundy was ostensibly a man. But if he had been put in a room with a dozen moderately intelligent persons, and those persons had been asked, 'Is this individual a man? Or is he a woman with short hair and dressed in man's clothing?' they would probably have decided unanimously that he was a woman. But the question never was asked. The issue was never raised. He was Mr. Bundy. One doesn't look at young men to see if they are women in disguise.

"Then consider the position of Strangeways – the chosen victim. He comes to a strange town to transact business with a firm of land agents. He goes into the office, and finds the partners – whose names are on the plate outside, and to whom he has been sent by his London agent – engaged in their normal avocations. He transacts his business with them in a normal way, and Mr. Bundy seems to be an ordinary, capable young man. He goes back later and interviews Mr. Bundy, who is just on the point of taking him to introduce him to Mrs. Frood, when he is called away. Then, within a few minutes, he is taken to Mrs. Frood's house, where he finds that lady calmly engaged in needlework. Supposing Mrs. Frood had been extremely like Bundy, could it possibly have entered Strangeways's head that they might be one and the same person? Remember that he had left Bundy in another place only a few minutes before, and here was Mrs. Frood in her own apartments, with the appearance of having been there for hours. Obviously no such thought could have occurred to any man. There was nothing to suggest it.

"But, in fact, Angelina was not perceptibly like Bundy on cursory inspection. They were markedly different in size. A woman always looks bigger than a man of the same height. Bundy was a little man and looked smaller than he was by reason of his very low heels, Angelina was a biggish woman and looked taller than she was by reason of her high heels and her hair. Disregarding her hair, she was fully two inches taller than Bundy.

"Then the facial resemblance must have been slight. Angelina had a mass of hair and wore it low down on her brows and temples, Bundy's hair was short and was brushed back from his forehead. Angelina had strong, black eyebrows, Bundy's eyebrows were thin – or rather, cut off short. Angelina was pale, careworn, dark under the eyes, with drooping mouth, melancholy expression, and depressed in manner, Bundy was fresh-coloured, smiling, gay and sprightly in manner, and he wore an eye-glass – which has a surprising effect on facial expression. Their voices and intonation were strikingly different. Finally, Strangeways never saw Angelina excepting in a very subdued light in which any small resemblances in features would be unnoticeable.

"And now observe another effect of suggestion. Strangeways had made the acquaintance of Mr. Bundy. Then he had made the acquaintance of Mrs. Frood. They were two separate persons, they were practically strangers to one another, they belonged to different sets of surroundings. He would never think of them in connexion with one another. They were two of his friends, mutually unacquainted. In this condition of separateness they would become established in his mind, and the conception of them as different persons would become confirmed by habit. It would be a permanent suggestion that would offer an obstacle to any future suggestion that they were the same. That was the advantage of introducing Bundy first, for if he had appeared only after Angelina had disappeared, there would have been no such opposing suggestion. The resemblances might have been noticed, and he might have been detected.

"In passing I may remark upon the tact and judgment that were shown in the disguise. The troublesome makeup, the wig, the false eyebrows, the grease-paint, the false voice, all were concentrated on the temporary Mrs. Frood, who was to disappear. Bundy was not disguised at all, excepting for the eye-glass. He was simply Angelina with her hair cut short and dressed as a man. He hadn't even an assumed voice, for as Angelina is a contralto, and habitually speaks in the lower register, her voice would pass quite well as a light tenor, so long as she kept off the 'head notes'.

"So much for the general aspects of the case. And now as to my own position. As I had never seen Angelina, I naturally should not perceive any resemblance to her in Bundy, but, equally with Strangeways, I was subject to the suggestion that Bundy was a man. The personal equation, however, was different. It is my professional habit to reject all mental suggestion so far as is possible, to sift out the facts and consider them with an open mind regardless of what they appear to suggest. And then you are to remember that when I first met Mr. Bundy, there was already in my mind a faint suspicion that this was not a genuine crime, that things were not quite what they appeared, and that if this were the case, the clues were being manipulated by somebody on the spot.

"When I met Mr. Bundy, I looked him over as I look over every person whom I meet for the first time, and that inspection yielded one or two rather remarkable facts. I noticed that he wore exceptionally low heels and that he had several physical characteristics that were distinctively feminine. The very low heels puzzled me somewhat. If they had been exceptionally high there would have been nothing in it. But why should a noticeably short man wear almost abnormally low heels? I could think of no reason, unless he wore them for greater comfort, but I noted the fact and reserved it for further consideration.

"Of his physical peculiarities, the first that attracted my attention was the shape of his hands. They were quite of the feminine type. Of course, hands vary, but still it was a fact to be noted, and the observation caused me to look him over a little more critically, and then I discovered a number of other feminine characteristics.

"Perhaps it may be useful to consider briefly the less obvious differences between the sexes – the more obvious ones would, of course, be provided for by the disguise. There are two principal groups of such differences, the one has reference to the distribution of bulk, the other to the direction of certain lines. Let us take the distribution of bulk. This exhibits opposite tendencies in the two sexes. In the female, the great mass is central – the hip region, and from this the form diminishes in both directions. The whole figure, including the arms, is contained in an elongated ellipse. And the tendency affects the individual members. The

228

limbs are bulky where they join the trunk, they taper pretty regularly towards the extremities, and they terminate in relatively small hands and feet. The hands themselves taper as a whole, and the individual fingers taper markedly from a comparatively thick base to a pointed tip.

"In the male figure the opposite condition prevails, it tends to be acromegalous. The central mass is relatively small, the peripheral masses is relatively large. The hip region is narrow, and there is a great widening towards the shoulders. The limbs taper much less towards the extremities, and they terminate in relatively large hands and feet. So, too, with the hands, they tend to be square in shape, and the individual fingers – excepting the index finger – are nearly as broad at the tips as at the base.

"Of the second group of differences we need consider only one or two instances. The general rule is that certain contour lines tend in the male to be vertical or horizontal in direction and in the female to be oblique. A man's neck, at the back, is nearly straight and vertical, a woman's shows a sweeping oblique curve. The angle of a man's lower jaw is nearly a right angle, there is a vertical and a horizontal ramus. A woman's lower jaw has an open angle and its contour forms an oblique line from the ear to the chin. But the most distinctive difference is in the ear itself. A man's ear has its long diameter vertical, a woman's has the long diameter oblique, and the obliquity is usually very marked.

"Bearing these differences in mind, and remembering that they are subject to variation in individual cases, let us now return to Mr. Bundy. His hands, as I have said, had the feminine character. His feet were small even for a small man, his ears were set obliquely, and the line of his jaw was oblique with an open angle. His shoulders had evidently been made up by the tailor, and he seemed rather wide across the hips for a man. In short, all those bodily characteristics which were not concealed or disguised by the clothing were feminine. It was a rather remarkable fact, so much so that I began to ask myself if it were possible that he might actually be a woman in disguise.

"I watched him narrowly. There was nothing distinctive in his walk, but there was in the movements of the arms. He flourished his stick jauntily enough, but he had not that 'nice conduct of a clouded cane' that is as much a social cachet in our day as it was in the days of good Queen Anne. It needs a skill born of years of practice to manage a stick properly, as one realizes when one sees the working man taking his Malacca for its Sunday morning walk. Mr. Bundy had not that skill. His stick was a thing consciously carried – it was not a part of himself. Then the movement of the free arm was feminine. When a woman swings her arm she swings it through a large arc, especially in the backward

229

direction – probably to avoid her hip – and the palm of the hand tends to be turned backward. A man's free arm either hangs motionless or swings slightly, unless he is walking very fast, it swings principally forward, and the palm of his hand inclines inwards. These are small matters, but their cumulative significance is great.

"Further, there was the mental habit. Bundy was jocose and playfully ironic. But a gentleman of twenty-five doesn't 'pull the leg' of a gentleman of fifty whom he knows but slightly, whereas a lady of twenty-five does. And very properly," he added, seeing that Angelina had turned rather pink. "That is a compliment in a young lady which would be an impertinence in a young man. No doubt, when the equality of the sexes is an accomplished fact, things will be different."

"It will never be an accomplished fact," said Angelina. "The equality of the sexes is like the equality of the classes. The people who roar for social equality are the under-dogs, and the women who shout for sex equality are the under-cats. Normal women are satisfied with things as they are."

"Hearken unto the wisdom of Angelina," said Thorndyke, with a smile. "But perhaps she is right. It may be that the women who are so eager to compete with men are those who can't compete with women. I can't say. I have never been a woman, whereas Angelina has the advantage of being able to view the question from both sides.

"The *prima facie* evidence, then, suggested that Mr. Bundy was a woman. But as this was a *prima facie* improbability, the matter had to be gone into further. On Mr. Bundy's cheeks and chin was a faint blue colouration, suggestive of such a growth of whiskers and beard as would be appropriate to his age. Now if those whiskers and that beard were genuine, the other signs were fallacious. Mr. Bundy must be a man. But his cheeks looked perfectly smooth and clean, and it was about seven o'clock in the evening. My own cheeks and Strangeways' were by this time visibly prickly, and as he had been with us all day, Mr. Bundy could not have shaved since the morning. I tried vainly to get a closer view, and was considering how it could be managed when Providence intervened."

"I know," said Angelina, "It was that beastly mosquito."

"Yes," agreed Thorndyke. "But even then I could not get a chance to look at the skin closely. But when we got Mr. Bundy into the surgery, and examined the bite through a lens, the murder was out."

"You could see there were no whiskers?" said Angelina.

"It wasn't that," replied Thorndyke. "It was something much more conclusive. You may know that the whole of the human body, excepting the palms of the hands, the soles of the feet, and the eyelids, is covered

230

with a fine down, technically called the *lanugo*. It consists of minute, nearly colourless hairs set quite closely together, and may be seen as a sort of halo on the face of a woman or child when the edge of the contour is against the light. On the face of a clean-shaved man it is, of course, absent, as it is shaved off with the whiskers. Now on Mr. Bundy's face the lanugo was intact all over the blue area. It followed that he had never been shaved. It further followed that the blue colouration was an artificial stain. But this made it practically a certainty that Mr. Bundy was a woman.

"The question now was: If Mr. Bundy was a woman, what woman was he? The obvious answer seemed to be: *Angelina Frood*. She was missing, but if the disappearance was an imposture, someone on the spot was planting the clues. That someone would most probably be Mrs. Frood, herself. But if she were lurking in the neighbourhood, she must be disguised, and here was a disguised woman. Nevertheless, obvious as the suggestion was, the thing suggested seemed to be impossible. Strangeways knew both Angelina and Bundy and he had not recognized the latter, and I had a vague impression that he had seen them together, which, of course, would absolutely exclude their identity. A little judicious conversation with him, however, showed that neither objection had any weight. He had never seen them both at one time, and his description of Mrs. Frood made it clear that she had appeared to him totally unlike Bundy.

"The next thing was to ascertain definitely if this woman really was Mrs. Frood, and fortunately I had the means of making a very simple test. Strangeways had given me a photograph of Angelina bearing the address of a theatrical photographer, and from him I obtained seven different photographs in various poses. Then I received from Strangeways the group-photograph that was taken of us by the city wall, which contained an excellent portrait of Mr. Bundy. Out of this photograph I cut a small square containing Bundy's head, soaked it in oil of bergamot, and mounted it in Canada balsam on a glass plate. This made the paper quite transparent, so I now had a transparent positive. I selected from the photographs of Angelina one that was in a pose exactly similar to the portrait, of Bundy – practically full face – and treated it in the same way. Then I handed the two transparencies to my assistant, and he, by means of our big copying camera, produced two life-sized negatives, exactly alike in dimensions. With prints from these negatives we were able to perform some experiments. From Angelina's portrait I carefully cut out the face, leaving the hair and neck, and slipped Bundy's portrait behind it, so that his face appeared through the hole. We could now see how Bundy looked with Angelina's hair and, on putting it beside an untouched portrait of Angelina, it was obvious, in spite of the eye-glass, that it was the same face. For you must remember that the Angelina that we had was the real person, not the made-up Angelina whom Strangeways had seen.

"This success encouraged us to take a little more trouble. My man, Polton, made some black paper masks, with the aid of which he produced two composite photographs, one of which had Bundy's face and Angelina's hair, neck, and bust, while the other had Angelina's face and Bundy's hair, forehead, neck, and bust. The eye-glass was the disturbing factor, though it showed very little, and Bundy managed it so skilfully that it hardly affected the shape of the eye and the set of the brow. Still, it was necessary to eliminate it, and as painting was out of our province, we invoked the aid of Mrs. Anstey, who is a very talented portrait painter and miniaturist. She touched out the joins in the composites, painted out the eye-glass in the one and painted an eye-glass into the other. And now the identity was complete. The Bundy-Angelina portrait was identical with the photographer's portrait, and the Angelina-Bundy photograph was Mr. Bundy to the life.

"However, we made a final test. Polton reduced the Bundy-Angelina portrait to cabinet size, and made a couple of carbon prints, which I brought down here and exhibited, and as Strangeways accepted them as portraits of Angelina, I considered the proof complete."

Here Angelina interrupted, "But what about that brooch? I never had a brooch like that."

Thorndyke smiled a grim smile. "I asked Mrs. Anstey to paint in a brooch of a characteristic design."

"What for?" asked Angelina.

"Ah!" said Thorndyke, "thereby hangs a tale."

"Oh! A serpent's tail, I suppose," said Angelina.

"You will be able to judge presently," he replied. "The brooch had its uses. Well, to continue: The identity of Mr. Bundy was now established as a moral certainty. But it was not certain enough for legal purposes. I wanted conclusive evidence, and I wanted to ascertain exactly how the transformation effects were worked. I had noted that Bundy and Angelina occupied adjoining houses which were virtually the two moieties of a double house with a common covered passageway. I assumed that the two houses communicated, but it was necessary to ascertain if they really did. The only way to establish the facts was to inspect the house in which Angelina had lived, and this I determined to do, in the very faint hope that I might be able, at the same time, to get one or more of Angelina's finger-prints. I made a pretext for visiting the house with Strangeways, and we had the extraordinary good luck to find

Mrs. Gillow just going out, so we had the house to ourselves. But this was not the only piece of luck, for we found that Angelina had taken a drink from the bedroom tumbler and water-bottle before going out, and had left on them a complete set of beautiful finger-prints, of which I secured a number of admirable photographs.

"Examination of the basement showed that I was right as to the communication. Both houses had a side door opening into the passage-way, and both doors were fitted with Yale latches which looked as if they were opened with the same key. The passage was little used, but the gravel between the two doors was a good deal trodden, and there were numerous finger-prints on Angelina's side-door. In the kitchen was a large cupboard fitted with a Yale lock on the door and pegs inside. I assumed that when Angelina was at home that cupboard contained a suit of Mr. Bundy's clothes, and that when Mr. Bundy was in the office it contained a wig and a dress and a pair of lady's shoes.

"Well, that made the evidence fairly complete with one exception. We had to get a set of Bundy's finger-prints to compare with Angelina's. That was where the brooch came in. I knew that when Mr. Bundy saw a portrait of his former self with a brooch that he had never possessed, his curiosity would be aroused, and he would examine that portrait closely. And so he did. And on my asking him to compare the two prints, he took the opportunity to pick them both up, one in each hand, to scrutinize them more minutely, and find out who the photographer was. When he put them down, they bore a complete, though invisible, set of his finger-prints. Later, Mr. Bundy went home, escorted by Strangeways. As soon as they were gone, I took the photographs up to my room, developed up the finger-prints with powder, and compared them minutely, line by line, with the photographs of those on the tumbler and bottle. They were identical. The finger-prints of Bundy were the finger-prints of Angelina Frood.

"That completed the case, and if I had known what Angelina's intentions were I should have notified Bundy that 'the game was up'. But I was in the dark. I could do nothing until I knew whether she was going to produce a body, and if so, whose body it would be. The City wall was in my mind as a possibility, since I had noted the curious disappearance of the gate-key on that significant date and I had heard of the story of Bill the bargee and knew that Bundy had heard it, and apparently taken it seriously. But one can't act on conjecture. I could only watch Angelina play her game and try to follow the moves. When the paper-chase turned up Black Boy Lane, I knew that the wall-burial was intended to be discovered. But I didn't know what was in the wall, and I may say that I was rather alarmed. For if Angelina had taken the story of Bill as a reliable precedent and had buried a real body in quicklime, there was going to be a catastrophe. It was an immense relief to me when I got Strangeways' report that only a skeleton had been found, for I knew then that only a skeleton had been buried and that no crime had been committed. That is all I have to tell, and now it is Angelina's turn to enter the confessional."

"You haven't left me much to tell," said Angelina. "I feel as if I had been doing the thimble-and-pea trick with glass thimbles. However, I will fill in a few details. This scheme first occurred to me when I came down here to take over the property that had been left to me. I put it confidentially to Uncle Japp, but he was so shocked that he has never been able to get his hair to lie down since. He wouldn't hear of it. So I asked him to lunch with poor Nicholas, and after that he was ready to agree to anything. Accordingly I made my preparations. I got a theatrical wig-maker to cut off my hair and make it into a wig (I told him I had a man's part and it was expected to be a long run), got a suit made by a theatrical costumier, and down I came as Mr. Bundy. Uncle J. had already had the new plate put up. The next door offices and basement were empty, so we got them furnished for Angelina, and as soon as the wig was ready, down she came and took possession.

"Up to this time the third act was a bit sketchy. I had arranged the disappearance, and the recovery of the clues from the river, and I had a plan of buying a mummy, dressing it in my clothes, and burying it in the marshes close to the shore, where I could discover it when it had matured sufficiently. But I didn't much like the plan. I didn't know enough about mummies, and some other people might know too much. It looked as if I should have to do without a body, and leave my death to mere rumour, which would be unsatisfactory. I did want a tombstone.

"About this time an angel of the name of Turcival – he lives in Adam and Eve Street, Adelphi, bless him! – sent a Dr. Strangeways down here. He was a regular windfall – a new doctor – and I gave him my entire attention. I took him to his own proposed premises, and kept him in conversation, to let my personality soak well in. That evening I interviewed him in the office, and let him suppose that I was going to take him to Mrs. Frood's house and introduce him to her. Then, when I suddenly remembered an engagement elsewhere, I went out, and as soon as the office door was shut, down I darted into our basement, out at the side door, in at the other side door, and into Mrs. Frood's kitchen. There I did a lightning change, slipped on my dress and wig, stuck on my eyebrows, and made up my complexion, flew up the stairs, lighted the lamp in the sitting-room, and spread myself out with my needle-work.

234

But I hadn't been settled more than two or three minutes when Uncle Japp arrived, leading the lamb to the slaughter.

"Then it turned out that I had struck a bit of luck that I hadn't bargained for. John had attended me in London and knew something of my affairs, so I appointed him my physician in ordinary on the spot. It was rare sport. The concern poor old John showed for my grease-paint was quite touching. I sat there squeaking complaints to him and receiving his sympathy until I was ready to screech with laughter. But I felt rather a pig all the same, for John was so sweet, and he was such a man and such a gentleman. However, I had to go on when once I had begun.

"But it was a troublesome business, worse than any stage job I ever had, to keep these two people going. I had to rush through from the office into the kitchen and cook things that I didn't want, just to make a noise and a smell of cooking, and listen to Mrs. Gillow so that I could pop up the stairs at the psychological moment and remind her that I lived there, and then to fly down and change and dart through into the office, so that people could see that I was occupied there. It was frightfully hard work, and anxious, too. I can tell you, it was a relief when I heard from Miss Cumbers that Nicholas was starting for Brighton, and that I could disappear without implicating him. However, there is no need for me to go into any more details. Your imaginations can fill those in."

"The man with the mole, I take it," said Thorndyke, "was – "

"Yes. I got a suit of slops in the Minories. The mole, of course, was built up, with toupee-paste."

"By the way," said Thorndyke, "was there any necessity for Bundy at all?"

"Well, I had to be somebody, you know, and I had to stay on the spot to work the clues and keep an eye on the developments. I couldn't be a woman because that would have required a heavy make-up that would almost certainly have been spotted, and would have been an intolerable bore, whereas Bundy, as you have pointed out, was not a disguise at all. When once I had got my hair cut and had provided myself with the clothes and eye-glass, there was no further trouble. I could have lived comfortably as Bundy for the rest of my life.

"So that is my story," Angelina concluded. "And," she added, with a sudden change of manner, "I am your grateful debtor forever. You have done far more for me even than you know. Only this morning, poor Peter Bundy was a forlorn little wretch, miserably anxious about the present and looking to a future that had nothing but empty freedom to offer. And now I am the happiest of women – for I should be a hypocrite if I pretended to have any regrets for poor Nicholas. I will say good-bye to him in his coffin and give him a decent funeral, and try to think of him as he was before he sank into the depths. But I am frankly glad that he is gone out of his own miserable life and out of mine. And his going, which would never have been known but for the wisdom of the benevolent serpent, has left me free – with a promise of a happiness that even he does not guess."

"I am not so sure of that," said Thorndyke, with a sly smile.

"Well, neither am I, now you come to mention it," said she, smiling at him in return. "He is an inquiring and observant serpent, with a way of nosing out all sorts of things that he is not supposed to be aware of. And, after all, perhaps he has a right to know. It is proper that the giver should have the satisfaction of realizing the preciousness of that which he has given."

Here endeth *The Mystery of Angelina Frood*. And yet it is not quite the end. Indeed, the end is not yet, for the blessed consequences still continue to develop like the growth of a fair tree. The story has dwindled to a legend, whose harmless whispers call but a mischievous smile to that face that, like the dial in our garden, acknowledges only the sunshine. Mrs. Dunk, it is true, still wages public war, but it is tempered by private adoration, and almost daily baskets of flowers, and even tomatoes and summer cabbages, arrive at our house accompanied by the beaming smile and portly person of Inspector Cobbledick.

1925 Hodder & Stoughton Cover

Chapter I
In Which Two Men Go Forth and One Arrives

About half-past-eight on a fine, sunny June morning a small yacht crept out of Sennen Cove, near the Land's End, and headed for the open sea. On the shelving beach of the Cove two women and a man, evidently visitors (or "foreigners" to use the local term), stood watching her departure with valedictory waving of cap or handkerchief, and the boatman who had put the crew on board, aided by two of his comrades, was hauling his boat up above the tide-mark.

A light northerly breeze filled the yacht's sails and drew her gradually seaward. The figures of her crew dwindled to the size of a doll's, shrank with the increasing distance to the magnitude of insects, and at last, losing all individuality, became mere specks merged in the form of the fabric that bore them. At this point the visitors turned their faces inland and walked away up the beach, and the boatman, having opined that "she be fetchin' a tidy offing", dismissed the yacht from his mind and reverted to the consideration of a heap of netting and some invalid lobster-pots.

On board the receding craft, two men sat in the little cockpit. They formed the entire crew, for the *Sandhopper* was only a ship's lifeboat, timber and decked of light draught and, in the matter of spars and canvas, what the art critics would call "reticent".

Both men, despite the fineness of the weather, wore yellow oilskins and sou'westers, and that was about all they had in common. In other respects they made a curious contrast: The one small, slender, sharp-featured, dark almost to swarthiness, and restless and quick in his movements, the other large, massive, red-faced, blue-eyed, with the rounded outlines suggestive of ponderous strength – a great ox of a man, heavy, stolid, but much less unwieldy than he looked.

The conversation incidental to getting the yacht under way had ceased, and silence had fallen on the occupants of the cockpit. The big man grasped the tiller and looked sulky, which was probably his usual aspect, and the small man watched him furtively. The land was nearly two miles distant when the latter broke the silence with a remark very similar to that of the boatman on the beach.

"You're not going to take the shore on board, Purcell. Where are we supposed to be going to?"

241

"I am going outside the Longships," was the stolid answer.

"So I see," rejoined the other. "It's hardly the shortest course for Penzance, though."

"I like to keep an offing on this coast," said Purcell, and once more the conversation languished.

Presently the smaller man spoke again, this time in a more cheerful and friendly tone. "Joan Haygarth has come on wonderfully the last few months, getting quite a fine-looking girl. Don't you think so?"

"Yes," answered Purcell, "and so does Phil Rodney."

"You're right," agreed the other. "But she isn't a patch on her sister, though, and never will be. I was looking at Maggie as we came down the beach this morning and thinking what a handsome girl she is. Don't you agree with me?"

Purcell stooped to look under the boom, and answered without turning his head, "Yes, she's all right."

"All right!" exclaimed the other. "Is that the way?"

"Look here, Varney," interrupted Purcell, "I don't want to discuss my wife's looks with you or any other man. She'll do for me, or I shouldn't have married her."

A deep coppery flush stole into Varney's cheeks. But he had brought the rather brutal snub on himself, and apparently had the fairness to recognize the fact, for he mumbled an apology and relapsed into silence.

When he next spoke he did so with a manner diffident and uneasy, as though approaching a disagreeable or difficult subject.

"There's a little matter, Dan, that I've been wanting to speak to you about when we got a chance of a private talk." He glanced a little anxiously at his stolid companion, who grunted, and then, without removing his gaze from the horizon ahead, replied, "You've a pretty fair chance now, seeing that we shall be bottled up together for another five or six hours. And it's private enough, unless you bawl loud enough to be heard at the Longships."

It was not a gracious invitation – but that Varney had hardly expected, and if he resented the rebuff he showed no signs of annoyance, for reasons which appeared when he opened his subject.

"What I wanted to say," he resumed, "was this. We're both doing pretty well now on the square. You must be positively piling up the shekels, and I can earn a decent living, which is all I want. Why shouldn't we drop this flash note business?"

Purcell kept his blue eye fixed on the horizon, and appeared to ignore the question, but after an interval, and without moving a muscle, he said gruffly, "Go on," and Varney continued. "The lay isn't what it was, you know. At first it was all plain sailing. The notes were first-class copies, and not a soul suspected anything until they were presented at the bank. Then the murder was out, and the next little trip that I made was a very different affair. Two or three of the notes were suspected quite soon after I had changed them, and I had to be precious fly, I can tell you, to avoid complications. And now that the second batch has come into the bank, the planting of fresh specimens is no sinecure. There isn't a money changer on the Continent of Europe that isn't keeping his weather eyeball peeled, to say nothing of the detectives that the bank people have sent abroad."

He paused and looked appealingly at his companion. But Purcell, still minding his helm, only growled, "Well?"

"Well, I want to chuck it, Dan. When you've had a run of luck and pocketed your winnings is the time to stop play."

"You've come into some money then, I take it," said Purcell.

"No, I haven't. But I can make a living now by safe and respectable means, and I'm sick of all this scheming and dodging with the gaol everlastingly under my lee."

"The reason I asked," said Purcell, "is that there is a trifle outstanding. You hadn't forgotten that, I suppose?"

"No, I hadn't forgotten it, but I thought that perhaps you might be willing to let me down a bit easily."

The other man pursed up his thick lips, but continued to gaze stonily over the bow.

"Oh, that's what you thought, hey?" he said, and then, after a pause, he continued, "I fancy you must have lost sight of some of the facts when you thought that. Let me just remind you how the case stands. To begin with, you start your career with a little playful forgery and embezzlement, you blew the proceeds, and you are mug enough to be found out. Then I come in. I compound the affair with old Marston for a couple-of-thousand, and practically clean myself out of every penny I possess, and he consents to regard your temporary absence in the light of a holiday.

"Now why do I do this? Am I a philanthropist? Devil a bit. I'm a man of business. Before I ladle out that two-thousand, I make a business contract with you. I happen to possess the means of making and the skill to make a passable imitation of the Bank of England paper. You are a skilled engraver and a plausible scamp. I am to supply you with paper blanks. You are to engrave plates, print the notes, and get them changed. I am to take two-thirds of the proceeds and, although I have done the most difficult part of the work, I agree to regard my share of the profits as constituting repayment of the loan. Our contract amounts to this: I lend you two-thousand without security – with an infernal amount of insecurity, in fact – you 'promise, covenant, and agree', as the lawyers say, to hand me back ten-thousand in instalments, being the products of our joint industry. It is a verbal contract which I have no means of enforcing, but I trust you to keep your word, and up to the present you have kept it. You have paid me a little over four-thousand. Now you want to cry off and leave the balance unpaid. Isn't that the position?"

"Not exactly," said Varney. "I'm not crying off the debt, I only want time. Look here, Dan: I'm making about five-fifty a year now. That isn't much, but I'll manage to let you have a hundred-a-year out of it. What do you say to that?"

Purcell laughed scornfully. "A hundred-a-year-to pay off six-thousand! That'll take just sixty years, and as I'm now forty-three, I shall be exactly a hundred-and-three years of age when the last instalment is paid. I think, Varney, you'll admit that a man of a hundred-and-three is getting a bit past his prime."

"Well, I'll pay you something down to start. I've saved about eighteen-hundred pounds out of the note business. You can have that now, and I'll pay off as much as I can at a time until I'm clear. Remember that if I should happen to get clapped in chokee for twenty years or so you won't get anything. And, I tell you, it's getting a risky business."

"I'm willing to take the risk," said Purcell.

"I dare say you are!" Varney retorted passionately, "because it's *my* risk. If I am grabbed, it's my racket. You sit out. It's I who passed the notes, and I'm known to be a skilled engraver. That'll be good enough for them. They won't trouble about who made the paper."

"I hope not," said Purcell.

"Of course they wouldn't, and you know I shouldn't give you away."

"Naturally. Why should you? Wouldn't do you any good."

"Well, give me a chance, Dan," Varney pleaded. "This business is getting on my nerves. I want to be quit of it. You've had four-thousand, that's a hundred-percent. You haven't done so badly."

"I didn't expect to do badly. I took a big risk. I gambled two-thousand for ten."

"Yes, and you got me out of the way while you put the screw on to poor old Haygarth to make his daughter marry you."

It was an indiscreet thing to say, but Purcell's stolid indifference to his danger and distress had ruffled Varney's temper somewhat.

244

Purcell, however, was unmoved. "I don't know," he said, "what you mean by getting you out of the way. You were never in the way. You were always hankering after Maggie, but I could never see that she wanted you."

"Well, she certainly didn't want you," Varney retorted, "and, for that matter, I don't much think she wants you now."

For the first time Purcell withdrew his eye from the horizon to turn it on his companion. And an evil eye it was, set in the great sensual face, now purple with anger.

"What the devil do you mean?" he exclaimed furiously, "you infernal sallow-faced little whipper-snapper! If you mention my wife's name again, I'll knock you on the head and pitch you over board."

Varney's face flushed darkly, and for a moment he was inclined to try the wager of battle. But the odds were impossible, and if Varney was not a coward, neither was he a fool. But the discussion was at an end. Nothing was to be hoped for now. Those indiscreet words of provocation had rendered further pleading impossible, and as Varney relapsed into sullen silence, it was with the knowledge that, for weary years to come, he was doomed, at best, to tread the perilous path of crime, or, more probably, to waste the brightest years of his life in a convict prison. For it is a strange fact, and a curious commentary on our current ethical notions, that neither of these rascals even contemplated as a possibility the breach of a merely verbal covenant. A promise had been given. That was enough. Without a specific release, the terms of that promise must be fulfilled to the letter. How many righteous men – prim lawyers or strait-laced, church-going men of business – would have looked at the matter in the same way?

The silence that settled down on the yacht and the aloofness that encompassed the two men were conducive to reflection. Each of the men ignored the presence of the other. When the course was altered southerly, Purcell slacked out the sheets with his own hand as he put up the helm. He might have been sailing single-handed. And Varney watched him askance, but made no move, sitting hunched up on the locker, nursing a slowly matured hatred and thinking his thoughts.

Very queer thoughts they were – rambling, but yet connected and very vivid. He was following out the train of events that might have happened, pursuing them to their possible consequences. Supposing Purcell had carried out his threat? Well, there would have been a pretty tough struggle, for Varney was no weakling. But a struggle with that solid fifteen-stone of flesh could end only in one way. He glanced at the great purple, shiny hand that grasped the knob of the tiller. Not the sort

245

of hand that you would want at your throat! No, there was no doubt: He would have gone overboard.

And what then? Would Purcell have gone back to Sennen Cove, or sailed alone into Penzance? In either case, he would have had to make up some sort of story, and no one could have contradicted him, whether the story was believed or not. But it would have been awkward for Purcell.

Then there was the body. That would have washed up sooner or later, as much of it as the lobsters had left. Well, lobsters don't eat clothes or bones, and a dent in the skull might take some accounting for. Very awkward, this, for Purcell. He would probably have had to clear out – to make a bolt for it, in short.

The mental picture of this great bully fleeing in terror from the vengeance of the law gave Varney appreciable pleasure. Most of his life he had been borne down by the moral and physical weight of this domineering brute. At school Purcell had fagged him, he had even bullied him up at Cambridge, and now he had fastened on for ever like The Old Man of the Sea. And Purcell always got the best of it. When he, Varney, had come back from Italy after that unfortunate little affair, behold! The girl whom they had both wanted (and who had wanted neither of them) had changed from Maggie Haygarth into Maggie Purcell. And so it was even unto this day. Purcell, once a book-keeper in a paper-mill, now a prosperous "financier" – a money-lender, as Varney more than suspected – spent a part of his secret leisure making, in absolute safety, those paper blanks, which he, Varney, must risk his liberty to change into money. Yes, it was quite pleasant to think of Purcell sneaking from town to town, from country to country, with the police at his heels.

But in these days of telegraphs and extradition there isn't much chance for a fugitive. Purcell would have been caught to a certainty, and he would have been hanged, no doubt of it. And, passing lightly over less attractive details, Varney considered luxuriously the circumstances of the execution. What a figure he would have made, that great human ox, turning round and round at the end of a taut rope, like a baron of beef on a colossal roasting-jack! Varney looked gloatingly at his companion, considered his large sullen face, and thought how it would swell and grow purple as the rope tightened round the thick crimson neck.

A disagreeable picture, perhaps, but not to Varney, who saw it through the distorting medium of years of accumulated dislike. Then, too, there was the consideration that in the very moment that those brawny limbs had ceased to twitch Maggie would have been free – would have been a widow. Not that that would have concerned him,

246

Varney – he would have been in some Cornish churchyard, with a dent in his skull. Still, it was a pleasant reflection.

The imagined picture of the execution gave him quite a lengthy entertainment. Then his errant thoughts began to spread out in search of other possibilities. For, after all, it was not an absolute certainty that Purcell could have got him overboard. There was just the chance that he might have gone overboard himself. That would have been a very different affair.

Varney settled himself composedly to consider the new and interesting train of consequences that would thus have been set going. They were more agreeable to contemplate than the others, because they did not include his own demise. The execution scene made no appearance in this version. The salient fact was that his oppressor would have vanished, that the intolerable burden of his servitude would have been lifted for ever, that he would have been free.

The thought of his regained freedom set him dreaming of the future – the future that might have been if he could have been rid of this monstrous parasite, the future that might even have held a place for Maggie – for she would have been free, too. It was all very pleasant to think about, though rather tantalizing. He almost wished he had let Purcell try to put him over.

Of course, some explanation would have to be given, some sort of story told, and people might not have believed him. Well, they could have pleased themselves about that. To be sure, there would have been the body, but if there were no marks of violence, what of it? Besides, it really need never have washed ashore – that could easily have been prevented, and if the body had never been found, who was to say that the man had gone overboard at all?

This, again, was a new view of the case, and it set his thoughts revolving afresh. He found himself roughly sketching out the conditions under which the body might have vanished for ever. It was mere idle speculation to while away a dull hour with an uncongenial companion, and he let his thoughts ramble at large. Now he was away in the imagined future, a future of peace and prosperity and honourable effort, and now his thoughts came back unbidden to fill in some forgotten detail. One moment he was dreamily wondering whether Maggie would ever have listened to him, ever have come to care for him. The next, he was back in the yacht's cabin, where hung from a hook on the bulkhead the revolver that the Rodneys used to practise at floating bottles. It was usually loaded, he knew, but if not, there was a canvas bag full of cartridges in the starboard locker. Again he found himself dreaming of the home that he would have had, a home very different from the cheerless lodgings in which he moped at present, and then his thoughts had flitted back to the yacht's hold, and were busying themselves with the row, of half-hundredweights that rested on the on either side of the kelson.

It was a curious mental state – rambling, seemingly incoherent, yet quite purposeful – the attention oscillating between the great general idea and its various component details. He was like a painter roughing the preliminary sketch of a picture, at first carelessly smearing in the general effect, then pausing from time to time to sharpen an edge, to touch in a crisp light, to define the shape of a shadow, but never losing sight of the central motive. And as in the sketch definable shapes begin to grow out of the formless expanse, and a vague suggestion crystallizes into an intelligible composition, so in Varney's mind a process of gradual integration turned a vague and general idea into a clear picture: Sharp, vivid, complete.

When Varney had thus brought his mental picture, so to speak, to a finish, its completeness surprised him. It was so simple, so secure. He had actually planned out the scheme of a murder, and behold! There was nothing in it. Anyone could have done it, and no one could have been any the wiser. Here he found himself wondering whether many murders passed undetected. They well might if murders were as easy and as safe as this. A dangerous reflection for an injured and angry man. And at this critical point his meditations were broken in on by Purcell, continuing the conversation as if there had been no pause.

"So you can take it from me, Varney, that I expect you to stick to your bargain. I paid down my money, and I'm going to have my pound of flesh."

"You won't agree to any sort of compromise?"

"No. There are six-thousand pounds owing. If you've got the money you can hand it over. If you haven't, you'll have to go on the lay and get it. That's all I've got to say. So now you know."

It was a brutal thing to say, and it was brutally said. But more than that – it was inopportune – or opportune, as you will. For it came as a sort of infernal doxology to the devil's anthem that had been, all unknown, ringing in Varney's soul.

Purcell had spoken without looking round. That was his unpleasant habit. Had he looked at his companion, he might have been startled. A change in Varney's face might have given him pause – a warm flush, a sparkle of the eye, a look of elation, of settled purpose, deadly, inexorable. The look of a man who has made a fateful resolution. But he never looked, and the warning of the uplifted axe passed him by.

It was so simple, so secure! That was the burden of the song that echoed in Varney's brain. So safe! And there abroad were the watchful money-changers waiting for the clever forger to come once too often. There were the detectives lurking in ambush for him. No safety there! Rather the certainty of swift disaster, with the sequel of judge and jury, the clang of an iron door, and thereafter the dreary prison eating up the years of his life.

He glanced over the sea. They had opened the South Coast now, and he could see, afar off, a fleet of black-sailed luggers heading east. They wouldn't be in his way. Nor would the big four-master that was creeping away to the west, for she was hull down already, and other ships there were none. There was one hindrance, though. Dead ahead the Wolf Rock lighthouse rose from the blue water, its red-and-white-ringed tower looking like some gaudily painted toy. The keepers of lonely light houses have a natural habit of watching the passing shipping through their glasses, and it was possible that one of their telescopes might be pointed at the yacht at this very moment. That was a complication.

Suddenly there came down the wind a sharp report like the firing of a gun, quickly followed by a second. Both men recognized the duplicate report and both looked round. It was the explosive signal from the Longships lighthouse, but when they looked there was no lighthouse to be seen, and the dark blue heaving water faded away at the foot of an advancing wall of vapour.

Purcell cursed volubly. A pretty place, this, to be caught in a fog! And then, as his eye lighted on his companion, he demanded angrily, "What the devil are you grinning at?" For Varney, drunk with suppressed excitement, snapped his fingers at rocks and shoals. He was thinking only of the light-keeper's telescope and of the revolver that hung on the bulkhead. He must make some excuse presently to go below and secure that revolver.

But no excuse was necessary. The opportunity came of itself. After a hasty glance at the vanishing land and another at the compass, Purcell put up the helm to jibe the yacht round on to an easterly course. As she came round, the single headsail that she carried in place of jib and foresail shivered for a few seconds and then filled suddenly on the opposite tack. And at this moment the halyard parted with a loud snap, the end of the rope flew through the blocks, and, in an instant, the sail was down and its upper half trailing in the water alongside.

Purcell swore furiously, but kept an eye to business. "Run below, Varney," said he, "and fetch up that coil of new rope out of the starboard locker while I haul the sail on board. And look alive. We don't want to drift down on to the Wolf."

Varney obeyed with silent alacrity and a curious feeling of elation. It was going to be even easier and safer than he had thought. He slipped through the hatch into the cabin, and, as he heard Purcell scrambling along the side-deck overhead, he quietly took the revolver from its hook and examined the chambers. Finding them all loaded, he cocked the hammer and slipped the weapon carefully into the inside breast-pocket of his oilskin coat. Then he took the coil of rope from the locker and went on deck.

As he emerged from the hatch he perceived that the yacht was already enveloped in fog, which drifted past in steamy clouds and swirling streamers, and that she had come up head to wind. Purcell was kneeling on the forecastle, tugging at the sail, which had caught under the forefoot, and punctuating his efforts with deep-voiced curses.

Varney stole silently along the deck, steadying himself by mast and shroud, softly laid down the coil of rope, and approached. Purcell was quite engrossed with his task, his back was towards Varney, his face over the side, intent on the entangled sail. It was a chance in a thousand.

With scarcely a moment's hesitation Varney stooped forward, steadying himself with a hand on the little windlass, and, softly drawing forth the revolver, pointed it at the back of Purcell's head, at the spot where the back seam of his sou'wester met the brim. The report rang out, but weak and flat in that open space, and a cloud of smoke mingled with the fog, but it blew away immediately, and showed Purcell almost unchanged in posture, crouching on the sail with his chin resting on the little rim of bulwark, while behind him his murderer, as if turned into bronze, still stood stooping forward, one hand grasping the windlass, the other still pointing the revolver.

Thus the two figures remained for some seconds motionless like some horrible waxworks, until the little yacht, lifting to the swell, gave a more than usually lively curvet, when Purcell rolled over on to his back, and Varney relaxed the rigidity of his posture like a golf player who has watched his ball drop. He bent over the prostrate figure with no emotion but curiosity. Looked into the wide-open, clear blue eyes, noted how the great red face had faded to a pallid mauve, against which the blood on lips and chin stood out like the painted patches on a clown's face, but he felt not a single twinge of compunction.

Purcell was dead. That was the salient fact. The head wagged to and fro as the yacht pitched and rolled, the limp arms and legs seemed to twitch, the limp body to writhe uneasily. But Varney was not disturbed. Lifeless things will move on an unsteady deck. He was only interested to notice how the passive movements produced the illusion of life. But it was only illusion. Purcell was dead. There was no doubt of that.

The double report from the Longships came down the wind, and then, as if in answer, a prolonged deep bellow. That was the fog-horn of the lighthouse on the Wolf Rock, and it sounded surprisingly near. But, of course, these signals were meant to be heard at a distance. Then a stream of hot sunshine, pouring down on deck, startled him and made him hurry. The body must be got overboard before the fog lifted. With an uneasy glance at the clear sky over head, he hastily cast off the broken halyard from its cleat and cut off a couple of fathoms. Then he hurried below and, lifting the trap in the cabin floor, hoisted out one of the iron half-hundredweights with which the yacht was ballasted. As he stepped on deck with the weight in his hand the sun was shining overhead, but the fog was still thick below, and the horn sounded once more from the Wolf. And again it struck him as surprisingly near. He passed the length of rope that he had cut off twice round Purcell's body, hauled it tight, and secured it with a knot. Then he made the ends fast to the handle of the iron weight.

Not much fear of Purcell drifting ashore now! That weight would hold him as long as there was anything to hold. But it had taken some time to do, and the warning bellow from the Wolf seemed to draw nearer and nearer. He was about to heave the body over when his eye fell on the dead man's sou' wester, which had fallen off when the body rolled over. That hat must be got rid of, for Purcell's name was worked in silk on the lining, and there was an unmistakable bullet-hole through the back. It must be destroyed, or, which would be simpler and quicker, lashed securely on the dead man's head.

Hurriedly, Varney ran aft and descended to the cabin. He had noticed a new ball of spun-yarn in the locker when he had fetched the rope. This would be the very thing.

He was back again in a few moments with the ball in his hand, unwinding it as he came, and without wasting time he knelt down by the body and fell to work. There was a curious absence of repugnance in his manner, horrible as his task would have seemed. He had to raise the dead man's head to fit on the hat, and in so doing covered his left hand with blood. But he appeared to mind no more than if he had been handling a seal that he had shot or a large and dirty fish. Quite composedly, and with that deftness in the handling of cordage that marks the sailor-man, whether amateur or professional, he proceeded with his task, intent only on making the lashing secure and getting it done quickly.

And every half-minute, the deep-voiced growl of the Wolf came to him out of the fog, and each time it sounded nearer and yet nearer.

By the time he had made the sou'wester secure, the dead man's face and chin were encaged in a web of spun-yarn that made him look like some old-time, grotesque-vizored Samurai warrior. But the hat was now immovable. Long after that burly corpse had dwindled to a mere skeleton it would hold, would still cling to the dead head when the face that looked through the lacing of cords was the face of a bare and grinning skull.

Varney rose to his feet. But his task was not finished yet. There was Purcell's suitcase. That must be sunk, too, and there was something in it that had figured in the detailed picture that his imagination had drawn. He ran to the cockpit, where the suitcase lay, and having tried its fastenings and found it unlocked, he opened it and took out with his right hand – the clean one – a letter that lay on top of the other contents. This he tossed through the hatch into the cabin. Then his eye caught Purcell's fountain-pen, slipped neatly through a loop in the lid. It was filled, he knew, with the peculiar black ink that Purcell always used. The thought passed swiftly through his mind that perchance it might be of use to him. In a moment he had drawn it from its loop and slipped it into his pocket. Then, having closed and fastened the suit case, he carried it forward and made it fast to the iron weight with a half-dozen turns of spun-yarn.

That was really all, and, indeed, it was time. As he rose, once more, to his feet, the growl of the fog horn burst out, as it seemed, right over the stern of the yacht, and she was drifting stern foremost, who could say how fast? Now, too, he caught a more ominous sound, which he might have heard sooner had he listened – the wash of water, the boom of breakers bursting on a rock.

A revulsion came over him. He burst into a wild sardonic laugh. And had it come to this, after all? Had he schemed and laboured only to leave himself alone on an unmanageable craft drifting down to shipwreck and certain death? Had he taken all this thought and care to secure Purcell's body, when his own might be resting beside it on the sea bottom within an hour?

But his reverie was brief. Suddenly from the white void over his very head, as it seemed, there issued a stunning, thunderous roar that shook the very deck-under his feet. The water around him boiled into a foamy chaos, the din of bursting waves was in his ears, the yacht plunged and wallowed amidst clouds of spray, and, for an instant, a dim, gigantic shadow loomed through the fog and was gone.

In that moment his nerve had come back. Holding on, with one hand, to the windlass, he dragged the body to the edge of the forecastle, hoisted the weight out-board, and then, taking advantage of a heavy lurch, gave the corpse a vigorous shove. There was a rattle and a hollow splash, and corpse and weight and suitcase had vanished into the seething water.

252

He clung to the swinging mast and waited. Breathlessly he told out the allotted seconds until, once again, the invisible Titan belched forth his thunderous warning. But this time the roar came over the yacht's bow. She had drifted past the Rock, then. The danger was over, and Purcell would have to go down to Davy Jones's Locker companionless after all.

Very soon the water around ceased to boil and tumble, and as the yacht's wild plunging settled down once more into the normal rise and fall on the long swell, Varney turned his attention to the refitting of the halyard. But what was this on the creamy duck sail? A pool of blood and a gory imprint of his own hand! That wouldn't do at all. He would have to clear that away before he could hoist the sail, which was annoying, as the yacht was helpless without her head-sail and was evidently drifting out to sea.

He fetched a bucket, a swab, and a scrubbing brush, and set to work. The bulk of the large blood stain cleared off pretty completely after he had drenched the sail with a bucketful or two and given it a good scrubbing. But the edge of the stain, where the heat of the deck had dried it, remained like the painted boundary on a map, and the hand-print, which had also dried, though it faded to a pale buff, continued clearly visible.

Varney began to grow uneasy. If those stains would not come out, especially the hand-print, it would be very awkward, they would take such a deal of explaining. He decided to try the effect of marine soap, and fetched a cake from the cabin, but even this did not obliterate the stains completely, though it turned them a faint greenish brown, very unlike the colour of blood. Still he scrubbed on, until at last the hand-print faded away entirely and the large stain was reduced to a faint green wavy line, and that was the best he could do, and quite good enough, for if that faint line should ever be noticed, no one would ever suspect its origin.

He put away the bucket and proceeded with the refitting. The sea had disengaged the sail from the forefoot, and he hauled it on board without difficulty. Then there was the reeving of the new halyard – a troublesome business, involving the necessity of his going aloft, where his weight, small man as he was, made the yacht roll most infernally, and set him swinging to-and-fro like the bob of a metronome. But he was a smart yachtsman and active, though not powerful, and a few minutes' strenuous exertion ended in his sliding down the shrouds with the new halyard running fairly through the upper block. A vigorous haul or two at the new hairy rope sent the head of the dripping sail aloft, and the yacht was once more under control.

The rig of the *Sandhopper* was not smart, but it was handy. She carried a short bowsprit to accommodate the single head-sail, and a relatively large mizzen, of which the advantage was that by judicious management of the mizzen-sheet, the yacht would sail with very little attention to the helm. Of this advantage Varney was keenly appreciative just now, for he had several things to do before entering port. The excitement of the last hour and the bodily exertions had left him shaky and faint. He wanted refreshment, he wanted a wash, and the various traces of recent events had to be removed. Also, there was that letter to be attended to. So that it was convenient to be able to leave the helm in charge of a lashing for a minute now and again.

When he had washed he put the kettle on the spirit-stove and, while it was heating, busied himself in cleaning the revolver, flinging the empty cartridge-case overboard, and replacing it with a cartridge from the bag in the locker. Then he picked up the letter that he had taken from Purcell's suitcase and examined it. It was addressed to "Joseph Penfield, Esq., George Yard, Lombard Street," and was unstamped, though the envelope was fastened up. He affixed a stamp from his pocket-book and, when the kettle began to boil, he held the envelope in the steam that issued from spout. Very soon the flap of the envelope loosened and curled back, when he laid it aside to mix himself a mug of hot grog which, together with the letter and a biscuit-tin, he took out into the cockpit. The fog was still dense, and the hoot of a steamer's whistle from somewhere to the westward caused him to reach the fog-horn out of the locker and blow a long blast on it. As if in answer to his treble squeak came the deep bass note from the Wolf, and, unconsciously, he looked round. He turned automatically, as one does towards a sudden noise, not expecting to see anything but fog, and what he did see startled him not a little.

For there was the lighthouse – or half of it, rather – standing up above the fogbank, clear, distinct, and hardly a mile away. The gilded vane, the sparkling lantern, the gallery, and the upper half of the red-and-white-ringed tower, stood sharp against the pallid sky, but the lower half was invisible. It was a strange apparition – like half a lighthouse suspended in mid-air – and uncommonly disturbing, too. It raised a very awkward question. If he could see the lantern the light-keepers could see him. But how long had the lantern been clear of the fog? That was the question, and the answer to it might come in a highly disagreeable form.

Thus he meditated as, with one hand on the tiller, he munched his biscuit and sipped his grog. Presently he picked up the stamped envelope and drew from it a letter, which he tore into fragments and dropped overboard. Then, from his pocket-book, he took a similar but

254

unaddressed envelope, from which he drew out its contents, and very curious those contents were. There was a letter, brief and laconic, which he read thoughtfully. *"These,"* it ran, *"are all I have by me, but they will do for the present, and when you have planted them I will let you have a fresh supply."* There was no date and no signature, but the rather peculiar handwriting, in jet-black ink, was similar to that on the envelope addressed to Joseph Penfield, Esq.

The other contents consisted of a dozen sheets of blank paper, each of the size of a Bank of England note. But they were not quite blank, for each bore an elaborate water-mark, identical with that of a twenty-pound banknote. They were, in fact, the "paper blanks" of which Purcell had spoken. The envelope with its contents had been slipped into his hand by Purcell, without remark, only three days ago.

Varney refolded the "blanks", enclosed them within the letter, and slipped letter and "blanks" together into the stamped envelope, the flap of which he licked and reclosed.

"I should like to see old Penfield's face when he opens that envelope," was his reflection as, with a grim smile, he put it away in his pocket-book "And I wonder what he will do," he added mentally. "However, I *shall* see before many days are over."

Varney looked at his watch. He was to meet Jack Rodney on Penzance Pier at a quarter-to-three. He would never do it at this rate, for when he opened Mount's Bay, Penzance would be right in the wind's eye. That would mean a long beat to windward. Then Rodney would be there first, waiting for him. Deuced awkward, this. He would have to account for his being alone on board, would have to invent some lie about having put Purcell ashore at Mousehole or Newlyn. But a lie is a very pernicious thing. Its effects are cumulative. You never know when you have done with it. Apart from moral considerations, lies should be avoided at all cost of present inconvenience – that is, unless they are absolutely unavoidable, and then they should be as probable as can be managed, and not calculated to provoke inquiry. Now, if he had reached Penzance before Rodney, he need have said nothing about Purcell – for the present, at any rate, and that would have been so much safer.

When the yacht was about abreast of Lamorna Cove, though some seven miles to the south, the breeze began to draw ahead, and the fog cleared off quite suddenly. The change of wind was unfavourable for the moment, but when it veered round yet a little more until it blew from east-north-east, Varney brightened up considerably. There was still a chance of reaching Penzance before Rodney arrived, for now, as soon as he had fairly opened Mount's Bay, he could head straight for his destination and make it on a single board.

Between two and three hours later the *Sandhopper* entered Penzance Harbour and, threading her way among an assemblage of luggers and small coasters, brought up alongside the Albert Pier, at the foot of a vacant ladder.

Having made the yacht fast to a couple of rings, Varney divested himself of his oilskins, locked the cabin scuttle, and climbed the ladder. The change of wind had saved him after all, and as he strode away along the pier he glanced complacently at his watch. He still had nearly half-an-hour to the good.

He seemed to know the place well and to have a definite objective, for he struck out briskly from the foot of the pier into Market Jew Street, and from thence, by a somewhat zigzag route, to a road which eventually brought him out about the middle of the esplanade. Continuing westward, he entered the Newlyn Road, along which he walked rapidly for about a third-of-a-mile, when he drew up opposite a small letter-box, which was let into a wall. Here he stopped to read the tablet, on which was printed the hours of collection, and then, having glanced at his watch, he walked on again, but at a less rapid pace.

When he reached the outskirts of Newlyn, he turned and began slowly to retrace his steps, looking at his watch from time to time with a certain air of impatience. Presently a quick step behind him caused him to look round. The newcomer was a postman, striding along, bag on shoulder, with the noisy tread of a heavily shod man and evidently collecting letters. Varney let him pass, watched him halt at the little letter-box, unlock the door, gather up the letters, and stow them in his bag, heard the clang of the iron door, and finally saw the man set forth again on his pilgrimage. Then he brought forth his pocket-book, and drawing from it the letter addressed to Joseph Penfield, Esq., stepped up to the letter-box. The tablet now announced that the next collection would be at 8.30 p.m. Varney read the announcement with a faint smile, glanced again at his watch, which stood at two-minutes-past-four, and dropped the letter into the box.

As he walked up the pier with a large paper bag under his arm, he became aware of a tall man who was doing sentry-go before a Gladstone bag that stood on the coping opposite the ladder, and who, observing his approach, came forward to meet him.

"Here you are, then, Rodney," was Varney's rather unoriginal greeting.

"Yes," replied Rodney, "and here I've been for nearly half-an-hour. Purcell gone?"

"Bless you! Yes, long ago," answered Varney.

"I didn't see him at the station. What train was he going by?"

"I don't know. He said something about taking Falmouth on the way, had some business or other there. But I expect he's gone to have a feed at one of the hotels. We got hung up in a fog, that's why I'm so late. I've been up to buy some grog."

"Well," said Rodney, "bring it on board. It's time we were under way. As soon as we are outside I'll take charge, and you can go below and stoke up at your ease."

The two men descended the ladder and proceeded at once to hoist the sails and cast off the shore ropes. A few strokes of an oar sent them clear of the lee of the pier, and in a few minutes the yacht *Sandhopper* was once more outside, heading south with a steady breeze from east-north-east.

Chapter II
In Which Margaret Purcell
Receives a Letter

Daylight dies hard in the month of June, and Night comes but tardily into her scanty reversion. The clock on the mantelpiece stood at half-past-nine, and candles twinkled on the supper table, but even now the slaty-grey band of twilight was only just stealing up behind the horizon to veil the fading glories of the western sky.

Varney sat at the old-fashioned, oval, gate-legged table with an air of placid contentment, listening to and joining in the rather disconnected talk (for hungry people are poor conversationalists) with quiet geniality but with a certain remoteness and abstraction. From where he sat he could see out through the open window, the great ocean stretching away to the south and west, the glittering horizon, and the gorgeous evening sky. With quiet pleasure he had watched the changing scene – the crimson disc of the setting sun, the flaming gold softening down into the sober tints of the afterglow – and now, as the grey herald of the night spread upwards, his eye dwelt steadily on one spot away in the south-west. At first faintly visible, then waxing as the daylight waned, a momentary spark flashed in the heart of the twilight grey, now white like the sparkle of a diamond, now crimson like the flash of a ruby. It was the light on the Wolf Rock.

He watched it thoughtfully as he talked: White – red, white – red, diamond – ruby, so it would go on every fifteen seconds through the short summer night – to mariners a warning and a guide, to him, a message of release, for another, a memorial.

As he looked at the changing light, he thought of his enemy lying out there in the chilly depths on the bed of the sea. It was strange how often he thought of Purcell. For the man was dead, had gone out of his life utterly. And yet, in the two days that had passed, every trivial incident had seemed to connect itself and him with the man who was gone. And so it was now. All roads seemed to lead to Purcell. If he looked out seaward, there was the lighthouse flashing its secret message, as if it should say, "We know, you and I, he is down here." If he looked around the table, still everything spoke of the dead man. There was Philip Rodney – Purcell and he had talked of him on the yacht. There was Jack Rodney, who had waited on the pier for the man who had not come. There, at the hostess's right hand, was the quiet, keen-faced stranger whom Purcell, for some reason, had not wished to meet, and there, at the head of the table, was Margaret herself, the determining cause of it all. Even the very lobsters on the table (lobsters are plentiful at the Land's End) set him thinking of dark crawling shapes down in that dim underworld, groping around a larger shape tethered to an iron weight.

He turned his face resolutely away from the sea. He would think no more of Purcell. The fellow had dogged him through life, but now he was gone. Enough of Purcell. Let him think of something more pleasant.

The most agreeable object of contemplation within his field of vision was the woman who sat at the head of the table, his hostess. And, in fact, Margaret Purcell was very pleasant to look upon, not only for her comeliness – though she was undoubtedly a pretty, almost a beautiful, woman – but because she was sweet-faced and gracious, and what men compliment the sex by calling "womanly". She was evidently under thirty, though she carried a certain matronly sedateness and an air of being older than she either looked or was, which was accentuated by the fashion in which she wore her hair, primly parted in the middle – a rather big woman, quiet and reposeful, as big women often are.

Varney looked at her with a kind of wonder. He had always thought her lovely, and now she seemed lovelier than ever. And she was a widow, little as she suspected it, little as anyone but he suspected it. But it was a fact. She was free to marry, if she only knew it.

He hugged himself at the thought and listened dreamily to the mellow tones of her voice. She was talking to her guest and the elder Rodney, but he had only a dim idea of what she was saying, he was enjoying the music of her speech rather than attending to the matter. Suddenly she turned to him and asked, "Don't you agree with me, Mr. Varney?"

He pulled himself together, and, after a momentarily vacant look, answered, "I always agree with you, Mrs. Purcell."

"And so," said Jack Rodney, "as the greater includes the less, he agrees with you now. I am admiring your self-possession, Varney. You haven't the least idea what we were talking about."

Varney laughed and reddened, and Margaret looked at him with playful reproach.

"Haven't you?" she asked. "But how deceitful of you to answer so readily! I was remarking that lawyers have a way of making a solemn parade of exactness and secrecy when there is no occasion. That was my statement."

"And it is perfectly correct," said Varney. "You know it is, Rodney. You're always doing it. I've noticed it constantly."

"Oh, this is mere vindictiveness, because he unmasked your deceit. I wasn't alluding to Mr. Rodney or anyone in particular. I was just speaking generally."

"But," said Varney, "something must have suggested the reflection."

"Certainly. Something did – a letter that I have just received from Mr. Penfield, a most portentous document, and all about nothing."

At the mention of the lawyer's name Varney's attention came to a sharp focus.

"It seems," Margaret continued, "that Dan, when he wrote to Mr. Penfield the other day, put the wrong letter in the envelope – a silly thing to do, but we all do silly things sometimes."

"I don't," said Rodney.

"Well, ordinary persons, I mean. Then Mr. Penfield, instead of simply stating the fact and returning the letter, becomes mysterious and alarming. He informs me that the envelope was addressed in Dan's handwriting, that the letter was posted at Penzance at eight-thirty p.m., that it was opened by him in person, and that the contents, which have been seen by no one but himself, are at present reposing in his private safe, of which he alone has the key. What he does not tell us is what the contents of the envelope were, which is the only thing that matters. It is most extraordinary. From the tone of his letter one would think that the envelope had contained something dreadful and incriminating."

"Perhaps it did," said Varney. "Dan's political views are distinctly revolutionary, and he is as secret as a whole barrel of oysters. That letter may have contained particulars of some sort of Guy Fawkes conspiracy, enclosing samples of suitable explosives. Who knows?"

Margaret was about to reply, when her glance happened to light on Jack Rodney, and something in that gentleman's expressive and handsome face gave her pause. Had she been chattering indiscreetly? And might Mr. Penfield have meant something after all? There were some curious points about his letter. She smilingly accepted the Guy Fawkes theory and then adroitly changed the subject.

"Speaking of Penzance, Mr. Varney, reminds me that you haven't told us what sort of voyage you had. There was quite a thick fog wasn't there?"

"Yes. It delayed us a lot. Purcell would steer right out to sea for fear of going ashore. Then the breeze failed for a time, and then it veered round easterly and headed us, and, as a wind up to the chapter of accidents, the jib-halyards carried away and we had to reeve a new one. Nice crazy gear you keep on your craft, Rodney."

"I suspected that rope," said Rodney. "In fact, I had meant to fit a new halyard before I went up to town. But I should have liked to see Purcell shinning up aloft."

"So should I – from the shore," said Varney. "He'd have carried away the mast or capsized the yacht. No, my friend, I left him below as a counterpoise and went aloft myself."

"Did Dan go straight off to the station?" Margaret asked.

"I should say not," replied Varney. "He was in a mighty hurry to be off – said he had some things to see to. I fancy one of them was a grilled steak and a bottle of Bass. We were both pretty ravenous."

"But why didn't you go with him if you were ravenous too?"

"I had to snug up the yacht and he wouldn't wait. He was up the ladder like a lamplighter almost before we had made fast. I can see him now, with that great suitcase in his hand, going up as light as a feather. He is wonderfully active for his size."

"Isn't he?" said Rodney. "But these big men often are. Look at the way those great lumping pilots will drop down into a boat, as light as cats."

"He is a big fellow, too," said Varney. "I was looking at him as he stopped at the top of the ladder to sing out 'So long'. He looked quite gigantic in his oilskins."

"He actually went up into town in his oilskins, did he?" exclaimed Margaret. "He must have been impatient for his meal! Oh, how silly of me! I never sewed on that button that had come off the collar of his oilskin coat. I hope you didn't have a wet passage."

"You need not reproach yourself, Mrs. Purcell," interposed Philip Rodney. "Your neglect was made good by my providence. I sewed on that button when I borrowed the coat on Friday evening to go to my diggings in."

"You told me you hadn't a spare oilskin button," said Margaret.

"I hadn't, but I made one – out of a cork."

"A cork?" Margaret exclaimed, with an incredulous laugh.

"Not a common cork, you know," Philip explained. "It was a flat circular cork from one of my collecting jars, waterproofed with paraffin wax, a most superior affair, with a beautiful round label – also waterproofed by the wax – on which was typed '*Marine Worms*'. The label was very decorative. It's my own invention, and I'm rather proud of it.".

"You may well be. And I suppose you sewed it on with rope-yarn and a sail-needle?" Margaret suggested.

"Not at all. It was secured with catgut, the fag end of an E string that I happened to have in my pocket. You see, I had no needle or thread, so I

261

made two holes in the cork with the marlin-spike in my pocket-knife, two similar holes in the coat, poked the ends of the fiddlestring through, tied a reef-knot inside, and there it was, tight as wax – paraffin wax."

"It was very ingenious and resourceful of you," Varney commented, "but the product wasn't very happily disposed of on Dan's coat – I mean as to your decorative label. I take it that Dan's interest in marine worms is limited to their use as bait. Now if you could have fitted out Dr. Thorndyke with a set there would have been some appropriateness in it, since marine worms are the objects of his devotion – at least, so I understand." And he looked interrogatively at Margaret's guest.

Dr. Thorndyke smiled. "You are draping me in the mantle of my friend, Professor D'Arcy," he said. "He is the real devotee. I have merely come down for a few days to stay with him and be an interested spectator of the chase. It is he who should have the buttons."

"Still," said Varney, "you aid and abet him. I suppose you help him to dig them up."

Philip laughed scornfully. "Why, you are as bad as Dan, Varney. You are thinking in terms of bait. Do you imagine Dr. Thorndyke and the professor go a-worming with a bully-beef tin and a garden fork as you do when you are getting ready for a fishing jaunt?"

"Well, how was I to know?" retorted Varney. "I am not a naturalist. What *do* they do? Set traps for 'em with bits of cheese inside?"

"Of course they don't," laughed Margaret. "How absurd you are, Mr. Varney! They go out with a boat and a dredge, and very interesting it must be to bring up all those curious creatures from the bottom of the sea."

She spoke rather absently, for her thoughts had gone back to Mr. Penfield's letter. There was certainly something a little cryptic in its tone, which she had taken for mere professional pedantry, but which she now recalled with vague uneasiness. Could the old lawyer have stumbled on something discreditable and written this ambiguously worded letter as a warning? Her husband was not a communicative man, and she could not pretend to herself that she had an exalted opinion of his moral character. It was all very disquieting.

The housekeeper, who had been retained with the furnished house, brought in the coffee, and as Margaret poured it out she continued her reflections, watching Varney with unconscious curiosity as he rolled a cigarette. The ring-finger of his left hand had a stiff joint, the result of an old injury, and was permanently bent at a sharp angle. It gave his hand an appearance of awkwardness, but she noted that he rolled his cigarette as quickly and neatly as if all his fingers were sound. The stiff finger had become normal to him. And she also noted that Dr. Thorndyke appeared quite interested in the contrast between the appearance of awkwardness and the actual efficiency of the maimed finger.

From Varney her attention – or inattention – wandered to her guest. Absently she dwelt on his powerful, intellectual face, his bold, clean-cut features, his shapely mouth, firm almost to severity, and all the time she was thinking of Mr. Penfield's letter.

"Have we all finished?" she asked at length, "and if so, where are we going to smoke our pipes and cigars?"

"I propose that we go into the garden," said Philip. "It is a lovely evening, and we can look at the moonlight on the sea while we smoke."

"Yes," Margaret agreed, "it will be more pleasant out there. Don't wait for me. I will join you in a few minutes, but I want first to have a few words with Mr. Rodney."

Philip, who, like the others, understood that this was a consultation on the subject of Mr. Penfield's letter, rose and playfully shepherded Varney out of the door which his brother held invitingly open. "Now then, Varney, out you go. No lagging behind and eavesdropping. The pronouncements of the oracle are not for the likes of you and me."

Varney took his dismissal with a smile and followed Dr. Thorndyke out, though, as he looked at the barrister's commanding figure and handsome face, he could not repress a twinge of jealousy. Why could not Maggie have consulted him? He was an old friend, and he knew more about old Penfield's letter than Rodney did. But, of course, she had no idea of that.

As soon as they were alone, Margaret and Rodney resumed their seats, and the former opened the subject without preamble.

"What do you really think of Mr. Penfield's letter?" she asked.

"Could you give me, in general terms, the substance of what he says?" Rodney answered cautiously.

"I had better show you the letter itself," said Margaret.

She rose and left the room, returning almost immediately with an official-looking envelope, which she handed to Rodney. The letter, which he extracted from it and spread out on the table, was not remarkably legible, an elderly solicitor's autograph letters seldom are. But barristers, like old-fashioned druggists, are usually expert decipherers, and Rodney read the letter without difficulty. It ran thus:

George Yard
Lombard Street, E.C.
2 July, 1911.
Dear Mrs. Purcell,

I have just received from your husband a letter with certain enclosures, which have caused me some surprise. The envelope is addressed to me in his handwriting, and the letter, which is unsigned, is also in his hand, but neither the letter nor the other contents could possibly have been intended for me, and it is manifest that they have been placed in the wrong envelope.

The postmark shows that the letter was posted at Penzance at 8:30 p.m. on the 23rd instant. It was opened by me, and the contents, which have been seen by no one but me, have been deposited in my private safe, of which I alone have the key.

Will you very kindly acquaint your husband with these facts and request him to call on me at his early convenience?

I am, dear Mrs. Purcell,

Yours sincerely,
Joseph Penfield

(Mrs. Daniel Purcell
Sennen, Cornwall)

Rodney read the solicitor's letter through twice, refolded it, replaced it in its envelope, and returned it to Margaret.

"Well, what do you think of it?" the latter asked.

Rodney reflected for some moments.

"It's a very careful letter," he replied at length.

"Yes, I know, and that is a very careful answer, but not very helpful. Now do drop the lawyer and tell me just what you think like a good friend."

Rodney looked at her quickly with a faint smile and yet very earnestly. He found it strangely pleasant to be called a good friend by Margaret Purcell.

"I gather," he said slowly, "from the tone of Mr. Penfield's letter, that he found something in that envelope that your husband would not have wished him to see – something that he had reasons for wishing no one to see but the person for whom it was meant."

"Do you mean something discreditable or compromising?"

"We mustn't jump at conclusions. Mr. Penfield is very reticent, so, presumably, he has some reasons for reticence, otherwise he would have

264

said plainly what the envelope contained. But why does he write to you? Doesn't he know your husband's address?"

"No, but he could have got it from Dan's office. I have been wondering myself why he wrote to me."

"Has your husband arrived at Oulton yet?"

"Heavens! Yes. It doesn't take two-days-and-a-half to get to Norfolk."

"Oh, then he wasn't staying at Falmouth?"

Margaret stared at him. "Falmouth!" she exclaimed. "What do you mean?"

"I understood Varney to say that he was going to call at Falmouth."

"No, certainly not. He was going straight to London and so on to Oulton the same night. I wonder what Mr. Varney can have meant."

"We must find out presently. Have you heard from your husband since he left?"

"No. Oddly enough, he hasn't written, which is unlike him. He generally sends me a line as soon as he arrives anywhere."

"You had better send him a telegram in the morning to make sure of his whereabouts, and then let him have a copy of Mr. Penfield's letter at once. And I think I wouldn't refer to the subject before any of our friends if I were you."

"No. I oughtn't to have said what I did. But, of course, I didn't dream that Mr. Penfield really meant anything. Shall we go out into the garden?"

Rodney opened the door for her, and they passed out to where their three companions sat in deck-chairs facing the sea. Two chairs had been placed for them, and, as they seated themselves, Varney remarked, "I take it that the oracle has spoken, and I hope he was more explicit than oracles are usually."

"He was explicit and discreet – especially discreet," Margaret replied.

"Oh, they are always that," said Varney. "Discretion is the oracular speciality. The explicitness is exceptional."

"I believe it is," replied Margaret, "and I am glad you set so much value on it, because I am coming to you now for information. Mr. Rodney tells me that Dan said something to you about Falmouth. What was it?"

"He said he was going to call in there – at least, so I understood."

"But he wasn't, you know. He was going direct to London and straight on to Oulton the same night. You must have misunderstood him."

"I may have done, but I don't think I did. Still, he only mentioned the matter casually, and I wasn't paying particular attention."

Margaret made no rejoinder, and the party became somewhat silent. Philip, realizing Margaret's uneasy preoccupation, engaged Dr. Thorndyke in an animated conversation respecting the natural history of the Cornish coast and the pleasures of dredging.

The other three became profoundly thoughtful. To each the solicitor's letter had its special message, though to one only was that message clearly intelligible. Rodney was puzzled and deeply suspicious. To him the letter had read like that of a man washing his hands of a disagreeable responsibility. The curious reticence as to the nature of the enclosures and the reference to the private safe sounded ominous. He knew little of Purcell – he had been a friend of the Haygarths' – and had no great opinion of him. Purcell was a financier, and financiers sometimes did queer things. At any rate, Penfield's excessive caution suggested something fishy – possibly something illicit. In fact, to speak colloquially, Rodney smelt a rat.

Margaret also was puzzled and suspicious but, womanlike, she allowed her suspicions to take a more special form. She, too, smelt a rat, but it was a feminine rat. The lawyer's silence as to the contents of that mysterious envelope seemed to admit of no other interpretation. It was so pointed. Of course he could not tell her, though he was an old friend and her trustee, so he had said nothing.

She reflected on the matter with lukewarm displeasure. Her relations with her husband were not such as to admit of jealousy in the ordinary sense, but still, she was married to him, and any affair on his part with another woman would be very disagreeable and humiliating to her. It might lead to a scandal, too, and from that her ingrained delicacy revolted.

Varney, meanwhile, sat with his head thrown back wrapped in thought of a more dreamy quality. He knew all about the letter, and his mind was occupying itself with speculation as to its effects. Rodney's view of it he gauged pretty accurately, but what did *she* think of it? Was she anxious – worried at the prospect of some unpleasant disclosure? He hoped not. At any rate, it could not be helped. And she was free, if she only knew it.

He had smoked out his cigarette, and now, as he abstractedly filled his pipe, his eye insensibly sought the spot where the diamond and ruby flashed out alternately from the bosom of the night. A cloud had crept over the moon, and the transitory golden and crimson gleam shone out bright and clear amidst the encompassing darkness, white – red, white –

red, diamond – ruby, a message in a secret code from the tall, unseen sentinel on that solitary, wave-washed rock, bidding him be of good cheer, reminding him again and again of the freedom that was his – and hers, made everlastingly secure by a friendly iron sinker.

The cloud turned silvery at the edge and the moon sailed out into the open. Margaret looked up at it thoughtfully.

"I wonder where Dan is to-night," she said, and in the pause that followed a crimson spark from the dim horizon seemed to Varney to signal, "Here," and instantly fade into discreet darkness.

"Perhaps," suggested Philip, "he is having a moonlight sail on the Broad, or, more probably, taking a whisky-and-soda with Bradford in the inn parlour where the stuffed pike is. You remember that stuffed pike, Jack?"

His brother nodded. "Can I ever forget it, or the landlord's interminable story of its capture? I wonder why people become so intolerably boresome about their fishing exploits. The angler is nearly as bad as the golfer."

"Still," said Varney, "he has more excuse. It is more of an achievement to catch a pike or a salmon than merely to whack a ball with a stick."

"Isn't that rather a crude description of the game?" asked Margaret. "It is to be hoped that Dr. Thorndyke is not an enthusiast."

"I am not," he assured her. "In fact, I was admiring Mr. Varney's simplification. His definition of the game is worthy of Dr. Johnson. But I must tear myself away. My host is an early bird, and I expect you are, too. Good-night, Mrs. Purcell. It has been very delightful to meet you again. I am only sorry that I should have missed your husband."

"So am I," said Margaret, shaking his hand warmly, "but I think it most kind of you to have remembered me after all these years."

As Dr. Thorndyke rose, the other three men stood up. "It is time for us to go, too," said Rodney, "so we will see you to the end of the road, Thorndyke. Good-night, Mrs. Purcell."

"Good-night, gentlemen all," she replied. "Eight o'clock breakfast, remember."

The four men went into the house to fetch their hats and took their departure, walking together as far as the cross-roads, where Thorndyke wished the other three "Good-night" and left them to pursue their way to the village.

The lodging accommodation in this neighbourhood was not sumptuous, but our three friends were not soft or fastidious. Besides, they only slept at their "diggings", taking their meals and making their home at the house which Purcell had hired, furnished, for the holiday. It was a somewhat unconventional arrangement, now that Purcell had gone, and spoke eloquently of his confidence in the discretion of his attractive wife.

The three men were not in the same lodgings. Varney was "putting up" at the First and Last Inn in the adjoining village – or "church-town", to give it its local title – of Sennen, while the Rodneys shared a room at the Ship down in Sennen Cove, more than a mile away. They proceeded together as far as Varney's hostel, when, having wished him "Good-night," the two brothers strode away along the moonlit road towards the Cove.

For a while neither spoke, though the thoughts of both were occupied by the same subject, the solicitor's letter. Philip had fully taken in the situation, although he had made no remark on it, and the fact that his brother had been consulted quasi-professionally on the subject made him hesitate to refer to it. For in spite of his gay, almost frivolous, manner, Philip Rodney was a responsible medical practitioner, and really a man of sound judgment and discretion.

Presently his scruples yielded to the consideration that his brother was not likely to divulge any confidence, and he remarked, "I hope Purcell hasn't been doing anything shady. It sounded to me as if there was a touch of Pontius Pilate in the tone of Penfield's letter."

"Yes, a very guarded tone, with a certain note of preparation for unpleasant possibilities. So it struck me. I do sincerely hope there isn't anything in it."

"So do I, by Jove! But I shouldn't be so very astonished. Of course we don't know anything against Purcell – at least, I don't – but somehow he doesn't strike me as a very scrupulous man. His outlook on life jars a bit, don't you feel that some times?"

"The commercial standard isn't quite the same as the professional, you know," Jack Rodney answered evasively, "and financial circles are not exactly of the higher morality. But I know of nothing to Purcell's discredit."

"No, of course not. But he isn't the same class as his wife. She's a lot too good for a coarse, bucolic fellow like that. I wonder why the deuce she married him. I used to think she rather liked you."

"A woman can't marry every man she rather likes, you know, Phil, unless she happens to live in Ladak, and even there I believe there are limits. But to come back to Purcell, we may be worrying ourselves about nothing. To-morrow we shall get into touch with him by telegraph, and then we may hear something from him."

Here the consideration of Purcell and his affairs dropped so far as conversation went, but in the elder man's mind certain memories had been revived by his brother's remark and occupied it during the remainder of the walk. For he, too, had once thought that Maggie Haygarth rather liked him, and he now recalled the shock of disagreeable surprise with which he had heard of her marriage. But that was over and done with long ago, and the question now was, how was the *Sandhopper*, at present moored in Whitesand Bay, to be got from the Land's End to her moorings above Westminster Bridge? – a problem that engaged the attention of the two brothers until they turned into their respective beds and the laggard, according to immemorial custom, blew out the light.

In spite of Mrs. Purcell's admonition, they were some minutes late on the following morning. Their two friends were already seated at the breakfast table, and it needed no extraordinary powers of observation to see that something had happened. Their hostess was pale and looked worried and some what frightened, and Varney was preternaturally grave. A telegram lay open on the table by Margaret's place, and as Rodney advanced to shake hands, she held it out to him without a word. He took the paper and read the brief but ominous message that confirmed but too plainly his misgivings of the previous night.

> *Where is Dan? Expected him here Tuesday night. Home nothing wrong.*
>
> *Bradford, Angler's Hotel*
> *Oulton*

Rodney laid down the telegram and looked at Margaret. "This is a queer business," said he. "Have you done anything?"

"No," she replied. "What can we do?" Rodney took a slip of paper and a pencil from his pocket. "If you will write down the name of the partner or clerk who is attending at the office and address, and that of the caretaker of your flat, I will go and send off reply-paid telegrams to them asking for information as to your husband's whereabouts, and I will also reply to Mr. Bradford. It is just possible that Purcell may have gone home after all."

"It's very unlikely," said Margaret. "The flat is shut up, and he would surely have written. Still, we may as well make sure, if you will be so kind. But won't you have your breakfast first?"

"We'd better waste no time," he answered, and, pocketing the paper, strode away on his errand.

Little was said until he returned, and even then the breakfast proceeded in a gloomy silence that contrasted strangely with the usual vivacity of the gatherings around that hospitable table. A feeling of tense expectation pervaded the party and a vivid sense of impending disaster. Dreary efforts were made to keep some kind of conversation going, but the talk was colourless and disjointed with long and awkward pauses.

Varney especially was wrapped in deep meditation. Outwardly he preserved an appearance of sympathetic anxiety, but inwardly he was conscious of a strange, rather agreeable excitement, almost of elation. When he looked at Margaret's troubled face he felt a pang of regret, of contrition, but principally he was sensible of a feeling of power, of knowledge. He sat apart, as it were, Godlike, omniscient. He knew all the facts that were hidden from the others. The past lay clear before him to the smallest detail. The involved present was as an open book which he read with ease, and he could even peer confidently into the future.

And these men and the woman before him, and those others afar off – the men at the office, the caretaker, Penfield the lawyer, and Bradford at his inn in Norfolk – what were they but so many puppets, moving feverishly hither and thither as he, the unseen master-spirit, directed them by a pull at the strings? It was he who had wound them up and set them going, and here he sat, motionless and quiet, watching them do his bidding. He was reminded of an occasion when he had been permitted for a short time to steer a five-thousand-ton steamer. What a sense of power it had given him to watch the stupendous consequences of his own trifling movements! A touch of the little wheel, the movement of a spoke or two to right or left, and what a commotion followed! How the steam gear had clanked with furious haste to obey, and the great ship had presently swerved round, responsive to the pressure of his fingers! What a wonderful thing it had been! There was that colossal structure with its enormous burden of merchandise, its teeming population sweating in the stokehold or sleeping in the dark forecastle, its unconscious passengers chatting on the decks, reading, writing, or playing cards in saloon or smoking-room, and he had had it all in the grasp of one hand, had moved it and turned it about with the mere touch of a finger.

And so it was now. The magical pressure of his finger on the trigger, a few turns of a rope, the hoisting of an iron weight, and behold! The whole course of a human life – probably of several human lives – was changed utterly.

It was a tremendous thought.

In a little over an hour the replies to Rodney's discreetly worded inquiries had come in. Mr. Purcell had not been home nor had he been heard of at the office. Mr. Penfield had been inquiring as to his whereabouts and so had Mr. Bradford. That was all. And what it amounted to was that Daniel Purcell had disappeared.

270

"Can't you remember exactly what Dan said about going to Falmouth, Mr. Varney?" Margaret asked.

"I am sorry to say I can't," replied Varney. "You see, he just threw the remark off casually, and I didn't ask any questions. He isn't very fond of being questioned, you know."

"I wonder what he could have been going to Falmouth for," she mused. In reality she did not wonder at all. She felt pretty certain that she knew. But pride would not allow her publicly to adopt that explanation until it was forced on her. "It seems to me that there is only one course," she continued. "I must go up to town and see Mr. Penfield. Don't you think so, Mr. Rodney?"

"Certainly. He is the only one who knows anything and is able to advise." He hesitated a moment, and then added, "Hadn't we better come up with you?"

"Yes," said Varney eagerly, "let us all go up."

Margaret considered for a few moments. "It is excessively kind and sympathetic of you all, and I am glad you offered, because it makes me feel that I have good loyal friends, which is a great deal to know just now. But, really, there would be no use in breaking up your holidays. What could you do? We can't make a search in person. Why not take over the house and stay on here?"

"We don't want the house if you're not in it," said Philip.

"No," agreed Jack Rodney, "if we can't be of use to you we shall get afloat and begin to crawl round the coast homewards."

"I think I shall run over to Falmouth and see if I can pick up any news," said Varney.

"Thank you," said Margaret. "I think that would be really useful," and Rodney agreed heartily, adding, "Why not come round in the yacht, Varney? We shall probably get there to-morrow night."

Varney reflected. And suddenly it was borne in upon him that he felt an unspeakable repugnance to the idea of going on board the yacht, and especially to making the voyage from Sennen to Penzance. The feeling came to him as an utter surprise, but there was no doubt of its reality.

"I think I'll go over by train," he said. "It will save a day, you know."

"Then we will meet you there," said Rodney, "and, Mrs. Purcell, will you send us a letter to the Green Banks Hotel, Falmouth, and let us know what Mr. Penfield says, and if you would like us to come up to town to help you?"

"Thank you, yes, I will," Margaret replied heartily. "And I promise that, if I want your help, I will ask for it."

"That is a solemn promise, mind," said Rodney.

"Yes, I mean it – a solemn promise."

So the matter was arranged. By twelve o'clock, the weather being calm, the yacht was got under way for Penzance. And even as on that other occasion, she headed seaward with her crew of two, watched from the shore by a woman and a man.

Chapter III
In Which Margaret Purcell
Consults Mr. Penfield

Mr. Joseph Penfield was undeniably in a rather awkward dilemma.
For he had hooked the wrong fish. His letter to Maggie Purcell had been
designed to put him immediately in touch with Purcell himself, whereas
it had evoked an urgent telegram from Maggie announcing her intention
of calling on him "on important business" and entreating him to arrange
an interview.

It was really most unfortunate. There was no one in the world whom
he had less desire to see, at the present moment, than Margaret Purcell.
And yet there was no possible escape, for not only was he her solicitor
and her trustee, but he was an old family friend, and not a little attached
to her in his dry way. But he didn't want her just now. He wanted
Purcell, and he wanted him very badly.

For a solicitor of irreproachable character and spotless reputation his
position was highly unpleasant. As soon as he had opened the letter from
Penzance he had recognised the nature of the enclosures, and had
instantly connected them with the forgeries of Bank of England notes of
which he had heard. The intricate water-marks on the "blanks" were
unmistakable. But so was the handwriting of the accompanying letter. It
was Daniel Purcell's beyond a doubt, and the peculiar, intensely black
ink was equally characteristic. And, short as the note was, it made
perfectly clear its connection with the incriminating enclosures. It wrote
down Daniel Purcell a banknote forger.

Now Mr. Penfield was, as we have said, a man of irreproachable
character. But he was a very secretive and rather casuistical old
gentleman, and his regard for Margaret had led him to apply his casuistry
to the present case, pretending to himself that his discovery of the illicit
blanks came within the category of "clients' secrets", which he need not
divulge. But in his heart he knew that he was conniving at a felony, that
he ought to give information to the police or to the Bank, and that he
wasn't going to. His plan was to get hold of Purcell, make him destroy
the blanks in his presence, and deliver such a warning as would put a
stop to the forgeries.

But if he did not propose to give Purcell away, neither did he intend
to give himself away. He would share his compromising secret with no

one – especially with a lady. And this consideration raised the difficult question: What on earth was he to say to Margaret Purcell when she arrived? A question which he was still debating, with her telegram spread out before him and his silver snuff-box in his hand, when a clerk entered his private office to announce the unwelcome visitor.

Fortifying himself with a pinch of snuff, he rose and advanced towards the door to receive her, and as she entered he made a quick mental note of her anxious and troubled expression.

"How do you do, Mrs. Purcell?" said he, with a ceremonious bow. "You have had a long journey and rather an early one. How very unfortunate that this business, to which you refer in your telegram, should have arisen while you were on holiday so far away!"

"You have guessed what the business is, I suppose?" said Margaret.

Mr. Penfield smiled deprecatingly. "We lawyers," said he, "are not much addicted to guessing, especially when definite information is available. Pray be seated. And now," he continued, as Margaret subsided into the clients' chair and he resumed his own, resting his elbows on the arms and placing his finger-tips together, "let us hear what this new and important business is."

"It is about that mysterious letter that you had from my husband," said Margaret.

"Dear, dear!" said Mr. Penfield. "What a pity that you should have taken this long journey for such a trifling affair! And I thought I gave you all the particulars."

"You didn't mention whom the letter was from."

"For several excellent reasons," replied Mr. Penfield, checking them off on his fingers. "First, I don't know. Second, it is not my business. Third, your husband, whose business it is, does know. My object in writing to you was to get into touch with him so that I could hand back to him this letter, which should never have come into my possession. Shall I take down his address now?"

"I haven't it myself," Margaret replied with a faint flush. "I have no idea where he is at present. He left Sennen on the 2nd to go to Oulton via Penzance. But he never arrived at Oulton. He has not been home, he has not been to the office, and he has not written. It is rather alarming, especially in connection with your mysterious letter."

"Was my letter mysterious?" said Mr. Penfield, rapidly considering this new but not very surprising development. "I hardly think so. It was not intended to be. What was there mysterious about it?"

"Everything," she replied, producing the letter from her bag and glancing at it as she spoke. "You emphasise that Dan's letter and the other contents have been seen by no eye but yours, and that they are in a

274

receptacle to which no one has access but yourself. There is a strong hint of something secret and compromising in the nature of Dan's letter and enclosures."

"I would rather say 'confidential'," murmured Mr. Penfield.

"And," Margaret continued, "you must see that there is an evident connection between this misdirected letter and Dan's disappearance."

Mr. Penfield saw the connection very plainly, but he was admitting nothing. He did, indeed, allow that "it was a coincidence", but would not agree to "a necessary connection".

"Probably you will hear from your husband in a day or two, and then the letter can be returned."

"Is there any reason why you should not show me Dan's letter?" Margaret demanded. "Surely I am entitled, as his wife, to see it."

Mr. Penfield pursed up his lips and took a deliberate pinch of snuff.

"We must not confuse," said he, "the theological relations of married people with their legal relations. Theologically they are one. Legally they are separate persons subject to a mutual contract. As to this letter, it is not mine, and consequently I can show it to no one, and I must assume that if your husband had desired you to see it he would have shown it to you himself."

"But," Margaret protested impatiently, "are not my husband's secrets my secrets?"

"That," replied the lawyer, "is a delicate question which we need not consider. There is the question of the secrets of a third party. If I had the felicity to be a married man, which unfortunately I have not, you would hardly expect me to communicate your private, and perhaps secret, affairs to my wife. Now would you?"

Margaret had to admit that she would not. But she instantly countered the lawyer by inquiring, "Then I was apparently right in inferring that this letter and the enclosures contained matter of a secret and compromising character?"

"I have said nothing to that effect," replied Mr Penfield uncomfortably, and then, seeing that he had no choice between a downright lie and a flat refusal to answer any questions, he continued. "The fact is that it is not admissible for me to make any statement. This letter came to me by an error, and my position must be as if I had not seen it."

"But it can't be," Margaret persisted, "because you *have* seen it. I want to know if Dan's letter was addressed to anyone whom I know. You could tell me that, surely?"

"Unfortunately, I cannot," replied the lawyer, glad to be able to tell the literal truth for once. "The letter was without any formal opening.

There was nothing to indicate the identity or even the sex of the person to whom it was addressed."

Margaret noted this curious fact and then asked, "With regard to the enclosures. Did they consist of money?"

"They did not," was the reply, "nor cheques." A brief silence followed, during which Margaret reflected rapidly on what she had learned and what she had not learned. At length she looked up with a somewhat wry smile and said, "Well, Mr. Penfield, I suppose that is all I shall get out of you?"

"I am afraid it is," he replied. "The necessity of so much reservation is most distasteful, I assure you, but it is the plain duty of a lawyer to keep not only his own counsel but other people's."

"Yes, of course, I quite understand that. And now, as we have finished with the letter, there is the writer to consider. What had I better do about Dan?"

"Why do anything? It is only four days since he left Sennen."

"Yes, but something has evidently happened. He may have met with an accident and be in some hospital. Do you think that I ought to notify the police that he is missing?"

"No, certainly not," Mr. Penfield replied emphatically, for, in his mind, Purcell's disappearance was quite simply explained. He had discovered the mistake of the transposed letter, and knew that Penfield held the means of convicting him of a felony, and he had gone into hiding until he should discover what the lawyer meant to do. To put the police on his track would be to convince him of his danger and drive him hopelessly out of reach. But Mr. Penfield could not explain this to Margaret, and to cover his emphatic rejection of police assistance he continued, "You see, he can hardly be said to be missing. He may merely have altered his plans and neglected to write. Have patience for a day or two, and if you still hear no tidings of him, send me a line, and I will take what measures seem advisable for trying to get into touch with him."

"Thank you," said Margaret, not very enthusiastically, rising to take her departure. She was in the act of shaking Mr. Penfield's hand when, with a sudden afterthought, she asked, "By the way, was there anything in Dan's letter that might account for his disappearance in this fashion?"

This was rather a facer for Mr. Penfield, who, like many casuists, hated telling a direct lie. For the answer was clearly "Yes," whereas the sense that he was compelled to convey was "No."

"You are forgetting that the letter was not addressed to me," he said. "And that reminds me that there must have been another letter – the one that was addressed to me and that must have been put into the other person's envelope. May I ask if that letter has been returned?"

"No, it has not," replied Margaret.

"Ha!" said Mr. Penfield. "But it probably will be in the course of a day or two. Then we shall know what he was writing to me about and who is the other correspondent. Good-day, good-day, Mrs. Purcell."

He shook her hand warmly, and hastened to open the door for her in the hope, justified by the result, that she would not realize until she had left that her very significant question had not been answered.

Indeed, she did not realize how adroitly the old solicitor had evaded that question until she was too far away to return and put it afresh, even if that had seemed worthwhile, for her attention was occupied by the other issue that he had so artfully raised. She had overlooked the presumable existence of the second transposed letter, the one that should have been in Mr. Penfield's envelope. It ought to have been returned at once. Possibly it was even now waiting at Sennen to be forwarded. If it arrived, it would probably disclose the identity of the mysterious correspondent. On the other hand, it might not, and if it were not returned at all, that would confirm the suspicion that there was something gravely wrong. And it was at this point that Margaret became conscious of Mr. Penfield's last evasion.

Its effect was to confirm the generally disagreeable impression that she had received from the interview. She was a little resentful of the lawyer's elaborate reticence, which, coupled with the strange precautionary terms of his letter to her, convinced her that her husband had embarked on some questionable transaction, and that Mr. Penfield knew it and knew the nature of that transaction. His instant rejection of the suggestion that an accident might have occurred and that the police should be notified seemed to imply that he had some inkling of Purcell's proceedings, and his final evasion of her question strongly suggested that the letter, or the enclosures, or both, contained some clue to the disappearance.

Thus, as she took her way home, Margaret turned over again and again the puzzling elements of the mystery, and at each reshuffling of the scanty facts the same conclusion emerged – her husband had absconded, and he had not absconded alone. The secret that Mr. Penfield was guarding was such a secret as might, if divulged, have pointed the way to the divorce court. And with this conclusion and a frown of disgust, she turned into the entry of her flat and ascended the stairs.

As she let herself in, the maid met her in the hakl. "Mr. Varney is in the drawing-room, ma'am," she said. "He came about ten minutes ago. I am getting tea for him."

"Thank you, Nellie," said Margaret, "and you might get me some, too."

She passed on to her bedroom for a hasty wash and change, and then joined her visitor in time to pour out the tea.

"How good of you, Mr. Varney," she said warmly, as they shook hands, "to come to me so quickly! You must have only just arrived."

"Yes," he replied, "I came straight on from the station. I thought you would be anxious to know if I had heard anything."

"And have you?"

"Well," Varney replied, hesitatingly, "I'm rather afraid not. I seem to have drawn a blank."

Margaret looked at him critically. There was something in his manner suggestive of doubt and reservation.

"Do you mean an absolute blank? Did you find out nothing at all?"

Again Varney seemed to hesitate, and Margaret's attention sharpened.

"There isn't much use in making guesses," said he. "I found no definite traces of Dan. He hadn't been at the Ship, where I put up, and where he used to stay when he went to Falmouth, and of course I couldn't go round the other hotels making inquiries. But I went down the quay-side and asked a few discreet questions about the craft that had left the port since Monday, especially the odd craft, bound for small ports. I felt that if Dan had any reason for slipping off quietly he wouldn't go by a passenger boat to a regular passenger port. He would go on a cargo boat bound to some out-of-the-way place. So I found out what I could about the cargo boats that had put out of Falmouth, but I didn't have much luck."

Again he paused irresolutely, and Margaret asked, with a shade of impatience, "Did you find out anything at all?"

"Well, no, I can't say that I did," Varney replied, in the same slow, inconclusive manner. "It's disappointing in a way, especially as I really thought at one time that I had got on his track. But that turned out a mistake after all."

"You are sure it was a mistake," said Margaret eagerly. "Tell me about it."

"I picked up the clue when I was asking about a Swedish steamer that had put out on Tuesday morning. She had a lading of china clay and was bound for Malmo, but she was calling at Ipswich to pick up some other cargo. I learned that she took one or two passengers on board, and one of them was described to me as a big red-faced man of about forty, who looked like a pilot or a ship's officer. That sounded rather like Dan, and when I heard that he was carrying a biggish suitcase and had a yellow oilskin coat on his arm, I made pretty sure that it was."

"And how do you know that it was not Dan?"

278

"Why," replied Varney, "it turned out that this man had a woman with him."

"I see," said Margaret hastily, flushing scarlet and turning her head away. For a while she could think of nothing further to say. To her, of course, the alleged disproof of the passenger's identity was "confirmation strong as Holy Writ". But her pride would not allow her to confess this – at any rate to Varney – and she was in difficulties as to how to pursue the inquiry without making the admission. At length she ventured, "Do you think that is quite conclusive? I mean, is it certain that the woman belonged to the man? There is the possibility that she may have been merely a fellow-passenger whom he had casually accompanied to the ship. Or did you ascertain that they were actually – er – companions?"

"No, by Jove!" exclaimed Varney. "I never thought of any other possibilities. I heard that the man went on board with a woman, and at once decided that he couldn't be Dan. But you are quite right. They may have just met at the hotel or elsewhere and walked down to the ship together. I wonder if it's worthwhile to make any further inquiries about the ship – I mean at Ipswich, or, if necessary, at Malmo."

"Do you remember the ship's name?"

"Yes, the *Hedwig* of Hernosand. She left Falmouth early on Tuesday morning, so she will probably have got to Ipswich some time yesterday. She may be there now, or, of course, she may have picked up her stuff and gone to sea the same day. Would you like me to run down to Ipswich and see if I can find out anything?"

Margaret turned on him with a look that set his heart thumping and his pulses throbbing.

"Mr. Varney," she said, in a low, unsteady voice, "you make me ashamed and proud – proud to have such a loyal, devoted friend, and ashamed to be such a tax on him."

"Not at all," he replied. "After all – " Here his voice, too, became a little unsteady. " – Dan was my pal. *Is* my pal still," he added huskily. He paused for a moment, and then concluded, "I'll go down to-night and try to pick up the scent while it is fresh."

"It is good of you!" she exclaimed, and as she spoke her eyes filled, but she still looked at him frankly as she continued. "Your faithful friendship is no little compensation for – " She was going to say "his unfaithfulness", but altered the words to "the worry and anxiety of this horrid mystery. But I am ashamed to let you take so much trouble, though I must confess that it would be an immense relief to me to get some news of Dan. I don't hope for good news, but it is terrible to be so completely in the dark."

"Yes, that is the worst part of it," Varney agreed, and then, setting his cup on the table, he rose. "I had better be getting along now," he said, "so that I can catch the earliest possible train. Good-bye, Mrs. Purcell, and good luck to us both."

The leave-taking almost shattered Varney's self-possession, for Margaret, in the excess of her gratitude, impulsively grasped both his hands and pressed them warmly as she poured out her thanks. Her touch made him tingle to the finger-ends. Heavens! How beautiful she looked, this lovely, unconscious young widow! And to think that she might in time be his own! A wild impulse surged through him to clasp her in his arms, to tell her that she was free and that he worshipped her. Of course, that was a mere impulse that interfered not at all with his decorous, deferential manner. And yet a sudden, almost insensible change in her made him suspect that his eyes had told her more than he had meant to disclose. Nevertheless, she followed him to the lobby to speed him on his errand, and when he looked back from the foot of the stairs, she was standing at the open door, smiling down on him.

The thoughts of these two persons, when each was alone, were strangely different. In Margaret's mind there was no doubt that the man on the steamer was her unworthy husband. But what did Varney think? That a man of the world should have failed to perceive that an unexplained disappearance was most probably an elopement seemed to her incredible. Varney could not be such an innocent as that. The only alternative was that he, like Mr. Penfield, was trying to shield Dan, to hush up the disreputable elements of the escapade. But whereas the lawyer's obstinate reticence had aroused some slight resentment, she felt no resentment towards Varney. For he was Dan's friend first of all, and it was proper that he should try to shield his "pal." And he was really serving husband and wife equally. To hush things up would be the best for both. She wanted no scandal. Loyal and faithful wife as she had been, her feelings towards her husband were of that some what tepid quality that would have allowed her to receive him back without reproaches, and to accept the lamest explanations without question or comment. Varney's assumed policy was as much to her interest as to Dan's, and he was certainly playing the part of a devoted friend to them both.

One thing did, indeed, rather puzzle her. Her marriage had been, on her husband's side, undoubtedly a love-match. It was for no mercenary reasons that he had forced the marriage on her and her father, and up to the last he had seemed to be, in his rather brutal way, genuinely in love with her. Why, then, had he suddenly gone off with another woman? To her constant, faithful nature, the thing was inexplicable.

Varney's reflections were more complex. A vague consciousness of the cumulative effects of actions was beginning to steal into his mind, a faint perception that he was being borne along on the current of circumstance. He had gone to Falmouth with the express purpose of losing Purcell. But it seemed necessary to pick up some trace of the imaginary fugitive, for the one essential to Varney's safety was that Purcell's disappearance must appear to date from the landing at Penzance. That landing must be taken as an established fact. There must be no inquiry into or discussion of the incidents of that tragic voyage. But to that end it was necessary that Purcell should make some reappearance on shore, must leave some traces for possible pursuers to follow. So Varney had gone to Falmouth to find such traces – and to lose them. That was to have been the end of the business so far as he was concerned.

But it was not the end, and as he noted this, he noted, too, with a curious interest unmixed with any uneasiness, how one event generates others. He had invented Purcell's proposed visit to Falmouth to give a plausible colour to the disappearance and to carry the field of inquiry beyond the landing at Penzance. Then the Falmouth story had seemed to commit him to a visit to Falmouth to confirm it. That visit had committed him to the fabrication of the required confirmatory traces, which were to be found and then lost. But he had not quite succeeded in losing them. Margaret's question had seemed to commit him to tracing them further, and now he had got to find and lose Purcell at Ipswich. That, however, would be the end. From Ipswich, Purcell would have to disappear for good.

The account that he had given Margaret was founded on facts. The ship that he had described was a real ship, which had sailed when he had said that she sailed and for the ports that he had named. Moreover, she had carried one or two passengers. But the red-faced man with the suitcase and his female companion were creatures of Varney's imagination.

Thus we see Varney already treading the well-worn trail left by multitudes of wrong-doers, weaving around him a defensive web of illusory appearances, laying down false tracks that lead always away from himself, never suspecting that the web may at last become as the fowler's snare, that the false tracks may point the way to the hounds of destiny. It is true that, as he fared on his way to Ipswich, he was conscious that the tide of circumstance was bearing him farther than he had meant to travel, but not yet did he recognize in this hardly perceived compulsion the abiding menace of accumulating consequences that encompasses the murderer.

Chapter IV
In Which Margaret Confers
With Dr. Thorndyke

The sun was shining pleasantly on the trees of King's Bench Walk, Inner Temple, when Margaret approached the handsome brick portico of No. 5A and read upon the jamb of the doorway the name of Dr. John Thorndyke under the explanatory heading "First Pair." She was a little nervous of the coming interview, partly because she had met the famous criminal lawyer only twice before, but more especially by reason of a vague fear that her uneasy suspicions of her husband might presently be turned into something more definite and disagreeable. Her nervousness on the first score was soon dispelled, for her gentle summons on the little brass knocker of the inner door – the "oak" was open – was answered by Dr. Thorndyke himself, who greeted her as an old friend and led her into the sittingroom, where tea-things were set out on a small table between two armchairs. The homely informality of the reception, so different from the official stiffness of Mr. Penfield, instantly put her at her ease, and when the teapot arrived in the custody of a small gentleman of archidiaconal aspect and surprising crinkliness of feature, she felt as if she were merely paying some rather unusual kind of afternoon call.

Dr. Thorndyke had what would, in his medical capacity, have been called a fine bedside manner – pleasant, genial, sympathetic, but never losing touch with the business on hand. Insensibly a conversation of pleasing generality slipped into a consultation, and Margaret found herself stating her case, apparently of her own initiative. Having described her interview with Mr. Penfield and commented on the old lawyer's very unhelpful attitude, she continued. "It was Mr. Rodney who advised me to consult you. As a civil lawyer with no experience of criminal practice, he felt hardly competent to deal with the case. That was what he said. It sounds rather ominous – as if he thought there might be some criminal element in the affair."

"Not necessarily," said Thorndyke. "But your husband is missing, and a missing man is certainly more in my province than in Rodney's. What did he suggest that you should ask me to do?"

"I should wish, of course," replied Margaret, "to get into communication with my husband. But if that is not possible, I should at least like to know what has become of him. Matters can't be left in their present uncertain state. There is the future to think of."

"Precisely," agreed Thorndyke, "and as the future must be based upon the present and the past, we had better begin by setting out what we actually know and can prove. First, I understand that on the 23rd of June your husband left Sennen, and was seen by several persons to leave, on a yacht in company with Mr. Varney, and that there was no one else on board. The yacht reached Penzance at about half-past two in the afternoon, and your husband went ashore at once. He was seen by Mr. Varney to land on the pier and go towards the town. Did anyone besides Mr. Varney see him go ashore?"

"No – at least, I have not heard of anyone. Of course, he may have been seen by some fishermen or strangers on the pier. But does it matter? Mr. Varney saw him land, and he certainly was not on the yacht when Mr. Rodney arrived half-an-hour later. There can't be any possible doubt that he did land at Penzance."

"No," Thorndyke agreed, "but as that is the last time that he was certainly seen alive, and as the fact that he landed may have to be proved in a court of law, additional evidence would be worth securing."

"But that was not the last time that he was seen alive," said Margaret, and here she gave him an account of Varney's expedition to Falmouth, explaining why he went and giving full particulars respecting the steamer, all of which Thorndyke noted down on the note-block which lay by his side on the table.

"This is very important," said he, when she had finished. "But you see that it is on a different plane of certainty. It is hearsay at the best, and there is no real identification. What luck did Mr. Varney have at Ipswich?"

"He went down there on the evening of the 27th, the day after his visit to Falmouth. He went straight to the quay-side and made inquiries about the steamer *Hedwig*, which he learned had left about noon, having come in about nine o'clock on the previous night. He talked to various quay-loafers, and from one of them ascertained that a single passenger had landed – a big man, carrying a large bag or portmanteau in his hand and a coat of some kind on his arm. The passenger landed alone. Nothing was seen of any woman."

"Did Mr. Varney take the name and address of his informant at Ipswich or the one at Falmouth?"

"I am afraid not. He said nothing about it."

"That is unfortunate," said Thorndyke, "because these witnesses may be wanted, as they might be able to identify a photograph of your husband. We must find out from Mr. Varney what he did in the matter."

Margaret looked at Dr. Thorndyke with a slightly puzzled expression. "You speak of witnesses and evidence," said she, "as if you had something definite in your mind. Some legal proceedings, I mean."

"I have," he replied. "If your husband makes no sign and if he does not presently appear, certain legal proceedings will become inevitable." He paused for a few moments and then continued.

"You must understand, Mrs. Purcell, that when a man of any position – and especially a married man – disappears from 'his usual places of resort,' as the phrase goes, he upsets all the social adjustments that connect him with his surroundings, and, sooner or later, those adjustments have to be made good. If he disappears completely, it becomes uncertain whether he is alive or dead, and this uncertainty communicates itself to his property and to his dependents and relatives. If he is alive, his property is vested in himself. If he is dead, it is vested in his executors or in his heirs or next of kin. Should he be named as a beneficiary in a will, and the person who has made that will die after his disappearance, the question immediately arises whether he was dead or alive at the time of the testator's death – a vitally important question, since it affects not only himself and his heirs, but also the other persons who benefit under the will. And then there is the status of the wife. If the missing man is married – the question whether she is a married woman or a widow has, in justice to her, to be settled if and when possible. So you see that the disappearance of a man like your husband sets going a process that generates all sorts of legal problems. You cannot simply write him off and treat him as non-existent. His life must be properly wound up so that his estate may be disposed of, and this will involve the necessity of presuming his death, and presumption of death may raise difficult questions of survivorship, although these may arise at any moment."

"What is meant by a question of survivorship?" Margaret asked.

"It is a question which arises in respect of two persons, both of whom are dead and concerning one or both of whom the exact date of death is unknown. One of them must have died before the other, unless they both died at the same instant. The question is, Which survived the other? Which of them died first? It is a question on which may turn the succession to an estate, a title, or even a kingdom."

"Well," said Margaret, "it is not likely to arise in respect of Dan."

"On the contrary," Thorndyke dissented, "it may arise to-morrow. If some person who has left him a legacy should die to-day, that person's will could not be administered until it had been decided whether your husband was or was not alive at the time the testator died, that is, whether or not he survived the testator. But, as matters stand, we can

284

give no answer to that question. We can prove that he was alive at half-past two on the 23rd of June. Thenceforward we have no knowledge of him."

"Excepting what Mr. Varney has told us."

"Mr. Varney's information is legally worthless unless he can produce the witnesses, and unless they can identify a photograph or otherwise prove that the man whom they saw was actually Mr. Purcell. You must ask Mr. Varney about it. However, at the moment you are more concerned to find out what has become of your husband. I suppose I may ask a few necessary questions?"

"Oh, certainly," she replied. "Pray don't have any scruples of delicacy. Ask anything you want to know."

"Thank you, Mrs. Purcell," said Thorndyke. "And to begin with the inevitable question: Do you know of, or suspect, any kind of entanglement with any woman?"

The direct, straightforward question came rather as a relief to Margaret, and she answered without embarrassment. "Naturally, I suspect, because I can think of no other reason for his leaving me in this way. But to be honest, I have never had the slightest grounds of complaint in regard to his behaviour with other women. He married me because he fell in love with me, and he has never seemed to change. Whatever he has been to other people, to me he has always appeared, in his rough, taciturn way, as devoted as his nature allowed him to be. This affair is an utter surprise to me."

Thorndyke made no comment on this but, following the hint that Margaret had dropped, asked, "As to his character in general, what sort of a man is he? Is he popular, for instance?"

"No," replied Margaret, "he is not very much liked – in fact, with the exception of Mr. Varney he has no really intimate friends, and I have often wondered how poor Mr. Varney put up with the way he treated him. The truth is that Dan is rather a bully. He is strong, big, and pugnacious, and used to having his own way, and is somewhat brutal, at times, in his manner of getting it. He is a very self-contained, taciturn, rather secretive man, and – well, perhaps he is not very scrupulous. I am not painting a very flattering picture, I am afraid."

"It sounds like a good portrait, though," said Thorndyke. "When you say that he is not very scrupulous, are you referring to his business transactions?"

"Well, yes, and to his dealings with people generally."

"By the way," asked Thorndyke, "what is his occupation?"

Margaret uttered a little apologetic laugh. "It sounds absurd, but I really don't quite know what his business is. He is so very uncommunicative. I have always understood that he is a financier, what ever that may be. I believe he negotiates loans and buys and sells stocks and shares, but he is not on the Stock Exchange. He has an office in Coleman Street, in the premises of a firm of outside brokers, and he keeps a clerk, a man named Levy. It seems to be quite a small establishment, though it appears to yield a fair income. That is all I can tell you, but I daresay Mr. Levy could give you other particulars if you wanted them."

"I will make a note of the address, at any rate," said Thorndyke, and having done so, he asked, "As to your husband's banking account – do you happen to know if any considerable sum has been drawn out quite lately, or if any cheques have been presented since he disappeared?"

"His current account is intact," she replied. "I have an account at the same bank, and I saw the manager a couple of days ago. Of course, he was not very expansive, but he did tell me that no unusual amounts had been withdrawn, and that no cheque has been presented since the 21st of June, when Dan drew a cheque for me. It is really rather odd, especially as the balance is somewhat above the average. Don't you think so?"

"I do," he answered. "It suggests that your husband's disappearance was unpremeditated, and that extreme precautions are being taken to conceal his present whereabouts. But the mystery is what he is living on if he took no considerable sum with him and has drawn no cheques since. However, we had better finish with the general questions. You don't appear to know much about your husband's present affairs. What do you know of his past?"

"Not a great deal, and I can think of nothing that throws any light on his extraordinary conduct in taking himself off as he has done. I met him at Maidstone about six years ago. He was then employed in the office of a large paper mill – Whichboy's Mill, I think it was – as a clerk or accountant. He had then recently come down from Cambridge, and seemed in rather low water. After a time, he left Whichboy's and went to London, and very shortly his circumstances began to improve in a remarkable way. It was then that he began his present business, which I know included the making of loans, because he lent my father money – in fact, it was through these transactions and his visits on business to my father that the intimacy grew which resulted finally in our marriage. He then seemed, as he always has, to be a keen business man, very attentive to the main chance, not at all sentimental in his dealings, and, as I have said, not over-scrupulous as to his methods."

Thorndyke nodded gravely but made no comment. The association of loans to the father with marriage with an evidently *not*-infatuated daughter seemed to throw a sufficiently suggestive light on Daniel Purcell's methods.

"And as to his personal habits and tastes?" he asked.

"He has always been reasonably temperate, though he likes good living and has a robust appetite, and he really has no vices beyond a rather unpleasant temper and excessive keenness on money. His principal interest is in boating, yachting, and fishing. He does not bet or gamble, and his relations with women have always seemed to be perfectly correct."

"You spoke of his exceptional intimacy with Mr. Varney. Is the friendship of long standing?"

"Yes, quite. They were schoolfellows. They were at Cambridge together, and they both came down about the same time and for a similar reason. Both their fathers got suddenly into financial difficulties. Dan's father was a stockbroker, and he failed suddenly, either through some unlucky speculations or through the default of a client. Mr. Varney's father was a clergyman, and he, too, lost all his money, and at about the same time. I have always suspected that there was some connection between the two failures, but I have never heard that there actually was. Dan is as close as an oyster, and, of course, Mr. Varney has never referred to the affair."

"Mr. Varney is not associated with your husband in business?"

"No. He is an artist, principally an etcher, and a very clever one, too. I think he is doing quite well now, but he had a hard struggle when he first came down from Cambridge. For a couple of years, he worked for an engraver doing ordinary copperplate work for the trade, and I understand that he is remarkably skilful at engraving. But now he does nothing but etchings and mezzotints."

"Then his activities are entirely concerned with art?"

"I believe so – now, at any rate. After he left the engraver, he went to a merchant in the City as a clerk. But he was only there quite a short time, and I fancy he left on account of some sort of unpleasantness, but I know nothing about it. After that, he went abroad and travelled about for a time, making sketches and drawings of the towns to do his etchings from – in fact, he only came back from Belgium a couple of months ago. But I am afraid I am wasting your time with a lot of irrelevant gossip."

"It is my fault if you are," said Thorndyke, "since I put the questions. But the fact is that nothing is irrelevant. Your husband has vanished into space in a perfectly unaccountable manner, and we have to find, if we can, something in his known circumstances which may give us a clue to the motive and the manner of his disappearance and his probable whereabouts at present. Has he any favourite haunts, abroad or at home?"

"He is very partial to the Eastern Counties, especially the Broads and rivers of Norfolk. You remember he was on his way to Oulton Broad when he disappeared?"

"Yes, and one must admit that the waterways of Norfolk and Suffolk, with all their endless communications, would form an admirable hiding-place. In a small yacht or covered boat, a man might lose himself in that network of rivers and lakes and lie hidden for months, creeping from end to end of the county without leaving a trace. We must bear that possibility in mind. By the way, have you brought me a copy of that very cautious letter of Mr. Penfield's?"

"I have brought the letter itself," she replied, producing it and laying it on the table.

"Thank you," said Thorndyke. "I will make a copy of it and let you have the original back. And there is another question. Has the letter which Mr. Penfield ought to have received been returned to you?"

"No," replied Margaret.

"Ha!" said Thorndyke. "That is important, because it is undoubtedly a remarkable circumstance and rather significant. A letter in the wrong envelope practically always implies another letter in another wrong envelope. Now a letter was almost certainly written to Mr. Penfield and almost certainly sent. It was presumably a business letter and of some importance. It ought certainly to have been returned to the sender, and under ordinary circumstances would have been. Why has it not been returned? The person to whom it was sent was the person to whom the mysterious communication that Mr. Penfield received was addressed. That communication, we judge from Mr. Penfield's letter, contained some highly confidential matter. But that implies some person who was in highly confidential relations with your husband. The suggestion seems to be that your husband discovered his mistake after he had posted the letter or letters, and that he went at once to this other person and informed him of what had happened."

"Informed her," Margaret corrected.

"I must admit," said Thorndyke, "that the circumstances give colour to your inference, but we must remember that they would apply equally to a man. They certainly point to an associate of some kind. The character of that associate and the nature of the association are questions that turn on the contents of that letter that Mr. Penfield received."

"Do you think," asked Margaret, "that Mr. Penfield would be more confidential with you than he was with me?"

"I doubt it," was the reply. "If the contents of that letter were of a secret nature, he will keep them to himself, and quite right, too. But I shall give him a trial all the same, and you had better let him know that you have consulted me."

This brought the conference to an end, and shortly afterwards Margaret went on her way, now more than ever convinced that the inevitable woman was at the bottom of the mystery. For some time after she had gone Thorndyke sat with his notes before him, wrapped in profound thought and deeply interested in the problem that he was called upon to solve. He did not share Margaret's suspicions, though he had not strongly contested them. To his experienced eye, the whole group of circumstances, with certain points which he had not thought fit to enlarge on, suggested something more sinister than a mere elopement.

There was Purcell's behaviour, for instance. It had all the appearances of an unpremeditated flight. No preparations seemed to have been made, no attempt to wind up his affairs. His banking account was left intact, though no one but he could touch it during his lifetime. He had left or sent no letter of farewell, explanation, or apology to his wife, and now that he was gone, he was maintaining a secrecy as to his whereabouts so profound that, apparently, he did not even dare to draw a cheque.

But even more significant was the conduct of Mr. Penfield. Taking from its envelope the mysterious letter that had come to Sennen and exploded the mine, Thorndyke spread it out and slowly read it though, and his interpretation of it now was the same as on the occasion when he heard Margaret's epitome of it at Sennen. It was a message to Purcell through his wife, telling him that something which had been discovered was not going to be divulged. What could that something be? The answer, in general terms, seemed to be given by Penfield's subsequent conduct. He had been absolutely uncommunicative to Margaret. Yet Margaret, as the missing man's wife, was a proper person to receive any information that could be given. Apparently, then, the information that Penfield possessed was of a kind that could not be imparted to anyone. Even its very nature could not be hinted at.

Now what kind of information could that be? The obvious inference was that the letter which had come to Penfield contained incriminating matter. That would explain everything. For if Penfield had thus stumbled on evidence of a crime, either committed or contemplated, he would have to choose between denouncing the criminal or keeping the matter to himself. But he was not entitled to keep it to himself, for, other considerations apart, this was not properly a client's secret. It had not been communicated to him – he had discovered it by accident. He was therefore not bound to secrecy, and he could not, consequently, claim a lawyer's privilege. In short, if he had discovered a crime and chose to suppress his discovery, he was, in effect, an accessory, before or after the fact, as the case might be, and he would necessarily keep the secret because he would not dare to divulge it.

This view was strongly supported by Purcell's conduct. The disappearance of the latter coincided exactly with the delivery of the mysterious letter to Penfield. The inference was that Purcell, having discovered his fatal mistake, and assuming that Penfield would immediately denounce him to the police, had fled instantly and was now in hiding. Purcell's and Penfield's conduct were both in complete agreement with this theory.

But there was a further consideration. If the contents of that letter were incriminating, they incriminated someone besides Purcell. The person for whom the letter was intended must have been a party to any unlawful proceedings referred to in it. He – or she – must, in fact, have been a confederate. Now, who could that confederate be? Someone, apparently, who was unknown to Margaret, unless it might be the somewhat shadowy Mr. Levy. And that raised yet a further question: What *was* Purcell? How did he get his living? His wife evidently did not know, which was a striking and rather suspicious fact. He had been described as a financier. But that meant nothing. The word "financier" covered a multitude of sins. The question was: What sins did it cover in the present instance? And the answer to that question seemed to involve a visit of exploration to Coleman Street.

As Thorndyke collected his notes to form the nucleus of a dossier of the Purcell Case, he foresaw that his investigations might well unearth some very unlovely skeletons. But that was no fault of his, nor need the disclosures be unnecessarily paraded. But Margaret Purcell's position must be secured and made regular. Her missing husband must either be found and brought back, or he must be written off and disposed of in a proper and legal fashion.

Chapter V
In Which Thorndyke Makes
A Few Inquiries

If Mr. Penfield had been reluctant to arrange an interview with Margaret Purcell, he was yet more unwilling to accept one with Dr. John Thorndyke. It is true that, as a lawyer of the old school, he regarded Thorndyke with a certain indulgent contempt, as a dabbler in law, an amateur, a mere doctor masquerading as a lawyer. But coupled with this contempt was an unacknowledged fear. For it was not unknown to him that this medico-legal hermaphrodite had strange and disconcerting methods – that he had a habit of driving his chariot through well-established legal conventions, and of using his eyes and ears in a fashion not recognized by orthodox legal precedents.

Accordingly, when he received a note from Thorndyke announcing the intention of the writer to call on him, he would have liked to decline the encounter. A less-courageous man would have absented himself. But Mr. Penfield was a sportsman to the backbone, and having got himself into difficulties by that very quality, elected to "face the music" like a man, and so it happened that when Thorndyke arrived in the clerks' office, he was informed that Mr. Penfield was at liberty, and was duly announced and ushered into the sanctum.

The old solicitor received him with a sort of stiff cordiality, helped himself to a pinch of snuff, and awaited the opening of the offensive.

"You have heard from Mrs. Purcell, I presume," said Thorndyke.

"Yes. I understand that you are commissioned by her to ascertain the whereabouts of her husband – a very desirable thing to do, and I wish you every success."

"I am sure you do," said Thorndyke, "and it is with that conviction that I have called on you to enable you to give effect to your good wishes."

Mr. Penfield paused, with his snuff-box open and an infinitesimal particle between his finger and thumb, to steal a quick glance at Thorndyke.

"In what way?" he asked.

"You received a certain communication, concerning which you wrote to Mrs. Purcell at – "

"I beg your pardon," interrupted Penfield, "but I received no communication. A communication was no doubt dispatched by Mr. Purcell, but it never reached me."

"I am referring to a letter which did reach you – a letter with certain enclosures, apparently put into the wrong envelope."

"And which," said Penfield, "is consequently no concern of mine, or, if you will pardon my saying so, of yours."

"Of that," said Thorndyke, "you are doubtless a better judge than I am, since you have read the letter and I have not. But I am instructed to investigate the disappearance of Mr. Purcell, and as this letter appears to be connected with this disappearance, it naturally becomes an object of interest to me."

"Why do you assume that it is connected with the disappearance?" Penfield demanded.

"Because of the striking coincidence of the time of its arrival and the time of the disappearance," replied Thorndyke.

"That seems a very insufficient reason," said Penfield.

"Not, I think," rejoined Thorndyke, "if taken in conjunction with the terms of your own letter to Mrs. Purcell. But do I understand you to say that there was no connection?"

"I did not say that. What I say is that I have inadvertently seen a letter which was not addressed to me and which I was not intended to see. You will agree with me that it would be entirely inadmissible for me to divulge or discuss its contents."

"I am not sure that I do agree with you, seeing that the writer of the letter is the husband of our client and the consignee is a person unknown to us both. But you will naturally act on your own convictions. Would it be admissible for you to indicate the nature of the enclosures?"

"It would be entirely inadmissible," replied Mr. Penfield.

There was a short silence, during which Mr. Penfield refreshed himself with a pinch of snuff and Thorndyke rapidly turned over the situation. Obviously, the old solicitor did not intend to give any information whatever, possibly for very good reasons. At any rate, his decision had to be accepted and this Thorndyke proceeded to acknowledge.

"Well, Mr. Penfield," he said, "I mustn't urge you to act against your professional conscience. I am sure you would help me if you could. By the way, I assume that there would be no objection to my inspecting the envelope in which that letter was contained?"

"The envelope!" exclaimed Penfield, considerably startled. "Why, what information could you possibly gather from the envelope?"

"That is impossible to say until I have seen it," was the reply.

"However," said Penfield, "I am afraid that the same objection applies, sorry as I am to refuse."

"But," persisted Thorndyke, "why should you refuse? The letter, as you say, was not addressed to you, but the envelope was. It is your own envelope, and is entirely at your disposal."

Mr. Penfield was cornered, and he had the wisdom to recognize the fact. Reluctant as he was to let Thorndyke examine even the envelope in which those incriminating blanks were enclosed, he saw that a refusal might arouse suspicion, and suspicion was what he must avoid at all costs. Nevertheless, he made a last effort to temporize.

"Was there any point on which I could enlighten you – in respect of the envelope? Can I give you any information?" he asked.

"I am afraid not," replied Thorndyke. "My experience has taught me always to examine the envelopes of letters closely. By doing so one often picks up unexpected crumbs of evidence, but, naturally, one cannot tell in advance what there may be to observe."

"No," agreed Penfield. "Quite so. It is like cross-examination. Well, I am afraid you won't pick up much this time, but if you really wish to inspect the envelope, I suppose, as you say, I need not scruple to place it in your hands."

With this he rose and walked over to the safe, opened it, opened an inner drawer, and, keeping his back towards Thorndyke, took out the envelope, which he carefully emptied of its contents. Thorndyke sat motionless, not looking at the lawyer's back but listening intently. Not a sound, however, reached his ears until the iron drawer slid back into its case, when Penfield turned and, without a word, laid the empty envelope on the table before him.

For a few moments Thorndyke looked at the envelope as it lay, noting that, although empty, it retained the bulge caused by its late contents, and that those contents must have been somewhat bulky. Then he picked it up and inspected it methodically, committing his observations to memory, since written notes seemed unadvisable under the circumstances. It was an oblong, "commercial" envelope, about six inches long by three and three-quarters wide. The address was written with a pen of medium width and unusually black ink in a rather small, fluent, legible hand, with elegant capitals of a distinctly uncial type. The post-mark was that of Penzance, dated the 23rd of June, 8:30 p.m. But of more interest to Thorndyke than the date, which he already knew, was an impression which the postmark stamp had made by striking the corner of the enclosure and thus defining its position in the envelope. From this, he was able to judge that the object enclosed was oblong in shape, about five inches long or a little more, and somewhat less than three inches wide, and that it consisted of some soft material, presumably folded paper, since the blow of the metal stamp had left but a blunt impression of the corner. He next examined the edge of the flap, first with the naked eye and then with his pocket lens, and finally, turning back the flap from the place where the envelope had been neatly cut open, he closely scrutinized its inner surface.

"Have you examined this envelope, Mr. Penfield?" he asked.

"Not in that exhaustive and minute manner," replied the solicitor, who had been watching the process with profound disfavour. "Why do you ask?"

"Because there appears to me a suggestion of its having been opened by moistening the flap and then reclosed. Just look at it through the glass, especially at the inside, where the gum seems to have spread more than one would expect from a single closing, and where there is a slight cockling of the paper."

He handed the envelope and the lens to Penfield, who seemed to find some difficulty in managing the latter, and after a brief inspection returned both the articles to Thorndyke.

"I have not your experience and skill," he said. "You may be right, but all the probabilities are against your suggestion. If Purcell had reopened the letter, it would surely have been to correct an error rather than to make one. And the letter certainly belonged to the enclosures."

"On the other hand," said Thorndyke, "when an envelope has been steamed or damped open, it will be laid down flap uppermost, with the addressed side hidden, and a mistake might occur in that way. However, there is probably nothing in it. That, I gather, is your opinion?"

Unfortunately it was. Very glad would Penfield have been to believe that the envelope had been opened and the blanks put in by another hand. But he had read Purcell's letter, and knew its connection with the enclosures.

"May I ask if you were expecting a letter from Purcell?" Thorndyke asked.

"Yes. I had written to him, and was expecting a reply."

"And would that letter have contained enclosures of about the same size as those which were sent?"

"I have no reason to suppose that it would have contained any enclosures," Penfield replied. "None were asked for."

Thorndyke made a mental note of this reply and of the fact that Penfield did not seem to perceive its bearing, and rose to depart.

"I am sorry to have had to be so reticent," said Penfield, as they shook hands, "but I hope your visit has not been entirely unfruitful, and I speed you on your quest with hearty good wishes."

Thorndyke replied in similarly polite terms and went on his way, leaving Mr. Penfield in a state of profound relief at having got rid of him, not entirely unmingled with twinges of apprehension lest some incriminating fact should have leaked out unnoticed by him. Meanwhile Thorndyke, as soon as he emerged into Lombard Street, halted and made a detailed memorandum in his pocket-book of the few facts that he had gleaned.

Having thus disposed of Mr. Penfield, he turned his steps in the direction of Coleman Street with the purpose of calling on Mr. Levy – not, indeed, with the expectation of extracting much information from him, but rather to ascertain, if possible, how Purcell got his living. Arrived at the number that Margaret had given him, he read through the list of occupants in the hall, but without finding among then the name of Purcell. There was, however, on the second floor a firm entitled Honeyball Brothers, who were described as "*Financial Agents*", and as this description was the only one that seemed to meet the case, he ascended the stairs and entered a small, well-furnished office bearing on its door the Honeyball superscription. The only occupant was a spectacled youth, who was busily directing envelopes.

"Is Mr. Levy in?" Thorndyke inquired.

"I'll see," was the cautious reply. "What name?"

Thorndyke gave his name, and the youth crossed to a door marked "Private," which he opened, and having passed through closed it behind him. His investigations in the sanctum resulted in the discovery that Mr. Levy was there, a fact which he announced when he reappeared, holding the door open and inviting Thorndyke to enter. The latter accordingly walked through into the private office, when the door immediately closed behind him, and a smartly dressed, middle-aged man rose from a writing-chair and received him with an outstretched hand.

"You are Mr. Levy?" inquired Thorndyke.

"I am Mr. Levy," was the answer, accompanied by an almost affectionate handshake and a smile of the most intense benevolence, "at your entire service, Dr. Thorndyke. Won't you sit down? This is the more comfortable chair and is nearer to my desk, and so more convenient for conversation. Ahem. We are always delighted to meet members of your profession, Doctor. We do business with quite a number of them, and I may say that we find them peculiarly appreciative of the delicacy with which our transactions are conducted. Ahem. Now, in what way can I have the pleasure of being of service to you?"

"The fact is," replied Thorndyke, "I have just called to make one or two inquiries."

"Quite so," interrupted Mr. Levy. "You are perfectly right. The wisdom of our ancestors, Dr. Thorndyke, expresses itself admirably in the old adage 'Look before you leap'. Don't be diffident, sir. The more inquiries you make the better we shall be pleased. Now, what is the first point?"

"Well," Thorndyke replied, "I suppose the first point to dispose of is whether I have or have not come to the right office. My business is concerned with Mr. Daniel Purcell."

"Then," said Mr. Levy, "I should say that you have come to the right office. Mr. Purcell is not here at the moment, but that is of no consequence. I am his authorized deputy. What is the nature of your business, Doctor?"

"I am acting for Mrs. Purcell, who has asked me to ascertain her husband's whereabouts, if possible."

"I see," said Levy. "Family doctor, hey? Well, I hope you'll find out where he is, because then you can tell me. But isn't Mr. Penfield looking into the matter?"

"Possibly. But Mr. Penfield is not very communicative, and it is not clear that he is taking any steps to locate Purcell. May I take it that you are willing to help us, so far as you can?"

"Certainly," replied Levy, "I'm willing enough. But if you want information, you are in the same position as myself. All I know is that I haven't got his present address, but I have no doubt I shall hear from him in due course. He is away on holiday, you must remember."

"You know of no reason for supposing that he has gone away for good?"

"Lord bless you, no," replied Levy. "The first I heard of anything unusual was when old Penfield came round to ask if he had been to the office. Of course he hadn't, but I gave Penfield his address at Oulton and I wrote to Oulton myself. Then it turned out that he hadn't gone to Oulton after all. I admit that it is queer he hasn't written, seeing how methodical he usually is, but there is nothing to make a fuss about. Purcell isn't the sort of man to go off on a jaunt that would involve his dropping money, I can tell you that."

"And meanwhile his absence is not causing any embarrassment in a business sense?"

Mr. Levy rose with a somewhat foxy smile. "Do I look embarrassed?" he asked. "Try me. I should like to do a bit of business with you. No? Well, then, I will wish you good-morning and good luck, and don't worry too much about the lost sheep. He is very well able to take care of himself."

296

He shook hands once more with undiminished cordiality, and personally escorted Thorndyke out on to the landing.

There was one other matter that had to be looked into. Mr. Varney's rather vague report of the voyage from Falmouth to Ipswich required to be brought into the region of ascertained fact. Accordingly, from Purcell's office Thorndyke took his way to Lloyd's, where a brief investigation put him in possession of the name and address of the owner of the steamship *Hedwig* of Hernosand. With this in his notebook, he turned homewards to the Temple with the immediate purpose of writing to the owner and the captain of the ship asking for a list of the passengers from Falmouth and of those who disembarked at Ipswich, and further giving a description of Purcell in case he should have travelled, as was highly probable, under an assumed name.

With these particulars it would be possible at least to attempt to trace the missing man, while if it should turn out that Varney had been misinformed, the trouble and expense of a search in the wrong place would be avoided.

Chapter VI
In Which Mr. Varney
Prepares a Deception

Varney's domestic arrangements were of the simplest. Unlike the majority of those who engage in dishonest transactions, he was frugal, thrifty, and content with little. Of what he earned, honestly or otherwise, he saved as much as he could, and now that he was free of the parasite who had clung to him for so long and had a future to look forward to, he was more than ever encouraged to live providently well within his modest means. For residence he occupied a couple of furnished rooms in Ampthil Square, Camden Town, but he spent little of his time in them, for he had a little studio in a quiet turning off the High Street, which he held on lease, and which contained his few household goods and formed his actual home. Thither he usually repaired as soon as he had breakfasted, buying a newspaper on the way and sitting in the Windsor armchair by the gas fire – alight or not, according to the season – to smoke his morning pipe and glance over the news before beginning work.

Following his usual custom, on a bright, sunny morning near the end of October, he arrived at the studio with a copy of *The Times* under his arm, and, letting himself in with his latch-key, laid the paper on the work-bench, hung up his hat, and put a match to the gas fire. Then, having drawn a chair up to the fire, he drew forth his pipe and pouch and sauntered over to the bench, where he stood, filling his pipe and gazing absently at the bench whereon the paper lay, while his thoughts travelled along a well-worn if somewhat vague track into a pleasant and tranquil future. Not for him alone was that future pleasant and tranquil. It held another figure – a sweet and gracious figure that lived in all his countless daydreams. She should be happy, too – freed, like himself, from that bloated parasite who had fastened upon her. Indeed, she was free now, if only she could be made to know it.

Again, for the thousandth time, he wondered, did she care for him? It was impossible to guess. She seemed always pleased to see him, she was warmly appreciative of his attentiveness and his efforts to help her, and her manner towards him was cordial and friendly. There was no doubt that she liked him, and what more could he ask until such time as the veil should be lifted and her freedom revealed to her? For Maggie Purcell was not only a pure-minded and innocent woman – she was the very soul of loyalty, even to the surly brute who had intruded unbidden into her life. And for this Varney loved her the more. But it left his question unanswered and unanswerable. For while her husband lived, in her belief, no thought of love for any other could be consciously admitted to that loyal heart.

He had filled his pipe, and taken a matchbox from his pocket, and was in the act of striking a match when, in an instant, his movement was arrested, and he stood, rigid and still, with the match poised in his hand and his eyes fixed on the newspaper. But no longer absently, for his wandering glance, travelling unheedingly over the printed page, had lighted by chance upon the name Purcell, printed in small capitals. For a few moments he stood with his eyes riveted on the familiar name, then he picked up the paper and read eagerly.

It was an advertisement in the *"Personal"* column, and read thus: *"PURCELL (D.) is requested to communicate at once with Mr. J. Penfield, who has important information to impart to him* in re *Catford, deceased. The matter is urgent, as the will has been proved and must now be administered."*

Varney read the advertisement through twice, and as he read it he smiled grimly – not, however, without a certain vague discomfort. There was nothing in the paragraph which affected him, but yet he found it, in some indefinable way, disquieting. And the more he reflected on the matter the more disturbing did it appear. Confound Purcell! The fellow was dead, and there was an end of it – at least, that was what he had intended and what he wished. But it seemed that it was not the end of it. Ever since that tragic voyage, when he had boldly cut the Gordian Knot of his entanglements, Purcell had continued to reappear in one way or another, still, as ever, seeming to dominate his life. From his unknown and unsuspected grave, fathoms deep in the ocean, mysterious and disturbing influences seemed to issue, as though, even in death, his malice was still active. When would it be possible to shake him off for good?

Varney laid down the paper, and, flinging himself into the chair, set himself to consider the bearings of this new incident. How did it affect him? At the first glance it appeared not to affect him at all. Penfield would get no reply, and after one or two more trials he would have to give it up. That was all. The affair was no concern of his.

But was that all? And was it no concern of his? Reflection did not by any means confirm these assumption. Varney knew little about the law, but he realized that a will which had been proved was a thing that had to be dealt with in some conclusive manner. When Penfield failed to get into touch with Purcell, what would he do? The matter, as he had said, was urgent. Something would have to be done. Quite probably Penfield would set some inquiries on foot. He would learn from Maggie, if he did not already know, of Purcell's supposed visit to Falmouth and the mythical voyage to Ipswich. Supposing he followed up those false tracks systematically? That might lead to complications. Those inventions had been improvised rather hastily, principally for Maggie's benefit. They might not stand such investigation as a lawyer might bring to bear on them. There was the ship, for instance. It would be possible to ascertain definitely what passengers she carried from Falmouth. And when it became certain that Purcell was not one of them, at the best the inquiry would draw a blank. At the worst there might be some suspicion of a fabrication of evidence on his part. In any case, the inquiry would be brought back to Penzance.

That would not do at all. Inquiries must be kept away from Penzance. He was the only witness of that mythical landing on the pier, and hitherto no one had thought of questioning his testimony. He believed that his own arrival on the pier had been unnoticed. But who could say? A vessel entering a harbour is always an object of interest to every nautical eye that beholds her. Who could say that some unseen watcher had not observed the yacht's arrival and noted that she was worked single-handed, and that one man only had gone ashore? It was quite possible, though he had seen no such watcher, and the risk was too great to be thought of. At all costs the inquiry must be kept away from Penzance.

How was that to be managed? The obvious way was to fabricate some sort of reply to the advertisement purporting to come from Purcell – a telegram, for instance, from France or Belgium, or even from some place in the Eastern Counties. The former was hardly possible, however. He could not afford the time or expense of a journey abroad, and, moreover, his absence from England would be known, and its coincidence with the arrival of the telegram might easily be noticed. Coincidences of that kind were much better avoided.

On reflection, the telegram did not commend itself. Penfield would naturally ask himself: "Why a telegram when a letter would have been equally safe and so much more efficient?" For both would reveal, approximately, the whereabouts of the sender. No, a telegram would not answer the purpose. It would not be quite safe, for telegrams, like typewritten letters, are always open to suspicion as to their genuineness. Such suspicions may lead to inquiries at the telegraph office. On the other hand, a letter, if it could be properly managed, would have quite the contrary effect. It would be accepted as convincing evidence, not only of the existence of the writer, but of his whereabouts at the time of writing – if only it could be properly managed. But could it be?

He struck a match and lit his pipe – to little purpose, for it went out and was forgotten in the course of a minute. Could he produce a letter from Purcell – a practicable letter which would pass with out suspicion the scrutiny, not only of Penfield himself, who was familiar with Purcell's handwriting, but also of Maggie, to whom it would almost certainly be shown? It was a serious question, and he gave it very serious consideration, balancing the chances of detection against the chances of success, and especially dwelling upon the improbability of any question arising as to its authenticity.

Now, Varney was endowed in a remarkable degree with the dangerous gift of imitating handwriting. Indeed, it was this gift, and its untimely exercise, that had been the cause of all his troubles. And the natural facility in this respect had been reinforced by the steadiness of hand and perfect control of line that had come from his years of practice as a copperplate engraver. In that craft his work had largely consisted of minute and accurate imitation of writing and other linear forms, and he was now capable of reproducing his "copy" with microscopic precision and fidelity. Reflecting on this, and, further, that he was in possession of Purcell's own fountain pen with its distinctive ink, he decided confidently that he could produce a letter which would not merely pass muster but would even defy critical examination, to which it was not likely to be subjected.

Having decided that the letter could be produced, the next question was that of ways and means. It would have been best for it to be sent from some place abroad, but that could not very well be managed. However, it would answer quite well if it could be sent from one of the towns or villages of East Anglia – in fact, that would perhaps be the best plan, as it would tend to confirm the Falmouth and Ipswich stories and be, in its turn, supported by them. But there was the problem of getting the letter posted. That would involve a journey down to Suffolk or Norfolk, and to this there were several objections. In the first place, he could ill spare the time, for he had a good deal of work on hand – he had an engagement with a dealer on the present evening, he had to arrange about an exhibition on the following day, and in the evening he was to dine with Maggie and Philip Rodney. None of these engagements, but especially the last, was he willing to cancel, and yet, if the letter was to be sent, there ought not to be much delay. But the most serious objection was the one that had occurred to him in relation to the telegram. His absence from town would probably be known and he might even be seen, either at his East Anglian destination or on his way thither or returning, and the coincidence of those movements with the arrival of the letter could hardly fail to be noticed. Indeed, if he were seen in the locality from whence the letter came, or going or returning, that would be a perilously striking coincidence.

What, then, was the alternative? He reflected awhile, and presently he had an idea. How would it answer if he should not post the letter at all, but simply drop it into Penfield's letter-box? There was something to be said for that. It would go to prove that Purcell must be lurking somewhere in London – not an unlikely thing in itself, for London is so large that it is hardly a locality at all, and it is admittedly one of the safest of hiding-places. But, for that matter, why not post the letter, say, in Limehouse or Ratcliff, and thus suggest a lurking-place in the squalid and nautical east? That did not seem a bad idea. But still his preferences leaned towards the Eastern Counties – somewhere in the neighbourhood of Ipswich, which would give consistency to the account of the voyage from Falmouth. It was something of a dilemma, and he turned over the alternative plans for some time without coming to any conclusion.

As he sat thus meditating, his eye roamed idly about the bare but homely studio, and presently it encountered an object that started a new and interesting train of thought. Pushed away in a corner was a small lithographic press, now mostly disused, for the little "auto-lithographs" that he used to produce had ceased to be profitable now that there was a fair demand for his etchings and mezzotints. But the press was in going order, and he was a moderately expert lithographer – quite expert enough to produce a perfectly convincing post-mark on a forged letter, especially if that post-mark were carefully indented after printing, to disguise the process by which it had been produced.

It was a brilliant idea. In his pleased excitement, he started up from his chair and began rapidly to pace up and down the studio. A most admirable plan! For it not only disposed of all the difficulties but actually turned them into advantages. He would get the letter prepared, he would keep his engagement with Maggie, then, after leaving her, he would make his way to George Yard and there drop the letter into Penfield's letter-box. It would be found on the following morning, and would appear to have been posted the previous evening and delivered by the first post. He would actually be present in Maggie's flat at the very moment when the letter was (apparently) being posted in Suffolk. A most excellent scheme!

Chuckling with satisfaction, he set himself forth with to carry it out. The means and appliances were in a cupboard that filled a recess – just a plain wall cupboard, but fitted with a Chubb lock of the highest class. Unlocking this, he cast his eye over the orderly shelves. Here, standing

302

upright in an empty ink-bottle, was the thick-barrelled fountain pen that had once been Purcell's. Varney took out the pen in its container and stood it on the table. Next, from the back of the cupboard, he reached out an expanding letter-file, and, opening it, took from the compartment marked "P" a small bundle of letters docketed "Purcell," which he also laid on the table. They were all harmless unimportant letters (saved for that very reason), and if one should have asked why Varney had kept them, the answer, applicable to most of the other contents of the file, would have been that they had been preserved in obedience to the forger's instinct to keep a few originals in stock on the chance that they might come in handy one day.

He drew a chair up to the table and began methodically to look through the letters, underlining with a lead pencil the words that he would probably want to copy. In the third letter that he read he had an unexpected stroke of luck, for it contained a reference to Mr. Penfield, to whom some enclosed document was to be sent, and it actually gave his full name and address. This was a windfall indeed! As he encircled the address with a pencil mark, Varney smiled complacently, and felt that Fortune was backing him up handsomely.

Having secured the "copy" for the handwriting, the next thing was to get the post-mark drawn and printed. The letters in the file had no envelopes, but he had in his pocket a letter that he had received that morning from an innkeeper at Tenterden, to whom he had written for particulars as to accommodation. It was probably a typical country letter, and its post-mark would serve as well as any other. He took it from his pocket, and, laying it on a small drawing board, pinned a piece of tracing paper over it and made a very careful tracing of the post-mark. Then he drew away the letter, and slipped in its place a small piece of lithographic transfer paper with a piece of black lead transfer paper over it, and went over the tracing carefully with a hard pencil. He now had a complete tracing of the post-mark on the lithographic paper, including the name "Tenterden" and the date and time, which he had included to give the dimensions and style of the lettering. But he now partially erased them, excepting the year date, and replaced them, in the same style and size, with the inscription *"Woodbridge, Oct. 28, 4:30 p.m."* drawn firmly with a rather soft pencil.

He now fetched his lithographic ink and pens from the cupboard, and, with the original before him, inked in the tracing, being careful to imitate all the accidental characters of the actual post-mark, such as the unequal thickness of the lines due to the uneven pressure of the marking stamp. When he had finished, he turned the envelope over and repeated the procedure with the London post-mark, only here he made an exact

303

facsimile excepting as to the date and time, which he altered to "*Oct. 29, 11:20 p.m.*."

The next proceeding was to transfer the inked tracings to a lithographic stone. He used a smallish stone, placing the two post-marks a convenient distance apart, so that they could be printed separately. When the transfer and the subsequent "etching" processes were completed and the stone was ready for printing, he inked up and took a trial proof of the two post-marks on a sheet of paper. The result was perfectly convincing. Ridiculously so. As he held the paper in his hand and looked at those absurd post-marks, he chuckled aloud. With a little ingenuity, how easy it was to sprinkle salt on the forensic tail of the inscrutable Penfield! He was disposed to linger and picture to himself the probable proceedings of that astute gentleman when he received the letter. But there was a good deal to do yet, and he must not waste time. There was the problem of printing the Woodbridge post-mark fairly on the stamp, and then there was the addressing and writing of the letter.

The first problem he solved by tracing the outline of an envelope on the sheet that he had printed, with the post-mark in the correct place for the stamp, cutting this piece out and using it to make register marks on the stone. Then he affixed a stamp exactly to the correct spot on the envelope, inked up the stone, laid the envelope against the register marks, and passed the stone under the roller. When he picked up the envelope, the stamp bore the Woodbridge post-mark with just that slight inaccuracy of imposition that made it perfectly convincing. The London post-mark presented no difficulty, as it did not matter to half-an-inch where it was placed. Another ink-up and another turn of the crank-handle, and the envelope was ready for the penmanship.

Although Varney was so expert a copyist, he decided to take no unnecessary risks. Accordingly, he made a careful tracing of Penfield's name and address from the original letter and transferred this in black lead to the envelope. Then with Purcell's pen, charged with its special black ink, and with the original before him, he inked in the tracing with a free and steady hand and quickly enough to avoid any tell-tale wavering or tremor of the line. It was certainly a masterly performance, and when it was done it would have puzzled a much greater expert than Penfield to distinguish between the copy and the original.

Varney regarded it with deep satisfaction. He was about to put it aside to dry, before he should rub out the tracing marks, when it occurred to him that Purcell would almost certainly have marked it "*Confidential*" or "*Personal*". It was, in fact, rather desirable that this missive should be opened by Penfield himself. The fewer hands it passed through the better, and then, of course, it was not worthwhile to let any of the clerks into the secret of Purcell's disappearance. Accordingly, with the original letter still before him, he wrote at the top of the envelope, in bold and rather large characters, the word "*Personal*". That ought to make it safe.

He put the envelope aside and began to think out the text of the letter that he was going to write. As he did so, his eyes rested gloatingly on the work that he had done, and done to such a perfect finish. It was really a masterpiece of deception. Even a post-office sorter would have been taken in by it. He took it up and again regarded it admiringly. Then he began to consider whether "*Confidential*" would not have been better than "*Personal*". It was certainly most desirable that this letter should not be opened even by the chief clerk, for it would let the cat out of the bag rather completely. He held the envelope irresolutely for a full minute, turning the question over. Finally, he picked up the pen, and, laying the envelope before him, turned the full stop into an "and" and followed this with the word "*Confidential*". There was not as much space as he would have liked, and in his anxiety to preserve the character of the handwriting while compressing the letters, the tail of the final *L* strayed on to the edge of the stamp, which to his critical eye looked a little untidy, but that was of no consequence – in fact, it was rather an additional realistic touch.

He now set to work upon the letter itself. It was to be but a short letter, and it took him only a few minutes to draft out the matter in pencil. Then, spreading Purcell's letter before him, he studied it word by word and letter by letter. When he had got the character of the writing well into his mind, he took a sheet of notepaper and, with a well-sharpened *H* pencil, made a very careful copy of his draft, constantly referring to Purcell's original and even making tracings of important words and of the signature. Having compared the lightly pencilled copy with Purcell's letter and made one or two corrections, he picked up the pen and traced over the pencil writing with the sureness and steadiness that his training as an engraver made possible.

The letter being finished with a perfect facsimile of the signature, he made a final comparison of the handwriting with Purcell's, and, finding it beyond criticism, read through the letter again, speculating on Mr. Penfield's probable proceedings when he received it. The text of the letter ran thus:

Dear Mr. Penfield,

I have just seen your advertisement in The Times, *and am writing to let you know that circumstances render it impossible for me to call on you, and for the same reason I am unable to give you my present address. If there is*

305

anything connected with the Catford business that you wish me to know, perhaps you could put it briefly in another advertisement, to which I could reply if necessary. Sorry to give you this trouble.

Yours sincerely,
Daniel Purcell

Laying down the letter, Varney once more turned to the envelope. First, with a piece of artist's soft rubber he removed the pencil marks of the tracing. Then, placing the envelope on a sheet of blotting-paper, he carefully traced over the post-marks with an agate tracing-style, following the two concentric circles of each with their enclosed letters and figures with minute accuracy and pressing somewhat firmly. The result was that each of the two post-marks was visibly indented, as if made by a sharply-struck marking stamp. It only remained to erase the pencil marks from the letter, to place it in the envelope, and close the latter, and when this was done, Varney rose and, having once more lit his pipe, began to replace the materials in the cupboard, where also he bestowed the letter for the present.

He was in the act of closing the cupboard door when his glance fell on a small deed-box on the top shelf. He looked at it thoughtfully for a few moments, then lifted it down, placed it on the table, and unlocked it. The contents were three paper packets, each sealed with his ring-seal. He broke the seals of all three and opened the packets. Two of them contained engraved copper plates, of a twenty-pound and a five-pound note respectively. The third contained a sheaf of paper blanks. Varney took out the latter and counted them, holding each one up to the light to examine the water-mark. There were twelve of them, all five-pound notes. He laid them down and cogitated profoundly, and unconsciously his eyes turned to the etching press at the end of the bench. A few minutes' work, a smear of ink, and a turn of the press, would convert those blanks into actual notes, so good that they could be passed with perfect safety. Twelve fives – sixty pounds. It was handsome pay for half-an-hour's work, and five-pound notes were so easy to get rid of.

It was a severe temptation to a comparatively poor man whose ethical standards were none of the highest. Prosperous as he now thought himself with the growing demand for his etchings, sixty pounds represented the product of nearly two months' legitimate work. It was a great temptation. There were the blanks, all ready for the magic change. It seemed a pity to waste them. There were only a dozen, and there

306

would be no more. This would really be the end of the lay. After this he could go straight and live a perfectly reputable life.

The gambler's lure, the attraction of easily won wealth, was beginning to take effect. He had actually picked up the five-pound plate, and was moving towards the bench, when something in his mind brought him suddenly to a stop. In that moment there had risen before his mental vision the sweet and gracious figure of Margaret Purcell. Instantly his feelings underwent a revulsion. That which, but a minute ago, had seemed natural and reasonable now looked unspeakably sordid and base. No compulsion now urged him on unwillingly to crime. It would be his own choice – the choice of mere greed. Was it for this that he had set her and himself free? Could he stand in her presence and cherish thoughts of honourable love with this mean crime, committed of his own free-will, on his conscience? Assuredly not. The very corpse of Purcell cried out from its dark tomb beneath the Wolf on this voluntary resumption of the chains which he had broken at the cost of murder.

Once more he turned towards the bench, but now with a different purpose. Hurriedly, as if fearful of another backsliding, he caught up a large graver and drove its point across the plate from corner to corner, ploughing up the copper in a deep score. That finished the matter. Never again could that plate be printed from. But he did not leave it at that. With a shaving scraper he pared off the surface of the plate until the engraving on it was totally obliterated. He fetched the other plate and treated it in a similar manner. Then he flung both plates into a porcelain dish and filled it with strong nitric acid mordant. Finally, as the malodorous red fumes began to rise from the dish, he took up the sheaf of blanks and held them in the flame of the gas-stove. When the last blackened fragments had fallen to the hearth, he drew a deep breath. Now at last he was free. Really free. Free even from the peril of his own weakness.

His labours had consumed the best part of the morning, but, in any case, he was in no mood for his ordinary work. Opening the window a little wider to let the fumes escape, he took his hat from the peg and went forth, turning his steps in the direction of Regent's Park.

Chapter VII
The Flash Note Factory

To the lover of quiet and the admirer of urban comeliness, the ever-increasing noise and turmoil of London and its ever-decreasing architectural interest and charm give daily an added value to the Inns of Court, in whose peaceful precincts quiet and comeliness yet survive. And of the Inns of Court, if we except Old Buildings, Lincoln's Inn, the Temple with its cloisters, its fountain, and its ancient church, makes the strongest appeal to the affections of that almost extinct creature the Londoner, of which class the last surviving genuine specimens are to be found in its obsolete chambers, living on amidst the amenities of a bygone age.

But it was neither the quiet nor the architectural charm of the old domestic buildings that had caused Mr. Superintendent Miller, of the Criminal Investigation Department, to take the Temple on his way from Scotland Yard to Fleet Street (though it was as short a way as any), nor was it a desire to contemplate the houses attributed to Wren that made him slow down when he reached King's Bench Walk and glance hesitatingly up and down that pleasant thoroughfare – if a thoroughfare it can be called. The fact is that Mr. Miller was engaged in certain investigations, which had led him, as investigations sometimes do, into a blind alley, and it was in his mind to see if the keen vision of Dr. John Thorndyke could detect a way out. But he did not want a formal consultation. Rather, he desired to let the matter arise, as it were, by chance, and he did not quite see how to manage it.

Here, as he stood hesitating opposite Thorndyke's chambers, Providence came to his aid, for at this moment a tall figure emerged from the shadow of the covered passage from Mitre Court and came with an easy, long-legged swing down the tree-shaded footway. Instantly the Superintendent strode forward to intercept the newcomer, and the two met halfway up the Walk.

"You were not coming to see me, by any chance?" Thorndyke asked, when the preliminary greetings had been exchanged.

"No," replied Miller, "though I had half-a-mind to look in on you, just to pass the time of day. I am on my way to Clifford's Inn to look into a rather queer discovery that has been made there."

Here the Superintendent paused with an attentive eye on Thorndyke's face, though experience should have told him that he might as well study the expression of a wigmaker's block. As Thorndyke showed no sign of rising to the bait, he continued. "A remarkably queer affair. Mysterious, in fact. Our people are rather stuck, so I am going to have a look round the chambers to see if I can pick up any traces."

"That is always a useful thing to do," said Thorndyke. "Rooms, like clothes, tend to take certain impressions from those who live in them. Careful inspection, eked out by some imagination, will usually yield something of interest."

"Precisely," agreed Miller. "I realized that long ago from watching your own methods. You were always rather fond of poking about in empty houses and abandoned premises. By the way," he added, forced into the open by Thorndyke's impassiveness, "I wonder if you would care to stroll up with me and have a look at these chambers?"

"Are the facts of the case available?" asked Thorndyke.

"Certainly," replied Miller, "to you – so far as they are known. If you care to walk up with me, I'll tell you about the case as we go along."

Thereupon Thorndyke (to whom the insoluble mystery and especially the untenanted chambers were as a hot scent to an eager fox-hound) turned and retraced his steps in company with the Supertendent.

"The history of the affair," the latter began, "is this: At No. 92, Clifford's Inn a man named Bromeswell had chambers on the second floor. He had been there several years, and was an excellent tenant, paying his rent and other liabilities with clockwork regularity on, or immediately after, Quarter Day. He had never been known to be even a week in arrear with rent, gas, or anything else. But at Midsummer he failed to pay up in his usual prompt manner, and, after a fortnight had passed, a polite reminder was dropped into his letter-box. But still nothing was done beyond dropping in another reminder. Once or twice the porter went to the door of the chambers but he always found the "oak" shut, and when he hammered on it with a stick, he got no answer.

"Well, the time ran on, and the porter began to think that things looked a bit queer, but still nothing was done. Then one day the postman brought a batch of letters, or, rather, circulars, to the lodge addressed to Bromeswell. He had tried to get them into Bromeswell's letter-box, but couldn't get them in, as the box was choke-full. Now this made it pretty clear that Bromeswell had not been in his chambers for some considerable time, unless he was dead and his body shut up in them, so the porter acquainted the treasurer with the state of affairs and consulted with him as to what was to be done. There were no means of getting into the chambers without breaking in, for the tenant had at some time fixed a new patent lock on the outer door, and the porter had no duplicate key. But the chambers couldn't be left indefinitely, especially at there was

309

possibly a dead man inside, so the treasurer decided to send a man up a ladder to break a window and let himself in. As a matter of fact, the porter went up himself, and as soon as he got into the chambers and had a look round, he began to smell a rat.

"The appearance of the place, and especially the even coating of dust that covered everything, showed that no one had been in those rooms for two or three months at least, but what particularly attracted the attention of the porter, who is a retired police sergeant, was a rather queer-looking set of apparatus that suggested to him the outfit of a maker of flash notes. On this he began to make some inquiries, and then it transpired that nobody knew anything about Bromeswell. Mr. Duskin, the late porter, must have known him, since he must have let him the chambers, but Duskin left the Inn some years ago, and the present porter has never met this tenant. It seems an incredible thing, but it appears to be a fact that no one even knows Bromeswell by sight."

"That does really seem incredible," said Thorndyke, "in the case of a man living in a place like Clifford's Inn."

"Ah, but he wasn't really living there. That was known, because no milk or bread was ever left there and no laundress ever called for washing. There are no resident chambers in No. 92. The porter had an idea that Bromeswell was a press artist or something of that kind, and used the premises to work in. But of course it wasn't any concern of his."

"How was the rent paid?"

"By post, in notes and cash. And the gas was paid in the same way, never by cheque. But to go on with the history: The porter's suspicions were aroused, and he communicated them to the treasurer, who agreed with him that the police ought to be informed. Accordingly, they sent us a note, and we instructed Inspector Monk, who is a first-class expert on flash notes, to go to Clifford's Inn and investigate, but to leave things undisturbed as far as possible. So Monk went to the chambers and had a look at the apparatus, and what he saw made him pretty certain that the porter was right. The apparatus was a complete paper-maker's plant in miniature, all except the moulds. There were no moulds to be seen, and until they were found it was impossible to say that the paper was not being made for some lawful purpose, though the size of the pressing plates – eighteen inches by seven – gave a pretty broad hint. However, there was an iron safe in the room, one of Wilkins' make, and Monk decided that the moulds were probably locked up in it. He also guessed what the moulds were like. You may have heard of a long series of most excellent forgeries of Bank of England notes."

"I have," said Thorndyke. "They were five-pound and twenty-pound notes, mostly passed in France, Belgium, Switzerland, and Holland."

"That's the lot," said Miller, "and first-class forgeries they were, and for a very good reason. They were made with the genuine moulds. Some six years ago two moulds were lost or stolen from the works at Maidstone, where the Bank of England makes its paper. They were the moulds for five-pound and twenty-pound notes respectively, and each mould would make a sheet that would cut into two notes – a long narrow sheet sixteen and three-quarter inches by five and five thirty-seconds in the case of a five-pound note. Well, we have been on the lookout for those forgers for years, but, naturally, they were difficult to trace, for the forgeries were so good that no one could tell them from the real thing but the experts at the Bank. You see, it is the paper that the forger usually comes a cropper over. The engraving is much easier to imitate. But this paper was not only made in the proper moulds with all the proper water-marks, but it seemed to be made by a man who knew his job. So you can reckon that Monk was as keen as mustard on getting those moulds.

"And get them he did. On our authority Wilkins made him a duplicate key – as we didn't want to blow the safe open – and sure enough, as soon as he opened the door, there were the two moulds. So that's that. There is an end of those forgeries. But the question is, Who and where the devil is this fellow Bromeswell? And there is another question. This only accounts for the paper. The engraving and printing were done somewhere else and by some other artist. We should like to find out who he is. But, for the present, he is a bird in the bush. Bromeswell is our immediate quarry."

"He seems to be pretty much in the bush, too," remarked Thorndyke. "Is there no trace of him at all? What about his agreement and his references?"

"Gone," replied Miller. "When the Inn was sold, most of the old papers were destroyed. They were of no use."

"It is astonishing," said Thorndyke, "that a man should have been in occupation of those chambers for years and remain completely unknown. And yet one sees how it can have happened with the change of porters. Duskin was the only link that we have with Bromeswell, and Duskin is gone. As to his not being known by sight, he probably came to the chambers only occasionally to make a batch of paper, and if there were no residents in his block, no one would be likely to notice him."

"No," Miller agreed, "Londoners are not inquisitive about their neighbours, especially in a business quarter. This is the place, and those are his rooms on the second floor."

As he paused by an ancient lamp-post near the postern gate that opens on Fetter Lane, the Superintendent indicated a small, dark entry, and then nodded at a range of dull windows at the top of the old house.

311

Then he crossed a tiny courtyard, plunged into the dark entry, and led the way up the narrow stairs, groping with his hands along the unseen handrail, and closely followed by Thorndyke.

At the first floor they emerged for a moment into modified daylight, and then ascended another flight of dark and narrow stairs, which opened on a grimy landing, whose only ornaments were an iron dust-bin and a gas-meter, and which displayed a single iron-bound door, above which appeared in faded white lettering the inscription "*Mr. Bromeswell*".

The Superintendent unlocked the massive outer door, which opened with a rusty creak, revealing an inner door fitted with a knocker. This Miller pushed open, and the two men entered the outer room of the "set" of chambers, halting just inside the door to make a general survey of the room, of which the most striking feature was its bareness. And this was really a remarkable feature when the duration of the tenancy was considered. In the course of some years of occupation, the mysterious tenant had accumulated no more furniture than a small kitchen table, a Windsor chair, a canvas seated camp armchair, a military camp bedstead with a sleeping-bag, and a couple of rugs and a small iron safe.

"It is obvious," said Thorndyke, "that Bromeswell never lived here. Apparently he visited the place only at intervals, but when he came he stayed until he had finished what he had come to do. Probably he brought a supply of food, and never went out between his arrival and departure."

He strolled into the tiny kitchen, where a gas ring, a teapot, a cup and saucer, one or two plates, a tin of milk-powder, one of sugar, another of tea, and a biscuit-tin containing an unrecognizable mildewy mass, bore out his suggestion. With a glance at the loaded letter-box, he crossed the room and, opening the door, entered what was intended to be the bedroom, but had been made into a workshop. And very complete it was, being fitted with a roomy sink and tap, a small boiler – apparently a dentist's vulcanizer – and a mixer or beater worked by a little electric motor, driven by a bichromate battery, there being no electric light in the premises. By the window was a strong bench, on which was a powerful office press, a stack of long, narrow copper plates, and a pile of pieces of felt of a similar shape but somewhat larger. Close to the bench was a trough made from a stout wooden box, lined with zinc and mounted on four legs, in which was a folded newspaper containing a number of neat coils of cow-hair cord, each coil having an eye-splice at either end, evidently to fit on the hooks which had been fixed in the walls.

"Those cords," Miller explained, as Thorndyke took them from the paper to examine them, "were used as drying lines to hang the damp sheets of paper on. They are always made of cow hair, because that is the only material that doesn't mark the paper. But I expect you know all about that. Is there anything that catches your eye in particular? You seem interested in those cords."

"I was looking at these two," said Thorndyke, holding out two cords which he had uncoiled. "This one, you see, was too long, it had been cut the wrong length, or, more probably, was the remainder of a long piece. But instead of cutting off the excess, our friend has thriftily shortened this rather expensive cord by working a sheep-shank on it. Now it isn't everyone who knows how to make a sheep-shank, and the persons who do are not usually papermakers."

"That's perfectly true, Doctor," assented Miller. "I'm one of the people who don't know how to make that particular kind of knot. What is the other point?"

"This other cord," replied Thorndyke, "which looks new, has an eye-splice at one end only, but it is, as you see, about five inches longer than the other, just about the amount that would be taken up by working the eye-splice. That looks as if Bromeswell had worked the splices himself, and if you consider the matter you will see that is probably the case. The length of these cords is roughly the width of this room. They have been cut to a particular measure, but the cord was most probably bought in a single length, as this extra long piece suggests."

"Yes," agreed Miller. "They wouldn't have been sold with the eye-splices worked on them, and, in fact, I don't see what he wanted with the eye-splices at all. A simple knotted loop would have answered the purpose quite as well."

"Exactly," said Thorndyke. "They were not necessary. They were a luxury, a refinement, and that emphasizes the point that they suggest, which is that Bromeswell is a man who has some technical knowledge of cordage, is probably a sailor, or in some way connected with the sea. As you say, a common knotted loop, such as a bowline knot, would have answered the purpose perfectly. But that is true of most of the cases in which a sailor uses an eye-splice. Then why does he take the trouble to work the splice? Principally for the sake of neatness of appearance, because, to an expert eye, a tied loop with its projecting end looks slovenly.

"Now this man will have had quite a lot of time on his hands. He will have had to wait about for hours while the pulp was boiling and while it was being beaten up. A sailor would very naturally spend a part of his idle time in tidying up the cordage."

The Superintendent nodded reflectively.

"Yes," he said, "I think you are right, Doctor, and it is an important point. This fellow was a fairly expert papermaker. He wasn't a mere amateur, like most of the note forgers. If he was some kind of sailor man as well, that would make him a lot easier to identify if we should get on his track. But that is just what we can't do. There is nothing to start from. He is a mere name, and pretty certainly a false name at that."

As he spoke, Miller looked about him discontentedly, running his eye over the bench and its contents. Suddenly he stepped over to the press and, diving into the shadowed space between it and the wall, brought up his hand grasping a silver-mounted briar pipe.

"Now, Doctor," he said with a grin, handing it to Thorndyke when he had inspected it, "here is something in your line. Just run your eye over that pipe and tell me what the man is like."

Thorndyke laughed as he took the pipe in his hand. "You are thinking of the mythical anatomist and the fossil bone," said he. "I am afraid this relic will not tell us much. It is a good pipe, it must have cost half-a-guinea, which would have meant more if its owner had been honest. The maker's name tells us that it was bought in Cheapside, near the Bank, its weight and the marks on the mouthpiece tell us that the owner has a strong jaw and a good set of teeth, its good condition suggests a careful, orderly man, and its presence here makes it likely that the owner was Mr. Bromeswell. That isn't much, but it confirms the other appearances."

"What other appearances?" demanded Miller.

"Those of the bed, the chair, the bench, the hooks, and the trough. They all point to a big, heavy man. The bedstead is about six-feet-six-inches long, but the heel-marks are near the foot and the pillow is right at the head. This bench and the trough have been put up for this man's use – they were apparently knocked up by himself – and they are both of a suitable height for you or me. A short man couldn't work at either. The hooks are over seven feet from the floor. The canvas seat of the chair is deeply sagged, although the woodwork looks in nearly new condition, and the canvas of the bed is in the same condition. Add this massive, hard-bitten pipe to those indications, and you have the picture of a tall, burly, powerful man. We must have a look at his pillow and rugs to see if we can pick up a stray hair or two and get an idea of his complexion. What did he make the pulp from? I don't see any traces of rags."

"He didn't use rags. He used Whatman's water-colour paper, which is a pure linen paper. Apparently he tore it up into tiny fragments and boiled it in soda lye until it was ready to go into the beater. Monk found a supply of the paper in a cupboard and some half-cooked stuff in the boiler." As he spoke, Miller unscrewed and raised the lid of the boiler, which was then seen to be half filled with a clear liquid, at the bottom of which was a mass of sodden fragments of shredded paper. From the boiler he turned to a small cupboard and opened the door. "That seems to be his stock of material," he said, indicating a large roll of thick white paper. He took out a sheet and handed it to Thorndyke, who held it up to the light and read the name "Whatman," which formed the water-mark.

"Yes," said Thorndyke, as he returned the sheet. "His method of work seems clear enough, but that is not of much interest, as you have the moulds. What we want is the man himself. You have no description of him, I suppose?"

"Not if your description of him is correct," replied Miller. "The suspected person, according to the Belgian police, is a smallish, slight, dark man. They may be on the wrong track, or there may be a confederate. There must have been a confederate, perhaps more than one. But Bromeswell only made the paper. Someone else must have done the engraving and printing. As to planting the notes, that may have been done by some other parties, or by either or both of these two artists. I should think they probably kept the game to themselves, judging by what we have seen here. This seems to be a one-man show, and it looks as if even the engraver didn't know where the paper was made, or the moulds wouldn't have been left in this way. Shall we go and look for those hairs that you spoke of?"

They returned to the outer room, where they both subjected the little pillow of the camp bed to a searching scrutiny. But though they examined both sides and even took off the dusty pillow-case, not a single hair was to be found. Then they turned their attention to the rugs, which had been folded neatly and placed on the canvas – there was no mattress – unfolding them carefully and going over them inch by inch. Here, too, they seemed to have drawn a blank, for they had almost completed their examination, when the Superintendent uttered an exclamation, and delicately picked a small object from near the edge of the rug.

"This seems to be a hair, Doctor," said he, holding it up between his finger and thumb. "Looks like a moustache hair, but it's a mighty short one."

Thorndyke produced his pocket lens and a sheet of notepaper, and holding the latter while Miller cautiously dropped the hair on it, he inspected the find through his lens.

"Yes," he said, "it is a moustache hair, about half an inch long, decidedly thick, cleanly cut, and of a lightish red-brown colour. Somehow it seems to fit the other characters. A closely-cropped, bristly, sandy moustache appears to go appropriately with the stature and weight of the man and that massive pipe. There is a tendency for racial characters to go together, and the blond races run to height and weight. Well, we have a fairly complete picture of the man, unless we have made

315

some erroneous inferences, and we seem to have finished our inspection. Have you been through the stuff in the letter-box?"

"Monk went through it, but we may as well have a look at it to make sure that he hasn't missed anything. I'll hand the things out if you will put them on the table and check them."

As Miller took out the letters in handfuls, Thorndyke received them from him and laid them out on the table. Then he and Miller examined the collection systematically.

"You see, Doctor," said the latter, "they are all circulars, not a private letter among them excepting the two notes from the treasurer about the rent. And they are quite a miscellaneous lot. None of these people knew anything about Bromeswell – apparently, they just copied the address out of the directory. Here's one from a money-lender. Bromeswell could have given him a tip or two. The earliest post-mark is the eleventh of June, so we may take it that he wasn't here after the tenth or the morning of the eleventh."

"There is a slight suggestion that he left at night," said Thorndyke, as he made a note of the date. "The place where you found the pipe would be in deep shadow by gaslight, but not by daylight. Certainly the blind was up, but he would probably have drawn it up after he had turned the gas out, as its being down during the day might attract attention."

"Yes," said Miller, "you are probably right about the time, and that reminds me that Monk found a small piece of paper under the bench – I've got it in my pocket – which seems to bear out your suggestion." He took from his pocket a bulky letter-case, from an inner recess of which he extracted a little scrap of Whatman paper. "Here it is," he said, handing it to Thorndyke. "He seems to have just jotted down the times of two trains, and, as you say, they were probably night trains."

Thorndyke looked with deep attention at the fragment, on which was written, hastily but legibly in very black ink, "*8:15 and 11:15*", and remarked, "Quite a valuable find in its way. The writing is very characteristic, and so is the ink. Probably it would be more so when seen through the microscope. Magnification brings out shades of colour that are invisible to the naked eye.

"Well, Doctor," said Miller, "if you can spare the time to have a look at it through the microscope, I wish you would, and let us know if you discover anything worth noting. And perhaps you wouldn't mind taking a glance at the hair, too, to settle the colour more exactly."

He transferred the latter, which he had carefully folded in paper and put in his pocket-book, to Thorndyke, who deposited it, with the scrap of paper, in his letter-case, after pencilling on the wrapper a note of the nature and source of the object.

"And that," said the Superintendent, "seems to be the lot. We haven't done so badly, after all. If you are right – and I expect you are – we have got quite a serviceable description of the man Bromeswell. But it is a most mysterious affair. I can't imagine what the deuce can have happened. It is pretty clear that he came here about the tenth of June, and probably made a batch of paper, which we shall hear of later. But what can have happened to the man? Something out of the common, evidently. He would never have stayed away voluntarily with the certainty that the premises would be entered, his precious moulds found, and the whole thing blown upon. If he had intended to clear out. he would certainly have taken the moulds with him, or at least destroyed them if he thought that the game was up. What do you think, Doctor?"

"It seems to me," replied Thorndyke, "that there are three possibilities. He may be dead, and if so he probably died suddenly, before he was able to make any arrangements. He may be in prison on some other charge, or he may have got a scare that we know nothing of and had to keep out of sight. You said that the Belgian police were taking some action."

"Yes, they have got an officer over here, by agreement with us, who is making inquiries about the man who planted the notes in Belgium. But he isn't after Bromeswell. He is looking for quite a different man, as I told you. But he doesn't pretend that he could recognize him."

"It doesn't follow that Bromeswell knows that. If the confederate has discovered that inquiries are being made, he may have given his friend a hint and the pair of them may have absconded. But that is a mere speculation. As you say, something extraordinary must have happened, and it must have been something sudden and unforeseen. And that is all that we can say at present."

By the time that this conclusion was reached, they had emerged from Clifford's Inn Passage into Fleet Street, and here they parted, the Superintendent setting a course westward and Thorndyke crossing the road to the gateway of Inner Temple Lane.

Chapter VIII
In Which Thorndyke
Tries Over the Moves

It was in a deeply meditative frame of mind that Thorndyke pursued his way towards his chambers after parting with the Superintendent, for the inspection which he had just made had developed points of interest other than those which he had discussed with the detective officer. To his acute mind, habituated to rapid inference, the case of the mysterious Mr. Bromeswell had inevitably presented a parallelism with that of Daniel Purcell. Bromeswell had disappeared without leaving a trace. If he had absconded, he had done so without premeditation or preparation, apparently under the compulsion of some unforeseen but imperative necessity. But that was precisely Purcell's case, and the instant the mere comparison was made, other points of agreement began to appear and multiply in the most startling manner.

The physical resemblance between Purcell and the hypothetical Bromeswell was striking but not conclusive. Both were big, heavy men, but such men are not uncommon, and the resemblance in the matter of the moustache had to be verified – or disproved. But the other points of agreement were very impressive – impressive alike by their completeness and by their number. Both men were connected with the making of paper and of the same kind – handmade paper. The banknote moulds had been stolen or lost at Maidstone about six years ago. But at that very time Purcell was at Maidstone, and was then engaged in the paper industry. Bromeswell appeared to have a sailor's knowledge and skill in respect of cordage. But Purcell was a yachtsman and had such knowledge and skill. Then the dates of the two disappearances coincided very strikingly. Bromeswell disappeared from London about the tenth of June, Purcell disappeared from Penzance on the twenty-third of June. Even in trivial circumstances there was curious agreement. For instance, it was a noticeable coincidence that Bromeswell's pipe should have been bought at a shop within a minute's walk of Purcell's office.

But there was another coincidence that Thorndyke had noted even while he was examining the premises at Clifford's Inn. Those premises were concerned exclusively with the making of the paper blanks on which the notes would later be printed. Of the engraving and printing activities there was no trace. Bromeswell was a papermaker pure and simple, but somewhere in the background there must have been a

318

confederate, who was an engraver and a printer, to whom Bromeswell supplied the paper blanks and who engraved the plates and printed the notes. But Purcell had one intimate friend, and that friend was a skilful engraver, who was able to print from engraved plates. Moreover, the rather vague description given by the Belgian police of the man who uttered the forged notes, while it obviously could not apply to Purcell, agreed very completely with Purcell's intimate friend.

And there was yet another agreement, perhaps more striking than any. If it were assumed that Bromeswell and Purcell were one and the same person, the whole of the mystery connected with Mr. Penfield's letter was resolved. Everything became consistent and intelligible – up to a certain point. If the mysterious "enclosures", were a batch of paper blanks with the Bank of England water-mark on them, it was easy to understand Mr. Penfield's reticence, for he had made himself an accessory to a felony, to say nothing of the offence that he was committing by having these things in his possession. It would also account completely for Purcell's sudden flight and his silence as to his whereabouts, for he would, naturally, assume that no lawyer would be such an imbecile as to accept the position of an accessory to a crime that he had no connection with. He would take it for granted that Penfield would forthwith hand the letter and the enclosures to the police.

But there were one or two difficulties. In the first place, the theory implied an incredible lack of caution on the part of Penfield, who was a lawyer of experience, and would fully appreciate the risk he was running. Then it assumed an equally amazing lack of care and caution in the case of Purcell – a carelessness quite at variance with the scrupulous caution and well-maintained secrecy of the establishment at Clifford's Inn. But the most serious discrepancy was the presence of the paper blanks in a letter. The letter into which they ought to have been put would be addressed to the confederate, and that confederate was assumed to be Varney. But why should they have been sent in a letter to Varney? On the very day on which the letter was posted, Varney and Purcell had been alone together for some hours on the yacht. The blanks could have been handed to Varney then, and naturally would have been. The discrepancy seemed to render the hypothesis untenable, or at any rate to rule out Varney as the possible confederate.

But it was impossible to dismiss the hypothesis as untenable. The agreement with the observed facts were too numerous, and as soon as the inquiry was transferred to a new field, a fresh set of agreements came into view. Very methodically Thorndyke considered the theory of the identity of Purcell with Bromeswell in connection with his interviews with Mr. Penfield and Mr. Levy.

319

Taking the latter first, what had it disclosed? It had shown that Purcell was a common money lender – not an incriminating fact, for the business of a money-lender is not in itself unlawful. But it is a vocation to which little credit attaches, and its practice is frequently associated with very unethical conduct. It is rather on the outside edge of lawful industry.

But what of Levy? Apparently he was not a mere employee. He appeared to be able to get on quite well without Purcell, and seemed to have the status of a partner. Was it possible that he was a partner in the other concern, too? It was not impossible. A money-lender has excellent opportunities for getting rid of good flash notes. His customers usually want notes in preference to cheques, and he could even get batches of notes from the Bank and number his forgeries to correspond, thus protecting himself in case of discovery. But even if Levy were a confederate he would not exclude Varney, for there was no reason to suppose that he was an engraver, whereas Varney was both an engraver and an old and constant associate of Purcell's. In short, Levy was not very obviously in the picture at all, and, for the time being, Thorndyke dismissed him and passed on to the other case. Taking now the interview with Penfield, there were the facts elicited by the examination of the envelope. That envelope had contained a rather bulky mass, apparently of folded paper, about five inches long or a little more, and somewhat less than three inches wide. Thorndyke rose, and, taking from the bookshelves a manuscript book labelled *Dimensions*, found in the index the entry *"Banknotes"*, and turned to the page indicated. Here the dimensions of a five-pound note were given as eight-inches-and-three-eighths long by five-inches-and-five-thirty-seconds wide. Folded lengthwise into three, it would thus be five-inches-and-five-thirty-seconds, or say five-and-an-eighth-long by two-and-three-quarters wide, if folded quite accurately, or a fraction more if folded less exactly. The enclosure in Penfield's envelope was therefore exactly the size of a small batch of notes folded into three. It did not follow that the enclosures actually were banknotes. They might have been papers of some other kind but of similar size. But the observed facts were in complete agreement with the supposition that they were banknotes, and taken in conjunction with Penfield's extraordinary secrecy and the wording of his letter to Margaret Purcell, they strongly supported that supposition.

Then there was the suggestion that the envelope had been steamed open and reclosed. It was only a suggestion, not a certainty. The appearances might be misleading. But to Thorndyke's expert eye the suggestion had been very strong. The gum had smeared upwards on the inside, which seemed impossible if the envelope had been closed once for all, and the paper showed traces of cockling, as if it had been damped. Mr. Penfield had rejected the suggestion, partly for the excellent reasons that he had given, but also, perhaps, because Purcell's flight implied that he had discovered the mistake, and that therefore the mistake was presumably his own.

But there was one important point that Penfield seemed to have overlooked. The letter that he expected to receive would (presumably) have contained no enclosures. The letter that he did receive contained a bulky enclosure which bulged the envelope. The two letters must therefore have been very different in appearance. Now, ordinarily, when two letters are put each into the envelope of the other, when once the envelopes are closed the mistake is covered up. There is nothing in their exterior to suggest that any mistake has occurred. But in the present case the error was blatantly advertised by the appearance of the closed letters. Penfield's envelope, which should have been flat, bulged with its contents. The other envelope – if there was one, as there almost certainly must have been – which should have bulged, was conspicuously flat. Of course, Penfield may have been wrong in assuming that no enclosures were to be sent to him. Both letters may have held enclosures. But taking the evidence as it was presented, it was to the effect that there were enclosures in only one of the letters. And if that were the case, the mistake appeared incredible. It became impossible to understand how Purcell could have handled the two letters and finally put them into the post without seeing that the enclosures were in the wrong envelope.

What was the significance of the point? Well, it raised the question whether Purcell could possibly have posted this letter himself, and this question involved the further question whether the envelope had been opened and reclosed. For if it had, the transposition of the contents must have taken place after the letters left Purcell's hands. Against this was the fact of Purcell's flight, which made it practically certain that he had become aware of the transposition. But it was not conclusive, and having noted the objection, Thorndyke proceeded to follow out the alternative theory. Accepting, for the moment, the hypothesis that the letter had been opened and the transposition made intentionally, certain other questions arose. First, who had the opportunity? Second, what could have been the purpose of the act? And, third, who could have had such a purpose? Thorndyke considered these questions in the same methodical fashion, taking them one by one and in the order stated.

Who had the opportunity? That depended, among other things, on the time at which the letter was posted. Penfield had stated that the letter had been posted at 8:30 p.m. If that were true, it put Varney out of the problem, for he had left Penzance some hours before that time. But it was not true. The time shown by the post-mark was not the time at which the letter was posted, but that at which it was sorted at the post office. It might have been posted at a pillar-box some hours previously. It was therefore not impossible that it might have been posted by Varney. And if it was physically possible, it at once became the most probable assumption, since there was no reasonable alternative. It was inconceivable that Purcell should have handed the letters to a stranger to post, and if he had, it was inconceivable that that stranger should have opened the letters and transposed their contents. There was, indeed, the possibility that Purcell had met a confederate at Penzance and had handed him the letters – one of which would be addressed to himself – to post, and that this confederate might have made the transposition. But this was pure speculation, without a particle of evidence to support it, whereas Varney, as an intimate friend, even if not a confederate, might conceivably have had the letters handed to him to post, though this was profoundly improbable, seeing that Purcell was going ashore and Varney was in charge of the yacht. In effect, there was no positive evidence that anybody had had the opportunity to make the transposition, but if it had not been done by Purcell, himself, then Varney appeared to be the only possible agent.

From this vague and unsatisfactory conclusion Thorndyke proceeded to the second question:

Assuming the transposition to have been made intentionally, what could have been the purpose of the act? To this question, so far as the immediate purpose was concerned, the answer was obvious enough, since only one was possible. The blanks must have been put into Mr. Penfield's envelope for the express purpose of notifying the solicitor that Purcell was a banknote forger – in short, for the purpose of exposing Purcell. This led at once to the third question: Who could have had such a purpose? But to this also the answer was obvious. The only person who could have had such a purpose would be a confederate, for no one else would have been in possession of the knowledge that would make such a purpose possible. The transposition could have been made only by someone who knew what the contents of the envelope were.

But why should any confederate have done this? The exposure of Purcell involved at least a risk of the exposure of his confederate, and it could be assumed that if Purcell suspected that he had been betrayed, he would certainly denounce his betrayer. The object, therefore, could not have been to secure the arrest of Purcell – a conclusion that was confirmed by the fact that Purcell had become aware of the transposition, and, if he had not done it himself, must apparently have been informed in time to allow of his escaping.

But what other object could there be? Was it possible that the confederate wished to get rid of Purcell, and made this exposure with the express purpose of compelling him to disappear? That raised the question: When did Purcell become aware that the transposition had been made? And the answer was somewhat perplexing. He could not have become aware of it immediately, or he would have telegraphed to Penfield and stopped the letter, and yet he seemed to have absconded at once, before the letter could have been delivered to Penfield. He was due at Oulton the following day, and he never arrived there. He was stated to have gone from Penzance to Falmouth. That might or might not be true, but the voyage to Ipswich was evidently a myth. The answer that he had received from the owners of the *Hedwig*, enclosing a report from the captain of the ship, showed that the only passengers who embarked at Falmouth were three distressed Swedish sailors, who travelled with the ship to Malmo, and that no one went ashore at Ipswich. It followed that Varney had either been misinformed or had invented the incidents, but when it was considered that he must, if he was telling the truth, have been misinformed in the same manner on both separate occasions, it seemed more probable that the story of the voyage was a fabrication. In that case, the journey to Falmouth, of which no one but Varney had heard, was probably a fabrication, too. This left Penzance as the apparent starting-point of the flight. Purcell had certainly landed at Penzance and had forthwith disappeared from view. What became of him thereafter it was impossible to guess. He seemed to have vanished into thin air.

Arrived at this point, Thorndyke's quietly reflective attitude suddenly gave place to one of intense attention. For a new and somewhat startling question had presented itself. With an expression of deep concentration he set himself to consider it.

Hitherto he had accepted Purcell's landing at Penzance as an undeniable fact, from which a secure departure could be taken. But was it an undeniable fact? The only witness of that landing was Varney, and Varney had shown himself a very unreliable witness. Apparently he had lied about the Ipswich voyage – probably, too, about the visit to Falmouth. What if the landing at Penzance were a fabrication, too? It seemed a wild suggestion, but it was a possibility, and Thorndyke proceeded carefully to develop the consequences that would follow if it were true.

Suppose that Purcell had never landed at Penzance at all. Then several circumstances hitherto incomprehensible became understandable. The fables of Purcell's appearance at Falmouth and Ipswich, which had seemed to be motiveless falsehoods, now showed a clear purpose, which was to create a certainty that Purcell had landed from the yacht as stated and to shift the search for the missing man from Penzance to Ipswich. Again, if Purcell had never landed at Penzance, the letter could not have been posted by him, and it became practically certain that it must have been posted there by Varney and the transposition made by him. And this made the transposition understandable by developing a very evident purpose. When Penfield opened the letter, and when, later, he heard of Purcell's disappearance, he would at once assume that Purcell had absconded to avoid being arrested. The purpose of the transposition, then, was to furnish a reasonable explanation of a disappearance that had already occurred.

But what had become of Purcell? If he had not landed at Penzance he certainly had not landed anywhere else, for there had not been time for the yacht to touch at any other port. Nor could it be supposed that he had trans-shipped on to another vessel during the voyage. There was no reason why he should. The letter had not been posted, and until it had been posted there was no reason for flight. The only reasonable inference from the facts, including Varney's false statements, was that something had happened during the voyage from Sennen, that Purcell had disappeared, presumably overboard, and that Varney had reasons for concealing the circumstances of his disappearance. In short, that Purcell was dead, and that Varney was responsible for his death.

It was an appalling theory. Thorndyke hardly dared even to propound it to himself. But there was no denying that it fitted the facts with the most surprising completeness. Once assume it to be true, and all the perplexing features of the case became consistent and understandable. Not only did it explain Varney's otherwise inexplicable anxiety to prove that Purcell had been seen alive at a date subsequent to that of the alleged landing at Penzance, it accounted for the facts that Purcell had taken no measures to provide himself with a stock of cash before disappearing, and that he had made no communication of any sort to his wife since his departure, though he could have done so with perfect safety. It was in perfect agreement with all the known facts and in disagreement with none. It was a complete solution of the mystery, and there was no other.

When Thorndyke reached this conclusion, he roused himself from his reverie, and, filling his pipe, took an impartial survey of the scheme of circumstantial evidence that he had been engaged in constructing. It was all very complete and consistent. There were, so far, no discrepancies or contradictions. All the evidence pointed in the one direction. The assumed actions of Varney were in complete agreement with the circumstances that were known and the others that were inferred, as well as with the assumed motives. But it was largely hypothetical, and might turn out to be entirely illusory. If only one of the assumed facts should prove to be untrue, the whole structure of inference would come tumbling down. He took out of his pocket-book the folded paper containing the single moustache hair that the Superintendent had found in the Clifford's Inn rooms. Laying it on a sheet of white paper, he once more examined it, first through his lens, then under the microscope, noting the length, thickness, and colour, and mentally visualizing the kind of moustache from which it had come. Here was an indispensable link in the chain of evidence. If Purcell had had such a moustache, that would not prove that he and Bromeswell were one and the same person, but it would be consistent with their identity. But if Purcell had no such moustache, then it was probable – indeed, nearly certain – that he and Bromeswell were different persons. And if they were, the whole hypothetical scheme that he had been working out collapsed. Both Purcell and Varney ceased to have any connection with the forged notes, the mysterious "enclosures" could not be of the nature that he had assumed, and all the deductions from those assumed facts ceased to be valid. It was necessary without delay to test this essential link, to ascertain whether this derelict hair could have been derived from Daniel Purcell.

Enclosed with it was the slip of paper with the notes of the trains, which he had, for the moment, forgotten. He now examined it minutely, and was once more struck by the intense blackness of the ink, and he recalled that a similar intensity of blackness had been noticeable in the address on Mr. Penfield's envelope. It had appeared almost like the black of a carbon ink, but he had decided that it was not. So it was with the present specimen, but now he had the means of deciding definitely. Fetching the microscope, he laid the paper on the stage and examined it, first by reflected, then by transmitted, light. The examination made it clear that this was an iron-tannin ink of unusual concentration, with a "provisional" blue pigment, probably methyl blue. There was only one letter, P. and this he tried to compare with the P on Mr. Penfield's envelope, so far as he could remember it, but he could not get beyond a belief that there was a resemblance – a belief that would have to be tested by a specimen of Purcell's handwriting.

Having finished with the paper he returned to the hair. He decided to write to Margaret, asking for a description of her missing husband, and had just reached out to the stationery case, when an elaborate and formal tattoo on the small brass knocker of the inner door arrested him. Rising, he crossed the room and threw the door open, thereby disclosing the dorsal aspect of a small elderly gentleman. As the door opened the visitor turned about, and Thorndyke immediately, not without surprise, recognized him. It was Mr. Penfield.

Chapter IX
In Which Mr. Penfield
Receives a Shock

Mr. Penfield greeted Thorndyke with a little stiff bow, and bestowed upon the extended hand a formal and somewhat rheumatic shake. "I must apologize," he said, as his host ushered him into the room, "for disturbing you by this visit, but I had a little matter to communicate to you, and thought it better to make that communication personally rather than by correspondence."

"You are not disturbing me at all," Thorndyke replied. "On the contrary, I expect that your visit will save me the necessity of writing a letter."

"To me?" asked Penfield.

"No, to Mrs. Purcell. I was on the point of writing to her to ask for a description of her husband. As I have never met him, I thought it as well that I should get from her such details of his appearance as might be necessary for purposes of identification."

"Quite so," said Mr. Penfield. "Very desirable indeed. Well, I think I can tell you all you want to know, unless you want very minute details. And it happens that your inquiry comes rather opportunely in respect of the matter that I have to communicate. Shall we dispose of your question first?"

"If you please," replied Thorndyke. He took from a drawer a pad of ruled paper and, uncapping his fountain pen, looked at Mr. Penfield, whom he had inducted into an easy chair. "May I offer you a cigar, Mr. Penfield?" he asked.

"I thank you," was the reply, "but I am not a smoker. Perhaps – " Here he held out his snuff-box tentatively. "No? Well, it is an obsolete vice, but I am a survivor from an obsolete age." He refreshed himself with a substantial pinch, and continued. "With regard to Purcell: His person is easy to describe and should be easy to identify. He is a big lump of a man, about six feet or a fraction over. Massive, heavy – but not fat, just elephantine. Rather slow in his movements, but strong, active, and not at all clumsy. As to his face, I would call it beefy – a full red face with thick, bright-red, crinkly ears and full lips. Eyes, pale blue, hair, yellowish or light brown, cropped short. No beard or whiskers, but a little, bristly, pale-reddish moustache, cut short like a sandy toothbrush. Expression surly, manner short, brusque, taciturn, and rather morose.

Big, thick, purple hands that look, in spite of their size, capable, neat, and useful hands. In fact, the hands are an epitome of Purcell – a combination of massive strength and weight with remarkable bodily efficiency. How will that do for you?"

"Admirably," replied Thorndyke, inwardly some what surprised at the old solicitor's powers of observation. "It is a very distinctive picture, and quite enough for what we may call *prima facie* identification. I take it that you know him pretty well?"

"I have seen a good deal of him since his marriage, when his wife introduced him to me, and I have managed his legal business for some years. But I know very little of his private affairs. Very few people do, I imagine. I never met a less communicative man. And now, if we have done with his appearance, let us come to the question of his present whereabouts. Have you any information on the subject?"

"There is a vague report that he was seen some months ago at Ipswich. It is quite unconfirmed, and I attach no importance to it."

"It is probably correct, though," said Penfield. "I have just had a letter from him, and the post-mark shows that it came from that very locality."

"There is no address on the letter, then?"

"No, and I am invited to reply by advertisement. The occasion of the letter was this: A client of mine, a Mrs. Catford, who is a relative of Mrs. Purcell's, had recently died, leaving a will of which I am the executor and residuary legatee. By the terms of that will, Mrs. Purcell and her husband each benefit to the extent of a thousand pounds. Now, as Mrs. Catford's death occurred subsequently to Purcell's disappearance, it became necessary to establish his survival of the testatrix or the contrary – in order that the will might be administered. As his whereabouts were unknown, the only method that I could think of was to put an advertisement in the '*Personal*' column of *The Times*, on the bare chance that he might see it, asking him to communicate with me. By a lucky chance he did see it and did communicate with me. But he gave no address, and any further communication from me will have to be by advertisement, as he suggests. That, however, is of no importance to me. His letter tells me all I want to know, that he is alive at a date subsequent to the death of the testatrix, and that the bequest in his favour can consequently take effect. I am not concerned with his exact whereabouts. That matter is in your province."

As he concluded, punctuating his conclusion with a pinch of snuff, the old lawyer looked at Thorndyke with a sly and slightly ironical smile.

Thorndyke reflected rapidly on Mr. Penfield's statement. The appearance of this letter was very remarkable, and the more so coming as it did on top of the confirmatory evidence respecting the moustache hair. It was now highly probable – almost certain – that Bromeswell and Purcell were one and the same person. But if that were so, all the probabilities went to show that Purcell must be dead. And yet here was a letter from him – not to a stranger, but to one who knew his handwriting well. It was very remarkable.

Again, the report of Purcell's voyage from Falmouth to Ipswich was certainly untrue. But if it was untrue, there was no reason for supposing that Purcell had ever been at Ipswich at all. Yet here was a letter sent by Purcell from that very locality. That was very remarkable, too. Clearly the matter called for further investigation, and that involved, in the first place, an examination of this letter that had come so mysteriously to confirm a report that was certainly untrue. He returned Mr. Penfield's smile, and then asked, "You accept this letter, then, as evidence of survival?"

Mr. Penfield looked astonished. "But, my dear sir, what else could I do? I may be insufficiently critical, and I have not your great special knowledge of this subject, but to my untrained intelligence, it would appear that the circumstance of a man's having written a letter affords good presumptive evidence that he was alive at the date when it was written. That is my own view, and I propose to administer the will in accordance with it. Do I understand that you dissent from it?"

Thorndyke smiled blandly. He was beginning rather to like Mr. Penfield.

"As you state the problem," said he, "you are probably right. At any rate, the administration of the will is your concern and not mine. As you were good enough to remark, my concern is with the person and the whereabouts of Mr. Purcell and not with his affairs. Were you proposing to allow me to inspect the envelope of this letter?"

"It was for that very purpose that I came," replied Penfield, with a smile and a twinkle of mischief in his eyes, "but I will not restrict you to the envelope this time. You shall inspect the letter as well, if a mere letter will not be superfluous when the envelope has given up its secrets."

He produced a wallet from his pocket and, opening it, took out a letter, which he gravely handed to Thorndyke. The latter took it from him, and as he glanced at the jet-black writing of the address said, "I take it that you are satisfied that the hand writing is Purcell's?"

"Certainly," was the reply. "But whose else should it be? The question does not seem to arise. However, I may assure you that it is undoubtedly Purcell's writing and also Purcell's ink, though that is less conclusive. Still, it is a peculiar ink. I have never seen any quite like it. My impression is that he prepares it himself."

As Penfield was speaking, Thorndyke examined the envelope narrowly. Presently he rose, and, taking a reading-glass from the mantelshelf, went over to the window, where, with the aid of the glass, he scrutinized the envelope inch by inch on both sides. Then, laying down the reading-glass, he took from his pocket a powerful doublet lens, through which he examined certain parts of the envelope, particularly the stamp and the London postmark. Finally, he took out the letter, opened the envelope, and carefully examined its interior, and then inspected the letter itself before unfolding it, holding it so that the light fell on it obliquely and scrutinizing each of the four corners in succession. At length he opened the letter, read it through, again examined the corners, and compared some portions of the writing with that on the envelope.

These proceedings were closely observed by Mr. Penfield, who watched them with an indulgent smile. He was better able than on the last occasion to appreciate the humour of Thorndyke's methods. There was nothing about this letter that he had need to conceal. He could afford to let the expert find out what he could this time, and Mr. Penfield, from a large and unfavourable experience of expert witnesses, suspected that the discovery would probably take the form of a mare's nest.

"Well," he said, as Thorndyke returned to his chair with the letter in his hand, "has the oracle spoken? Have we made any startling discoveries?"

"I wouldn't use the word 'discoveries'," replied Thorndyke, "which seems to imply facts definitely ascertained, but there are certain appearances which suggest a rather startling inference."

"Indeed!" said Mr. Penfield, taking snuff with great enjoyment. "I somehow expected that they would when I decided to show you the letter. What is the inference that is suggested?"

"The inference is," replied Thorndyke, "that this letter has never been through the post."

Mr. Penfield paused with his hand uplifted, holding a minute pinch of snuff, and regarded Thorndyke in silent astonishment.

"That," he said, at length, "is certainly a startling inference, and it would be still more startling if there were any possibility that it could be true. Unfortunately, the letter bears a postmark showing that it was posted at Woodbridge, and another showing that it was sorted at the London office. But no doubt you have observed and allowed for those facts."

"The appearances," said Thorndyke, "suggest that when the post-marks were made the envelope was empty and probably unaddressed."

330

"But, my dear sir," protested Penfield, "that is a manifest impossibility. You must see that for yourself. How could such a thing possibly have happened?"

"That is a separate question," replied Thorndyke. "I am now dealing only with the appearances. Let me point them out to you. First, you will notice that the words '*Personal and Confidential*' have been written at the top of the envelope. Apparently the word '*Personal*' was first written alone and the words '*and Confidential*' added as an after thought. That is suggested by the change in the writing and the increasingly condensed form of the letters towards the end, due to the want of space. But in spite of the squeezing up of the letters the tail of the final L has been forced on to the stamp, and actually touches the circle of the post-mark, and if you examine it through this lens you can see plainly that the written line is on *top* of the post-mark. Therefore the post-mark was already there when that word was written."

He handed the envelope and the lens to Mr. Penfield, who, after some ineffectual struggles, rejected the lens and had recourse to his spectacles.

"It has somewhat the appearance that you suggest," he said at length, "but I have not your expert eye, and therefore not your confidence. I should suppose it to be impossible to say with certainty whether one written mark was on top of or underneath another."

"Very well," said Thorndyke, "then we will proceed to the next point. You will notice that both of the post-marks are deeply indented, unusually so. As a matter of fact, post-marks are usually not visibly indented at all, and it is a noticeable coincidence that this envelope should bear two different post-marks, each unusually indented."

"Still," said Penfield, "that might easily have happened. The laws of chance are not applicable to individual cases."

"Quite so," Thorndyke agreed. "But now observe another point. These post-marks are so deeply indented that, in both cases, the impression is clearly visible on the opposite side of the envelope, especially inside. That is rather remarkable, seeing that, if the letter was inside, the impression must have penetrated four thicknesses of paper."

"Still," said Penfield, "it is not impossible."

"Perhaps not," Thorndyke admitted. "But what does seem impossible is that it should have done so without leaving any trace on the letter itself. But that is what has happened. If you will examine the letter you will see that there is not a vestige of an indentation on any part of it. From which you must agree with me that the only reasonable inference is that when the indentations were made the letter was not in the envelope."

331

Mr. Penfield took the letter and the envelope and compared them carefully. There was no denying the obvious facts. There was the envelope with the deeply indented post-marks showing plainly on the reverse sides, and there was the letter with never a sign of any mark at all. It was certainly very odd. Mr. Penfield was a good deal puzzled and slightly annoyed. To his orthodox legal mind, this prying into concrete facts and physical properties was rather distasteful. He was accustomed to sworn testimony, which might be true or might be untrue (but that was the witnesses' lookout), but which could be accepted as admitted evidence. He could not deny that the facts were apparently as Thorndyke had stated. But that unwilling admission produced no conviction. He was a lawyer, not a scientific observer.

"Yes," he agreed reluctantly, "the appearances are as you say. But they must be in some way illusory. Perhaps some difference in the properties of the paper may be the explanation. At any rate, I cannot accept your inference, for the simple reason that it predicates an impossibility. It assumes that this man, or some other, posted a blank, empty envelope, got it back, put a letter in it, addressed it, and then delivered it by hand, having travelled up from Woodbridge to do so. That would be an impossibility, unless the person were a post office official, and then, what on earth could be the object of such an insane proceeding? Have you asked yourself that question?"

As a matter of fact, Thorndyke had, and he had deduced a completely sufficient answer. But he did not feel called upon to explain this. It was not his concern to convince Mr. Penfield. That gentleman's beliefs were a matter of perfect indifference to him. He had considered it fair to draw Mr. Penfield's attention to the observed facts and even to point out the inferences that they suggested. But if Mr. Penfield chose to shut his eyes to the facts, or to reject the obvious inferences, that was his affair.

"At the moment," he replied, "I am concerned with the appearances and the immediate inferences from them. When I am sure of my facts I shall go on to consider their bearing – those questions of motive, for instance, to which you have referred. That would be premature until I have verified the facts by a more searching examination. Would it be convenient for you to leave this letter with me for a few hours, that I might examine it more completely?"

Mr. Penfield would have liked to refuse, but there was no pretext for such refusal. He therefore made a virtue of necessity, and replied graciously, "Certainly, certainly. By all means. I will just take a copy, and then you can do as you please with the original, short of destroying it. But don't, pray don't let it lead you astray."

"In what respect?"

"Well," said Mr. Penfield, taking a deprecating pinch of snuff, "it has sometimes seemed to me that the specialist has a tendency – just a tendency, mark you – to mislead himself. He looks for a certain thing, which might be there, and – well, he finds it. I cannot but remark your own unexpected successes in your search for the – Ha! – the unusual, shall we say. On two occasions I have shown you an envelope. On both occasions you have made most surprising discoveries, involving the strangest aberrations of conduct on the part of Purcell and others. To-day you have found unheard-of anomalies in the post-marks, from which you infer that Purcell or another has exerted immense ingenuity and overcome insuperable obstacles in order to behave like a fool. On the previous occasion you discovered that Purcell had been at the trouble of ungumming the envelope, which he had undoubtedly addressed with his own hand, for the express purpose of taking out the right contents, which were already in it, and putting in the wrong ones. Perhaps you made some other discoveries which you did not mention," Mr. Penfield added, after a slight pause, and as Thorndyke only bowed slightly, which was not very explicit, he further added, "Would it be indiscreet or impertinent to inquire whether you did, in fact, make any further discoveries? Whether, for instance, you arrived at any opinion as to the nature of the enclosures, which were, I think, the objects of your investigations?"

Thorndyke hesitated. For a moment he was disposed to take the old solicitor into his confidence. But experience had taught him, as it teaches most of us, that when the making or withholding of confidences are alternatives, he chooses the better part who keeps his own counsel. Nevertheless, he gave Penfield a cautionary hint.

"Those enclosures," said he, "have ceased to interest me. Any opinions that I formed as to their nature had better be left unstated. I seek no verification of them. Opinions held but not disclosed commit the holder to nothing, whereas actual knowledge has its responsibilities. I do not know what those enclosures were and I do not want to know."

For some moments after Thorndyke finished speaking there was a slightly uncomfortable silence. Mr. Penfield's dry facetiousness evaporated rather suddenly, and he found himself reading a somewhat alarming significance into Thorndyke's ambiguous and even cryptic reply. He did not know and he did not want to know. Now, Mr. Penfield *did* know, and would have given a good deal to be without that knowledge, for to possess the knowledge was to be an accessory. Was that what Thorndyke meant? Mr. Penfield had a dark suspicion that it was.

"Probably you are right," he said presently. "You know what opinions you formed and I do not. But there is one point that I should like to have made clear. We are both acting in Mrs. Purcell's interest, but her husband is also my client. Is there any conflict in our purposes with regard to him?"

"I think not," replied Thorndyke. "At any rate, I will say this much: That I should under no circumstances take any action that might be prejudicial to him without your concurrence, or at least without placing you in possession of all the facts. But I feel confident that no such necessity will arise. We are dealing with separate aspects of the case, but it would be foolish for us to get at cross-purposes."

"Exactly," said Mr. Penfield. "That is my own feeling. And with regard to this letter: If it should yield any further suggestions and you should consider them as being of any interest to me, perhaps you would be so good as to inform me of them."

"I will, certainly," Thorndyke replied, "and, by the way, what are you going to do? Shall you issue any further advertisement?"

"I had not intended to," said Mr. Penfield, "but perhaps it would be well to try to elicit a further reply. I might ask Purcell to send a receipt for the legacy, which I shall pay into his bank. He knows the amount, so that I need not state it."

"I think that would be advisable," said Thorndyke, "but my impression is that there will be no reply."

"Well, we shall see," said Penfield, rising and drawing on his gloves. "If an answer comes, you shall see it, and if there is no answer, I will advise you to that effect. You will agree with me that we keep our own counsel about the matters that we have discussed." And as Thorndyke assented, he added, "Of course the actual receipt of the letter is no secret."

With this and a stiff handshake, Mr. Penfield took his departure, cogitating profoundly as he wended his way eastward, wondering how much Thorndyke really knew about those unfortunate enclosures and how he came by his knowledge.

Meanwhile Thorndyke, as soon as he was alone, resumed his examination of the letter, calling in now the aid of more exact methods. Placing on the table a microscope specially constructed for examining documents, he laid the envelope on the stage and inspected the post-mark at the point where the tail of the L touched it. The higher magnification at once resolved any possible uncertainty. The written line was on top of the post-mark beyond all doubt. But it also brought another anomaly into view. It was now evident that the indentation of the post-mark did not coincide exactly with the whole width of the printed line. The indented line was somewhat narrower. It consisted of a furrow, deepest in the middle, which followed the printed line but did not completely occupy, it, and in one or two places strayed slightly outside it. On turning the envelope over and testing the other post-mark, the same peculiarity was observable. The indentation was a thing separate from the printed mark, and had been produced by a separate operation, apparently with a bluntly pointed tool, which would account for its excessive depth.

It was an important discovery in two respects. First, it confirmed the other evidence that the letter had never been posted, and, secondly, it threw some light on the means by which the postmark had been produced. What was the object of the indentation? Evidently to imitate the impression of metal types and disguise the method that had actually been used.

What was that method? It was not photography, for the marks were in printers' ink. It was not copperplate, for the engraved plate throws up a line in relief, whereas these lines were flat, like the lines of a lithograph. In fact, lithography appeared to be the only alternative, and with this view the appearances agreed completely, particularly the thick black ink, quite different from the rather fluid ink used by the post office.

From the post-marks, Thorndyke now transferred his attention to the writing. He had been struck by the exact resemblance of the name *"Penfield"* on the envelope to the same name in the letter. Each was a perfect facsimile of the other. Placing them together, he could not see a single point of difference or variation between them. With a delicate caliper gauge he measured the two words, taking the total length, the height of each letter, and the distance between various points. In all cases the measurements were practically identical. Now such perfect repetition as this does not happen in natural writing. It is virtually diagnostic of forgery – of a forgery by means of a careful tracing from an original. And Thorndyke had no doubt that this was such a forgery.

Confirmation was soon forthcoming. An exploration with the microscope of the surfaces of the envelope and the letter showed in both a number of minute spindle-shaped fragments of rubber. Something had been rubbed out. Then, on examining the words by transmitted light powerful enough to turn the jet-black writing into a deep purple, there could be seen through the ink a broken grey line, the remains of a pencil line, which the ink had partly protected from the rubber. Similar remains of a pencil tracing were to be seen in other parts of the letter, especially in the signature. In short, there was no possible doubt that the whole production, letter and post-marks alike, was a forgery.

The next question was: Who was the forger? But the answer to that seemed to be contained in the further question, What was the purpose of the forgery? For the evident purpose of this letter was to furnish evidence that Purcell was still alive, and as such it had been accepted by Mr. Penfield. That distinctly pointed to Varney, who had already made two false, or at least incorrect, statements, apparently with the same object. The skill with which the forgery had been executed also pointed to him, for an engraver must needs be a skilful copyist. There was only one doubtful point. Whoever had prepared this letter was a lithographer – not a mere draughtsman, but a printer as well. Now was Varney a lithographer? It was extremely probable. Many etchers and mezzotinters work also on the stone. But until it had been ascertained that he was, the authorship of the letter must be left in suspense. But assuming the letter to be Varney's work, it was evident that Mr. Penfield's visit had added materially to the body of circumstantial evidence. It had established that Purcell had worn a moustache apparently identical in character with that of the missing Bromeswell, which, taken in conjunction with all the other known facts, made it nearly a certainty that Bromeswell and Purcell were one and the same person. But that assumption had been seen to lead to the inference that Purcell was dead, and that Varney was responsible for, or implicated in, the circumstances of his death.

Then there was this letter. It was a forged letter, and its purpose was to prove that Purcell was alive. But the fact that it was necessary to forge a letter to prove that he was alive was in itself presumptive evidence that he was *not* alive. Subject to proof that Varney was a lithographer and therefore capable of producing this forgery, the evidence that Mr. Penfield had brought furnished striking confirmation of the hypothesis that Thorndyke had formed as to what had become of Daniel Purcell.

Chapter X
In Which Thorndyke
Sees a New Light

"We shall only be three at dinner, after all," said Margaret. "Mr. Rodney will be detained somewhere, but he is coming in for a chat later in the evening."

Varney received the news without emotion. He could do without Rodney. He would not have been desolated if the other guest had been a defaulter, too. At any rate, he hoped that he would not be needlessly punctual, and thus shorten unduly the *tête-à-têete* with Margaret which he, Varney, had secured by exercising the privilege of an old friend to arrive considerably before his time.

"You have only met Dr. Thorndyke once before, I think?" said Margaret.

"Yes, at Sennen, you know, the day that queer letter came from Mr. Penfield, and I didn't see much of him then. I remember that I was a little mystified about him – couldn't quite make out whether he was a lawyer, a doctor, or a man of science."

"As a matter of fact, he is all three. He is what is called a 'medical jurist' – a sort of lawyer who deals with legal cases that involve medical questions. I understand that he is a great authority on medical evidence."

"What legal cases do involve medical questions?"

"I don't know much about it," replied Margaret, "but I believe they include questions of survivorship and cases of presumption of death."

"Presumption of death!" repeated Varney. "What on earth does that mean?"

"I am not very clear about it myself," she replied, "but from what I am told, I gather that it is a sort of legal proceeding that takes place when a person disappears permanently and there is uncertainty as to whether he or she is dead or alive. An application is made to the court for permission to presume that the person is dead, and if the court gives the permission, the person is then legally presumed to be dead, and his will can be administered and his affairs wound up. That is an instance of the kind of case that Dr. Thorndyke undertakes. He must have had quite a lot of experience of persons who have disappeared, and for that reason Mr. Rodney advised me to consult him about Dan."

"Do you mean with a view to presuming his death?" asked Varney, inwardly anathematizing Dan for thus making his inevitable appearance in the conversation, but keenly interested nevertheless.

"No," replied Margaret. "I consulted him quite soon after Dan went away. What I asked him to do was to find out, if possible, what had become of him, and if he could discover his whereabouts to get into touch with him."

"Well," said Varney, "he doesn't seem to have had much luck up to the present. He hasn't been able to trace Dan, has he?"

"No," she replied – "at least, I suppose not. But we know where the lost sheep is now. Had you heard about the letter?"

"The letter?"

"Yes. From Dan. He wrote to Mr. Penfield a few days ago."

"Did he, though?" said Varney, with well-simulated surprise. "From somewhere abroad, I suppose?"

"No. The post-mark was Woodbridge – there was no address," and here Margaret briefly explained the circumstances.

"It sounds rather as if he were afloat," said Varney. "That is an ideal coast for lurking about in a smallish yacht. There is endless cover in the rivers and the creeks off the Come, the Roach, the Crouch, and the Blackwater. But it looks as if he had made more preparation for the flitting than we thought at the time. He hasn't written to you?"

Margaret shook her head. The affront was too gross for comment.

"It was beastly of him," said Varney. "He might have sent you just a line. However, Dr. Thorndyke will have something to go on now. He will know whereabouts to look for him."

"As far as I am concerned," Margaret said coldly, "the affair is finished. This insult was the last straw. I have no further interest in him, and I hope I may never see him again. But," she added earnestly, after a brief pause, "I should like to be rid of him completely. I want my freedom."

As she spoke – with unusual emphasis and energy – she looked, for a moment, straight into Varney's eyes. Then suddenly she flushed scarlet and turned her head away.

Varney was literally overwhelmed. He felt the blood rush to his head and tingle in the tips of his fingers. After one swift glance he, too, turned away his head. He did not dare to look at her. Nor, for some seconds, did he dare to trust his voice. At last it had come! In the twinkling of an eye his dim hopes, more than half-distrusted, had changed into realities. For there could be no doubt. That look into his eyes, that sudden blush – what could they be but an unpremeditated, unintended confession? She wanted her freedom. That unguarded glance told him why, and then her mantling cheeks, while they rebuked the glance, but served to interpret its significance.

With an effort he regained his normal manner. His natural delicacy told him that he must not be too discerning. He must take no cognizance of this confidence that was never intended. She must still think that her secret was locked up in her own breast, secure from every eye, even from his.

And yet what a pitiful game of cross-purposes they were playing! She wanted her freedom! And behold! She was free, and he knew it and could not tell her. What a tangle it was! And how was it ever going to be straightened out? In life, Purcell had stood between him and liberty, and now the ghost – nay, less than the ghost, the mere unsubstantial name – of Purcell stood between him and a lifelong happiness that Fortune was actually holding out to him.

It was clear that, sooner or later, the ghost of Purcell would have to be laid. But how? And here it began to dawn upon him that the ingenious letter, on which he had been congratulating himself, had been a tactical mistake. He had not known about Dr. Thorndyke, and he had never heard before of the possibility of presuming a person's death. He had been busying himself to produce convincing evidence that Purcell was alive, whereas it was possible that Thorndyke had been considering the chances of being able to presume his death. It was rather a pity, for Purcell had got to be disposed of before he could openly declare himself to Maggie, and this method of legal presumption of death appeared to be the very one that suited the conditions. He wished he had known about it before.

These reflections flashed through his mind in the silence that had followed Margaret's unguarded utterance. For the moment Varney had been too overcome to reply. And Margaret suddenly fell silent with an air of some confusion. Recovering himself, Varney now replied in a tone of conventional sympathy, "Of course you do. The bargain is off on the one side, and it is not reasonable that it should hold on the other. You don't want to be shackled for ever to a man who has gone out of your life. But I don't quite see what is to be done."

"Neither do I," said Margaret. "Perhaps the lawyers will be able to make some suggestion – and I think I hear one of them arriving."

A moment or two later the door opened and the housemaid announced, "Dr. Thorndyke." Varney stood up, and as the guest was ushered in he looked with deep curiosity, not entirely unmingled with awe, at this tall, imposing man, who held in his mind so much recondite knowledge and doubtless so many strange secrets.

339

"I think you know Mr. Varney," said Margaret, as she shook hands, "though you hadn't much opportunity to improve his acquaintance at Sennen."

"No," Thorndyke agreed. "Mr. Penfield's bombshell rather distracted our attention from the social aspects of that gathering. However, we are free from his malign influence this evening."

"I am not sure that we are," said Varney. "Mrs. Purcell tells me that he has just produced another mysterious letter."

"I shouldn't call it 'mysterious'," said Thorndyke. "On the contrary, it resolves the mystery. We now know, approximately, where Mr. Purcell is."

"Yes, it ought to be easy to get on his track now. That, I understand, is what you have been trying to do. Do you propose to locate him more exactly?"

"I see no reason for doing so," replied Thorndyke. "His letter answers Mr. Penfield's purpose, which was to produce evidence that he is alive. But his letter does raise certain questions that will have to be considered. We shall hear what Mr. Rodney has to say on the subject. He is coming to-night, isn't he?"

"He is not coming to dinner," said Margaret, "but he is going to drop in later. There goes the gong. Shall we go into the dining room?"

Thorndyke held the door open, and they crossed the corridor to the pleasant little room beyond. As soon as they had taken their places at the table, Margaret led off the conversation with a rather definite change of subject.

"Have you brought any of your work to show us, Mr. Varney?" she asked.

"Yes," he replied, "I have brought one or two etchings that I don't think you have seen and a couple of aquatints."

"Aquatints," said Margaret. "Isn't that a new departure?"

"No. It is only a revival. I used to do a good deal of aquatint work, but I have not done any for quite a long time until I attacked these two. I like a change of method now and again. But I always come back to etchings."

"Do you work much with the dry point?" asked Thorndyke.

"Not the pure dry point," was the reply. "Of course, I use it to do finishing work on my etchings, but that is a different thing. I have done very few dry points proper. I like the bitten line."

"I suppose," said Thorndyke, "an etcher rather looks down on lithography?"

"I don't think so," replied Varney. "I don't certainly. It is a fine process and an autograph process, like etching and mezzotint. The

340

finished print is the artist's own work, every bit of it, as much as an oil painting."

"Doesn't the printer take some of the credit?" Thorndyke asked.

"I am assuming that the artist does his own printing. If he doesn't, I should not call him a lithographer. He is only a lithographic draughtsman. When I used to work at lithography I always did my own printing. It is more than half the fun. I have the little press still."

"Then perhaps you will revive that process, too, one day?"

"I don't think so," Varney replied. "The flat surface of a lithograph is rather unsatisfying after the rich raised lines of an etching. I shall never go back to lithography – except, perhaps, for some odd jobs," and here a spirit of mischievous defiance impelled him to add, "I did a little lithograph only the other day, but I didn't keep it. It was a crude little thing."

Thorndyke noted the statement with a certain grim appreciation. In spite of himself, he could not but like Varney, and this playful, sporting attitude in respect of a capital crime appealed to him as a new experience. It established him and Varney as opposing players in a sort of grim and tragic game, and it confirmed him in certain opinions that he had formed as to the antecedents and motives of the crime. For as to the reality of the crime he now had no doubt. The statement that Varney had just made in all the insolence of his fancied security had set the keystone on the edifice that Thorndyke had built up. Circumstantial evidence has a cumulative quality. It advances by a sort of geometrical progression, in which each new fact multiplies the weight of all the others. The theory that Varney had made away with Purcell involved the assumption that Varney was a lithographer who was able to print. It was now established that Varney was a lithographer and that he owned a press. Thus the train of circumstantial evidence was complete.

It was a most singular situation. In the long pauses which tend to occur when good appetites coincide with a good dinner, the two men, confronting one another across the table, sat, each busy with his thoughts behind the closed shutters of his mind, each covertly observant of the other, and each the object of the other's meditations. To Varney had come once more that queer feeling of power that he had experienced at Sennen when Mr. Penfield's letter had arrived, the sense of an almost godlike superiority and omniscience. Here were these simple mortals, full of wonder, perplexity, and speculation as to the vanished Purcell. And they were all wrong. But he knew everything. And he was the motive power behind all their ineffectual movements. It was he who, by the pressure of a finger, had set this puppet-show in motion, and he had but to tweak a string in his quiet studio and they were all set dancing

341

again. Every one of them was obedient to his touch: Maggie, Penfield, Rodney, even this strong-faced, inscrutable man whose eye he had just met – all of them were the puppets whose movements, joint or separate, were directed by his guiding hand.

Thorndyke's reflections were more complex. From time to time he glanced at Varney – he was too good an observer to need to stare – profoundly interested in his appearance. No man could look less like a murderer than this typical artist with his refined face, dreamy yet vivacious, and his suave, gentle manners. Yet that, apparently, was what he was. Moreover, he was a forger of bank notes – perhaps of other things, too, as suggested by the very expert production of this letter – and had almost certainly uttered the forged notes. That was, so to speak, the debit side of his moral account, and there was no denying that it was a pretty heavy one.

On the other hand, he was evidently making a serious effort to earn an honest living. His steady industry was clear proof of that. It was totally unlike a genuine criminal to work hard and with enthusiasm for a modest income. Yet that was what he was evidently doing. It was a very singular contradiction. His present mode of life, which was evidently adapted to his temperament, seemed totally irreconcilable with his lurid past. There seemed to be two Varneys: The criminal Varney, practising felonies and not stopping short of murder, and the industrious, artistic Varney, absorbed in his art and content with the modest returns that it yielded.

Which of them was the real Varney? As he debated this question, Thorndyke turned to the consideration of the other partner in the criminal firm. And this seemed to throw an appreciable light on the question. Purcell had clearly been the senior partner. The initiative must have been his. The starting-point of the banknote adventure must have been the theft of the note-moulds at Maidstone. That had been Purcell's exploit, probably a lucky chance of which he had taken instant advantage. But the moulds were of no use to him without an engraver, so he had enlisted Varney's help. Now, to what extent had that help been willingly given?

It was, of course, impossible to say. But it was possible to form a reasonable opinion by considering the characters of the two men. On the one hand, Varney, a gentle, amiable, probably pliable man. On the other, Purcell, a strong, masterful bully, brutal, selfish, unscrupulous, ready to trample ruthlessly on any rights or interests that conflicted with his own desires. That was, in effect, the picture of him that his wife had painted – the wife whom he had married, apparently against her inclination, by putting pressure on her father, who was his debtor. Purcell was a money-lender, a usurer, and even at that a hard case, as Mr. Levy's observations seemed to hint. Now, a usurer has certain affinities with a blackmailer. Their methods are somewhat similar. Both tend to fasten on their victim and bleed him continuously. Both act by getting a hold on the victim and putting on the screw when necessary, and both are characterized by a remorseless egoism.

Now, Purcell was clearly of the stuff of which blackmailers are made. Was it possible that there was an element of blackmail in his relations with Varney? The appearances strongly suggested it. Here were two men jointly engaged in habitual crime. Suddenly one of them is eliminated by the act of the other, and forthwith the survivor rids himself of the means of repeating the crime and settles down to a life of lawful industry. That was what had happened. The instant Varney had got rid of Purcell he had proceeded to get rid of the paper blanks by sending them to Mr. Penfield instead of printing them and turning them into money, and by thus denouncing the firm had made it impossible, in any case, to continue the frauds. Then he had settled down to regular work in his studio. That seemed to be the course of events.

It was extremely suggestive. Purcell's disappearance coincided with the end of the criminal adventure and the beginning of a reputable mode of life. That seemed to supply the motive for the murder – if it had been a murder. It suggested that no escape from the life of crime had been possible so long as Purcell was alive, that Purcell had obtained some kind of hold on Varney which enabled him to compel the latter to continue in the criminal partnership, and that Varney had taken the only means that were possible to rid himself of his parasite. That was what it looked like.

Of course, this was mere guesswork. No proof was possible. But it agreed with all the facts, and it made Varney's apparent dual personality understandable. The real and essential Varney appeared to be the artist, not the criminal. He appeared to be a normal man who had committed a murder under exceptional circumstances. With the bank-note business Thorndyke was not concerned, and he had no knowledge of its circumstances. But the murder was his concern, and he set himself to consider it.

The hypothesis was that Purcell had been, in effect, a blackmailer, and that Varney had been his victim. Now, it must be admitted that Thorndyke held somewhat unconventional views on the subject of blackmail. He considered that a blackmailer acts entirely at his own risk, and that the victim (since the law can afford him but a very imperfect protection) is entitled to take any available measures for his own defence, including the elimination of the blackmailer. But if the blackmailer acts at his own risk, so does the victim who elects to make away with him.

343

Morally, the killing of a blackmailer may be justifiable homicide, but it has no such legal status. In law, self-defence means defence against bodily injury. It does not include defence against moral injury. Whoever elects to rid himself of a blackmailer by killing him accepts the risk of a conviction on a charge of murder. But that appeared to be Varney's position. He had accepted the risk. It was for him to avoid the consequences if he could. As to Thorndyke himself, though he might, like the Clerk of Arraigns at the Old Bailey, wish the offender "a good deliverance", his part was to lay bare the hidden facts. He and Varney were players on opposite sides. He would play impersonally, without malice and with a certain good will to his opponent. But he must play his own hand and leave his opponent to do the same.

These reflections passed swiftly through his mind in the intervals of a very desultory conversation. As he reached his conclusion, he once more looked up at Varney. And then he received something like a shock. At the moment no one was speaking, and Varney was sitting with his eyes somewhat furtively fixed on Margaret's downcast face. Now, to an experienced observer there is something perfectly unmistakable in the expression with which a man looks at a woman with whom he is deeply in love. And such was the expression that Thorndyke surprised on Varney's face. It was one of concentrated passion, of adoration.

Thorndyke was completely taken aback. This was an entirely new situation, calling for a considerable revision of his conclusions and also of his sympathies. An eliminated blackmailer is one thing, Uriah's wife is another and a very different one. Thorndyke was rather puzzled, for though the previous hypothesis hung fairly together, it was now weakened by the possibility that the murder had been committed merely to remove a superfluous husband. Not that it made any practical difference. He was concerned with the fact of Purcell's murder. The motives were no affair of his.

His reflections were interrupted by a question from Margaret.

"You haven't been down to Cornwall, I suppose, since you came to see us at Sennen in the summer?"

"No, I have not, but Professor D'Arcy has, and he is starting for another trip at the end of next month."

"Is he still in search of worms? It was worms that you were going to look for, wasn't it?"

"Yes, marine worms. But he is not fanatical on the subject. All marine animals are fish that come to his net."

"You are using the word 'net' in a metaphorical sense, I presume," said Varney. "Or does he actually use a net?"

"Sometimes," replied Thorndyke. "A good many specimens can be picked up by searching the shore at low tide, but the most productive work is done with the dredge. Many species are found only below low-water mark."

"Is there anything particularly interesting about marine worms?" Margaret asked. "There always seems something rather disgusting about a worm, but I suppose that is only vulgar prejudice."

"It is principally unacquaintance with worms," replied Thorndyke. "They are a highly interesting group of animals, both in regard to structure and habits. You ought to read Darwin's fascinating book on earthworms and learn what an important part they play in the fashioning of the earth's surface. But the marine worms are not only interesting – some of them are extraordinarily beautiful creatures."

"That was what Philip Rodney used to say," said Margaret, "but we didn't believe him, and he never showed us any specimens."

"I don't know that he ever got any," said Varney. "He made great preparations in the way of bottles and jars, and then he spent most of his time sailing his yacht or line-fishing from a lugger. The only tangible result of his preparations was that remarkable jury button that he fixed on Dan's oil-skin coat. You remember that button, Mrs. Purcell?"

"I remember something about a button, but I have forgotten the details. What was it?"

"Why, Dan lost the top button from his oiler and never got it replaced. One day he lent the coat to Philip to go home in the wet, and as Phil was going out line-fishing the next day and his own oilers were on the yacht, he thought he would take Dan's. So he proceeded to fix on a temporary button, and a most remarkable job he made of it. It seems that he hadn't got either a button or a needle and thread, so he extemporized. He took the cork out of one of his little collecting bottles – it was a flat cork, waterproofed with paraffin wax and it had a round label inscribed 'Marine Worms.' Well, as he hadn't a needle or thread, he bored two holes through the cork with the little marlinspike in his pocket-knife, passed through them the remains of a fiddle-string that he had in his pocket, made two holes in the oilskin, threaded the catgut through them, and tied a reef-knot on the inside."

"And did it answer?" asked Margaret. "It sounds rather clumsy."

"It answered perfectly. So well that it never got changed. It was on the coat when Dan went up the ladder at Penzance, and it is probably on it still. Dan seemed quite satisfied with it."

There was a brief silence, during which Thorndyke looked down thoughtfully at his plate. Presently he asked, "Was the label over the wax or under it?"

345

Varney looked at him in surprise, as also did Margaret. What on earth could it matter whether the label were over or under the wax?

"The label was under the wax," the former replied. "I remember Philip mentioning the fact that the label was waterproofed as well as the cork. He made quite a point of it, though I didn't see why. Do you?"

"If he regarded the label as a decorative adjunct," replied Thorndyke, "he would naturally make a point of the impossibility of its getting washed off, which was the object of the waxing."

"I suppose he would," Varney agreed in an absent tone, and still looking curiously at Thorndyke. He had a feeling that the latter's mildly facetious reply was not quite "in key" with the very definite question. Why had that question been asked? Had Thorndyke anything in his mind? Probably not. What could he have? At any rate, it was of no consequence to him, Varney.

In which he was, perhaps, mistaken. Thorndyke had been deeply interested in the history of the button. Here was one of those queer, incalculable trivialities which so often crop up in the course of a criminal trial. By this time, no doubt, that quaint button was detached and drifting about in the sea, or lying unnoticed on some lonely beach among the high-water jetsam. The mere cork would be hardly recognizable, but if the label had been protected by the wax it would be identifiable with absolute certainty. And if ever it should be identified, its testimony would go to prove the improbability that Daniel Purcell ever went ashore at Penzance.

Chapter XI
In Which Varney
Has an Inspiration

The adjournment to the drawing-room was the signal for Varney to fetch his portfolio and exhibit his little collection, which he did with a frank interest and pleasure in his works that was yet entirely free from any appearance of vanity. Thorndyke examined the proofs with a curiosity that was not wholly artistic. Varney interested him profoundly. There was about him a certain reminiscence of Benvenuto Cellini: A combination of the thoroughgoing rascal with the sincere and enthusiastic artist. But Thorndyke could not make up his mind how close the parallel was. From Cellini's grossness Varney appeared to be free, but how about the other vices? Had Varney been forced into wrongdoing by the pressure of circumstances on a weak will? Or was he a criminal by choice and temperament? That was what Thorndyke could not decide.

An artist's work may show only one side of his character, but it shows that truthfully and unmistakably. A glance through Varney's works made it clear that he was an artist of no mean talent. There was not only skill, which Thorndyke had looked for, but a vein of poetry, which he noted with appreciation and almost with regret.

"You don't seem to value your aquatints," he said, "but I find them very charming. This sea cape with the fleet of luggers half hidden in the mist, and the lighthouse peeping over the top of the fogbank, is really wonderful. You couldn't have done that with the point."

"No," Varney agreed, "every process has its powers and its limitations."

"The lighthouse, I suppose, is no lighthouse in particular?"

"Well, no, but I had the Wolf in my mind when I planned this plate. As a matter of fact, I saw a scene very like this when I was sailing round with Purcell to Penzance the day he vanished. The lighthouse looked awfully ghostly with its head out of the fog and its body invisible."

"Wasn't that the time you had to climb up the mast?" asked Margaret.

"Yes, when the jib halyard parted and the jib went overboard. It was rather a thrilling experience, for the yacht was out of control for the moment and the Wolf rock was close under our lee. Dan angled for the sail while I went aloft."

Thorndyke looked thoughtfully at the little picture, and Varney watched him with outward unconcern but with secret amusement and a sort of elfish mischief.

And again he was conscious of a sense of power, of omniscience. Here was this learned, acute lawyer and scientist looking in all innocence at the very scene on which he, Varney, had looked as he was washing the stain of Purcell's blood from the sail. Little did he dream of the event which this aquatint commemorated! For all his learning and his acuteness, he, Varney, held him in the hollow of his hand.

To Thorndyke the state of mind revealed by this picture was as surprising as it was illuminating. This was, in effect, a souvenir of that mysterious and tragic voyage. Whatever had happened on that voyage was clearly the occasion of no remorse. There was no shrinking from the memory of that day, but rather evidence that it was recalled with a certain satisfaction. In that there seemed a most singular callousness. But what did that callous indifference, or even satisfaction, suggest? A man who had made away with a friend with the express purpose of getting possession of that friend's wife would surely look back on the transaction with some discomfort – indeed, would avoid looking back on it at all – whereas one who had secured his liberty by eliminating his oppressor could hardly be expected to feel either remorse or regrets. It looked as if the blackmail theory were the true one, after all.

"That will be Mr. Rodney," Margaret said, looking expectantly at the door.

"I didn't hear the bell," said Varney. Neither had Thorndyke heard it, but he had not been listening, whereas Margaret apparently had, which perhaps accounted for the slightly preoccupied yet attentive air that he had noticed once or twice when he had looked at her.

A few moments later John Rodney entered the room unannounced, and Margaret went forward quickly to welcome him. And for the second time that evening Thorndyke found himself looking, all unsuspected, into the secret chamber of a human heart.

As Margaret had advanced towards the door, he and Varney stood up. They were thus both behind her when Rodney entered the room. But on the wall by the door was a small mirror, and in this Thorndyke had caught an instantaneous glimpse of her face as she met Rodney. That glimpse had told him what, perhaps, she had hardly guessed herself, but the face which appeared for a moment in the mirror and was gone was a face transfigured. Not, indeed, with the expression of passionate adoration that he had seen on Varney's face. That meant passion consciously recognized and accepted. What Thorndyke saw on Margaret's face was a softening, a tender, joyful welcome such as a mother might bestow on a beloved child. It spoke of affection rather than passion. But it was unmistakable. Margaret Purcell loved John Rodney. Nor, so far as Thorndyke could judge, was the affection only on one side. Rodney, facing the room, naturally made no demonstration, but still, his greeting had in it something beyond mere cordiality.

It was an extraordinarily complex situation, and there was in it a bitter irony such as De Maupassant would have loved. Thorndyke glanced at Varney, from whom Margaret's face had been hidden, with a new interest. Here was a man who had made away with an unwanted husband, perhaps with the sole purpose of securing the reversion of the wife, and behold! He had only created a vacancy for another man.

"This is a great pleasure, Thorndyke," said Rodney, shaking hands heartily. "Quite an interesting experience, too, to see you in evening clothes, looking almost human. I am sorry I couldn't get here to dinner. I should like to have seen you taking food like an ordinary mortal."

"You shall see him take some coffee presently," said Margaret. "But doesn't Dr. Thorndyke usually look human?"

"Well," replied Rodney, "I won't say that there isn't a certain specious resemblance to a human being. But it is illusory. He is really a sort of legal abstraction like John Doe or Richard Roe. Apart from the practice of the law, there is no such person."

"That sounds to me like a libel," said Margaret.

"Yes," agreed Varney. "You've done it now, Rodney. It must be actionable to brand a man as a mere hallucination. There will be wigs on the green – barrister's wigs – when Dr. Thorndyke begins to deal out writs."

"Then I shall plead justification," said Rodney, "and I shall cite the present instance. For what do these pretences of customary raiment and food consumption amount to? They are mere camouflage, designed to cover a legal inquiry into the disappearances from his usual places of resort of one Daniel Purcell."

"Now you are only making it worse," said Margaret, "for you are implicating me. You are implying that my little dinner party is nothing more than a camouflaged legal inquisition."

"And you are implicating me, too," interposed Varney, "as an accessory before, during, and after the fact. You had better be careful, Rodney. It will be a joint action, and Dr. Thorndyke will produce scientific witnesses who will prove anything he tells them to."

"I call this intimidation," said Rodney. "The circumstances seem to call for the aid of tobacco – I see that permission has been given to smoke."

"And perhaps a cup of coffee might help," said Margaret, as the maid entered with the tray.

"Yes, that will clear my brain for the consideration of my defence. But still, I must maintain that this is essentially a legal inquisition. We have assembled primarily to consider the position which is created by this letter that Penfield has received."

"Nothing of the kind," said Margaret. "I asked you primarily that I might enjoy the pleasure of your society, and, secondly, that you might enjoy the pleasure of one another's."

"And yours."

"Thank you. But as to the letter, I don't see that there is anything to discuss. We now know where Dan is, but that doesn't seem to alter the situation."

"I don't agree with you in either respect," said Rodney. "There seems to me a good deal to discuss, and our knowledge as to Dan's whereabouts alters the situation to this extent: That we can get into touch with him if we want to – or at least Dr. Thorndyke can, I presume."

"I am not so sure of that," said Thorndyke. "But we could consider the possibility if the necessity should arise. Had you anything in your mind that would suggest such a necessity?"

"What I have in my mind," replied Rodney, "is this. Purcell has left his wife for reasons known only to himself. He has never sent a word of excuse, apology, or regret. Until this letter arrived, it was possible to suppose that he might be dead, or have lost his memory, or in some other way be incapable of communicating with his friends. Now we know that he is alive, that he has all his faculties – except the faculty of behaving like a decent and responsible man – and that he has gone away and is staying away of his own free will and choice. If there was ever any question as to his coming back, there is none now, and if there could ever have been any excuse or extenuation of his conduct, there is now none. We see that although he has never sent a message of any kind to his wife, yet, when the question of a sum of money arises, he writes to his solicitor with the greatest promptitude. That letter is a gross and callous insult to his wife."

Thorndyke nodded. "That seems to be a fair statement of the position," said he. "And I gather that you consider it possible to take some action?"

"My position is this," said Rodney. "Purcell has deserted his wife. He has shaken off all his responsibilities as a husband. But he has left her with all the responsibilities and disabilities of a wife. He has taken to himself the privileges of a bachelor, but she remains a married woman. That is an in tolerable position. My contention is that, since he has gone for good, the tow-rope ought to be cut. He should be set adrift finally and completely and she should be liberated."

"I agree with you entirely and emphatically," said Thorndyke. "A woman whose husband has left her should, if she wishes it, revert to the status of a spinster."

"And she does wish it," interposed Margaret.

"Naturally," said Thorndyke. "The difficulty is in respect of ways and means. Have you considered the question of procedure, Rodney?"

"It seems to me," was the reply, "that the ways and means are provided by the letter itself. I suggest that the terms of that letter and the circumstances in which it was written afford evidence of desertion, or at least good grounds of action."

"You may be right," said Thorndyke, "but I doubt if it would be accepted as evidence of an intention not to return. It seems to me that a court would require something more definite. I suppose an action for restitution, as a preliminary, would not be practicable?"

Rodney shook his head emphatically, and Margaret pronounced a most decided refusal.

"I don't want restitution," she exclaimed, "and I would not agree to it. I would not receive him back on any terms."

"He wouldn't be likely to come back," said Thorndyke, "and if he did not, his failure to comply with the order of the court would furnish definite grounds for further action."

"But he might come back, at least temporarily," objected Margaret, "if only by way of retaliation."

"Yes," agreed Rodney, "it is perfectly possible. In fact, it is rather the sort of thing that Purcell would do – come back, make himself unpleasant, and then go off again. No, I am afraid that cat won't jump."

"Then," said Thorndyke, "we are in difficulties. We want the marriage dissolved, but we haven't as much evidence as the court would require."

"Probably more evidence could be obtained," suggested Rodney, "and of a different kind. Didn't Penfield say something about an associate or companion? Well, that is where our knowledge of Purcell's whereabouts should help us. If it were possible to locate him exactly and keep him under observation, evidence of the existence of that companion might be forthcoming, and then the case would be all plain sailing."

Thorndyke had been expecting this suggestion and considering how he should deal with it. He could not undertake to search the Eastern Counties for a man who was not there, nor could he give his reasons for not undertaking that search. Until his case against Varney was complete he would make no confidences to anybody. And as he reflected he watched Varney (who had been a keenly interested listener to the discussion), wondering what he was thinking about it all, and noting idly how neatly and quickly he rolled his cigarettes and how little he was inconvenienced by his contracted finger, the third finger of his left hand.

"I think, Rodney," he said, "that you overestimate the ease with which we could locate Purcell. The Eastern Counties offer a large area in which to search for a man – who may not be there, after all. The post-mark on the letter tells us nothing of his permanent abiding-place, if he has one. Varney suggests that he may be afloat, and if he is, he will be very mobile and difficult to trace. And it would be possible for him to change his appearance – by growing a beard, for instance, to make a circulated description useless."

Rodney listened to these objections with hardly veiled impatience. He had supposed that Thorndyke's special practice involved the capacity to trace missing persons, yet as soon as a case calling for this special knowledge arose, he raised difficulties. That was always the way with these confounded experts. Now, to him – though, to be sure, it was out of his line – the thing presented no difficulties at all. To no man does a difficult thing look so easy as to one who is totally unable to do it.

Meanwhile Thorndyke continued to observe Varney, who was evidently reflecting profoundly on the impasse that had arisen. He, of course, could see the futility of Rodney's scheme. He, moreover, since he was in love with Margaret, would be at least as keen on the dissolution of this marriage as Rodney. Thorndyke, watching his eager face, began to hope that he might make some useful suggestion. Nor was he disappointed. Suddenly Varney looked up, and, addressing himself to Rodney, said, "I've got an idea. You may think it bosh, but it is really worth considering. It is this. There is no doubt that Dan has cleared out for good, and it is rather probable that he has made some domestic arrangements of a temporary kind. You know what I mean. And he might be willing to have the chance of making them permanent, because he is not free in that respect any more than his wife is. Now what I propose is that we put in an advertisement asking him to write to his wife, or to Penfield, stating what his intentions are. It is quite possible that he might, in his own interests, send a letter that would enable you to get a divorce without any other evidence. It is really worth trying."

Rodney laughed scornfully. "You've missed your vocation, Varney," said he. "You oughtn't to be tinkering about with etchings. You ought to be in the Law. But I'm afraid the mackerel wouldn't rise to your sprat."

Thorndyke could have laughed aloud. But he did not. On the contrary, he made a show of giving earnest consideration to Varney's

352

suggestion, and finally said, "I am not sure that I agree with you, Rodney. It doesn't seem such a bad plan."

In this he spoke quite sincerely. But then he knew, which Rodney did not, that if the advertisement were issued there would certainly be a reply from Purcell, and, moreover, that the reply would be of precisely the kind that would be most suitable for their purpose.

"Well," said Rodney, "it seems to me rather a wild-cat scheme. You are proposing to ask Purcell to give himself away completely. If you knew him as well as I do, you would know that no man could be less likely to comply. Purcell is one of the most secretive men I have ever known, and you can see for yourself that he has been pretty secret over this business."

"Still," Thorndyke persisted, "it is possible, as Varney suggests, that it might suit him to have the tow-rope cut, as you express it. What do you think, Mrs. Purcell?"

"I am afraid I agree with Mr. Rodney. Dan is as secret as an oyster, and he hasn't shown himself at all well disposed. He wouldn't make a statement for my benefit. As to the question of another woman, I have no doubt that there is one, but my feeling is that Dan would prefer to have a pretext for not marrying her."

"That is exactly my view," said Rodney. "Purcell is the sort of man who will get as much as he can and give as little in exchange."

"I don't deny that," said Varney, "but I still think that it would be worth trying. If nothing came of it, we should be no worse off."

"Exactly," agreed Thorndyke. "It is quite a simple proceeding. It commits us to nothing and it is very little trouble, and if by any chance it succeeded, see how it would simplify matters. In place of a crowd of witnesses collected at immense trouble and cost you would have a letter which could be put in evidence, and which would settle the whole case in a few minutes."

Rodney shrugged his shoulders and secretly marvelled how Thorndyke had got his great reputation.

"There is no answering a determined optimist," said he. "Of course, Purcell may rise to your bait. He may even volunteer to go into the witness-box and make a full confession and offer to pay our costs. But I don't think he will."

"Neither do I," said Thorndyke. "But it is bad practice to reject a plan because you think it probably will not succeed when it is possible and easy to give it a trial. Have you any objection to our carrying out Mr. Varney's suggestion?"

"I have no objection to your carrying it out," replied Rodney, "and I don't suppose Mrs. Purcell has, but I don't feel inclined to act on it myself."

Thorndyke looked interrogatively at Margaret. "What do you say, Mrs. Purcell?" he asked.

"I am entirely in your hands," she replied. "It is very good of you to take so much trouble, but I fear you will have your trouble for nothing."

"We shan't lose much on the transaction even then," Thorndyke rejoined, "so we will leave it that I insert the advertisement in the most alluring terms that I can devise. If anything comes of it, you will hear before I shall."

This brought the discussion to an end. If Rodney had any further ideas on the subject, he reserved them for the benefit of Margaret or Mr. Penfield, having reached the conclusion that Thorndyke was a pure specialist – and probably overrated at that – whose opinions and judgment on general law were not worth having. The conversation thus drifted into other channels, but with no great vivacity, for each of the four persons was occupied inwardly with the subject that had been outwardly dismissed.

Presently Varney, who had been showing signs of restlessness, began to collect his etchings in preparation for departure. Thereupon Thorndyke also rose to make his farewell.

"I have had a most enjoyable evening, Mrs. Purcell," he said, as he shook his hostess's hand. And he spoke quite sincerely. He had had an extremely enjoyable evening, and he hoped that the entertainment was even now not quite at an end. "May we hope that our plottings and schemings will not be entirely unfruitful?"

"You can hope as much as you like," said Rodney, "if hopefulness is your speciality, but if anything comes of this plan of Varney's, I shall be the most surprised man in London."

"And I hope you will give the author of the plan all the credit he deserves," said Thorndyke.

"He has got that now," Rodney replied with a grin.

"I doubt if he has," retorted Thorndyke. "But we shall see. Are we walking the same way, Varney?"

"I think so," replied Varney, who had already decided, for his own special reasons, that they were, in which he was in complete, though unconscious, agreement with Thorndyke.

"Rodney seems a bit cocksure," the former remarked, as they made their way towards the Brompton Road, "but it is no use taking things for granted. I think it quite possible that Purcell may be willing to cut his cable. At any rate, it is reasonable to give him the chance."

"Undoubtedly," agreed Thorndyke. "There is no greater folly than to take failure for granted and reject an opportunity. Now, if this plan of yours should by any chance succeed, Mrs. Purcell's emancipation is as good as accomplished."

"Is it really?" Varney exclaimed eagerly.

"Certainly," replied Thorndyke. "That is, if Purcell should send a letter the contents of which should disclose a state of affairs which would entitle his wife to a divorce. But that is too much to hope for unless Purcell also would like to have the marriage dissolved."

"I think it quite possible that he would, you know," said Varney. "He must have had strong reasons for going off in this way, and we know what those strong reasons usually amount to. But would a simple letter, without any witnesses, be sufficient to satisfy the court?"

"Undoubtedly," replied Thorndyke. "A properly attested letter is good evidence enough. It is just a question of what it contains. Let us suppose that we have a suitable letter. Then our procedure is perfectly simple. We produce it in court, and it is read and put in evidence. We say to the judge: 'Here is a letter from the respondent to the petitioner, or her solicitor, as the case may be. It is in answer to an advertisement, also read and put in evidence. The handwriting has been examined by the petitioner, by her solicitor, and by the respondent's banker, and each of them swears that the writing and the signature are those of the respondent. In that letter the respondent clearly and definitely states that he has left his wife for good, that under no circumstances will he ever return to her, that he refuses hereafter to contribute to her support, and that he has transferred his affections to another woman, who is now living with him as his wife.' On that evidence I think we should have no difficulty in obtaining a decree."

Varney listened eagerly. He would have liked to make a few notes, but that would hardly do, though Thorndyke seemed to be a singularly simple-minded and confiding man. And he was amazingly easy to pump.

"I don't suppose Purcell would give himself away to that extent," he remarked, "unless he was really keen on a divorce."

"It is extremely unlikely in any case," Thorndyke agreed. "But we have to bear in mind that if he writes at all it will be with the object of stating his intentions as to the future and making his position clear. I shall draft the advertisement in such a way as to elicit this information, if possible. If he is not prepared to furnish the information, he will not reply. If he replies it will be because, for his own purposes, he is willing to furnish the information."

"Yes, that is true. So that he may really give more information than one might expect. I wonder if he will write. What do you think?"

"It is mere speculation," replied Thorndyke. "But if I hadn't some hopes of his writing I shouldn't be at the trouble of putting in the advertisement. But perhaps Rodney is right: I may be unreasonably optimistic."

At Piccadilly Circus they parted and went their respective ways, each greatly pleased with the other and both highly amused. As soon as Thorndyke was out of sight, Varney whipped out his notebook, and by the light of a street lamp made a careful note of the necessary points of the required letter. That letter also occupied Thorndyke's mind, and he only hoped that the corresponding agent of Daniel Purcell, deceased, would not allow his enthusiasm to carry him to the extent of producing a letter the contents of which would stamp the case as one of rank collusion. For in this letter Thorndyke saw a way, and the only way, out for Margaret Purcell. He knew, or at least was fully convinced, that her husband was dead. But he had no evidence that he could take into court, nor did he expect that he ever would have. It would be years before it would be possible to apply to presume Purcell's death, and throughout those years Margaret's life would be spoiled. This letter was a fiction. The erring husband was a fiction. But it would be better that Margaret should be liberated by a fiction than that she should drag out a ruined life shackled to a husband who was himself a fiction.

Chapter XII
In Which Varney Once More Pulls the Strings

For the second time in connection with the death of Daniel Purcell, Mr. Varney found it necessary to give an attentive eye to the movements of the postman. He had ascertained from the post office the times at which letters were delivered in the neighbourhood of Margaret's flat, and now, in the gloom of a December evening, he lurked in the vicinity until he saw the postman approaching down the street and delivering letters at the other flats on his way. Then he entered the now familiar portals, and made his way quietly up the stairs until he reached Margaret's outer door. Here he paused for a few moments, standing quite still and listening intently. If he had been discovered he would have simply come to pay a call. But he was not, and the silence from within suggested that there was nobody in the hall. With a furtive look round, he drew a letter from his pocket and silently slipped it into the letter-box, catching the flap on his finger as it fell to prevent it from making any sound. Then he turned and softly stole down the stairs, and as he reached the ground floor the postman walked into the entry.

It was not without reluctance that he came away, for she was behind that door, almost certainly – she, his darling, for whose freedom from the imaginary shackles that she wore he was carrying out this particular deception. But his own guilty conscience made it seem to him that he had better not be present when the fabricated letter arrived. So he tore himself from the beloved precincts and went his way, thinking his thoughts and dreaming his dreams.

Varney's surmise was correct. Margaret was within. But it was perhaps as well that he had refrained from paying a call, for she was not alone, and his visit would not have been entirely welcome. About half-an-hour before his arrival Jack Rodney had ascended those stairs, and had been admitted in time to join Margaret at a somewhat belated tea.

"My excuse for coming to see you," said Rodney, "is in my pocket – the front page of *The Times*."

"I don't know what you mean by an excuse," Margaret replied. "You know perfectly well that I am always delighted to see you. But perhaps you mean an excuse to yourself for wasting your time in gossiping with me."

"Indeed, I don't," said he. "I count no time so profitably employed as that which I spend here."

"I don't quite see what profit you get," she rejoined, "unless it is the moral benefit of doing a kindness to a lonely woman."

"I should like to take that view if I honestly could. But the fact is that I come here for the very great pleasure of seeing you and talking to you, and the profit that I get is that very great pleasure. I only wish the proprieties allowed me to come oftener."

"So do I," she said frankly. "But you know that, too. And now tell me what there is in the front page of *The Times* that gave you this sorely needed excuse."

Rodney laughed in a boisterous, schoolboy fashion as he drew from his pocket a folded leaf of the newspaper. "It's the great advertisement," said he. "The Thorndyke-Varney or Varney-Thorndyke advertisement. It came out yesterday morning. Compose yourself to listen, and I'll read it out to you."

He opened the paper out, refolded it into a convenient size, and with a portentous preliminary "Ahem!" read aloud in a solemn sing-song:

Purcell, D., is earnestly requested to communicate to M. or her solicitor his intentions with regard to the future. If his present arrangements are permanent, she would be grateful if he would notify her to that effect, in order that she may make the necessary modifications in her own.

As he finished, he looked up at her and laughed contemptuously.

"Well, Maggie," said he, "what do you think of it?"

She laughed merrily, and looked at him with hardly disguised fondness and admiration. "What a schoolboy you are, John!" she exclaimed. "How annoyed Dr. Thorndyke would be if he could hear you! But it is rather funny. I can imagine Dan's face when he reads it – if he ever does read it."

"So can I," chuckled Rodney. "I can see him pulling down his lower lip and saying, 'Gur!' in that pleasant way that he has. But isn't it a perfectly preposterous exhibition? Just imagine a man of Thorndyke's position doing a thing like this! Why, it is beneath the dignity of a country attorney's office-boy. I can't conceive how he got his reputation. He seems to be an absolute greenhorn."

"Probably he is quite good at his own speciality," suggested Margaret.

"But this *is* his own speciality! The truth is that the ordinary lawyer's prejudice against experts is to a great extent justified. They are really humbugs and pretenders. You saw what his attitude was when I suggested that he should get Dan under observation. Of course it was the obvious thing to do, and one would suppose that it would be quite in his line. Yet as soon as I made the suggestion he raised all sorts of difficulties, whereas a common private inquiry agent would have made no difficulty about it at all."

"Do you think not?" Margaret asked, a little eagerly. "Perhaps it might be worthwhile to employ one. It would be such a blessed thing to get rid of Dan for good."

"It would, indeed," Rodney agreed heartily. "But perhaps we had better see if Thorndyke gets a bite. If he fails we can try the other plan."

Margaret was slightly disappointed. She wanted to see some progress made, and was a little impatient of the law's delays. But the truth was that Rodney had been speaking rather at random. When he came to consider what information he had to give to a private detective, the affair did not look quite such plain sailing.

"Perhaps," said Margaret, "Dr. Thorndyke was right in giving Mr. Varney's plan a trial. We are no worse off if it fails, and if it were by any chance to succeed, oh, what a relief it would be! Not that there is the slightest chance that it will."

"Not a dog's chance," agreed Rodney, "and Thorndyke was an ass to have anything to do with the advertisement. He should have let Varney put it in. No one expects an artist to show any particular legal acumen."

"Poor Mr. Varney!" murmured Margaret with a faint smile, and at this moment the housemaid entered the room with a couple of letters on a salver. Margaret took the letters, and, having thanked the maid, laid them on the table by her side.

"Won't you read your letters?" said Rodney. "You are not going to make a stranger of me, I hope."

"Thank you," she replied. "If you will excuse me, I will just see whom they are from."

She took up the top letter, opened it, glanced through it, and laid it down. Then she picked up the second letter, and as her glance fell on the address she uttered a little cry of amazement.

"What is it?" asked Rodney.

She held the envelope out for him to see. "It's from Dan!" she exclaimed, and forthwith she tore it open and eagerly took out the letter.

As she read it, Rodney watched her with mingled amusement, vexation, and astonishment. The utterly inconceivable thing had happened. Thorndyke had taken odds of a million to one against and it had come off. That was just a piece of pure luck. It reflected no particular credit on Thorndyke's judgment, but still, Rodney rather wished he had been less dogmatic.

When she had quickly read through the letter, Margaret handed it to him without comment. He took it from her and rapidly ran through the contents.

> *Dear Maggie* (it ran),
>
> *I have just seen your quaint advertisement, and send you a few lines, as requested. I don't know what you mean by "modifying your arrangements", but I can guess. However, that is no concern of mine, and whatever your plans may be, I don't want to stand in your way. So I will give you a plain statement, and you can do what you like.*
>
> *My present arrangements are quite permanent. You have seen the last of yours truly. I have no intention of ever coming back – and I don't suppose you particularly want me. It may interest you to know that I have made fresh domestic arrangements – necessarily a little unorthodox, but also quite permanent.*
>
> *With regard to financial questions, I am afraid I can't contribute to your "arrangements", what ever they may be. You have enough to live on, and I have new responsibilities, but if you can get anything out of Levy you are welcome to it. You will be the first person who ever has. You can also try Penfield, and I wish you the best of luck. And that is all I have got to say on the subject.*
>
> *With best wishes,*
>
> *Yours sincerely,*
> *Daniel Purcell*

Rodney returned the letter with an expression of disgust. "It is a brutal, hoggish letter," said he, "typical of the writer. Where does he write from?"

"The post-mark is Wivenhoe. It was posted last night at seven-thirty."

"That looks as if Varney were right and he were afloat, but it is a queer time of year for yachting on the East Coast. Well, I suppose you are not much afflicted by the tone of that letter?"

360

"Not at all. The more brutal the better. I shall have no qualms now. But the question is, will the letter do? What do you think?"

"It ought to do well enough – if it isn't a little too good to be true."

"I don't quite understand. You don't doubt the truth of what he says, do you?"

"Not at all. What I mean is this: Divorce judges are pretty wary customers. They have to be. The law doesn't allow married people who are tired of one another and would like to try a fresh throw of the dice to make nice little mutual arrangements to get their marriage dissolved. That is called collusion. And then there is a mischievous devil called the King's Proctor, whose function is to 'prevent us, O Lord, in all our doings' and to trip up poor wretches who have got a decree and think they have escaped, and to send them back to cat-and-dog matrimony until death do them part. Now, the only pitfall about this letter of Dan's is that it is so very complete. He makes things so remarkably easy for us. He leaves us nothing to prove. He admits everything in advance, and covers the whole of our case in our favour. That letter might have been dictated by a lawyer in our interest."

Margaret looked deeply disappointed. "You don't mean to say that we shan't be able to act on it!" she exclaimed in dismay.

"I don't say that," he replied, "and I certainly think it will be worth trying. But I do wish that we could produce evidence that he is living with some woman, as he appears to state. That would be so much more convincing. However, I will get an opinion from a counsel who has had extensive experience of divorce practice – a man like Barnby, for instance. I could show him a copy of the letter and hear what he thinks."

"Why not Dr. Thorndyke?" said Margaret. "He was really right, after all, and we shall have to show him the letter."

"Yes, and he must see the original. But as to taking his opinion – well, we shall have to do that as a matter of courtesy, but I don't set much value on his judgment. You see, he chose to go double Nap on this letter, and he happened to win. Events prove that he was right to take the chance, but it was primitive strategy. It doesn't impress me."

Margaret made no immediate rejoinder. She was not a lawyer, and to her the fact that the plan had succeeded was evidence that it was a good plan. Accordingly, her waning faith in Thorndyke was strongly revived.

"I can't help hoping," she said presently, "that this letter will secure a decision in our favour. It really ought to. You see, there is no question of arrangement or collusion on my side. Our relations were perfectly normal and pleasant up to the moment of Dan's disappearance. There were no quarrels, no differences, nothing to hint at any desire for a

361

change in our relations, and I have waited six months for him to come back, and have taken no action until he made it clear that he had gone for good. Don't you think that I have a fair chance of getting my freedom?"

"Perhaps you are right, Maggie," he replied. "I may be looking out for snags that aren't there. Of course, you could call me and Philip and Varney to prove that all was normal up to the last, and Penfield and Thorndyke to give evidence of your efforts to trace Dan. Yes, perhaps it is a better case than I thought. But all the same, I will show the letter to Barnby when Thorndyke has seen it and get his opinion without prejudice."

He paused and reflected profoundly for a while. Suddenly he looked up at Margaret, and in his eyes there was a new light.

"Supposing, Maggie," he said in a low, earnest voice, "you were to get this marriage dissolved. Then you would be free – free to marry. You know that years ago, when you were free, I loved you. You know that, because I told you, and I thought, and I still think, that you cared for me then. The fates were against us at that time, but in the years that have passed there has been no change in me. You are the only woman I have ever wanted, Of course, I have kept my feelings to myself. That had to be. But if we can win back your freedom, I shall ask you to be my wife, unless you forbid me. What shall you say to me, Maggie?"

Margaret sat with downcast eyes as Rodney was speaking. For a few moments she had appeared pale and agitated, but she was now quite composed, and nothing but a heightened colour hinted at any confusion. At the final question she raised her head and looked Rodney frankly in the face.

"At present, John," she said quietly, "I am the wife of Daniel Purcell, and as such have no right to contemplate any other marriage. But I will be honest with you. There is no reason why I should not be. You are quite right, John. I loved you in those days that you speak of, and if I never told you, you know why. You know how I came to marry Dan. It seemed to me then that I had no choice. Perhaps I was wrong, but I did what I thought was my duty to my father.

"In the years that have passed since then – the long, grey years – I have kept my covenant with Dan loyally in every respect. If I have ever looked back with regret, it has been in secret. But through those years you have been a faithful friend to me, and of all my friends the best beloved. And so you are now. That is all I can say, John."

"It is enough, Maggie," he said, "and I thank you from my heart for saying so much. Whatever your answer might have been, I would have done everything in my power to set you free. But now I shall venture to have a hope that I hold a stake in your freedom."

She made no answer to this, and for some time both sat silently engrossed with their own thoughts, and each thinking much the same thoughts as the other. The silence was at length broken by Rodney.

"It was an awful blow to me when I came home from my travels and found you married. Of course, I guessed what had happened, though I never actually knew. I assumed that Dan had put the screw on your father in some way."

"Yes. He had lent my father money, and the bills could not be met."

"What a Juggernaut the fellow is!" exclaimed Rodney. "An absolutely ruthless egoist. By the way, was he in the habit of lending money? I notice that he refers in this letter to a person named Levy. Who is Levy? And what does Dan do for a livelihood? He is out of the paper trade, isn't he?"

"I think so. The truth is, I have never known what his occupation is. I have suspected that he is principally a money-lender. As to Mr. Levy, I have always thought he was a clerk or manager, but it rather looks as if he were a partner."

"We must find out," said Rodney. "And there is another thing that we must look into – that mysterious letter that Penfield received from Dan. Did you ever learn what was in it?"

"Never. Mr. Penfield refused to divulge the slightest hint of its contents. But I feel convinced that it was in some way connected with Dan's disappearance. You remember it arrived on the very day that Dan went away. I think Dr. Thorndyke called on Mr. Penfield to see if he could glean any information, but I assume that he didn't succeed."

"We can take that for granted," said Rodney. "I don't think Thorndyke would get much out of a wary old bird like Penfield. But we must find out what was in that letter. Penfield will have to produce it if we put him in the witness-box, though he will be a mighty slippery witness. However, I will see Thorndyke and ask him about it when I have consulted Barnby. Perhaps I had better take charge of the letter."

Margaret handed him the letter, which he put securely in his wallet, and the plan of action being now settled, he stayed only for a little further gossip, and then took his leave.

On the following afternoon he called by appointment on Thorndyke, who, having admitted him, closed the "oak", and connected the bell with the laboratory upstairs, where his assistant, Polton, was at work.

"So," he said, "our fish has risen to the tin minnow, as I gather from your note."

"Yes. You have had better luck than I expected."

"Or than I deserved, you might have added if you had been less polite. Well, I don't know that I should agree. I consider it bad practice to treat an improbability as an impossibility. But what does he say?"

"All that we could wish – and perhaps a little more. That is the only difficulty. He makes things a little too easy for us – at least, that is my feeling. But you had better see the letter."

He took it from his wallet and passed it to Thorndyke, who glanced at the post-mark, and when he had taken out the letter looked quickly into the interior of the envelope.

"Wivenhoe," he remarked. "Some distance from Woodbridge, but in the same district."

He read carefully through the text, noting at the same time the peculiarities that he had observed in the former letter. In this case, too, the postmarks had been made when the envelope was empty – a curious oversight on the part of Varney in view of the care and ingenuity otherwise displayed. Indeed, as he read through the letter, Thorndyke's opinion of that cunning artificer rose considerably. It was a most skilful and tactful production. It did certainly make things almost suspiciously easy, but then that was its function. The whole case for the petition rested on it. But the brutal attitude of the imaginary truant was admirably rendered, and, so far as he could judge, the personality of the missing man convincingly represented.

"It is not a courteous epistle," he remarked tentatively.

"No," agreed Rodney, "but it is exactly the sort of letter that one would expect from Purcell. It gives you his character in a nutshell."

This was highly satisfactory and very creditable to Varney.

"You mentioned in your note that you were going to take Barnby's opinion on it. Have you seen him?"

"Yes, and he thinks the same as I do: That it would be a little risky to base a petition on this letter alone. The judge might smell a rat. He considers that if we could produce evidence that Purcell is actually living with another woman, this letter would be good evidence of desertion. He suggested putting a private inquiry agent on Purcell's tracks. What do you say to that?"

"In the abstract it is an excellent suggestion. But how are you going to carry it out? You speak of putting the agent on Purcell's tracks. But there are no tracks. There is no place in which he is known to have been staying, and there is no person known to us who has seen him since he landed at Penzance. You would start your sleuth without a scent to wander about Essex and Suffolk looking for a man whom he had never seen and would probably not recognize if he met him, and who is possibly not in either of those counties at all. It really is not a practicable scheme."

Rodney emitted a discontented grunt. "Doesn't sound very encouraging certainly," he admitted. "But how do the police manage in a case of the kind?"

"By having, not one agent but a thousand, and all in communication through a central office. And even the police fail if they haven't enough data. But with regard to Barnby, of course his opinion has great weight. He knows the difficulties of these cases, and his outlook will probably be the judge's outlook. But did you make clear to him the peculiarities of this case? The character of the petitioner, her excellent relations with her husband, the sudden, unforeseen manner of the disappearance, and the total absence of any grounds for a suspicion of collusion? Did you present these points to him?"

"No, I didn't. We merely discussed the letter."

"Well, see him again and put the whole case to him. My feeling is that a petition would probably succeed."

"I hope you are right," said Rodney, more encouraged than he would have liked to admit. "I'll see Barnby again. Oh, and there is another point. That letter that Purcell sent to Penfield by mistake in June. It probably throws some light on the disappearance, and might be important as evidence on our side. I suppose Penfield did not tell you what was in it or show it to you?"

"No, he would say nothing about it, but he allowed me, at my request, to examine the envelope."

Rodney grinned. "He might also have shown you the postman who delivered the letter. But if he won't tell us anything, we might put him in the witness-box and make him disgorge his secret."

"Yes, and you may have to if the court demands to have the letter produced. But I strongly advise you to avoid doing so if you can. I have the impression that the production of that letter would be very much the reverse of helpful – might, in fact, be fatal to the success of the case and would in addition be very disagreeable to Mrs. Purcell."

Rodney looked at him in astonishment. "Then you know what was in the letter?" said he.

"No, but I have formed certain opinions which I have no doubt are correct, but which I do not feel at liberty to communicate. I advise you to leave Mr. Penfield alone. Remember that he is a lawyer, that he is Mrs. Purcell's friend, that he does know what is in the letter, and that he thinks it best to keep his knowledge to himself. But he will have to be approached on the question as to whether he is willing to act for Mrs. Purcell against her husband. If you undertake that office you can raise the question of the letter with him, but I would urge you most strongly not to force his hand."

Rodney listened to this advice with a slightly puzzled expression. Like Mr. Penfield, he viewed Thorndyke with mixed feelings, now thinking of him as an amateur, a doctor who dabbled in effectively in law, and now considering the possibility that he might command some means of acquiring knowledge that were not available to the orthodox legal practitioner. Here was a case in point. He had examined the envelope of that mysterious letter "at his own request" and evidently for a specific purpose, and from that inspection he had in some unaccountable way formed a very definite opinion as to what the envelope had contained. That was very curious. Of course, he might be wrong, but he seemed to be pretty confident. Then there was the present transaction. Rodney himself had rejected Varney's suggestion with scorn. But Thorndyke had adopted it quite hopefully, and the plan had succeeded in the face of all probabilities. Could it be that Thorndyke had some odd means of gauging those probabilities? It looked rather like it.

"You are only guessing at the nature of that letter," he said tentatively, "and you may have got it wrong."

"That is quite possible," Thorndyke agreed. "But Penfield isn't guessing. Put the case to him, hear what he says, and follow his advice. And if you see Barnby again it would be better to say nothing about that letter. Penfield will advise you to keep it out of the case if you can, and that is my advice, too."

When Rodney took his departure, which he did a few minutes later, he carried with him a growing suspicion that he had under-estimated Thorndyke – that the latter, perhaps, played a deeper game than at first sight appeared, and that he played with pieces unknown to traditional legal practice.

For some time after his visitor had left, Thorndyke remained wrapped in profound thought. In his heart he was sensible of a deep distaste for this case that he was promoting. If it were to succeed, it could only be by misleading the court. It is true that the parties were acting in good faith, that the falsities which they would present were falsities that they believed to be true. But the whole case was based on a fiction, and Thorndyke detested fictions. Nor was he satisfied with his own position in an ethical sense. He knew that the case was fictitious, that the respondent was a dead man, and that the documents to be produced in evidence were forgeries. He was, in fact, an accessory to those forgeries. He did not like it at all. And he was not so optimistic as to the success of the petition as he had led Rodney to believe, though he was not very uneasy on that score. What troubled him was that this was, in effect, a bogus case, and that he was lending it his support.

But what was the alternative? His thoughts turned to Margaret: Sweet-faced, sweet-natured, gracious-mannered, the perfect type of an English gentlewoman, and he thought of the fine, handsome, high-minded gentleman who had just gone away. These two loved one another – loved as only persons of character can love. Their marriage, if it could be achieved, would secure to them a lifelong happiness, in so far as such happiness is attainable by mortals. But between them and their happiness stood the fiction of Daniel Purcell. In order that they might marry, Purcell must either be proved to be dead or assumed to be alive.

Could he be proved to be dead? If he could, that were the better way, because it would demonstrate the truth. But was it possible? In a scientific sense it probably was. Science can accept a conclusion with reservations. But the law has to say "yes" or "no" without any reservations at all. This was not a case of death merely presumed. It was a death alleged to have occurred at a specific time and place and in a specific manner, and inseparably bound up with it was a charge of murder. If Purcell was dead, Varney had murdered him, and the murder was the issue that would be tried. But no jury would entertain for a moment the guilt of the accused on such evidence as Thorndyke could offer. And an acquittal would amount to a legal decision that Purcell was not dead. On that decision Margaret's marriage to Rodney would be impossible.

Thus Thorndyke's reflections led him back, as they always did, to the conclusion that Purcell's death was incapable of legal proof, and must ever remain so, unless by some miracle new and conclusive evidence should come to light. But to wait for a miracle to happen was an unsatisfactory policy. If Purcell could not be proved to be dead, and if such failure of proof must wreck the happiness of two estimable persons, then it would appear that it might be allowable to accept what was the actual legal position and assume that he was alive.

So, once again, Thorndyke decided that he had no choice but to continue to share with Varney the secret of Purcell's death and to hold his peace.

And if this must be, the petition must take its course, aided and abetted, if necessary, by him. After all, nobody would be injured and nothing done which was contrary either to public policy or private morals. There were only two alternatives, as matters stood: The fiction of Purcell as a living man would either keep Margaret and Rodney apart, as it was doing now, or it would be employed (with other fictions) to enable them to be united. And it was better that they should be united.

367

Chapter XIII
In Which the Medico-Legal Worm Arrives

Romance lurks in unsuspected places. As we go our daily round, we are apt to look distastefully upon the scenes made dull by familiarity, and to seek distraction by letting our thoughts ramble far away into time and space, to ages and regions in which life seems more full of colour. In fancy, perchance, we thread the ghostly aisles of some tropical forest, or linger on the white beach of some lonely coral island, where the coconut palms, shivering in the sea breeze, patter a refrain to the song of the surf, or we wander by moonlight through the narrow streets of some Southern city and hear the thrum of the guitar serenading to the shrouded balcony, and behold! All Romance is at our very doors.

It was on a bright afternoon early in March that Thorndyke sat, with Philip Rodney by his side, on one of the lower benches of the lecture theatre of the Royal College of Surgeons. Not a likely place, this, to encounter Romance. Yet there it was – and Tragedy, too – lying unnoticed at present on the green baize cover of the lecturer's table, its very existence unsuspected.

Meanwhile Thorndyke and Philip conversed in quiet undertones, for it still wanted some minutes to the hour at which the lecture would commence.

"I suppose," said Philip, "you have had no report from that private detective fellow – I forget his name?"

"Bagwell. No, excepting the usual weekly note stating that he is still unable to pick up any trace of Purcell."

"Ah," commented Philip, "that doesn't sound encouraging. Must be costing a lot of money, too. I fancy my brother and Maggie Purcell are both beginning to wish they had taken your advice and relied on the letter by itself. But Jack was overborne by Barnby's insistence on corroborative evidence, and Maggie let him decide. And now they are sorry they listened to Barnby. They hadn't bargained for all this delay."

"Barnby was quite right as to the value of the additional evidence," said Thorndyke. "What he didn't grasp was the very great difficulty of getting it. But I think I hear the big-wigs approaching."

As he spoke, the usher threw open the lecturer's door. The audience stood up, the president entered, preceded by the mace-bearer and followed by the officers and the lecturer, and took his seat, the audience sat down, and the lecture began without further formalities.

The theatre was nearly full. It usually was when Professor D'Arcy lectured, for that genial savant had the magnetic gift of infusing his own enthusiasm into the lecture and so into his audience, even when, as on this occasion, his subject lay on the outside edge of medical science. To-day he was lecturing on the epidermic appendages of the marine worms, and from the opening sentence he held his audience as by a spell, standing before the great blackboard with a bunch of coloured chalks in either hand, talking with easy eloquence – mostly over his shoulder – while he covered the black surface with those delightful drawings that added so much to the charm of his lectures. Philip watched his flying fingers with fascination, and struggled frantically to copy the diagrams into a large notebook with the aid of a handful of coloured pencils, while Thorndyke, not much addicted to note-taking, listened and watched with concentrated attention, mentally docketing and pigeon-holing any new or significant facts in what was to him a fairly familiar subject.

The latter part of the lecture dealt with those beautiful sea worms that build themselves tubes to live in – worms like the Serpula, that make their shelly or stony tubes by secretion from their own bodies, or, like the Sabella or Terebella, build them up with sand-grains, little stones, or fragments of shell. Each, in turn, appeared in lively portraiture on the blackboard, and the trays on the table were full of specimens which were exhibited by the lecturer, and which the audience were invited to inspect more closely after the lecture.

Accordingly, when the last words of the peroration had been pronounced, the occupants of the benches trooped down into the arena to look at the exhibits and seek further details from the genial Professor. Thorndyke and Philip held back for a while on the outskirts of the crowd, but the Professor had seen them on their bench, and now approached, greeting them with a hearty hand shake and a facetious question.

"What are you doing here, Thorndyke? Is it possible that there are medico-legal possibilities even in a marine worm?"

"Oh, come, D'Arcy!" protested Thorndyke, "don't make me such a hidebound specialist. May I have no rational interests in life? Must I live for ever in the witness-box like a marine worm in its tube?"

"I suspect you don't get very far out of your tube," said the Professor, with a chuckle and a sly glance at Philip.

"I got far enough out last summer," retorted Thorndyke, "to come and aid and abet you in your worm-hunting. Have you forgotten Cornwall?"

"No, to be sure," was the reply. "But that was only a momentary lapse, and I expect you had ulterior motives. However, the association of Cornwall, worm-hunting, and medical jurisprudence reminds me that I have something in your line. A friend of mine, who was wintering in Cornwall, picked it up on the beach at Morte Hoe and sent it to me. Now, where is it? It is on this table somewhere. It is a ridiculous thing – a small, flat cork, evidently from a zoologist's collecting-bottle, for it has a label stuck on it with the inscription 'Marine Worms.' It seems that our zoologist was a sort of Robinson Crusoe, for he had bored a couple of holes through it and evidently used it as a button. But the most ludicrous thing about it is that a Terebella has built its tube on it, as if the worm had been prowling about, looking for lodgings, and had read the label and forthwith had engaged the apartments. Ah! Here it is."

He pounced on a little cardboard box, and, opening it, took out the cork button and laid it in Thorndyke's palm.

As the Professor was describing the object, Philip looked at him with a distinctly startled expression, and uttered a smothered exclamation. He was about to speak, but suddenly checked himself and looked at Thorndyke, who flashed at him a quick glance of understanding.

"Isn't that a quaint coincidence?" chuckled the Professor. "I mean that the worm should have taken up its abode and actually built his tube on the label?"

"Very quaint," replied Thorndyke, still looking with deep interest at the object that lay in his hand.

"You realize," Philip said in a low voice, as the Professor turned away to answer a question, "that this button came from Purcell's oilskin coat?"

"Yes, I remember the incident. I realized what it was as soon as D'Arcy described the button."

He glanced curiously at Philip, wondering whether he, too, realized exactly what this queer piece of jetsam was. For to Thorndyke its message had been conveyed even before the Professor had finished speaking. In that moment it had been borne to him that the unlooked-for miracle had happened, and that Margaret Purcell's petition need never be filed.

"Well, Thorndyke," said the Professor, "my friend's treasure trove seems to interest you. I thought it would as an instance of the possibilities of coincidence. Quite a useful lesson to a lawyer, by the way."

"Exactly," said Thorndyke. "In fact, I was going to ask you to allow me to borrow it to examine at my leisure."

The Professor was delighted. "There, now," he chuckled, with a mischievous twinkle at Philip, "what did I tell you? He hasn't come here for the comparative anatomy at all. He has just come to grub for legal data. And now, you see, the medico-legal worm has arrived, and is instantly collared by the medical jurist. Take him, by all means, Thorndyke. You needn't borrow him. I present him as a gift to your black museum. You needn't return him."

Thorndyke thanked the Professor, and, having packed the specimen with infinite tenderness in its cotton wool, bestowed the box in his waistcoat pocket. A few minutes later he and Philip took their leave of the Professor and departed, making their way through Lincoln's Inn to Chancery Lane.

"That button gave me quite a shock for a moment," said Philip, "appearing out of the sea on the Cornish coast, for, of course, it was on Purcell's coat when he went ashore – at least, I suppose it was. I understood Varney to say so."

"He did," said Thorndyke. "He mentioned the incident at dinner one evening, and he then said definitely that the cork button was on the coat when Purcell went up the ladder."

"Yes, and it seemed rather mysterious at first, as Purcell went right away from Cornwall. But there is probably quite a simple explanation. Purcell went to the East Coast by sea, and it is most likely that, when he got on board the steamer, he obtained a proper button from the steward, cut off the jury button, and chucked it overboard. But it is a queer chance that it should have come back to us in this way."

Thorndyke nodded. "A very queer chance," he agreed.

As he spoke, he looked at Philip with a somewhat puzzled expression. He was, in fact, rather surprised. Philip Rodney was a doctor, a man of science, and an unquestionably intelligent person. He knew all the circumstances that were known, and he had seen and examined the button, and yet he had failed to observe the one vitally important fact that stared him in the face.

"What made you want to borrow the button?" Philip asked presently. "Was it that you wanted to keep it as a relic of the Purcell case?"

"I want to examine the worm-tube," replied Thorndyke. "It is a rather unusual one, very uniform in composition. Mostly, Terebella tubes are very miscellaneous as to their materials – sand, shell, little pebbles, and so forth. The material of this one seems to be all alike."

"Probably the stuff that the worm was able to pick up in the neighbourhood of Morte Hoe."

"That is possible," said Thorndyke, and the conversation dropped for a moment, each man occupying himself with reflections on the other.

To Philip it seemed rather surprising that a man like Thorndyke, full of important business, should find time, or even inclination, to occupy himself with trivialities like this. For, after all, what did it matter whether this worm-tube was composed of miscellaneous gatherings or of a number of similar particles? No scientific interest attached to the question. It seemed rather a silly quest. And yet Thorndyke had thought it worth while to borrow the specimen for this very purpose.

Thorndyke, for his part, was more than ever astonished at the mental obtuseness of this usually acute and intelligent man. Not only had he failed in the first place to observe a most striking and significant fact: He could not see that fact even when his nose was rubbed hard on it.

As they passed through Old Buildings and approached the main gateway, Philip slowed down.

"I am going into my brother's chambers here to have tea with him. Do you care to join us? He will be glad to see you."

Thorndyke, however, was in no mood for tea and gossip. He had got a first-class clue – a piece of really conclusive evidence. How conclusive it was and how far its conclusiveness went he could not tell at present, and he was eager to get to work on the assay of this specimen in an evidential sense – to see exactly what was the amount and kind of evidence that the sea had cast up on the shore of Morte Hoe. He therefore excused himself, and having bidden Philip *adieu*, he strode out into Chancery Lane and bore south towards the Temple.

On entering his chambers, he discovered his assistant, Polton, in the act of transferring boiling water from a copper kettle to a small silver teapot, whereby he was able to infer that his approach had been observed by the said Polton from his lookout in the laboratory above. The two men, master and man, exchanged friendly greetings, and Thorndyke then observed, "I have got a job to do later on, Polton, when I have finished up the evening's work. I shall want to grind some small sections of a mineral that I wish to identify. Would you put out one or two small hones and the other things that I shall need?"

"Yes, sir," replied Polton. "I will put the mineral section outfit on a tray and bring it down after tea. But can't I grind the sections? It seems a pity for you to be wasting your time on a mechanical job like that."

"Thank you, Polton," replied Thorndyke. "Of course you could cut the sections as well as, or better than, I can. But it is possible that I may have to produce the sections in evidence, and in that case it will be better if I can say that I cut them myself and that they were never out of my own hands. The courts don't know you as I do, you see, Polton."

Polton acknowledged the compliment with a gratified smile, and departed to the laboratory. As soon as he was gone, Thorndyke brought forth the little cardboard box, and, having taken out the button, carried it over to the window, where, with the aid of his pocket lens, he made a long and careful examination of the worm-tube, the result of which was to confirm his original observation. The mineral particles of which the tube was built up were of various shapes and sizes, from mere sand-grains up to quite respectable little pebbles. But, so far as he could see, they were all of a similar material. What that material was an expert mineralogist would have been able, no doubt, to say offhand, and an expert opinion would probably have to be obtained. But in the meantime his own knowledge was enough to enable him to form a fairly reliable opinion when he had made the necessary investigations.

As he drank his tea, he reflected on this extra ordinary windfall. Circumstances had conspired in the most singular manner against Varney. How much they had conspired remained to be seen. That depended on how much the worm-tube had to tell. But even if no further light were thrown on the matter by the nature of the mineral, there was evidence enough that Purcell had never landed at Penzance. The Terebella had already given that much testimony. And the cross-examination was yet to come.

Having finished tea, he fell to work on the reports and written opinions which had to be completed and sent off by the last post, and it was characteristic of the man that, though the button and its as yet half-read message lurked in the sub-conscious part of his mind as the engrossing object of interest, he was yet able to concentrate the whole of his conscious attention on the matters with which he was outwardly occupied. Twice during the evening Polton stole silently into the room, once to deposit on a side-table the little tray containing the mineral section appliances, and the second time to place on a small table near the fire a large tray bearing the kind of frugal, informal supper that Thorndyke usually consumed when alone and at work.

"If you wait a few moments, Polton, I shall have these letters ready for the post. Then we shall both be free. I don't want to see anybody to-night unless it is something urgent."

"Very well, sir," replied Polton. "I will switch the bell on to the laboratory, and I'll see that you are not disturbed unnecessarily."

With this he took up the letters which Thorndyke had sealed and stamped and reluctantly withdrew, not without a last wistful glance at the apparatus on the tray.

As the door closed behind him, Thorndyke rose and, bringing forth the button from the drawer in which he had bestowed it, began operations at once. First, with a pair of fine forceps he carefully picked off the worm-tube half-a-dozen of the largest fragments and laid them on a glass slide. This he placed on the stage of the microscope, and, having fitted on a two-inch objective, made a preliminary inspection under various conditions of light, both transmitted and reflected. When he had got clearly into his mind the general character of the unknown rock, he fetched from a store cabinet in the office a number of shallow drawers filled with labelled specimens of rocks and minerals, and he also placed on the table in readiness for reference one or two standard works on geology and petrology. But before examining either the books or the specimens in the drawers, he opened out a geological chart of the British Isles and closely scrutinized the comparatively small area with which the button was concerned – the Land's End and the north and south coast of Cornwall. A very brief scrutiny of the map showed him that the inquiry could now be narrowed down to a quite small group of rocks, the majority of which he could exclude at once by his own knowledge of the more familiar types, which was highly satisfactory. But there was evidently something more than this. Anyone who should have been observing him as he pored over the chart would have seen, by a suddenly increased attention, with a certain repressed eagerness, that some really illuminating fact had come into view, and his next proceedings would make clear to such an observer that the problem had already changed from one of search to a definite and particular identification.

From the chart he turned to the drawers of specimens, running his eye quickly over their contents, as if looking for some specific object, and this object he presently found in a little cardboard tray – a single fragment of a grey, compact rock, which he pounced upon at once, and, picking it out of its tray, laid it on the slide with the fragment from the worm-tube. Careful comparison gave the impression that they were identical in character, but the great difference in the size of the fragments compared was a source of possible error. Accordingly, he wrapped the specimen lightly in paper, and with a hammer from the tool drawer struck it a sharp blow, which broke it into a number of smaller fragments, some of them quite minute. Picking out one or two of the smallest from the paper and carefully noting the "conchoidal" character of the fracture, he placed them on a separate slide, which he at once labelled "*Stock Specimen*", labelling the other slide "*Worm Tube*". Having taken this precaution against possible confusion, he laid the two slides on the stage of the microscope and once more made a minute comparison. And again the conclusion emerged that the fragments from the worm-tube were identical in all their characters with the fragment of the stock specimen.

It now remained to test this conclusion by more exact methods. Two more labelled slides having been prepared, Thorndyke laid them, label downwards, on the table and dropped on each a large drop of melted Canada balsam. In one drop, while it was still soft, he immersed two or three fragments from the worm-tube, in the other a like number of fragments of the stock specimen. Then he heated both slides over a spirit-lamp to liquefy the balsam and completely immerse the fragments, and laid them aside to cool while he prepared the appliances for grinding the sections.

This process was, as Polton had hinted, a rather tedious one. It consisted in rubbing the two slides backwards and forwards upon a wetted Turkey stone until the fragments of rock were ground to a flat surface. The flattened surfaces had then to be polished upon a smoother stone, and when this had been done the slides were once more heated over a spirit-lamp, the balsam liquefied, and each of the fragments neatly turned over with a needle on to its flat side. When the balsam was cool and set hard, the grinding process was repeated until each of the fragments was worn down to a thin plate or film with parallel sides. Then the slides were again heated, a fresh drop of balsam applied, and a cover-glass laid on top. The specimens were now finished and ready for examination.

On this, the final stage of the investigation, he bestowed the utmost care and attention. The two specimens were examined exhaustively and compared again and again by every possible method, including the use of the polariscope and the spectroscope, and the results of each observation were at once written down. Finally, Thorndyke turned to the books of reference and, selecting a highly technical work on petrology, checked his written notes by the very detailed descriptions that it furnished of rocks of volcanic origin. And once again the results were entirely confirmatory of the opinion that he had at first formed. No doubt whatever was left in his mind as to the nature of the particles of rock of which the worm had built its tube. But if his opinion was correct, he held evidence producible in a court of law that Daniel Purcell had never landed at Penzance – that, in fact, his dead body was even now lying at the bottom of the sea.

As he consumed his frugal supper, Thorndyke turned over the situation in his mind. He had no doubts at all. But it would be necessary to get his identification of the rock confirmed by a recognized authority who could be called as a witness, and whose statement would be accepted by the court as establishing the facts. There was no difficulty about that. He had a friend who was connected with the Geological Museum, and who was recognized throughout the world as a first-class authority on everything relating to the physical and chemical properties of rocks and minerals. He would take the specimens to-morrow to this expert, and ask him to examine them, and when the authoritative opinion had been pronounced, he would consider what procedure he should adopt. Already there was growing up in his mind a doubt as to the expediency of taking action on purely scientific evidence, and in answer to that doubt a new scheme began to suggest itself.

But for the moment he put it aside. The important thing was to get the expert identification of the rock, and so put his evidence on the basis of established fact. The conversion of scientific into legal evidence was a separate matter that could be dealt with later. And having reached this conclusion, he took a sheet of notepaper from the rack and wrote a short letter to his friend at the Museum, making an appointment for the following afternoon. A few minutes later he dropped it into the box of the Fleet Street Post Office, and for the time being dismissed the case from his mind.

Chapter XIV
In Which Mr. Varney is Disillusioned

Thorndyke's visit to the Geological Museum was not a protracted affair, for his friend, Mr. Burston, made short work of the investigation.

"You say you have examined the specimens yourself," said he. "Well, I expect you know what they are, just come to me for an official confirmation, hmm? However, don't tell me what your conclusion was. I may as well start with an open mind. Write it down on this slip of paper and lay it on the table face downwards. And now let us have the specimens."

Thorndyke produced from his pocket a cigar-case, from which he extracted a pill-box and the labelled microscope-slide.

"There are two little water-worn fragments in the pill-box," he explained, "and three similar ones which I have ground into sections. I am sorry the specimens are so small, but they are the largest I had."

Mr. Burston took the pill-box, and, tipping the two tiny pebbles into the palm of his hand, inspected them through a Coddington lens.

"Yes," said he, "I don't think it will be very difficult to decide what this is. I think I could tell you offhand. But I won't. I'll put it through the regular tests and make quite sure of it, and meanwhile you had better have a browse round the Museum."

He bustled off to some inner sanctum of the curator's domain, and Thorndyke adopted his advice by straying out into the galleries. But he had little opportunity to study the contents of the cases, for in a few minutes Mr. Burston returned with a slip of paper in his hand.

"Now," he said facetiously, as they re-entered the room, "you see there's no deception."

He laid his slip of paper on the table beside Thorndyke's, and invited the latter to "turn up the cards." Thorndyke accordingly turned over the two slips of paper. Each bore the single word "*Phonolite*".

"I knew you had spotted it," said Burston. "However, you have now got corroborative evidence, and I suppose you are happy. I only hope I haven't helped to send some poor devil to chokee or worse. Good-bye. Glad you brought the things to me."

He restored the pill-box and slide, and having shaken hands heartily returned to his lair, while Thorndyke went forth into Jermyn Street and took his way thoughtfully eastward.

In a scientific sense, the Purcell case was now complete. But the more he thought about it, the more did he feel the necessity for bringing the scheme of evidence into closer conformity with traditional legal practice. Even to a judge a purely theoretical train of evidence might seem inconclusive. To a jury, who had been well pounded by a persuasive counsel, it would probably appear quite unconvincing. It would be necessary to obtain corroboration along different lines and in a new direction, and the direction in which it would be well to explore in the first place was the ancient precinct of Lincoln's Inn, where, at 62, Old Buildings, Mr. John Rodney had his professional chambers.

Now, at the very moment when Thorndyke was proceeding with swift strides from the neighbourhood of Jermyn Street towards Lincoln's Inn on business of the most critical importance to Mr. Varney, it was decreed by the irony of Fate that the latter gentleman should be engaged in bringing his affairs to a crisis of another kind. For some time past he had been watching with growing impatience the dilatory proceedings of the lawyers in regard to Margaret's petition. Especially had he chafed at the farce of the private detective, searching, as he knew, for a man whose body was lying on the bed of the sea hundreds of miles away from the area of the search. He was deeply disappointed, too. For when his advertisement scheme had been adopted by Thorndyke, he had supposed that all was plain sailing. He had but to send the necessary letter, and the dissolution of the marriage could be proceeded with at once. That was how it had appeared to him. And as soon as the marriage was dissolved he would make his declaration, and in due course his heart's desire would be accomplished.

Very differently had things turned out. Months had passed, and not a sign of progress had been made. The ridiculous search for the missing man – ridiculous to him only, however – dragged on interminably, and made him gnash his teeth in secret. His omniscience was now a sheer aggravation, for it condemned him to look on at the futile activities that Barnby had suggested and Rodney initiated, recognizing all their futility, but unable to utter a protest. To a man of his temperament it was maddening.

But there was another source of trouble. His confidence in Margaret's feelings towards him had been somewhat shaken of late. It had seemed to him there had been a change in her bearing towards him – a slight change, subtle and indefinable, but a change. She seemed as friendly, as cordial as ever. She welcomed his visits and appeared always glad to see him, and yet there was a something guarded, so he felt, as if she were consciously restraining any further increase of intimacy.

The thought of it troubled him profoundly. Of course, it might be nothing more than a little extra carefulness, due to her equivocal position. She had need to keep clear of anything in the slightest degree compromising – that he realized clearly. But still, the feeling lurked in his mind that she had changed, at least in manner, and sometimes he was aware of a horrible suspicion that he might have been over-confident. More than once he had been on the point of saying something indiscreet, and as time went on he felt ever growing a yearning to have his doubts set at rest.

On this present occasion he was taking tea with Margaret by invitation, with the ostensible object of showing her a set of etchings of some of the picturesque corners of Maidstone. He always enjoyed showing her his works, because he could see that she enjoyed looking at them, and these etchings of her native town would, he knew, have a double appeal.

"What a lovely old place it is!" she exclaimed, as she sipped her tea with her eyes fixed on the etchings that Varney had placed before her on a music-stand. "Why is it, Mr. Varney, that an etching or a drawing of any kind is so much more like the place than a photograph? It can't be a question of accuracy, for the photograph is at least as accurate as a drawing, and contains a great deal more detail."

"Yes," agreed Varney, "and that is probably the explanation. An artist puts down what he sees and what anyone else would see and recognize. A photograph puts down what is there, regardless of how the scene would look to a spectator. Consequently, it is full of irrelevant detail, which gets in the way of the real effect as the eye would see it, and it may show appearances that the eye never sees at all, as in the case of Muybridge's instantaneous photographs of galloping horses. A photograph of a Dutch clock might catch the pendulum in the middle of its swing, and then the clock would appear to have stopped. But an artist would always draw it at the end of its swing, where it pauses for an instant, and that is where the eye sees it when the clock is going."

"Yes, of course," said Margaret, "and now I understand why your etchings of the old streets and lanes show just the streets and lanes that I remember, whereas the photographs that I have all look more or less strange and unfamiliar. I suppose they are full of details that I never noticed, but your etchings pick out and emphasize the things that I used to look at with pleasure and which live in my memory. It is a long time since I have been to Maidstone. I should like to see it again. Indeed, I am not sure that, if I were free to choose, I shouldn't like to live there again. It is a dear old town."

"Yes, isn't it? But you say 'if you were free to choose'. Aren't you free to choose where you will live?"

"In a sense I am, I suppose," she replied, "but I don't feel that I can make any definite arrangements for the future until – well, until I know what my own future is to be."

"But surely you know that now. You have got that letter of Dan's. That practically releases you. The rest is only a matter of time and legal formalities. If Jack Rodney had only got Penfield or some other solicitor to get the case started as soon as you had that letter, you would have had your decree by now and have been your own mistress. At least, that is my feeling on the subject. Of course, I am not a lawyer, and I may be wrong."

"I don't think you are," said Margaret. "I have thought the same all along, and I fancy Mr. Rodney is beginning to regret that he did not follow Dr. Thorndyke's advice and rely on the letter only. But he felt that he could hardly go against Mr. Barnby, who has had so much experience in this kind of practice. And Mr. Barnby was very positive that the letter was not enough."

"Yes, Barnby has crabbed the whole business, and now after all these months you are just where you were, excepting that you have dropped a lot of money on this ridiculous private detective. Can't you get Rodney to send the fellow packing and get the case started in earnest?"

"I am inclined to think that he is seriously considering that line of action, and I hope he is. Of course, I have not tried to influence him in the matter. It is silly for a lay person to embarrass a lawyer by urging him to do this or that against his judgment. But I must say that I have grown rather despondent as the time has dragged on and nothing has been done, and I shall be very relieved when a definite move is made. I have an impression that it will be quite soon."

"That is good hearing," exclaimed Varney, "because when a move is made it can't fail to be successful. How can it? On that letter Dan could offer no defence, and it is pretty obvious that he has no intention of offering any. And if there is no defence, the case must go in your favour."

"Unless the judge suspects collusion, as Mr. Barnby seems to think he may."

"But," protested Varney, "judges don't give their decisions on what they suspect, do they? I thought they decided on the evidence. Surely collusion would have to be proved like anything else, and it couldn't be, because there has been no collusion. And I don't see why anyone should suspect that there has been."

"I agree with you entirely, Mr. Varney," said Margaret, "and I do hope you are right. You are making me feel quite encouraged."

"I am glad of that," said he, "and I am encouraging myself at the same time. This delay has been frightfully disappointing. I had hoped that by this time the affair would have been over and you would have been free. However, we may hope that it won't be so very long now."

"It will take some months, in any case," said Margaret.

"Yes, of course," he admitted, "but that is a mere matter of waiting. We can wait patiently when we see the end definitely in view. And what a relief it will be when it is over! Just think of it! When the words are spoken and the shackles are struck off! Won't that be a joyful day?"

As Varney was speaking, Margaret watched him furtively and a little uneasily. For there had come into his face an expression that she had seen more than once of late – an expression that filled her gentle soul with forebodings of trouble for this impulsive, warm-hearted friend. And now the note of danger was heightened by something significant in the words that he had used – something that expressed more than mere friendly solicitude.

"It will certainly be a relief when the whole business is over," she said quietly, "and it is most kind and sympathetic of you to take such a warm interest in my future."

"It isn't kind at all," he replied, "nor particularly sympathetic. I feel that I am an interested party. In a sense, your future is my future."

He paused for a few moments, and she looked at him in something like dismay. Vainly she cast about for some means of changing the current of the conversation, of escaping to some less perilous topic. Before she had time to recover from her confusion, he looked up at her and burst out passionately, "Maggie, I want to ask you a question. I know I oughtn't to ask it, but you must try to forgive me. I can't bear the suspense any longer. I think about it day and night, and it is eating my heart out. What I want to ask you is this: When it is all over – when that blessed day comes and you are free, will you – can I hope that you may be willing to listen to me if I ask you to let me be your devoted servant, your humble worshipper, and to try to make up to you by love and faithful service all that has been missing from your life in the past? For years – for many years, Maggie – I have been your friend – a friend far more loving and devoted than you have ever guessed, for in those days I hardly dared to dream even of intimate friendship. But now the barrier between us is no longer immovable. Soon it will be cast down for ever. And then – can it be, Maggie, that my dream will come true? That you will grant me a lifelong joy by letting me be the guardian of your happiness and peace?"

For a moment there had risen to Margaret's face a flush of resentment, but it faded almost instantly and was gone, extinguished by a deep sense of the tragedy of this unfortunate but real and great passion. She had always liked Varney, and she had recognized and valued his quiet, unobtrusive friendship and the chivalrous deference with which he had been used to treat her. And now she was going to make him miserable, to destroy his cherished hopes of a future made happy in the realization of his great love for her. The sadness of it left no room for resentment, and her eyes filled as she answered unsteadily, "You know, Mr. Varney, that, as a married woman, I have no right to speak or think of the making of a new marriage. But I feel that your question must be answered, and I wish, dear Mr. Varney, I wish from my heart that it could be answered differently. I have always valued your friendship – with very good reason, and I value your love, and am proud to have been thought worthy of it. But I cannot accept it. I can never accept it. It is dreadful to me, dear friend, to make you unhappy – you whom I like and admire so much. But it must be so. I have nothing but friendship to offer you, and I shall never have."

"Why do you say you will never have, Maggie?" he urged. "May it not be that you will change? That the other will come if I wait long enough? And I will wait patiently – wait until I am an old man if need be, so that only the door is not shut. I will never weary you with importunities, but just wait your pleasure. Will you not let me wait and hope, Maggie?"

She shook her head sadly. "No, Mr. Varney," she answered. "Believe me, it can never be. There is nothing to wait for. There will be no change. The future is certain so far as that. I am so sorry, dear generous friend. It grieves me to the heart to make you unhappy. But what I have said is final. I can never say anything different."

Varney looked at her in incredulous despair. He could not believe in this sudden collapse of all his hopes, for his doubts of her had been but vague misgivings, born of impatience and unrest. But suddenly a new thought flashed into his mind.

"How do you know that?" he asked. "Why are you so certain? Is there anything now that you know of that – that must keep us apart for ever? You know what I mean, Maggie. Is there anything?"

She was silent for a few moments. Naturally, she was reluctant to disclose to another the secret that she had held so long locked in her own heart, and that even now she dared but to whisper to herself. But she felt that to this man, whose love she must reject and whose happiness she must shatter, she owed a sacred duty. He must not be allowed to wreck his life if a knowledge of the truth would save him.

382

"I will tell you, Mr. Varney," she said. "You know how I came to marry Dan?"

"I think so," he replied. "He never told me, but I guessed."

"Well, if I had not married Dan, I should have married John Rodney. There was no engagement and nothing was said, but we were deeply attached to one another, and we both understood. Then circumstances compelled me to marry Dan. Mr. Rodney knew what those circumstances were. He cherished no resentment against me. He did not even blame me. He has remained my friend ever since, and he has formed no other attachment. I know that he has never forgotten what might have been, and neither have I. Need I say any more?"

Varney shook his head. "No," he replied gruffly. "I understand."

For some moments there was a deep silence in the room. Margaret glanced timidly at her companion, shocked at the sudden change in his appearance. In a moment all the enthusiasm, the eager vivacity, had died out of his face, leaving it aged, drawn, and haggard. He had understood, and his heart was filled with black despair. At a word all his glorious dream-castles had come crashing down, leaving the world that had been so sunny a waste of dust and ashes. So he sat for a while silent, motionless, stunned by the suddenness of the calamity. At length he rose and began, in a dull, automatic way, to collect his etchings and bestow them in his portfolio. When he had secured them and tied the ribbons of the portfolio, he turned to Margaret and, standing before her, looked earnestly in her face.

"Good-bye, Maggie," he said in a strange, muffled voice, "I expect I shan't see you again for some time."

She stood up, and with a little smothered sob held out her hand. He took it in both of his and, stooping, kissed it reverently. "Good-bye again," he said, still holding her hand. "Don't be unhappy about me. It couldn't be helped. I shall often think of you and of how sweet you have been to me to-day, and I shall hope to hear soon that you have got your freedom. And I do hope to God that Rodney will make you happy. I think he will. He is a good fellow, an honest man, and a gentleman. He is worthy of you, and I wish you both long years of happiness."

He kissed her hand once more, and then, releasing it, made his way gropingly out into the hall and to the door. She followed him with the tears streaming down her face, and watched him, as she had watched him once before, descending the stairs. At the landing he turned and waved his hand, and even as she returned his greeting he was gone. She went back to the drawing-room still weeping silently, very sad at heart at this half-foreseen tragedy. For the time being, she could see, Varney was a broken man. He had come full of hope and he had gone away in despair,

383

and something seemed to hint – it may have been the valedictory tone of his last words – that she had looked on him for the last time, that the final wave of his hand was a last farewell.

Meanwhile Varney, possessed by a wild unrest, hurried through the streets, yearning, like a wounded animal, for the solitude of his lair. He wanted to shut himself in his studio and be alone with his misery. Presently he hailed a taxicab, and from its window gazed out impatiently to measure its progress. Soon it drew up at the familiar entry, and when he had paid the driver he darted in and shut the door, but hardly had he attained the sanctuary that he had longed for than the same unrest began to engender a longing to escape. Up and down the studio he paced, letting the unbidden thoughts surge chaotically through his mind, mingling the troubled past with the future of his dreams – the sunny future that might have been – and this with the empty reality that lay before him.

On the wall he had pinned an early proof of the aquatint that Thorndyke had liked and that he himself rather liked. He had done it partly from bravado and partly as a memorial of the event that had set both him and Maggie free. Presently he halted before it and let it set the tune to his meditations. There was the lighthouse looking over the fog-bank just as it had looked on him when he was washing the bloodstain from the deck. By that time Purcell was overboard, at the bottom of the sea. His oppressor was gone. His life was now his own, and her life was her own.

He looked at the memorial picture, and in a moment it seemed to him to have become futile. The murder itself was futile, so far as he was concerned, though it had set Maggie free. To what purpose had he killed Purcell? It had been to ensure a future for himself, and behold! There was to be no future for him after all. Thus in the bitterness of his disappointment he saw everything out of proportion and in false perspective. He forgot that it was not to win Margaret but to escape from the clutches of his parasite that he had pulled the trigger on that sunny day in June. He forgot that he had achieved the very object that was in his mind when he fired the shot: Freedom to live a reputable life safe from the menace of the law. His passion for Margaret had become so absorbing that it had obscured all the other purposes of his life, and now that it was gone, it seemed to him that nothing was left.

As he stood thus gloomily reflecting with his eyes fixed on the little picture, he began to be aware of a new impulse. The lighthouse, the black-sailed luggers, the open sea, seemed to take on an unwonted friendliness. They were the setting of something besides tragedy. There, in Cornwall, he had been happy in a way, despite the abiding menace of

384

Purcell's domination. There, at Sennen, he had lived under the same roof with her, had sat at her table, had been her guest and her accepted friend. It had not really been a happy period, but memory, like the sundial, numbers only the sunny hours, and Varney looked back on it with wistful eyes. At least his dream had not been shattered then. So, as he looked at the picture, he felt stirring within him a desire to go back and look upon those scenes again. Falmouth and Penzance and Sennen – especially Sennen – seemed to draw him. He wanted to look out across the sea to the Longships, and in the gathering gloom of the horizon to see the diamond and the ruby sparkle as they did that evening when he and the distant lighthouse seemed to hold secret converse.

It was, perhaps, a strange impulse. Whence it came he neither knew nor asked. It may have been the effect of memory and association. It may have been mere unrest. Or it may have been that a dead hand beckoned to him to come. Who shall say? He only knew that he was sensible of the impulse, and that it grew from moment to moment.

To a man in his condition, to feel an impulse is to act on it. No sooner was he conscious of the urge to go back and look upon the well-remembered scenes than he began to make his simple preparations for the journey. Like most experienced travellers he travelled light. Most of his kit, including his little case of sketching materials, was in the studio. The rest could be picked up at his lodgings en route for Paddington. Within ten minutes of his having formed the resolve to go, he stood on the threshold, locking the studio door from without with the extra key that he used when he was absent for more than a day. At the outer gate he paused to pocket the key, and stood for a few moments with his portmanteau in his hand, looking back at the studio with a curiously reflective air. Then, at last, he turned and went on his way. But if he could have looked, as the clairvoyant claims to look, through the bricks and mortar of London, he might at this very time have seen Dr. John Thorndyke striding up Chancery Lane from Fleet Street, might have followed him to the great gateway of Lincoln's Inn (on the masonry whereof tradition has it that Ben Jonson worked as a bricklayer), and seen him pass through into the little square beyond, and finally plunge into the dark and narrow entry of one of the ancient red brick houses that have looked down upon the square for some three or four centuries – an entry on the jamb of which was painted the name of Mr. John Rodney.

But Varney was not a clairvoyant, and neither was Thorndyke. And so it befell that each of them went his way unconscious of the movements of the other.

Chapter XV
In Which Thorndyke
Opens the Attack

$\mathbf{A}$s Thorndyke turned the corner at the head of the stairs, he encountered Philip Rodney with a kettle in his hand, which he had apparently been filling at some hidden source of water.

"This is a bit of luck," said Philip, holding out his disengaged hand. "For me, at least. Not, perhaps, for you. I have only just arrived, and Jack hasn't come over from the courts yet. I hope this isn't a business call."

"In a sense it is," replied Thorndyke, "as I am seeking information. But I think you can probably tell me all I want to know."

"That's all right," said Philip. "I'll just plant 'Polly' on the gas-stove, and while she is boiling we can smoke a preparatory pipe and you can get on with the examination-in-chief. Go in and take the presidential chair."

Thorndyke entered the pleasant, homely room, half-office, half-sitting room, and seating himself in the big armchair, began to fill his pipe. In a few moments Philip entered and sat down on a chair which commanded a view of the tiny kitchen and of "Polly", seated on a gas-ring.

"Now," said he, "fire away. What do you want to know?"

"I want," replied Thorndyke, "to ask you one or two questions about your yacht."

"The deuce you do!" exclaimed Philip. "Are you thinking of going in for a yacht yourself?"

"Not at present," was the reply. "My questions have reference to that last trip that Purcell made in her, and the first one is: When you took over the yacht after that trip, did you find her in every respect as she was before? Was there anything missing that you could not account for, or any change in her condition, or anything about her that was not quite as you expected it to be?"

Philip looked at his visitor with undissembled surprise. "Now I wonder what makes you ask that. Have you any reason to expect that I should have found any change in her condition?"

"If you don't mind," said Thorndyke, "we will leave that question unanswered for the moment. I would rather not say, just now, what my object is in seeking this information. We can go into that later.

386

Meanwhile, do you mind just answering my questions as if you were in the witness-box?"

A shade of annoyance crossed Philip's face. He could not imagine what possible concern Thorndyke could have with his yacht, and he was inclined to resent the rather cryptic attitude of his questioner. Nevertheless, he answered readily. "Of course I don't mind. But, in fact, there is nothing to tell. I don't remember noticing any thing unusual about the yacht, and there was nothing missing, so far as I know."

"No rope or cordage of any kind, for instance?"

"No – at least, nothing to speak of. A new ball of spun-yarn had been broached. I noticed that, and I meant to ask Varney what he used it for. But there wasn't a great deal of it gone, and I know of nothing else. Oh, wait! If I am in the witness-box I must tell the whole truth, be it never so trivial. There was a mark or stain or dirty smear of some kind on the jib. Is that any good to you?"

"Are you sure it wasn't there before that day?"

"Quite. I sailed the yacht myself the day before, and I will swear that the jib was spotlessly clean then. So the mark must have been made by Purcell or Varney, because I noticed it the very next day."

"What was the mark like?"

"It was just a faint wavy line, as if some dirty water had been spilt on the sail and allowed to dry partly before it was washed off."

"Did you form any opinion as to how the mark might have been caused?"

Philip struggled, not quite successfully, to suppress a smile. To him there seemed something extremely ludicrous in this solemn interrogation concerning these meaningless trifles. But he answered as gravely as he could. "I could only make a vague guess. I assumed that it was caused in some way by the accident that occurred. You may remember that the jib-halyard broke, and the sail went overboard and got caught under the yacht's forefoot. That is when it must have happened. Perhaps the sail may have picked some dirt off the keel. Usually a dirty mark on the jib means mud on the fluke of the anchor, but it wasn't that. The anchor hadn't been down since it was scrubbed. The yacht rode at moorings in Sennen Cove. However, there was the mark. How it came there you are as well able to judge as I am."

"And that is all you know – this mark on the sail and the spun-yarn? There is no other cordage missing?"

"No, not so far as I know."

"And there is nothing else missing? No iron fittings or heavy objects of any kind?"

387

"Good Lord, no! How should there be? You don't suspect Purcell of having hooked off with one of the anchors in his pocket, do you?"

Thorndyke smiled indulgently, but persisted in his questions.

"Do you mean that you know there was nothing missing, or only that you are not aware of any thing being missing?"

The persistence of the questions impressed Philip with a sudden suspicion that Thorndyke had something definite in his mind, that he had some reason for believing that something had been removed from the yacht. He ventured to suggest this to Thorndyke, who answered frankly enough. "You are so far right, Philip, that I am not asking these questions at random. I would rather not say more than that just now."

"Very well," said Philip, "I won't press you for an explanation. But I may say that we dismantled the yacht in rather a hurry, and hadn't time to check the inventory, so I can't really say whether there was anything missing or not. But you have come at a most opportune time, for it happens that we had arranged to go over to the place where she is laid up, at Battersea, to-morrow afternoon for the very purpose of checking the inventory and generally overhauling the boat and the gear. If you care to come over with us, or meet us there, we can settle your questions quite definitely. How will that suit you?"

"It will suit me perfectly," replied Thorndyke. "If you will give me the address and fix a time, I will meet you there."

"It is a disused wharf with some empty work shops," said Philip. "I will write down the directions, and if you will be at the gate at three o'clock to-morrow, we can go through the gear and fittings together."

Thorndyke made a note of the whereabouts of the wharf, and having thus despatched the business on which he had come, he took an early opportunity to depart, not having any great desire to meet John Rodney and be subjected to the inevitable cross-examination. He could see that Philip was, naturally enough, extremely curious as to the object of his inquiries, and he preferred to leave the two brothers to discuss the matter. On the morrow his actions would be guided by the results, if any, of the survey of the yacht.

Three o'clock on the following afternoon found him waiting at a large wooden gate in a narrow thoroughfare close to the river. On the pavement by his side stood the green canvas-covered "research case", which was his constant companion whenever he went abroad on professional business. It contained a very complete outfit of such reagents and apparatus as he might require in a preliminary investigation, but on the present occasion its usual contents had been reinforced by two large bottles, to obtain which Polton had that morning made a special visit to a wholesale chemist's in the Borough. A church clock somewhere across the river struck the hour, and almost at the same moment John and Philip Rodney emerged from a tributary alley and advanced towards the gate.

"You are here first, then," said Philip, "but we are not late. I heard a clock strike a moment ago."

He produced a key from his pocket, with which he unlocked a wicket in the gate and, having pushed it open, invited Thorndyke to enter. The latter passed through and the two brothers followed, locking the wicket after them, and conducted Thorndyke across a large yard to a desolate looking wharf, beyond which was a stretch of unreclaimed shore. Here, drawn up well above high-water mark, a small, sharp-sterned yacht stood on chocks under a tarpaulin cover.

"This is the yacht," said Philip, "but there is nothing on board of her. All the stores and gear and loose fittings are in the workshop behind us. Which will you see first?"

"Let us look at the gear," replied Thorndyke, and they accordingly turned towards a large disused workshop at the rear of the wharf.

"Phil was telling me about your visit last night," said Rodney, with an inquisitive eye on the research case, "and we are both fairly flummoxed. He gathered that these inquiries of yours are in some way connected with Purcell."

"Yes, that is so. I want to ascertain whether, when you resumed possession of the yacht after Purcell left her, you found her in the same condition as before, and whether her stores, gear, and fittings were intact."

"Did you suppose that Purcell might have taken some of them away with him?"

"I thought it not impossible," Thorndyke replied.

"Now, I wonder why on earth you should think that," said Rodney, "and what concern it should be of yours if he had."

Thorndyke smiled evasively. "Everything is my concern," he replied. "I am an Autolycus of the Law, a collector of miscellaneous trifles of evidence and unclassifiable scraps of information."

"Well," said Rodney, with a somewhat sour smile, "I have no experience of legal curiosity shops and oddment repositories. But I don't know what you mean by 'evidence'. Evidence of what?"

"Of whatever it may chance to prove," Thorndyke replied blandly.

"What did you suppose Purcell might have taken with him?" Rodney asked, with a trace of irritability in his tone.

"I had thought it possible that there might be some cordage missing and perhaps some iron fittings or other heavy objects. But, of course, that is mere surmise. My object is, as I have said, to ascertain whether the

389

yacht was in all respects in the same condition when Purcell left her as when he came on board."

Rodney gave a grunt of impatience, but at this moment Philip, who had been wrestling with a slightly rusty lock, threw open the door of the workshop, and they all entered. Thorndyke looked curiously about the long, narrow interior with its prosaic contents, so little suggestive of the tragedy which his thoughts associated with them. Overhead, the yacht's spars rested on the tie-beams, from which hung bunches of blocks. On the floor reposed a long row of neatly painted half-hundred weights, a pile of chain cable, two anchors, a stove, and other oddments such as water-breakers, buckets, mops, etcetera., and on the long benches at the side folded sails, locker cushions, sidelight lanterns, the binnacle, the cabin lamp, and other more delicate fittings. After a long look round, in the course of which his eye travelled along the row of ballast-weights, Thorndyke deposited his case on a bench and asked. "Have you still got the broken jib-halyard that Philip was telling me about last night?"

"Yes," answered Rodney, "it is here under the bench."

He drew out a coil of rope, and, flinging it on the floor, began to uncoil it, when it separated into two lengths.

"Which are the broken ends?" asked Thorndyke.

"It broke near the middle," replied Rodney, "where it chafed on the cleat when the sail was hoisted. This is the one end, you see, frayed out, like a brush in breaking, and the other – " He picked up the second half, and passing it rapidly through his hands held up the end. He did not finish the sentence, but stood, with a frown of surprise, staring at the rope in his hand.

"This is queer," he said, after a pause. "The broken end has been cut off. Did you cut it off, Phil?"

"No," replied Philip, "it is just as I took it from the locker, where, I suppose, you or Varney stowed it."

"I wonder," said Thorndyke, "how much has been cut off. Do you know what the original length of the rope was?"

"Yes," replied Rodney, "forty-two feet. It is down in the inventory, but I remember working it out. Let us see how much there is here."

He laid the two lengths of rope along the floor, and with Thorndyke's spring tape care fully measured them. The combined length was exactly thirty-one feet.

"So," said Thorndyke, "there are eleven feet missing, without allowing for the lengthening of the rope by stretching."

The two brothers glanced at one another, and both looked at Thorndyke with very evident surprise.

"Well," said Philip, "you seem to be right about the cordage. But what made you go for the jib-halyard in particular?"

"Because if any cordage had been cut off, it would naturally be taken from a broken rope in preference to a whole one."

"Yes, of course. But I can't understand how you came to suspect that any rope was missing at all."

"We will talk about that presently," said Thorndyke. "The next question is as to the iron fittings, chain, and so forth."

"I don't think any of those can be missing," said Rodney. "You can't very well cut a length of chain off with your pocket-knife."

"No," agreed Thorndyke, "but I thought you might have some odd piece of chain among the ballast."

"We have no chain except the cable. Our only ballast is in the form of half-hundredweights. They are handier to stow than odd stuff."

"How many half-hundred weights have you?"

"Twenty-four," replied Rodney.

"There are only twenty-three in that row," said Thorndyke. "I counted them as we came in and noted the odd number."

The two brothers simultaneously checked Thorndyke's statement and confirmed it. Then they glanced about the floor of the workshop, under the benches, and by the walls, but the missing weight was nowhere to be seen, nor was there any place in which an object of this size could have got hidden.

"It is very extraordinary," said Philip. "There is certainly one weight missing. And no one has handled them but Jack and I. We hired a barrow and brought up all the gear ourselves."

"There is just the chance," said Thorndyke, "that one of them may have been overlooked and left in the yacht's hold."

"It is very unlikely," replied Philip, "seeing that we took out the floor-boards, so that you can see the whole of the bilges from end to end. But I will run down and make sure."

He ran out, literally, and crossing the wharf disappeared over the edge. In a couple of minutes he was back, breathing fast, and evidently not a little excited.

"It isn't there," he said. "Of course it couldn't be. But the question is, what has become of it? It is a most mysterious affair."

"It is," agreed Rodney. "And what is still more mysterious is that Thorndyke seemed to suspect that it was missing even before he came here. Now didn't you, Thorndyke?"

"I suspected that some heavy object was missing, as I mentioned," was the reply, "and a ballast-weight was a likely object. By the way, can you fix a date on which you know that all the ballast-weights were in place?"

"Yes, I think I can," replied Philip. "A few days before Purcell went to Penzance, we beached the yacht to give her a scrape. Of course we had to take out the ballast, and when we launched her again I helped to put it back. I am certain that all the weights were there then, because I counted them after they were stowed in their places."

"Then," said Thorndyke, "it is virtually certain that they were all on board when Purcell and Varney started from Sennen."

"I should say it is absolutely certain," said Philip.

Thorndyke nodded gravely and appeared to reflect a while. But his reflections were broken in upon by John Rodney.

"Look here, Thorndyke, we have answered your questions and given you facilities for verifying certain opinions that you held, and now it is time that you were a little less reserved with us. You evidently connected the disappearance of this rope and this weight in some way with Purcell. Now, we are all interested in Purcell. You have got something up your sleeve, and we should like to know what that something is. It is perfectly obvious that you don't imagine that Purcell, when he went up the pier ladder at Penzance, had a couple of fathoms of rope and a half-hundred weight concealed about his person."

"As a matter of fact," said Thorndyke, "I don't imagine that Purcell ever went up the ladder at Penzance at all."

"But Varney saw him go up," protested Philip.

"Varney *says* he saw him go up," Thorndyke corrected. "I do not accept Mr. Varney's statement."

"Then what on earth do you suggest?" demanded Philip. "And why should Varney say what isn't true?"

"Let us sit down on this bench," said Thorndyke, "and thrash the matter out. I will put my case to you, and you can give me your criticisms on it. I will begin by stating that some months ago I came to the conclusion that Purcell was dead."

Both the brothers started and gazed at Thorndyke in utter astonishment. Then Rodney said, "You say 'some months ago'. You must mean within the last three months."

"No," replied Thorndyke. "I decided that he died on the twenty-third of last June, before the yacht reached Penzance."

An exclamation burst simultaneously from both of his hearers, and Rodney protested impatiently. "But this is sheer nonsense, if you will pardon me for saying so. Have you forgotten that two persons have received letters from him less than four months ago?"

"I suggest that we waive those letters and consider the other evidence."

"But we can't waive them!" exclaimed Rodney. "They are material evidence of the most conclusive kind."

"I may say that I have ascertained that both those letters were forgeries. The evidence can be produced, if necessary, as both the letters are in existence, but I don't propose to produce it now. I ask you to accept my statement for the time being and to leave the letters out of the discussion."

"It is leaving out a good deal," said Rodney. "I find it very difficult to believe that they were forgeries or to imagine who on earth could have forged them. However, we won't contest the matter now. When did you come to this extraordinary conclusion?"

"A little over four months ago," replied Thorndyke.

"And you never said anything to any of us on the subject?" said Rodney. "And, what is more astonishing, you actually put in an advertisement, addressed to a man whom you believed to be dead."

"And got an answer from him," added Philip, with a derisive smile.

"Exactly," said Thorndyke. "It was an experiment, and it was justified by the result. But let us get back to the matter that we have been investigating. I came to the conclusion, as I have said, that Purcell met his death during that voyage from Sennen to Penzance, and that Varney, for some reason, had thought it necessary to conceal the occurrence, but I decided that the evidence in my possession would not be convincing in a court of law."

"I have no doubt that you were perfectly right in that," Rodney remarked dryly.

"I further considered it very unlikely that any fresh evidence would ever be forthcoming, and that, since the death could not be proved, it was, for many reasons, undesirable that the question should ever be raised. Accordingly, I never communicated my belief to anybody."

"Then," said Rodney, "are we to understand that some new evidence has come to light, after all?"

"Yes. It came to light the other day at the College of Surgeons. I dare say Philip told you about it."

"He told me that, by an extraordinary coincidence, that quaint button of Purcell's had turned up, and that some sort of sea-worm had built a tube on it. But if that is what you mean, I don't see the bearing of it as evidence."

"Neither do I," said Philip.

"You remember that Varney distinctly stated that when Purcell went up the ladder at Penzance he was wearing his oilskin coat, and that the button was then on it?"

"Yes. But I don't see anything in that. Purcell went ashore, it is true, and he went away from Cornwall. But he seems to have gone by sea, and, as I suggested the other day, he probably got a fresh button when he went on board the steamer and chucked this cork one overboard."

"I remember your making that suggestion," said Thorndyke, "and very much astonished I was to hear you make it. I may say that I have ascertained that Purcell was never on board that steamer."

"Well, he might have thrown it into the sea somewhere else. There is no particular mystery about its having got into the sea. But what was there about my suggestion that astonished you so much?"

"It was," replied Thorndyke, "that you completely overlooked a most impressive fact which was staring you in the face and shouting aloud for recognition."

"Indeed!" said Philip. "What fact was it that I overlooked?"

"Just consider," replied Thorndyke, "what it was that Professor D'Arcy showed us. It was a cork button with a Terebella tube on it. Now an ordinary cork, if immersed long enough, will soak up water until it is waterlogged and then sink to the bottom. But this one was impregnated with paraffin wax. It could not get waterlogged and it could not sink. It would float forever."

"Well?" queried Philip.

"But it had sunk. It had been lying at the bottom of the sea for months – long enough for a Terebella to build a tube on it. Then at last it had broken loose, risen to the surface and drifted ashore."

"You are taking the worm-tube as evidence," said John Rodney, "that the button had sunk to bottom. Is it impossible – I am no naturalist – but is it impossible that the worm could have built its tube while the button was floating about in the sea?"

"It is quite impossible," replied Thorndyke, "in the case of this particular worm, since the tube is built up of particles of rock gathered by the worm from the sea bottom. You will bear me out in that, Philip?"

"Oh, certainly," replied Philip. "There is no doubt that the button has been at the bottom for a good many months. The question is how the deuce it can have got there, and what was holding it down."

"You are not overlooking the fact that it is a button," said Thorndyke. "I mean that it was attached to a garment?"

Both men looked at Thorndyke a little uncomfortably. Then Rodney replied, "Your suggestion obviously is that the button was attached to a garment and that the garment contained a body. I am disposed to concede

394

the garment, since I can think of no other means by which the button could have been held down, but I see no reason for assuming the body. I admit that I do not quite understand how Purcell's oilskin coat could have got to the bottom of the sea, but still less can I imagine how Purcell's body could have got to the bottom of the sea. What do you say, Phil?"

"I agree with you," answered Philip. "Something must have held the button down, and I can think of nothing but the coat to which it was attached. But as to the body, it seems a gratuitous assumption, to say nothing of the various reasons for believing that Purcell is still alive. There is nothing wildly improbable in the supposition that the coat might have blown overboard and been sunk by something heavy in the pocket. As a matter of fact, it would have sunk by itself as soon as it got thoroughly soaked. You must admit, Thorndyke, that that is so."

But Thorndyke shook his head. "We are not dealing with general probabilities," said he. "We are dealing with a specific case. An empty oilskin coat, even if sunk by some object in the pocket, would have been comparatively light, and, like all moderately light bodies, would have drifted about the sea bottom, impelled by currents and tide-streams. But that is not the condition in the present case. There is evidence that this button was moored immovably to some very heavy object."

"What evidence is there of that?" demanded Rodney.

"There is the conclusive fact that it has been all these months lying continuously in one place."

"Indeed!" said Rodney, with hardly concealed scepticism. "That seems a bold thing to say. But if you know that it has been lying all the time in one place, perhaps you can point out the spot where it has been lying."

"As a matter of fact I can," said Thorndyke. "That button, Rodney, has been lying all these months on the sea bottom at the base of the Wolf Rock."

The two brothers started very perceptibly. They stared at Thorndyke, then looked at one another, and then Rodney challenged the statement.

"You make this assertion very confidently," he said. "Can you produce any evidence to support it?"

"I can produce perfectly convincing and conclusive evidence," replied Thorndyke. "A very singular conjunction of circumstances enables us to fix with absolute certainty the place where that button has been lying. Do you happen to be acquainted with the peculiar resonant volcanic rock known as phonolite, or clink-stone?"

Rodney shook his head a little impatiently. "No," he answered, "I have never heard of it before."

"It is not a very rare rock," said Thorndyke, "but in the neighbourhood of the British Isles it occurs in only two places. One is inland in the North, and may be disregarded. The other is the Wolf Rock."

Neither of his hearers made any comment on this statement, though it was evident that both were deeply impressed, and he continued. "This Wolf Rock is a very remarkable structure. It is what is called a 'volcanic neck' – that is, it is a mass of altered lava that once filled the funnel of a volcano. The volcano has disappeared, but this cast of the funnel remains standing up from the bottom of the sea like a great column. It is a single mass of phonolite, and thus entirely different in composition from the sea bed around or anywhere near these islands. But, of course, immediately at its base the sea bottom must be covered with decomposed fragments which have fallen from its sides, and it is with these fragments that our Terebella has built its tube. You remember, Philip, my pointing out to you, as we walked home from the College, that the worm-tube appeared to be built of fragments that were all alike. Now, that was a very striking and significant fact. It furnished *prima facie* evidence that the button had been moored in one place, and that it had therefore been attached to some very heavy object. That night I made an exhaustive examination of the material of the tube, and then the further fact emerged that the material was phonolite. This, as I have said, fixed the locality with exactness and certainty. And I may add that, in view of the importance of the matter in an evidential sense, I submitted the fragments yesterday to one of the greatest living authorities on petrology, who recognized them at once as phonolite."

For some time after Thorndyke had finished speaking, the two brothers sat wrapped in silent reflection. Both were deeply impressed, but each in a markedly different way. To John Rodney, the lawyer, accustomed to sworn testimony and documentary evidence, this scientific demonstration appeared amazingly ingenious, but somewhat fantastic and unconvincing. In the case of Philip, the doctor, it was quite otherwise. Accustomed to acting on inferences from facts of his own observing, he gave full weight to each item of evidence, and his thoughts were already stretching out to the as yet unstated corollaries.

John Rodney was the first to speak. "What inference," he asked, "do you wish us to draw from this very ingenious theory of yours?"

"It is rather more than a theory," said Thorndyke, "but we will let that pass. The inference I leave to you, but perhaps it would help you if I were to recapitulate the facts."

"Perhaps it would," said Rodney.

"Then," said Thorndyke, "I will take them in their order. This is the case of a man who was seen to start on a voyage for a given destination in company with one other man. His start out to sea was witnessed by a number of persons. From that moment he was never seen again by any person excepting his one companion. He is said to have reached his destination, but his arrival there rests upon the unsupported verbal testimony of one person, the said companion. Thereafter he vanished utterly, and since then has made no sign of being alive, he has drawn no cheques, though he has a considerable balance at his bank, he has communicated with no one, and he has never been seen by anybody who could recognize him."

"Is that quite correct?" interposed Philip. "He is said to have been seen at Falmouth and Ipswich, and then there are those letters."

"His alleged appearance, embarking at Falmouth and disembarking at Ipswich," replied Thorndyke, "rest, like his arrival at Penzance, upon the unsupported testimony of one person, his sole companion on the voyage. That statement I can prove to be untrue. He was never seen either at Falmouth or at Ipswich. As to the letters. I can prove them both to be forgeries and for the present I ask you to admit them as such pending the production of proof. But if we exclude the alleged appearances and the letters, what I have said is correct: From the time when this man put out to sea from Sennen he has never been seen by anyone but Varney, and there has never been any corroboration of Varney's statement that he landed at Penzance.

"Some eight months later a portion of this man's clothing is found. It bears evidence of having been lying at the bottom of the sea for many months, so that it must have sunk to its resting-place within a very short time of the man's disappearance. The place where it has been lying is one over, or near, which the man must have sailed in the yacht. It has been moored to the bottom by some very heavy object, and a very heavy object has disappeared from the yacht. That heavy object had apparently not disappeared when the yacht started, and it is not known to have been on the yacht afterwards. The evidence goes to show that the disappearance of that object coincided in time with the disappearance of the man, and a quantity of cordage disappeared certainly on that day.

"Those are the facts at present in our possession with regard to the disappearance of Daniel Purcell, to which we may add that the disappearance was totally unexpected, that it has never been explained or accounted for excepting in a letter which is a manifest forgery, and that even in the latter, apart from the fictitious nature of the letter, the explanation is utterly inconsistent with all that is known of the missing man in respect of his character, his habits, his intentions, and his circumstances."

Chapter XVI
In Which John Rodney is Convinced

Once more, as Thorndyke concluded, there was a long, uncomfortable silence, during which the two brothers cogitated profoundly and with a very disturbed expression. At length John Rodney spoke.

"There is no denying, Thorndyke, that the body of circumstantial evidence that you have produced and expounded so skilfully and lucidly is extra ordinarily complete. Of course, it is subject to your being able to prove that Varney's reports as to Purcell's appearance at Falmouth and Ipswich were false reports, and that the letters which purported to be written and sent by Purcell were in fact not written or sent by him. If you can prove those assertions, there will undoubtedly be a very formidable case against Varney, because those reports and those letters would then be evidence that someone was endeavouring to prove, falsely, that Purcell is alive. But this would amount to presumptive evidence that he is *not* alive, and that someone has reasons for concealing the fact of his death. But we must look to you to prove what you have asserted. You could hardly suggest that we should charge a highly respectable gentleman of our acquaintance with having murdered his friend and made away with the body – for that is obviously your meaning – on a mass of circumstantial evidence, which is, you must admit, rather highly theoretical."

"I agree with you completely," replied Thorndyke. "The evidence respecting the reports and the letters is obviously essential. But in the meantime, it is of the first importance that we carry this investigation to an absolute finish. It is not merely a question of justice or our duty on grounds of public policy to uncover a crime and secure the punishment of the criminal. There are individual rights and interests to be guarded – those, I mean, of the missing man's wife. If her husband is dead, common justice to her demands that his death should be proved and placed on public record."

"Yes, indeed," Rodney agreed heartily. "If Purcell is dead, then she is a widow, and the petition becomes unnecessary. By the way, I understand now why you were always so set against the private detective, but what I don't understand is why you put in that advertisement."

"It is quite simple," was the reply. "I wanted another forged letter, written in terms dictated by myself – and I got it."

"Ha!" exclaimed Rodney. And now, for the first time, he began to understand how Thorndyke had got his great reputation.

"You spoke just now," Rodney continued, "of carrying this investigation to a finish. Haven't you done so? Is there anything more to investigate?"

"We have not yet completed our examination of the yacht," replied Thorndyke. "The facts that we have elicited enable us to make certain inferences concerning the circumstances of Purcell's death – assuming his death to have occurred. We infer, for instance, that he did not fall overboard, nor was he pushed overboard. He met his death on the yacht, and it was his dead body which was cast into the sea with the sinker attached to it. That we may fairly infer. But we have, at present, no evidence as to the way in which he came by his death. Possibly a further examination of the yacht may show some traces from which we may form an opinion. By the way, I have been looking at that revolver that is hanging from the beam. Was that on board at the time?"

"Yes," answered Rodney. "It was hanging on the cabin bulkhead. Be careful," he added, as Thorndyke lifted it from its hook. "I don't think it has been unloaded."

Thorndyke opened the breech of the revolver and, turning out the cartridges into his hand, peered down the barrel and into each chamber separately. Then he looked at the cartridges in his hand.

"This seems a little odd," he remarked. "The barrel is quite clean and so is one chamber, but the other five chambers are extremely foul. And I notice that the cartridges are not all alike. There are five Eleys and one Curtis and Harvey. That is quite a suggestive coincidence."

Philip looked with a distinctly startled expression at the little heap of cartridges in Thorndyke's hand, and, picking out the odd one, examined it with knitted brows.

"When did you fire the revolver last, Jack?" he asked, looking up at his brother.

"On the day when we potted at those champagne bottles," was the reply.

Philip raised his eyebrows. "Then," said he, "this is a very remarkable affair. I distinctly remember on that occasion, when we had sunk all the bottles, reloading the revolver with Eleys, and that there were then three cartridges left over in the bag. When I had loaded I opened the new box of Curtis and Harvey's, tipped them into the bag, and threw the box overboard."

"Did you clean the revolver?" asked Thorndyke.

400

"No, I didn't. I meant to clean it later, but forgot to."

"But," said Thorndyke, "it has undoubtedly been cleaned, and very thoroughly as to the barrel and one chamber. Shall we check the cartridges in the bag? There ought to be forty-nine Curtis and Harveys and three Eleys if what you have told us is correct."

Philip searched among the raffle on the bench, and presently unearthed a small linen bag. Untying the string, he shot out on the bench a heap of cartridges, which he counted one by one. There were fifty-two in all, and three of them were Eleys.

"Then," said Thorndyke, "it comes to this: Since you used that revolver, it has been used by someone else. That someone fired only a single shot, after which he carefully cleaned the barrel and the empty chamber and reloaded. Incidentally, he seems to have known where the cartridge-bag was kept, but he did not know about the change in the make of cartridges or that the revolver had not been cleaned. You notice, Rodney," he added, "that the circumstantial evidence accumulates."

"I do, indeed," Rodney replied gloomily. "Is there anything else that you wish to examine?"

"Yes, there is the sail. Philip mentioned a stain on the jib. Shall we see if we can make any thing of that?"

"I don't think you will make much of it," said Philip. "It is very faint. However, you shall see it and judge for yourself."

He picked out one of the bundles of white duck, and while he was unfolding it Thorndyke dragged an empty bench into the middle of the floor under the skylight. Over this the sail was spread so that the mysterious mark was in the middle of the bench. It was very inconspicuous – just a faint grey-green, wavy line, like the representation of an island on a map. The three men looked at it curiously for a few moments, then Thorndyke asked, "Would you mind if I made a further stain on the sail? I should like to apply some reagents."

"Of course you must do what is necessary," said Rodney. "The evidence is more important than the sail."

On this Thorndyke opened his research case and brought forth the two bottles that Polton had procured from the Borough, of which one was labelled "*Tinct. Guaiaci Dil.*", and the other "*Ozon.*". As they emerged from the case, Philip commented, "I shouldn't have thought that the guaiacum test would be of any use after all these months, especially as the sail seems to have been scrubbed."

"It will act, I think, if the pigment or its derivatives is there," said Thorndyke, and as he spoke he poured a quantity of the tincture on the middle of the stained area. The pool of liquid rapidly spread considerably beyond the limits of the stain, growing paler as it extended. Then

401

Thorndyke cautiously dropped small quantities of the ozonic ether at various points around the stained area, and watched closely as the two liquids mingled in the fabric of the sail. Gradually the ether spread towards the stain, and, first at one point and then at another, approached and finally crossed the wavy grey line, and at each point the same change occurred: First the faint grey line turned into a strong blue line, and then the colour extended to the enclosed space until the entire area of the stain stood out a conspicuous blue patch. Philip and Thorndyke looked at one another significantly, and the latter said, "You understand the meaning of this reaction, Rodney. This is a bloodstain, and a very carefully washed bloodstain."

"So I supposed," Rodney replied, and for a while no one spoke.

There was something very dramatic and solemn, they all felt, in the sudden appearance of this staring blue patch on the sail with the sinister message that it brought. But what followed was more dramatic still. As they stood silently regarding the blue stain, the mingled liquids continued to spread, and suddenly, at the extreme edge of the wet area, they became aware of a new spot of blue. At first a mere speck, it grew slowly, as the liquid spread over the canvas, into a small oval, and then a second spot appeared by its side. At this point Thorndyke poured out a fresh charge of the tincture, and when it had soaked into the cloth cautiously applied a sprinkling of ether. Instantly the blue spots began to elongate, fresh spots and patches appeared, and as they ran together there sprang out of the blank surface the clear impression of a hand – a left hand, complete in all its details excepting the third finger, which was represented by a round spot at some two-thirds of its length.

The dreadful significance of this apparition, and the uncanny and mysterious manner of its emergence from the white surface, produced a most profound impression on all the observers, but especially on Rodney, who stared at it with an expression of the utmost horror, but spoke not a word. His brother was hardly less appalled, and when he at length spoke it was in a hushed voice that was little above a whisper.

"It is horrible," he murmured. "It seems almost supernatural, that accusing hand springing into existence out of the blank surface after all this time. I wonder," he added, after a pause, "why the third finger made no mark, seeing that the others are so distinct."

"I think," said Thorndyke, "that the impression is there. That small round spot looks like the mark of a finger-tip, and its position rather suggests a finger with a stiff joint."

As he made this statement, both brothers simultaneously uttered a smothered exclamation.

"It is Varney's hand!" gasped Philip. "You recognize it, Jack, don't you? That is just where the tip of his stiff finger would come. Have you ever noticed Varney's left hand, Thorndyke?"

"You mean the ankylosed third finger? Yes, and I agree with you that this is undoubtedly the print of Varney's hand."

"Then," said Rodney, "the case is complete. There is no need for any further investigation. On the evidence that is before us, to say nothing of the additional evidence that you can produce, there cannot be the shadow of a doubt that Purcell was murdered by Varney and his body sunk in the sea. You agree with me, I am sure, Thorndyke?"

"Certainly," was the reply. "I consider the evidence so far conclusive that I have not the slightest doubt on the subject."

"Very well," said Rodney. "Then the next question is, what is to be done? Shall I lay a sworn information or will you? Or had we better go to the police together and make a joint statement?"

"Whatever we do," replied Thorndyke, "don't let us be premature. The evidence, as you say, is perfectly convincing. It leaves us with no doubt as to what happened on that day last June. It would probably be, in an intellectual sense, quite convincing to a judge. It might even be to a jury. But would it be sufficient to secure a conviction? I think it extremely doubtful."

"Do you really?" exclaimed Philip. "I should have thought it impossible that anyone who had heard the evidence could fail to come to the inevitable conclusion."

"You are probably right," said Thorndyke. "But a jury who are trying an accused person on a capital charge have got to arrive at something more than a belief that the accused is guilty. They have got to be convinced that there is, humanly speaking, no possible doubt as to the prisoner's guilt. No jury would give an adverse verdict on a balance of probabilities, nor would any judge encourage them to do so."

"But surely," said Philip, "this is something more than a mere balance of probabilities. The evidence all points in the same direction, and there is nothing to suggest a contrary conclusion."

Thorndyke smiled dryly. "You might think differently after you have heard a capable counsel for the defence. But the position is this: We are dealing with a charge of murder. Now, in order to prove that a particular person is guilty of murder, it is necessary first to establish the *corpus delicti*, as the phrase goes – that is, to prove that a murder has been committed by someone. But the proof that a person has been murdered involves the antecedent proof that he is dead. If there is any doubt that the alleged deceased is dead, no murder charge can be sustained. But proof of death usually involves the production of the body

403

or of some identifiable part of it, or at least the evidence of some person who has seen it and can swear to its identity. There are exceptional cases, of course, and this might be accepted as one. But you can take it that the inability of the prosecution to produce the body or any part of it, or any witness who can testify to having seen it, or any direct evidence that the person alleged to have been murdered is actually dead, would make it extremely difficult to secure the conviction of the accused."

"Yes, I see that," said Philip. "But, after all, that is not our concern. If we give the authorities all the information that we possess, we shall have done our duty as citizens. As to the rest, we must leave the court to convict or acquit, according to its judgment."

"Not at all," Thorndyke dissented. "You are losing sight of our position in the case. There are two different issues, which are, however, inseparably connected. One is the fact of Purcell's death, the other is Varney's part in compassing it. Now it is the first issue that concerns us, or at least concerns me. If we could prove that Purcell is dead without bringing Varney into it at all, I should be willing to do so, for I strongly suspect that there were extenuating circumstances."

"So do I," said Rodney. "Purcell was a brute, whereas Varney has always seemed to be a perfectly decent, gentlemanly fellow."

"That is the impression that I have received," said Thorndyke, "and I feel no satisfaction in proceeding against Varney. My purpose all along has been, not to convict Varney, but to prove that Purcell is dead. And that is what we have to do now, for Margaret Purcell's sake. But we cannot leave Varney out of the case. For if Purcell is dead, he is dead because Varney killed him, and our only means of proving his death is to charge Varney with having murdered him. But if we charge Varney, we must secure a conviction. We cannot afford to fail. If the court is convinced that Purcell is dead, it will convict Varney, for the evidence of his death is evidence of his murder, but if the court acquits Varney, it can do so only on the ground that there is no conclusive evidence that Purcell is dead. Varney's acquittal would therefore leave Margaret Purcell still bound by law to a hypothetical husband, with the insecure chance of obtaining her release at some future time either by divorce or presumption of death. That would not be fair to her. She is a widow, and she is entitled to have her status acknowledged."

Rodney nodded gloomily. A consciousness of what he stood to gain by Varney's conviction lent an uncomfortable significance to Thorndyke's words.

"Yes," he agreed, half-reluctantly, "there is no denying the truth of what you say, but I wish it might have been the other way about. If Purcell had murdered Varney I could have raised the hue and cry with a

404

good deal more enthusiasm. I knew both the men well, and I like Varney, but detested Purcell. Still, one has to accept the facts."

"Exactly," said Thorndyke, who had realized and sympathized with Rodney's qualms. "The position is not of our creating, and whatever our private sentiments may be, the fact remains that a man who elects to take the life of another must accept the consequences. That is Varney's position so far as we can see, and if he is innocent it is for him to clear himself."

"Yes, of course," Rodney agreed, "but I wish the accusation had come through different channels."

"So do I," said Philip. "It is horrible to have to denounce a man with whom one has been on terms of intimate friendship. But apparently Thorndyke considers that we should not denounce him at present. That is what I don't quite understand. You seemed to imply, Thorndyke, that the case was not complete enough to warrant our taking action, and that some further evidence ought to be obtained in order to make sure of a conviction. But what further evidence is it possible to obtain?"

"My feeling," replied Thorndyke, "is that the case is at present, as your brother expressed it just now, somewhat theoretical, or, rather, hypothetical. The evidence is circumstantial from beginning to end. There is not a single item of direct evidence to furnish a starting-point. It would be insisted by the defence that Purcell's death is a matter of mere inference, and that you cannot convict a man of the murder of another who may conceivably be still alive. We ought, if possible, to put Purcell's death on the basis of demonstrable fact."

"But how is that possible?" demanded Philip.

"The conclusive method of proving the death of a person is, as I have said, to produce that person's body or some recognizable part of it."

"But Purcell's body is at the bottom of the sea."

"True. But we know its whereabouts. It is a small area, with the lighthouse as a landmark. If that area were systematically worked over with a trawl or dredge, or, better still, with a set of creepers attached to a good-sized spar, there should be a very fair chance of recovering the body, or at least the clothing and the weight."

Philip reflected for a few moments. "I think you are right," he said at length. "The body appears, from what you say, to be quite close to the Wolf Rock, and almost certainly on the east side. With a good compass and the lighthouse as a sailing mark, it would be possible to ply up and down and search every inch of the bottom in the neighbourhood of the Rock."

"There is only one difficulty," said Rodney. "Your worm-tube was composed entirely of fragments of the Rock. But how large an area of the sea bottom is covered with those fragments? We should have to ascertain that if we are to work over the whole of it."

"It would not be difficult to ascertain," replied Thorndyke. "If we take soundings with a hand-lead as we approach the Rock, the samples that come up on the arming of the lead will tell us when we are over a bottom covered with phonolite debris."

"Yes," Rodney agreed, "that will answer if the depth is within the range of a hand-lead. If it isn't we shall have to rig the tackle for a deep-sea lead. It will be rather a gruesome quest. Do I gather that you are prepared to come down with us and lend a hand? I hope you are."

"So do I!" exclaimed Philip. "We shall be quite at home with the navigation, but if – er – if anything comes up on the creepers, it will be a good deal more in your line than ours."

"I should certainly wish to come," said Thorndyke, "and, in fact, I think it rather desirable that I should, as Philip suggests. But I can't get away from town just at present, nor, I imagine, can you. We had better postpone the expedition for a week or so until the commencement of the spring vacation. That will give us time to make the necessary arrangements, to charter a suitable boat, and so forth. And, in any case, we shall have to pick our weather, having regard to the sort of sea that one may encounter in the neighbourhood of the Wolf."

"Yes," agreed Philip, "it will have to be a reasonably calm day when we make the attempt, so I suggest that we put it off until you and Jack are free, and meanwhile I will get on with the preliminary arrangements, the hiring of the boat and getting together the necessary gear."

While they had been talking the evening had closed in, and the workshop was now almost in darkness. It being too late for the brothers to carry out the business that had brought them to the wharf, even if they had been in a state of mind suitable to the checking of inventories, they postponed the survey to a later date, locked up the workshop, and in company with Thorndyke made their way homeward.

Chapter XVII
In Which There is a
Meeting and a Farewell

It was quite early on a bright morning at the beginning of April when Thorndyke and the two Rodneys took their way from their hotel towards the harbour of Penzance. Philip had been in the town for a day or two, completing the arrangements for the voyage of exploration, the other two had come down from London only on the preceding evening.

"I hope the skipper will be punctual," said Philip. "I told him to meet us on the pier at eight o'clock sharp. We want to get off as early as possible, for it is a longish run out to the Rock, and we may have to make a long day of it."

"We probably shall," said Rodney. "The Wolf Rock is a good departure for purposes of navigation, but when it comes to finding a spot of sea bottom only a foot or two in extent, our landmark isn't very exact. It will take us a good many hours to search the whole area."

"I wonder," said Thorndyke, "what took them out there. According to Varney's description and the evidence of the button, they must have had the Rock close aboard. But it was a good deal out of their way from Sennen to Penzance."

"It was," agreed Philip. "But you can't make a bee-line in a sailing craft. That's why I chartered a motor-boat for this job. Under canvas you can only keep as near to your course as the wind will let you. But Purcell was a deuce of a fellow for sea room. He always liked to keep a good offing. I remember that on that occasion he headed straight out to sea and got well outside the Longships before he turned south. I watched the yacht from the shore, and wondered how much longer he was going to hold on. It looked as if he were heading for America. Then, you remember, the fog came down, and they may have lost their bearings a bit, and the tides are pretty strong about here."

"Yes," said Thorndyke, "and as we may take it that the trouble, whatever it was, came to a head while they were enveloped in fog, it is likely that the yacht was left to take care of herself for a time, and may have drifted a good deal off her course. At any rate, it is clear that at one time she had the Rock right under her lee, and must have drifted past within a few feet."

"It would have been a quaint position," said Philip, "if she had bumped on to it and gone to the bottom. Then they would have kept one another company in Davy Jones's locker."

"It would have saved a lot of trouble if they had gone down together," his brother remarked. "But from what you have just said, Thorndyke, it seems that you have a more definite idea as to the position of the body than I thought. Where do you suppose it to be?"

"Judging from all the facts taken together," replied Thorndyke, "I should say that it is lying close to the base of the Rock on the east side. We have it from Varney that the yacht drifted down towards the Rock during the fog, and I gathered that she drifted past close to the east side. And we also learned from him that the jib had then come down, which was, in fact, the cause of her being adrift. But the bloodstains on the sail prove that the tragedy occurred either before the halyard broke or while the sail was down – almost certainly the latter. And we may take it that it occurred during the fog, that the fog created the opportunity, for we must remember that they were close to the lighthouse, and therefore, apart from the fog, easily within sight of it. For the same reason we may assume that the body was put overboard before the fog lifted. All these circumstances point to the body being close to the Rock, and the worm-tube emphatically confirms that inference."

"Then," said Philip, "in that case there is no great point in taking soundings."

"Not in the first instance," Thorndyke agreed. "But if we get no result close to the Rock, we may have to sample the bottom to see how far from the base the conditions indicated by the worm-tube extend."

They walked on in silence for some time.

Presently Rodney remarked, "This reminds me of the last time I came down to a rendezvous on Penzance pier, when I expected to find Varney waiting for me and he wasn't there. I wonder where he was, by the way."

"He had probably gone to post a letter to Mr. Penfield at some remote pillar-box, where collections were not too frequent," said Thorndyke.

Rodney looked at him quickly, once more astonished at his intimate knowledge of the details of the case. He was about to remark on it when Thorndyke asked, "Have you seen much of Varney lately?"

"I haven't seen him at all," replied Rodney. "Have you, Phil?"

"No," replied Philip, "not for quite a long time. Which is rather odd, for he used to look in at Maggie's flat pretty often to have tea and show her his latest work. But he hasn't been there for weeks, I know, because I was speaking to her about him only a day or two ago. She seemed to have an idea that he might have gone away on a sketching tour, though I don't think she had anything to go on."

"He can't have smelt a rat and cleared out," mused Rodney. "I don't see how he could, though I shouldn't be altogether sorry if he had. It will be a horrid business when we have to charge him and give evidence against him But it isn't possible that he can have seen or heard anything."

This was also Thorndyke's opinion, but he was deeply interested in the report of Varney's disappearance. Nor was he entirely without a clue to it. His observations of Margaret and Varney suggested a possible explanation, which he did not think it necessary to refer to. And, in fact, the conversation was here interrupted by their arrival at the pier, where an elderly fisherman, who had been watching their approach, came forward and saluted them.

"Here you are then, skipper," said Philip, "Punctual to the minute. We've got a fine day for our trip, haven't we?"

"Aye, sir," replied the skipper. "'Tis a wonderful calm day for the time of year. And glad I am to see it, if we are to work close into the Wolf, for it's a lumpy bit of water at the best of times around the Rock."

"Is everything ready?" asked Philip.

"Aye, sir. We are all ready to cast off this moment." And in confirmation he preceded the party to the head of the ladder and indicated the craft lying alongside the pier beneath it – a small converted Penzance lugger with a large open cock pit, in the fore part of which was the engine.

The four men descended the ladder, and while the skipper and the second fisherman, who constituted the crew, were preparing to cast off the shore ropes, Philip took a last look round to see that all was in order. Then the crew, who was named Joe Tregenna, pushed off and started the engine, the skipper took the tiller, and the boat got under way.

"You see," said Philip, as the boat headed out to sea, "we have got good strong tackle for the creeping operations."

He pointed over the boat's side to a long stout spar which was slung outside the bulwarks. It was secured by a chain bridle to a trawl-rope, and to it were attached a number of creepers – lengths of chain fitted with rows of hooks – which hung down into the water and trailed alongside. The equipment also included a spirit-compass, fitted with sight-vanes, a sextant, a hand-lead, which lay on the cockpit floor, with its line neatly coiled round it, and a deep-sea lead, stowed away forward with its long line and the block for lowering and hoisting it.

The occupants of the cockpit were strangely silent. It was a beautiful spring day, bright and sunny, with a warm blue sky overhead and a tranquil sea, heaving quietly to the long swell from the Atlantic, showing

409

a sunlit sparkle on the surface and clear sapphire in the depths. "Nature painted all things gay," excepting the three men who sat on the side benches of the cockpit, whose countenances were expressive of the deepest gravity and even, in the case of the two Rodneys, of profound gloom.

"I shall be glad when this business is over," said Philip. "I feel as nervous as a cat."

"So do I," his brother agreed. "It is a gruesome affair. I find myself almost hoping that nothing will come of it. And yet that would only leave us worse off than ever."

"We mustn't be prepared to accept failure," said Thorndyke. "The thing is there, and we have got to find it, if not to-day, then to-morrow or some other day."

The two brothers looked at Thorndyke, a little daunted by his resolute attitude. "Yes, of course you are right," the elder admitted, "and it is only cowardice that makes me shrink from what we have to do. But when I think of what may come up, hanging from those creepers, I – Bah! It is too horrible to think of! But I suppose it doesn't make that sort of impression on you? You don't find anything repulsive in the quest that we are engaged in?"

"No," Thorndyke admitted. "My attention is occupied by the scientific and legal interest of the search. But I can fully sympathize with your feelings on the matter. To you Purcell is a real person, whom you have known and talked with, to me he is a mere abstraction connected with a very curious and interesting case. The really unpleasant part of that case. To me – will come when we have completed our evidence, if we are so fortunate. I mean when we have to set the criminal law in motion."

"Yes," said Philip. "That will be perfectly beastly."

Once more silence fell upon the boat, broken only by the throb of the engine and the murmur of the water as it was cloven by the boat's stern. And meanwhile the distant coast slipped past until they were abreast of the Land's End, and far away to the south-west the solitary lighthouse rose on the verge of the horizon. Soon afterwards they began to overtake the scattered members of a fleet of luggers, some with lowered mainsails and hand-lines down, others with their black sails set, heading for some distant fishing-ground. Through the midst of them the boat was threading her way, when her occupants suddenly became aware that one of the smaller luggers was steering so as to close in. Observing this, the skipper was putting over the helm to avoid her, when a seafaring voice from the little craft was heard to hail.

"Motor-boat ahoy! Gentleman aboard wants to speak to you!"

The two Rodneys looked at one another in surprise and then at the approaching lugger.

"Who the deuce can it be?" exclaimed Rodney. "But perhaps it is a stranger who wants a passage. If it is we shall have to refuse. We can't take anyone on board."

The boat slowed down, for at a word from the skipper Joe Tregenna had reversed the propeller. The lugger closed in rapidly, watched anxiously by the two Rodneys and Thorndyke. Suddenly a man appeared standing on the bulwark rail and holding on by the mast stay, while with his free hand he held a binocular to his eyes. Nearer and nearer the lugger approached, and still the two Rodneys gazed with growing anxiety at the figure on the bulwark. At length the man removed the glasses from his eyes and waved them above his head, and as his face became visible both brothers uttered a cry of amazement.

"God!" exclaimed Philip. "It's Varney! Sheer off, skipper! Don't let him come along side."

But it was too late. The boat had lost way and failed to answer her helm. The lugger sheered in, sweeping abreast within a foot, and as she crept past Varney sprang lightly from her gunwale and dropped on the side bench beside Jack Rodney.

"Well!" he exclaimed, "this is a queer meeting. I couldn't believe my eyes when I first spotted you through the glasses. Motor-boat, too! Rather a come down, isn't it, for seasoned yachtsmen?"

He looked curiously at his hosts, evidently a little perplexed by their silence and their unresponsive bearing. The Rodneys were, in fact, stricken dumb with dismay, and even Thorndyke was for the moment disconcerted. The lugger which had brought Varney had already gone about and was standing out to sea, leaving to them the alternative of accepting this most unwelcome passenger or of pursuing the lugger and insisting on his returning on board of her. But the Rodneys were too paralyzed to do anything but gaze at Varney in silent consternation, and Thorndyke did not feel that his position on the boat entitled him to take any action. Indeed, no action seemed to be practicable.

"This is an odd show," said Varney, looking inquisitively about the boat. "What is the lay? You can't be going out to fish in this craft. And you seem to be setting a course for the Scillies. What is it? Dredging? I see you've got a trawl-rope."

As the Rodneys were still almost stupefied by the horror of the situation, Thorndyke took upon himself to reply.

"The occasion of this little voyage was a rather remarkable marine worm that was sent to Professor D'Arcy, and which came from the

411

locality to which we are bound. We are going to explore the bottom there."

Varney nodded. "You seem mighty keen on marine worms. I remember when I met you down here before you were in search of them, and so was Phil, though I don't fancy he got many. He had the bottles labelled ready for them, and that was about as far as he went. Do you remember that button you made, Phil, from the cork of one?"

"Yes," Philip replied huskily, "I remember."

During this conversation Thorndyke had been observing Varney with close attention, and he noted a very appreciable change in his appearance. He looked aged and worn, and there was in his expression a weariness and dejection that seemed to confirm certain opinions that Thorndyke had formed as to the reasons for his sudden disappearance from surroundings which had certainly not been without their attractions to him. And, not for the first time, a feeling of compunction and of some distaste for this quest contended with the professional interest and the sense of duty that had been the impelling force behind the long, patient investigation.

Philip's curt reply was followed by a rather long, uncomfortable silence. Varney, quick and sensitive by nature, perceived that there was something amiss, that in some way his presence was a source of embarrassment. He sat on the side bench by Jack Rodney, gazing with a far-away look over the sea towards the Longships, wishing that he had stayed on board the lugger or that there were some means of escaping from this glum and silent company. And as he meditated he brought forth from his pocket his tobacco-pouch and cigarette-book, and half-unconsciously, with a dexterity born of long practice, rolled a cigarette, all unaware that three pairs of eyes were riveted on his strangely efficient maimed finger, that three minds were conjuring up the vivid picture of a blue handprint on a white sail.

When he had lit the cigarette, Varney once more looked about the boat, and again his eye lighted on the big coil of trawl-rope, with its end passed out through a fair-lead. He rose, and, crossing the cockpit, looked over the side.

"Why," he exclaimed, "you've got a set of creepers! I thought you were going dredging. You won't pick up much with creepers, will you?"

"They will pick up anything with weeds attached to it," said Thorndyke.

Varney went back to his seat with a thoughtful, somewhat puzzled expression. He smoked in silence for a minute or two, and then suddenly asked, "Where is the place that you are going to explore for these worms?"

412

"Professor D'Arcy's specimen," replied Thorndyke, "came from the neighbourhood of the Wolf Rock. That is where we are going to work."

Varney made no comment on this answer. He looked long and steadily at Thorndyke, then he turned away his head, and once more gazed out to sea. Evidently he was thinking hard, and his companions, who watched him furtively, could have little doubt as to the trend of his thoughts. Gradually, as the nature of the exploration dawned on him, his manner changed more and more. A horrible pallor overspread his face, and a terrible restlessness took possession of him. He smoked furiously cigarette after cigarette. He brought various articles out of his pockets, fidgeted with them awhile, and put them back. He picked up the hand-lead, looking at its arming, ran the line through his fingers, and made fancy knots on the bight. And ever and anon his glance strayed to the tall lighthouse, standing out of the sea with its red-and-white ringed tower, and drawing inexorably nearer and nearer.

So the voyage went on until the boat was within half-a-mile of the Rock, when Philip, having caught a glance and a nod from Thorndyke, gave the order to stop the engine and lower the creepers. The spar was cast loose and dropped into the water with a heavy splash, the trawl-rope ran out through the fair-lead, and meanwhile Jack Rodney took a pair of cross-bearings on the lighthouse and a point of the distant land. Then the engine was restarted, the boat moved forward at half-speed, and the search began.

It was an intensely disagreeable experience for all excepting the puzzled but discreet skipper and the unconscious Joe. Varney – pale, haggard, and wild in aspect – fidgeted about the boat, now silent and moody, now making miserable efforts to appear interested or unconcerned, picking up and handling loose objects or portions of the gear, but constantly returning to the hand-lead, counting up the "marks" on the line, or making and pulling out various knots with his restless but curiously skilful fingers. And as his mood changed, Thorndyke watched him furtively, as if to judge by his manner how near they were to the object of the search.

It was a long and wearisome quest. Slowly the boat plied up and down on the eastern side of the Rock, gradually approaching it nearer and nearer at each return. From time to time the creepers caught on the rocky bottom, and had to be eased off, from time to time the dripping trawl-rope was hauled in and the creepers brought to the surface, offering to the anxious eyes that peered over the side nothing on the hooks but, perchance, a wisp of Zostera or a clinging spider-crab.

Calm as the day was and quiet as was the ocean, stirred only by the slumberous echoes of the great Atlantic swell, the sea was breaking heavily over the Rock, and as the boat closed in nearer and nearer, the water around boiled and eddied in an unpleasant and even dangerous manner. The lighthouse keepers, who had for some time past been watching from the gallery the movements of the boat, now began to make warning signs, and one of them bellowed through a megaphone to the searchers to keep farther away.

"What do you say?" Rodney asked in a low voice. "We can't go any nearer? We shall be swamped or stove in? Shall we try another side?"

"Better try one more cast this side," said Thorndyke, and he spoke so definitely that all the others, including Varney, looked at him curiously. But no one answered, and as the skipper made no demur the creepers were dropped for a fresh cast still nearer the Rock. The boat was then to the north of the lighthouse, and the course set was to the south, so as to pass the Rock again on the east side. As they approached, the man with the megaphone bawled out fresh warnings and continued to roar at them and flourish his arm until they were abreast of the Rock in a wild tumble of confused waves. At this moment, Philip, who had his hand on the trawl-rope between the bollard and the fair-lead, reported that he had felt a pull, but that it seemed as if the creepers had broken away. As soon, therefore, as the boat was clear of the backwash and in comparatively smooth water, the order was passed to haul in the trawl-rope and examine the creepers.

The two Rodneys looked over the side eagerly but fearfully, for both had noticed something new – a definite expectancy – in Thorndyke's manner. Varney, too, who had hitherto taken but little notice of the creepers, now knelt on the side bench, gazing earnestly into the clear water whence the trawl-rope was rising. And still he toyed with the hand-lead, and absently made clove-hitches on the line and slipped them over his arm.

At length the spar came into view, and below it, on one of the creepers, a yellowish object, dimly visible through the wavering water.

"There's somethin' on this time," said the skipper, craning over the side and steadying himself by the tiller, which he still held. All eyes were riveted on the half-seen yellowish shape, moving up and down to the rise and fall of the boat. Apart from the others, Varney knelt on the bench, not fidgeting now, but still, rigid, pale as wax, staring with dreadful fascination at the slowly rising object. Suddenly the skipper uttered an exclamation.

"Why, 'tis a sou 'wester! And all laced about wi' spun-y'n! Surely 'tis – Steady, sir, you'll be overboard! My God!"

The others looked round quickly, and even as they looked Varney fell, with a heavy splash, into the water alongside. There was a

414

tumultuous rush to the place whence he had fallen, and arms were thrust into the water in vain efforts to grasp the sinking figure. Rodney darted forward for the boat-hook, but by the time he was back with it the doomed man was far out of reach, yet for a long time, as it seemed, the horror-stricken onlookers could see him through the clear, blue-green water, sinking, sinking, growing paler, more shadowy, more shapeless, but always steadily following the lead sinker, until at last he faded from their sight into the darkness of the ocean.

Not until some time after he had vanished did they haul on board the creeper with its dreadful burden. Indeed, that burden, in its entirety, was never hauled on board. As it reached the surface, Tregenna stopped hauling and held the rope steady, and for a sensible time all eyes were fixed upon a skull, with a great jagged hole above the brows, that looked up at them beneath the peak of the sou'wester, through the web of spun-yarn, like the face of some phantom warrior looking out through the bars of his helmet. Then as Philip, reaching out an unsteady hand, unhooked the sou'wester from the creeper, the encircling coils of spun-yarn slipped, and the skull dropped into the water. Still the fascinated eyes watched it as it sank, turning slowly over and over, and seeming to cast back glances of horrid valediction, watched it grow green and pallid and small, until it vanished into the darkness, even as Varney had vanished.

When it was quite invisible, Philip turned, and, flinging the hat down on the floor of the cockpit, sank on the bench with a groan. Thorndyke picked up the hat and unwound the spun-yarn.

"Do you identify it?" he asked, and then, as he turned it over, he added, "But I see it identifies itself."

He held it towards Rodney, who was able to read in embroidered, lettering on the silk lining "Dan Purcell."

Rodney nodded. "Yes," he said, "but, of course, there was no doubt. Is it necessary for us to do anything more?" He indicated the creepers with a gesture of weariness and disgust.

"No," replied Thorndyke. "We have seen the body and can swear to its identity, and I can certify as to the cause of death. We can produce this hat, with a bullet-hole, as I perceive, in the back, corresponding to the injury that we observed in the skull. I can also certify as to the death of Varney, and can furnish a sworn declaration of the facts that are within my knowledge. That may possibly be accepted by the authorities, having regard to the circumstances, as rendering any further inquiry unnecessary. But that is no concern of ours. We have established the fact that Daniel Purcell is dead, and our task is accomplished.

415

"Yes," said Rodney, "our quest has been successful beyond my expectations. But it has been an awful experience. I can't get the thought of poor Varney out of my mind."

"Nor I," said Philip. "And yet it was the best that could have happened. And there is a certain congruity in it, too. They are down there together. They had been companions – in a way, friends – the best part of their lives, and in death they are not divided."

The End

1926 Hodder & Stoughton Cover

Chapter I
The Pool in the Wood

There are certain days in our lives which, as we recall them, seem to detach themselves from the general sequence as forming the starting-point of a new epoch. Doubtless, if we examined them critically, we should find them to be but links in a connected chain. But in a retrospective glance their continuity with the past is unperceived, and we see them in relation to the events which followed them rather than to those which went before.

Such a day is that on which I look back through a vista of some twenty years, for on that day I was, suddenly and without warning, plunged into the very heart of a drama so strange and incredible that in the recital of its events I am conscious of a certain diffidence and hesitation.

The picture that rises before me as I write is very clear and vivid. I see myself, a youngster of twenty-five, the owner of a brand-new medical diploma, wending my way gaily down Wood Lane, Highgate, at about eight o'clock on a sunny morning in early autumn. I was taking a day's holiday, the last I was likely to enjoy for some time, for on the morrow I was to enter on the duties of my first professional appointment. I had nothing in view to-day but sheer, delightful idleness. It is true that a sketch-book in one pocket and a box of collecting-tubes in another suggested a bare hint of purpose in the expedition, but primarily it was a holiday, a pleasure jaunt, to which art and science were no more than possible sources of contributory satisfaction.

At the lower end of the Lane was the entrance to Churchyard Bottom Wood, then open and unguarded save by a few hurdles. (It has since been enclosed and renamed "Queen's Wood".) I entered and took my way along the broad, rough path, pleasantly conscious of the deep silence and seeming remoteness of this surviving remnant of the primeval forest of Britain, and letting my thoughts stray to the great plague-pit in the haunted bottom that gave the wood its name. The foliage of the oaks was still unchanged, despite the waning of the year. The low-slanting sunlight spangled it with gold and made rosy patterns on the path, where lay a few prematurely fallen leaves, but in the hollows among the undergrowth traces of the night-mists lingered, shrouding tree-bole, bush, and fern in a mystery of gauzy blue.

421

A turn of the path brought me suddenly within a few paces of a girl who was stooping at the entrance to a side track and seemed to be peering into the undergrowth as if looking for something. As I appeared, she stood up and looked round at me with a startled, apprehensive manner that caused me to look away and pass as if I had not seen her. But the single glance had shown me that she was a strikingly handsome girl – indeed, I should have used the word "beautiful" – that she seemed to be about my own age, and that she was evidently a lady.

The apparition, pleasant as it was, set me speculating as I strode forward. It was early for a girl like this to be afoot in the woods, and alone, too. Not so very safe, either, as she had seemed to realize, judging by the start that my approach seemed to have given her. And what could it be that she was looking for? Had she lost something at some previous time and come to search for it before anyone was about? It might be so. Certainly she was not a poacher, for there was nothing to poach, and she hardly had the manner or appearance of a naturalist.

A little farther on I struck into a side-path which led, as I knew, in the direction of a small pond. That pond I had had in my mind when I put the box of collecting-tubes in my pocket, and I now made my way to it as directly as the winding track would let me. But still, it was not the pond or its inmates that occupied my thoughts, but the mysterious maiden whom I had left peering into the undergrowth. Perhaps if she had been less attractive I might have given her less consideration. But I was twenty-five, and if a man at twenty-five has not a keen and appreciative eye for a pretty girl, there must be something radically wrong with his mental make-up.

In the midst of my reflections, I came out into a largish opening in the wood, at the centre of which, in a slight hollow, was the pond – a small oval piece of water, fed by the trickle of a tiny stream, the continuation of which carried away the overflow towards the invisible valley. Approaching the margin, I brought out my box of tubes and, uncorking one, stooped and took a trial dip. When I held the glass tube against the light and examined its contents through my pocket-lens, I found that I was in luck. The "catch" included a green hydra, clinging to a rootlet of duckweed, several active water-fleas, a scarlet water-mite, and a beautiful sessile rotifer. Evidently this pond was a rich hunting-ground.

Delighted with my success, I corked the tube, put it away, and brought out another, with which I took a fresh dip. This was less successful, but the naturalist's ardour and the collector's cupidity being thoroughly aroused, I persevered, gradually enriching my collection and working my way slowly round the margin of the pond, forgetful of everything – even of the mysterious maiden – but the objects of my search. Indeed, so engrossed was I with my pursuit of the minute denizens of this watery world that I failed to observe a much larger object which must have been in view most of the time. Actually, I did not see it until I was right over it. Then, as I was stooping to clear away the duckweed for a fresh dip, I found myself confronted by a human face, just below the surface and half-concealed by the pondweed.

It was a truly appalling experience. Utterly unprepared for this awful apparition, I was so overcome by astonishment and horror that I remained stooping, with motion arrested, as if petrified, staring at the thing in silence and hardly breathing. The face was that of a man of about fifty or a little more, a handsome, refined, rather intellectual face with a moustache and Vandyke beard, and surmounted by a thickish growth of iron-grey hair. Of the rest of the body little was to be seen, for the duckweed and water-crowfoot had drifted over it, and I had no inclination to disturb them. Recovering somewhat from the shock of this sudden and fearful encounter, I stood up and rapidly considered what I had better do. It was clearly not for me to make any examination or meddle with the corpse in any way. Indeed, when I considered the early hour and the remoteness of this solitary place, it seemed prudent to avoid the possibility of being seen there by any chance stranger. Thus reflecting, with my eyes still riveted on the pallid, impassive face, so strangely sleeping below the glassy surface and conveying to me somehow a dim sense of familiarity, I pocketed my tubes and, turning back, stole away along the woodland track, treading lightly, almost stealthily, as one escaping from the scene of a crime.

Very different was my mood, as I retraced my steps, from that in which I had come. Gone was all my gaiety and holiday spirit. The dread meeting had brought me into an atmosphere of tragedy, perchance even of something more than tragedy. With death I was familiar enough – death as it comes to men, prefaced by sickness or even by injury. But the dead man who lay in that still and silent pool in the heart of the wood had come there by none of the ordinary chances of normal life. It seemed barely possible that he could have fallen in by mere misadventure, for the pond was too shallow and its bottom shelved too gently for accidental drowning to be conceivable. Nor was the strange, sequestered spot without significance. It was just such a spot as might well be chosen by one who sought to end his life – or another's.

I had nearly reached the main path when an abrupt turn of the narrow track brought me once more face to face with the girl whose existence I had till now forgotten. She was still peering into the dense undergrowth as if searching for something, and again, on my sudden appearance, she turned a startled face towards me. But this time I did not look away. Something in her face struck me with a nameless fear. It was not only that she was pale and haggard, that her expression betokened anxiety and even terror. As I looked at her, I understood in a flash the dim sense of familiarity of which I had been conscious in the pallid face beneath the water. It was her face that it had recalled.

With my heart in my mouth, I halted, and, taking off my cap, addressed her.

"Pray pardon me, you seem to be searching for something. Can I help you in any way or give you any information?"

She looked at me a little shyly and, as I thought, with slight distrust, but she answered civilly enough though rather stiffly, "Thank you, but I am afraid you can't help me. I am not in need of any assistance."

This, under ordinary circumstances, would have brought the interview to an abrupt end. But the circumstances were not ordinary, and, as she made as if to pass me, I ventured to persist.

"Please," I urged, "don't think me impertinent, but would you mind telling me what you are looking for? I have a reason for asking, and it isn't curiosity."

She reflected for a few moments before replying and I feared that she was about to administer another snub. Then, without looking at me, she replied, "I am looking for my father." (And at these words my heart sank.) "He did not come home last night. He left Hornsey to come home and he would ordinarily have come by the path through the wood. He always came that way from Hornsey. So I am looking through the wood in case he missed his way, or was taken ill, or – "

Here the poor girl suddenly broke off, and, letting her dignity go, burst into tears. I huskily murmured a few indistinct words of condolence, but, in truth, I was little less affected than she was. It was a terrible position, but there was no escape from it. The corpse that I had just seen was almost certainly her father's corpse. At any rate, the question whether it was or was not had to be settled now, and settled by me – and her. That was quite clear, but yet I could not screw my courage up to the point of telling her. While I was hesitating, however, she forced the position by a direct question.

"You said just now that you had a reason for asking what I was searching for. Would it be – ?" She paused and looked at me inquiringly as she wiped her eyes.

I made a last, frantic search for some means of breaking the horrid news to her. Of course there was none. Eventually I stammered, "The reason I asked was – er – the fact is that I have just seen the body of a man lying – "

"Where?" she demanded. "Show me the place!"

Without replying, I turned and began quickly to retrace my steps along the narrow track. A few minutes brought me to the opening in which the pond was situated, and I was just beginning to skirt the margin, closely followed by my companion, when I heard her utter a low, gasping cry. The next moment she had passed me and was running along the bank towards a spot where I could now see the toe of a boot just showing through the duckweed. I stopped short and watched her with my heart in my throat. Straight to the fatal spot she ran, and for a moment stood on the brink, stooping over the weedy surface. Then, with a terrible, wailing cry she stepped into the water.

Instantly, I ran forward and waded into the pond to her side. Already she had her arms round the dead man's neck and was raising the face above the surface. I saw that she meant to bring the body ashore, and, useless as it was, it seemed a natural thing to do. Silently I passed my arms under the corpse and lifted it, and as she supported the head, we bore it through the shallows and up the bank, where I laid it down gently in the high grass.

Not a word had been spoken, nor was there any question that need be asked. The pitiful tale told itself only too plainly. As I stood looking with swimming eyes at the tragic group, a whole history seemed to unfold itself – a history of love and companionship, of a happy, peaceful past made sunny by mutual affection, shattered in an instant by the hideous present, with its portent of a sad and lonely future. She had sat down on the grass and taken the dead head on her lap, tenderly wiping the face with her handkerchief, smoothing the grizzled hair and crooning or moaning words of endearment into the insensible ears. She had forgotten my presence – indeed, she was oblivious of everything but the still form that bore the outward semblance other father.

Some minutes passed thus. I stood a little apart, cap in hand, more moved than I had ever been in my life, and, naturally enough, unwilling to break in upon a grief so overwhelming and, as it seemed to me, so sacred. But presently it began to be borne in on me that something had to be done. The body would have to be removed from this place, and the proper authorities ought to be notified. Still, it was some time before I could gather courage to intrude on her sorrow, to profane her grief with the sordid realities of everyday life. At last I braced myself up for the effort and addressed her.

"Your father," I said gently – I could not refer to him as "the body" – "will have to be taken away from here, and the proper persons will have to be informed of what has happened. Shall I go alone, or will you come with me? I don't like to leave you here."

425

She looked up at me and, to my relief, answered me with quiet composure. "I can't leave him here all alone. I must stay with him until he is taken away. Do you mind telling whoever ought to be told – " Like me, she instinctively avoided the word *police*. " – and making what arrangements are necessary?"

There was nothing more to be said, and loath as I was to leave her alone with the dead, my heart assented to her decision. In her place, I should have had the same feeling. Accordingly, with a promise to return as quickly as I could, I stole away along the woodland track. When I turned to take a last glance at her before plunging into the wood, she was once more leaning over the head that lay in her lap, looking with fond grief into the impassive face and stroking the dank hair.

My intention had been to go straight to the police-station, when I had ascertained its whereabouts, and make my report to the officer in charge. But a fortunate chance rendered this proceeding unnecessary, for, at the moment when I emerged from the top of Wood Lane, I saw a police officer, mounted on a bicycle – a road patrol, as I assumed him to be – approaching along the Archway Road. I hailed him to stop, and as he dismounted and stepped on to the footway, I gave him a brief account of the finding of the body and my meeting with the daughter of the dead man. He listened with calm, businesslike interest, and, when I had finished, said, "We had better get the body removed as quickly as possible. I will run along to the station and get the wheeled stretcher. There is no need for you to come. If you will go back and wait for us at the entrance to the wood, that will save time. We shall be there within a quarter-of-an-hour."

I agreed gladly to this arrangement, and when I had seen him mount his machine and shoot away along the road, I turned back down the Lane and re-entered the wood. Before taking up my post, I walked quickly down the path and along the track to the opening by the pond. My new friend was sitting just as I had left her, but she looked up as I emerged from the track and advanced towards her. I told her briefly what had happened, and was about to retire when she asked, "Will they take him to our house?"

"I am afraid not," I replied. "There will have to be an inquiry by the coroner, and until that is finished, his body will have to remain in the mortuary."

"I was afraid it might be so," she said with quiet resignation, and as she spoke she looked down with infinite sadness at the waxen face in her lap. A good deal relieved by her reasonable acceptance of the painful necessities, I turned back and made my way to the rendezvous at the entrance to the wood.

As I paced to-and-fro on the shady path, keeping a lookout up the Lane, my mind was busy with the tragedy to which I had become a party. It was a grievous affair. The passionate grief which I had witnessed spoke of no common affection. On one life at least this disaster had inflicted irreparable loss, and there were probably others on whom the blow had yet to fall. But it was not only a grievous affair, it was highly mysterious. The dead man had apparently been returning home at night in a customary manner and by a familiar way. That he could have strayed by chance from the open, well-worn path into the recesses of the wood was inconceivable, while the hour and the circumstances made it almost as incredible that he should have been wandering in the wood by choice. And again, the water in which he had been lying was quite shallow – so shallow as to rule out accidental drowning as an impossibility.

What could the explanation be? There seemed to be but three possibilities, and two of them could hardly be entertained. The idea of intoxication I rejected at once. The girl was evidently a lady, and her father was presumably a gentleman who would not be likely to be wandering abroad drunk. Nor could a man who was sober enough to have reached the pond have been so helpless as to be drowned in its shallow waters. To suppose that he might have fallen into the water in a fit was to leave unexplained the circumstance of his being in that remote place at such an hour. The only possibility that remained was that of suicide, and I could not but admit that some of the appearances seemed to support that view. The solitary place – more solitary still at night – was precisely such as an intending suicide might be expected to seek, the shallow water presented no inconsistency, and when I recalled how I had found his daughter searching the wood with evident foreboding of evil, I could not escape the feeling that the dreadful possibility had not been entirely unforeseen.

My meditations had reached this point when, as I turned once more towards the entrance and looked up the Lane, I saw two constables approaching, trundling a wheeled stretcher, while a third man, apparently an inspector, walked by its side. As the little procession reached the entrance and I turned back to show the way, the latter joined me and began at once to interrogate me. I gave him my name, address, and occupation, and followed this with a rapid sketch of the facts as known to me, which he jotted down in a large notebook, and he then said, "As you are a doctor, you can probably tell me how long the man had been dead when you first saw him."

"By the appearance and the rigidity," I replied, "I should say about nine or ten hours, which agrees pretty well with the account his daughter gave of his movements."

427

The inspector nodded. "The man and the young lady," said he, "are strangers to you, I understand. I suppose you haven't picked up anything that would throw any light on the affair?"

"No," I answered, "I know nothing but what I have told you."

"Well," he remarked, "it's a queer business. It is a queer place for a man to be in at night, and he must have gone there of his own accord. But there, it is no use guessing. It will all be thrashed out at the inquest."

As he reached this discreet conclusion, we came out into the opening and I heard him murmur very feelingly, "Dear, dear! Poor thing!" The girl seemed hardly to have changed her position since I had last seen her, but she now tenderly laid the dead head on the grass and rose as we approached, and I saw with great concern that her skirts were soaked almost from the waist downwards.

The officer took off his cap and as he drew near looked down gravely but with an inquisitive eye at the dead man. Then he turned to the girl and said in a singularly gentle and deferential manner, "This is a very terrible thing, miss. A dreadful thing. I assure you that I am more sorry for you than I can tell, and I hope you will forgive me for having to intrude on your sorrow by asking questions. I won't trouble you more than I can help."

"Thank you," she replied quietly. "Of course I realize your position. What do you want me to tell you?"

"I understand," replied the inspector, "that this poor gentleman was your father. Would you mind telling me who he was and where he lived and giving me your own name and address?"

"My father's name," she answered, "was Julius D'Arblay. His private address was Ivy Cottage, North Grove, Highgate. His studio and workshop, where he carried on the profession of a modeller, is in Abbey Road, Hornsey. My name is Marion D'Arblay and I lived with my father. He was a widower and I was his only child."

As she concluded, with a slight break in her voice, the inspector shook his head and again murmured, "Dear, dear!" as he rapidly entered her answers in his notebook. Then, in a deeply apologetic tone, he asked, "Would you mind telling what you know as to how this happened?"

"I know very little," she replied. "As he did not come home last night, I went to the studio quite early this morning to see if he was there. He sometimes stayed there all night when he was working very late. The woman who lives in the adjoining house and looks after the studio told me that he had been working late last night, but that he left to come home soon after ten. He always used to come through the wood, because it was the shortest way and the most pleasant. So when I learned that he had started to come home, I came to the wood to see if I could find any traces

428

of him. Then I met this gentleman and he told me that he had seen a dead man in the wood and – " Here she suddenly broke down and, sobbing passionately, flung out her hand towards the corpse.

The inspector shut his notebook and, murmuring some indistinct words of sympathy, nodded to the constables, who had drawn up the stretcher a few paces away and lifted off the cover. On this silent instruction, they approached the body and, with the inspector's assistance and mine, lifted it on to the stretcher without removing the latter from its carriage. As they picked up the cover, the inspector turned to Miss D'Arblay and said gently but finally, "You had better not come with us. We must take him to the mortuary, but you will see him again after the inquest, when he will be brought to your house if you wish it."

She made no objection, but as the constables approached with the cover, she stooped over the stretcher and kissed the dead man on the forehead.

Then she turned away, the cover was placed in position, the inspector and the constables saluted reverently, and the stretcher was wheeled away along the narrow track.

For some time after it had gone, we stood in silence at the margin of the pond with our eyes fixed on the place where it had disappeared. I considered in no little embarrassment what was to be done next. It was most desirable that Miss D'Arblay should be got home as soon as possible, and I did not at all like the idea of her going alone, for her appearance, with her drenched skirts and her dazed and rather wild expression, was such as to attract unpleasant attention. But I was a total stranger to her and I felt a little shy of pressing my company on her. However, it seemed a plain duty, and, as I saw her shiver slightly, I said, "You had better go home now and change your clothes. They are very wet. And you have some distance to go."

She looked down at her soaked dress and then she looked at me.

"You are rather wet, too," she said. "I am afraid I have given you a great deal of trouble."

"It is little enough that I have been able to do," I replied. "But you must really go home now, and if you will let me walk with you and see you safely to your house, I shall be much more easy in my mind."

"Thank you," she replied. "It is kind of you to offer to see me home, and I am glad not to have to go alone."

With this, we walked together to the edge of the opening and proceeded in single file along the track to the main path, and so out into Wood Lane, at the top of which we crossed the Archway Road into Southwood Lane. We walked mostly in silence, for I was unwilling to disturb her meditations with attempts at conversation, which could only have seemed banal or impertinent. For her part, she appeared to be absorbed in reflections the nature of which I could easily guess, and her grief was too fresh for any thought of distraction. But I found myself speculating with profound discomfort on what might be awaiting her at home. It is true that her own desolate state as an orphan without brothers or sisters had its compensation in that there was no wife to whom the dreadful tidings had to be imparted, nor any fellow-orphans to have their bereavement broken to them. But there must be someone who cared, or if there were not, what a terrible loneliness would reign in that house!

"I hope," I said as we approached our destination, "that there is someone at home to share your grief and comfort you a little."

"There is," she replied. "I was thinking of her and how grievous it will be to have to tell her – an old servant and a dear friend. She was my mother's nurse when the one was a child and the other but a young girl. She came to our house when my mother married and has managed our home ever since. This will be a terrible shock to her, for she loved my father dearly – everyone loved him who knew him. And she has been like a mother to me since my own mother died. I don't know how I shall break it to her."

Her voice trembled as she concluded and I was deeply troubled to think of the painful homecoming that loomed before her, but still it was a comfort to know that her sorrow would be softened by sympathy and loving companionship, not heightened by the empty desolation that I had feared.

A few minutes more brought us to the little square – which, by the way, was triangular – and to a pleasant little old-fashioned house, on the gate of which was painted the name, "Ivy Cottage". In the bay window on the ground-floor I observed a formidable-looking elderly woman who was watching our approach with evident curiosity, which, as we drew nearer and the state of our clothing became visible, gave place to anxiety and alarm. Then she disappeared suddenly, to reappear a few moments later at the open door, where she stood viewing us both with consternation and me in particular with profound disfavour.

At the gate Miss D'Arblay halted and held out her hand. "Good-bye," she said. "I must thank you some other time for all your kindness." And with this she turned abruptly and, opening the gate, walked up the little paved path to the door where the old woman was waiting.

Chapter II
A Conference with
Dr. Thorndyke

The sound of the closing door seemed, as it were, to punctuate my experiences and to mark the end of a particular phase. So long as Miss D'Arblay was present, my attention was entirely taken up by her grief and distress, but now that I was alone I found myself considering at large the events of this memorable morning. What was the meaning of this tragedy? How came this man to be lying dead in that pool? No common misadventure seemed to fit the case. A man may easily fall into deep water and be drowned, may step over a quay-side in the dark or trip on a mooring-rope or ring-bolt. But here there was nothing to suggest any possible accident. The water was hardly two feet deep where the body was lying and much less close to the edge. If he had walked in in the dark, he would simply have walked out again. Besides, how came he there at all? The only explanation that was intelligible was that he went there with the deliberate purpose of making away with himself.

I pondered this explanation and found myself unwilling to accept it, notwithstanding that his daughter's presence in the wood, her obvious apprehension, and her terrified searching among the underwood, seemed to hint at a definite expectation on her part. But yet that possibility was discounted by what his daughter had told me of him. Little as she had said, it was clear that he was a man universally beloved. Such men, in making the world a pleasant place for others, make it pleasant for themselves. They are usually happy men, and happy men do not commit suicide. Yet, if the idea of suicide were rejected, what was left? Nothing but an insoluble mystery.

I turned the problem over again and again as I sat on the top of the tram (where I could keep my wet trousers out of sight), not as a matter of mere curiosity but as one in which I was personally concerned. Friendships spring up into sudden maturity under great emotional stress. I had known Marion D'Arblay but an hour or two, but they were hours which neither of us would ever forget, and in that brief space she had become to me a friend who was entitled, as of right, to sympathy and service. So, as I revolved in my mind the mystery of this man's death, I found myself thinking of him not as a chance stranger but as the father of a friend, and thus it seemed to devolve upon me to elucidate the mystery, if possible.

It is true that I had no special qualifications for investigating an obscure case of this kind, but yet I was better equipped than most young medical men. For my hospital, St. Margaret's, though its medical school was but a small one, had one great distinction: The chair of Medical Jurisprudence was occupied by one of the greatest living authorities on the subject. Dr. John Thorndyke. To him and his fascinating lectures my mind naturally turned as I ruminated on the problem, and presently, when I found myself unable to evolve any reasonable suggestion, the idea occurred to me to go and lay the facts before the great man himself.

Once started, the idea took full possession of me, and I decided to waste no time but to seek him at once. This was not his day for lecturing at the hospital, but I could find his address in our school calendar, and as my means, though modest, allowed of my retaining him in a regular way, I need have no scruples as to occupying his time. I looked at my watch. It was even now but a little past noon. I had time to change and get an early lunch and still make my visit while the day was young.

A couple of hours later found me walking slowly down the pleasant, tree-shaded footway of King's Bench Walk in the Inner Temple, looking up at the numbers above the entries. Dr. Thorndyke's number was 5A, which I presently discovered inscribed on the keystone of a fine, dignified brick portico of the seventeenth century, on the jamb whereof was painted his name as the occupant of the "*1ˢᵗ Pair*". I accordingly ascended the first pair and was relieved to find that my teacher was apparently at home, for a massive outer door, above which his name was painted, stood wide open, revealing an inner door, furnished with a small, brilliantly-burnished brass knocker, on which I ventured to execute a modest rat-tat. Almost immediately the door was opened by a small, clerical-looking gentleman who wore a black linen apron – and ought, from his appearance, to have had black gaiters to match – and who regarded me with a look of polite inquiry.

"I wanted to see Dr. Thorndyke," said I, adding discreetly, "on a matter of professional business."

The little gentleman beamed on me benevolently. "The Doctor," said he, "has gone to lunch at his club, but he will be coming in quite shortly. Would you like to wait for him?"

"Thank you," I replied, "I should, if you think I shall not be disturbing him."

The little gentleman smiled – that is to say, the multitudinous wrinkles that covered his face arranged themselves into a sort of diagram of geniality. It was the crinkliest smile that I have ever seen, but a singularly pleasant one.

"The Doctor," said he, "is never disturbed by professional business. No man is ever disturbed by having to do what he enjoys doing."

As he spoke, his eyes turned unconsciously to the table, on which stood a microscope, a tray of slides and mounting material, and a small heap of what looked like dressmaker's cuttings.

"Well," I said, "don't let me disturb you, if you are busy."

He thanked me very graciously and, having installed me in an easy-chair, sat down at the table and resumed his occupation, which apparently consisted in isolating fibres from the various samples of cloth and mounting them as microscopic specimens. I watched him as he worked, admiring his neat, precise, unhurried methods and speculating on the purpose of his proceedings – whether he was preparing what one might call museum specimens, to be kept for reference, or whether these preparations were related to some particular case. I was considering whether it would be admissible for me to ask a question on the subject when he paused in his work, assuming a listening attitude with one hand – holding a mounting-needle – raised and motionless.

"Here comes The Doctor," said he.

I listened intently and became aware of footsteps, very faint and far away, and only barely perceptible. But my clerical friend – who must have bad the auditory powers of a watch-dog – had no doubts as to their identity, for he began quietly to pack all his material on the tray. Meanwhile the footsteps drew nearer, they turned in at the entry, and ascended the "first pair", by which time my crinkly-faced acquaintance had the door open. The next moment Dr. Thorndyke entered and was duly informed that "a gentleman was waiting to see" him.

"You underestimate my powers of observation, Polton," he informed his subordinate, with a smile. "I can see the gentleman distinctly with my naked eye. How do you do, Gray?" and he shook my hand cordially.

"I hope I haven't come at the wrong time, sir," said I. "If I have, you must adjourn me. But I want to consult you about a rather queer case."

"Good," said Thorndyke. "There is no wrong time for a queer case. Let me hang up my hat and fill my pipe and then you can proceed to make my flesh creep."

He disposed of his hat, and when Mr. Polton had departed with his tray of material, he filled his pipe, laid a note-block on the table, and invited me to begin, whereupon I gave him a detailed account of what had befallen me in the course of the morning, to which he listened with close attention, jotting down an occasional note, but not interrupting my

433

narrative. When I had finished, he read through his notes and then said, "It is, of course, evident to you that all the appearances point to suicide. Have you any reasons, other than those you have mentioned, for rejecting that view?"

"I am afraid not," I replied gloomily. "But you have always taught us to beware of too ready acceptance of the theory of suicide in doubtful cases."

He nodded approvingly. "Yes," he said, "'that is a cardinal principle in medico-legal practice. All other possibilities should be explored before suicide is accepted. But our difficulty in this case is that we have hardly any of the relevant facts. The evidence at the inquest may make everything clear. On the other hand, it may leave things obscure. But what is your concern with the case? You are merely a witness to the finding of the body. The parties are all strangers to you, are they not?"

"They were," I replied. "But I feel that someone ought to keep an eye on things for Miss D'Arblay's sake, and circumstances seem to have put the duty on me. So, as I can afford to pay any costs that are likely to be incurred, I proposed to ask you to undertake the case – on a strict business footing, you know, sir."

"When you speak of my undertaking the case," said he, "what is it that is in your mind? What do you want me to do in the matter?"

"I want you to take any measures that you may think necessary," I replied, "to ascertain definitely, if possible, how this man came by his death."

He reflected a while before answering. At length he said, "The examination of the body will be conducted by the person whom the coroner appoints, probably the police surgeon. I will write to the coroner for permission to be present at the *post mortem* examination. He will certainly make no difficulties. I will also write to the police surgeon, who is sure to be quite helpful. If the *post mortem* throws no light on the case – in fact, in any event – I will instruct a first-class shorthand writer to attend at the inquest and make a verbatim report of the evidence, and you, of course, will be present as a witness. That, I think, is about all that we can do at present. When we have heard all the evidence, including that furnished by the body itself, we shall be able to judge whether the case calls for further investigation. How will that do?"

"It is all that I could wish," I answered, "and I am most grateful to you, sir, for giving your time to the case. I hope you don't think I have been unduly meddlesome."

"Not in the least," he replied warmly. "I think you have shown a very proper spirit in the way you have interpreted your neighbourly duties to this poor, bereaved girl who, apparently, has no one else to

434

watch over her interests. And I take it as a compliment from an old pupil that you should seek my help."

I thanked him again, very sincerely, and had risen to take my leave, when he held up his hand.

"Sit down, Gray, if you are not in a hurry," said he. "I hear the pleasant clink of crockery. Let us follow the example of the eminent Mr. Pepys – though it isn't always a safe thing to do – and taste of the '*China drinke called Tee*' while you tell me what you have been doing since you went forth from the fold."

It struck me that the sense of hearing was uncommonly well developed in this establishment, for I had heard nothing, but a few moments later the door opened very quietly and Mr. Polton entered with a tray on which was a very trim, and even dainty, tea service, which he set out, noiselessly and with a curious neatness of hand, on a small table placed conveniently between our chairs.

"Thank you, Polton," said Thorndyke. "I see you diagnosed my visitor as a professional brother."

Polton crinkled benevolently and admitted that he "thought the gentleman looked like one of us", and with this he melted away, closing the door behind him without a sound.

"Well," said Thorndyke, as he handed me my teacup, "what have you been doing with yourself since you left the hospital?"

"Principally looking for a job," I replied, "and now I've found one – a temporary job, though I don't know how temporary. To-morrow I take over the practice of a man named Cornish in Mecklenburgh Square. Cornish is a good deal run down and wants to take a quiet holiday on the East Coast. He doesn't know how long he will be away. It depends on his health, but I have told him that I am prepared to stay as long as he wants me to. I hope I shan't make a mess of the job, but I know nothing of general practice."

"You will soon pick it up," said Thorndyke, "but you had better get your principal to show you the ropes before he goes, particularly the dispensing and book-keeping. The essentials of practice you know, but the little practical details have to be learnt, and you are doing well to make your first plunge into professional life in a practice that is a going concern. The experience will be valuable when you make a start on your own account."

On this plane of advice and comment our talk proceeded until I thought that I had stayed long enough, when I once more rose to depart. Then, as we were shaking hands, Thorndyke reverted to the object of my visit.

"I shall not appear in this case unless the coroner wishes me to," said he. "I shall consult with the official medical witness and he will probably give our joint conclusions in his evidence – unless we should fail to agree, which is very unlikely. But you will be present, and you had better attend closely to the evidence of all the witnesses and let me have your account of the inquest as well as the shorthand writer's report. Good-bye, Gray. You won't be far away if you should want my help or advice."

I left the precincts of the temple in a much more satisfied frame of mind. The mystery which seemed to me to surround the death of Julius D'Arblay would be investigated by a supremely competent observer, and I need not further concern myself with it. Perhaps there was no mystery at all. Possibly the evidence at the inquest would supply a simple explanation. At any rate, it was out of my hands and into those of one immeasurably more capable, and I could now give my undivided attention to the new chapter of my life that was to open on the morrow.

Chapter III
The Doctor's Revelations

It was in the evening of the very day on which I took up my duties at number 61 Mecklenburgh Square that the little blue paper was delivered summoning me to attend at the inquest on the following day. Fortunately, Dr. Cornish's practice was not of a highly strenuous type, and the time of year tended to a small visiting list, so that I had no difficulty in making the necessary arrangements. In fact, I made them so well that I was the first to arrive at the little building in which the inquiry was to be held and was admitted by the caretaker to the empty room. A few minutes later, however, the inspector made his appearance, and while I was exchanging a few words with him, the jury began to straggle in, followed by the reporters, a few spectators and witnesses, and finally the coroner, who immediately took his place at the head of the table and prepared to open the proceedings.

At this moment I observed Miss D'Arblay standing hesitatingly in the doorway and looking into the room as if reluctant to enter. I at once rose and went to her, and as I approached, she greeted me with a friendly smile and held out her hand, and then I perceived, lurking just outside, a tall, black-apparelled woman, whose face I recognized as that which I had seen at the window.

"This," said Miss D'Arblay, presenting me, "is my friend Miss Boler, of whom I spoke to you. This, Arabella, dear, is the gentleman who was so kind to me on that dreadful day."

I bowed deferentially and Miss Boler recognized my existence by a majestic inclination, remarking that she remembered me. As the coroner now began his preliminary address to the jury, I hastened to find three chairs near the table and, having inducted the ladies into two of them, took the third myself, next to Miss D'Arblay. The coroner and the jury now rose and went out to the adjacent mortuary to view the body, and during their absence I stole an occasional critical glance at my fair friend.

Marion D'Arblay was, as I have said, a strikingly handsome girl. The fact seemed now to dawn on me afresh, as a new discovery, for the harrowing circumstances of our former meeting had so preoccupied me that I had given little attention to her personality. But now, as I looked her over anxiously to see how the grievous days had dealt with her, it was with a sort of surprised admiration that I noted the beautiful, thoughtful face, the fine features, and the wealth of dark, gracefully disposed hair. I was relieved, too, to see the change that a couple of days had wrought. The wild, dazed look was gone. Though she was pale and heavy-eyed and looked tired and infinitely sad, her manner was calm, quiet, and perfectly self-possessed.

"I am afraid," said I, "that this is going to be rather a painful ordeal for you."

"Yes," she agreed, "it is all very dreadful. But it is a dreadful thing in any case to be bereft in a moment of the one whom one loves best in all the world. The circumstances of the loss cannot make very much difference. It is the loss itself that matters. The worst moment was when the blow fell – when we found him. This inquiry and the funeral are just the drab accompaniments that bring home the reality of what has happened."

"Has the inspector called on you?" I asked.

"Yes," she replied. "He had to, to get the particulars, and he was so kind and delicate that I am not in the least afraid of the examination by the coroner. Everyone has been kind to me, but none so kind as you were on that terrible morning."

I could not see that I had done anything to call for so much gratitude, and I was about to enter a modest disclaimer when the coroner and the jury returned and the inspector approached somewhat hurriedly.

"It will be necessary," said he, "for Miss D'Arblay to see the body – just to identify the deceased, a glance will be enough. And, as you are a witness, Doctor, you had better go with her to the mortuary. I will show you the way."

Miss D'Arblay rose without any comment or apparent reluctance and we followed the inspector to the adjoining mortuary, where, having admitted us, he stood outside awaiting us. The body lay on the slate-topped table, covered with a sheet excepting the face, which was exposed and was undisfigured by any traces of the examination. I watched my friend a little nervously as we entered the grim chamber, fearful that this additional trial might be too much for her self-control. But she kept command of herself, though she wept quietly as she stood beside the table looking down on the still, waxen-faced figure. After standing thus for a few moments, she turned away with a smothered sob, wiped her eyes, and walked out of the mortuary.

When we re-entered the courtroom, we found our chairs moved up to the table and the coroner waiting to call the witnesses. As I had expected, my name was the first on the list, and on being called, I took my place by the table near to the coroner and was duly sworn.

"Will you give us your name, occupation and address?" the coroner asked.

"My name is Stephen Gray," I replied. "I am a medical practitioner and my temporary address is 61 Mecklenburgh Square, London."

"When you say your 'temporary address' you mean – ?"

"I am taking charge of a medical practice at that address. I shall be there six weeks or more."

"Then that will be your address for our purposes. Have you viewed the body that is now lying in the mortuary, and, if so, do you recognize it?"

"Yes. It is the body which I saw lying in a pond in Churchyard Bottom Wood on the morning of the 16th instant – last Tuesday."

"Can you tell us how long the deceased had been dead when you first saw the body?"

"I should say he had been dead nine or ten hours."

"Will you relate the circumstances under which you discovered the body?"

I gave a circumstantial account of the manner in which I made the tragic discovery, to which not only the jury but also the spectators listened with eager interest. When I had finished my narrative, the coroner asked, "Did you observe anything which led you, as a medical man, to form any opinion as to the cause of death?"

"No," I replied. "I saw no injuries or marks of violence or anything which was not consistent with death by drowning."

This concluded my evidence, and when I had resumed my seat, the name of Marion D'Arblay was called by the coroner, who directed that a chair should be placed for the witness. When she had taken her seat, he conveyed to her, briefly but feelingly, his own and the jury's sympathy.

"It has been a terrible experience for you," he said, "and we are most sorry to have to trouble you in your great affliction, but you will understand that it is unavoidable."

"I quite understand that," she replied, "and I wish to thank you and the jury for your kind sympathy."

She was then sworn, and having given her name and address, proceeded to answer the questions addressed to her, which elicited a narrative of the events substantially identical with that which she had given to the inspector and which I have already recorded.

"You have told us," said the coroner, "that when Dr. Gray spoke to you, you were searching among the bushes. Will you tell us what was in your mind – what you were searching for and what induced you to make that search?"

"I was very uneasy about my father," she replied. "He had not been home that night, and he had not told me that he intended to stay at the studio – as he sometimes did when he was working very late. So in the morning I went to the studio in Abbey Road to see if he was there, but the caretaker told me that he had started for home about ten o'clock. Then I began to fear that something had happened to him, and as he always came home by the path through the wood, I went there to see if – if anything had happened to him."

"Had you in your mind any definite idea as to what might have happened to him?"

"I thought he might have been taken ill or have fallen down dead. He once told me that he would probably die quite suddenly. I believe that he suffered from some affection of the heart, but he did not like speaking about his health."

"Are you sure that there was nothing more than this in your mind?"

"There was nothing more. I thought that his heart might have failed and that he might have wandered, in a half-conscious state, away from the main path and fallen dead in one of the thickets."

The coroner pondered this reply for some time. I could not see why, for it was plain and straightforward enough. At length he said, very gravely and with what seemed to me unnecessary emphasis, "I want you to be quite frank and open with us. Miss D'Arblay. Can you swear that there was no other possibility in your mind than that of sudden illness?"

She looked at him in surprise, apparently not understanding the drift of the question. As to me, I assumed that he was endeavouring delicately to ascertain whether the deceased was addicted to drink. "I have told you exactly what was in my mind," she replied.

"Have you ever had any reason to suppose, or to entertain the possibility, that your father might take his own life?"

"Never," she answered emphatically. "He was a happy, even-tempered man, always interested in his work and always in good spirits. I am sure he would never have taken his own life."

The coroner nodded with a rather curious air of satisfaction, as if he were concurring with the witness's statement. Then he asked in the same grave, emphatic manner, "So far as you know, had your father any enemies?"

"No," she replied confidently. "He was a kindly, amiable man who disliked nobody, and everyone who knew him loved him."

As she uttered this panegyric (and what prouder testimony could a daughter have given?), her eyes filled, and the coroner looked at her with deep sympathy but yet with a somewhat puzzled expression.

"You are sure," he said gently, "that there was no one whom he might have injured – even inadvertently – or who bore him any grudge or ill-will?"

"I am sure," she answered, "that he never injured or gave offence to anyone, and I do not believe that there was any person in the whole world who bore him anything but goodwill."

The coroner noted this reply, and as he entered it in the depositions, his face bore the same curious puzzled or doubtful expression. When he had written the answer down, he asked, "By the way, what was the deceased's occupation?"

"He was a sculptor by profession, but in late years he worked principally as a modeller for various trades – pottery manufacturers, picture-frame makers, carvers and the makers of high-class wax figures for shop windows."

"Had he any assistants or subordinates?"

"No. He worked alone. Occasionally I helped him with his moulds when he was very busy or had a very large work on hand, but usually he did everything himself. Of course, he occasionally employed models."

"Do you know who those models were?"

"They were professional models. The men, I think, were all Italians and some of the women were, too. I believe my father kept a list of them in his address book."

"Was he working from a model on the night of his death?'

"No. He was making the moulds for a porcelain statuette."

"Did you ever hear that he had any kind of trouble with his models?"

"Never. He seemed always on the best of terms with them and he used to speak of them most appreciatively."

"What sort of persons are professional models? Should you say they are a decent, well-conducted class?"

"Yes. They are usually most respectable, hard-working people, and, of course, they are sober and decent in their habits or they would be of no use for their professional duties."

The coroner meditated on these replies with a speculative eye on the witness. After a short pause, he began along another line.

"Did the deceased ever carry about with him property of any considerable value?"

"Never, to my knowledge."

"No jewellery, plate, or valuable material?"

"No. His work was practically all in plaster or wax. He did no goldsmith's work and he used no precious material."

"Did he ever have any considerable sums of money about him?"

"No. He received all his payments by cheque and he made his payments in the same way. His habit was to carry very little money on his person – usually not more than one or two pounds."

Once more the coroner reflected profoundly. It seemed to me that he was trying to elicit some fact – I could not imagine what – and was failing utterly. At length, after another puzzled look at the witness, he turned to the jury and inquired if any of them wished to put any questions, and when they had severally shaken their heads, he thanked Miss D'Arblay for the clear and straightforward way in which she had given her evidence and released her.

While the examination had been proceeding, I had allowed my eyes to wander round the room with some curiosity, for this was the first time that I had ever been present at an inquest. From the jury, the witnesses in waiting and the reporters – among whom I tried to identify Dr. Thorndyke's stenographer – my attention was presently transferred to the spectators. There were only a few of them, but I found myself wondering why there should be any. What kind of person attends as a spectator at an ordinary inquest such as this appeared to be? The newspaper reports of the finding of the body were quite unsensational and promised no startling developments. Finally, I decided that they were probably local residents who had some knowledge of the deceased and were just indulging their neighbourly curiosity.

Among them my attention was particularly attracted by a middle-aged woman who sat near me – at least I judged her to be middle-aged, though the rather dense black veil that she wore obscured her face to a great extent. Apparently she was a widow, and advertised the fact by the orthodox, old-fashioned "weeds". But I could see that she had white hair and wore spectacles. She held a folded newspaper on her knee, apparently dividing her attention between the printed matter and the proceedings of the court. She gave me the impression of having come in to spend an idle hour, combining a somewhat perfunctory reading of the paper with a still more perfunctory attention to the rather gruesome entertainment that the inquest afforded.

The next witness called was the doctor who had made the official examination of the body, on whom the – presumed – widow bestowed a listless, incurious glance and then returned to her newspaper. He was a youngish man, though his hair was turning grey, with a quiet but firm and confident manner and a very clear, pleasant voice. The preliminaries having been disposed of, the coroner led off with the question, "You have made an examination of the body of the deceased?"

"Yes. It is that of a well-proportioned, fairly muscular man of about sixty, quite healthy with the exception of the heart, one of the valves of which – the mitral valve – was incompetent and allowed some leakage of blood to take place."

"Was the heart affection sufficient to account for the death of the deceased?"

"No. It was quite a serviceable heart. There was good compensation – that is to say, there was extra growth of muscle to make up for the leaky valve. So far as his heart was concerned, the deceased might have lived for another twenty years."

"Were you able to ascertain what actually was the cause of death?"

"Yes. The cause of death was aconitine poisoning."

At this reply a murmur of astonishment arose from the jury, and I heard Miss D'Arblay suddenly draw in her breath. The spectators sat up on their benches, and even the veiled lady was so far interested as to look up from her paper.

"How had the poison been administered?" the coroner asked.

"It had been injected under the skin by means of a hypodermic syringe."

"Can you give an opinion as to whether the poison was administered to the deceased by himself or by some other person?"

"It could not have been injected by the deceased himself," the witness replied. "The needle-puncture was in the back, just below the left shoulder-blade. It is, in my opinion, physically impossible for anyone to inject with a hypodermic syringe into his own body in that spot. And, of course, a person who was administering an injection to himself would select the most convenient spot – such as the front of the thigh. But apart from the question of convenience, the place in which the needle-puncture was found was actually out of reach." Here the witness produced a hypodermic syringe, the action of which he demonstrated with the aid of a glass of water, and having shown the impossibility of applying it to the spot that he had described, passed the syringe round for the jury's inspection.

"Have you formed any opinion as to the purpose for which this drug was administered in this manner?"

"I have no doubt that it was administered for the purpose of causing the death of the deceased."

"Might it not have been administered for medicinal purposes?"

"That is quite inconceivable. Leaving out of consideration the circumstances – the time and place where the administration occurred – the dose excludes the possibility of medicinal purposes. It was a lethal dose. From the tissues round the needle-puncture we recovered the twelfth-of-a-grain of aconitine. That alone was more than enough to cause death. But a quantity of the poison had been absorbed, as was shown by the fact that we recovered a recognizable trace from the liver."

"What is the medicinal dose of aconitine?"

"The maximum medicinal dose is about the four-hundredth of a grain, and even that is not very safe. As a matter of fact, aconitine is very seldom used in medical practice. It is a dangerous drug and of no particular value."

"How much aconitine do you suppose was injected?"

"Not less than the tenth-of-a-grain – that is, about forty times the maximum medicinal dose. Probably more."

"There can, I suppose, be no doubt as to the accuracy of the facts that you have stated as to the nature and quantity of the poison?"

"There can be no doubt whatever. The analysis was made in my presence by Professor Woodford of St. Margaret's Hospital after I had removed the tissues from the body in his presence. He has not been called because, in accordance with the procedure under Coroners Law, I am responsible for the analysis and the conclusions drawn from it."

"Taking the medical facts as known to you, are you able to form an opinion as to what took place when the poison was administered?"

"That," the witness replied, "is a matter of inference or conjecture. I infer that the person who administered the poison thrust the needle violently into the back of the deceased, intending to inject the poison into the chest. Actually, the needle struck a rib and bent up sharply, so that the contents of the syringe were delivered just under the skin. Then I take it that the assailant ran away – probably towards the pond – and the deceased pursued him. Very soon the poison would take effect, and then the deceased would have fallen. He may have fallen into the pond, or more probably was thrown in. He was alive when he fell into the pond, as is proved by the presence of water in the lungs, but he must then have been insensible and in a dying condition, for there was no water in the stomach, which proves that the swallowing reflex had already ceased."

"Your considered opinion, then, based on the medical facts ascertained by you, is, I understand, that the deceased died from the effects of a poison injected into his body by some other person with homicidal intent?"

"Yes, that is my considered opinion, and I affirm that the facts do not admit of any other interpretation."

The coroner looked towards the jury. "Do any of you gentlemen wish to ask the witness any questions?" he inquired, and when the foreman had replied that the jury were entirely satisfied with the doctor's explanations, he thanked the witness, who thereupon retired. The medical witness was succeeded by the inspector, who made a short statement respecting the effects found on the person of the deceased. They comprised a small sum of money – under two pounds – a watch, keys and other articles – none of them of any appreciable value, but such as

444

they were, furnishing evidence that at least petty robbery had not been the object of the attack.

When the last witness had been heard, the coroner glanced at his notes and then proceeded to address the jury.

"There is little, gentlemen," he began, "that I need say to you. The facts are before you and they seem to admit of only one interpretation. I remind you that, by the terms of your oath, your finding must be 'according to the evidence'. Now, the medical evidence is quite dear and definite. It is to the effect that the deceased met his death by poison administered violently by some other person – that is, by homicide. Homicide is the killing of a human being, and it may or may not be criminal. But if the homicidal act is done with the intent to kill, if that intention has been deliberately formed – that is to say, if the homicidal act has been premeditated – then that homicide is wilful murder.

"Now, the person who killed the deceased came to the place where the act was done provided with a solution of a very powerful and uncommon vegetable poison. He was also provided with a very special appliance – to wit, a hypodermic syringe – for injecting it into the body. The fact that he was furnished with the poison and the appliance creates a strong presumption that he came to this place with the deliberate intention of killing the deceased. That is to say, this fact constitutes strong evidence of premeditation.

"As to the motive for this act, we are completely in the dark, nor have we any evidence pointing to the identity of the person who committed that act. But a coroner's inquest is not necessarily concerned with motives, nor is it our business to fix the act on any particular person. We have to find how and by what means the deceased met his death, and for that purpose we have clear and sufficient evidence. I need say no more, but will leave you to agree upon your finding."

There was a brief interval of silence when the coroner had finished speaking. The jury whispered together for a few seconds, then the foreman announced that they had agreed upon their verdict.

"And what is your decision, gentlemen?" the coroner asked.

"We find," was the reply, "that the deceased met his death by wilful murder, committed by some person unknown."

The coroner bowed. "I am in entire agreement with you, gentlemen," said he. "No other verdict was possible, and I am sure you will join with me in the hope that the wretch who committed this dastardly crime may be identified and in due course brought to justice."

This brought the proceedings to an end. As the court rose, the spectators filed out of the building and the coroner approached Miss D'Arblay to express once more his deep sympathy with her in her tragic bereavement. I stood apart with Miss Boler, whose rugged face was wet with tears, but set in a grim and wrathful scowl.

"Things have taken a terrible turn," I ventured to observe.

She shook her head and uttered a sort of low growl. "It won't bear thinking of," she said gruffly. "There is no possible retribution that would meet the case. One has thought that some of the old punishments were cruel and barbarous, but if I could lay my hands on the villain that did this – " She broke off, leaving the conclusion to my imagination, and in an extraordinarily different voice, said, "Come, Miss Marion, let us get out of this awful place."

As we walked away slowly and in silence, I looked at Miss D'Arblay, not without anxiety. She was very pale, and the dazed expression that her face had borne on the fatal day of the discovery had, to some extent, reappeared. But now the signs of bewilderment and grief were mingled with something new. The rigid face, the compressed lips, and lowered brows spoke of a deep and abiding wrath.

Suddenly she turned to me and said, abruptly, almost harshly, "I was wrong in what I said to you before the inquiry. You remember that I said the circumstances of the loss could make no difference, but they make a whole world of difference. I had supposed that my dear father had died as he had thought he would die, that it was the course of Nature, which we cannot rebel against. Now I know, from what the doctor said, that he might have lived on happily for the full span of human life but for the malice of this unknown wretch. His life was not lost, it was stolen – from him and from me."

"Yes," I said somewhat lamely. "It is a horrible affair."

"It is beyond bearing!" she exclaimed. "If his death had been natural, I would have tried to resign myself to it. I would have tried to put my grief away. But to think that his happy, useful life has been snatched from him, that he has been torn from us who loved him, by the deliberate act of this murderer – it is unendurable. It will be with me every hour of my life until I die. And every hour I shall call on God for justice against this wretch."

I looked at her with a sort of admiring surprise. A quiet, gentle girl as I believed her to be at ordinary times, now, with her flushed cheeks, her flashing eyes and ominous brows, she reminded me of one of the heroines of the French Revolution. Her grief seemed to be merged in a longing for vengeance.

While she had been speaking. Miss Boler had kept up a running accompaniment in a deep, humming bass. I could not catch the words – if there were any – but was aware only of a low, continuous bourdon. She now said with grim decision, "God will not let him escape. He shall pay the debt to the uttermost farthing." Then, with sudden fierceness, she added, "If I should ever meet with him, I could kill him with my own hand."

After this, both women relapsed into silence, which I was loath to interrupt. The circumstances were too tragic for conversation. When we reached their gate. Miss D'Arblay held out her hand and once again thanked me for my help and sympathy.

"I have done nothing," said I, "that any stranger would not have done, and I deserve no thanks. But I should like to think that you will look on me as a friend, and if you should need any help will let me have the privilege of being of use to you."

"I look on you as a friend already," she replied, "and I hope you will come and see us sometimes – when we have settled down to our new conditions of life."

As Miss Boler seemed to confirm this invitation, I thanked them both and took my leave, glad to think that I had now a recognized status as a friend and might pursue a project which had formed in my mind even before we had left the court-house.

The evidence of the murder, which had fallen like a thunderbolt on us all, had a special significance for me, for I knew that Dr. Thorndyke was behind this discovery, though to what extent I could not judge. The medical witness was an obviously capable man, and it might be that he would have made the discovery without assistance. But a needle-puncture in the back is a very inconspicuous thing. Ninety-nine doctors in a hundred would almost certainly have overlooked it, especially in the case of a body apparently "found drowned" and seeming to call for no special examination beyond the search for gross injuries. The revelation was very characteristic of Thorndyke's methods and principles. It illustrated in a most striking manner the truth which he was never tired of insisting on – that it is never safe to accept obvious appearances, and that every case, no matter how apparently simple and commonplace, should be approached with suspicion and scepticism and subjected to the most rigorous scrutiny. That was precisely what had been done in this case, and thereby an obvious suicide had been resolved into a cunningly-planned and skilfully-executed murder. It was quite possible that, but for my visit to Thorndyke, those cunning plans would have succeeded and the murderer have secured the cover of a verdict of "Death by misadventure" or "Suicide while Temporarily Insane". At any rate, the results had justified me in invoking Dr. Thorndyke's aid, and the question now arose whether it would be possible to retain him for the further investigation of the case.

This was the project that had occurred to me as I listened to the evidence and realized how completely the unknown murderer had covered up his tracks. But there were difficulties. Thorndyke might consider such an investigation outside his province. Again, the costs involved might be on a scale entirely beyond my means. The only thing to be done was to call on Thorndyke and hear what he had to say on the subject, and this I determined to do on the first opportunity. And having formed this resolution, I made my way back by the shortest route to Mecklenburgh Square, where the evening consultations were now nearly due.

Chapter IV
Mr. Bendelow

There are certain districts in London the appearance of which conveys to the observer the impression that the houses, and indeed the entire streets, have been picked up second-hand. There is in their aspect a grey, colourless, mouldy quality, reminiscent not of the antique shop, but rather of the marine-store dealers, a quality which even communicates itself to the inhabitants, so that one gathers the impression that the whole neighbourhood was taken as a going concern.

It was on such a district that I found myself looking down from the top of an omnibus a few days after the inquest (Dr. Cornish's brougham being at the moment under repairs and his horse "out to grass" during the slack season), being bound for a street in the neighbourhood of Hoxton – Market Street by name – which abutted, as I had noticed when making out my route, on the Regent's Canal. The said route I had written out, and now, in the intervals of my surveys of the unlovely prospect, I divided my attention between it and the note which had summoned me to these remote regions.

Concerning the latter I was somewhat curious, for the envelope was addressed, not to Dr. Cornish but to "Dr. Stephen Gray". This was really quite an odd circumstance. Either the writer knew me personally or was aware that I was acting as *locum tenens* for Cornish. But the name – James Morris – was unknown to me, and a careful inspection of the index of the ledger had failed to bring to light anyone answering to the description. So Mr. Morris was presumably a stranger to my principal also. The note, which had been left by hand in the morning, requested me to call "*as early in the forenoon as possible*", which seemed to hint at some degree of urgency. Naturally, as a young practitioner, I speculated with interest, not entirely unmingled with anxiety, on the possible nature of the case, and also on the patient's reason for selecting a medical attendant whose residence was so inconveniently far away.

In accordance with my written route, I got off the omnibus at the corner of Shepherdess Walk and, pursuing that pastoral thoroughfare for some distance, presently plunged into a labyrinth of streets adjoining it and succeeded most effectually in losing myself. However, inquiries addressed to an intelligent fish-vendor elicited a most lucid direction and I soon found myself in a little, drab street which justified its name by giving accommodation to a row of stationary barrows loaded with what

449

looked like the "throw-outs" from a colossal spring-clean. Passing along this kerb-side market and reflecting (like Diogenes, in similar circumstances) how many things there were in the world that I did not want, I walked slowly up the street looking for Number 23 – my patient's number – and the canal which I had seen on the map. I located them both at the same instant, for Number 23 turned out to be the last house on the opposite side, and a few yards beyond it the street was barred by a low wall, over which, as I looked, the mast of a sailing-barge came into view and slowly crept past. I stepped up to the wall and looked over. Immediately beneath me was the towing-path, alongside which the barge was now bringing up and beginning to lower her mast, apparently to pass under a bridge that spanned the canal a couple of hundred yards farther along.

From these nautical manoeuvres I transferred my attention to my patient's house – or at least, so much of it as I could see, for Number 23 appeared to consist of a shop with nothing over it. There was, however, in a wall which extended to the canal wall, a side door with a bell and knocker, so I inferred that the house was behind the shop and that the latter had been built on a formerly existing front garden. The shop itself was somewhat reminiscent of the stalls down the street, for though the fascia was newly painted (with the inscription *J. Morris, Dealer in Antiques*), the stock-in-trade exhibited in the window was in the last stage of senile decay. It included, I remember, a cracked Toby jug, a mariner's sextant of an obsolete type a Dutch clock without hands, a snuff-box, one or two planter statuettes, an invalid punchbowl, a shiny, dark and inscrutable oil-painting, and a plaster mask – presumably the death mask of some celebrity whose face was unknown to me.

My examination of this collection was brought to a sudden end by the apparition of a face above the half-blind of the glazed shop-door, the face of a middle-aged woman who seemed to be inspecting me with malevolent interest. Assuming – rather too late – a brisk, professional manner, I opened the shop-door, thereby setting a bell jangling within, and confronted the owner of the face.

"I am Dr. Gray," I began to explain.

"Side-door," she interrupted brusquely. "Ring the bell and knock."

I backed out hastily and proceeded to follow the directions, giving a tug at the bell and delivering a flourish on the knocker. The hollow reverberations of the latter almost suggested an empty house, but my vigorous pull at the bell-handle produced no audible result, from which I inferred – wrongly, as afterwards appeared – that it was out of repair.

After waiting quite a considerable time, I was about to repeat the performance when I heard sounds within, and then the door was opened, to my surprise, by the identical sour-faced woman whom I had seen in the shop. As her appearance and manner did not invite conversation, and as she uttered no word, I followed her in silence through a long passage, or covered way, which ran parallel to the side of the shop and presumably crossed the site of the garden. It ended at a door which opened into the hall proper, a largish square space into which the doors of the ground-floor rooms opened. It contained the main staircase and was closed in at the farther end by a heavy curtain which extended from wall to wall.

We proceeded in this funereal manner up the stairs to the first floor, on the landing of which my conductress halted and for the first time broke the silence.

"You will probably find Mr. Bendelow asleep or dozing," she said in a rather gruff voice. "If he is, there is no need for you to disturb him."

"Mr. Bendelow!" I exclaimed. "I understood that his name was Morris."

"Well, it isn't," she retorted. "It is Bendelow. My name is Morris and so is my husband's. It was he who wrote to you."

"By the way," said I, "how did he know my name? I am acting for Dr. Cornish, you know."

"I didn't know," said she, "and I don't suppose he did. Probably the servant told him. But it doesn't matter. Here you are, and you will do as well as another. I was telling you about Mr. Bendelow. He is in a pretty bad way. The specialist whom Mr. Morris took him to – Dr. Artemus Cropper – said he had cancer of the bilorus, whatever that is – "

"Pylorus," I corrected.

"Well, pylorus, then, if you prefer it," she corrected impatiently. "At any rate, whatever it is, he's got cancer of it, and as I said before, he is in a pretty bad way. Dr. Cropper told us what to do, and we are doing it. He wrote out full directions as to diet – I will show them to you presently – and he said that Mr. Bendelow was to have a dose of morphia if he complained of pain – which he does, of course – and that, as there was no chance of his getting better, it didn't matter how much morphia he had. The great thing was to keep him out of pain. So we give it to him twice a day – at least, my husband does – and that keeps him fairly comfortable. In fact, he sleeps most of the time and is probably dozing now, so you are not likely to get much out of him, especially as he is rather hard of hearing even when he is awake. And now you had better come in and have a look at him."

She advanced to the door of a room and opened it softly, and I followed in a somewhat uncomfortable frame of mind. It seemed to me that I had no function but that of a mere figure-head. Dr. Cropper, whom

I knew by name as a physician of some reputation, had made the diagnosis and prescribed the treatment, neither of which I, as a mere beginner, would think of contesting. It was an unsatisfactory, even an ignominious position, from which my professional pride revolted, but apparently it had to be accepted.

Mr. Bendelow was a most remarkable-looking man. Probably he had always been, but now the frightful emaciation (which strongly confirmed Cropper's diagnosis) had so accentuated his original peculiarities that he had the appearance of some dreadful, mirthless caricature. Under the influence of the remorseless disease, every shrinkable structure had shrunk to the vanishing-point, leaving the unshrinkable skeleton jutting out with a most horrible and grotesque effect. His great hooked nose, which must always have been strikingly prominent, stuck out now, thin and sharp, like the beak of some bird of prey. His heavy beetling brows, which must always have given to his face a frowning sullenness, now overhung sockets which had shrunk away into mere caverns. His naturally-high cheek-bones were now not only prominent, but exhibited the details of their structure as one sees them in a dry skull. Altogether, his aspect was at once pitiable and forbidding. Of his age I could form no estimate. He might have been a hundred. The wonder was that he was still alive, that there was yet left in that shrivelled body enough material to enable its mechanism to continue its functions.

He was not asleep, but was in that somnolent, lethargic state that is characteristic of the effects of morphia. He took no notice of me when I approached the bed, nor even when I spoke his name somewhat loudly.

"I told you you wouldn't get much out of him," said Mrs. Morris, looking at me with a sort of grim satisfaction. "He doesn't have a great deal to say to any of us nowadays."

"Well," said I, "there is no need to rouse him, but I had better just examine him, if only as a matter of form. I can't take the case entirely on hearsay."

"I suppose not," she agreed. "You know best. Do what you think necessary, but don't disturb him more than you can help."

It was not a prolonged examination. The first touch of my fingers on the shrunken abdomen made me aware of the unmistakable hard mass and rendered further exploration needless. There could be no doubt as to the nature of the case or of what the future held in store. It was only a question of time, and a short time at that.

The patient submitted to the examination quite passively, but he seemed to be fully aware of what was going on, for he looked at me in a sort of drunken, dreamy fashion, but without any sign of interest in my proceedings. When I had finished, I looked him over again, trying to reconstitute him as he might have been before this deadly disease fastened on him. I observed that he seemed to have a fair crop of hair of a darkish iron-grey. I say seemed because the greater part of his head was covered by a skull-cap of black silk, but a fringe of hair straying from under it on to the forehead suggested that he was not bald. His teeth, too, which were rather conspicuous, were natural teeth and in good preservation. In order to confirm this fact, I stooped and raised his lip the better to examine them. But at this point Mrs. Morris intervened.

"There, that will do," she said impatiently. "You are not a dentist, and his teeth will last as long as he will want them. If you have finished, you had better come with me and I will show you Dr. Cropper's prescriptions. Then you can tell me if you have any further directions to give."

She led the way out of the room, and when I had made a farewell gesture to the patient (of which he took no notice), I followed her down the stairs to the ground floor, where she ushered me into a small, rather elegantly furnished room. Here she opened the top of a bureau and from one of the little drawers took an open envelope, which she handed to me. It contained one or two prescriptions for occasional medicines and a sheet of directions relative to the diet and general management of the patient, including the administration of morphia. The latter read, under the general heading, "*Simon Bendelow, Esq.*":

> *As the case progresses, it will probably be necessary to administer morphine regularly, but the amount given should, if possible, be restricted to 14 gr. Morph. Sulph, not more than twice a day, but, of course, the hopeless prognosis and probable early termination of the case make some latitude admissible.*

Although I was in complete agreement with the writer, I was a little puzzled by these documents. They were signed "*Artemus Cropper, MD*", but they were not addressed to any person by name. They appeared to have been given to Mr. Morris, in whose possession they now were, but the use of the word "*morphine*" instead of the more familiar "*morphia*" and the general technical phraseology seemed inappropriate to directions addressed to lay persons. As I returned them I remarked, "These directions read as if they had been intended for the information of a medical man."

"They were," she replied. "They were meant for the doctor who was attending Mr. Bendelow at the time. When we moved to this place, I got them from him to show to the new doctor. You are the new doctor."

"Then you haven't been here very long?"

"No," she replied. "We have only just moved in. And that reminds me that our stock of morphia is running out. Could you bring a fresh tube of the tabloids next time you call? My husband left an empty tube for me to give you to remind you what size the tabloids are. He gives Mr. Bendelow the injections."

"Thank you," said I, "but I don't want the empty tube. I read the prescription and shan't forget the dose. I will bring a new tube to-morrow – that is, if you want me to call every day. It seems hardly necessary."

"No, it doesn't," she agreed. "I should think twice a week would be quite enough. Monday and Thursday would suit me best, if you could manage to come about this time I should be sure to be in. My time is rather taken up, as I haven't a servant at present."

It was a bad arrangement. Fixed appointments are things to avoid in medical practice. Nevertheless I agreed to it – subject to unforeseen obstacles – and was forthwith conducted back along the covered way and launched into the outer world with a farewell which it would be inadequate to describe as unemotional.

As I turned away from the door, I cast a passing glance at the shop-window, and once again I perceived a face above the half-blind. It was a man's face this time, presumably the face of Mr. Morris. And like his wife, he seemed to be taking stock of me. I returned the attention and carried away with me the instantaneous mental photograph of a man in that unprepossessing transitional state between being clean-shaved and wearing a beard which is characterized by a sort of grubby prickliness that disfigures the features without obscuring them. His stubble was barely a week old, but as his complexion and hair were dark, the effect was very untidy and disreputable. And yet, as I have said, it did not obscure the features. I was even able, in that momentary glance, to note a detail which would probably have escaped a non-medical eye – the scar of a hare-lip which had been very neatly and skilfully mended and which a moustache would probably have concealed altogether.

I did not, however, give much thought to Mr. Morris. It was his dour-faced wife with her gruff, overbearing manner who principally occupied my reflections. She seemed to have divined in some way that I was but a beginner – perhaps my youthful appearance gave her the hint – and to have treated me with almost open contempt. In truth, my position was not a very dignified one. The diagnosis of the case had been made for me, the treatment had been prescribed for me, and was being carried out by other hands than mine. My function was to support a kind of legal fiction that I was conducting the case, but principally to supply the morphia (which a chemist might have refused to do) and, when the time came, to sign the death certificate. It was an ignominious role for a young and ambitious practitioner and my pride was disposed to boggle at it. But yet there was nothing to which I could object. The diagnosis was undoubtedly correct and the treatment and management of the case exactly such as I should have prescribed. Finally, I decided that my dissatisfaction was principally due to the unattractive personality of Mrs. Morris, and with this conclusion I dismissed the case from my mind and let my thoughts wander into more agreeable channels.

Chapter V
Inspector Follett's Discovery

To a man whose mind is working actively, walking is a more acceptable mode of progression than riding in a vehicle. There is a sort of reciprocity between the muscles and the brain – possibly due to the close association of the motor and psychical centres – whereby the activity of the one appears to act as a stimulus to the other. A sharp walk sets the mind working, and, conversely, a state of lively reflection begets an impulse to bodily movement.

Hence, when I had emerged from Market Street and set my face homewards, I let the omnibuses rumble past unheeded. I knew my way now. I had but to retrace the route by which I had come and, preserving my isolation amidst the changing crowd, let my thoughts keep pace with my feet. And I had, in fact, a good deal to think about – a general subject for reflection which arranged itself around two personalities: Miss D'Arblay and Dr. Thorndyke.

To the former I had written suggesting a call on her, "*subject to the exigencies of the service*", on Sunday afternoon, and had received a short but cordial note definitely inviting me to tea. So that matter was settled and really required no further consideration, though it did actually occupy my thoughts for an appreciable part of my walk. But that was mere self-indulgence, the preliminary savouring of an anticipated pleasure. My cogitations respecting Dr. Thorndyke were, on the other hand, somewhat troubled. I was eager to invoke his aid in solving the hideous mystery which his acuteness had (I felt convinced) brought into view. But it would probably be a costly business and my pecuniary resources were not great. To apply to him for services of which I could not meet the cost was not to be thought of. The too-common meanness of sponging on a professional man was totally abhorrent to me.

But what was the alternative? The murder of Julius D'Arblay was one of those crimes which offer the police no opportunity – at least, so it seemed to me. Out of the darkness this fiend had stolen to commit this unspeakable atrocity, and into the darkness he had straightway vanished, leaving no trace of his identity nor any hint of his diabolical motive. It might well be that he had vanished for ever, that the mystery of the crime was beyond solution. But if any solution was possible, the one man who seemed capable of discovering it was John Thorndyke.

This conclusion, to which my reflections led, again and again, committed me to the dilemma that either this villain must be allowed to go his way unmolested, if the police could find no clue to his identity – a position that I utterly refused to accept – or that the one supremely skilful investigator should be induced, if possible, to take up the inquiry. In the end I decided to call on Thorndyke and frankly lay the facts before him, but to postpone the interview until I had seen Miss D'Arblay and ascertained what view the police took of the case and whether any new facts had transpired.

The train of reflection which brought me to this conclusion had brought me also, by way of Pentonville, to the more familiar neighbourhood of Clerkenwell, and I had just turned into a somewhat squalid by-street which seemed to bear in the right direction, when my attention was arrested by a brass plate affixed to the door of one of those hybrid establishments, intermediate between a shop and a private house, known by the generic name of *"Open Surgery"*. The name upon the plate – *Dr. Solomon Usher* – awakened certain reminiscences. In my freshman days there had been a student of that name at our hospital, a middle-aged man (elderly, we considered him, seeing that he was near upon forty) who, after years of servitude as an unqualified assistant, had scraped together the means of completing his curriculum. I remembered him very well – a facetious, seedy, slightly bibulous but entirely good-natured man, invincibly amiable (as he had need to be), and always in the best of spirits. I recalled the quaint figure that furnished such rich material for our school-boy wit: The solemn spectacles, the ridiculous side-whiskers, the chimney-pot hat, the formal frock-coat (too often decorated with a label secretly pinned to the coat-tail and bearing some such inscription as *"This style 10s. 6d."* or other scintillations of freshman humour), and, looking over the establishment, decided that it seemed to present a complete congruity with that well-remembered personality. But the identification was not left to mere surmise, for even as my eye roamed along a range of stoppered bottles that peeped over the wire blind, the door opened and there he was, spectacles, side-whiskers, top-hat and frock-coat, all complete, plus an oedematous-looking umbrella.

He did not recognise me at first – naturally, for I had changed a good deal more than he had in the five or six years that had slipped away – but inquired gravely if I wished to see him. I replied that it had been the dearest wish of my heart, now at length gratified. Then, as I grinned in his face, my identity suddenly dawned on him.

"Why, it's Gray!" he exclaimed, seizing my hand. "God bless me, what a surprise! I didn't know you. Getting quite a man. Well, I am delighted to see you. Come in and have a drink."

He held the door open invitingly, but I shook my head.

"No, thanks," I replied. "Not at this time in the day."

"Nonsense," he urged. "Do you good. I've just had one myself. Can't say more than that, excepting that I am ready to have another. Won't you really? Pity. Should never waste an opportunity. Which way are you going?"

It seemed that we were going the same way for some distance and we accordingly set off together.

"So you've flopped out of the nest," he remarked, looking me over. "At least, so I judge by the adult clothes that you are wearing. Are you in practice in these parts?"

"No," I replied, "I am doing a *locum*. Only just qualified, you know."

"Good," said he. "A *locum*'s the way to begin. Try your 'prentice hand on somebody else's patients and pick up the art of general practice, which they don't teach you at the hospital."

"You mean book-keeping and dispensing and the general routine of the day's work?" I suggested.

"No, I don't," he replied. "I mean *practice*, the art of pleasing your patients and keeping your end up. You've got a lot to learn, my boy. *Experientia* does it. Scientific stuff is all very well at the hospital, but in practice it is experience, gumption, tact, knowledge of human nature, that counts."

"I suppose a little knowledge of diagnosis and treatment is useful?" I suggested.

"For your own satisfaction, yes," he admitted, "but for practical purposes, a little knowledge of men and women is a good deal better. It isn't your scientific learning that brings you kudos, nor is it out-of-the-way cases. It is just common sense brought to bear on common ailments. Take the case of an aurist. You think that he lives by dealing with obscure and difficult middle and internal ear cases. Nothing of the kind. He lives on wax. Wax is the foundation of his practice. Patient comes to him as deaf as a post. He does all the proper jugglery — tuning-fork, otoscope, speculum and so on, for the moral effect. Then he hikes out a good old plug of cerumen and the patient hears perfectly. Of course, he is delighted. Thinks a miracle has been performed. Goes away convinced that the aurist is a genius, and so he is if he has managed the case properly. I made my reputation here on a fish-bone."

"Well, a fish-bone isn't always so very easy to extract,' said I.

"It isn't," he agreed. "Especially if it isn't there."

"What do you mean?" I asked.

458

"I'll tell you about it," he replied. "A chappie here got a fish-bone stuck in his throat. Of course it didn't stay there. They never do. But the prick in his soft palate did, and he was convinced that the bone was still there. So he sent for a doctor. Doctor came, looked in his throat. Couldn't see any fish-bone and, like a fool, said so. Tried to persuade the patient that there was no bone there. But the chappie said it was his throat and he knew better. He could *feel* it there. So he sent for another doctor and the same thing happened. No go. He had four different doctors and they hadn't the sense of an infant among them. Then he sent for me.

"Now, as soon as I heard how the land lay, I nipped into the surgery and got a fish-bone that I keep there in a pillbox for emergencies, stuck it into the jaws of a pair of throat-forceps, and off I went. 'Show me whereabouts it is,' says I, handing him a probe to point with. He showed me the spot and nearly swallowed the probe. 'All right,' said I. 'I can see it. Just shut your eyes and open your mouth wide and I will have it out in a jiffy.' I popped the forceps into his mouth, gave a gentle prod with the point on the soft palate, patient hollered out, 'Hoo!' I whisked out the forceps and held them up before his eyes with the fish-bone grasped in their jaws.

"'Ha!' says he. 'Thank Gawd! What a relief! I can swallow quite well now.' And so he could. It was a case of suggestion and counter-suggestion. Imaginary fish-bone cured by imaginary extraction. And it made my local reputation. Well, good-bye, old chap. I've got a visit to make here. Come in one evening and smoke a pipe with me. You know where to find me. And take my advice to heart. Never go to extract a fish-bone without one in your pocket, and it isn't a bad thing to keep a dried earwig by you. I do. People will persist in thinking they've got one in their ears. So long. Look me up soon." And with a farewell flourish of the umbrella, he turned to a shabby street-door and began to work the top bell-pull as if it were the handle of an air-pump.

I went on my way, not a little amused by my friend's genial cynicism, nor entirely uninstructed. For "there is a soul of truth in things erroneous", as the philosopher reminds us, and if the precepts of Solomon Usher did not sound the highest note of professional ethics, they were based on a very solid foundation of worldly wisdom.

When, having finished my short round of visits, I arrived at my temporary home, I was informed by the housemaid in a mysterious whisper that a police officer was waiting to see me. "Name of Follett," she added. "He's waiting in the consulting room."

Proceeding thither, I found my friend, the Highgate inspector, standing with one eye closed before a card of test-types that hung on the

459

wall. We greeted one another cordially and then, as I looked at him inquiringly, he produced from his pocket without remark an official envelope, from which he extracted a coin, a silver pencil-case, and a button. These objects he laid on the writing-table and silently directed my attention to them. A little puzzled by his manner, I picked up the coin and examined it attentively. It was a Charles the Second guinea, dated 1663, very clean and bright and in remarkably perfect preservation. But I could not see that it was any concern of mine.

"It is a beautiful coin," I remarked, "but what about it?"

"It doesn't belong to you, then?" he asked.

"No. I wish it did."

"Have you ever seen it before?"

"Never, to my knowledge."

"What about the pencil-case?"

I picked it up and turned it over in my fingers. "No," I said, "it is not mine and I have no recollection of ever having seen it before."

"And the button?"

"It is apparently a waistcoat button," I said after having inspected it, "which seems to belong to a tweed waistcoat, and judging by the appearance of the thread and the wisp of cloth that it still holds, it must have been pulled off with some violence. But it isn't off my waistcoat, if that is what you want to know."

"I didn't much think it was," he replied, "but I thought it best to make sure. And it didn't come from poor Mr. D'Arblay's waistcoat, because I have examined that and there is no button missing. I showed these things to Miss D'Arblay and she is sure that none of them belonged to her father. He never used a pencil-case – artists don't, as a rule – and as to the guinea, she knew nothing about it. If it was her father's, he must have come by it immediately before his death. Otherwise she felt sure he would have shown it to her, seeing that they were both interested in anything in the nature of sculpture."

"Where did you get these things?' I asked.

"From the pond in the wood," he replied. "I will tell you how I came to find them – that is, if I am not taking up too much of your time."

"Not at all," I assured him, and even as I spoke, I thought of Solomon Usher. He wouldn't have said that. He would have anxiously consulted his engagement-book to see how many minutes he could spare. However, Inspector Follett was not a patient, and I wanted to hear his story. So having established him in the easy-chair, I sat down to listen.

"The morning after the inquest," he began, "an officer of the CID came up to get particulars of the case and see what was to be done. Well, as soon as I had told him all I knew and shown him our copy of the depositions, it was pretty clear to me that he didn't think there was anything to be done but wait for some fresh evidence. Mind you, Doctor, this is in strict confidence."

"I understand that. But if the Criminal Investigation Department doesn't investigate crime, what the deuce is the good of it?"

"That is hardly a fair way of putting it," he protested. "The people at Scotland Yard have got their hands pretty full and they can't spend their time in speculating about cases in which there is no evidence. They can't create evidence, and you can see for yourself that there isn't the ghost of a clue to the identity of the man who committed this murder. But they are keeping the case in mind, and meanwhile we have got to report any new facts that may turn up. Those were our instructions, and when I heard them I decided to do a bit of investigating on my own – with the superintendent's permission, of course.

"Well, I began by searching the wood thoroughly, but I got nothing out of that excepting Mr. D'Arblay's hat, which I found in the undergrowth not far from the main path.

"Then I thought of dragging the pond, but I decided that, as it was only a small pond and shallow, it would be best to empty it and expose the bottom completely. So I dammed up the little stream that feeds it and deepened the outflow, and very soon I had it quite empty excepting a few small puddles. And I think it was well worth the trouble. These things don't tell us much, but they may be useful one day for identification. And they do tell us something. They suggest that this man was a collector of coins, and they make it fairly clear that there was a struggle in the pond before Mr. D'Arblay fell down."

"That is, assuming that the things belonged to the murderer," I interposed. "There is no evidence that they did."

"No, there isn't," he admitted, "but if you consider the three things together, they suggest a very strong probability. Here is a waistcoat button violently pulled off, and here are two things such as would be carried in a waistcoat pocket and might fall out if the waistcoat were dragged at violently when the wearer was stooping over a fallen man and struggling to avoid being pulled down with him. And then there is this coin. Its face-value is a guinea, but it must be worth a good deal more than that. Do you suppose anybody would leave a thing of that kind in a shallow pond from which it could be easily recovered with a common landing-net? Why, it would have paid to have had the pond dragged or even emptied. But, as I say, that wouldn't have been necessary."

"I am inclined to think you are right. Inspector," said I, rather impressed by the way in which he had reasoned the matter out, "but even so, it doesn't seem to me that we are much more forward. The things don't point to any particular person."

"Not at present," he rejoined. "But a fact is a fact and you can never tell in advance what you may get out of it. If we should get a hint of any other kind pointing to some particular person, these things might furnish invaluable evidence connecting that person with the crime. They may even give a clue now to the people at the CID, though that isn't very likely."

"Then you are going to hand them over to the Scotland Yard people?"

"Certainly. The CID are the lions, you know. I'm only a jackal."

I was rather sorry to hear this, for the idea had floated into my mind that I should have liked Thorndyke to see these waifs, which, could they have spoken, would have had much to tell. To me they conveyed nothing that threw any light on the ghastly events of that night of horror. But to my teacher, with his vast experience and his wonderful power of analysing evidence, they might convey some quite important significance.

I reflected rapidly on the matter. It would not be wise to say anything to the inspector about Thorndyke, and it was quite certain that a loan of the articles would not be entertained. Probably a description of them would be enough for the purpose, but still I had a feeling that an inspection of them would be better. Suddenly I had a bright idea and proceeded cautiously to broach it.

"I should rather like to have a record of these things," said I, "particularly of the coin. Would you object to my taking an impression of it in sealing-wax?"

Inspector Follett looked doubtful. "It would be a bit irregular," he said. "It is a bit irregular for me to have shown it to you, but you are interested in the case, and you are a responsible person. What did you want the impression for?"

"Well," I said, "we don't know much about that coin. I thought I might be able to pick up some further information. Of course, I understand hat what you have told me is strictly confidential. I shouldn't go showing the thing about, or talking. But I should like to have the impression to refer to, if necessary."

"Very well," said he. "On that understanding, I have no objection. But see that you don't leave any wax on the coin, or the CID people will be asking questions."

With this permission, I set about the business gleefully, determined to get as good an impression as possible. From the surgery I fetched an ointment slab, a spirit-lamp, a stick of sealing-wax, a teaspoon, some powder-papers, a bowl of water and a jar of vaseline. Laying a paper on the slab, I put the coin on it and traced its outline with a pencil. Then I broke off a piece of sealing-wax, melted it in the teaspoon and poured it out carefully into the marked circle so that it formed a round, convex button of the right size. While the wax was cooling to the proper consistency, I smeared the coin with vaseline and wiped the excess off with my handkerchief. Then I carefully laid it on the stiffening wax and made steady pressure. After a few moments, I cautiously lifted the paper and dropped it into the water, leaving it to cool completely. When, finally, I turned it over under water, the coin dropped away by its own weight.

"It is a beautiful impression," the inspector remarked, as he examined it with the aid of my pocket-lens, while I prepared to operate on the reverse of the coin. "As good as the original. You seem rather a dab at this sort of thing, Doctor. I wonder if you would mind doing another pair for me?"

Of course, I complied gladly, and when the inspector departed a few minutes later he took with him a couple of excellent wax impressions to console him for the necessity of parting with the original.

As soon as he was gone, I proceeded to execute a plan that had already formed in my mind. First, I packed the two wax impressions very carefully in lint and bestowed them in a tin tobacco box, which I made up into a neat parcel and addressed it to Dr. Thorndyke. Then I wrote him a short letter giving him the substance of my talk with Inspector Follett and asking for an appointment early in the following week to discuss the situation with him. I did not suppose that the wax impressions would convey, even to him, anything that would throw fresh light on this extraordinarily obscure crime. But one never knew. And the mere finding of the coin might suggest to him some significance that I had overlooked. In any case, the new incident gave me an excuse for reopening the matter with him.

I did not trust the precious missive to the maid, but as soon as the letter was written I took it and the parcel in my own hands to the post, dropping the letter into the box, but giving the parcel the added security of registration. This business being thus dispatched, my mind was free to occupy itself with pleasurable anticipations of the projected visit to Highgate on the morrow and to deal with whatever exigencies might arise in the course of the Saturday-evening consultations.

Chapter VI
Marion D'Arblay at Home

Most of us have, I imagine, been conscious at times of certain misgivings as to whether the Progress of which we hear so much has done for us all that it is assumed to have done, whether the undoubted gain of advancing knowledge has not a somewhat heavy counterpoise of loss. We moderns are accustomed to look upon a world filled with objects that would have made our forefathers gasp with admiring astonishment, and we are accordingly a little puffed up by our superiority. But the museums and galleries and ancient buildings sometimes tell a different tale. By them we are made aware that the same "rude forefathers" were endowed with certain powers and aptitudes that seem to be denied to the present generation.

Some such reflections as these passed through my mind as I sauntered about the ancient village of Highgate, having arrived in the neighbourhood nearly an hour too early. Very delightful the old village was to look upon, and so it had been even when the mellow red brick was new and the plaster on the timber houses was but freshly laid, when the great elms were saplings and the stage-wagon with its procession of horses rumbled along the road which now resounds to the thunder of the electric tram. It was not Time that had made beautiful its charming old houses and pleasant streets and closes, but fine workmanship guided by unerring taste.

At four o'clock precisely, by the chime of the church dock, I pushed open the gate of Ivy Cottage, and as I walked up the flagged path, read the date, 1709, on a stone tablet let into the brickwork. I had no occasion to knock, for my approach had been observed, and as I mounted the threshold the door opened and Miss D'Arblay stood in the opening.

"Miss Boler saw you coming up the Grove," she explained, as we shook hands. "It is surprising how much of the outer world you can see from a bay window. It is as good as a watch-tower." She disposed of my hat and stick and then preceded me into the room to which the window appertained, where, beside a bright fire. Miss Boler was at the moment occupied with a brilliantly-burnished copper kettle and a silver teapot. She greeted me with an affable smile and as much of a bow as was possible under the circumstances, and then proceeded to make the tea with an expression of deep concentration.

"I do like punctual people," she remarked, placing the teapot on a carved wooden stand. "You know where you are with them. At the very moment when you turned the corner, sir, Miss Marion finished buttering the last muffin and the kettle boiled over. So you won't have to wait a moment."

Miss D'Arblay laughed softly. "You speak as if Dr. Gray had staggered into the house in a famished condition, roaring for food," said she.

"Well," retorted Miss Boler, "you said 'tea at four o'clock', and at four o'clock the tea was ready and Dr. Gray was here. If he hadn't been, he would have had to eat leathery muffins, that's all."

"Horrible!" exclaimed Miss D'Arblay. "One doesn't like to think of it, and there is no need to as it hasn't happened. Remember that this is a gate-legged table, Dr. Gray, when you sit down. They are delightfully picturesque, but exceedingly bad for the knees of the unwary."

I thanked her for the warning and took my seat with due caution. Then Miss Boler poured out the tea and uncovered the muffins with the grave and attentive air of one performing some ceremonial rite.

As the homely, simple meal proceeded, to an accompaniment of desultory conversation on everyday topics, I found myself looking at the two women with a certain ill-defined surprise. Both were garbed in unobtrusive black, and both, in moments of repose, looked somewhat tired and worn. But in their manner and the subjects of their conversation they were astonishingly ordinary and normal. No stranger, looking at them and listening to their talk, would have dreamed of the tragedy that overshadowed their lives. But so it constantly happens. We go into a house of mourning and are almost scandalized by its cheerfulness, forgetting that whereas to us the bereavement is the one salient fact, to the bereaved there is the necessity of taking up afresh the threads of their lives. Food must be prepared even while the corpse lies under the roof, and the common daily round of duty stands still for no human affliction.

But, as I have said, in the pauses of the conversation when their faces were in repose, both women looked strained and tired. Especially was this so in the case of Miss D'Arblay. She was not only pale, but she had a nervous, shaken manner which I did not like. And as I looked anxiously at the delicate, pallid face, I noticed, not for the first time, several linear scratches on the cheek and a small cut on the temple.

"What have you been doing to yourself?" I asked. "You look as if you have had a fall."

"She has," said Miss Boler in an indignant tone. "It is a marvel that she is here to tell the tale. The wretches!"

465

I looked at Miss D'Arblay in consternation. "What wretches?" I asked.

"Ah! Indeed!" growled Miss Boler. "I wish I knew. Tell him about it. Miss Marion."

"It was really rather a terrifying experience," said Miss D'Arblay, "and most mysterious. You know Southwood Lane and the long, steep hill at the bottom of it?" I nodded, and she continued, "I have been going down to the studio every day on my bicycle, just to tidy up, and of course I went by Southwood Lane. It is really the only way. But I always put on the brake at the top of the hill and go down quite slowly because of the crossroads at the bottom. Well, three days ago I started as usual, and ran down the Lane pretty fast until I got on the hill. Then I put on the brake, and I could feel at once that it wasn't working."

"Has your bicycle only one brake?" I asked.

"It had. I am having a second one fixed now. Well, when I found that the brake wasn't acting, I was terrified. I was already going too fast to jump off, and the speed increased every moment. I simply flew down the hill, faster and faster, with the wind whistling about my ears and the trees and houses whirling past like express trains. Of course, I could do nothing but steer straight down the hill, but at the bottom there was the Archway Road with the trams and buses and wagons. I knew that if a tram crossed the bottom of the Lane as I reached the road, it was practically certain death. I was horribly frightened.

"However, mercifully the Archway Road was clear when I flew across it, and I steered to run on down Muswell Hill Road, which is nearly in a line with the Lane. But suddenly I saw a steam roller and a heavy cart, side by side and taking up the whole of the road. There was no room to pass. The only possible thing was to swerve round, if I could, into Wood Lane. And I just managed it. But Wood Lane is pretty steep, and I flew down it faster than ever. That nearly broke down my nerve, for at the bottom of the Lane is the wood – the horrible wood that I can never even think of without a shudder. And there I seemed to be rushing towards it to my death."

She paused and drew a deep breath, and her hand shook so that the cup which it held rattled on the saucer.

"Well," she continued, "down the Lane I flew with my heart in my mouth and the entrance to the wood rushing to meet me. I could see that the opening in the hurdles was just wide enough for me to pass through, and I steered for it. I whizzed through into the wood and the bicycle went bounding down the steep, rough path at a fearful pace until it came to a sharp turn, and then I don't quite know what happened. There was a crash of snapping branches and a violent shock, but I must have been

466

partly stunned, for the next thing that I remember is opening my eyes and looking stupidly at a lady who was stooping over me. She had seen me fly down the Lane and had followed me into the wood to see what happened to me. She lived in the Lane and she very kindly took me to her house and cared for me until I was quite recovered, and then she saw me home and wheeled the bicycle."

"It is a wonder you were not killed outright!" I exclaimed.

"Yes," she agreed, "it was a narrow escape. But the odd thing is that, with the exception of these scratches and a few slight bruises, I was not hurt at all, only very much shaken. And the bicycle was not damaged a bit."

"By the way," said I, "what had happened to the brake?"

"Ah!" exclaimed Miss Boler. "There you are. The villains!"

Miss D'Arblay laughed softly. "Ferocious Arabella!" said she. "But it is really a most mysterious affair. Naturally, I thought that the wire of the brake had snapped. But it hadn't. It had been *cut*."

"Are you quite sure of that?" I asked.

"Oh, there is no doubt at all," she replied. "The man at the repair shop showed it to me. It wasn't merely cut in one place. A length of it had been cut right out. And I can tell within a few minutes when it was done, for I had been riding the machine in the morning and I know the brake was all right then. But I left it for a few minutes outside the gate while I went into the house to change my shoes, and when I came out, I started on my adventurous journey. In those few minutes someone must have come along and just snipped the wire through in two places and taken away the piece."

"Scoundrel!" muttered Miss Boler, and I agreed with her most cordially.

"It was an infamous thing to do," I exclaimed, "and the act of an abject fool. I suppose you have no idea or suspicion as to who the idiot might be?"

"Not the slightest," Miss D'Arblay replied. "I can't even guess at the kind of person who would do such a thing. Boys are sometimes very mischievous, but this is hardly like a boy's mischief."

"No," I agreed, "it is more like the mischief of a mentally defective adult, the sort of half-baked larrikin who sets fire to a rick if he gets the chance."

Miss Boler sniffed. "Looks to me more like deliberate malice," said she.

"Mischievous acts usually do," I rejoined, "but yet they are mostly the outcome of stupidity that is indifferent to consequences."

467

"And it is of no use arguing about it," said Miss D'Arblay, "because we don't know who did it or why he did it, and we have no means of finding out. But I shall have two brakes in future and I shall test them both every time I take the machine out."

"I hope you will," said Miss Boler, and this closed the topic so far as conversation went, though I suspect that, in the interval of silence that followed, we all continued to pursue it in our thoughts. And to all of us, doubtless, the mention of Churchyard Bottom Wood had awakened memories of that fatal morning when the pool gave up its dead. No reference to the tragedy had yet been made, but it was inevitable that the thoughts which were at the back of all our minds should sooner or later come to the surface. They were in fact brought there by me, though unintentionally, for, as I sat at the table, my eyes had strayed more than once to a bust – or rather a head, for there were no shoulders – which occupied the centre of the mantelpiece. It was apparently of lead and was a portrait, and a very good one, of Miss D'Arblay's father. At the first glance I had recognized the face which I had first seen through the water of the pool. Miss D'Arblay, who was sitting facing it, caught my glance and said, "You are looking at that head of my dear father. I suppose you recognized it?"

"Yes, instantly. I should take it to be an excellent likeness."

"It is," she replied, "and that is something of an achievement in a self-portrait in the round."

"Then he modelled it himself?"

"Yes, with the aid of one or two photographs and a couple of mirrors. I helped him by taking the dimensions with callipers and drawing out a scale. Then he made a wax cast and a fireproof mould and we cast it together in type-metal, as we had no means of melting bronze. Poor Daddy! How proud he was when we broke away the mould and found the casting quite perfect!"

She sighed as she gazed fondly on the beloved features, and her eyes filled. Then, after a brief silence, she turned to me and asked, "Did Inspector Follett call on you? He said he was going to."

"Yes, he called yesterday to show me the things that he had found in the pond. Of course they were not mine, and he seemed to have no doubt – and I think he is right – that they belonged to the – to the – "

"Murderer," said Miss Boler.

"Yes. He seemed to think that they might furnish some kind of clue, but I am afraid he had nothing very clear in his mind. I suppose that coin suggested nothing to you?"

Miss D'Arblay shook her head. "Nothing," she replied. "As it is an ancient coin, the man may be a collector or a dealer – "

"Or a forger," interposed Miss Boler.

"Or a forger. But no such person is known to us. And even that is mere guess-work."

"Your father was not interested in coins, then?"

"As a sculptor, yes, and more especially in medals and plaquettes. But not as a collector. He had no desire to possess, only to create. And so far as I know, he was not acquainted with any collectors. So this discovery of the inspector's, so far from solving the mystery, only adds a fresh problem."

She reflected for a few moments with knitted brows. Then, turning to me quickly, she asked, "Did the inspector take you into his confidence at all? He was very reticent with me, though most kind and sympathetic. But do you think that he, or the others, are taking any active measures?"

"My impression," I answered reluctantly, "is that the police are not in a position to do anything. The truth is that this villain seems to have got away without leaving a trace."

"That is what I feared," she sighed. Then with sudden passion, though in a quiet, suppressed voice, she exclaimed, "But he must not escape! It would be too hideous an injustice. Nothing can bring back my dear father from the grave, but if there is a God of Justice, this murderous wretch must be called to account and made to pay the penalty of his crime."

"He must," Miss Boler assented in deep, ominous tones, "and he shall, though God knows how it is to be done."

"For the present," said I, "there is nothing to be done but to wait and see if the police are able to obtain any fresh information, and meanwhile to turn over every circumstance that you can think of, to recall the way your father spent his time, the people he knew and the possibility in each case that some cause of enmity may have arisen."

"That is what I have done," said Miss D'Arblay. "Every night I lie awake, thinking, thinking, but nothing comes of it. The thing is incomprehensible. This man must have been a deadly enemy of my father's. He must have hated him with the most intense hatred, or he must have had some strong reason, other than mere hatred, for making away with him. But I cannot imagine any person hating my father, and I certainly have no knowledge of any such person, nor can I conceive of any reason that any human creature could have had for wishing for my father's death. I cannot begin to understand the meaning of what has happened."

"But yet," said I, "there must be a meaning. This man – unless he was a lunatic, which he apparently was not – must have had a motive for committing the murder. That motive must have had some background,

469

some connexion with circumstances of which somebody has knowledge. Sooner or later those circumstances will almost certainly come to light, and then the motive for the murder will come into view. But, once the motive is known, it should not be difficult to discover who could be influenced by such a motive. Let us, for the present, be patient and see how events shape, but let us also keep a constant watch for any glimmer of light, for any fact that may bear on either the motive or the person."

The two women looked at me earnestly and with an expression of respectful confidence of which I knew myself to be wholly undeserving.

"It gives me new courage," said Miss D'Arblay, "to hear you speak in that reasonable, confident tone. I was in despair, but I feel that you are right. There must be some explanation of this awful thing, and if there is, it must be possible to discover it. But we ought not to put the burden of our troubles on you, though you have been so kind."

"You have done me the honour," said I, "to allow me to consider myself your friend. Surely friends should help to bear one another's burdens."

"Yes," she replied, "in reason, and you have given most generous help already. But we must not put too much on you. When my father was alive, he was my great interest and chief concern. Now that he is gone, the great purpose of my life is to find the wretch who murdered him and to see that justice is done. That is all that seems to matter to me. But it is my own affair. I ought not to involve my friends in it."

"I can't admit that." said I. "The foundation of friendship is sympathy and service. If I am your friend, then what matters to you matters to me, and I may say that in the very moment when I first knew that your father had been murdered, I made the resolve to devote myself to the discovery and punishment of his murderer by any means that lay in my power. So you must count me as your ally as well as your friend."

As I made this declaration – to an accompaniment of approving growls from Miss Boler – Marion D'Arblay gave me one quick glance and then looked down, and once more her eyes filled. For a few moments she made no reply, and when, at length, she spoke, her voice trembled.

"You leave me nothing to say," she murmured, "but to thank you from my heart. But you little know what it means to us, who felt so helpless, to know that we have a friend so much wiser and stronger than ourselves."

I was a little abashed, knowing my own weakness and helplessness, to find her putting so much reliance on me. However, there was Thorndyke in the background, and now I was resolved that, if the thing was in any way to be compassed, his help must be secured without delay.

470

A longish pause followed, and as it seemed to me that there was nothing more to say on this subject until I had seen Thorndyke, I ventured to open a fresh topic.

"What will happen to your father's practice?" I asked. "Will you be able to get anyone to carry it on for you?"

"I am glad you asked that," said Miss D'Arblay, "because, now that you are our counsellor, we can take your opinion. I have already talked the matter over with Arabella – with Miss Boler."

"There's no need to stand on ceremony," the latter lady interposed. "Arabella is good enough for me."

"Arabella is good enough for anyone," said Miss D'Arblay. "Well, the position is this. The part of my father's practice that was concerned with original work – pottery figures and reliefs and models for goldsmith's work – will have to go. No one but a sculptor of his own class could carry that on. But the wax figures for the shop-windows are different. When he first started, he used to model the heads and limbs in clay and make plaster casts from which to make the gelatine moulds for the waxwork. But as time went on, these casts accumulated and he very seldom had need to model fresh beads or limbs. The old casts could be used over and over again. Now there is a large collection of plaster models in the studio – heads, arms, legs and faces, especially faces – and as I have a fair knowledge of the waxwork, from watching my father and sometimes helping him, it seemed that I might be able to carry on that part of the practice."

"You think you could make the wax figures yourself?" I asked.

"Of course she could," exclaimed Miss Boler. "She's her father's daughter. Julius D'Arblay was a man who could do anything he turned his hand to and do it well. And Miss Marion is just like him. She is quite a good modeller – so her father said, and she wouldn't have to make the figures. Only the wax parts."

"Then they are not wax all over?" said I.

"No," answered Miss D'Arblay. "They are just dummies, wooden frameworks covered with stuffed canvas, with wax heads, busts and arms and shaped legs. That was just what poor Daddy used to hate about them. He would have liked to model complete figures."

"And as to the business side. Could you dispose of them?"

"Yes, if I could do them satisfactorily. The agent who dealt with my father's work has already written to me asking if I could carry on. I know he will help me so far as he can. He was quite fond of my father."

"And you have nothing else in view?"

"Nothing by which I could earn a real living. For the last year or two I have worked at writing and illuminating – addresses, testimonials, and church services when I could get them – and filled in the time writing special window-tickets. But that isn't very remunerative, whereas the wax figures would yield quite a good living. And then," she added, after a pause, "I have the feeling that Daddy would have liked me to carry on his work, and I should like it myself. He taught me quite a lot, and I think he meant me to join him when he got old."

As she had evidently made up her mind, and as her decision seemed quite a wise one, I concurred with as much enthusiasm as I could muster.

"I am glad you agree," said she, "and I know Arabella does. So that is settled, subject to my being able to carry out the plan. And now, if we have finished, I should like to show you some of my father's works. The house is full of them and so, even, is the garden. Perhaps we had better go there first before the light fails."

As the treasures of this singularly interesting home were presented, one after another, for my inspection, I began to realize the truth of Miss Boler's statement. Julius D'Arblay had been a remarkably versatile man. He had worked in all sorts of mediums and in all equally well. From the carved stone sundial and the leaden garden figures to the clock-case decorated with gilded gesso and enriched with delicate bronze plaquettes, all his works were eloquent of masterly skill and a fresh, graceful fancy. It seems to me little short of a tragedy that an artist of his ability should have spent the greater part of his time in fabricating those absurd, posturing effigies that simper and smirk so grotesquely in the enormous windows of Vanity Fair.

I had intended, in compliance with the polite conventions, to make this, my first visit, a rather short one, but a tentative movement to depart only elicited protests and I was easily persuaded to stay until the exigencies of Dr. Cornish's practice seemed to call me. When at last I shut the gate of Ivy Cottage behind me and glanced back at the two figures standing in the lighted doorway, I had the feeling of turning away from a house with which, and its inmates, I had been familiar for years.

On my arrival at Mecklenburgh Square, I found a note which had been left by hand earlier in the evening. It was from Dr. Thorndyke, asking me, if possible, to lunch with him at his chambers on the morrow. I looked over my visiting-list, and finding that Monday would be a light day – most of my days here were light days – I wrote a short letter accepting the invitation and posted it forthwith.

472

Chapter VII
Thorndyke Enlarges his Knowledge

"I am glad you were able to come," said Thorndyke, as we took our places at the table. "Your letter was a shade ambiguous. You spoke of discussing the D'Arblay case, but I think you had something more than discussion in your mind."

"You are quite right," I replied. "I had it in my mind to ask if it would be possible for me to retain you – I believe that is the correct expression – to investigate the case, as the police seem to think there is nothing to go on, and if the costs would be likely to be within my means."

"As to the costs," said he, "we can dismiss them. I see no reason to suppose that there would be any costs."

"But your time, sir – " I began.

He laughed derisively. "Do you propose to pay me for indulging in my pet hobby? No, my dear fellow, it is I who should pay you for bringing a most interesting and intriguing case to my notice. So your questions are answered. I shall be delighted to look into this case, and there will be no costs unless we have to pay for some special services. If we do, I will let you know."

I was about to utter a protest, but he continued, "And now, having disposed of the preliminaries, let us consider the case itself, Your very shrewd and capable inspector believes that the Scotland Yard people will take no active measures unless some new facts turn up. I have no doubt he is right, and I think they are right, too. They can't spend a lot of time – which means public money – on a case in which hardly any data are available and which holds out no promise of any result. But we mustn't forget that we are in the same boat. Our chances of success are infinitesimal. This investigation is a forlorn hope. That, I may say, is what commends it to me, but I want you to understand clearly that failure is what we have to expect."

"I understand that," I answered gloomily, but nevertheless rather disappointed at this pessimistic view. "There seems to be nothing whatever to go upon."

"Oh, it isn't so bad as that," he rejoined. "Let us just run over the data that we have. Our object is to fix the identity of the man who killed Julius D'Arblay. Let us see what we know about him. We will begin with the evidence at the inquest. From that we learned – One: That he is a man of some education. Ingenious, subtle, resourceful. This murder was planned with extraordinary ingenuity and foresight. The body was found in the pond with no tell-tale mark on it but an almost invisible pin-prick in the back. The chances were a thousand-to-one, or more, against that tiny puncture ever being observed, and if it had not been observed, the verdict would have been 'found drowned' or 'found dead', and the fact of the murder would never have been discovered.

"Two: We also learned that he has some knowledge of poisons. The common, vulgar poisoner is reduced to flypapers, weed-killer, or rat-poison – arsenic or strychnine. But this man selects the most suitable of all poisons for his purpose and administers it in the most effective manner – with a hypodermic syringe.

"Three: We learned further that he must have had some extraordinarily strong reason for making away with D'Arblay. He made most elaborate plans, he took endless trouble – for instance, it must have been no easy matter to get possession of that quantity of aconitine (unless he were a doctor, which God forbid!). That strong reason – the motive, in fact – is the key of the problem. It is the murderer's one vulnerable point, for it can hardly be beyond discovery, and its discovery must be our principal objective."

I nodded, not without some self-congratulation as I recalled how I had made this very point in my talk with Miss D'Arblay.

"Those," Thorndyke continued, "are the data that the inquest furnished. Now we come to those added by Inspector Follett."

"I don't see that they help us at all," said I. "The ancient coin was a curious find, but it doesn't appear to tell us anything new excepting that this man may have been a collector or a dealer. On the other hand, he may not. It doesn't seem to me that the coin has any significance."

"Doesn't it really?" said Thorndyke, as he refilled my glass. "You are surely overlooking the very curious coincidence that it presents?"

"What coincidence is that?" I asked, in some surprise.

"The coincidence," he replied, "that both the murderer and the victim should be, to a certain extent, connected with a particular form of activity. Here is a man who commits a murder and who at the time of committing it appears to have been in possession of a coin, which is not a current coin but a collector's piece, and behold! The murdered man is a sculptor – a man who, presumably, was capable of making a coin, or at least the working model."

"There is no evidence," I objected, "that D'Arblay was capable of cutting a die. He was not a die-sinker."

"There was no need for him to be," Thorndyke rejoined. "Formerly, the medallist who designed the coin cut the die himself. But that is not the modern practice. Nowadays, the designer makes the model, first in wax and then in plaster, on a comparatively large scale. The model of a shilling may be three inches or more in diameter. The actual die-sinking is done by a copying machine which produces a die of the required size by mechanical reduction. I think there can be no doubt that D'Arblay could have modelled the design for a coin on the usual scale, say three or four inches in diameter."

"Yes," I agreed, "he certainly could, for I have seen some of his small relief work, some little plaquettes, not more than two inches long and most delicately and beautifully modelled. But still I don't see the connexion, otherwise than as a rather odd coincidence."

"There may be nothing more," said he. "There may be nothing in it at all. But odd coincidences should always be noted with very special attention."

"Yes, I realize that. But I can't imagine what significance there could be in the coincidence."

"Well," said Thorndyke, "let us take an imaginary case, just as an illustration. Suppose this man to have been a fraudulent dealer in antiquities, and suppose him to have obtained enlarged photographs of a medal or coin of extreme rarity and of great value, which was in some museum or private collection. Suppose him to have taken the photographs to D'Arblay and commissioned him to model from them a pair of exact replicas in hardened plaster. From those plaster models he could, with a copying machine, produce a pair of dies with which he could strike replicas in the proper metal and of the exact size, and these could be sold for large sums to judiciously-chosen collectors."

"I don't believe D'Arblay would have accepted such a commission," I exclaimed indignantly.

"We may assume that he would not, if the fraudulent intent had been known to him. But it would not have been, and there is no reason why he should have refused a commission merely to make a copy. Still, I am not suggesting that anything of the kind really happened. I am simply giving you an illustration of one of the innumerable ways in which a perfectly honest sculptor might be made use of by a fraudulent dealer. In that case, his honesty would be a source of danger to him, for if a really great fraud were perpetrated by means of his work, it would clearly be to the interest of the perpetrator to get rid of him. An honest and unconscious collaborator in a crime is apt to be a dangerous witness if questions arise."

I was a good deal impressed by this demonstration. Here, it seemed to me, was something very like a tangible clue. But at this point Thorndyke again applied a cold *douche*.

"Still," he said, "we are only dealing with generalities, and rather speculative ones. Our assumptions are subject to all sorts of qualifications. It is possible, for instance, though very improbable, that D'Arblay may have been murdered in error by a perfect stranger, that he may have walked into an ambush prepared for someone else. Again, the coin may not have belonged to the murderer at all, though that is also most improbable. But there are numerous possibilities of error, and we can eliminate them only by following up each suggested clue and seeking verification or disproof. Every new fact that we learn is a multiple gain. For as money makes money, so knowledge begets knowledge."

"That is very true," I answered dejectedly – for it sounded rather like a platitude, "but I don't see any means of following up any of these clues."

"We are going to follow up one of them after lunch, if you have time," said he. As he spoke, he took from the table-drawer a paper packet and a jeweller's leather case. "This," he said, handing me the packet, "contains your sealing-wax moulds. You had better take care of them and keep the box with the marked side up to prevent the wax from warping. Here are a pair of casts in hardened plaster – '*fictile ivory*' as it is called – which my assistant, Polton, has made."

He opened the case and passed it to me, when I saw that it was lined with purple velvet and contained what looked like two old ivory replicas of the mysterious coin.

"Mr. Polton is quite an artist," I said, regarding them admiringly. "But what are you going to do with these?"

"I had intended to take them round to the British Museum and show them to the Keeper of the Coins and Medals, or one of his colleagues. But I think I will just ask a few questions and hear what he says before I produce the casts. Have you time to come round with me?"

"I shall make time. But what do you want to know about the coin?"

"It is just a matter of verification," he replied. "My books on the British coinage describe the Charles the Second guinea as having a tiny elephant under the bust on the obverse, to show that the gold from which it was minted came from the Guinea Coast."

"Yes," said I. "Well, there is a little elephant under the bust in this coin."

"True," he replied. "But this elephant has a castle on his back and would ordinarily be described as an elephant and castle, to distinguish him from the plain elephant which appeared on some coins. What I want to ascertain is whether there were two different types of guinea. The books make no mention of a second variety."

476

"Surely they would have referred to it if there had been," said I.

"So I thought," he replied, "but it is better to make sure than to think."

"I suppose it is," I agreed without much conviction, "though I don't see that, even if there were two varieties, that fact would have any bearing on what we want to know."

"Neither do I," he admitted. "But then you can never tell what a fact will prove until you are in possession of the fact. And now, as we seem to have finished, perhaps we had better make our way to the Museum."

The Department of Coins and Medals is associated in my mind with an impassive-looking Chinese person in bronze who presides over the upper landing of the main staircase. In fact, we halted for a moment before him to exchange a final word.

"It will probably be best," said Thorndyke, "to say nothing about this coin, or, indeed, about anything else. We don't want to enter into any explanations."

"No," I agreed. "It is best to keep one's own counsel," and with this we entered the hall, where Thorndyke led the way to a small door and pressed the electric bell-push. An attendant admitted us, and when we had signed our names in the visitors' book, he ushered us into the keeper's room. As we entered, a keen-faced, middle-aged man who was seated at a table inspected us over his spectacles, and apparently recognizing Thorndyke, rose and held out his hand.

"Quite a long time since I have seen you," he remarked after the preliminary greetings. "I wonder what your quest is this time."

"It is a very simple one," said Thorndyke. "I am going to ask you if you can let me look at a Charles the Second guinea dated 1663."

"Certainly I can," was the reply, accompanied by an inquisitive glance at my friend. "It is not a rarity, you know."

He crossed the room to a large cabinet, and having run his eye over the multitudinous labels, drew out a small, very-shallow drawer. With this in his hand, he returned, and picking a coin out of its circular pit, held it out to Thorndyke, who took it from him, holding it delicately by the edges. He looked at it attentively for a few moments, and then silently presented the obverse for my inspection. Naturally my eye at once sought the little elephant under the bust, and there it was, but there was no castle on its back.

"Is this the only type of guinea issued at that date?" Thorndyke asked.

"The only type – with or without the elephant, according to the source of the gold."

"There was no variation or alternative form?"

477

"No."

"I notice that this coin has a plain elephant under the bust, but I seem to have heard of a guinea, bearing this date, which had an elephant and castle under the bust. You are sure there was no such guinea?"

Our official friend shook his head as he took the coin from Thorndyke and replaced it in its cell. "As sure," he replied, "as one can be of a universal negative." He picked up the drawer and was just moving away towards the cabinet when there came a sudden change in his manner.

"Wait!" he exclaimed, stopping and putting down the drawer. "You are quite right. Only it was not an issue, it was a trial piece, and only a single coin was struck. I will tell you about it. There is a rather curious story hanging to that piece.

"This guinea, as you probably know, was struck from dies cut by John Roettier, and was one of the first coined by the mill-and-screw process in place of the old hammer-and-pile method. Now, when Roettier had finished the dies, a trial piece was struck, and in striking that piece, the obverse die cracked right across, but apparently only at the last turn of the screw, for the trial piece was quite perfect. Of course Roettier had to cut a new die, and for some reason he made a slight alteration. The first die had an elephant and castle under the bust. In the second one he changed this to a plain elephant. So your impression was, so far, correct, but the coin, if it still exists, is absolutely unique."

"Is it not known, then, what became of that trial piece?"

"Oh, yes – up to a point. That is the queerest part of the story. For a time it remained in the possession of the Slingsby family – Slingsby was the Master of the Mint when it was struck. Then it passed through the hands of various collectors and finally was bought by an American collector named Van Zellen. Now, Van Zellen was a millionaire and his collection was a typical millionaire's collection. It consisted entirely of things of enormous value which no ordinary man could afford or of unique things of which nobody could possibly have a duplicate. It seems that he was a rather solitary man and that he spent most of his evenings alone in his museum, gloating over his possessions.

"One morning Van Zellen was found dead in the little study attached to the museum. That was about eighteen months ago. There was an empty champagne bottle on the table and a half-emptied glass, which smelt of bitter almonds, and in his pocket was an empty phial labelled 'Hydrocyanic Acid'. At first it was assumed that he had committed suicide, but when, later, the collection was examined, it was found that a considerable part of it was missing. A clean sweep had been made of the gems, jewels, and other portable objects of value, and, among other

478

things, this unique trial guinea had vanished. Surely you remember the case?"

"Yes," replied Thorndyke. "I do, now you mention it, but I never heard what was stolen. Do you happen to know what the later developments were?"

"There were none. The identity of the murderer was never discovered, and not a single item of the stolen property has ever been traced. To this day the crime remains an impenetrable mystery – unless you know something about it?", and again our friend cast an inquisitive glance at Thorndyke.

"My practice," the latter, plied, "does not extend to the United States. Their own very efficient investigators seem to be able to do all that is necessary. But I am very much obliged to you for having given us so much of your time, to say nothing of this extremely interesting information. I shall make a note of it, for American crime occasionally has its repercussions on this side."

I secretly admired the adroit way in which Thorndyke had evaded the rather pointed question without making any actual misstatement. But the motive for the evasion was not very obvious to me. I was about to put a question on the subject, but he anticipated it, for, as soon as we were outside, he remarked with a chuckle, "It is just as well that we didn't begin by exhibiting the casts. We could hardly have sworn our friend to secrecy, seeing that the original is undoubtedly stolen property."

"But aren't you going to draw the attention of the police to the fact?"

"I think not," he replied. "They have got the original, and no doubt they have a list of the stolen property. We must assume that they will make use of their knowledge, but if they don't, it may be all the better for us. The police are very discreet, but they do sometimes give the Press more information than I should. And what is told to the Press is told to the criminal."

"And why not?" I asked. "What is the harm of his knowing?"

"My dear Gray!" exclaimed Thorndyke. "You surprise me. Just consider the position. This man aimed at being entirely unsuspected. That failed. But still his identity is unknown, and he is probably confident that it will never be ascertained. Then he is, so far, off his guard. There is no need for him to disappear or go into hiding. But let him know that he is being tracked and he will almost certainly take fresh precautions against discovery. Probably he will slip away beyond our reach. Our aim must be to encourage him in a feeling of perfect security, and that aim commits us to the strictest secrecy. No one must know what cards we hold or that we hold any, or even that we are taking a hand."

"What about Miss D'Arblay?" I asked anxiously. "May I not tell her that you are working on her behalf?"

He looked at me somewhat dubiously. "It would obviously be better not to," he said, "but that might seem a little unfriendly and unsympathetic."

"It would be an immense relief to her to know that you are trying to help her, and I think you could trust her to keep your secrets."

"Very well," he conceded. "But warn her very thoroughly. Remember that our antagonist is hidden from us. Let us remain hidden from him, so far as our activities are concerned."

"I will make her promise absolute secrecy," I agreed, and then, with a slight sense of anti-climax, I added, "But we don't seem to have so very much to conceal. This curious story of the stolen coin is interesting, but it doesn't appear to get us any more forward."

"Doesn't it?" he asked. "Now, I was just congratulating myself on the progress that we had made, on the way in which we are narrowing down the field of inquiry. Let us trace our progress. When you found the body, there was no evidence as to the cause of death, no suspicion of any agent whatever. Then came the inquest demonstrating the cause of death and bringing into view a person of unknown identity but having certain distinguishing characteristics. Then Follett's discovery added some further characteristics and suggested certain possible motives for the crime. But still there was no hint as to the person's identity or position in life. Now we have good evidence that he is a professional criminal of a dangerous type, that he is connected with another crime and with a quantity of easily-identified stolen property. We also know that he was in America about eighteen months ago, and we can easily get exact information as to dates and locality. This man is no longer a mere formless shadow. He is in a definite category of possible persons."

"But," I objected, "the fact that he had the coin in his possession does not prove that he is the man who stole it."

"Not by itself," Thorndyke agreed. "But taken in conjunction with the crime, it is almost conclusive. You appear to be overlooking the striking similarity of the two crimes. Each was a violent murder committed by means of poison, and in each case the poison selected was the most suitable one for the purpose. The one, aconitine, was calculated to escape detection, the other, hydrocyanic acid – the most rapidly-acting of all poisons – was calculated to produce almost instant death in a man who was probably struggling and might have raised an alarm. I think we arc fairly justified in assuming that the murderer of Van Zellen was the murderer of D'Arblay. If that is so, we have two groups of circumstances to investigate, two tracks by which to follow him, and sooner or later, I

480

feel confident, we shall be able to give him a name. Then, if we have kept our own counsel, and he is unconscious of the pursuit, we shall be able to lay our hands on him. But here we are at the Foundling Hospital. It is time for each of us to get back to the routine of duty."

Chapter VIII
Simon Bendelow, Deceased

It was near the close of my incumbency of Dr. Cornish's practice – indeed, Cornish had returned on the previous evening – that my unsatisfactory attendance on Mr. Simon Bendelow came to an end. It had been a wearisome affair. In medical practice, perhaps even more than in most human activities, continuous effort calls for the sustenance of achievement. A patient who cannot be cured or even substantially relieved is of all patients the most depressing. Week after week I had made my fruitless visits, had watched the silent, torpid sufferer grow yet more shrivelled and wasted, speculating even a little impatiently on the possible duration of his long-drawn-out passage to the grave. But at last the end came.

"Good morning, Mrs. Morris," I said as that grim female opened the door and surveyed me impassively. "And how is our patient to-day?"

"He isn't our patient any longer," she replied. "He's dead."

"Ha!" I exclaimed. "Well, it had to be, sooner or later. Poor Mr. Bendelow! When did he die?"

"Yesterday afternoon, about five," she answered.

"Hmm! If you had sent me a note, I could have brought the certificate. However, I can post it to you. Shall I go up and have a look at him?"

"You can if you like," she replied. "But the ordinary certificate won't be enough in his case. He is going to be cremated."

"Oh, indeed," said I, once more unpleasantly conscious of my inexperience. "What sort of certificate is required for cremation?"

"Oh, all sorts of formalities have to be gone through," she answered. "Just come into the drawing room and I will tell you what has to be done."

She preceded me along the passage and I followed meekly, anathematizing myself for my ignorance, and my instructors for having sent me forth crammed with academic knowledge but with the practical business of my profession all to learn.

"Why are you having him cremated?" I asked, as we entered the room and shut the door.

"Because it is one of the provisions of his will," she answered. "I may as well let you see it."

482

She opened a bureau and took from it a foolscap envelope from which she drew out a folded document. This she first unfolded and then re-folded so that its concluding clauses were visible, and laid it on the flap of the bureau. Placing her finger on it, she said, "That is the cremation clause. You had better read it."

I ran my eye over the clause, which read: "*I desire that my body shall be cremated, and I appoint Sarah Elizabeth Morris, the wife of the aforesaid James Morris, to be the residuary legatee and sole executrix of this my will.*" Then followed the attestation clause, underneath which was the shaky but characteristic signature of Simon Bendelow, and opposite this the signatures of the witnesses, Anne Dewsnep and Martha Bonnington, both described as spinsters and both of a joint address which was hidden by the folding of the document.

"So much for that," said Mrs. Morris, returning the will to its envelope. "And now as to the certificate. There is a special form for cremation which has to be signed by two doctors, and one of them must be a hospital doctor or a consultant. So I wrote off at once to Dr. Cropper, as he knew the patient, and I have had a telegram from him this morning saying that he will be here this evening at eight o'clock to examine the body and sign the certificate. Can you manage to meet him at that time?"

"Yes," I replied, "fortunately I can, as Dr. Cornish is back."

"Very well," said she. "Then in that case you needn't go up now. You will be able to make the examination together. Eight o'clock, sharp, remember."

With this she re-conducted me along the passage and – I had almost said ejected me, but she sped the parting guest with a business-like directness that was perhaps accounted for by the presence opposite the door of one of those grim parcels-delivery vans in which undertakers distribute their wares, and from which a rough-looking coffin was at the moment being hoisted out by two men.

The extraordinary promptitude of this proceeding so impressed me that I remarked, "They haven't been long making the coffin."

"They didn't have to make it," she replied. "I ordered it a month ago. It's no use leaving things to the last moment."

I turned away with somewhat mixed feelings. There was certainly a horrible efficiency about this woman. Executrix indeed! Her promptness in carrying out the provisions of the will was positively appalling. She must have written to Cropper before the breath was fairly out of poor Bendelow's body, but her forethought in the matter of the coffin fairly made my flesh creep.

Dr. Cornish made no difficulty about taking over the evening consultations – in fact he had intended to do so in any case. Accordingly, after a rather early dinner, I made my way in leisurely fashion back to Hoxton, where, after all, I arrived fully ten minutes too soon. I realized my prematureness when I halted at the corner of Market Street to look at my watch, and as ten additional minutes of Mrs. Morris's society offered no allurement, I was about to turn back and fill up the time with short walk when my attention was arrested by a mast which had just appeared above the wall at the end of the street. With its black-painted truck and halyard blocks, and its long tricolour pennant, it looked like the mast of a Dutch *schuyt* or *galliot*, but I could hardly believe it possible that such a craft could make its appearance in the heart of London. All agog with curiosity, I hurried up the street and looked over the wall at the canal below, and there, sure enough, she was – a big Dutch sloop, broad-bosomed, massive and mediaeval, just such a craft as one may see in the pictures of old Vandervelde, painted when Charles the Second was king.

I leaned on the low wall and watched her with delighted interest as she crawled forward slowly to her berth, bringing with her, as it seemed, a breath of the distant sea and the echo of the surf murmuring on sandy beaches. I noted appreciatively her old-world air, her antique build, her gay and spotless paint and the muslin curtains in the little windows of her deck-house, and was, in fact, so absorbed in watching her that the late Simon Bendelow had passed completely out of my mind. Suddenly, however, the chiming of a clock recalled me to my present business. With a hasty glance at my watch, I tore myself away reluctantly, darted across the street and gave a vigorous pull at the bell.

Dr. Cropper had not yet arrived, but the deceased had not been entirely neglected, for when I had spent some five minutes staring inquisitively about the drawing room into which Mrs. Morris had shown me, that lady returned, accompanied by two other ladies whom she introduced to me somewhat informally by the names of Miss Dewsnep and Miss Bonnington respectively. I recognized the names as those of the two witnesses to the will and inspected them with furtive curiosity, though, indeed, they were quite unremarkable excepting as typical specimens of the genus elderly spinster.

"Poor Mr. Bendelow!" murmured Miss Dewsnep, shaking her head and causing an artificial cherry on her bonnet to waggle idiotically. "How beautiful he looks in his coffin!"

She looked at me as if for confirmation, so that I was fain to admit that his beauty in this new setting had not yet been revealed to me.

"So peaceful," she added, with another shake of her head, and Miss Bonnington chimed in with the comment, "Peaceful and restful." Then they both looked at me and I mumbled indistinctly that I had no doubt he did, the fact being that the inmates of coffins are not in general much addicted to boisterous activity.

"Ah!" Miss Dewsnep resumed, "how little did I think when I first saw him, sitting up in bed so cheerful in that nice, sunny room in the house at – "

"Why not?" interrupted Mrs. Morris. "Did you think he was going to live forever?"

"No, Mrs. Morris, ma'am," was the dignified reply, "I did not. No such idea ever entered my head. I know too well that we mortals are all born to be gathered in at last as the – er – as the – "

"Sparks fly upwards," murmured Miss Bonnington. "As the corn is gathered in at harvest-time," Miss Dewsnep continued with slight emphasis. "But not to be cast into a burning fiery furnace. When I first saw him in the other house at – "

"I don't see what objection you need have to cremation," interrupted Mrs. Morris. "It was his own choice, and a good one, too. Look at those great cemeteries. What sense is there in letting the dead occupy the space that is wanted for the living?"

"Well," said Miss Dewsnep, "I may be old-fashioned, but it does seem to me that a nice quiet funeral with plenty of flowers and a proper, decent grave in a churchyard is the natural end to a human life. That is what I look forward to, myself."

"Then you are not likely to be disappointed," said Mrs. Morris, "though I don't quite see what satisfaction you expect to get out of your own funeral."

Miss Dewsnep made no reply, and an interval of dismal silence followed. Mrs. Morris was evidently impatient of Dr. Cropper's unpunctuality. I could see that she was listening intently for the sound of the bell, as she had been even while the conversation was in progress. Indeed I had been dimly conscious all the while of a sense of tension and anxiety on her part. She had seemed to me to watch her two friends with a sort of uneasiness and to give a quite uncalled-for attention to their rather trivial utterances.

At length her suspense was relieved by a loud ringing of the bell. She started up and opened the door, but she had barely crossed the threshold when she suddenly turned back and addressed me.

"That will be Dr. Cropper. Perhaps you had better come out with me and meet him."

It struck me as an odd suggestion, but I rose without comment and followed her along the passage to the street door, which we reached just as another loud peal of the bell sounded in the house behind us. She

485

flung the door wide open and a small, spectacled man charged in and seized my hand, which he shook with violent cordiality.

"How do you do, Mr. Morris?" he exclaimed. "So sorry to keep you waiting, but I was unfortunately detained at a consultation."

Here Mrs. Morris sourly intervened to explain who I was, upon which he shook my hand again and expressed his joy at making my acquaintance. He also made polite inquiries as to our hostess's health, which she acknowledged gruffly over her shoulder as she preceded us along the passage, which was now pitch-dark and where Cropper dropped his hat and trod on it, finally bumping his head against the unseen wall in a frantic effort to recover it.

When we emerged into the dimly-lighted hall, I observed the two ladies peering inquisitively out of the drawing room door. But Mrs. Morris took no notice of them, leading the way directly up the stairs to the room with which I was already familiar. It was poorly illuminated by a single gas-bracket over the fireplace, but the light was enough to show us a coffin resting on three chairs, and beyond it the shadowy figure of a man whom I recognized as Mr. Morris.

We crossed the room to the coffin, which was plainly finished with zinc fastenings, in accordance with the regulations of the crematorium authorities, and had let into the top what I first took to be a pane of glass, but which turned out to be a plate of clear celluloid. When we had made our salutations to Mr. Morris, Cropper and I looked in through the celluloid window. The yellow, shrunken face of the dead man, surmounted by the skull-cap which he had always worn, looked so little changed that he might still have been in the drowsy, torpid state in which I had been accustomed to see him. He had always looked so like a dead man that the final transition was hardly noticeable.

"I suppose," said Morris, "you would like to have the coffin-lid taken off?"

"God bless my soul, yes!" exclaimed Cropper. "What are we here for? We shall want him out of the coffin, too."

"Are you proposing to make a *post mortem*?" I asked, observing that Dr. Cropper had brought a good-sized handbag. "It seems hardly necessary, as we both know what he died of."

Cropper shook his head. "That won't do," said he. "You mustn't treat a cremation certificate as a mere formality. We have got to certify that we have verified the cause of death. Looking at a body through a window is not verifying the cause of death. We should cut a pretty figure in a court of law if any question arose and we bad to admit that we had certified without any examination at all. But we needn't do much, you know. Just get the body out on the bed and a single small incision will

486

settle the nature of the growth. Then everything will be regular and in order. I hope you don't mind, Mrs. Morris," he added suavely, turning to that lady.

"You must do what you think necessary," she replied indifferently. "It is no affair of mine." And with this she went out of the room and shut the door.

While we had been speaking, Mr. Morris, who apparently had kept a screw-driver in readiness for the possible contingency, had been neatly extracting the screws and now lifted off the coffin-lid. Then the three of us raised the shrivelled body – it was as light as a child's – and laid it on the bed. I left Cropper to do what he thought necessary, and while he was unpacking his instruments, I took the opportunity to have a good look at Mr. Morris, for it is a singular fact that in all the weeks of my attendance at this house I had never come into contact with him since that first morning when I had caught a momentary glimpse of him as he looked out over the blind through the glazed shop-door. In the interval, his appearance had changed considerably for the better. He was no longer a merely unshaved man. His beard had grown to respectable length, and, so far as I could judge in the uncertain light, the hare-lip scar was completely concealed by his moustache.

"Let me see," said Cropper, as he polished a scalpel on the palm of his hand. "When did you say Mr. Bendelow died?"

"Yesterday afternoon at about five o'clock," replied Mr. Morris.

"Did he really?" said Cropper, lifting one of the limp arms and letting it drop on the bed. "Yesterday afternoon! Now, Gray, doesn't that show how careful one should be in giving opinions as to the time that has elapsed since death? If I had been shown this body and asked how long the man had been dead, I should have said three or four days. There isn't the least trace of rigor mortis left, and the other appearances – but there it is. You are never safe in giving dogmatic opinions."

"No," I agreed. "I should have said he had been dead more than twenty-four hours. But I suppose there is a good deal of variation."

"There is," he replied. "You can't apply averages to particular cases."

I did not consider it necessary to take any active part in the proceedings. It was his diagnosis and it was for him to verify it. At his request, Mr. Morris fetched a candle and held it as he was directed, and while these preparations were in progress I looked out of the window, which commanded a partial view of the canal. The moon had now risen and its light fell on the white-painted hull of the Dutch sloop, which had come to rest and made fast alongside a small wharf. It was quite a pleasant picture, strangely at variance with the squalid neighbourhood around. As I looked down on the little vessel, with the ruddy light glowing from the deck-house windows and casting shimmering reflections in the quiet water, the sight seemed to carry me far away from the sordid streets around into the fellowship of the breezy ocean and the far-away shores whence the little craft had sailed, and I determined, as soon as our business was finished, to seek some access to the canal and indulge myself with a quiet stroll in the moonlight along the deserted towing-path.

"Well, Gray," said Cropper, standing up with the scalpel and forceps in his hands, "there it is, if you want to see it. Typical carcinoma. Now we can sign the certificates with a clear conscience. I'll just put in a stitch or two and then we can put him back in his coffin. I suppose you have got the forms?"

"They are downstairs," said Mr. Morris. "When we have got him back, I will show you the way down."

This, however, was unnecessary, as there was only one staircase and I was not a stranger. Accordingly, when we had replaced the body, we took our leave of Mr. Morris and departed, and glancing back as I passed out of the door, I saw him driving in the screws with the ready skill of a cabinet-maker.

The filling up of the forms was a portentous business which was carried out in the drawing room under the superintendence of Mrs. Morris, and was watched with respectful interest by the two spinsters. When it was finished and I had handed the registration certificate to Mrs. Morris, Cropper gathered up the forms *B* and *C* and slipped them into a long envelope on which the Medical Referee's address was printed.

"I will post this off to-night," said he, "and you will send in *Form A*, Mrs. Morris, when you have filled it in."

"I have sent it off already," she replied.

"Good," said Dr. Cropper. "Then that is all, and now I must run away. Can I put you down anywhere. Gray?"

"Thank you, no," I replied. "I thought of taking a walk along the tow-path, if you can tell me how to get down to it, Mrs. Morris."

"I can't," she replied. "But when Dr. Cropper has gone, I will run up and ask my husband. I daresay he knows."

We escorted Cropper along the passage to the door, which he reached without mishap, and having seen him into his brougham, turned back to the hall, where Mrs. Morris ascended the stairs and I went into the drawing room, where the two spinsters appeared to be preparing for departure. In a couple of minutes Mrs. Morris returned, and seeing both the ladies standing, said, "You are not going yet. Miss Dewsnep. You must have some refreshment before you go. Besides, I thought you wanted to see Mr. Bendelow again."

"So we should," said Miss Dewsnep. "Just a little peep, to see how he looks after – "

"I will take you up in a minute," interrupted Mrs. Morris. "When Dr. Gray has gone." Then addressing me, she said, "My husband says that you can get down to the tow-path through that alley nearly opposite. There is a flight of steps at the end which come right out on the path."

I thanked her for the direction, and, having bidden farewell to the spinsters, was once more escorted along the passage and finally launched into the outer world.

Chapter IX
A Strange Misadventure

Although I had been in harness but a few weeks, it was with a pleasant sense of freedom that I turned from the door and crossed the road towards the alley. My time was practically my own, for, though I was remaining with Dr. Cornish until the end of the week, he was now in charge and my responsibilities were at an end.

The alley was entered by an arched opening so narrow that I had never suspected it of being a public thoroughfare, and I now threaded it with my shoulders almost touching the walls. Whither it finally led I have no idea, for when I reached another arched opening in the left-hand wall and saw that this gave on a flight of stone steps, I descended the latter and found myself on the tow-path. At the foot of the steps, I stood awhile and looked about me. The moon was nearly full and shone brightly on the opposite side of the canal, but the tow-path was in deep shadow, being flanked by a high wall, behind which were the houses of the adjoining streets. Looking back – that is, to my left – I could just make out the bridge and the adjoining buildings, all their unlovely details blotted out by the thin night-haze, which reduced them to mere flat shapes of grey. A little nearer, one or two spots of ruddy light with wavering reflections beneath them marked the cabin windows of the sloop, and her mast, rising above the grey obscurity, was clearly visible against the sky.

Naturally, I turned in that direction, sauntering luxuriously and filling my pipe as I went. Doubtless by day the place was sordid enough in aspect – though it is hard to vulgarize a navigable waterway – but now, in the moonlit haze, the scene was almost romantic. And it was astonishingly quiet and peaceful. From above, beyond the high wall, the noises of the streets came subdued and distant like sounds from another world, but here there was neither sound nor movement. The tow-path was utterly deserted, and the only sign of human life was the glimmer of light from the sloop.

It was delightfully restful. I found myself treading the gravel lightly, not to disturb the grateful silence, and as I strolled along, enjoying my pipe, I let my thoughts ramble idly from one topic to another. Somewhere above me, in that rather mysterious house, Simon Bendelow was lying in his narrow bed, the wasted, yellow face looking out into the darkness through that queer little celluloid window – or perhaps Miss

Dewsnep and her friend were even now taking their farewell peep at him. I looked up but, of course, the house was not visible from the tow-path, nor was I now able to guess at its position.

A little farther and the hull of the sloop came clearly into view, and nearly opposite to it, on the tow-path, I could see some kind of shed or hut against the wall, with a derrick in front of it overhanging a little quay. When I had nearly reached the shed, I passed a door in the wall, which apparently communicated with some house in one of the streets above. Then I came to the shed, a small wooden building which probably served as a lighterman's office, and I noticed that the derrick swung from one of the corner-posts. But at this moment my attention was attracted by sounds of mild revelry from across the canal. Someone in the sloop's deck-house had burst into song.

I stepped out on to the little quay and stood at the edge, looking across at the homely curtained windows and wondering what the interior of the deck-house looked like at this moment. Suddenly my ear caught an audible creak from behind me. I was in the act of turning to see whence it came when something struck me a heavy, glancing blow on the arm, crashed to the ground, and sent me flying over the edge of the quay.

Fortunately the water here as not more than four feet deep, and as I had plunged in feet first and am a good swimmer, I never lost control of myself. In a moment I was standing up with my head and shoulders out of water, not particularly alarmed, though a good deal annoyed and much puzzled as to what had happened. My first care was to recover my hat, which was floating forlornly close by, and the next was to consider how I should get ashore. My left arm was numb from the blow and was evidently useless for climbing. Moreover, the face of the quay was of smooth concrete, as was also the wall below the tow-path. But I remembered having passed a pair of boat-steps some fifty yards back and decided to make for them. I had thought of hailing the sloop, but as the droning song still came from the deck-house, it was clear that the Dutchmen had heard nothing, and I did not think it worthwhile to disturb them. Accordingly I set forth for the steps, walking with little difficulty over the soft, muddy bottom, keeping close to the side and steadying myself with my right hand, with which I could just reach the edge of the coping.

It seemed a long journey, for one cannot progress very fast over soft mud with the water up to one's armpits, but at last I reached the steps and managed to scramble up on to the tow-path. There I stood for a moment or two irresolute. My first impulse was to hurry back as fast as I could and seek the Morris's hospitality, for I was already chilled to the bone and felt as physically wretched as the proverbial cat in similar circumstances. But I was devoured by curiosity as to what had happened, and, moreover, I believed that I had dropped my stick on the quay. The latter consideration decided me, for it was a favourite stick, and I set out for the quay at a very different pace from that at which I had approached it the first time.

The mystery was solved long before I arrived at the quay – at least it was solved in part. For the derrick, which had overhung the quay, now lay on the ground. Obviously it had fallen – and missed my head only by a matter of inches. But how had it come to fall? Again, obviously, the guy-rope had given way. As it could not have broken, seeing that the derrick was unloaded and the rope must have been strong enough to bear the last load, I was a good deal puzzled as to how the accident could have befallen. Nor was I much less puzzled when I had made my inspection. The rope was, of course, unbroken and its 'fall' – the part below the pulley-blocks – passed into the shed through a window-like hole. This I could see as I approached, and also that a door in the end of the shed nearest to me was ajar. Opening it, I plunged into the dark interior, and partly by touch and partly by the faint glimmer that came in at the window, I was able to make out the state of affairs. Just below the hole through which the rope entered was a large cleat, on which the fall must have been belayed. But the cleat was vacant, the rope hung down from the hole and its end lay in an untidy raffle on the floor. It looked as if it had been cast off the cleat, but as there had apparently been no one in the shed, the only possible supposition was that the rope had been badly secured, that it had gradually worked loose and had at last slipped off the cleat. But it was difficult to understand how it had slipped right off.

I found my stick lying at the edge of the quay and close by it my pipe. Having recovered these treasures, I set off to retrace my steps along the tow-path, sped on my way by a jovial chorus from the sloop. A very few minutes brought me to the steps, which I ascended two at a time, and then, having traversed the alley, I came out sheepishly into Market Street. To my relief, I saw a light in Mr. Morris's shop and could even make out a moving figure in the background. I hurried across and, opening the glazed door, entered the shop, at the back of which Mr. Morris was seated at a bench filing some small object which was fixed in a vice. He looked round at me with no great cordiality, but suddenly observing my condition, he dropped his file on the bench and exclaimed, "Good Lord, Doctor! What on earth have you been doing?"

"Nothing on earth," I replied with a feeble grin, "but something in the water. I've been into the canal."

"But what for?" he demanded.

"Oh, I didn't go in intentionally," I replied, and then I gave him a sketch of the incident, as short as I could make it, for my teeth were chattering and explanations were chilly work. However, he rose nobly to the occasion. "You'll catch your death of cold!" he exclaimed, starting up. "Come in here and slip off your things at once while I go for some blankets."

He led me into a little den behind the shop, and, having lighted a gas fire, went out by a back door. I lost no time in peeling off my dripping clothes, and by the time that he returned I was in the state in which I ought to have been when I took my plunge.

"Here you are," said he. "Put on this dressing-gown and wrap yourself in the blankets. We'll draw this chair up to the fire and then you will be all right for the present."

I followed his directions, pouring out my thanks as well as my chattering teeth would let me.

"Oh, that's all right," said he. "If you will empty your pockets, the missus can put some of the things through the wringer and then they'll soon dry. There happens to be a good fire in the kitchen, some advance cooking on account of the funeral. You can dry your hat and boots here. If anyone comes to the shop, you might just press that electric bell-push."

When he had gone, I drew the Windsor arm-chair close to the fire and made myself as comfortable as I could, dividing my attention between my hat and my boots, which called for careful roasting, and the contents of the room. The latter appeared to be a sort of store for the reserve stock-in-trade and certainly this was a most amazing collection. I could not see a single article for which I would have given sixpence. The array on the shelves suggested that the shop had been stocked with the sweepings of all the stalls in Market Street, with those of Shoreditch High Street thrown in. As I ran my eye along the ranks of dial-less clocks, cracked fiddles, stopperless decanters and tattered theological volumes, I found myself speculating profoundly on how Mr. Morris made a livelihood. He professed to be a "dealer in antiques", and there was assuredly no question as to the antiquity of the goods in this room. But there is little pecuniary value in the kind of antiquity that is unearthed from a dust-bin.

It was really rather mysterious. Mr. Morris was a somewhat superior man and he did not appear to be poor. Yet this shop did not seem capable of yielding an income that would have been acceptable to a rag-picker. And during the whole of the time in which I sat warming myself, there was not a single visitor to the shop. However, it was no concern of mine, and I had just reached this sage conclusion when Mr. Morris returned with my clothes.

493

"There," he said, "they are very creased and disreputable but they are quite dry. They would have had to be cleaned and pressed in any case."

With this he went out into the shop and resumed his filing while I put on the stiff and crumpled garments. When I was dressed, I followed him and thanked him effusively for his kind offices, leaving also a grateful message for his wife. He took my thanks rather stolidly, and having wished me "Good night", picked up his file and fell to work again.

I decided to walk home – principally, I think, to avoid exhibiting myself in a public vehicle. But my self-consciousness soon wore off, and when, in the neighbourhood of Clerkenwell, I perceived Dr. Usher on the opposite side of the street, I crossed the road and touched his arm. He looked round quickly, and recognizing me, shook hands cordially. "What arc you doing on my beat at this time of night?" he asked. "You are not still at Cornish's, are you?"

"Yes," I answered, "but not for long. I have just made my last visit and signed the death certificate."

"Good man," said he. "Very methodical. Nothing like finishing a case up neatly. They didn't invite you to the funeral, I suppose?"

"No," I replied, "and I shouldn't have gone if they had."

"Quite right," he agreed. "Funerals are rather outside medical practice. But you have to go sometimes. Policy, you know. I had to go to one a couple of days ago. Beastly nuisance it was. Chappie would insist on putting me down at my own door in the mourning coach. Meant well, of course, but it was very awkward. All the neighbours came to their shop-doors and grinned as I got out. Felt an awful fool, couldn't grin back, you see. Had to keep up the farce to the end."

"I don't see that it was exactly a farce," I objected.

"That is because you weren't there," he retorted. "It was the silliest exhibition you ever saw. Just think of it! The parson who ran the show actually got a lot of school-children to stand round the grave and sing a blooming hymn – something about gathering at the river. I expect you know the confounded doggerel."

"Well, why not?" I protested. "I daresay the friends of the deceased liked it."

"No doubt," said he. "I expect they put the parson up to it. But it was sickening to hear those kids bleating that stuff. How did they know where he was? An old rip with malignant disease of the pancreas, too!"

"Really, Usher," I exclaimed, laughing at his quaint cynicism, "you are unreasonable. There are no pathological disqualifications for the better land, I hope."

494

"I suppose not," he agreed with a grin. "Don't have to show a clean bill of health before they let you in. But it was a trying business, you must admit. I hate cant of that sort, and yet one had to pull a long face and join in the beastly chorus."

The picture that his last words suggested was too much for my gravity. I laughed long and joyously. However, Usher was not offended. Indeed I suspect that he appreciated the humour of the situation as much as I did. But he had trained himself to an outward solemnity of manner that was doubtless a valuable asset in his particular class of practice and he walked at my side with unmoved gravity, taking an occasional quick, critical look at me. When we came to the parting of our ways, he once more shook my hand warmly and delivered a little farewell speech.

"You've never been to see me, Gray. Haven't had time, I suppose. But when you are free you might look me up one evening to have a smoke and a glass and talk over old times. There's always a bit of grub going, you know."

I promised to drop in before long, and he then added, "I gave you one or two tips when I saw you last. Now I'm going to give you another. Never neglect your appearance. It's a great mistake. Treat yourself with respect and the world will respect you. No need to be a dandy. But just keep an eye on your tailor and your laundress – especially your laundress. Clean collars don't cost much, and they pay, and so does a trousers-press. People expect a doctor to be well turned out. Now, you mustn't think me impertinent. We are old pals and I want you to get on. So long, old chap. Look me up as soon as you can." And without giving me the opportunity to reply, he turned about and bustled off, swinging his umbrella and offering, perhaps, a not very impressive illustration of his own excellent precepts. But his words served as a reminder which caused me to pursue the remainder of my journey by way of side-streets neither too well lighted nor too much frequented.

As I let myself in with my key and closed the street-door, Cornish stepped out of the dining room.

"I thought you were lost, Gray," said he. "Where the deuce have you been all this time?" Then, as I came into the light of the hall-lamp, he exclaimed, "And what in the name of Fortune have you been up to?"

"I have had a wetting," I explained. "I'll tell you all about it presently."

"Dr. Thorndyke is in the dining room," said he. "Came in a few minutes ago to see you." He seized me by the arm and ran me into the room, where I found Thorndyke methodically filling his pipe. He looked up as I entered and regarded me with raised eyebrows.

"Why, my dear fellow, you've been in the water!" he exclaimed. "But yet your clothes are not wet. What has been happening to you?"

"If you can wait a few minutes," I replied, "while I wash and change, I will relate my adventures. But perhaps you haven't time."

"I want to hear all about it," he replied, "so run along and be as quick as you can."

I bustled up to my room and, having washed and executed a lightning change, came down to the dining room, where I found Cornish in the act of setting out decanters and glasses.

"I've told Dr. Thorndyke what took you to Hoxton," said he, "and he wants a full account of everything that happened. He is always suspicious of cremation cases, as you know from his lectures."

"Yes, I remember his warnings," said I. "But this was a perfectly commonplace, straightforward affair."

"Did you go for your swim before or after the examination?" Thorndyke asked.

"Oh, after," I replied.

"Then let us hear about the examination first," said he.

On this I plunged into a detailed account of all that had befallen since my arrival at Market Street, to which Thorndyke listened, not only patiently but with the closest attention, and even cross-examined me to elicit further details. Everything seemed to interest him, from the construction of the coffin to the contents of Mr. Morris's shop. When I had finished, Cornish remarked, "Well, it is a queer affair. I don't understand that rope at all. Ropes don't uncleat themselves. They may slip, but they don't come right off the cleat. It looks more as if some mischievous fool had cast it off for a joke."

"But there was no one there," said I. "The shed was empty when I examined it and there was not a soul in sight on the tow-path."

"Could you see the shed when you were in the water?" Thorndyke asked.

"No. My head was below the level of the tow-path. But if anyone had run out and made off, I must have seen him on the path when I came out. He couldn't have got out of sight in the time. Besides, it is incredible that even a fool should play such a trick as that."

"It is," he agreed. "But every explanation seems incredible. The only plain fact is that it happened. It is a queer business altogether, and not the least queer feature in the case is your friend Morris. Hoxton is an unlikely place for a dealer in antiques, unless he should happen to deal in other things as well – things, I mean, of ambiguous ownership."

"Just what I was thinking," said Cornish. "Sounds uncommonly like a fence. However, that is no business of ours."

"No," agreed Thorndyke, rising and knocking out his pipe. "And now I must be going. Do you care to walk with me to the bottom of Doughty Street, Gray?"

I assented at once, suspecting that he had something to say to me that he did not wish to say before Cornish. And so it turned out, for as soon as we were outside he said, "What I really called about was this: It seems that we have done the police an injustice. They were more on the spot than we gave them credit for. I have learned – and this is in the strictest confidence – that they took that coin round to the British Museum for the expert's report. Then a very curious fact came to light. That coin is not the original which was stolen. It is an electrotype in gold, made in two halves very neatly soldered together and carefully worked on the milled edge to hide the join. That is extremely important in several respects. In the first place it suggests an explanation of the otherwise incredible circumstance that it was being carried loose in the waistcoat pocket. It had probably been recently obtained from the electrotyper. That suggests the question, is it possible that D'Arblay might have been that electrotyper? Did he ever work the electrotype process? We must ascertain whether he did."

"There is no need," said I. "It is known to me as a fact that he did. The little plaquettes that I took for castings are electrotypes, made by himself. He worked the process quite a lot and was very skilful in finishing. For instance, he did a small bust of his daughter in two parts and brazed them together."

"Then you see, Gray," said Thorndyke, "that advances us considerably. We now have a plausible suggestion as to the motive and a new field of investigation. Let us suppose that this man employed D'Arblay to make electrotype copies of certain unique objects with the intention of disposing of them to collectors. The originals, being stolen property, would be almost impossible to dispose of with safety, but a copy would not necessarily incriminate the owner. But when D'Arblay had made the copies, he would be a dangerous person, for he would know who had the originals. Here, to a man whom we know to be a callous murderer, would be a sufficient reason for making away with D'Arblay."

"But do you think that D'Arblay would have undertaken such a decidedly fishy job? It seems hardly like him."

"Why not?" demanded Thorndyke. "There was nothing suspicious about the transaction. The man who wanted the copies was the owner of the originals, and D'Arblay would not know or suspect that they were stolen."

497

"That is true," I admitted. "But you were speaking of a new field of investigation."

"Yes. If a number of copies of different objects have been made, there is a fair chance that some of them have been disposed of. If they have and can be traced, they will give us a start along a new line which may bring us in sight of the man himself. Do you ever see Miss D'Arblay now?"

"Oh, yes," I replied. "I am quite one of the family at Highgate. I have been there every Sunday lately."

"Have you!" he exclaimed with a smile. "You are a pretty *locum tenens*. However, if you are quite at home there you can make a few discreet inquiries. Find out, if you can, whether any electros had been made recently, and if so, what they were and who was the client. Will you do that?"

I agreed readily, only too glad to take an active part in the investigation, and having by this time reached the end of Doughty Street, I took leave of Thorndyke and made my way back to Cornish's house.

Chapter X
Marion's Peril

The mist, which had been gathering since the early afternoon, began to thicken ominously as I approached Abbey Road, Hornsey, from Crouch End station, causing me to quicken my pace so that I might make my destination before the fog closed in, for this was my first visit to Marion D'Arblay's studio and the neighbourhood was strange to me. And in fact I was none too soon, for hardly had I set my hand on the quaint bronze knocker above the plate inscribed *Mr. J. D'Arblay*, – when the adjoining houses grew pale and shadowy and then vanished altogether.

My elaborate knock – in keeping with the distinguished knocker – was followed by soft, quick footsteps, the sound whereof set my heart ticking in double-quick time, the door opened and there stood Miss D'Arblay, garbed in a most alluring blue smock or pinafore, with sleeves rolled up to the elbow, with a smile of friendly welcome on her comely face and looking so sweet and charming that I yearned then and there to take her in my arms and kiss her. This, however, being inadmissible, I shook her hand warmly and was forthwith conducted through the outer lobby into the main studio, where I stood looking about me with amused surprise. She looked at me inquiringly as I emitted an audible chuckle.

"It is a queer-looking place," said I, "something between a miracle-shrine hung with votive offerings from sufferers who have been cured of sore heads and arms and legs, and a meat emporium in a cannibal district."

"It is nothing of the kind!" she exclaimed indignantly. "I don't mind the votive offerings, but I reject the cannibal meat-market as a gross and libellous fiction. But I suppose it does look rather queer to a stranger."

"To a what?" I demanded fiercely.

"Oh, I only meant a stranger to the place, of course, and you know I did. So you needn't be cantankerous."

She glanced smilingly round the studio and for the first time, apparently, the oddity of its appearance dawned on her, for she laughed softly and then turned a mischievous eye on me as I gaped about me like a bumpkin at a fair. The studio was a very large and lofty room or hall with a partially-glazed roof and a single large window just below the skylight. The walls were fitted partly with rows of large shelves and the remainder with ranks of pegs. From the latter hung row after row of casts of arms, hands, legs, and faces – especially faces – while the shelves supported a weird succession of heads, busts, and a few half-length but armless figures. The general effect was very strange and uncanny, and what made it more so was the fact that all the heads presented perfectly smooth, bare craniums.

"Are artists' models usually bald?" I inquired, as I noted this latter phenomenon.

"Now you are being foolish," she replied – "wilfully and deliberately foolish. You know very well that all these heads have got to be fitted with wigs, and you couldn't fit a wig to a head that already had a fine covering of plaster curls. But I must admit that it rather detracts from the beauty of a girl's head if you represent it without hair. The models used to hate it when they were shown with heads like old gentlemen's, and so did poor Dad – in fact he usually rendered the hair in the clay, just sketchily, for the sake of the model's feelings and his own and took it off afterwards with a wire tool. But there is the kettle boiling over. I must make the tea."

While this ceremony was being performed, I strolled round the studio and inspected the casts, more particularly the heads and faces. Of these latter the majority were obviously modelled, but I noticed quite a number with closed eyes, having very much the appearance of death masks. When we had taken our places at the little table near the great gas-ring, I inquired what they were.

"They do look rather cadaverous, don't they?" she said as she poured out the tea, "but they are not death masks. They are casts from living faces, mostly from the faces of models, but my father always used to take a cast from anyone who would let him. They are quite useful to work from, though, of course, the eyes have to be put in from another cast or from life."

"It must be rather an unpleasant operation," I said, "having the plaster poured all over the face. How does the victim manage to breathe?"

"The usual plan is to put little quills or tubes into the nostrils. But my father could keep the nostrils free without any tubes. He was a very skilful moulder, and then he always used the best plaster, which sets very quickly, so that it only took a few minutes."

"And how are you getting on, and what were you doing when I came in?"

"I am getting on quite well," she replied. "My work has been passed as satisfactory and I have three new commissions. When you came in, I was just getting ready to make a mould for a head and shoulders. After tea I shall go on with it and you shall help me. But tell me about yourself. You have finished with Dr. Cornish, haven't you?"

"Yes, I am a gentleman at large for the time being, but that won't do. I shall have to look out for another job."

"I hope it will be a London job," she said. "Arabella and I would feel quite lonely if you went away, even for a week or two. We both look forward so much to our little family gathering on Sunday afternoon."

"You don't look forward to it as much as I do," I said warmly. "It is difficult for me to realize that there was ever a time when you were not a part of my life. And yet we are quite new friends."

"Yes," she said, "only a few weeks old. But I have the same feeling. I seem to have known you for years, and as for Arabella, she speaks of you as if she had nursed you from infancy. You have a very insinuating way with you."

"Oh, don't spoil it by calling me insinuating!" I protested.

"No, I won't," she replied. "It was the wrong word. I meant sympathetic. You have the gift of entering into other people's troubles and feeling them as if they were your own, which is a very precious gift – to the other people."

"Your troubles are my own," said I, "since I have the privilege to be your friend. But I have been a happier man since I shared them."

"It is very nice of you to say that," she murmured with a quick glance at me and just a faint heightening of colour, and then for a while neither of us spoke.

"Have you seen Dr. Thorndyke lately?" she asked, when she had refilled our cups, and thereby, as it were, punctuated our silence.

"Yes," I answered. "I saw him only a night or two ago. And that reminds me that I was commissioned to make some inquiries. Can you tell me if your father ever did any electrotype work for outsiders?"

"I don't know," she answered. "He used latterly to electrotype most of his own work instead of sending it to the bronze-founders, but it is hardly likely that he would do electros for outsiders. There are firms who do nothing else, and I know that, when he was busy, he used to send his own work to them. But why do you ask?"

I related to her what Thorndyke had told me and pointed out the importance of ascertaining the facts, which she saw at once.

"As soon as we have finished tea," she said, "we will go and look over the cupboard where the electro moulds were kept – that is, the permanent ones. The gelatine moulds for works in the round couldn't be kept. They were melted down again. But the water-proofed-plaster moulds were stored away in this cupboard, and the gutta-percha ones too until they were wanted to soften down to make new moulds. And even if the moulds were destroyed, Father usually kept a cast."

501

"Would you be able to tell by looking through the cupboard?" I asked.

"Yes. I should know a strange mould, of course, as I saw all the original work that he did. Have we finished? Then let us go and settle the question now."

She produced a bunch of keys from her pocket and crossed the studio to a large, tall cupboard in a corner. Selecting a key, she inserted it and was trying vainly to turn it when the door came open. She looked at it in surprise and then turned to me with a somewhat puzzled expression.

"This is really very curious," she said. "When I came here this morning I found the outer door unlocked. Naturally I thought I must have forgotten to lock it, though that would have been an extraordinary oversight. And now I find this door unlocked. But I distinctly remember locking it before going away last night, when I had put back the box of modelling wax. What do you make of that?"

"It looks as if someone had entered the studio last night with false keys or by picking the lock. But why should they? Perhaps the cupboard will tell. You will know if it has been disturbed."

She ran her eyes along the shelves and said at once, "It has been. The things are all in disorder and one of the moulds is broken. We had better take them all out and see if anything is missing – so far as I can judge, that is, for the moulds were just as my father left them."

We dragged a small work-table to the cupboard and emptied the shelves one by one. She examined each mould as we took it out, and I jotted down a rough list at her dictation. When we had been through the whole collection and rearranged the moulds on the shelves – they were mostly plaques and medallions – she slowly read through the list and reflected for a few moments. At length she said, "I don't miss anything that I can remember. But the question is, were there any moulds or casts that I did not know about? I am thinking of Dr. Thorndyke's question. If there were any, they have gone, so that question cannot be answered."

We looked at one another gravely and in both our minds was the same unspoken question: "Who was it that had entered the studio last night?"

We had just closed the cupboard and were moving away when my eye caught a small object half-hidden in the darkness under the cupboard itself – the bottom of which was raised by low feet about an inch and a half from the floor. I knelt down and passed my hand into the shallow space and was just able to hook it out. It proved to be a fragment of a small plaster mould, saturated with wax and black-leaded on the inside. Miss D'Arblay stooped over it eagerly and exclaimed, "I don't know that one. What a pity it is such a small piece. But it is certainly part of a coin."

"It is part of the coin," said I. "There can be no doubt of that. I examined the cast that Mr. Polton made and I recognize this as the same. There is the lower part of the bust, the letters CA – the first two letters of Carolus – and the tiny elephant and castle. That is conclusive. This is the mould from which that electrotype was made. But I had better hand it to Dr. Thorndyke to compare with the cast that he has."

I carefully bestowed the fragment in my tobacco pouch as the safest place for the time being, and meanwhile e Miss D'Arblay looked fixedly at me with a very singular expression.

"You realize," she said in a hushed voice, "what this means. He was in here last night."

I nodded. The same conclusion had instantly occurred to me, and a very uncomfortable one it was. There was something very sinister and horrid in the thought of that murderous villain quietly letting himself into this studio and ransacking its hiding-places in the dead of the night. So unpleasantly suggestive was it that, for a time, neither of us spoke a word, but stood looking blankly at one another in silent dismay. And in the midst of the tense silence there came a knock at the door.

We both started as if we had been struck. Then Miss D'Arblay, recovering herself quickly, said, "I had better go," and hurried down the studio to the lobby.

I listened nervously, for I was a little unstrung. I heard her go into the lobby and open the outer door. I heard a low voice, apparently asking a question, the outer door closed and then came a sudden scuffling sound and a piercing shriek. With a shout of alarm, I raced down the studio, knocking over a chair as I ran, and darted into the lobby just as the outer door slammed.

For a moment I hesitated. Miss D'Arblay had shrunk into a corner and stood in the semi-darkness with both her hands pressed tightly to her breast. But she called out excitedly, "Follow him! I am not hurt!", and on this I wrenched open the door and stepped out.

But the first glance showed me that pursuit was hopeless. The fog had now become so dense that I could hardly see my own feet. I dared not leave the threshold for fear of not being able to find my way back. Then she would be alone – and he was probably lurking close by even now.

I stood irresolutely, stock-still, listening intently. The silence was profound. All the natural noises of a populous neighbourhood seemed to be smothered by the dense blanket of dark yellow vapour. Not a sound came to my ear, no stealthy foot-fall, no rustle of movement. Nothing but stark silence.

Uneasily I crept back until the open doorway showed as a dim rectangle of shadow, crept back and peered fearfully into the darkness of the lobby. She was still standing in the corner – an upright smudge of deeper darkness in the obscurity. But even as I looked the shadowy figure collapsed and slid noiselessly to the floor.

In an instant the pursuit was forgotten and I darted into the lobby, shutting the outer door behind me, and dropped on my knees at her side. Where she had fallen a streak of light came in from the studio, and the sight that it revealed turned me sick with terror. The whole front of her smock, from the breast downwards, was saturated with blood, both her hands were crimson and gory, and her face was dead-white to the lips.

For an instant I was paralysed with horror. I could see no movement of breathing, and the white face with its parted lips and half-closed eyes was as the face of the dead. But when I dared to search for the wound, I was a little reassured, for, closely as I scrutinized it, the gory smock showed no sign of a cut excepting on the blood-stained right sleeve. And now I noticed a deep gash on the left hand, which was still bleeding freely, and was probably the source of the blood which had soaked the smock. There seemed to be no vital wound.

With a deep breath of relief, I hastily tore my handkerchief into strips and applied the improvised bandage tightly enough to control the bleeding. Then with the scissors from my pocket-case, which I now carried from habit, I laid open the blood-stained sleeve. The wound on the arm just above the elbow was quite shallow, a glancing wound which tailed off upwards into a scratch. A turn of the remaining strip of bandage secured it for the time being, and this done, I once more explored the front of the smock, pulling its folds tightly apart in search of the dreaded cut. But there was none, and now, the bleeding being controlled, it was safe to take measures of restoration. Tenderly – and not without effort – I lifted her and carried her into the studio where there was a shabby but roomy couch, on which poor D'Arblay had been accustomed to rest when he stayed for the night. On this I laid her, and fetching some water and a towel, dabbed her face and neck. Presently she opened her eyes and heaved a deep sigh, looking at me with a troubled, bewildered expression and evidently only half-conscious. Suddenly her eye caught the great blood-stain on her smock and her expression grew wild and terrified. For a few moments she gazed at me with eyes full of horror, then, as the memory other dreadful experience rushed back on her, she uttered a little cry and burst into tears, moaning and sobbing almost hysterically.

I rested her head on my shoulder, and tried to comfort her, and she, poor girl, weak and shaken by the awful shock, clung to me, trembling, and wept passionately with her face buried in my breast. As for me, I was almost ready to weep, too, if only from sheer relief and revulsion from my late terrors.

"Marion darling!" I murmured into her ear as I stroked her damp hair. "Poor dear little woman! It was horrible. But you mustn't cry any more now. Try to forget it, dearest."

She shook her head passionately. "I can never do that," she sobbed. "It will haunt me as long as I live. Oh! and I am so frightened, even now. What a coward I am!"

"Indeed you are not!" I exclaimed. "You are just weak from loss of blood. Why did you let me leave you, Marion?"

"I didn't think I was hurt, and I wasn't particularly frightened then, and I hoped that if you followed him, he might be caught. Did you see him?"

"No. There is a thick fog outside. I didn't dare to leave the threshold. Were you able to see what he was like?"

She shuddered and choked down a sob. "He is a dreadful-looking man," she said, "I loathed him at the first glance – a beetle-browed, hook-nosed wretch with a face like that of some horrible bird of prey. But I couldn't see him very distinctly, for it is rather dark in the lobby and he wore a wide-brimmed hat, pulled down over his brows."

"Would you know him again? And can you give a description of him that would be of use to the police?"

"I am sure I should know him again," she said with a shudder. "It was a face that one could never forget. A hideous face! The face of a demon! I can see it now and it will haunt me, sleeping and waking, until I die."

Her words ended with a catch of the breath and she looked piteously into my face with wide, terrified eyes. I took her trembling hand and once more drew her head to my shoulder.

"You mustn't think that, dear," said I. "You are all unstrung now, but these terrors will pass. Try to tell me quietly just what this man was like. What was his height for instance?"

"He was not very tall. Not much taller than me. And he was rather slightly built."

"Could you see whether he was dark or fair?"

"He was rather dark. I could see a shock of hair sticking out from under his hat and he had a moustache with turned-up ends and a beard – a rather short beard."

"And now as to his face. You say he had a hooked nose?"

505

"Yes, a great, high-bridged nose like the beak of some horrible bird. And his eyes seemed to be deep-set under heavy brows with bushy eyebrows. The face was rather thin with high cheek-bones – a fierce, scowling, repulsive face."

"And the voice? Should you know that again?"

"I don't know," she answered. "He spoke in quite a low tone, rather indistinctly. And he said only a few words – something about having come to make some inquiries about the cost of a wax model. Then he stepped into the lobby and shut the outer door, and immediately, without another word, he seized my right arm and struck at me. But I saw the knife in his hand and, as I called out, I snatched at it with my left hand, so that it missed my body and I felt it cut my right arm. Then I got hold of his wrist. But he had heard you coming and wrenched himself free. The next moment he had opened the door and rushed out, shutting it behind him."

She paused and then added in a shaking voice, "If you had not been here – if I had been alone – "

"We won't think of that, Marion. You were not alone, and you will never be again in this place. I shall see to that."

At this she gave a little sigh of satisfaction, and looked into my face with the pallid ghost of a smile. "Then I shan't be frightened any more," she murmured, and closing her eyes she lay for a while, breathing quietly as if asleep. She looked very delicate and frail with her waxen checks and the dark shadows under her eyes, but still I noted a faint tinge of colour stealing back into her lips. I gazed down at her with fond anxiety, as a mother might look at a sleeping child that had just passed the crisis of a dangerous illness. Of the bare chance that had snatched her from imminent death I would not allow myself to think. The horror of that moment is too fresh for the thought to be endurable. Instead I began to occupy myself with the practical question as to how she was to be got home. It was a long way to North Grove – some two miles, I reckoned – too far for her to walk in her present weak state, and then there was the fog. Unless it lifted it would be impossible for her to find her way, and I could give her no help, as I was a stranger to this locality. Nor was it by any means safe, for our enemy might still be lurking near, waiting for the opportunity that the fog would offer.

I was still turning over these difficulties when she opened her eyes and looked up at me a little shyly.

"I'm afraid I've been rather a baby," she said, "but I am much better now. Hadn't I better get up?"

"No," I answered. "Lie quiet and rest. I am trying to think how you are to be got home. Didn't you say something about a caretaker?"

506

"Yes, a woman in the little house next door, which really belongs to the studio. Daddy used to leave the key with her at night so that she could clean up. But I just fetch her in when I want her help. Why do you ask?"

"Do you think she could get a cab for us?"

"I am afraid not. There is no cab-stand anywhere near here. But I think I could walk, unless the fog is too thick. Shall we go and see what it is like?"

"I will go," said I, rising. But she clung to my arm.

"You are not to go alone," she said, in sudden alarm. "He may be there still."

I thought it best to humour her and accordingly helped her to rise. For a few moments she seemed rather unsteady on her feet, but soon she was able to walk, supported by my arm, to the studio door, which I opened, and through which wreaths of vapour drifted in. But the fog was perceptibly thinner, and even as I was looking across the road at the now faintly visible houses, two spots of dull yellow light appeared up the road and my ear caught the muffled sound of wheels. Gradually the lights grew brighter and at length there stole out of the fog the shadowy form of a cab with a man leading the horse at a slow walk. Here seemed a chance to escape from our dilemma.

"Go in and shut the door while I speak to the cabman," said I. "He may be able to take us. I shall give four knocks when I come back."

She was unwilling to let me go, but I gently pushed her in and shut the door and then advanced to meet the cab. A few words set my anxieties at rest, for it appeared that the cabman had to set down a fare a little way along the street and was very willing to take a return fare, on suitable terms. As any terms would have been suitable to me under the circumstances, the cabman was able to make a good bargain and we parted with mutual satisfaction and a cordial *au revoir*. Then I steered back along the fence to the studio door, on which I struck four distinct knocks and announced myself vocally by name. Immediately the door opened and a hand drew me in by the sleeve.

"I am so glad you have come back," she whispered. "It was horrid to be alone in the lobby even for a few minutes. What did the cabman say?"

I told her the joyful tidings and we at once made ready for our departure. In a minute or two the welcome glare of the cab-lamps reappeared, and when I had locked up the studio and pocketed the key I helped her into the rather ramshackle vehicle.

I don't mind admitting that the cabman's charges were extortionate, but I grudged him never a penny. It was probably the slowest journey

507

that I had ever made, but yet the funereal pace was all too swift. Half-ashamed as I was to admit it to myself, this horrible adventure was bearing sweet fruit to me in the unquestioned intimacy that had been born in the troubled hour. Little enough was said, but I sat happily by her side, holding her uninjured hand in mine (on the pretence of keeping it warm), blissfully conscious that our sympathy and friendship had grown to something sweeter and more precious.

"What are we to say to Arabella?" I asked. "I suppose she will have to be told?"

"Of course she will," replied Marion, "you shall tell her. But," she added in a lower tone, "you needn't tell her everything – I mean what a baby I was and how you had to comfort and soothe me. She is as brave as a lion and she thinks I am, too. So you needn't undeceive her too much."

"I needn't undeceive her at all," said I, "because you are." And we were still arguing this weighty question when the cab drew up at Ivy Cottage. I sent the cabman off rejoicing, and then escorted Marion up the path to the door, where Miss Boler was waiting, having apparently heard the cab arrive.

"Thank goodness!" she exclaimed. "I was wondering how on earth you would manage to get home." Then she suddenly observed Marion's bandaged hand and uttered an exclamation of alarm.

"Miss Marion has cut her hand rather badly," I explained. "We won't talk about it just now. I will tell you everything presently when you have put her to bed. Now I want some stuff to make dressings and bandages."

Miss Boler looked at me suspiciously, but made no comment. With extraordinary promptitude she produced a supply of linen, warm water and other necessaries, and then stood by to watch the operation and give assistance.

"It is a nasty wound," I said, as I removed the extemporized dressing, "but not so bad as I feared. There will be no lasting injury."

I put on the permanent dressing and then exposed the wound on the arm, at the sight of which Miss Boler's eyebrows went up. But she made no remark, and when a dressing had been put on this, too, she took charge of the patient to conduct her up to the bedroom.

"I shall come up and see that she is all right before I go," said I, "and meanwhile, no questions, Arabella."

She cast a significant look at me over her shoulder and departed with her arm about the patient's waist.

The rites and ceremonies above-stairs were briefer than I had expected – perhaps the promised explanations had accelerated matters.

At any rate, in a very few minutes Miss Boler bustled into the room and said, "You can go up now, but don't stop to gossip. I am bursting with curiosity."

Thereupon, I ascended to my lady's chamber, which I entered as diffidently and reverently as though such visits were not the commonplace of my professional life. As I approached the bed, she heaved a little sigh of content and murmured, "What a fortunate girl I am! To be petted and cared for and pampered in this way! Arabella is a perfect angel, and you. Dr. Gray – "

"Oh, Marion!" I protested. "Not Dr. Gray."

"Well, then, Stephen," she corrected with a faint blush.

"That is better. And what am I?"

"Never mind," she replied, very pink and smiling. "I expect you know. If you don't, ask Arabella when you go down."

"I expect she will do most of the asking," said I. "And I have strict orders not to stop to gossip, so let me see the bandages and then I must go."

I made my inspection, without undue hurry, and having seen that all was well, I took her hand.

"You are to stay here until I have seen you to-morrow morning, and you are to be a good girl and try not to think of unpleasant things."

"Yes, I will do everything that you tell me."

"Then I can go away happy. Good night, Marion."

"Good night, Stephen."

I pressed her hand and felt her fingers close on mine. Then I turned away and, with only a moment's pause at the door for a last look at the sweet, smiling face, descended the stairs to confront the formidable Arabella.

Of my cautious statement and her keen cross-examination I will say nothing. I made the proceedings as short as was decent, for I wanted, if possible, to take counsel with Thorndyke. On my explaining this, the brevity of my account was condoned, and even my refusal of food.

"But remember, Arabella," I said as she escorted me to the gate, "she has had a very severe shock. The less you say to her about the affair for the present, the quicker will be her recovery."

With this warning I set forth through the rapidly-thinning fog to catch the first conveyance that I could find to bear me southward.

Chapter XI
Arms and the Man

The fog had thinned to a mere haze when the porter admitted me at the Inner Temple Gate, so that, as I passed the Cloisters and looked through into Pump Court, I could see the lighted windows of the residents' chambers at tile far end. The sight of them encouraged me to hope that the chambers in King's Bench Walk might throw out a similar hopeful gleam. Nor was I disappointed, and the warm glow from the windows of number 5A sent me tripping up the stairs profoundly relieved though a trifle abashed at the untimely hour of my visit.

The door was opened by Thorndyke, himself, who instantly cut short my apologies.

"Nonsense, Gray!" he exclaimed, shaking my hand. "It is no interruption at all. On the contrary – how beautiful upon the staircase are the feet of him that bringeth – well, what sort of tidings?"

"Not good, I am afraid, sir."

"Well, let us have them. Come and sit by the fire." He drew up an easy-chair, and having installed me in it and taken a critical look at me, invited me to proceed. I accordingly proceeded bluntly to inform him that an attempt had been made to murder Miss D'Arblay.

"Ha!" he exclaimed. "These are bad tidings indeed! I hope she is not injured in any way."

I reassured him on this point and gave him the details as to the patient's condition, and he then asked, "When did the attempt occur and how did you hear of it?"

"It happened this evening and I was present."

"You were present!" he repeated, gazing at me in the utmost astonishment. "And what became of the assailant?"

"He vanished into the fog," I replied.

"Ah, yes. The fog. I had forgotten that. But now let us drop this question-and-answer method. Give me a narrative from the beginning with the events in their proper sequence. And omit nothing, no matter how trivial."

I took him at his word – up to a certain point. I described my arrival at the studio, the search in the cupboard, the sinister interruption, the attack and the unavailing attempt at pursuit. As to what befell thereafter I gave him a substantially complete account – with certain reservations – up to my departure from Ivy Cottage.

"Then you never saw the man at all?"

"No, but Miss D'Arblay did," and here I gave him such details of the man's appearance as I had been able to gather from Marion.

"It is quite a vivid description," he said as he wrote down the details. "And now shall we have a look at that piece of the mould?"

I disinterred it from my tobacco-pouch and handed it to him. He glanced at it and then went to a cabinet, from a drawer in which he produced the little case containing Polton's casts of the guinea and a box which he placed on the table and opened. From it he took a lump of moulding-wax and a bottle of powdered French chalk. Pinching off a piece of the wax, he rolled it into a ball, dusted it lightly with the chalk powder and pressed it with his thumb into the mould. It came away on his thumb bearing a perfect impression of the inside of the mould.

"That settles it," said he, taking the obverse cast from the case and laying it on the table beside the wax "squeeze". "The squeeze and the cast are identical. There is now no possible doubt that the electrotype guinea that was found in the pond was made by Julius D'Arblay. Probably it had been delivered by him to the murderer on the very evening of his death. So we are undoubtedly dealing with that same man. It is a most alarming situation."

"It would be alarming if it were any other man," I remarked.

"No doubt," he agreed. "But there is something very special about this man. He is a criminal of a type that is almost unknown here, but is not uncommon in South European and Slav countries. You find him, too, in the United States. He is not a normal human being. He is an inveterate murderer, to whom a human life does not count at all. And this type of man continually grows more and more dangerous, for two reasons: First, the murder habit becomes more confirmed with each crime. Second, there is virtually no penalty for the succeeding murders, for the first one entails the death sentence and fifty murders can involve no more. This man killed Van Zellen as a mere incident of a robbery. Then he appears to have killed D'Arblay to secure his own safety, and he is now attempting to kill Miss D'Arblay, apparently for the same reason. And he will kill you and he will kill me if our existence is inconvenient or dangerous to him. We must bear that in mind and take the necessary measures."

"I can't imagine," said I, "what motive he can have for wanting to kill Miss D'Arblay."

"Probably he believes that she knows something that would be dangerous to him – something connected with those moulds, or perhaps something else. We are rather in the dark. We don't know for certain what it was he came to look for when he entered the studio, or whether or

511

not he found what he wanted. But to return to the danger. It is obvious that he knows the Abbey Road district well, for he found his way to the studio in the fog. He may be living close by. There is no reason why he should not be. His identity is quite unknown."

"That is a horrid thought!" I exclaimed.

"It is," he agreed, "but it is the assumption that we have to act upon. We must not leave a loophole unwatched. He mustn't get another chance."

"No," I concurred warmly, "he certainly must not – if we can help it. But it is an awful position. We carry that poor girl's life in our hands, and there is always the possibility that we may be caught off our guard, just for a moment."

He nodded gravely. "You are quite right. Gray. An awful responsibility rests on us. I am very unhappy about this poor young lady. Of course, there is the other side – but at present we are concerned with Miss D'Arblay's safety."

"What other side is there?" I demanded.

"I mean," he replied, "that if we can hold out, this man is going to deliver himself into our hands."

"What makes you think that?" I asked eagerly.

"I recognize a familiar phenomenon," he replied. "My large experience and extensive study of crimes against the person have shown me that in the overwhelming majority of cases of obscure crime, the discovery has been brought about by the criminal's own efforts to make himself safe. He is constantly trying to hide his tracks – and making fresh ones. Now, this man is one of those criminals who won't let well alone. He kills Van Zellen and disappears, leaving no trace. He seems to be quite safe. But he is not satisfied. He can't keep quiet. He kills D'Arblay, he enters the studio, he tries to kill Miss D'Arblay – all to make himself more safe. And every time he moves, he tells us something fresh about himself. If we can only wait and watch, we shall have him."

"What has he told us about himself this time?" I asked.

"We won't go into that now, Gray. We have other business on hand. But you know all that I know as to the facts. If you will turn over those facts at your leisure, you will find that they yield some very curious and striking inferences."

I was about to press the question when the door opened and Mr. Polton appeared on the threshold. Observing me, he crinkled benevolently and then, in answer to Thorndyke's inquiring glance, said, "I thought I had better remind you, sir, that you have not had any supper."

"Dear me, Polton," Thorndyke exclaimed, "now you mention it, I believe you are right. And I suspect that Dr. Gray is in the same case. So we place ourselves in your hands. Supper and pistols are what we want."

"Pistols, sir!" exclaimed Polton, opening his eyes to an unusual extent and looking at us suspiciously.

"Don't be alarmed, Polton," Thorndyke chuckled. "It isn't a duel. I just want you to go over our stock of pistols and ammunition."

At this I thought I detected a belligerent gleam in Polton's eye, but even as I looked, he was gone. Not for long, however. In a couple of minutes he was back with a large hand-bag, which he placed on the table and again retired. Thorndyke opened the bag and took out quite a considerable assortment of weapons – single pistols, revolvers and automatics – which he laid out on the table, each with its box of appropriate cartridges.

"I hate fire-arms!" he exclaimed as he viewed the collection distastefully. "They are dangerous things, and when it comes to business they are scurvy weapons. Any poltroon can pull a trigger. But we must put ourselves on equal terms with our opponent, who is certain to be provided. Which will you have? I recommend this Baby Browning for portability. Have you had any practice?"

"Only target practice. But I am a fair shot with a revolver. I have never used an automatic."

"We will go over the mechanism after supper," said he. "Meanwhile, I hear the approach of Polton and am conscious of a voracious interest in what he is bringing. When did you feed last?"

"I had tea at the studio about half-past-four."

"My poor Gray!" he exclaimed, "you must be starving. I ought to have asked you sooner. However, here comes relief." He opened a folding table by the fire just as Polton entered with the tray, on which I was gratified to observe a good-sized dish-cover and a claret-jug. Polton rapidly laid the little table and then, whisking off the cover, retired with a triumphant crinkle.

"You have a regular kitchen upstairs, I presume," said I as we took our seats at the table, "as well as a laboratory? And a pretty good cook, too, to judge by the results."

Thorndyke chuckled. "The kitchen and the laboratory are one," he replied, "and Polton is the cook. An uncommonly good cook, as you suggest, but his methods are weird. These cutlets were probably grilled in the cupel furnace, but I have known him to do a steak with the brazing-jet. There is nothing conventional about Polton. But whatever he does, he does to a finish, which is fortunate, because I thought of calling in his aid in our present difficulty."

513

I looked at him inquiringly and he continued, "If Miss D'Arblay is to go on with her work, which she ought to, as it is her livelihood, she must be guarded constantly. I had considered applying to Inspector Follett, and we may have to later, but for the present it will be better for us to keep our own counsel and play our own hand. We have two objects in view. First – and paramount – is the necessity of securing Miss D'Arblay's safety. But, second, we want to lay our hands on this man, not to frighten him away, as we might do if we put the police on his track. When once we have him, her safety is secured forever, whereas if he were merely scared away, he would be an abiding menace. We have got to catch him, and at present he is catchable. Secure in his unknown identity, he is lurking within reach, ready to strike, but also ready to be pounced upon when we are ready to pounce. Let us keep him confident of his safety while we are gathering up the clues."

"Hmm, yes," I assented, without much enthusiasm. "What is it that you propose to do?"

"Somebody," he replied, "must keep watch over Miss D'Arblay from the moment when she leaves her house until she returns to it. How much time – if any – can you give up to this duty?"

"My whole time," I answered promptly. "I shall let everything else go."

"Then," said he, "I propose that you and Polton relieve one another on duty. It will be better than for you to be there all the time."

I saw what he meant and agreed at once. The conventions must be respected as far as possible.

"But," I suggested, "isn't Polton rather a light-weight – if it should come to a scrap, I mean?"

"Don't undervalue small men, even physically," he replied. "They are commonly better built than big men and more enduring and energetic. Polton is remarkably strong and he has the pluck of a bulldog. But we must see how he is placed as regards work."

The question was put to him and the position of affairs explained when he came down to clear the table, whereupon it appeared (from his own account) that he was absolutely without occupation of any kind and pining for something to do. Thorndyke laughed incredulously but did not contest this outrageous and barefaced untruth, merely remarking, "I am afraid it will be rather an idle time for you."

"Oh, no, it won't, sir," Polton assured him emphatically. "I've always wanted to learn something about sculptor's moulding and wax-casting, but I've never had a chance. Now I shall have. And that opportunity isn't going to be wasted."

Thorndyke regarded his assistant with a twinkling eye. "So it was mere self-seeking that made you so enthusiastic," said he. "But you are quite a good moulder already."

"Not a sculptor's moulder, sir," replied Polton, "and I know nothing about waxwork. But I shall, before I have been there many days."

"I am sure you will," said Thorndyke. "Miss D'Arblay will have an apprentice and journeyman in one. You will be able to give her quite a lot of help, which will be valuable just now while her hand is disabled. When do you think she will be able to go back to work, Gray?"

"I can't say. Not to-morrow certainly. Shall I send you a report when I have seen her?"

"Do," he replied. "Or better still, come in to-morrow evening and give me the news. So, Polton, we shall want you for another day or so."

"Ah!" said Polton, "then I shall be able to finish that recording-clock before I go," upon which Thorndyke and I laughed aloud and Polton, his mendacity thus unmasked, retired with the tray, crinkling but unabashed.

The short remainder of the evening – or rather, of the night – was spent in the study of the mechanism and mode of use of automatic pistol. When I finally bestowed the "Baby", fully loaded, in my hip-pocket and rose to go, Thorndyke sped me on my way with a few words of warning and advice.

"Be constantly on your guard. Gray. You are going to make a bitter enemy of a man who knows no scruples, indeed, you have done so already, and something tells me that he is aware of it. Avoid all solitary or unfrequented places. Keep to main thoroughfares and well-lighted streets and maintain a vigilant look-out for any suspicious appearances. You have said truly that we carry Miss D'Arblay's life in our hands. But to preserve her life we must preserve our own, which we should probably prefer to do in any case. Don't get jumpy – I don't much think you will, but keep your attention alert and your weather eyelid lifting."

With these encouraging words and a hearty handshake, he let me out and stood watching me as I descended the stairs.

Chapter XII
A Dramatic Discovery

About eleven o'clock in the forenoon of the third day after the terrible events of that unforgettable night of the great fog, Marion and I drew up on our bicycles opposite the studio door. She was now outwardly quite recovered, excepting as to her left hand, but I noticed that, as I inserted the key into the door, she cast a quick, nervous glance up and down the road, and as we passed through the lobby, she looked down for one moment at the great bloodstain on the floor and then hastily averted her face.

"Now," I said, assuming a brisk, cheerful tone, "we must get to work. Mr. Polton will be here in half-an-hour and we must be ready to put his nose on the grindstone at once."

"Then your nose will have to go on first," she replied with a smile, "and so will mine, with two raw apprentices to teach and an important job waiting to be done. But, dear me! What a lot of trouble I am giving!"

"Nothing of the kind, Marion," I exclaimed. "You are a public benefactor. Polton is delighted at the chance to come here and enlarge his experience, and as for me – "

"Well? As for you?" She looked at me half-shyly, half-mischievously. "Go on. You've stopped at the most interesting point."

"I think I had better not," said I. "We don't want the forewoman to get too uppish."

She laughed softly, and when I had helped her out of her overcoat and rolled up the sleeve of her one serviceable arm, I went out to the lobby to stow away the bicycles and lock the outer door. When I returned, she had got out from the cupboard a large box of flaked gelatine and a massive spouted bucket which she was filling at the sink.

"Hadn't you better explain to me what we are going to do?" I asked.

"Oh, explanations are of no use," she replied. "You just do as I tell you and then you will know all about it. This isn't a school, it's a workshop. When we have got the gelatine in to soak, I will show you how to make a plaster case."

"It seems to me," I retorted, "that my instructress has graduated in the academy of Squeers. 'W-i-n-d-e-r, winder, now go and clean one.' Isn't that the method?"

"Apprentices are not allowed to waste time in wrangling," she rejoined severely. "Go and put on one of Daddy's blouses and I will set you to work."

This practical method of instruction justified itself abundantly. The reasons for each process emerged at once as soon as the process was completed. And it was withal a pleasant method, for there is no comradeship so sympathetic as the comradeship of work, nor any which begets so wholesome and friendly an intimacy. But though there were playful and frivolous interludes – as when the forewoman's working hand became encrusted with clay and had to be cleansed with a sponge by the apprentice – we worked to such purpose that by the time Mr. Polton was due, the plaster bust (of which a wax replica had to be made) was firmly fixed on the work-table on a clay foundation and surrounded by a carefully-levelled platform of clay, in which it was embedded to half its thickness. I had just finished smoothing the surface when there came a knock at the outer door, on which Marion started violently and clutched my arm. But she recovered in a moment and exclaimed in a tone of vexation, "How silly I am! Of course it is Mr. Polton."

It was. I found him on the threshold in rapt contemplation of the knocker and looking rather like an archdeacon on tour. He greeted me with a friendly crinkle, and I then conducted him into the studio and presented him to Marion, who shook his hand warmly and thanked him so profusely for coming to her aid that he was quite abashed. However, he did not waste time in compliments, but, producing an apron from his hand-bag, took off his coat, donned the apron, rolled up his sleeves, and beamed inquiringly at the bust.

"We are going to make a plaster case for the gelatine mould, Mr. Polton," Marion explained, and proceeded to a few preliminary directions, to which the new apprentice listened with respectful attention. But she had hardly finished when he fell to work with a quiet, unhurried facility that filled me with envy. He seemed to know where to find everything. He discovered the wastepaper with which to cover the model to prevent the clay from sticking to it, he pounced on the clay-bin at the first shot, and when he had built up the shape for the case, found the plaster-bin, mixing-bowl, and spoon as if he had been born-and-bred in the workshop, stopping only for a moment to test the condition of the gelatine in the bucket.

"Mr. Polton," Marion said after watching him for a while, "you are an impostor – a dreadful impostor. You pretend to come here as an improver, but you really know all about gelatine moulding, now, don't you?"

517

Polton admitted apologetically that he "had done a little in that way. But," he added, in extenuation, "I have never done any work in wax. And talking of wax, The Doctor will be here presently."

"Dr. Thorndyke?" Marion asked.

"Yes, miss. He had some business in Holloway, so he thought he would come on here to make your acquaintance and take a look at the premises."

"All the same," Mr. Polton' said I, "I don't quite see the connexion between Dr. Thorndyke and wax."

He crinkled with a slightly embarrassed air and explained that he must have been thinking of something that The Doctor had said to him, but his explanations were cut short by a knock at the door.

"That is his knock," said Polton, and he and I together proceeded to open the door, when I inducted the distinguished visitor into the studio and presented him to the presiding goddess. I noticed that each of them inspected the other with some curiosity and that the first impressions appeared to be mutually satisfactory, though Marion was at first a little overawed by Thorndyke's impressive personality.

"You mustn't let me interrupt your work," the latter said, when the preliminary politenesses had been exchanged. "I have just come to fill in Dr. Gray's outline sketches with details of my own observing. I wanted to see you – to convert a name into an actual person, to see the studio for the same reason, and to get as precise a description as possible of the man whom we are trying to identify. Will it distress you to recall his appearance?"

She had turned a little pale at the mention of her late assailant, but she answered stoutly enough, "Not at all. Besides, it is necessary."

"Thank you," said he, "then I will read out the description that I had from Dr. Gray and we will see if you can add anything to it."

He produced a notebook from which he read out the particulars that I had given him, at the conclusion of which he looked at her inquiringly.

"I think that is all that I remember," she said. "There was very little light and I really only glanced at him."

Thorndyke looked at her reflectively. "It is a fairly full description," said he. "Perhaps the nose is a little sketchy. You speak of a hooked nose with a high bridge. Was it a curved nose, or a squarer Roman nose?"

"It was rather square in profile – a Wellington nose, but with a rather broad base. Like a vulture's beak, and very large."

"Was it actually a hook-nose – I mean, had it a drooping tip?"

"Yes, the tip projected downwards and it was rather sharp – not bulbous."

518

"And the chin? Should you call it a pronounced or a retreating chin?"

"Oh, it was quite a projecting chin, rather of the Wellington type."

Thorndyke reflected once more. Then, having jotted down the answers to his questions, he closed the book and returned it to his pocket.

"It is a great thing to have a trained eye," he remarked. "In your one glance you saw more than an ordinary person would have noted in a leisurely inspection in a good light. You have no doubt that you would know this man again if you should meet him?"

"Not the slightest," she replied with a shudder. "I can see him now, if I shut my eyes."

"Well," he rejoined, with a smile, "I wouldn't recall that unpleasant vision too often, if I were you. And now, may I, without disturbing you further, just take a look round the premises?"

"But, of course. Dr. Thorndyke," she replied. "Do exactly what you please."

With this permission he drew away and stood for some moments letting a very reflective eye travel round the interior, and meanwhile I watched him curiously and wondered what he had really come for. His first proceeding was to walk slowly round the studio and examine closely, one by one, all the casts which hung on pegs. Next, in the same systematic manner, he inspected all the shelves, mounting a chair to examine the upper ones. It was after scrutinizing one of the latter that he turned towards Marion and asked, "Have you moved these casts lately. Miss D'Arblay?"

"No," she replied. "So far as I know, they have not been touched for months."

"Someone has moved them within the last day or two," said he. "Apparently the nocturnal explorer went over the shelves as well as the cupboard."

"I wonder why?" said Marion. "There were no moulds on the shelves."

Thorndyke made no rejoinder, but as he stood on the chair he once more ran his eye round the studio. Suddenly he stepped down from the chair, picked it up, carried it over to the tall cupboard, and once more mounted it. His stature enabled him easily to look over the cornice on to the top of the cupboard, and it was evident that something there had attracted his attention.

"Here is a derelict of some sort," he announced, "which certainly has not been moved for some months." As he spoke, he reached over the cornice into the enclosed space and lilted out an excessively grimy plaster mask, from which he blew the thick coating of dust, and then stood for a while looking at it thoughtfully.

"A striking face, this," he remarked, "but not attractive. It rather suggests a Russian or Polish Jew. Do you recognize the person, Miss D'Arblay?"

He stepped down from the chair and handed the mask to Marion, who had advanced to look at it and who now held it in her hand, regarding it with a frown of perplexity.

"This is very curious," she said. "I thought I knew all the casts that have been made here. But I have never seen this one before, and I don't know the face. I wonder who he was. It doesn't look like an English face, but I should hardly have taken it for a foreign face, with that rather small and nearly straight nose."

"You will see many a face of that type in Whitechapel High Street."

At this point, deserting the work-table, I came and looked over Marion's shoulder at the mask which she was holding at arm's length. And then I got a surprise of the most singular kind, for I recognized the face at a glance.

"What is it, Gray?" asked Thorndyke, who had apparently observed my astonishment.

"This is a most extraordinary coincidence!" I exclaimed. "Do you remember my speaking to you about a certain Mr. Morris?"

"The dealer in antiques?" he queried.

"Yes. Well, this is his face."

He regarded me for some moments with a strangely intent expression. Then he asked, "When you say that this is Morris's face, do you mean that it resembles his face, or that you identify it positively?"

"I identify it positively. I can swear to the identity. It isn't a face that one would forget. And if any doubt were possible, there is this hare-lip scar, which you can see quite plainly on the cast."

"Yes, I noticed that. And Morris has a hare-lip scar, has he?"

"Yes, and in the same position and of the same character. I think you can take it as a fact that this cast was undoubtedly taken from Morris's face."

"Which," said Thorndyke, "is a really important fact and one that is worth looking into."

"In what way is it important?" I asked.

"In this respect," he answered. "This man, Morris, is unknown to Miss D'Arblay, but he was not unknown to her father. Here we have evidence that Mr. D'Arblay had dealings with people of whom his daughter had no knowledge. The circumstances of the murder made it clear that there must be such people, but here we have proof of their existence and we can give to one of them a local habitation and a name. And you will notice that this particular person is a dealer in curios and possibly in more questionable things. There is just a hint that he may have had some rather queer acquaintances."

"He seemed to have had rather a fancy for plaster masks," I remarked. "I remember that he had one in his shop window."

"Did your father make many life or death masks as commissions, Miss D'Arblay?" Thorndyke asked.

"Only one or two, so far as I know," she replied. "There is very little demand for portrait masks nowadays. Photography has superseded them."

"That is what I should have supposed," said he. "This would be just a chance commission. However, as it establishes the fact that this man Morris was in some way connected with your father, I think I should like to have a record of his appearance. May I take this mask away with me to get a photograph of it made? I will take great care of it and let you have it back safely."

"Certainly," replied Marion, "but why not keep it, if it is of any interest to you? I have no use for it."

"That is very good of you," said he, "and if you will give me some rag and paper to wrap it in, I will take myself off and leave you to finish your work in peace."

Marion took the cast from him and, having procured some rag and paper, began very carefully to wrap it up. While she was thus engaged, Thorndyke stood letting his eye travel once more round the studio.

"I see," he remarked, "that you have quite a number of masks moulded from life or death. Do I understand that they were not commissions?"

"Very few of them were," Marion replied. "Most of them were taken from professional models, but some from acquaintances whom my father bribed with the gift of a duplicate mask."

"But why did he make them? They could not have been used for producing wax faces for the show figures, for you could hardly turn a shop-window into a waxwork exhibition with lifelike portraits of real persons."

"No," Marion agreed, "that wouldn't do at all. These masks were principally used for reference as to details of features when my father was modelling a head in clay. But he did sometimes make moulds for the wax from these masks, only he obliterated the likeness, so that the wax face was not a portrait."

"By working on the wax, I suppose?"'

"Yes, or more usually by altering the mask before making the mould. It is quite easy to alter a face. Let me show you."

She lifted one of the masks from its peg and laid it on the table.

"You see," she said, "that this is the face of a young girl-one of my father's models. It is a round, smooth, smiling face with a very short, weak chin and a projecting upper lip. We can change all that in a moment."

She took up a lump of clay, and pinching off a pellet, laid it on the right cheek-bone and spread it out. Having treated the other side in the same manner, she rolled an elongated pellet with which she built up the lower lip. Then, with a larger pellet, she enlarged the chin downwards and forwards, and having added a small touch to each of the eyebrows, she dipped a sponge in thick clay-water, or 'slip', and dabbed the mask all over to bring it to a uniform colour.

"There," she said, "it is very rough, but you see what I mean."

The result was truly astonishing. The weak, chubby, girlish face had been changed by these few touches into the strong, coarse face of a middle – aged woman.

"It really is amazing!" I exclaimed. "It is a perfectly different face. I wouldn't have believed that such a thing was possible."

"It is a most striking and interesting demonstration," said Thorndyke. "But yet I don't know that we need be so surprised. If we consider that of all the millions of persons in this island alone, each one has a face which is different from any other and yet that all those faces are made up of the same anatomical parts, we realize that the differences which distinguish one face from another must be excessively subtle and minute."

"We do," agreed Marion, "especially when we are modelling a portrait bust and the likeness won't come, although every part appears to be correct and all the measurements seem to agree. A true likeness is an extraordinarily subtle and exact piece of work."

"So I have always thought," said Thorndyke. "But I mustn't delay you any longer. May I have my precious parcel?"

Marion hastily put the finishing touches to the not very presentable bundle and handed it to him with a smile and a bow. He then took his leave of her and I escorted him to the door, where he paused for a moment as we shook hands.

"You are bearing my advice in mind, I hope. Gray," he said.

"As to keeping clear of unfrequented places? Yes, I have been very careful in that respect, and I never go abroad without the pistol. It is in my hip-pocket now. But I have seen no sign of anything to justify so much caution. I doubt if our friend is even aware of my existence, and in any case, I don't see that he has anything against me, excepting as Miss D'Arblay's watch-dog."

"Don't be too sure, Gray," he rejoined earnestly. "There may be certain little matters that you have overlooked. At any rate, don't relax your caution. Give all unfrequented places a wide berth and keep a bright look-out."

With this final warning, he turned away and strode off down the road, while I re-entered the studio just in time to see Polton mix the first bowl of plaster, as Marion, having washed the clay from the transformed mask, dried it and rehung it on its peg.

Chapter XIII
A Narrow Escape

The statement that I had made to Thorndyke was perfectly true in substance, but it was hardly as significant in fact as the words implied. I had, it is true, in my journeyings abroad, restricted myself to well-beaten thoroughfares. But then I had had no occasion to do otherwise. Until Polton's arrival on the scene, my time had been wholly taken up in keeping a watch on Marion, and so it would have continued if I had followed my own inclination. But at the end of the first day's work she intervened resolutely.

"I am perfectly ashamed," she said, "to occupy the time of two men, both of whom have their own affairs to attend to, though I can't tell you how grateful I am to you for sacrificing yourselves."

"We are acting under The Doctor's orders, miss," said Polton – thereby, in his opinion, closing the subject.

"You mean Dr. Thorndyke's?" said Marion, not realizing – or not choosing to realize – that, to Polton, there was no other doctor in the world who counted.

"Yes, miss. The Doctor's orders must be carried out."

"Of course they must," she agreed warmly, "since he has been so very good as to take all this trouble about my safety. But there is no need for both of you to be here together. Couldn't you arrange to take turns on duty – alternate days or a half-day each? I hate the thought that I am wasting the whole of both your times."

I did not look on the suggestion with favour, for I was reluctant to yield up to any man – even to Polton – the privilege of watching over the safety of one who was so infinitely dear to me. Nor was Polton much less unwilling to agree, for he loathed to leave a piece of work uncompleted. However, Marion refused to accept our denials (as is the way of women), and the end of it was that Polton and I had to arrange our duties in half-day shifts, changing over at the end of each week, the first spell allotting the mornings to me and the latter half of the day – with the duty of seeing Marion home – to him.

Thus, during each of the following six working days, I found myself with the entire afternoon and evening free. The former I usually spent at the hospital, but in the evenings, feeling too unsettled for study, I occupied myself very pleasantly with long walks through the inexhaustible streets, extending my knowledge of the town and making systematic explorations of such distant regions as Mile End, Kingsland, Dalston, Wapping, and the Borough.

One evening I bethought me of my promise to look in on Usher. I did not find myself yearning for his society, but a promise is a promise. Accordingly, when I had finished my solitary dinner, I set forth from my lodgings in Camden Square and made a bee-line for Clerkenwell, so far, that is to say, as was possible, while keeping to the wider streets. For in this respect, I followed Thorndyke's instructions to the letter, though, as to the other matter – that of keeping a bright look-out – I was less attentive, my mind being much more occupied with thoughts of Marion (who would, just now, be on her way home under Polton's escort) than with any considerations of my own personal safety. Indeed, to tell the truth, I was inclined to be more than a little sceptical as to the need for these extraordinary precautions.

I found Usher in the act of bowing out the last of the "evening consultations" and was welcomed by him with enthusiasm.

"Delighted to see you, old chap!" he exclaimed, shaking my hand warmly. "It is good of you to drop in on an old fossil like me. Didn't much think you would. I suppose you don't often come this way?"

"No," I replied. "It is rather off my beat. I've finished with Hoxton – for the present, at any rate."

"So have I," said Usher, "since poor old Crile went off to the better land."

"Crile?" I repeated. "Who was he?"

"Don't you remember me telling you about his funeral, when they had those Sunday School kids yowling hymns round the grave? That was Mr. Crile – Christian name, Jonathan."

"I remember, but I didn't realize that he was a Hoxton aristocrat."

"Well, he was. Fifty-two Field Street was his earthly abode. I used to remember it by the number of weeks in the year. And glad enough I was when he hopped off his perch, for his confounded landlady, a Mrs. Pepper, would insist on fixing the times for my visits, and deuced inconvenient times, too. Between four and six on Tuesdays and Fridays. I hate patients who turn your visits into appointments. Upsets your whole visiting-list."

"It seems to be the fashion in Hoxton," I remarked. "I had to make my visits at appointed times, too. It would have been frightfully inconvenient if I had been busy. Is it often done?"

"They will always do it if you let 'em. Of course it is a convenience to a woman who doesn't keep a servant, to know what time the doctor is going to call, but it doesn't do to give way to 'em."

525

I assented to this excellent principle, noting, however, that he seemed to have "given way to 'em" all the same.

As we had been talking, we had gradually drifted from the surgery up a flight of stairs to a shabby, cosy little room on the first floor, where a cheerful fire was burning and a copper kettle on a trivet purred contentedly and breathed forth little clouds of steam. Usher inducted me into a large easy-chair, the depressed seat of which suggested its customary use by an elephant of sedentary habits, and produced from a cupboard a spirit-decanter, a high-shouldered Dutch gin-bottle, a sugar-basin, and a couple of tumblers and sugar-crushers.

"Whisky or Hollands?" he demanded, and as curiosity led me to select the latter, he commented, "That's right, Gray. Good stuff, Hollands. Touches up the cubical epithelium – What! I am rather partial to a drop of Hollands."

It was no empty profession. The initial dose made me open my eyes, and that was only a beginning. In a twinkling, as it seemed, his tumbler was empty and the collaboration of the bottle and the copper kettle was repeated. And so it went on for nearly an hour, until I began to grow quite uneasy, though without any visible cause, so far as Usher was concerned. He did not turn a hair (he hadn't very many to turn for that matter, but I speak figuratively). The only effect that I could observe was an increasing fluency of speech with a tendency to discursiveness, and I must admit that his conversation was highly entertaining. But his evident intention to "make a night of it" set me planning to make my escape without appearing to slight his hospitality. How I should have managed it, unaided by the direct interposition of Providence, I cannot guess, for his conversation had now taken the form of an interminable sentence punctuated by indistinguishable commas, but in the midst of this steadily-flowing stream of eloquence the outer silence was rent by the sudden jangling of a bell.

Usher stopped short, stared at me solemnly, deliberately emptied his tumbler, and stood up.

"Night bell, ol' chappie," he explained. "Got to go out. But don't you disturb yourself. Be back in a few minutes. Soon polish 'em off."

"I'll walk round with you as far as your patient's house," said I, "and then I shall have to get home. It is past ten, and I have a longish walk to Camden Square."

He was disposed to argue the point, but another violent jangling cut his protests short and lent him hurrying down the stairs, with me close at his heels. A couple of minutes later we were out in the street, following in the wake of a hurrying figure, and, looking at Usher as he walked sedately at my side, with his top-hat, his whiskers, and his inevitable umbrella, I had the feeling that all those jorums of Hollands had been consumed in vain. In appearance, in manner, in speech, and in gait he was just his normal self, with never a hint of any change from the *status quo ante bellum*.

Our course led us into the purlieus of St. John Street Road, where we presently turned into a narrow, winding and curiously desolate little street, along which we proceeded for a few hundred yards, when our "fore-runner" halted at a door into which he inserted a latch-key. When we arrived at the open door, inside which a shadowy figure was lurking, Usher stopped and held out his hand.

"Good night, old chap," he said. "Sorry you can't come back with me. If you keep straight on and turn to the left at the cross-roads, you will come out presently into the King's Cross Road. Then you'll know your way. So long."

He turned into the dark passage, the door was closed, and I went on my way.

The little meandering street was singularly silent and deserted, and its windings cut off the light from the scanty street-lamps, so that stretches of it were in almost total darkness. As I strode forward, the echoes of my foot-falls resounded with hollow reverberations which smote my ear – and ought have smitten my conscience – causing me to wonder, with grim amusement, what Thorndyke would have said if he could have seen me thus setting his instructions at defiance. Indeed, I was so far sensible of the impropriety of my being in such a place at such an hour that I was about to turn to take a look back along the street, but at the very moment that I halted within a few feet of a street-lamp, something struck the brim of my hat with a sharp, weighty blow like the stroke of a hammer, and I heard a dull thud from the lamp-post.

In an instant I spun round, mighty fierce, whipping out my pistol, cocking it and pointing it down the street as I raced back towards the spot from whence the missile had appeared to come. There was not a soul in sight nor any sound of movement, and the shallow doorways seemed to offer no possible hiding-place. But some thirty yards back, I came suddenly on a narrow opening like an empty doorway, but actually the entrance to a covered alley not more than three feet wide and as dark as a pocket. This was evidently the ambush (which I had passed, like a fool, without observing it), and I halted beside it, with my pistol still pointed, listening intently and considering what I had better do. My first impulse had been to charge into the alley, but a moment's reflection showed the futility of such a proceeding. Probably my assailant had made off by some well-known outlet, but in any case it would be sheer insanity for me to plunge into that pitch-dark passage. For if he were still lurking there, he would be invisible to me, whereas I should be a clear silhouette against the dim light of the street. Moreover, I had seen no one and I could not shoot at any chance stranger whom I might find there. Reluctantly, I recognized that there was nothing for it but to retreat cautiously and be more careful in future.

My retirement would have looked an odd proceeding to an observer, if there had been one, for I had to retreat crab-wise in order that I might keep the entrance of the alley covered with my pistol and yet see where I was going. When I reached the lamp-post, I scanned the area of lighted ground beneath it, and, almost at the first glance, perceived an object like a largish marble lying in the road. It proved, when I picked it up, to be a leaden ball, like an old-fashioned musket-ball, with one flattened side, which had prevented it from rolling away from the spot where it had fallen. I dropped it into my pocket and resumed my masterly retreat until, at length, the cross-roads came into view. Then I quickened my pace, and as I reached the corner, put away my pistol after slipping in the safety-catch.

Once more out in the lighted and frequented main streets, my thoughts were free to turn over this extraordinary experience, but I did not allow them to divert me from a very careful look-out. All my scepticism was gone now. I realized that Thorndyke had not been making mere vague guesses, but that he had clearly foreseen that something of this kind would probably happen. That was, to me, the most perplexing feature of this incomprehensible affair.

I turned it over in my mind again and again and could make nothing of it. I could see no adequate reason why this man should want to make away with me. True, I was Marion's protector, but that – even if he were aware of it – did not seem an adequate reason. Indeed, I could not see why he was seeking to make away with her – nor, even, was it clear to me that there had been a reasonable motive for murdering her father. But as to myself, I seemed to be out of the picture altogether. The man had nothing to fear from me or to gain by my death.

That was how it appeared to me, and yet I saw plainly that I must be mistaken. There must be something behind all this – something that was unknown to me but was known to Thorndyke. What could it be? I found myself unable to make any sort of guess. In the end, I decided to call on Thorndyke the following evening, report the incident and see if I could get any enlightenment from him.

The first part of this programme I carried out successfully enough, but the second presented more difficulties.

Thorndyke was not a very communicative man, and a perfectly impossible one to pump. What be chose to tell, he told freely, and beyond that, no amount of ingenuity could extract the faintest shadow of a hint.

"I am afraid I am disturbing you, sir," I said in some alarm, as I noted a portentous heap of documents on the table.

"No," he replied. "I have nearly finished, and I shall treat you as a friend and keep you waiting while I do the little that is left." He turned to his papers and took up his pen, but paused to cast one of his quick, penetrating glances at me.

"Has anything fresh happened?" he asked.

"Our unknown friend has had a pot at me," I answered. "That is all."

He laid down his pen and, leaning back in his chair, demanded particulars. I gave him an account of what had happened on the preceding night, and taking the leaden ball from my pocket, laid it on the table. He picked it up, examined it curiously and then placed it on the letter-balance.

"Just over half-an-ounce," he said. "It is a mercy it missed your head. With that weight and the velocity indicated by the flattening, it would have dropped you insensible with a fractured skull."

"And then he would have come along and put the finishing touches, I suppose. But I wonder how he shot the thing. Could he have used an air-gun?"

Thorndyke shook his head. "An air-gun that would discharge a ball of that weight would make quite a loud report, and you say you heard nothing. You are quite sure of that, by the way?"

"Perfectly. The place was as silent as the grave."

"Then he must have used a catapult, and an uncommonly efficient weapon it is in skilful hands, and as portable as a pistol. You mustn't give him another chance, Gray."

"I am not going to if I can help it. But what the deuce does the fellow want to pot at me for? It is a most mysterious thing. Do you understand what it is all about, sir?"

"I do not," he replied. "My knowledge of the facts of this case is nearly all second-hand knowledge, derived from you. You know all that I know and probably more."

"That is all very well, sir," said I, "but you foresaw that this was likely to happen. I didn't. Therefore you must know more about the case than I do."

He chuckled softly. "You are confusing knowledge and inference," said he. "We had the same facts, but our inferences were not the same. It is just a matter of experience. You haven't squeezed out of the facts as much as they are capable of yielding. Come, now, Gray, while I am finishing my work, you shall look over my notes of this case, and then you should take a sort of bird's-eye view of the whole case and see if anything new occurs to you. And you must add to those notes that this man has been at the enormous trouble of stalking you continuously, that he shadowed you to Usher's, that he waited patiently for you to come out, that he followed you most skillfully and took instant advantage of the first opportunity that you gave him. You might also note that he did not elect to overtake you and make a direct attack on you as he did on Miss D'Arblay. Note those facts and consider what their significance may be. And now just go through this little dossier. It won't take you many minutes."

He took out of a drawer a small portfolio, on the cover of which was written "*J. D'Arblay, Decd.*" and, passing it to me, returned to his documents. I opened it and found it to contain a number of separate abstracts, each duly headed with its descriptive title, and an envelope marked "*Photographs*". Glancing over the abstracts, I saw that they dealt respectively with J. D'Arblay, the Inquest, the Van Zellen Case, Miss D'Arblay, Dr. Gray, and Mr. Morris, the last containing, somewhat to my surprise, all the details that I had given Thorndyke respecting that rather mysterious person together with an account of my dealings with him and cross-references to the abstract bearing my name. It was all very complete and methodical, but none of the abstracts contained any information that was new to me. If this represented all the facts that were known to Thorndyke, then he was no better informed than I was. But he had evidently got a great deal more out of the information than I had.

Returning the abstracts with some disappointment to the portfolio, I turned to the photographs, and then I got a very thorough surprise. There were only three, and the first two were of no great interest, one representing the two casts of the guinea and the other the plaster mask of Morris. But the third fairly took away my breath. It was a very bad photograph, apparently an enlargement from a rather poor snap-shot portrait, but, bad as it was, it gave a very vivid presentment of one of the most evil-looking faces that I have ever looked on: A lean, bearded face with high cheekbones, with heavy, frowning brows that overhung deep-shadowed, hollow eye-sockets, and an almost grotesquely large nose, thin, curved and sharp, that jutted out like a great predatory beak.

I stared at the photograph in speechless amazement. At the first glance I had been struck by the perfect way in which this crude portrait realized Marion's description of the man who had tried to murder her. But that was not all. There was another resemblance which I now perceived with even more astonishment. Indeed, it was so incredible that the perception of it reduced me to something like stupefaction. I sat for fully a minute with the portrait in my hand and my thoughts surging confusedly in a vain effort to grasp the meaning of this extraordinary likeness. Then, happening to glance up at Thorndyke, I found him quietly regarding me with undisguised interest.

"Well?" he said, as he caught my eye.

"Who is he?" I demanded, holding up the photograph.

"That is what I want to know," he replied. "The photograph came to me without any description. The identity of the subject is unknown. Who do you think he is?"

"To begin with," I answered, "he exactly corresponds in appearance with Miss D'Arblay's description of her would-be murderer. Don't you think so?"

"I do," he replied. "The correspondence seems complete in every detail, so far as I can judge. That was why I secured the photograph. But the actual resemblance will have to be settled by her. I suggest that you take the portrait and let her see it, but you had better not show it to her pointedly for identification. It would be better to put it in some place where she will see it without previous suggestion or preparation. But you said just now 'to begin with'. Was there anything else that struck you about this photograph?"

"Yes," I answered, "there was – a most amazing thing. You remember my telling you about the patient I attended in Morris's house?"

"The man who died of gastric cancer and was eventually cremated?"

"Yes. His name was Bendelow. Well, this photograph might have been a portrait of Bendelow, taken with a beard and moustache before the disease got hold of him. Excepting for the emaciation and the beard – Bendelow was clean-shaved – I should think it would be quite an excellent likeness of him."

Thorndyke made no immediate reply or comment, but sat quite still, looking at me with a very singular expression. I could see that he was thinking rapidly and intensely, but I suspected that his thoughts were in a good deal less confusion than mine had been.

"It is," he remarked at length, "as you say, a most amazing affair. The face is no ordinary face. It would be difficult to mistake it, and one would have to go far to find another with which it could be confused. Still, one must not forget the possibility of a chance resemblance. Nature doesn't take out a letters-patent, even for a human face. But I will ask you, Gray, to write down and send to me all that you know about the late Mr. Bendelow, including all the details of your attendance on him, dead and alive."

"I will," said I, "though it is difficult to imagine what connexion he could have had with the D'Arblay case."

"It seems incredible that he could have had any," Thorndyke agreed. "But at present we are collecting facts, and we must note everything impartially. It is a fatal mistake to select your facts in accordance with the apparent probabilities. By the way, if Bendelow was like this photograph, he must have corresponded pretty exactly with Miss D'Arblay's very complete and lucid description. I wonder why you did not realize that at the time."

"That is what I have been wondering. But I suppose it was the beard and the absence of any kind of association between Bendelow and the D'Arblays."

"Probably," he agreed. "A beard and moustache alter very greatly even a striking face like this. Incidentally, it illustrates the superiority of a picture over a verbal description for purposes of identification. No mere description will enable you to visualize correctly a face which you have never seen. I shall be curious to hear what Miss D'Arblay has to say about this photograph."

"I will let you know without delay," said I, and then, as he seemed to have completed his work and put the documents aside, I made a final effort to extract some definite information from him.

"It is evident," I said, "that the body of facts in your notes has conveyed a good deal more to you than it has to me."

"Probably," he agreed. "If it had not, I should seem to have profited little by years of professional practice."

"Then," I said persuasively, "may I ask, if you have formed a really satisfactory theory as to who this man is and why he murdered D'Arblay?"

Thorndyke reflected for a few moments and then replied, "My position. Gray, is this: I have arrived at a very definite theory as to the motive of the murder, and a most extraordinary motive it is. But there are one or two points that I do not understand. There are some links missing from the chain of evidence. So with the identity of the man. We know pretty certainly that he is the murderer of Van Zellen and we know what he is like to look at, but we can't give him a name and a definite personality. There are links missing there, too. But I have great hopes of finding those missing links. If I find them, I shall have a complete case against this man and I shall forthwith set the law in motion. I can't tell you more than that at present, but I repeat that you are in possession of all the facts and that if you think over all that has happened and ask yourself what it can mean, though you will not arrive at a complete solution any more than I have, you will at least begin to see the light."

This was all that I could get out of him, and as it was growing late I presently rose to take my departure. He walked with me as far as the

Middle Temple Gate and stood outside the wicket watching me as I strode away westward.

Chapter XIV
The Haunted Man

When I arrived at the studio on the following afternoon, I found the door open and Polton waiting just inside with his hat and overcoat on and his bag in his hand.

"I am glad you are punctual, sir," he said, with his benevolent smile. "I wanted to get back to the chambers in good time to-day. It won't matter to-morrow, which is fortunate, as you may be late."

"Why may I be late to-morrow?" I asked.

"I have a message for you from The Doctor," he replied. "It is about what you were discussing last night. He told me to tell you that he is expecting a visit from an officer of the Criminal Investigation Department and he would like you to be present, if it would be convenient. About half-past-ten, sir."

"I will certainly be there," said I.

"Thank you, sir," said he. "And The Doctor told me to warn you, in case you should arrive after the officer, not to make any comment on anything that may be said, or to seem to know anything about the subject of the interview."

"This is very mysterious, Polton," I remarked.

"Why, not particularly, sir," he replied. "You see, the officer is coming to give certain information, but he will try to get some for himself if he can. But he won't get anything out of The Doctor, and the only way for you to prevent his pumping you is to say nothing and appear to know nothing."

I laughed at his ingenuous wiliness. "Why," I exclaimed, "you are as bad as the doctor, Polton. A regular Machiavelli."

"I never heard of him," said Polton, "but most Scotchmen are pretty close. Oh, and there is another little matter that I wanted to speak to you about – on my own account this time. I gathered from The Doctor, in confidence, that someone has been following you about. Now, sir, don't you think it would be very useful to be able to see behind you without turning your head?"

"By Jove!" I exclaimed. "It would indeed! Capital! I never thought of it. I will have a supplementary eye fixed in the back of my head without delay."

Polton crinkled deprecatingly. "No need for that, sir," said he. "I have invented quite a lot of different appliances for enabling you to see behind you – reflecting spectacles and walking-sticks with prisms in the handle and so on. But for use at night I think this will answer your purpose best."

He produced from his pocket an object somewhat like a watchmaker's eye-glass, and having fixed it in his eye to show me how it worked, handed it to me with the request that I would try it. I did so and was considerably surprised at the efficiency of the appliance, for it gave me a perfectly dear view of the street almost directly behind me.

"I am very much obliged to you, Polton," I said enthusiastically. "This is a most valuable gift, especially under the present circumstances."

He was profoundly gratified "I think you will find it useful, sir," he said. "The Doctor uses these things sometimes, and so do I if the occasion arises. You see, sir, if you are being shadowed, it is a fatal thing to turn round and look behind you. You never get a chance of seeing what the stalker is like, and you put him on his guard."

I saw this clearly enough and once more thanked him for his timely gift. Then, having shaken his hand and sped him on his way, I entered the lobby and shut the outer door, at the same time transferring Thorndyke's photograph from my letter-case to my jacket-pocket. When I passed through into the studio, I found Marion putting the finishing touches to a plaster case. She greeted me with a smile as I entered and then plunged her hand once more into the bowl of rapidly-thickening plaster, whereupon I took the opportunity to lay the photograph on a side-bench as I walked towards the table on which she was working.

"Good afternoon, Marion," said I.

"Good afternoon, Stephen," she responded, adding, "I can't shake hands until I have washed," and held out her emplastered hands in evidence.

"That will be too late," said I, and as she looked up at me inquiringly, I stooped and kissed her.

"You are very resourceful," she remarked with a smile and a warm blush, as she scooped up another handful of plaster, and then, as if to cover her slight confusion, she asked, "What was all that solemn pow-wow about with Mr. Polton? And why did he wait for you at the door in that suspicious manner? Had he some secret message for you?"

"I don't know whether it was intended to be secret," I answered, "but it isn't going to be so far as you are concerned," and I repeated to her the substance of Thorndyke's message, to which she listened with an eagerness that rather surprised me, until her further inquiries explained it.

535

"This sounds rather encouraging," she said, "as if Dr. Thorndyke had been making some progress in his investigations. I wonder if he has. Do you think he really knows much more than we do?"

"I am sure he does," I replied, "but how much more, I cannot guess. He is extraordinarily close. But I have a feeling that the end is not so very far off. He seems to be quite hopeful of laying his hand on this villain."

"Oh! I hope you are right, Stephen," she exclaimed. "I have been getting so anxious. There has seemed to be no end to this deadlock. And yet it can't go on indefinitely."

"What do you mean, Marion?" I asked.

"I mean," she answered, "that you can't go on wasting your time here and letting your career go. Of course, it is delightful to have you here. I don't dare to think what the place will be like without you. But it makes me wretched to think how much you are sacrificing for me."

"I am not really sacrificing anything," said I. "On the contrary, I am spending my time most profitably in the pursuit of knowledge and most happily in a sweet companionship which I wouldn't exchange for anything in the world."

"It is very nice of you to say that," she said, "but still, I shall be very relieved when the danger is over and you are free."

"Free!" I exclaimed. "I don't want to be free. When my apprenticeship has run out, I am coming on as journeyman. And now I had better get my blouse on and start work."

I went to the further end of the studio, and taking the blouse down from its peg, proceeded to exchange it for my coat. Suddenly I was startled by a sharp cry, and turning round, beheld Marion stooping over the photograph with an expression of the utmost horror.

"Where did this come from?" she demanded, turning a white, terror-stricken face on me.

"I put it there, Marion," I answered somewhat sheepishly, hurrying to her side. "But what is the matter? Do you know the man?"

"Do I know him?" she repeated. "Of course I do. It is he – the man who came here that night."

"Are you quite sure?" I asked. "Are you certain that it is not just a chance resemblance?"

She shook her head emphatically. "It is he, Stephen. I can swear to him. It is no mere resemblance. It is a likeness, and a perfect one, though it is such a bad photograph. But where did you get it? And why didn't you show it to me when you came in?"

I told her how I came by it and explained Thorndyke's instructions. "Then," she said, "Dr. Thorndyke knows who the man is."

536

"He says he doesn't, and he was very close and rather obscure as to how the photograph came into his possession."

"It is very mysterious," said she, with another terrified glance at the photograph. Then suddenly she snatched it up and, with averted face, held it out to me. "Put it away, Stephen," she entreated. "I can't bear the sight of that horrible face. It brings back afresh all the terrors of that awful night."

I hastily returned the photograph to my letter-case, and taking her arm, led her back to the work-table. "Now," I said, "let us forget it and get on with our work." And I proceeded to turn the case over and fix it in the new position with lumps of clay. For a little while she watched me in silence, and I could see by her pallor that she was still suffering from the shock of that unexpected encounter. But presently she picked up a scraper and joined me in trimming up the edges of the case, cutting out the "key-ways" and making ready for the second half, and by degrees her colour came back and the interest of the work banished her terrors.

We were, in fact, extremely industrious. We not only finished the case – it was an arm from the shoulder which was to be made – cut the pouring-holes and varnished the inside with knotting, but we filled one half with the melted gelatine which was to form the actual mould in which the wax would be cast. This brought the day's work to an end, for nothing more could be done until the gelatine had set – a matter of at least twelve hours.

"It is too late to begin anything fresh," said Marion. "You had better come and have supper with me and Arabella."

I agreed readily enough to this proposal, and when we had tidied up in readiness for the morning's work, we set forth at a brisk pace – for it was a cold evening – towards Highgate, gossiping cheerfully as we went. By the time we reached Ivy Cottage, eight o'clock was striking and "the village" was beginning to settle down for the night. The premature quiet reminded me that the adjacent town would presently be settling down, too, and that I should do well to start for home before the streets had become too deserted.

Nevertheless, so pleasantly did the time slip away in the cosy sitting room with my two companions that it was close upon half-past-ten when I rose to take my departure. Marion escorted me to the door, and as I stood in the hall buttoning up my overcoat, she said, "You needn't worry if you are detained to-morrow. We shall be making the wax cast of the bust, and I am certain Mr. Polton won't leave the studio until it is finished, whether you are there or not. He is perfectly mad on waxwork. He wormed all the secrets of the trade out of me the very first time we were alone and he is extraordinarily quick at learning. But I can't imagine what use the knowledge will be to him."

"Perhaps he thinks of starting an opposition establishment," I suggested, "or he may have an eye to a partnership. But if he has, he will have a competitor, and one with a prior claim. Good night, dear child. Save some of the waxwork for me to-morrow."

She promised to restrain Polton's enthusiasm as far as possible and, wishing me "Good night", held out her hand, but submitted without demur to being kissed, and I took my departure in high spirits, more engrossed with the pleasant leave-taking than with the necessity of keeping a bright look-out.

I was nearing the bottom of the High Street when the prevailing quiet recalled me to the grim realities of my position, and I was on the point of stopping to take a look round when I bethought me of Polton's appliance and also of that cunning artificer's advice not to put a possible Stalker on his guard. I accordingly felt in my pocket and, having found the appliance carefully fixed it in my eye without altering my pace. The first result was a collision with a lamp-post, which served to remind me of the necessity of keeping both eyes open. The instrument was, in fact, not very easy to use while walking and it took me a minute or two to learn how to manage it. Presently, however, I found myself able to divide my attention between the pathway in front and the view behind, and then it was that I became aware of a man following me at a distance of about a hundred yards. Of course, there was nothing remarkable or suspicious in this, for it was a main thoroughfare and by no means deserted at this comparatively early tour. Nevertheless, I kept the man in view, noting that he wore a cloth cap and a monkey-jacket, that he carried no stick or umbrella, and that when I slightly slackened my pace he did not seem to overtake me. As this suggested that he was accommodating his pace to mine, I decided to put the matter to the test by giving him an opportunity to pass me at the next side-turning.

At this moment the Roman Catholic church came into view, and I recalled that at its side a narrow lane – Dartmouth Park Hill – ran down steeply between high fences towards Kentish Town. Instantly I decided to turn into the lane – which bent sharply to the left behind the church – walk a few yards down it and then return slowly. If my follower were a harmless stranger, he would then have passed on down Highgate Hill, whereas if he were stalking me I should meet him at the entrance to the lane and could then see what he was like.

But I was not very well satisfied with this plan, for the obvious manoeuvre would show him that he was suspected, and as I approached the church, a better plan suggested itself.

538

On one side by the entrance to the lane were some low railings and a gate with large brick piers. In a moment I had vaulted over the railings and taken up a position behind one of the piers, where I stood motionless, listening intently. Very soon I caught the sound of distinctly rapid footsteps, which suddenly grew louder as my follower came opposite the entrance to the lane, and louder still as, without a moment's hesitation, he turned into it.

From my hiding-place in the deep shadow of the pier I could safely peep out into the wide space at the entrance of the lane, and as this space was well lighted by a lamp I was able to get an excellent view of my follower. And very much puzzled I was therewith. Naturally I had expected to recognize the man whose photograph I had in my pocket. But this was quite a different type of man. It is true that he was shortish and rather slightly built and that he had a beard – but there the resemblance ended. His face, which I could see plainly by the lamp-light, so far from being of an aquiline or vulturine cast, was rather of the blunt and bibulous type. The short, though rather bulbous nose made up in colour what it lacked in size, and its florid tint extended into the cheek on either side in the form of what dermatologists call *acne rosacea*.

I say that his appearance puzzled me, but it was not his appearance alone. For the latter showed that he was a stranger to me, and suggested that he was going down the lane on his lawful occasions, but his movements did not support that suggestion. He had turned into the lane and passed my hiding-place at a very quick walk. But just as he reached the sharp turn he slackened his pace, stepping lightly, and then stopped for a moment, listening intently and peering forward into the darkness of the lane. At length he started again and disappeared round the corner, and by the sound of his retreating footsteps I could tell that he was once more putting on the pace.

I listened until these sounds had nearly died away and was just about to emerge from my shelter when I became aware of footsteps approaching from the opposite direction, and as I did not choose to be seen in the act of climbing the railings, I decided to remain perdu until this person had passed. These footsteps, too, had a distinctly hurried sound, a fact which I noted with some surprise, but I was a good deal more surprised when the new-comer turned sharply into the entrance, walked swiftly past my ambush, and then, as he approached the corner, suddenly slowed down, advancing cautiously on tip-toe, and finally halted to listen and stare into the obscurity of the lane.

I peered out at this new arrival with an amazement that I cannot describe. Like the first man, he was a complete stranger to me – a tallish, athletic-looking man of about thirty-five, not ill-looking and having something of a military air, fair-complexioned with a sandy moustache, but otherwise clean-shaved, and dressed in a suit of thick tweed with no overcoat. I could see these details clearly by the light of the lamp, and even as I was noting them, he disappeared round the corner and I could hear him walking quickly but lightly down the lane.

As soon as he was gone, I looked out from my hiding-place and listened attentively. There was no one in sight, nor could I hear anyone approaching. I accordingly came forth and, quickly climbing over the railings, stood for a few moments irresolute. The obviously reasonable thing to do was to make off down Highgate Hill as fast as I could and take the first conveyance that I could get homeward. But the appearance of that second man had inflamed me with curiosity. What was he here for? Was he shadowing me or was he in pursuit of the other man? Either supposition was incredible, but one of them must be true. The end of it was that curiosity got the better of discretion and I, too, started down the lane, walking as fast as I could and treading as lightly as circumstances permitted.

The second man was some considerable distance ahead, for his footsteps came to me but faintly, and I did not seem to be gaining on him, and I took it that his speed was a fair measure of that of the man in front. Keeping thus within hearing of my quarry, I sped on, turning over the amazing situation in my bewildered mind. The first man was a mystery to me, though apparently not to Thorndyke. Who could he be, and why on earth was he taking this prodigious amount of trouble to get rid of a harmless person like myself? For there could be no mistake as to the magnitude of the efforts that he was making. He must have waited outside the studio, followed Marion and me to her home and there kept a patient vigil of over two hours, waiting for me to come out. It was a stupendous labour. And what was it all about? I could not form the most shadowy guess, while as to the other man, the very thought of him reduced me to a state of hopeless bewilderment.

As my reflections petered out to this rather nebulous conclusion, I halted for a moment to listen for the footsteps ahead. They were still audible, though they sounded somewhat farther away. But now I caught the sound of other footsteps, approaching from behind. Someone else was coming down the lane. Of course, there was nothing surprising in that circumstance, for, after all, this was a public thoroughfare, little frequented as it was, especially after dark. Nevertheless, something in the character of those footsteps put me on the *qui vive*. For this man, too, was walking quickly – very quickly – and with a certain stealthiness, as if he had rubber-soled boots and, like the rest of us, were making as little noise as possible.

I walked on at my previous rapid pace, keeping my ears cocked now both fore and aft, and as I went, my mind surged with wild speculations. Could it be that I had yet another follower? The thing was becoming grotesque. My bewilderment began to mingle with a spice of grim amusement, but still I listened, not without anxiety, to those foot-steps from behind, which seemed to be growing rapidly more distinct. Whoever this newcomer might be, he was no mean walker, for he was overtaking me apace, and this fact gave a pretty broad hint as to his size and strength.

I looked back from time to time, but without stopping or slackening my pace, trying to pierce the deep obscurity of the narrow, closed-in lane. But it was a dark winter's night, and the high fences shut out even the glimmer from the murky sky. It was not until the approaching footfalls sounded quite near that I was able, at length, to make out a smear of deeper darkness on the general obscurity. Then I drew out my pistol and, withdrawing the safety-catch, put my hand, grasping it, into my overcoat pocket. Having thus made ready for possible contingencies, I watched the black shape emerge from the darkness until it developed into a tall, portly man, bearing down on me with long, swinging strides, when I halted and drew back against the fence to let him pass.

But he had no intention of passing. As he came up to me, he, too, halted, and, looking into my face with undissembled curiosity, he addressed me in a brusque though not uncivil tone.

"Now, sir, I must ask you to explain what is going on."

"What do you mean?" I demanded.

"I'll tell you," he replied. "I saw you, a little time ago, climb over the railings and hide behind a gate-post. Then I saw a man come up in a deuce of a hurry, and turn into the lane. I saw him stop and listen for a moment and then bustle off down the hill. Close on this fellow's heels comes another man, also in a devil of a hurry. He turns into the lane, too, and suddenly he pulls up and creeps forward on tip-toe like a cat on hot bricks. He stops and listens, too, and then off he goes down the lane like a lamplighter. Then out you come from behind the gate-post, over the railings you climb, and then you creep up to the corner and listen, and then off you go down the lane like another lamplighter. Now, sir, what's it all about?"

"I assume," said I, repressing a strong tendency to giggle, "that you have some authority for making these inquiries?"

"I have, sir," he replied. "I am a police officer on plain-clothes duty. I happened to be at the corner of Hornsey Lane when I saw you coming down the High Street walking in a queer sort of way as if you couldn't see where you were going. So I drew back into the shadow and had a look at you. Then I saw you nip into the lane and climb over the railings, so I waited to see what was going to happen next. And then those other two came along. Well, now, I ask you again, sir, what's going on? What is it all about?"

"The fact is," I said a little sheepishly, "I thought the first man was following me, so I hid just to see what he was up to."

"What about the second man?"

"I don't know anything about him."

"What do you know about the first man?"

"Nothing, except that he certainly was following me."

"Why should he be following you?"

"I can't imagine. He is a stranger to me and so is the other man."

"Hmm!" said the officer, regarding me with a distrustful eye. "Damn funny affair. I think you had better walk up to the station with me and give us a few particulars about yourself."

"I will with pleasure," said I. "But I am not altogether a stranger there. Inspector Follett knows me quite well. My name is Gray – Dr. Gray."

The officer did not reply for a few moments. He seemed to be listening to something. And now my ear caught the sound of footsteps approaching hurriedly from down the lane. As they drew near, my friend peered into the darkness and muttered in an undertone, "Will that be one of 'em coming back?" He listened again for a moment or two and then, resuming his inquiries, said aloud, "You say Inspector Follett knows you. Well, perhaps you had better come and see Inspector Follett."

As he finished speaking, he again listened intently, and his mouth opened slightly. I suspect my own did, too. For the footsteps had ceased. There was now a dead silence in the lane.

"That chap has stopped to listen," my new friend remarked in a low voice. "We had better see what his game is. Come along, sir," and with this he strode off at a pace that taxed my powers to keep up with him.

But at the very moment that he started, the footsteps became audible again, only now they were obviously retreating, and straining my ears I caught the faint sound of other and more distant foot-falls, also retreating, so far as I could judge, and in the same hurried fashion.

For a couple of minutes the officer swung along like a professional pedestrian and I struggled on just behind him, perspiring freely and wishing that I could shed my overcoat. Still, despite our efforts, there was no sign of our gaining on the men ahead. My friend evidently realized this, for he presently growled over his shoulder, "This won't do," and forthwith broke into a run.

542

Instantly this acceleration communicated itself to the men in front. The rhythm of both sets of foot-falls showed that our fore-runners were literally justifying that description of them, and as both had necessarily given up any attempt to move silently, the sounds of their retreat were borne to us quite distinctly. And from those sounds, the unsatisfactory conclusion emerged that they were drawing ahead pretty rapidly. My friend the officer was, as I have said, an uncommonly fine walker. But he was no runner. His figure was against him. He was fully six feet in height, and he had a presence. He could have walked me off my legs, but when it came to running, I found myself ambling behind him with such ease that I was able to get out my pistol and, after replacing the safety-catch, stow the weapon in my hip-pocket out of harm's way.

However, if my friend was no sprinter he was certainly a stayer, for he lumbered on doggedly until the lane entered the new neighbourhood of Dartmouth Park, and here it was that the next act opened. We had just passed the end of the first of the streets when I saw a surprisingly agile policeman dart out from a shady corner and follow on in our wake in proper Lilliebridge style. I immediately put on a spurt and shot past my companion, and a few moments later, sounds of objurgation arose from behind. I stopped at once and turned back just in time to hear an apologetic voice exclaim, "I'm sure I beg your pardon, Mr. Plonk. I didn't reckernize you in the dark."

"No, of course you wouldn't," replied the plain-clothes officer. "Did you see two men run past here just now?"

"I did," answered the constable, "one after the other, and both running as if the devil was after them. I was halfway up the street, but I popped down to have a look at them, and when I got to the corner I heard you coming. So I just kept out of sight and waited for you."

"Quite right too," said Mr. Plonk. "Well, I don't see or hear anything of those chaps now."

"No," agreed the constable, "and you are not likely to. There's a regular maze of new streets about here. You can take it that they've got clear away."

"Yes, I'm afraid they have," said Plonk. "Well, it can't be helped and there's nothing much in it. Good night, Constable."

He moved off briskly, not wishing, apparently, to discuss the affair, and in a few minutes we came to the wide crossroads. Here he halted and looked me over by the light of a street-lamp. Apparently the result was satisfactory, for he said, "It's hardly worthwhile to take you all the way back to the station at this time of night. Where do you live?"

I told him Camden Square and offered a card in corroboration.

"Then you are pretty close home," said he, inspecting my card. "Very well, Doctor. I'll speak to Inspector Follett about this affair, and if you have any further trouble of this sort you had better let us know. And you had better let us have a description of the men in any case."

I promised to send him the particulars on the following day, and we then parted with mutual good wishes, he making his way towards Holloway Road and I setting my face homeward by way of the Brecknock Road and keeping an uncommonly sharp look-out as I went.

Chapter XV
Thorndyke Proposes a New Move

On the following morning, in order to make sure of arriving before the detective officer, I presented myself at King's Bench Walk a good half-hour before I was due. The door was opened by Thorndyke himself, and as we shook hands, he said, "I am glad you have come early. Gray. No doubt Polton explained the programme to you, but I should like to make our position quite clear. The officer who is coming here presently is Detective-Superintendent Miller of the Criminal Investigation Department. He is quite an old friend and he is coming at my request to give me certain information. But, of course, he is a detective officer, with his own duties to his department, and an exceedingly shrewd, capable man. Naturally, if he can pick up any crumbs of information from us, he will, and I don't want him to learn more, at present, than I choose to tell him."

"Why do you want to keep him in the dark?" I asked.

"Because," he replied, "we are doing quite well, and I want to get the case complete before I call in the police. If I were to tell him all I know and all I think, he might get too busy and scare our man away before we have enough evidence to justify an arrest. As soon as the investigation is finished and we have such evidence as will secure a conviction, I shall turn the case over to him. Meanwhile, we keep our own counsel. Your role this morning will be that of listener. Whatever happens, make no comment. Act as if you knew nothing that is not of public knowledge."

I promised to follow his directions to the letter, though I could not get rid of the feeling that all this secrecy was somewhat futile. Then I began to tell him of my experiences of the previous night, to which he listened at first with grave interest, but with growing amusement as the story developed. When I came to the final chase and the pursuing policeman, he leaned back in his chair and laughed heartily.

"Why," he exclaimed, wiping his eyes, "it was a regular procession! It only wanted a string of sausages and a harlequin to bring it up to pantomime form."

"Yes," I admitted with a grin, "It was a ludicrous affair. But it was a mighty mysterious affair too. You see, neither of the men was the man I had expected. There must be more people in this business than we had supposed. Have you any idea who these men can be?"

"It isn't much use making vague guesses," he replied. "The important point to note is that this incident, farcical as it turned out, might easily have taken a tragical turn, and the moral is that, for the present, you can't be too careful in keeping out of harm's way."

It was obvious to me that he was evading my question, that those two sinister strangers were not the mystery to him that they were to me, and I was about to return to the charge with a more definitely pointed question when an elaborate flourish on the little brass knocker of the inner door announced a visitor.

The tall, military-looking man whom Thorndyke admitted was evidently the superintendent, as I gathered from the mutual greetings. He looked rather hard at me until Thorndyke introduced me, which he did with characteristic reticence.

"This is Dr. Gray, Miller, you may remember his name. It was he who discovered the body of Mr. D'Arblay."

"Yes, I remember," said the superintendent, shaking my hand unemotionally and still looking at me with a slightly dubious air.

"He is a good deal interested in the case," Thorndyke continued, "not only professionally, but as a friend of the family – since the catastrophe."

"I see," said the superintendent, taking a final inquisitive look at me and obviously wondering why the deuce I was there. "Well, there is nothing of a very secret nature in what I have to tell you, and I suppose you can rely on Dr. Gray to keep his own counsel and ours."

"Certainly," replied Thorndyke. "He quite understands that our talk is confidential, even if it is not secret."

The officer nodded and, having been inducted into an easy-chair, by the side of which a decanter, a siphon, and a box of cigars had been placed, settled himself comfortably, lit a cigar, mixed himself a modest refresher, and drew from his pocket a bundle of papers secured with red tape.

"You asked me, Doctor," he began, "to give you all particulars up to date of the Van Zellen case. Well, I can do that without difficulty, as the case – or at least what is left of it – is in my hands. The circumstances of the actual crime I think you know already, so I will take up the story from that point.

"Van Zellen, as you know, was found dead in his room, poisoned with prussic acid, and a quantity of very valuable portable properly was missing. It was not clear whether the murderer had let himself in with false keys or whether Van Zellen had let him in, but the place hadn't been broken into. The job had been done with remarkable skill, so that not a trace of the murderer was left. Consequently, all that was left for the police to do was to consider whether they knew of anyone whose methods agreed with those of this murderer.

"Well, they did know of such a person, but they had nothing against him but suspicion. He had never been convicted of any serious crime, though he had been in chokee once or twice for receiving. But there had been a number of cases of robbery with murder – or rather murder with robbery, for this man seemed to have committed the murder as a preliminary precaution – and they were all of this kind: A solitary crime, very skilfully carried out by means of poison. There was never any trace of the criminal, but gradually the suspicions of the police settled down on a rather mysterious individual of the name of Bendelow – Simon Bendelow. Consequently, when the Van Zellen crime came to light, they were inclined to put it on this man Bendelow, and they began making fresh inquiries about him. But presently it transpired that someone had seen a man, on the morning of the crime, coming away from the neighbourhood of Van Zellen's house just about the time when the murder must have been committed."

"Was there anything to connect him with the crime?" Thorndyke asked.

"Well, there was the time – the small hours of the morning – and the man was carrying a good-sized handbag which seemed to be pretty heavy and which would have held the stuff that was missing. But the most important point was the man's appearance. He was described as a smallish man, clean-shaven, with a big hooked nose and very heavy eyebrows set close down over his eyes.

"Now, this put Bendelow out of it as the principal suspect, because the description didn't fit him at all." (Here I caught Thorndyke's eye for an instant and was warned afresh, and not unnecessarily, to make no comment.) "But," continued the superintendent, "it didn't put him out altogether. For the man whom the description did fit – and it fitted him to a T – was a fellow named Crile – Jonathan Crile – who was a pal of Bendelow's and was known to have worked with him as a confederate in the receiving business and had been in prison once or twice. So the police started to make inquiries about Crile, and before long they were able to run him to earth. But that didn't do them much good, for it turned out that Crile wasn't in New York at all. He was in Philadelphia, and it was clearly proved that he had been there on the day of the murder, on the day before, and the day after. So they seemed to have drawn a blank, but they were still a bit suspicious of Mr. Crile, who seems to have been as downy a bird as his friend Bendelow, and of the other chappie, too. But they hadn't a crumb of evidence against either.

"So there the matter stands. A complete deadlock. There was nothing to be done, for you can't arrest a man on mere suspicion with not a single fact to support it. But the police kept their eye on both gents, so far as they could, and presently they got a chance. Bendelow made a slip – or at any rate they said he did. It was a little trumpery affair, something in the receiving line, and of no importance at all. Probably a faked charge, too. But they thought that if they could get him arrested they might be able to squeeze something out of him – the police in America can do things that we aren't allowed to. So they tried to pounce on him. But Mr. Bendelow was a slippery customer and he got wind of their intentions just in time. When they got into his rooms they found that he had left – in a deuce of a hurry, too, and only a few minutes before they arrived. They searched the place, but found nothing incriminating, and they tried to get on Bendelow's track, but they didn't succeed. He had managed to get dear away, and Crile seemed to have disappeared, too.

"Well, that seemed to be the end of the affair. Both of these crooks had made off without leaving a trace, and the police – having no evidence – didn't worry any more about them. And so things went on for about a year, until the Van Zellen case had been given up and nearly forgotten. Then something happened quite recently that gave the police a fresh start.

"It appears that there was a fire in the house in which Bendelow's rooms were and a good deal of damage was done, so that they had to do some rebuilding, and in the course of the repairs the builder's men found, hidden under the floor-boards, a small parcel containing part of the Van Zellen swag. There was nothing of real value, just coins and medals and seal-rings and truck of that kind. But the things were all identified by means of Van Zellen's catalogue, and, of course, the finding of them in what had been Bendelow's rooms put the murder pretty clearly on to him.

"On this, as you can guess, the police and the detective agencies got busy. They searched high and low for the missing man, but for a long time they could pick up no traces of him. At last they discovered that he and Crile had taken a passage, nearly a year ago, on a tramp-steamer bound for England. Thereupon they sent a very smart, experienced detective over to work at the case in conjunction with our own detective department.

"But we didn't have much to do with it. The American – Wilson was his name – had all the particulars, with the prison photographs and finger-prints of both the men, and he made most of the inquiries himself. However, there were two things that we did for him. We handed over to him the Van Zellen guinea and the particulars of the D'Arblay murder, and we were able to inform him that his friend Bendelow was dead."

"How did you find that out?" Thorndyke asked.

"Oh, quite by chance. One of our men happened to be at Somerset House looking up some details of a will when in the list of wills he came across the name of Simon Bendelow, which he had heard from Wilson himself. He at once got out the will, copied out the address of the executrix and the names and addresses of the witnesses and handed them over to Wilson, who was mightily taken aback, as you may suppose. However, he wasn't taking anything for granted. He set off instantly to look up the executrix – a Mrs. Morris. But there he got another disappointment, for the Morrises had gone away and no one knew where they had gone."

"I take it," said Thorndyke, "that probate of the will had been granted."

"Yes, everything in that way had been finished up. Well, on this, Wilson set off in search of the witnesses, and he had better luck this time. They were two elderly spinsters who lived together in a house in Turnpike Lane, Hornsey. They didn't know much about Bendelow, for they had only made his acquaintance after he had taken to his bed. They were introduced to him by his friend and landlady, Mrs. Morris, who used to take them up to his room to talk to him and cheer him up a bit. However, they knew all about his death, for they had seen him in his coffin and they followed him to the Ilford Crematorium."

"Ha!" said Thorndyke. "So he was cremated."

"Yes," chuckled the superintendent with a sly look at Thorndyke. "I thought that would make you prick up your ears, Doctor. Yes, there were no half-measures for Mr. Bendelow. He had gone literally to ashes. But it was all right, you know. There couldn't have been any hanky-panky. These two ladies had not only seen him in his coffin, they actually had a last look at him through a little celluloid window in the coffin-lid, just before the coffin was passed through into the cremation furnace."

"And there was no doubt as to his identity?"

"None whatever. Wilson showed the old ladies his photograph and they recognized him instantly, picked his photograph out of a dozen others."

"Where was Bendelow living when they made his acquaintance?"

"Not far from their house – in Abbey Road, Hornsey. But the Morrises moved afterwards to Market Street, Hoxton, and that is where he died and where the will was signed."

"I suppose Wilson ascertained the cause of death?"

"Oh, yes. The old ladies told him that. But he went to Somerset House and got a copy of the death certificate. I haven't got that, as he took it back with him, but the cause of death was cancer of the pylorus – that's some part of the gizzard, I believe, but you'll know all about it. At any rate, there was no doubt on the subject, as the two doctors made a *post mortem* before they signed the death certificate. It was all perfectly plain and straightforward.

"Well, so much for Mr. Bendelow. When Wilson had done with him, he turned his attention to Crile. And then he really did get a proper shake-up. When he was at Somerset House, looking up Bendelow's death certificate, it occurred to him just to run his eye down the list and make sure that Crile was still in the land of the living. And there, to his astonishment, he found Crile's name. He was dead, too! And not only was he dead – he, also, had died of cancer – it was the pancreas this time, another part of the gizzard – and he had died at Hoxton, too, and he had died just four days before Bendelow. The thing was ridiculous. It looked like a conspiracy. But here again everything was plain and above-board. Wilson got a copy of the certificate and called on the doctor who had signed it, a man named Usher. Of course, Dr. Usher remembered all about the case as it had occurred quite recently. There was not a shadow of doubt that Crile was dead. Usher had helped to put him in his coffin and had attended at his funeral, and he, too, had no difficulty in picking out Crile's photograph, and he had no doubt at all as to what Crile died of. So there it was. Queer as it was, there was no denying the plain facts. Those two crooks had slipped through the fingers of the law, so far as it was possible to see.

"But I must admit that I was not quite satisfied, the circumstances were so remarkably odd. I told Wilson so, and I advised him to look further into the matter. I reminded him of the D'Arblay murder and the finding of that guinea, but he said that the murder was our affair, that the men he had come to look for were dead and that was all that concerned him. So back he went to New York, taking with him the death certificates and the two photographs with the certificates of recognition on the backs of them. But he left the notes of the case with me, on the chance that they might be useful to me, and the two sets of finger-prints, which certainly don't seem likely to be of much use under the circumstances."

"You never know," said Thorndyke, with an enigmatical smile.

The superintendent gave him a quick, inquisitive look and agreed. "No, you don't, especially when you are dealing with Dr. John Thorndyke." He pulled out his watch and, staring at it anxiously, exclaimed, "What a confounded nuisance! I've got an appointment at the

550

Law Courts in five minutes. It is quite a small matter. Won't take me more than half-an-hour. May I come back when I have finished? I should like to hear what you think of this extraordinary story."

"Come back, by all means," said Thorndyke, "and I will turn over the facts in my mind while you are gone. Probably some suggestion may present itself in the interval."

He let the officer out, and when the hurried footsteps had died away on the stairs, he closed the door and turned to me with a smile.

"Well, Gray," he said, "what do you think of that? Isn't it a very pretty puzzle for a medical jurist?"

"It is a hopeless tangle to me," I replied. "My brain is in a whirl. You can't dispute the facts and yet you can't believe them. I don't know what to make of the affair."

"You note the fact that, whoever may be dead, there is somebody alive – very much alive, and that that somebody is the murderer of Julius D'Arblay."

"Yes, I realize that. But obviously he can't be either Crile or Bendelow. The question is, who is he?"

"You note the link between him and the Van Zellen murder – I mean the electrotype guinea?"

"Yes, there is evidently some connexion, but I can't imagine what it can be. By the way, you noticed that the American police had got muddled about the personal appearance of these two men. The description of that man who was seen coming away from Van Zellen's house, and who was said to be quite unlike Bendelow, actually fitted him perfectly. They had evidently made a mistake of some kind."

"Yes, I noticed that. But the description may have fitted Crile better. We must get into touch with this man Usher. I wonder if he will be the Usher who used to attend at St. Margaret's."

"He is, and I am in touch with him already. In fact, he was telling me about this very patient, Jonathan Crile."

"Indeed! Can you remember the substance of what he told you?"

"I think so. It wasn't very thrilling." And here I gave him, as well as I could remember them, the details with which Usher had entertained me of his attendance on the late Jonathan Crile, his dealings with the landlady, Mrs. Pepper, and the incidents of the funeral, including Usher's triumphant return in the mourning-coach. It seemed a dull and trivial story, but Thorndyke listened to it with the keenest interest, and when I had finished, he asked, "He didn't happen to mention where Crile lived, I suppose?"

"Yes, curiously enough, he did. The address, I remember, was 52 Field Street, Hoxton."

"Ha!" said Thorndyke. "You are a mine of information, Gray."

He rose and, taking down from the bookshelves Philip's *Atlas of London*, opened it and pored over one of the maps. Then, replacing the atlas, he go out his notes of the D'Arblay case and searched for a particular entry. It was evidently quite a short one, for when he had found it he gave it but a single glance and closed the portfolio. Then, returning to the bookshelves, he took out the *Post Office Directory*, and opened it at the "Streets" section. Here, also, his search was but a short one, though it appeared to be concerned with two separate items, for having examined one, he turned to a different part of the section to find the other. Finally he closed the unwieldy volume and, having replaced it on the shelf, turned and once more looked at me inquiringly.

"Reflecting on what Miller has told us," he said, "does anything suggest itself to you? Any sort of hypothesis as to what the real facts may be?"

"Nothing whatever," I replied. "The confusion that was already in my mind is only the worse confounded. But that is not your case, I take it?"

"Not entirely," he admitted. "The fact is that I had already formed a hypothesis as to the motives and circumstances which lay behind the murder of Julius D'Arblay, and I find this new matter not inconsistent with it. But that hypothesis may, nevertheless, turn out to be quite wrong when we put it to the test of further investigation."

"You have some further investigation in view, then?"

"Yes. I am going to make a proposal to Superintendent Miller – and here he comes, before his time, by which I judge that he, also, is keen on the solution of this puzzle."

Thorndyke's opinion seemed to be justified, for the superintendent entered all agog and opened the subject at once.

"Well, Doctor, I suppose you have been thinking over Wilson's story? How does it strike you? Have you come to any conclusion?"

"Yes," replied Thorndyke. "I have come to the conclusion that I can't accept that story at its face-value as representing the actual facts."

Miller laughed with an air of mingled amusement and vexation. "That is just my position," said he. "The story seems incredible, but yet you can't raise any objection. The evidence in support of it is absolutely conclusive at every point. There isn't a single weak spot in it – at least I haven't found one. Perhaps you have?" And here he looked at Thorndyke with eager inquiry in his eyes.

"I won't say that," Thorndyke replied. "But I put it to you, Miller, that the alleged facts that are offered are too abnormal to be entertained. We cannot accept that string of coincidences. It must be obvious to you

552

that there is a fallacy somewhere and that the actual facts are not what they seem."

"Yes, I feel that myself," rejoined Miller. "But what are we to do? How are we to find the flaw in the evidence, if there is one? Can you see where to look for it? I believe you can."

"I think there is one point which ought to be verified," said Thorndyke. "The identification of Crile doesn't strike me as perfectly convincing."

"How does his case differ from Bendelow's?" Miller demanded.

"In two respects," was the reply. "First, Bendelow was identified by two persons who had known him well for some time and who gave a circumstantial account of his illness, his death, and the disposal of his body, and second, Bendelow's remains have been cremated and are therefore, presumably, beyond our reach for purposes of identification."

"Well," Miller objected, "Crile isn't so very accessible, being some few feet under ground."

"Still, he is there, and he has been buried only a few weeks. It would be possible to exhume the body and settle the question of his identity once for all."

"Then you are not satisfied with Dr. Usher's identification?"

"No. Usher saw him only after a long, wasting illness, which must have altered his appearance very greatly, whereas the photograph was taken when Crile was in his normal health. It couldn't have been so very like Usher's patient."

"That's true," said Miller, "and I remember that Usher wasn't so very positive, according to Wilson. But he agreed that it seemed to be the same man, and all the other facts seemed to point to the certainty that it was really Crile. Still, you are not satisfied? It's a pity Wilson took the photograph back with him."

"The photograph is of no consequence," said Thorndyke. "You have the finger-prints – properly authenticated finger-prints, actually taken from the man in the presence of witnesses. After this short time it will be possible to get perfectly recognizable finger-prints from the body, and those finger-prints will settle the identity of Usher's patient beyond any possible doubt."

The superintendent scratched his chin thoughtfully. "It's a bit of a job to get an exhumation order," said he. "Before I raise the question with the Commissioner, I should like to have a rather more definite opinion from you. Do you seriously doubt that the man in that coffin is Jonathan Crile?'

"It is my opinion," replied Thorndyke. "Of course, I may be wrong, but it is my considered opinion that the Crile who is in that coffin is not the Crile whose fingerprints are in your possession."

"Very well, Doctor," said Miller, rising and picking up his hat. "That is good enough for me. I won't ask you for your reasons, because I know you won't give them. But I have known you long enough to feel sure that you wouldn't give a definite opinion like that unless you had got something pretty solid to go on. And I don't think we shall have any difficulty about the exhumation order after what you have said."

With this the superintendent took his leave, and very shortly afterwards Thorndyke carried me off to lunch at his club before dismissing me to take up my duties at the studio.

Chapter XVI
A Surprise for the Superintendent

It appeared that Thorndyke was correct in his estimate of the superintendent's state of mind, for that officer managed to dispose in a very short time of the formalities necessary for the obtaining of an exhumation licence from the Home Office. It was less than a week after the interview that I have recorded when I received a note from Thorndyke asking me to join him and Miller at King's Bench Walk on the following morning at the unholy hour of half-past-six. He offered to put me up for the night at his chambers, but I declined this hospitality, not wishing to trouble him unnecessarily, and after a perfunctory breakfast by gaslight, a ride on an early tram, and a walk through the dim, lamplit streets, I entered the Temple just as the subdued notes of an invisible clock-bell announced a quarter-past-six. On my arrival at Thorndyke's chambers, I observed a roomy hired carriage drawn up at the entry, and ascending the stairs, found the doctor and Miller ready to start, each provided with a good-sized handbag.

"This is a queer sort of function," I remarked, as we took our way down the stairs. "A sort of funeral the wrong way about."

"Yes," Thorndyke agreed, "it is what Lewis Carroll would have called an 'unfuneral' – and very appropriately too. I didn't give you any particulars in my note, but you understand the object of this expedition?"

"I assume that we are going to resurrect the late Jonathan Crile," I replied. "It isn't very dear to me what I have to do with the business, as I never knew Mr. Crile, though I am delighted to have this rather uncommon experience. But I should have thought that Usher would be the proper person to accompany you."

"So the superintendent thought," said Thorndyke, "and quite rightly, so I have arranged to pick up Usher and take him with us. He will be able to identify the body as that of his late patient, and you and I will help the superintendent to take the finger-prints."

"I am taking your word for it, Doctor," said Miller, "that the finger-prints will be recognizable, and that they will be the wrong ones."

"I don't guarantee that," Thorndyke replied, "but still, I shall be surprised if you get the right ones."

Miller nodded with an air of satisfaction, and nothing more was said on the subject until we drew up before Dr. Usher's surgery. That discreet practitioner was already waiting at the open door and at once took his place in the carriage, watched curiously by observers from adjacent windows.

"This is a rum go," he remarked, diffusing a vinous aroma into the atmosphere of the carriage. "I really did think I had paid my last visit to Mr. Crile. But there's no such thing as certainty in this world." He chuckled softly and continued, "A bit different this journey from the last. No hat-bands this time and no Sunday-school children. Lord! When I think of those kids piping round the open grave, and that our dear departed brother was wanted by the police so badly that they are actually going to dig him up, it makes me smile – it does indeed."

In effect, it made him cackle, and as Miller had not heard the account of the funeral, it was repeated for his benefit in great detail. Then the anecdotal ball was set rolling in a fresh direction by one or two questions from Thorndyke, with the result that the entire history of Usher's attendance on the deceased, including the misdeeds of Mrs. Pepper, was retailed with such a wealth of circumstance that the narration lasted until we stopped at the cemetery gate.

Our arrival was not unexpected, for, as we got out of the carriage, two gentlemen approached the entrance and one of them unlocked a gate to admit us. He appeared to be the official in charge of the cemetery, while the other, to whom he introduced us, was no less a person than Dr. Garroll, the Medical Officer of Health.

"The Home Office licence," the latter explained, "directs that the removal shall be carried out under my supervision and to my satisfaction – very necessary in a populous neighbourhood like this."

"Very necessary," Thorndyke agreed gravely.

"I have provided a supply of fresh ground-lime, according to the directions," Dr. Garroll continued, "and as a further precaution, I have brought with me a large formalin spray. That, I think, would satisfy all sanitary requirements."

"It certainly should be sufficient," Thorndyke agreed, "to meet the requirements of the present case. Has the excavation been commenced yet?"

"Oh, yes," replied the cemetery official. "It was started quite early and has been carried down nearly to the full depth, but I thought that the coffin had better not be uncovered until you arrived. I have had a canvas screen put up round the grave so that the proceedings may be quite private. We can send the labourers outside before we unscrew the coffin-lid. You said, Superintendent, that you were anxious to avoid any kind of publicity, and I have warned the men to say nothing to anyone about the affair."

"Quite right," said Miller. "We don't want this to get into the papers, in case – well, in any case."

"Exactly, sir," agreed the official, who was evidently bursting with curiosity himself. "Exactly. Here is the screen. If you will step inside, the excavation can be proceeded with."

We passed inside the screen, where we found four men reposefully contemplating a coil of stout rope, a basket, attached to another rope, and a couple of spades. The grave yawned in the middle of the enclosure, flanked on one side by the mound of newly-dug earth and on the other by a tub of lime and a Winchester quart bottle fitted with a spray nozzle and large rubber bellows.

"You can get on with the digging now," said the official, whereupon one of the men was let down into the grave, together with a spade and the basket, and set to work briskly. Then Dr. Garroll directed one of the other men to sprinkle in a little lime, which he did, with a pleased smile and so little discretion that the man below was seen to stop digging, and after looking up indignantly, take off his cap, shake it violently and ostentatiously dust his shoulders with it.

When about a dozen basketfuls of earth had been hoisted up, a hollow, woody sound accompanying the thrusts of the spade announced that the coffin had been reached. Thereupon more lime was sprinkled in, and Dr. Garroll, picking up the formalin bottle, sprayed vigorously into the cavity until a plaintive voice from below – accompanied by an unnaturally loud sneeze – was heard to declare that "he'd 'ave brought his umbrella if he'd knowed he was goin' to be squirted at." A few minutes' more work exposed the coffin and enabled us to read the confirmatory inscription on the plate. Then the rope slings were let down and with some difficulty worked into position by the excavator below who, when he had completed his task, climbed to the surface and grasped one end of a sling in readiness to haul on it.

"It's a good deal easier letting 'em down than hoisting 'em up," Usher remarked, as a final shower of lime descended and the men began to haul, "but poor old Crile oughtn't to take much lifting. There was nothing of him but skin and bone."

However this might be, it took the united efforts of the four men to draw the coffin up to the surface and slew it round clear of the yawning grave. But at last this was accomplished and it was lifted, for convenience of inspection, on to one of the mounds of newly-dug earth.

"Now," said the presiding official, "you men had better go outside and wait down at the end of the path until you are wanted again," – an order that was received with evident disfavour and complied with rather sulkily. As soon as they were gone, our friend produced a couple of screw-drivers, with which he and Miller proceeded in a very workmanlike manner to extract the screws, while Dr. Garroll enveloped them in a cloud of spray and Thorndyke, Usher, and I stood apart to keep out of range. It was not a long process. Indeed, it came to an end sooner than I had expected, for the first intimation that I received of its completion was a loud exclamation (consisting of the single word "Snakes!") in the voice of Superintendent Miller. I turned quickly and saw that officer standing with the raised coffin-lid in his hand, staring into the interior with a look of perfectly indescribable amazement. Instantly I rushed forward and looked into the coffin, and then I was no less amazed. For in place of the mortal remains of the late Jonathan Crile was a portly sack oozing sawdust from a hole in its side, through which coyly peeped a length of thick lead pipe.

For a sensible time we all stood in breathless silence gazing down at that incredible sack. Suddenly Miller looked up eagerly at Thorndyke, whose sphinx-like countenance showed the faintest shadow of a smile. "You knew this coffin was empty. Doctor," said he.

Thorndyke shook his head. "If I had known," he replied, "I should have told you."

"Well, you suspected that it was empty."

"Yes," Thorndyke admitted, "I don't deny that."

"I wonder why you did and why it never occurred to me."

"It did not occur to you, perhaps, because you were not in possession of certain suggestive facts which are known to me. Still, if you consider that the circumstances surrounding the alleged deaths of these two men were so incredible as to make us both feel certain that there was some fallacy or deception in regard to the apparent facts, you will see that this was a very obvious possibility. Two men were alleged to have died, and one of them was certainly cremated. It followed that either the other man had died, as alleged, or that his funeral was a mock funeral. There was no other alternative. You must admit that, Miller."

"I do, I do," the superintendent replied ruefully. "It is always like this. Your explanations are so obvious when you have given them, and yet no one thinks of them but yourself. All the same, this isn't so very obvious, even now. There are some extraordinary discrepancies that have yet to be explained. But we can discuss them on the way back. The question now is, what is to be done with this coffin?"

"The first thing to be done," replied Thorndyke, "is to screw on the lid. Then we can leave the cemetery authorities to deal with it. But those men must be sworn to absolute secrecy. That is vitally important, for if this exhumation should get reported in the press, we should probably lose the whole advantage of this discovery."

"Yes, by Jove!" the superintendent agreed emphatically. "It would be a disaster. At present the late Mr. Crile is at large, perfectly happy and secure and entirely off his guard. We can just follow him up at our leisure and take him unawares. But if he got wind of this, he would be out of reach in a twinkling – that is, if he is alive, which I suppose – " And here the superintendent suddenly paused, with knitted brows.

"Exactly," said Thorndyke. "The advantage of surprise is with us and we must keep it at all costs. You realize the position," he added, addressing the cemetery official and the Medical Officer.

"Perfectly," the latter replied – a little glumly, I thought, "and you may rely on us both to do everything that we can to keep the affair secret."

With this we all emerged from the screen and walked back slowly towards the gate, and as we went, I strove vainly to get my ideas into some kind of order. But the more I considered the astonishing event which had just happened, the more incomprehensible did it appear. And yet I saw plainly that it could not really be incomprehensible since Thorndyke had actually arrived at its probability in advance. The glaring discrepancies and inconsistencies which chased one another through my mind could not be real. They must be susceptible of reconciliation with the observed facts. But by no effort was I able to reconcile them.

Nor, evidently, was I alone the subject of these difficulties and bewilderments. The superintendent walked with corrugated brows and an air of profound cogitation, and even Usher – when he could detach his thoughts from the juvenile choir at the funeral – was obviously puzzled. In fact it was he who opened the discussion as the carriage moved off.

"This job," he observed with conviction, "is what the sporting men would call a fair knock-out. I can't make head nor tail of it. You talk of the late Mr. Crile being at large and perfectly happy. But the late Mr. Crile died of cancer of the pancreas. I attended him in his illness. There was no doubt about the cancer, though I wouldn't swear to the pancreas. But he died of cancer all right. I saw him dead, and what is more, I helped to put him into that coffin. What do you say to that, Dr. Thorndyke?"

"What is there to say?" was the elusive reply, "You are a competent observer and your facts are beyond dispute. But inasmuch as Mr. Crile was not in that coffin when we opened it, the unavoidable inference is that after you had put him in, somebody else must have taken him out."

"Yes, that is clear enough," rejoined Usher. "But what has become of him? The man was dead, that I am ready to swear to. But where is he?"

"Yes," said Miller. "That is what is bothering me. There has evidently been some hanky-panky. But I can't follow it. It isn't as though we were dealing with a supposititious body. There was a real dead man. That isn't disputed – at least, I take it that it isn't."

"It certainly is not disputed by me," said Thorndyke.

"Then what the deuce became of him? And why, in the name of blazes, was he taken out of the coffin? That's what I want to know. Can you tell me. Doctor? But there! What is the good of asking you? Of course you know all about it! You always do. But it is the old story. You have got the ace of trumps up your sleeve, but you won't bring it out until it is time to take the trick. Now, isn't that the position, Doctor?"

Thorndyke's impassive face softened with a faint, inscrutable smile.

"We hold a promising hand. Miller," he replied quietly, "but if the ace is there, it is you who will have the satisfaction of playing it. And I hope to see you put it down quite soon."

Miller grunted. "Very well," said he. "I can see that I am not going to get any more out of you than that, so I must wait for you to develop your plans. Meanwhile I am going to ask Dr. Usher for a signed statement."

"Yes, that is very necessary," said Thorndyke. "You two had better go on together and set down Gray and me in the Kingsland Road, where he and I have some other business to transact."

I glanced at him quickly as he made this astonishing statement, for we had no business there, or anywhere else that I knew of. But I said nothing. My recent training had not been in vain.

A few minutes later, near to Dalston Junction, he stopped the carriage, and having made our *adieux*, we got out. Then Thorndyke strode off down the Kingsland Road, but presently struck off westward through a bewildering maze of seedy suburban streets and shabby squares in which I was as completely lost as if I had been dropped into the midst of the Sahara.

"What is the nature of the business that we are going to transact?" I ventured to ask as we turned yet another corner.

"In the first place," he replied, "I wanted to hear what conclusions you had reached in view of this discovery at the cemetery."

"Well, that won't take long," I said, with a grin. "They can be summed up in half-a-dozen words: I have come to the conclusion that I am a fool."

He laughed good-humouredly. "There is no harm in thinking that," he said, "provided you are not right – which you are not. But did that empty coffin suggest no new ideas to you?"

"On the contrary," I replied, "it scattered the few ideas that I had. I am in the same condition as Superintendent Miller – an inextricable muddle."

"But," he objected, "you are not in the same position as the superintendent. If he knew all that you and I know, he wouldn't be in a muddle at all. What is your difficulty?"

"Primarily the discrepancies about this man Crile. There seems to be no possible doubt that he died. But apparently he was never buried, and you and Miller seem to believe that he is still alive. Further, I don't see what business Crile is of ours at all."

"You will see that presently," said he, "and meanwhile you must not confuse Miller's beliefs with mine. However," he added as we crossed a bridge over a canal – presumably the Regent's Canal – "we will adjourn the discussion for the moment. Do you know what street that is ahead of us?"

"No," I answered, "I have never been here before, so far as I know."

"That is Field Street," said he.

"The street that the late Mr. Crile lived in?"

"Yes," he answered, and as we passed on into the street from the foot of the bridge, he added, pointing to a house on our left hand, "And that is the residence of the late Mr. Crile – empty, and to let, as you observe."

As we walked past I looked curiously at the house, with its shabby front and its blank, sightless windows, its desolate condition emphasized by the bills which announced it, but I made no remark until we came to the bottom of the street, when I recognized the cross-roads as the one along which I used to pass on my way to the Morrises' house. I mentioned the fact to Thorndyke, and he replied, "Yes. That is where we are going now. We are going to take a look over the premises. That house also is empty, and I have got a permit from the agent to view it and have been entrusted with the keys."

In a few minutes we turned into the familiar little thoroughfare, and as we took our way past its multitudinous stalls and barrows, I speculated on the object of this exploration. But it was futile to ask questions, seeing that I had but to wait a matter of minutes or the answer to declare itself. Soon we reached the house and halted for a moment to look through the glazed door into the empty shop. Then Thorndyke inserted the key into the side-door and pushed it open.

There is always something a little melancholy in the sight of an empty house which one has known in its occupied state. Nothing, indeed, could be more cheerless than the Morris household, yet it was with a certain feeling of depression that I looked down the long passage (where Cropper had bumped his head in the dark) and heard the clang of the closing door. This was a dead house – a mere empty shell. The feeble life that I had known in it was no more. So I reflected as I walked slowly down the passage at Thorndyke's side, recalling the ungracious personalities of Mrs. Morris and her husband and the pathetic figure of poor Mr. Bendelow.

When from the passage we came out into the hall, the sense of desolation was intensified, for here not only the bare floor and vacant walls proclaimed the untenanted state of the house. The big curtain that had closed in the end of the hall and to a great extent furnished it was gone, leaving the place very naked and chill. Incidentally, its disappearance revealed a feature of whose existence I had been unaware.

"Why," I exclaimed, "they had a second street-door. I never saw that. It was hidden by a curtain. But it can't open into Market Street."

"It doesn't," replied Thorndyke. "It opens on Field Street."

"On Field Street!" I repeated in surprise. "I wonder why they didn't let me in that way. It is really the front of the house."

"I think," answered Thorndyke, "that if you open the door and look out, you will understand why you were admitted at the back."

I unbolted the door and, opening it, stepped out on the wide threshold and looked up and down the street. Thorndyke was right. The thoroughfare was undoubtedly Field Street, down which we had passed only a few minutes ago, and close by, on the right hand, was the canal bridge. Strongly impressed with the oddity of the affair, I turned to re-enter, and as I turned I glanced up at the number on the door. As my eye lighted on it, I uttered a cry of astonishment. For the number was Fifty-two!

"But this is amazing!" I exclaimed, re-entering the hall – where Thorndyke stood watching me with quiet amusement – and shutting the door. "It seems that Usher and I were actually visiting at the same house!"

"Evidently," said he.

"But it almost looks as if we were visiting the same patient!"

"There can be practically no doubt that you were," he agreed. "It was on that assumption that I induced Miller to apply for the exhumation order, and the empty coffin seems to confirm it completely."

I was thunderstruck, not only by the incredible thing that had happened, but by Thorndyke's uncanny knowledge of all the circumstances.

"Then," I said, after a pause, "if Usher and I were attending the same man, we were both attending Bendelow."

"That is certainly what the appearances suggest," he agreed.

"It was undoubtedly Bendelow who was cremated," said I.

"All the circumstances seem to point to that conclusion," he admitted, "'unless you can think of any that point in the opposite direction."

"I cannot," I replied. "Everything points in the same direction. The dead man was seen and identified as Bendelow by those two ladies. Miss Dewsnep and Miss Bonnington, and they not only saw him here, but they actually saw him in his coffin just before it was passed through into the crematorium. And there is no doubt that they knew Bendelow by sight, for you remember that they recognized the photograph of him that the American detective showed them."

"Yes," he admitted, "that is so. But their identification is a point that requires further investigation. And it is a vitally important point. I have my own hypothesis as to what took place, but that hypothesis will have to be tested, and that test will be what the logicians would call the *Experimentum Crucis*. It will settle one way or the other whether my theory of this case is correct. If my hypothesis as to their identification is true, there will be nothing left to investigate. The case will be complete and ready to turn over to Miller."

I listened to this statement in complete bewilderment. Thorndyke's reference to the case conveyed nothing definite to me. It was all so involved that I had almost lost count of the subjects of our investigation.

"When you speak of 'the case'," said I, "what case are you referring to?"

"My dear Gray!" he protested. "Do you not realize that we are trying to discover who murdered Julius D'Arblay?"

"I thought you were," I answered, "but I can't connect this new mystery with his death in any way."

"Never mind," said he. "When the case is completed, we will have a general elucidation. Meanwhile, there is something else that I have to show you before we go. It is through this side-door."

He led me out into a large neglected garden and along a wide path that was all overgrown with weeds. As we went I tried to collect and arrange my confused ideas, and suddenly a new discrepancy occurred to me. I proceeded to propound it.

563

"By the way, you are not forgetting that the two alleged deaths were some days apart? I saw Bendelow dead on a Monday. He had died on the preceding afternoon. But Crile's funeral had already taken place a day or two previously."

"I see no difficulty in that," Thorndyke replied. "Crile's funeral occurred, as I have ascertained, on a Saturday. You saw Bendelow alive for the last time on Thursday morning. Usher was sent for and saw Crile dead on Thursday evening, he having evidently died – with or without assistance – soon after you left. Of course, the date of death given to you was false, and you mention in your notes of the case that both you and Cropper were surprised at the condition of the body. The previous funeral offers no difficulty, seeing that we know that the coffin was empty. This is what I thought you might be interested to see."

He pointed to a flight of stone steps, at the bottom of which was a wooden gate set in the wall that enclosed the garden. I looked at the steps – a little vacantly, I am afraid – and inquired what there was about them that I was expected to find of interest.

"Perhaps," he replied, "you will see better if we open the gate."

We descended the steps and he inserted a key into the gate, drawing my attention to the fact that the lock had been oiled at no very distant date and was in quite good condition. Then he threw the gate open and we both stepped out on to the tow-path of the canal. I looked about me in considerable surprise, for we were within a few yards of the hut with the derrick and the little wharf from which I had been flung into the canal.

"I remember this gate," said I. "In fact, I think I mentioned it to you in my account of my adventure here. But I little imagined that it belonged to the Morrises' house. It would have been a short way in, if I had known. But I expect it was locked at the time."

"I expect it was," Thorndyke agreed, and thereupon turned and re-entered. We passed once more down the long passage, and came out into Market Street, when Thorndyke locked the door and pocketed the key.

"That is an extraordinary arrangement," I remarked, "one house having two frontages on separate streets."

"It is not a very uncommon one," Thorndyke replied. "You see how it comes about. A house fronting on one street has a long back garden extending to another street which is not yet fully built on. As the new street fills up, a shop is built at the end of the garden. A small house may be built in connexion with it and cut off from the garden or the shop may be connected with the original house, as in this instance. But in either case, the shop belongs to the new street and has its own number. What are you going to do now?"

"I am going straight on to the studio," I replied.

"You had better come and have an early lunch with me first," said he. "There is no occasion to hurry. Polton is there and you won't easily get rid of him, for I understand that Miss D'Arblay is doing the finishing work on a wax bust."

"I ought to see that, too," said I.

He looked at me with a mischievous smile. "I expect you will have plenty of opportunities in the future," said he, "whereas Polton must make hay while the sun shines. And, by the way, he may have something to tell you. I have instructed him to make arrangements with those two ladies, Miss Dewsnep and her friend, to go into the question of their identification of Bendelow. I want you to be present at the interview, but I have left him to fix the date. Possibly he has made the arrangement by now. You had better ask him."

At this moment an eligible omnibus making its appearance, we both climbed on board and were duly conveyed to King's Cross, where we alighted and lunched at a modest restaurant, thereafter separating to go our respective ways north and south.

Chapter XVII
A Chapter of Surprise

In answer to my knock, the studio door was opened by Polton, and as I met his eyes for a moment I was conscious of something unusual in his appearance. I had scanty opportunity to examine him, for he seemed to be in a hurry, bustling away after a few hasty words of apology and returning whence he had come. Following close on his heels, I saw what was the occasion of his hurry. He was engaged with a brush and a pot of melted wax in painting a layer of the latter on the insides of the moulds of a pair of arms, while Marion, seated on a high stool, was working at a wax bust, which was placed on a revolving modelling-stand, obliterating the seams and other irregularities with a steel tool which she heated from time to time at a small spirit-lamp.

When I had made my salutations, I offered my help to Polton, which he declined – without looking up from his work – saying that he wanted to carry the job through by himself. I sympathized with this natural desire, but it left me without occupation, for the work which Marion was doing was essentially a one-person job, and in any case was far beyond the capabilities of either of the apprentices. For a minute or two I stood idly looking on at Polton's proceedings, but noticing that my presence seemed to worry him, I presently moved away – again with a vague impression that there was something unusual in his appearance – and drawing up another high stool beside Marion's, settled myself to take a lesson in the delicate and difficult technique of surface finishing.

We were all very silent. My two companions were engrossed by their respective occupations and I must needs refrain from distracting them by untimely conversation, so I sat, well-content to watch the magical tool stealing caressingly over the wax surface, causing the disfiguring seams to vanish miraculously into an unbroken contour. But my own attention was somewhat divided, for even as I watched the growing perfection of the bust there would float into my mind now and again an idle speculation as to the change in Polton's appearance. What could it be? It was something that seemed to have altered, to some extent, his facial expression. It couldn't be that he had shaved off his moustache or whiskers, for he had none to shave. Could he have parted his hair in a new way? It seemed hardly sufficient to account for the change, and looking round at him cautiously, I could detect nothing unfamiliar about his hair.

At this point he picked up his wax-pot and carried it away to the farther end of the studio, to exchange it for another which was heating in a water-bath. I took the opportunity to lean towards Marion and ask in a whisper, "Have you noticed anything unusual about Polton?"

She nodded emphatically and cast a furtive glance over her shoulder in his direction.

"What is it?" I asked in the same low tone.

She took another precautionary glance and then, leaning towards me with an expression of exaggerated mystery, whispered, "He has cut his eyelashes off."

I gazed at her in amazement, and was about to put a further question, but she held up a warning fore-finger and turned again to her work. However, my curiosity was now at boiling-point. As soon as Polton returned to his bench, I slipped off my stool and sauntered over to it on the pretence of seeing how his wax cast was progressing.

Marion's report was perfectly correct. His eyelids were as bare of lashes as those of a marble bust. And this was not all. Now that I came to look at him critically, his eyebrows had a distinctly moth-eaten appearance. He had been doing something to them, too.

It was an amazing affair. For one moment I was on the point of demanding an explanation, but good sense and good manners conquered the inquisitive impulse in time. Returning to my stool, I cast an inquiring glance at Marion, from whom, however, I got no enlightenment but such as I could gather from a most alluring dimple that hovered about the corner of her mouth, and that speedily diverted my thoughts into other channels.

My two companions continued for some time to work silently, leaving me to my meditations – which concerned themselves alternately with Polton's eyelashes and the dimple aforesaid. Suddenly Marion turned to me and asked, "Has Mr. Polton told you that we are all to have a holiday to-morrow?"

"No," I answered, "but Dr. Thorndyke mentioned that Mr. Polton might have something to tell us. Why are we all to have a holiday?"

"Why, you see, sir," said Polton, standing up and forgetting all about his eyelashes, "The Doctor instructed me to make an appointment with those two ladies, Miss Dewsnep and Miss Bonnington, to come to our chambers on a matter of identification. I have made the appointment for ten o'clock to-morrow morning, and as The Doctor wants you to be present at the interview and wants me to be in attendance, and we can't leave Miss D'Arblay here alone, we have arranged to shut up the studio for to-morrow."

567

"Yes," said Marion, "and Arabella and I are going to spend the morning looking at the shops in Regent Street, and then we are coming to lunch with you and Dr. Thorndyke. It will be quite a red-letter day."

"I don't quite see what these ladies are coming to the chambers for," said I.

"You will see, all in good time, sir," replied Polton and, as if to head me off from any further questions, he added, "I forgot to ask how your little party went off this morning."

"It went off with a bang," I answered. "We got the coffin up all right, but Mr. Fox wasn't at home. The coffin was empty."

"I rather think that was what The Doctor expected," said Polton.

Marion looked at me with eager curiosity. "This sounds rather thrilling," she said. "May one ask who it was that you expected to find in that coffin?"

"My impression is," I replied, "that the missing tenant was a person who bore a strong resemblance to that photograph that I showed you."

"Oh, dear!" she exclaimed. "What a pity! I wish that coffin hadn't been empty. But, of course, it could hardly have been occupied, under the circumstances. I suppose I mustn't ask for fuller details?"

"I don't imagine that there is any secrecy about the affair, so far as you are concerned," I answered, "but I would rather that you had the details from Dr. Thorndyke, or at least with his express authority. He is conducting the investigations, and what I know has been imparted to me in confidence."

This view was warmly endorsed by Polton (who had by now either forgotten his eyelashes or abandoned concealment as hopeless). The subject was accordingly dropped and the two workers resumed their occupations. When Polton had painted a complete skin of wax over the interior of both pairs of moulds, I helped him to put the latter together and fasten them with cords. Then into each completed mould we poured enough melted wax to fill it, and after a few seconds poured it out again, leaving a solid layer to thicken the skin and unite the two halves of the wax cast. This finished Polton's job, and shortly afterwards he took his departure. Nor did we remain very much longer, for the final stages of the surface finishing were too subtle to be carried out by artificial light and had to be postponed until daylight was available.

As we walked homewards, we discussed the situation so far as was possible without infringing Thorndyke's confidences.

"I am very confused and puzzled about it all," she said. "It seems that Dr. Thorndyke is trying to get on the track of the man who murdered my father. But whenever I hear any details of his investigations, they

568

always seem to be concerned with somebody else or with something that has no apparent connexion with the crime."

"That is exactly my condition," said I. "He seems to be busily working at problems that are totally irrelevant. As far as I can make out, the murderer has never once come into sight, excepting when he appeared at the studio that terrible night. The people in whom Thorndyke has interested himself are mere outsiders – suspicious characters, no doubt, but not suspected of the murder. This man, Crile, for instance, whose empty coffin was dug up, was certainly a shady character. But he was not the murderer, though he seems to have been associated with the murderer at one time. Then there is that Morris, whose mask was found at the studio. He is another queer customer. But he is certainly not the murderer, though he was also probably an associate. Thorndyke has taken an immense interest in him. But I can't see why. He doesn't seem to me to be in the picture, or at any rate, not in the foreground of it. Of the actual murderer we seem to know nothing at all – at least that is my position."

"Do you think Dr. Thorndyke has really got anything to go on?" she asked.

"My dear Marion!" I exclaimed, "I am confident that he has the whole case cut and dried and perfectly clear in his mind. What I was saying referred only to myself. My ideas are all in confusion, but his are not. He can see quite clearly who is in the picture and in what part of it. The blindness is mine. But let us wait and see what to-morrow brings forth. I have a sort of feeling – in fact he hinted – that this interview is the final move. He may have something to tell you when you arrive."

"I do hope he may," she said earnestly, and with this we dismissed the subject. A few minutes later we parted at the gate of Ivy Cottage and I took my way (by the main thoroughfares) home to my lodgings.

On the following morning I made a point of presenting myself at Thorndyke's chambers well in advance of the appointed time in order that I might have a few words with him before the two ladies arrived. With the same purpose, no doubt, Superintendent Miller took a similar course, the result being that we converged simultaneously on the entry and ascended the stairs together. The "oak" was already open and the inner door was opened by Thorndyke, who smilingly remarked that he seemed thereby to have killed two early birds with one stone.

"So you have, Doctor," assented the superintendent, "two early birds who have come betimes to catch the elusive worm – and I suspect they won't catch him."

569

"Don't be pessimistic, Miller," said Thorndyke with a quiet chuckle. "He isn't such a slippery worm as that. I suppose you want to know something of the programme?"

"Naturally, I do, and so, I suppose, does Dr. Gray."

"Well," said Thorndyke, "I am not going to tell you much – "

"I knew it,' groaned Miller.

" – Because it will be better for everyone to have an open mind – "

"Well," interposed Miller, "mine is open enough, wide open, and nothing inside."

"And then," pursued Thorndyke, "there is the possibility that we shall not get the result we hope for, and in that case, the less you expect the less you will be disappointed."

"But," persisted Miller, "in general terms, what are we here for? I understand that those two ladies, the witnesses to Bendelow's will, are coming presently. What are they coming for? Do you expect to get any information out of them?"

"I have some hopes," he replied, "of learning something from them. In particular, I want to test them in respect of their identification of Bendelow."

"Ha! Then you have got a photograph of him?"

Thorndyke shook his head. "No," he replied. "I have not been able to get a photograph of him."

"Then you have an exact description of him?"

"No," was the reply. "I have no description of him at all."

The superintendent banged his hat on the table. "Then what the deuce have you got, sir?" he demanded distractedly. "You must have something, you know, if you are going to test these witnesses on the question of identification. You haven't got a photograph, you haven't got a description, and you can't have the man himself because he is at present reposing in a little terra-cotta pot in the form of bone-ash. Now, what have you got?"

Thorndyke regarded the exasperated superintendent with an inscrutable smile and then glanced at Polton, who had just stolen into the room and was now listening with an expression of such excessive crinkliness that I wrote him down an accomplice on the spot.

"You had better ask Polton," said Thorndyke. "He is the stage manager on this occasion."

The superintendent turned sharply to confront my fellow-apprentice, whose eyes thereupon disappeared into a labyrinth of crow's feet.

"It's no use asking me, sir," said he. "I'm only an accessory before the fact, so to speak. But you'll know all about it when the ladies arrive – and I rather think I hear 'em coming now."

In corroboration, light footsteps and feminine voices became audible, apparently ascending the stairs. We hastily seated ourselves while Polton took his station by the door and Thorndyke said to me in a low voice, "Remember, Gray, no comments of any kind. These witnesses must act without any sort of suggestion from anybody."

I gave a quick assent, and at that moment Polton threw open the door with a flourish and announced majestically, "Miss Dewsnep, Miss Bonnington."

We all rose, and Thorndyke advanced to receive his visitors while Polton placed chairs for them.

"It is exceedingly good of you to take all this trouble to help us," said Thorndyke. "I hope it was not in any way inconvenient for you to come here this morning."

"Oh, not at all," replied Miss Dewsnep, "only we are not quite clear as to what it is that you want us to do."

"We will go into that question presently," said Thorndyke. "Meanwhile, may I introduce to you these two gentlemen, who are interested in our little business: Mr. Miller and Dr. Gray."

The two ladies bowed, and Miss Dewsnep remarked, "We are already acquainted with Dr. Gray. We had the melancholy pleasure of meeting him at Mrs. Morris's house on the sad occasion when he came to examine the mortal remains of poor Mr. Bendelow, who is now with the angels."

"And no doubt," added Miss Bonnington, "in extremely congenial society."

At this statement of Miss Dewsnep's the superintendent turned and looked at me sharply with an expression of enlightenment, but he made no remark, and the latter lady returned to her original inquiry. "You were going to tell us what it is that you want us to do."

"Yes," replied Thorndyke. "It is quite a simple matter. We want you to look at the face of a certain person who will be shown to you and to tell us if you recognize and can give a name to that person."

"Not an insane person, I hope!" exclaimed Miss Dewsnep.

"No," Thorndyke assured her, "not an insane person."

"Nor a criminal person in custody, I trust," added Miss Bonnington.

"Certainly not," replied Thorndyke. "In short, let me assure you that the inspection of this person need not cause you the slightest embarrassment. It will be a perfectly simple affair, as you will see. But perhaps we had better proceed at once. If you two gentlemen will follow Polton, I will conduct the ladies upstairs myself."

On this we rose, and Miller and I followed Polton out on to the landing, where he turned and began to ascend the stairs at a slow and solemn pace, as if he were conducting a funeral. The superintendent walked at my side and muttered as he went, being evidently in a state of bewilderment fully equal to my own.

"Now, what the blazes," he growled, "can the doctor be up to now? I never saw such a man for springing surprises on one. But who the deuce can he have up there?"

At the top of the second flight we came on to a landing and, proceeding along it, reached a door which Polton unlocked and opened.

"You understand, gentlemen," he said, halting in the doorway, "that no remarks or comments are to be made until the witnesses have gone. Those were my instructions."

With this he entered the room, closely followed by Miller, who, as he crossed the threshold, set at naught Polton's instructions by exclaiming in a startled voice, "Snakes!" I followed quickly, all agog with curiosity, but whatever I had expected to see – if I had expected anything – I was totally unprepared for what I did see.

The room was a smallish room, completely bare and empty of furniture save for four chairs – on two of which Polton firmly seated us, and in the middle of the floor, raised on a pair of trestles, was a coffin covered with a black linen cloth. At this gruesome object Miller and I gazed in speechless astonishment, but, apart from Polton's injunction, there was no opportunity for an exchange of sentiments, for we had hardly taken our seats when we heard the sound of ascending footsteps mingled with Thorndyke's bland and persuasive accents. A few moments later the party reached the door, and as the two ladies came in sight of the coffin, both started back with a cry of alarm.

"Oh, dear!" exclaimed Miss Dewsnep. "It's a dead person! Who is it, sir? Is it anyone we know?"

"That is what we want you to tell us," Thorndyke replied.

"How mysterious!" exclaimed Miss Bonnington, in a hushed voice. "How dreadful! Some poor creature who has been found dead, I suppose? I hope it won't be very – er – you know what I mean, sir – when the coffin is opened."

"There will be no need to open the coffin," Thorndyke reassured her. "There is an inspection window in the coffin-lid through which you can see the face. All you have to do is to look through the window and tell us if the face that you see is the face of anyone who is known to you. Are you ready, Polton?"

Polton replied that he was, having taken up his position at the head of the coffin with an air of profound gravity, approaching to gloom. The two ladies shuddered audibly, but their nervousness being now overcome by a devouring curiosity, they advanced, one on either side of the coffin and, taking up a position close to Polton, gazed eagerly at the covered coffin. There was a solemn pause as Polton carefully gathered up the two comers of the linen pall. Then, with a quick movement, he threw it back. The two witnesses simultaneously stooped and peered in at the window. Simultaneously their mouths opened and they sprang back with a shriek.

"Why, it's Mr. Bendelow!"

"You are quite sure it is Mr. Bendelow?" Thorndyke asked.

"Perfectly," replied Miss Dewsnep. "And yet," she continued with a mystified look, "it can't be, for I saw him pass through the bronze doors into the cremation furnace. I saw him with my own eyes," she added, somewhat unnecessarily. "And what's more, I saw his ashes in the casket."

She gazed with wide-open eyes at Thorndyke and then at her friend, and the two women tip-toed forward and once more stared in at the window with starting eyes and dropped chins.

"It *is* Mr. Bendelow," said Miss Bonnington, in an awe-stricken voice.

"But it can't be," Miss Dewsnep protested in tremulous tones. "You saw him put through those doors yourself, Susan, and you saw his ashes afterwards."

"I can't help that, Sarah," the other lady retorted. "This is Mr. Bendelow. You can't deny that it is."

"Our eyes must be deceived," said Miss Dewsnep, the said eyes being still riveted on the face behind the window. "It can't be – and yet it is – but yet it is impossible – "

She paused suddenly and raised a distinctly alarmed face to her friend.

"Susan," she said, in a low, rather shaky voice, "there is something here with which we, as Christian women, are better not concerned. Something against nature. The dead has been recalled from a burning fiery furnace by some means which we may not inquire into. It were better, Susan, that we should now depart from this place."

This was evidently Susan's opinion, too, for she assented with uncommon alacrity and with a distinctly uncomfortable air, and the pair moved with one accord towards the door. But Thorndyke gently detained them.

"Do we understand," he asked, "that, apart from the apparently impossible circumstances, the body in that coffin is, in your opinion, the body of the late Simon Bendelow?"

"You do," Miss Dewsnep replied in a resentfully nervous tone and regarding Thorndyke with very evident alarm. "If it were possible that it could be, I would swear that those unnatural remains were those of my poor friend Mr. Bendelow. As it is not possible, it cannot be."

"Thank you," said Thorndyke, with the most extreme suavity of manner. "You have done us a great service by coming here to-day, and a great service to humanity – how great a service you will learn later. I am afraid it has been a disagreeable experience to both of you, for which I am sincerely sorry, but you must let me assure you that there is nothing unlawful or supernatural in what you have seen. Later, I hope you will be able to realize that. And now I trust you will allow Mr. Polton to accompany you to the dining room and offer you a little refreshment."

As neither of the ladies raised any objection to this programme, we all took our leave of them and they departed down the stairs, escorted by Polton. When they had gone, Miller stepped across to the coffin and cast a curious glance in at the window.

"So that is Mr. Bendelow," said he. "I don't think much of him, and I don't see how he is going to help us. But you have given those two old girls a rare shake-up, and I don't wonder. Of course, this can't be a dead body that you have got in this coffin, but it is a most life-like representation of one, and it took in those poor old Judies properly. What have you got to tell us about this affair, Doctor? I can see that your scheme, whatever it was, has come off. They always do. But what about it? What has this experiment proved?"

"It has turned a mere name into an actual person," was the reply.

"Yes, I know," rejoined Miller, "Very interesting, too. Now we know exactly what he looked like. But what about it? And what is the next move?"

"The next move on my part is to lay a sworn information against him as the murderer of Julius D'Arblay, which I will do now, if you will administer the oath and witness my signature." As he spoke, Thorndyke produced a paper from his pocket and laid it on the coffin.

The superintendent looked at the paper with a surprised grin.

"A little late, isn't it," he said, "to be swearing an information? Of course you can if you like, but when you've done it, what then?"

"Then," replied Thorndyke, "it will be for you to arrest him and bring him to trial."

At this reply the superintendent's eyes opened until his face might have been a symbolic mask of astonishment. Grasping his hair with both hands, he rose slowly from his chair, staring at Thorndyke as if at some alarming apparition.

"You'll be the death of me, Doctor!" he exclaimed. "You really will. I am not fit for these shocks at my time of life. What is it you ask me to do? I am to arrest this man! What man? Here is a waxwork gentleman in a coffin – at least, I suppose that is what he is – that might have come straight from Madame Tussaud's. Am I to arrest him? And there is a casket full of ashes somewhere. Am I to arrest those? Or am I off my head or dreaming?"

Thorndyke smiled at him indulgently. "Now, Miller," said he, "don't pretend to be foolish, because you are not. The man whom you are to arrest is a live man, and what is more, he is easily accessible whenever you choose to lay your hands on him."

"Do you know where to find him?'

"Yes," Thorndyke replied. "I, myself, will conduct you to his house, which is in Abbey Road, Hornsey, nearly opposite Miss D'Arblay's studio."

I gave a gasp of amazement on hearing this, which directed the superintendent's attention to me.

"Very well, Doctor," he said, "I will take your information, but you needn't swear to it, just sign your name. I must be off now, but I will look in to-night about nine, if that will do, to get the necessary particulars and settle the arrangements with you. Probably to-morrow afternoon will be a good time to make the arrest. What do you think?"

"I should think it would be an excellent time," Thorndyke replied, "but we can settle definitely to-night."

With this, the superintendent, having taken the signed paper from Thorndyke, shook both our hands and bustled away with the traces of his late surprise still visible on his countenance.

The recognition of the tenant of the coffin as Simon Bendelow had come on me with almost as great a shock as it had on the two witnesses, but for a different reason. My late experiences enabled me to guess at once that the mysterious tenant was a waxwork figure, presumably of Polton's creation. But what I found utterly inexplicable was that such a waxwork should have been produced in the likeness of a man whom neither Polton nor Thorndyke had ever seen. The astonishing conversation between the latter and Miller had, for the moment, driven this mystery out of my mind, but as soon as the superintendent had gone, I stepped over to the coffin and looked in at the window. And then I was more amazed than ever. For the face that I saw was not the face that I had expected to see. There, it is true, was the old familiar skull-cap, which Bendelow had worn, pulled down over the temples above the jaw-bandage. But it was the wrong face. (Incidentally I now understood what had become of Polton's eyelashes. That conscientious realist had evidently taken no risks.)

"But," I protested, "this is not Bendelow. This is Morris."

Thorndyke nodded. "You have just heard two competent witnesses declare with complete conviction and certainty that this is Simon Bendelow, and, as you yourself pointed out, there can be no doubt as to their knowledge of Bendelow, since they recognized the photograph of him that was shown to them by the American detective."

"That is perfectly true," I admitted. "But it is a most incomprehensible affair. This is not the man who was cremated."

"Evidently not, since he is still alive."

"But these two women saw Bendelow cremated – at least they saw him pass through into the crematorium, which is near enough. And they had seen him in the coffin a few minutes before I saw him in the coffin, and they saw him again a few minutes after Cropper and Morris and I had put him back in the coffin. And the man whom we put into the coffin was certainly not this man."

"Obviously not, since he helped you to put the corpse in."

"And again," I urged, "if the body that we put into the coffin was not the body that was cremated, what has become of it? It wasn't buried, for the other coffin was empty. Those women must have made some mistake."

He shook his head. "The solution of the mystery is staring you in the face," said he. "It is perfectly obvious, and I am not going to give you any further hints now. When we have made the arrest, you shall have a full exposition of the case. But tell me, now, did those two women ever meet Morris?"

I considered for a few moments and then replied, "I have no evidence that they ever met him. They certainly never did in my presence. But even if they had, they would hardly have recognized him as the person they have identified to-day. He had grown a beard and moustache, you will remember, and his appearance was very much altered from what it was when I first saw him."

Thorndyke nodded. "It would be," he agreed. Then, turning to another subject, he said, "I am afraid it will be necessary for you to be present at the arrest. I would much rather that you were not, for he is a dangerous brute and will probably fight like a wild cat, but you are the only one of us who really knows him by sight in his present state."

"I should like to be in at the death," I said eagerly.

"That is well enough," said he, "so long as it is *his* death. You must bring your pistol and don't be afraid to use it."

"And how shall I know when I am wanted?" I asked.

"You had better go to the studio to-morrow morning," he replied. "I will send a note by Polton giving you particulars of the time when we shall call for you. And now we may as well help Polton to prepare for

576

our other visitors, and I think, Gray, that we will say as little as possible about this morning's proceedings or those of to-morrow. Explanations will come better after the event."

With this, we went down to the dining room, where we found Polton sedately laying the table, having just got rid of the two ladies. We made a show of assisting him and I ventured to inquire, "Who is doing the cooking to-day, Polton? Or is it to be a cold lunch?"

He looked at me almost reproachfully as he replied, "It is to be a hot lunch, and I am doing the cooking, of course."

"But," I protested, "you have been up to your eyes in other affairs all the morning."

He regarded me with a patronizing crinkle. "You can do a good deal," said he, "with one or two casseroles, a hay-box, and a four-storey cooker on a gas stove. Things don't cook any better for your standing and staring at them."

Events went to prove the soundness of Polton's culinary principles, and the brilliant success of their application in practice gave a direction to the conversation which led it comfortably away from other and less discussable topics.

Chapter XVIII
The Last Act

Shortly before leaving Thorndyke's chambers with Marion and Miss Boler, I managed to secure his permission to confide to them, in general terms, what was to happen on the morrow, and very relieved I was thereat, for I had little doubt that questions would be asked which it would seem ungracious to evade. Events proved that I was not mistaken, indeed, we were hardly clear of the precincts of the Temple when Marion opened the inquisition.

"You said yesterday," she began, "that Dr. Thorndyke might have something to tell us to-day, and I hoped that he might. I even tried to pluck up courage to ask him, but then I was afraid that it might seem intrusive. He isn't the sort of man that you can take liberties with. So I suppose that whatever it was that happened this morning is a dead secret?"

"Not entirely," I replied. "I mustn't go into details at present, but I am allowed to give you the most important item of information. There is going to be an arrest tomorrow."

"Do you mean that Dr. Thorndyke has discovered the man?" Marion demanded incredulously.

"He says that he has, and I take it that he knows. What is more, he offered to conduct the police to the house. He has actually given them the address."

"I would give all that I possess," exclaimed Miss Boler, "to be there and see the villain taken."

"Well," I said, "you won't be far away, for the man lives in Abbey Road, nearly opposite the studio."

Marion stopped and looked at me aghast. "What a horrible thing to think of!" she gasped. "Oh, I am glad I didn't know! I could never have gone to the studio if I had. But now we can understand how he managed to find his way to the place that foggy night, and to escape so easily."

"Oh, but it is not *that* man," I interposed, with a sudden ease of hopeless bewilderment, for I had forgotten this absolute discrepancy when I was talking to Thorndyke about the identification.

"Not that man!" she repeated, gazing at me in wild astonishment. "But that man was my father's murderer. I feel certain of it."

"So do I," was my rather lame rejoinder.

578

"Besides," she persisted, "if he was not the murderer, who was he, and why should he want to kill me?"

"Exactly," I agreed. "It seems conclusive. But apparently it isn't. At any rate, the man they are going to arrest is the man whose mask Thorndyke found at the studio."

"Then they are going to arrest the wrong man," said she, looking at me with a deeply troubled face. I was uncomfortable, too, for I saw what was in her mind. The memory of the ruffian who had made that murderous attack on her still lingered in her mind as a thing of horror. The thought that he was still at large and might at any moment reappear made it impossible for her ever to work alone in the studio, or even to walk abroad without protection. She had looked, as I had, to the discovery of the murderer to rid her of this abiding menace. But now it seemed that even after the arrest of the murderer this terrible menace would remain.

"I can't understand it," she said dejectedly. "When you showed me that photograph of the man who tried to kill me, I naturally hoped that Dr. Thorndyke had discovered who he was. But now it appears that he is at large and still untraced, yet I am convinced that he is the man who ought to have been followed."

"Never mind, my dear," I said cheerfully. "Let us see the affair out. You don't understand it and neither do I. But Thorndyke does. I have absolute faith in him, and so, I can see, have the police."

She assented without much conviction, and then Miss Boler began to press for further particulars. I mentioned the probable time of the arrest and the part that I was required to play in identifying the accused.

"You don't mean that you are asked to be present when the actual arrest is made, do you?" Marion asked anxiously.

"Yes," I answered. "You see, I am the only person who really knows the man by sight."

"But," she urged, "you are not a policeman. Suppose this man should be violent, like that other man, and he probably will be."

"Oh," I answered airily, "that will be provided for. Besides, I am not asked to arrest him, only to point him out to the police."

"I wish," she said, "you would stay in the studio until they have secured him. Then you could go and identify him. It would be much safer."

"No doubt," I agreed. "But it might lead to their arresting the wrong man and letting the right one slip. No, Marion, we must make sure of him if we can. Surely you are at least as anxious as any of us that he should be caught and made to pay the penalty?"

"Yes," she answered, "if he is really the right man – which I can hardly believe. But still, punishing him will not bring poor Daddy back, whereas if anything were to happen to you, Stephen – Oh! I don't dare to think of it!"

"You needn't think of it, Marion," I rejoined, cheerfully. "I shall be all right. And you wouldn't have your – *apprentice* hang back when the bobbies are taking the affair as a mere every-day job."

She made no reply beyond another anxious glance, and I was glad enough to let the subject drop, bearing in mind Thorndyke's words with regard to the pistol. As a diversion, I suggested a visit to the National Gallery, which we were now approaching, and the suggestion being adopted, without acclamation, we drifted in and rather listlessly perambulated the galleries, gazing vacantly at the exhibits and exchanging tepid comments. It was a spiritless proceeding, of which I remember very little but some rather severe observations by Miss Boler concerning a certain "hussy" (by one Bronzino) in the great room. But we soon gave up this hollow pretence and went forth to board a yellow bus which was bound for the Archway Tavern, and so home to an early supper.

On the following morning I made my appearance betimes at Ivy Cottage, but it was later than usual when Marion and I started to walk in leisurely fashion to the studio.

"I don't know why we are going at all," said she. "I don't feel like doing any work."

"Let us forget the arrest for the moment," said I. "There is plenty to do. Those arms of Polton's have got to be taken out of the moulds and worked. It will be much better to keep ourselves occupied."

"I suppose it will,' she agreed, and then, as we turned a corner and came in sight of the studio, she exclaimed, "Why, what on earth is this? There are some painters at work on the studio! I wonder who sent them. I haven't given any orders. There must be some extraordinary mistake."

There was not, however. As we came up, one of the two linen-coated operators advanced, brush in hand, to meet us and briefly explained that he and his mate had been instructed by Superintendent Miller to wash down the paint-work and keep an eye on the premises opposite. They were, in fact, "plain-clothes" men on special duty.

"We have been here since seven o'clock," our friend informed us, as we made a pretence of examining the window-sashes, "and we took over from a man who had been watching the house all night. My nabs is there all right. He came home early yesterday evening and he hasn't come out since."

"Then you know the man by sight?" Marion asked eagerly.

"Well, miss," was the reply, "we have a description of him, and the man who went into the house seemed to agree with it, and, as far as we know, there isn't any other man living there. But I understand that we are relying on Dr. Gray to establish the identity. Could I have a look at the inside woodwork?"

Marion unlocked the door and we entered, followed by the detective, whose interest seemed to be concerned exclusively with the woodwork of windows, and from windows in general finally became concentrated on a small window in the lobby which commanded a view of the houses opposite. Having examined the sashes of this, with his eye cocked on one of the houses aforesaid, he proceeded to operate on it with his brush, which, being wet and dirty and used with a singular lack of care, soon covered the glass so completely with a mass of opaque smears that it was impossible to see through it at all. Then he cautiously raised the sash about an inch, and whipping out a prism binocular from under his apron, stood back a couple of feet and took a leisurely survey through the narrow opening of one of the opposite houses.

"Hallo!" said he. "There is a woman visible at the first-floor window. Just have a look at her, sir. She can't see us through this narrow crack."

He handed me the glass, indicating the house, and I put the instrument to my eyes. It was a powerful glass, and seemed to bring the window and the figure of the woman within a dozen feet of me. But at the moment she had turned her head away, apparently to speak to someone inside the room, and all that I could see was that she seemed to be an elderly woman who wore what looked like an old-fashioned widow's cap. Suddenly she turned and looked out over the half-curtain, giving me a perfectly clear view of her face, and then I felt myself lapsing into the old sense of confusion and bewilderment.

I had, of course, expected to recognize Mrs. Morris. But this was evidently not she, although not such a very different-looking woman, an elderly, white-haired widow in a crape cap and spectacles – reading-spectacles they must be, since she was looking over and not through them. She seemed to be a stranger – and yet not quite a stranger, for as I looked at her some chord of memory stirred. But the cup of my confusion was not yet full. As I stared at her, trying vainly to sound a clearer note on that chord of memory, a man slowly emerged from the darkness of the room behind and stood beside her, and him I recognized instantly as the bottle-nosed person whom I had watched from my ambush at the top of Dartmouth Park Hill.

"Well, sir," said the detective, as the man and woman turned away from the window and vanished, "what do you make of 'em? Do you recognize 'em?"

"I recognize the man," I replied, "and I believe I have seen the woman before, but they aren't the people I expected to see."

"Oh, dear!" said he. "That's a bad look-out. Because I don't think there is anybody else there."

"Then," I said, "we have made a false shot, and yet – well, I don't know. I had better think this over and see if I can make anything of it."

I turned into the studio, where I found Marion – who had been listening attentively to this dialogue – in markedly better spirits.

"It seems a regular muddle," she remarked cheerfully. "They have come to arrest the wrong man and now it appears that he isn't there."

"Don't talk to me for a few minutes, Marion, dear," said I. "There is something behind this and I want to think what it can be. I have seen that woman somewhere, I feel certain. Now, where was it?"

I cudgelled my brains for some time without succeeding in recovering the recollections connected with her. I re-visualized the face that I had seen through the glass, with its deep-set, hollow eyes and strong, sharply sloping eyebrows, and tried to connect it with some person whom I had seen, but in vain. And then in a flash it came to me. She was the widow whom I had noticed at the inquest. The identification, indeed, was not very complete, for the veil that she had worn on that occasion had considerably obscured her features. But I had no doubt that I was right, for her present appearance agreed in all that I could see with that of the woman at the inquest.

The next question was, who could she be? Her association with the bottle-nosed man connected her in some way with what Thorndyke would have called "the case", for that man, whoever he was, had certainly been shadowing me. Then her presence at the inquest had now a sinister suggestiveness. She would seem to have been there to watch developments on behalf of others. Could she be a relative of Mrs. Morris? A certain faint resemblance seemed to support this idea. As to the man, I gave him up. Evidently there were several persons concerned in this crime, but I knew too little about the circumstances to be able to make even a profitable guess. Having reached this unsatisfactory conclusion, I turned, a little irritably, to Marion, exclaiming, "I can make nothing of it. Let us get on with some work to pass the time."

Accordingly we began, in a half-hearted way, upon Polton's two moulds. But the presence of the two detectives was disturbing, especially when, having finished the exterior, they brought their pails and ladders inside and took up their station at the lobby window. We struggled on for a time, but when, about noon. Miss Boler made her appearance with a basket of provisions and a couple of bottles of wine, we abandoned the attempt and occupied ourselves in tidying up and laying a table.

"Don't you think, Marion," I said, as we sat down to lunch (having provided for the needs of the two "painters", who lunched in the lobby), "that it would be best for you and Arabella to go home before any fuss begins?"

"Whatever Miss Marion thinks," Arabella interposed firmly, "I am not going home. I came down expressly to see this villain captured, and here I stay until he is safely in custody."

"And I," said Marion, "am going to stay with Arabella. You know why, Stephen. I couldn't bear to go away and leave you here after what you have told me. We shall be quite safe in here."

"Well," I temporised, seeing plainly that they had made up their minds, "you must keep the door bolted until the business is over."

"As to that," said Miss Boler, "we shall be guided by circumstances." And from this ambiguous position neither she nor Marion would budge.

Shortly after lunch I received a farther shock of surprise. In answer to a loud single knock, I hurried out to open the door. A tradesman's van had drawn up at the kerb and two men stood on the threshold, one of them holding a good-sized parcel. I stared at the latter in astonishment, for I recognized him instantly as the second shadower of the Dartmouth Park Hill adventure, but before I could make any comment, both men entered – with the curt explanation "police business"– and the last-comer shut the door, when I heard the van drive off.

"I am Detective-Sergeant Porter," the stranger explained. "You know what I am here for, of course."

"Yes," I replied, and turning to the other man, I said, "I think I have seen you before. Are you a police-officer, too?"

My acquaintance grinned. "Retired Detective-Sergeant," he explained, "name of Barber. At present employed by Dr. Thorndyke. I think I have seen you before, sir," and he grinned again, somewhat more broadly.

"I should like to know bow you were employed when I saw you last," said I. But here Sergeant Porter interposed, "Better leave explanations till later, sir. You've got a back gate, I think."

"Yes," said one of the "painters". "At the bottom of the garden. It opens on an alley that leads into the next road – Chilton Road."

"Can we get into the garden through the studio?" the sergeant asked, and on my answering in the affirmative, he requested permission to inspect the rear premises. I conducted both men to the back door and let

583

them out into the garden, where they passed out at the back gate to reconnoitre the alley. In a minute or two they returned, and they had hardly re-entered the studio when another knock at the door announced more visitors. They turned out to be Thorndyke and Superintendent Miller, of whom the latter inquired of the senior painter, "Is everything in going order, Jenks?"

"Yes, sir," was the reply. "The man is there all right. Dr. Gray saw him, but I should mention, sir, that he doesn't think it's the right man."

"The devil he doesn't!" exclaimed Miller, looking at me uneasily and then glancing Thorndyke.

"That man isn't Morris," said I. "He is that red-nosed man whom I told you about. You remember."

"I remember," Thorndyke replied calmly. "Well, I suppose we shall have to content ourselves with the red-nosed man," upon which ex-Sergeant Barber's countenance became wreathed in smiles and the superintendent looked relieved.

"Are all the arrangements complete, Sergeant?" Miller inquired, turning to Sergeant Porter.

"Yes, sir," the latter replied. "Inspector Follett has got some local men, who know the neighbourhood well, posted in the rear watching the back garden, and there are some uniformed men waiting round both the corners to stop him, in case he slips past us. Everything is ready, sir."

"Then," said the superintendent, "we may as well open the ball at once. I hope it will go off quietly. It ought to. We have got enough men on the job."

He nodded to Sergeant Porter, who at once picked up his parcel and went out into the garden, accompanied by Barber. Miller, Thorndyke, and I now adjourned to the lobby window, where, with the two painter-detectives, we established a look-out. Presently we saw the sergeant and Barber advancing separately on the opposite side of the road, the latter leading and carrying the parcel. Arrived at the house, he entered the front garden and knocked a loud single knock. Immediately, the mysterious woman appeared at the ground-floor window – it was a bay-window – and took a long, inquisitive look at ex-Sergeant Barber. There ensued a longish pause, during which Sergeant Porter walked slowly past the house. Then the door opened a very short distance – being evidently chained – and the woman appeared in the narrow opening. Barber offered the parcel, which was much too large to go through the opening without unchaining the door, and appeared to be giving explanations. But the woman evidently denied all knowledge of it, and having refused to receive it, tried to shut the door, into the opening of which Barber had inserted his foot, but he withdrew it somewhat hastily as a coal-hammer

584

descended, and before he could recover himself the door shut with a bang and was immediately bolted.

The ball was opened, as Miller had expressed it, and the developments followed with a bewildering rapidity that far out-paced any possible description.

The sergeant returning and joining Barber, the two men were about to force the ground-floor window, when pistol-shots and police whistles from the rear announced a new field of operations. At once Miller opened the studio door and sallied forth, with the two detectives and Thorndyke, and when I had called out to Marion to bolt the door, I followed, shutting it after me. Meanwhile, from the rear of the opposite houses came a confused noise of police-whistles, barking dogs and women's voices, with an occasional report. Following three rapid pistol-shots there came a brief interval. Then, suddenly, the door of a house farther down the street burst open and the fugitive rushed out, wild-eyed and terrified, his white face contrasting most singularly with his vividly-red nose. Instantly, the two detectives and Miller started in pursuit, followed by the sergeant and Barber, but the man ran like a hare and was speedily drawing ahead when suddenly a party of constables appeared from a side-turning and blocked the road. The fugitive zigzagged and made as if he would try to dodge between them, flinging away his empty pistol and drawing out another. The detectives and Miller were close on him, when in an instant he turned and, with extraordinary agility, avoided them. Then, as the two sergeants bore down on him, he fired at them at close range, stopping them both, though neither actually fell. Again he out-ran his pursuers, racing down the road towards us, yelling like a maniac and firing his pistol wildly at Thorndyke and me. And suddenly my left leg doubled up and I fell heavily to the ground nearly opposite the studio door.

The fall confused me for a moment and as I lay, half-dazed, I was horrified to see Marion dart out of the studio. In an instant she was kneeling by my side with her arm around my neck. "Stephen! Oh, Stephen, darling!" she sobbed and gazed into my face with eyes full of terror and affection, oblivious of everything but my peril. I besought her to go back, and struggled to get out my pistol, for the man, still gaining on his pursuers, was now rapidly approaching. He had flung away his second pistol and had drawn a large knife, and as bore down on us, mad with rage and terror, he gibbered and grinned like a wild cat.

When he was but a couple of dozen paces away, I saw Thorndyke raise his pistol and take a careful aim. But before he had time to fire, a most singular diversion occurred. From the open door of the studio Miss Boler emerged, swinging a massive stool with amazing ease. The man, whose eyes were fixed on me and Marion, did not observe her until she was within a few paces of him, when, gathering all her strength, she hurled the heavy stool with almost incredible force. It struck him below the knees, knocking his feet from under him, and he fell with a sort of dive or half-somersault, falling with the hand that grasped the knife under him.

He made no attempt to rise, but lay with slightly twitching limbs but otherwise motionless. Miss Boler stalked up to him and stood looking down on him with grim interest until Thorndyke, still holding his pistol, stooped and, grasping one arm, gently turned him over. Then we could see the handle of the knife sticking out from his chest near the right shoulder.

"Ha!" said Thorndyke. "Bad luck to the last. It must have gone through the arch of the aorta. But perhaps it is just as well."

He rose and, stepping across to where I sat, supported by Marion and still nursing my pistol, bent over me with an anxious face.

"What is it, Gray?" he asked. "Not a fracture, I hope?"

"I don't think so," I replied. "Damaged muscle and perhaps nerve. It is all numb at present, but it doesn't seem to be bleeding much. I think I could hobble if you would help me up."

He shook his head and beckoned to a couple of constables, with whose aid he carried me into the studio and deposited me on the sofa. Immediately afterwards the two wounded officers were brought in, and I was relieved to hear that neither of them was dangerously hurt, though the sergeant had a fractured arm and Barber a flesh-wound of the chest and a cracked rib. The ladies having been politely ejected into the garden, Thorndyke examined the various injuries and applied temporary dressings, producing the materials from a very business-like-looking bag which he had providently brought with him. While he was thus engaged, three constables entered carrying the corpse, which, with a few words of apology, they deposited on the floor by the side of the sofa.

I looked down on the ill-omened figure with lively curiosity, and especially was I impressed and puzzled by the very singular appearance of the face. Its general colour was of that waxen pallor characteristic of the faces of the dead, particularly of those who have died from haemorrhage. But the nose and the acne patches remained unchanged. Indeed, their colour seemed intensified, for their vivid red "stared" from the surrounding white like the painted patches on a down's face.. The mystery was solved when, the surgical business being concluded, Barber came and seated himself on the edge of the sofa.

586

"Masterly make-up, that," said he, nodding at the corpse. "Looks queer enough now, but when he was alive you couldn't spot it, even in daylight."

"Make-up!" I exclaimed. "I didn't know you could make-up off the stage."

"You can't wear a celluloid nose off the stage, or a tie-on beard," he replied. "But when it is done as well as this – a touch or two of nose-paste or toupee-paste, tinted carefully with grease-paint and finished up with powder – it's hard to spot. These experts in make-up are a holy terror to the police."

"Did you know that he was made up?" I asked, looking at Thorndyke.

"I inferred that he was," the latter replied, "and so did Sergeant Barber. But now we had better see what his natural appearance is."

He stooped over the corpse and, with a small ivory paper-knife, scraped from the end of the nose and the parts adjacent a layer of coloured plastic material about the consistency of modelling-wax. Then with vaseline and cotton-wool, he cleaned away the red pigment until the pallid skin showed unsullied.

"Why, it is Morris after all!" I exclaimed. "It is perfectly incredible, and you seemed to remove such a very small quantity of paste, too! I wouldn't have believed that it would make such a change."

"Not after that very instructive demonstration that Miss D'Arblay gave us with the day and the plaster mask?" he asked with a smile.

I smiled sheepishly in return. "I told you I was a fool, sir." And then, as a new idea burst upon me, I asked, "And that other man – the hook-nosed man?"

"Morris – that is to say, *Bendelow* – " he replied, "with a different, more exaggerated make-up."

I was pondering with profound relief on this answer when one of the painter-detectives entered in search of the superintendent.

"We got into the house from the back, sir," he reported. "The woman is dead. We found her lying on the bed in the first-floor front, and we found a tumbler half-full of water and this by the bedside."

He exhibited a small, wide-mouthed bottle labelled "*Potassium Cyanide*", which the superintendent took from him.

"I will come and look over the house presently," the latter said. "Don't let anybody in, and let me know when the cabs are here."

"There are two here now, sir," the detective announced, "and they have sent down three wheeled stretchers."

587

"One cab will carry our two casualties, and I expect the doctor will want the other. The bodies can be put on two of the stretchers, but you had better send the woman here for Dr. Gray to see."

The detective saluted and retired, and in a few minutes a stretcher dismounted from its carriage was borne in by two constables and placed on the floor beside Morris's corpse. But even now, prepared as I was, and knowing who the new arrival must be, I looked doubtfully at the pitiful effigy that lay before me so limp and passive, that but an hour since had been a strong, courageous, resourceful woman. Not until the white wig, the cap and the spectacles had been removed, the heavy eyebrows detached with spirit and the dark pigment cleaned away from the eyelids, could I say with certainty that this was the corpse of Mrs. Morris.

"Well, Doctor," said the superintendent, when the wounded and the dead had been borne away and we were alone in the studio, "you have done your part to a finish, as usual, but ours is a bit of a failure. I should have liked to bring that fellow to trial."

"I sympathize with you. Miller," replied Thorndyke. "The gallows ought to have had him. But yet I am not sure that what has happened is not all for the best. The evidence in both cases – the D'Arblay and the Van Zellen murders – is entirely circumstantial and extremely intricate. That is not good evidence for a jury. A conviction would not have been a certainty either here or in America, and an acquittal would have been a disaster that I don't dare to think of. No, Miller, I think that, on the whole, I am satisfied, and I think that you ought to be, too."

"I suppose I ought," Miller conceded, "but it would have been a triumph to put him in the dock, after he had been written off as dead and cremated. However, we must take things as we find them, and now I had better go and look over that house."

With a friendly nod to me, he took himself off, and Thorndyke went off to notify the ladies that the intruders had departed.

As he returned with them I heard Marion cross-examining him with regard to my injuries and listened anxiously for his report.

"So far as I can see. Miss D'Arblay," he answered, "the damage is confined to one or two muscles. If so, there will be no permanent disablement and he should soon be quite well again. But he will want proper surgical treatment without delay. I propose to take him straight to our hospital, if he agrees."

"Miss Boler and I were hoping," said Marion, "that we might have the privilege of nursing him at our house."

"That is very good of you," said Thorndyke, "and perhaps you might look after him during his convalescence. But for the present he needs skilled surgical treatment. If it should not be necessary for him to stay in the hospital after the wound has been attended to, it would be best for him to occupy one of the spare bedrooms at my chambers, where he can be seen daily – the surgeon and I can keep an eye on him. Come," he added coaxingly, "let us make a compromise. You or Miss Boler shall come to the Temple every day for as long as you please and do what nursing is necessary. There is a spare room of which you can take possession, and as to your work here, Polton will give you any help that he can. How will that do?"

Marion accepted the offer gratefully (with my concurrence), but begged to be allowed to accompany me to the hospital.

"That was what I was going to suggest," said Thorndyke. "The cab will hold the four of us, and the sooner we start the better."

Our preparations were very soon made. Then the door was opened, I was assisted out through a lane of hungry-eyed spectators, held at bay by two constables, and deposited in the cab, and when the studio had been locked up, we drove off, leaving the neighbourhood to settle down to its normal condition.

Chapter XIX
Thorndyke Disentangles the Threads

The days of my captivity at Number 5A Kings Bench Walk passed with a tranquillity that made me realize the weight of the incubus that had been lifted. Now, in the mornings, when Polton ministered to me – until Arabella arrived and was ungrudgingly installed in office – I could let my untroubled thoughts stray to Marion, working alone in the studio with restored security, free for ever from the hideous menace which hung over her. And later, when she herself, released by her faithful apprentice, came to take her spell of nursing, what a joy it was to see her looking so fresh and rosy, so youthful and buoyant!

Of Thorndyke – the giver of these gifts – I saw little in the first few days, for he had heavy arrears of work to make up. However, he paid me visits from time to time, especially in the mornings and at night, when I was alone, and very delightful those visits were. For he had now dropped the investigator and there had come into his manner something new – something fatherly or elder-brotherly, and he managed to convey to me that my presence in his chambers was a source of pleasure to him – a refinement of hospitality that filled up the cup of my gratitude to him.

It was on the fifth day, when I was allowed to sit up in bed – for my injury was no more than a perforating wound of the outer side of the calf, which had missed every important structure – that I sat watching Marion making somewhat premature preparations for tea, and observed with interest that a third cup had been placed on the tray.

"Yes," Marion replied to my inquiry, "'The Doctor' is coming to tea with us to-day. Mr. Polton gave me the message when he arrived." She gave a few further touches to the teaset and continued, "How sweet Dr. Thorndyke has been to us, Stephen! He treats me as if I were his daughter, and however busy he is, he always walks with me to the Temple gate and puts me into a cab. I am infinitely grateful to him – almost as grateful as I am to you."

"I don't see what you have got to be grateful to me for," I remarked.

"Don't you?" said she. "Is it nothing to me, do you suppose, that in the moment of my terrible grief and desolation, I found a noble chivalrous friend whom I trusted instantly, that I have been guarded through all the dangers that threatened me, and that at last I have been rescued from them and set free to go my ways in peace and security?

Surely, Stephen, dear, all this is abundant matter for gratitude. And I owe it all to you."

"To me!" I exclaimed in astonishment, recalling secretly what a consummate donkey I had been. "But there, I suppose it is the way of a woman to imagine that her particular gander is a swan."

She smiled a superior smile. "Women," said she, "are very intelligent creatures. They are able to distinguish between swans and ganders, whereas the swans themselves are apt to be muddle-headed and self-depreciatory."

"I agree to the muddle-headed factor," I rejoined, "and I won't be unduly ostentatious as to the ganderism. But to return to Thorndyke, it is extraordinarily good of him to allow himself to be burdened with me."

"With us," she corrected.

"It is the same thing, sweetheart. Do you know if he is going to give us a long visit?"

"I hope so," she replied. "Mr. Polton said that he had got through his arrears of work and had this afternoon free."

"Then," said I, "perhaps he will give us the elucidation that he promised me some time ago. I am devoured by curiosity as to how he unravelled the web of mystification that the villain, Bendelow, spun round himself."

"So am I," said she, "and I believe I can hear his footsteps on the stair."

A few moments later Thorndyke entered the room and, having greeted us with quiet geniality, seated himself in the easy-chair by the table and regarded us with a benevolent smile.

"We were just saying, sir," said I, "how very kind it is of you to allow your chambers to be invaded by a stray cripple and his – his belongings."

"I believe you were going to say 'baggage'," Marion murmured.

"Well," said Thorndyke, smiling at the interpolation, "I may tell you both in confidence that you were talking nonsense. It is I who am the beneficiary."

"It is a part of your goodness to say so, sir," I said.

"But," he rejoined, "it is the simple truth. You enable me to combine the undoubted economic advantages of bachelordom with the satisfaction of having a family under my roof, and you even allow me to participate in a way, as a sort of supercargo, in a certain voyage of discovery which is to be undertaken by two young adventurers in the near future – in the very near future, as I hope."

"As I hope, too," said I, glancing at Marion, who had become a little more rosy than usual and who now adroitly diverted the current of the conversation.

"We were also wondering," said she, "if we might hope for some enlightenment on things which have puzzled us so much lately."

"That," he replied, "was in my mind when I arranged to keep this afternoon and evening free. I wanted to give Stephen – who is my professional offspring, so to speak – a full exposition of this very intricate and remarkable case. If you, my dear, will keep my cup charged as occasion arises, I will begin forthwith. I will address myself to Stephen, who has all the facts first-hand, and if, in my exposition, I should seem somewhat callously to ignore the human aspects of this tragic story – aspects which have meant so much in irreparable loss and bereavement to you, poor child – remember that it is an exposition of evidence, and necessarily passionless and impersonal."

"I quite realize that," said Marion, "and you may trust me to understand."

He bowed gravely, and, after a brief pause, began, "I propose to treat the subject historically, so to speak, to take you over the ground that I traversed myself, recounting my observations and inferences in the order in which they occurred. The inquiry falls naturally into certain successive stages, corresponding to the emergence of new facts, of which the first was concerned with the data elicited at the inquest. Let us begin with them.

"First, as to the crime itself. It was a murder of a very distinctive type. There was evidence, not only of premeditation in the bare legal sense, but of careful preparation and planning. It was a considered act and not a crime of impulse or passion. What could be the motive for such a crime? There appeared to be only two alternative possibilities: Either it was a crime of revenge or a crime of expediency. The hypothesis of revenge could not be explored, because there were no data excepting the evidence of the victim's daughter, which was to the effect that the deceased had no enemies, actual or potential, and this evidence was supported by the very deliberate character of the crime.

"We were therefore thrown back on the hypothesis of expediency, which was, in fact, the more probable one, and which became still more probable as the circumstances were further examined. But having assumed, as a working hypothesis, that this crime had been committed in pursuit of a definite purpose which was not revenge, the next question was: What could that purpose have been? And that question could be answered only by a careful consideration of all that was known of the parties to the crime – the criminal and the victim and their possible relations to one another.

"As to the former, the circumstances indicated that he was a person of some education, that he had an unusual acquaintance with poisons, and such social position and personal qualities as would enable him to get possession of them. That he was subtle, ingenious, and resourceful, but not far-sighted, since he took risks that could have been avoided. His mentality appeared to be that of the gambler, whose attention tends to be riveted on the winning chances and who makes insufficient provision for possible failure. He staked everything on the chance of the needle-puncture being overlooked and the presence of the poison being undiscovered.

"But the outstanding and most significant quality was his profound criminality. Premeditated murder is the most atrocious of crimes, and murder for expediency is the most atrocious form of murder. This man, then, was of a profoundly criminal type and was, most probably, a practising criminal.

"Turning now to the victim, the evidence showed that he was a man of high moral qualities: Honest, industrious, thrifty, kindly, and amiable and of good reputation – the exact reverse of the other. Any illicit association between these two men was therefore excluded, and yet there must have been an association of some kind. Of what kind could it have been?

"Now, in the case of this man, as in that of the other, there was one outstanding fact. He was a sculptor. And not only a sculptor but an artist in the highest class of waxwork. And not only this. He was probably the only artist of this kind practising in this country, for waxwork is almost exclusively a French art. So far as I know, all the wax figures and high-class lay figures that are made are produced in France. This man, therefore, appeared to be the unique English practitioner of this very curious art.

"The fact impressed me profoundly. To realize its significance we must realize the unique character of the art. Waxwork is a fine art, but it differs from all other fine arts in that its main purpose is one that is expressly rejected by all those other arts. An ordinary work of sculpture, no matter how realistic, is frankly an object of metal, stone, or pottery. Its realism is restricted to truth of form. No deception is aimed at, but, on the contrary, is expressly avoided. But the aim of waxwork is complete deception, and its perfection is measured by the completeness of the deception achieved. How complete that may be can be judged by incidents that have occurred at Madame Tussaud's. When that exhibition was at the old Baker Street Bazaar, the snuff-taker – whose arms, head,

593

and eyes were moved by clock-work – used to be seated on an open bench, and it is recorded that, quite frequently, visitors would sit down by him on the bench and try to open conversation with him. So, too, the waxwork policeman near the door was occasionally accosted with questions by arriving visitors.

"Bearing this fact in mind, it is obvious that this art is peculiarly adapted to employment in certain kinds of fraud, such as personation, false alibi, and the like, and it is probable that the only reason why it is not so employed is the great difficulty of obtaining first-class waxworks.

"Naturally, then, when I observed this connexion of a criminal with a waxwork artist, I asked myself whether the motive of the murder was not to be sought in that artist's unique powers. Could it be that an attempt had been made to employ the deceased on some work designed for a fraudulent purpose? If such an attempt had been made, whether it had or had not been successful, the deceased would be in possession of knowledge which would be highly dangerous to the criminal, but especially if a work had actually been executed and used as an instrument of fraud.

"But there were other possibilities in the case of a sculptor who was also a medallist. He might have been employed to produce – quite innocently – copies of valuable works which were intended for fraudulent use, and the second stage of the investigation was concerned with these possibilities. That stage was ushered in by Follett's discovery of the guinea, the additional facts that we obtained at the Museum, and later, when we learned that the guinea that had been found was an electrotype copy, and that the deceased was an expert electrotyper, all seemed to point to the production of forgeries as the crime in which Julius D'Arblay had been implicated. That was the view to which we seemed to be committed, but it did not seem to me satisfactory, for several reasons. First, the motive was insufficient – there was really nothing to conceal. When the forgeries were offered for sale, it would be obvious that someone had made them and that someone could be traced by the purchaser through the vendor. The killing of the actual maker would give no security to the man who sold the forgeries and who would have to appear in the transaction. And then, although the deceased was unique as a waxworker, he was not as a copyist or electrotyper. For those purposes, much more suitable accomplices might have been found. The execution of copies by the deceased appeared to be a fact, but my own feeling was that they had been a mere by-product – that they had been used as a means of introduction to the deceased for some other purpose connected with waxwork.

"At the end of this stage we had made some progress. We had identified this unknown man with another unknown man, who was undoubtedly a professional criminal. We had found, in the forged guinea, a possible motive for the murder. But, as I have said, that explanation did not satisfy me, and I still kept a look-out for new evidence connected with the waxworks.

"The next stage opened on that night when you arrived at Cornish's, looking like a resuscitated 'found drowned'. Your account of your fall into the canal and the immediately antecedent events made a deep impression on me, though I did not, at the time, connect them with the crime that we were investigating. But the whole affair was so abnormal that it seemed to call for very careful consideration, and the more I considered it, the more abnormal did it appear.

"The theory of an accident could not be entertained, nor could the dropping of that derrick have been a practical joke. Your objection that no one was in sight had no weight, since there was a gate in the wall by which a person could have made his escape. Someone had attempted to murder you, and that attempt had been made immediately after you had signed a cremation certificate. That was a very impressive fact. As you know, it is my habit to look very narrowly at cremation cases, for the reason that cremation offers great facilities for certain kinds of crime. Poisoners – and particularly arsenic and antimony poisoners – have repeatedly been convicted on evidence furnished by an exhumed body. If such poisoners can get the corpse of the victim cremated, they are virtually safe, for whatever suspicions may thereafter arise, no conviction is possible, since the means of proving the administration have been destroyed.

"Accordingly, I considered very carefully your account of the proceedings, and as I did so, strong suggestions of fraud arose in all directions. There was, for instance, the inspection window in the coffin. What was its object? Inspection windows are usually provided only in cases where the condition of the body is such that it has to be enclosed in a hermetically sealed coffin. But no such condition existed in this case. There was no reason why the friends should not have viewed the body in the usual manner in an open coffin. Again, there was the curious alternation of you and the two witnesses. First they went up and viewed the deceased – through the window. Then, after a considerable interval, you and Cropper went up and viewed the deceased – through the window. Then you took out the body, examined it and put it back. Again, after a considerable interval, the witnesses went up a second time and viewed the deceased – through the window.

"It was all rather queer and suspicious, especially when considered in conjunction with the attempt on your life. Reflecting on the latter, the question of the gate in the wall by the canal arose in my mind, and I examined the map to see if I could locate it. It was not marked, but the wharf was, and from this and your description it appeared certain that the gate must be in the wall of the garden of Morris's house. Here was another suspicious fact. For Morris – who could have let you out by this side-gate – sent you by a long, roundabout route to the tow-path. He knew which way you must be going – westward – and could have slipped out of the gate and waited for you in the hut by the wharf. It was possible, and there seemed to be no other explanation of what had happened to you. Incidentally, I made another discovery. The map showed that Morris's house had two frontages – one on Field Street and one on Market Street – and that you appeared to have been admitted by the back entrance. Which was another slightly abnormal circumstance.

"I was very much puzzled by the affair. There was a distinct suggestion that some fraud – some deception – had been practised, and that what the spinsters saw through the coffin window was not the same thing as that which you saw. And yet, what could the deception have been? There was no question about the body. It was a real body. The disease was undoubtedly genuine and was, at least, the effective cause of death. And the cremation was necessarily genuine, for though you can bury an empty coffin, you can't cremate one. The absence of calcined bone would expose the fraud instantly.

"I considered the possibility of a second body, that of a murdered person, for instance. But that would not do. For if a substitution had been effected, there would still have been a redundant body to dispose of and account for. Nothing would have been gained by the substitution.

"But there was another possibility to which no such objection applied. Assuming a fraud to have been perpetrated, here was a case adapted in the most perfect manner to the use of a waxwork. Of course, a full-length figure would have been impossible because it would have left no calcined bones. But the inspection window would have made it unnecessary. A wax head would have done, or better still, a wax mask, which could have been simply placed over the face of the real corpse. The more I thought about it the more was I impressed by the singular suitability of the arrangements to the use of a wax mask. The inspection window seemed to be designed for the very purpose – to restrict the view to a mere face and to prevent the mask from being touched and the fraud thus discovered – and the alternate inspections by you and the spinsters were quite in keeping with a deception of that kind.

"There was another very queer feature in the case. These people, living at Hoxton, elected to employ a doctor who lived miles away at Bloomsbury. Why did they not call in a neighbouring practitioner? Also, they arranged the days and even the hours at which the visits were to be made. Why? There was an evident suggestion of something that the doctor was not to know – something or somebody that he was not desired to see, that some preparations had to be made for his visits.

"Again, the note was addressed to Dr. Stephen Gray, not to Dr. Cornish. They knew your name and address, although you had only just come there, and they did not know Dr. Cornish, who was an old resident. How was this? The only explanation seemed to be that they had read the report of the inquest, or even been present at it. You there stated publicly that your temporary address was at 61 Mecklenburgh Square, that you were, in fact, a bird of passage, and you gave your full name and your age. Now, if any fraud was being carried out, a bird of passage, who might be difficult to find later, and a young one at that, was just the most suitable kind of doctor.

"To sum up the evidence at this stage: The circumstances, taken as a whole, suggested in the strongest possible manner that there was something fraudulent about this cremation. That fraud must be some kind of substitution or personation with the purpose of obtaining a certificate that some person had been cremated, who in fact had *not* been cremated. In that case it was nearly certain that the dead man was *not* Simon Bendelow, for the certificates would be required to agree with false appearances, not true. There was a suggestion – but only a speculative one – that the deception might have been effected by means of a wax mask.

"There were, however two objections. As to the wax mask, there was the great difficulty of obtaining one. A perfect portrait mask could have been obtained only either from an artist in Paris or from Julius D'Arblay. The objection to the substitution theory was that there was a real body – the body of a real person. If the cremation was in a name which was not the name of that person, then the disappearance of that person would remain unaccounted for.

"So you see that the whole theory of the fraud was purely conjectural. There was not a single particle of direct evidence. You also see that at two points there was a faint hint of a connexion between this case and the murder of Mr. D'Arblay. These people seemed to have read of, or attended at, the inquest, and if a wax mask existed, it was quite probably made by him.

"The next stage opens with the discovery of the mask at the studio. But there are certain antecedent matters that must first be glanced at.

When the attempt was made to murder Marion, I asked myself the questions:

"1. Why did this man want to kill Marion?

"2. What did he come to the studio on the preceding night to search for?

"3. Did he find it, whatever it was?

"4. Why had he delayed so long to make the search?'

"Let us begin with the second question. What had he come to look for? The obvious suggestion was that he had come to get possession of some incriminating object. But what was that object? Could it be the mould of some forged coin or medal? I did not believe that it was. For since the forgery or forgeries were extant, the moulds had no particular significance, and what little significance they had, applied to Mr. D'Arblay, who was, technically, the forger. My feeling was that the object was in some way connected with waxwork, and in all probability with a wax portrait mask, as the most likely thing to be used for a fraudulent purpose. And I need hardly say that the cremation case lurked in the back of my mind.

"This view was supported by consideration of the third question: Did he find what he came to seek? If he came for moulds of coins or medals, he must have found them, for none remained. But the fact that he came the next night and attempted to murder Marion – believing her to be alone – suggested that his search had failed. And consideration of the fourth question led – less decisively – to the same conclusion as to the nature of the object sought.

"Why had he waited all this time to make the search? Why had he not entered the studio immediately after the murder, when the place was mostly unoccupied? The most probable explanation appeared to me to be that he had only recently become aware that there was any incriminating object in existence. Proceeding on the hypothesis that he had commissioned Mr. D'Arblay to make a wax portrait mask, I further assumed that he knew little of the process, and – perhaps misunderstanding Mr. D'Arblay – confused the technique of wax with that of plaster. In making a plaster mask from life – as you probably know by this time – you have to destroy the mould to get the mask out. So when the mask has been delivered to the client, there is nothing left.

"But to make a wax mask, you must first make one of plaster to serve as a matrix from which to make the gelatine mould for the wax. Then, when the wax mask has been delivered to the client, the plaster matrix remains in the possession of the artist.

"The suggestion, then, was that this man had supposed that the mould had been destroyed in making the mask, and that only some time after the murder had he, in some way, discovered his mistake. When he did discover it, he would see what an appalling blunder he had made, for the plaster matrix was the likeness of his own face.

"You see that all this was highly speculative. It was all hypothetical and it might all have been totally fallacious. We still had not a single solid fact, but all the hypothetical matter was consistent, and each inference seemed to support the others."

"And what," I asked, "did you suppose was his motive for trying to make away with Marion?"

"In the first place," he replied, "I inferred that he looked on her as a dangerous person who might have some knowledge of his transactions with her father. This was probably the explanation of his attempt when he cut the brake-wire of her bicycle But the second, more desperate attack, was made, I assume, when he had realized the existence of the plaster mask, and supposed that she knew of it, too. If he had killed her, he would probably have made another search with the studio fully lighted up.

"To return to our inquiry. You see that I had a mass of hypothesis but not a single real fact. But I still had a firm belief that a wax mask had been made and that – if it had not been destroyed – there must be a plaster mask somewhere in the studio. That was what I came to look for that morning, and as it happens that I am some six inches taller than Bendelow was, I was able to see what had been invisible to him. When I discovered that mask, and when Marion had disclaimed all knowledge of it, my hopes began to rise. But when you identified the face as that of Morris, I felt that our problem was solved. In an instant my card-house of speculative hypothesis was changed into a solid edifice. What had been but bare possibilities had now become so highly probable that they were almost certainties.

"Let us consider what the finding of this mask proved – subject, of course, to verification. It proved that a wax mask of Morris had been made – for here was the matrix – varnished, as you will remember, in readiness for the gelatine mould – and that mask was obviously obtained for the purpose of a fraudulent cremation. And that mask was made by Julius D'Arblay.

"What was the purpose of the fraud? It was perfectly obvious. Morris was clearly the *real* Simon Bendelow, and the purpose of the fraud was to create undeniable evidence that he was dead. But why did he want to prove that he was dead? Well, we knew that he was the murderer of Van Zellen, for whom the American police were searching, and he might be in more danger than we knew. At any rate, a death certificate would make him absolutely secure – on one condition: That the body was cremated. Mere burial would not be enough, for an exhumation would discover the fraud. But perfect security could be secured only by destruction of all evidence of the fraud. Julius D'Arblay held such evidence. Therefore Julius D'Arblay must be got rid of. Here, then, was an amply sufficient motive for the murder. The only point which remained obscure was the identity of your patient and the means by which his disappearance had been accounted for.

"My hypothesis, then, had been changed into highly probable theory. The next stage was the necessary verification. I began with a rather curious experiment. The man who tried to murder Marion could have been no other than her father's murderer. Then he must have been Morris. But it seemed that he was totally unlike Morris, and the mask evidently suggested to her no resemblance. But yet it was probable that the man was Morris, for the striking features – the hook nose and the heavy brows – would be easily 'made up', especially at night. The question was whether the face was Morris's with these additions. I determined to put that question to the test. And here Polton's new accomplishment came to our aid.

"First, with a pinch of clay, we built up on Morris's mask a nose of the shape described and slightly thickened the brows. Then Polton made a gelatine mould and from this produced a wax mask. He fitted it with glass eyes and attached it to a rough plaster head, with ears which were casts of my own painted. We then fixed on a moustache, beard and wig, and put on a shirt, collar and jacket. It was an extraordinarily crude affair, suggestive of the Fifth of November. But it answered the purpose, which was to produce a photograph, for we made the photograph so bad – so confused and ill-focused – that the crudities disappeared, while the essential likeness remained. As you know, that photograph was instantly recognized, without any sort of suggestion. So the first test gave a positive result. Marion's assailant was pretty certainly Morris."

"I should like to have seen Mr. Polton's prentice effort," said Marion, who had been listening, enthralled by this description.

"You shall see it now," Thorndyke replied with a smile. "It is in the next room, concealed in a cupboard."

He went out, and presently returned, carrying what looked like an excessively crude hair-dresser's dummy, but a most extraordinarily horrible and repulsive one. As he turned the face towards us, Marion gave a little cry of horror and then tried to laugh – without very striking success.

"It is a dreadful-looking thing!" she exclaimed, "and so hideously like that fiend." She gazed at it with the most extreme repugnance for a

600

while and then said, apologetically: "I hope you won't think me very silly, but – "

"Of course I don't," Thorndyke interrupted. "It is going back to its cupboard at once," and with this he bore it away, returning in a few moments with a smaller object, wrapped in a cloth, which he laid on the table. "Another 'exhibit', as they say in the courts," he explained, "which we shall want presently. Meanwhile we resume the thread of our argument.

"The photograph of this waxwork, then, furnished corroboration of the theory that Morris was the man whom we were seeking. My next move was to inquire at Scotland Yard if there were any fresh developments of the Van Zellen case. The answer was that there were, and Superintendent Miller arranged to come and tell me all about them. You were present at the interview and will remember what passed. His information was highly important, not only by confirming my inference that Bendelow was the murderer, but especially by disposing of the difficulty connected with the disappearance of your patient. For now there came into view a second man – Crile – who had died at Hoxton of an abdominal cancer and had been duly buried, and when you were able to give me this man's address, a glance at the map and at the Post Office Directory showed that the two men had died in the same house. This fact, with the farther facts that they had died of virtually the same disease and within a day or two of the same date, left no reasonable doubt that we were really dealing with one man who had died and for whom two death certificates, in different names, and two corresponding burial orders had been obtained. There was only one body, and that was cremated in the name of Bendelow. It followed that the coffin which was buried at Mr. Crile's funeral must have been an empty coffin. I was so confident that this must be so that I induced Miller to apply for an exhumation, with the results that you know.

"There now remained only a single point requiring verification: The question as to what face it was that those two ladies saw when they looked into the coffin of Simon Bendelow. Here again Polton's new accomplishment came to our aid. From the plaster mask your apprentice made a most realistic wax mask, which I offer for your critical inspection."

He unfolded the cloth and produced a mask of thin, yellowish wax and of a most cadaverous aspect, which he handed to Marion.

"Yes," she said approvingly, "it is an excellent piece of work, and what beautiful eyelashes. They look exactly like real ones."

"They are real ones," Thorndyke explained with a chuckle.

She looked up at him inquiringly, and then, breaking into a ripple of laughter, exclaimed, "Of course! They are his own! Oh! How like Mr. Polton! But he was quite right, you know. He couldn't have got the effect any other way."

"So he declared," said Thorndyke. "Well, we hired a coffin and had an inspection window put in the lid, and we got a black skull-cap. We put a dummy head in the coffin with a wig on it, we laid the mask where the face should have been and we adjusted the jaw-bandage and the skull-cap so as to cover up the edges of the mask, and we got the two ladies here and showed them the coffin. When they had identified the tenant as Mr. Bendelow, the verification was complete, the hypothesis was now converted into ascertained fact, and all that remained to be done was to lay hands on the murderer."

"How did you find out where Morris was living?" I asked.

"Barber did that," he replied. "When I learned that you were being stalked, I employed Barber to shadow you. He, of course, observed Morris on your track and followed him home."

"That was what I supposed," said I, and for a while we were all silent. Presently Marion said, "It is all very involved and confusing. Would you mind telling us exactly what happened?"

"In a direct narrative, you mean?" said he. "Yes, I will try to reconstruct the events in the order of their occurrence. It began with the murder of Van Zellen by Bendelow. There was no evidence against him at the time, but he had to fly from America for other reasons and he left behind him incriminating traces which he knew must presently be discovered and which would fix the murder on him. His friend Crile, who fled with him, developed gastric cancer and only had a month or two to live. Then Bendelow decided that when Crile should die, he would make believe to die at that same time. To this end, he commissioned your father to make a wax mask – a portrait mask of himself with his eyes closed. His wife must then have persuaded the two spinsters to visit him – he, of course, taking to his bed when they called and being represented as a mortally sick man. Then they moved from Hornsey to Hoxton, taking Crile with him. There he engaged two doctors – Usher and Gray, both of whom lived at a distance – to attend Crile and to visit him on alternate days. Crile seems to have been deaf, or at least, hard of hearing, and was kept continuously under the influence of morphia. Usher, who was employed by Mrs. Bendelow – whom he knew as Mrs. Pepper – came to the front of the house in Field Street to visit Mr. Crile, while Stephen, who was employed by the Bendelows – whom he knew by the name of Morris – entered at the rear of the house in Market Street to visit the same man under the name of Bendelow. About

602

the time of the move, Bendelow committed the murder in order to destroy all evidence of the making of the wax mask.

"Eventually Crile died – or was finished off with an extra dose of morphia – on a Thursday. Usher gave the certificate and the funeral took place on the Saturday. But previously – probably on the Friday night – the coffin-lid was unscrewed by Bendelow, the body taken out and replaced by a sack of sawdust with some lead pipe in it.

"On the Monday the body was again produced, this time as that of Simon Bendelow, who was represented as having died on the Sunday afternoon. It was put in a cremation coffin with a celluloid window in the lid. The wax mask was placed over the face, the jaw-bandage and the skull-cap adjusted to hide the place where the wax face joined the real face, and the two spinsters were brought up to see Mr. Bendelow in his coffin. They looked in through the window and, of course, saw the wax mask of Bendelow. Then they retired. The coffin-lid was taken off, the wax mask removed, the coffin-lid screwed on again, and then the two doctors were brought up. They removed the body from the coffin, examined it and put it back, and Bendelow – or Morris – put on the coffin-lid.

"As soon as the doctors were gone, the coffin-lid was taken off again, the wax mask was put back and adjusted and the coffin-lid replaced and screwed down finally. Then the two ladies were brought up again to take a last look at poor Mr. Bendelow – not actually the last look, for, at the funeral, they peeped in at the window and saw the wax face just before the coffin was passed through into the crematorium."

"It was a diabolically clever scheme," said I.

"It was," he agreed. "It was perfectly convincing and consistent. If you and those two ladies had been put in the witness-box, your testimony and theirs would have been in complete agreement. They had seen Simon Bendelow (whom they knew quite well) in his coffin. A few minutes later, you had seen Simon Bendelow in his coffin, had taken the body out, examined it thoroughly and put it back, and had seen the coffin-lid screwed down, and again a few minutes later they had looked in through the coffin-window and had again seen Simon Bendelow. The evidence would appear to be beyond the possibility of a doubt. Simon Bendelow was proved conclusively to be dead and cremated and was doubly certified to have died from natural causes. Nothing could be more complete.

"And yet," he continued, after a pause, "while we are impressed by the astonishing subtlety and ingenuity displayed, we are almost more impressed by the fundamental stupidity exhibited along with it – a stupidity that seems to be characteristic of this type of criminal. For all the security that was gained by one part of the scheme was destroyed by the idiotic efforts to guard against dangers that had no existence. The murder was not only a foul crime, it was a tactical blunder of the most elementary kind. But for that murder, Bendelow would now be alive and in unchallenged security. The cremation scheme was completely successful. It deceived everybody. Even the two detectives, though they felt vague suspicions, saw no loophole. They had to accept the appearances at their face value.

"But it was the old story. The wrong-doer could not keep quiet. He must be for ever making himself safer and yet more safe. At each move he laid down fresh tracks. And so, in the end, he delivered himself into our hands."

He paused and for a while seemed to be absorbed in reflection on what he had been telling us. Presently he looked up, and, addressing Marion, said in quiet, grave tones, "We have ended our quest and we have secured retribution. Justice was beyond our reach, for complete justice implies restitution, and to attain that, the dead must have been recalled from beyond the grave. But, at least sometimes, out of evil cometh good. Surely it will seem to you when, in the happy years which I trust and confidently believe lie before you, your thoughts turn back to the days of your mourning and grief, that the beloved father, who, when living, made your happiness his chief concern, even in dying bequeathed to you a blessing."

The End

About the Author

Richard Austin Freeman was born on April 11th, 1862 in the Soho district of London. He was the son of a skilled tailor and the youngest of five children. As he grew, it was expected that he would become a tailor as well, but instead he had an interest in natural history and medicine, and so he obtained employment in a pharmacist's shop. While there, he qualified as an apothecary and could have gone on to manage the shop, but instead he began to study medicine at Middlesex Hospital.

Austin Freeman qualified as a physician in 1887, and in that same year he married. Faced with the twin facts of his new marital responsibilities and his very limited resources as a young doctor, he made the unusual decision to join the Colonial Service, spending the next seven years in Africa as an Assistant Colonial Surgeon. This continued until the early 1890's, when he contracted Blackwater Fever, an illness that eventually forced him to leave the service and return permanently to England.

For several years, he served as a *locum tenens* for various physicians, a bleak time in his life as he moved from job to job, his income low, and his health never quite recovered. However, he supplemented his meager income and exercised his creativity during these years by beginning to write. His early publications included *Travels and Live in Ashanti and Jaman* (1898), recounting some of his African sojourns.

In 1900, Freeman obtained work as an assistant to Dr. John James Pitcairn (1860-1936) at Holloway Prison. Although he wasn't there for very long, the association between the two men was enough to turn Freeman's attention toward writing mysteries. Over the next few years, they co-wrote several under the pseudonym *Clifford Ashdown*, including *The Adventures of Romney Pringle* (1902), *The Further Adventures of Romney Pringle* (1903), *From a Surgeon's Diary* (1904-1905), and *The Queen's Treasure* (written around 1905-1906, and published posthumously in 1975.)

In approximately 1904, Freeman began developing a mystery novella based on a short job that he had held at the Western Ophthalmic Hospital. This effort, "31 New Inn", was published in 1905, and it is the true first Dr. Thorndyke story. In 1907, the first Thorndyke novel, *The Red Thumb Mark*, was published.

From Thorndyke's creation until 1914, Freeman wrote four novels and two volumes of short stories. Then, with the commencement of the

First World War, he entered military service. In February 1915, at the age of fifty-two, he joined the Royal Army Medical Corps. Due to his health, which had never entirely recovered from his time in Africa, he spent the duration of the war involved with various aspects of the ambulance corps, having been promoted very early to the rank of Captain. He wrote nothing about Thorndyke during this period, but he did publish one book concerning the adventures of a scoundrel, *The Exploits of Danby Croker* (1916).

Following the war, he resumed his previous life, writing approximately one Thorndyke novel per year, as well as three more volumes of Thorndyke short stories and a number of other unrelated items, until his death on September 28th, 1943 – likely related to Parkinson's Disease, which had plagued him in later years. He is buried in Gravesend.

If you enjoy Dr. Thorndyke, then you'll love
The MX Book of New Sherlock Holmes Stories
Edited by David Marcum
(MX Publishing, 2015-   )

"This is the finest volume of Sherlockian fiction I have ever read, and I have read, literally, thousands." – Philip K. Jones

"Beyond Impressive . . . This is a splendid venture for a great cause!
– Roger Johnson, Editor, *The Sherlock Holmes Journal,*
The Sherlock Holmes Society of London

Part I: 1881-1889
Part II: 1890-1895
Part III: 1896-1929
Part IV: 2016 Annual
Part V: Christmas Adventures
Part VI: 2017 Annual
Part VII: Eliminate the Impossible (1880-1891)
Part VIII – Eliminate the Impossible (1892-1905)
Part IX – 2018 Annual (1879-1895)
Part X – 2018 Annual (1896-1916)
Part XI – Some Untold Cases (1880-1891)
Part XII – Some Untold Cases (1894-1902)
Part XIII – 2019 Annual (1881-1890)
Part XIV – 2019 Annual (1891-1897)
Part XV – 2019 Annual (1898-1917)
Part XVI – Whatever Remains . . . Must be the Truth (1881-1890)
Part XVII – Whatever Remains . . . Must be the Truth (1891-1898)
Part XVIII – Whatever Remains . . . Must be the Truth (1898-1925)

In Preparation
Part XIX – 2020 Annual

. . . and more to come!

The MX Book of New Sherlock Holmes Stories
Edited by David Marcum
(MX Publishing, 2015-   )

Publishers Weekly says:

Part VI: *The traditional pastiche is alive and well . . . .*

Part VII: *Sherlockians eager for faithful-to-the-canon plots and characters will be delighted.*

Part VIII: *The imagination of the contributors in coming up with variations on the volume's theme is matched by their ingenious resolutions.*

Part IX: *The 18 stories . . . will satisfy fans of Conan Doyle's originals. Sherlockians will rejoice that more volumes are on the way.*

Part X: *. . . new Sherlock Holmes adventures of consistently high quality.*

Part XI: *. . . an essential volume for Sherlock Holmes fans.*

Part XII: *. . . continues to amaze with the number of high-quality pastiches . . .*

Part XIII: *. . . Amazingly, Marcum has found 22 superb pastiches . . . This is more catnip for fans of stories faithful to Conan Doyle's original*

Part XIV: *. . . this standout anthology of 21 short stories written in the spirit of Conan Doyle's originals.*

Part XV: *Stories pitting Sherlock Holmes against seemingly supernatural phenomena highlight Marcum's 15th anthology of superior short pastiches.*

The MX Book of New Sherlock Holmes Stories
Edited by David Marcum
(MX Publishing, 2015-   )

Also From MX Publishing

Traditional Canonical Sherlock Holmes Adventures by
David Marcum
Creator and editor of
The MX Book of New Sherlock Holmes Stories

The Papers of Sherlock Holmes
"The Papers of Sherlock Holmes by David Marcum contains nine intriguing mysteries . . . very much in the classic tradition . . . He writes well, too."
– Roger Johnson, Editor, *The Sherlock Holmes Journal*,
The Sherlock Holmes Society of London

"Marcum offers nine clever pastiches."
– Steven Rothman, Editor, *The Baker Street Journal*

Sherlock Holmes and A Quantity of Debt
"This is a welcome addendum to Sherlock lore that respectfully fleshes out Doyle's legendary crime-solving couple in the context of new escapades . . . ."
– Peter Roche, Examiner.com

"David Marcum is known to Sherlockians as the author of two short story collections . . . In Sherlock Holmes and A Quantity of Debt, *he demonstrates mastery of the longer form as well."*
– Dan Andriacco, Author

Sherlock Holmes – Tangled Skeins
(Included in Randall Stock's, 2015 Top Five Sherlock Holmes Books – Fiction)
"Marcum's collection will appeal to those who like the traditional elements of the Holmes tales"
– Randall Stock, BSI

"There are good pastiche writers, there are great ones, and then there is David Marcum who ranks among the very best . . . I cannot recommend this book enough."
– Derrick Belanger, Author and Publisher of Belanger Books

Sherlock Holmes in Montague Street
by Arthur Morrison
Edited, Holmes-ed, and with Original Material
by David Marcum

Separate Paperback Editions

Combined Hardcover Edition

*"It's been suggested that Hewitt was the young Mycroft Holmes,
but David Marcum has a more plausible and attractive theory
– that he was Sherlock, early in his career as an investigator
. . . these are remarkably convincing in their new guise."*
– Roger Johnson, Editor, *The Sherlock Holmes Journal*,
The Sherlock Holmes Society of London

MX Publishing

MX Publishing is the world's largest specialist Sherlock Holmes publisher, with several hundred titles and over a hundred authors creating the latest in Sherlock Holmes fiction and non-fiction.

From traditional short stories and novels to travel guides and quiz books, MX Publishing caters to all Holmes fans.

The collection includes leading titles such as *Benedict Cumberbatch In Transition* and *The Norwood Author*, which won the 2011 *Tony Howlett Award* (Sherlock Holmes Book of the Year).

MX Publishing also has one of the largest communities of Holmes fans on *Facebook*, with regular contributions from dozens of authors.

www.mxpublishing.co.uk (UK) and *www.mxpublishing.com* (USA)

www.ingramcontent.com/pod-product-compliance
Lightning Source LLC
Chambersburg PA
CBHW030739030726
47497CB00001B/45